Quicksand: Marion's Memories Married to a Sex Addict Minister

Melanie J. Barton Bragg

Table of Contents

Preface

IN MY THREE plus decades counseling addiction clients and their loved ones, I have witnessed heartbreak, devastation, and renewed hope. My own addiction journey involved many fits and starts. I have been both the one causing pain as the chemical abuser and as the judge of my loved one struggling to escape their own addiction nightmare. I do not pass judgment on anyone involved in this debacle. This book is a fictional composite based on my experience personally and professionally. Names, characters, businesses, places, events, and incidents are either products of my imagination or used in a fictitious manner. Any resemblance to actual persons, living or dead, or actual events is coincidental.

Acknowledgments

QUICKSAND CAME INTO existence because my friend Mike Nash urged me to create a book based on my personal and professional experiences. Seeing me through that process was my editor, Maureen Yoder. She was kind in her constructive criticism expecting me to vanish after our first meeting. Not only did she help me to perfect my craft, but the journey became cathartic for me and others as the characters came to life. Draft readers Ray Hardy, Dan Pearson, Anita Nash, Dr. Yvonne Siddall, Garth Duke-Barton, and Miriam Wilkinson pointed out inconsistencies and grammatical errors. Connie Stoutamire of Keep It Simple Photography took the author photo. My sister, Robin Pearson created the artwork for the cover. I thank all of you for being part of this endeavor. As you enter the Quicksand with Marion, I hope you will explore your own life "stuckedness" and emerge stronger, wiser, and better equipped to make decisions that bring out the best in you.

Quicksand Introduction

Session One

MARION'S WHOLE BODY trembled turning the doorknob as she entered Dr. Weinstein's psychotherapy reception room. Her ninety-six-pound frame could barely stand erect. Holding onto the wall she eased herself into a maroon upholstered chair. Fidgeting in her seat she wondered how she would impart her Quicksand journey to the therapist. Her train of thought derailed as Dr. Weinstein towering over asked, "You must be Marion, right?"

Shakily rising she shook the practitioner's hand and answered, "Yes, I am."

"Good, step into my office," he said leading the way.

Marion perched herself at the edge of the white swivel leather seat in case she decided to make a hasty exit. Dr. Weinstein's soothing voice unloosed Marion's fears and increased her trust to unwind the tightly sealed memories of her life.

"Well, Marion you said on the phone when we set this appointment that you wanted therapy because of extreme long-term stress in your life. Is that what you want to work on?" he asked in a caring tone.

Nodding she said, "Yes my life and my health are a total disaster. It's hard for me to even fathom how I got to this point," she said as tears mixed with mascara stung her eyes."

Dr. Weinstein's calm voice urged Marion to trust him to unburden her pain. "It's okay, Marion. Your life did not get this way over night and it will take time to unwind it and reshape it in a new direction. At times, it will seem like you have made no progress and at other times it will seem like you don't recognize where you were.

Why don't you start by giving me some of your family background? Sometimes that makes it easier to get the process started."

Marion inhaled and stared off into space. Dr. Weinstein waited patiently recognizing her behavior as consistent with someone who has been traumatized.

Half smiling, she returned her eyes to face his and said, "How many years do you have for me to tell you all of it?"

"As many as it takes. For my clients who have lived through trauma, it makes it less emotionally triggering to describe it, if they tell it like they are a narrator. Do you think that might help?"

"I don't know," she said, "but I can try. So here goes."

"I think I'll start with my dad's family."

"Good idea," Dr. Weinstein said attentively leaning in.

The Groundwork

Eleven-year-old bow-legged Andrew, dressed in his plus four pants and his round-necked schoolboy sweater, slammed the black, spindly porch screen door as he hollered back to his mom in the kitchen.

"Ma, I'm going now."

Peering through the screen mesh wiping her hands on a floral terrycloth dishtowel, she called after him, "Andy, you be careful. You know Officer Murphy, walking his beat, will tell you to skedaddle home if he sees you hanging around in the alley."

He looked back over his shoulder, and answered, "I know Ma. I'll be back as quick as I can," and hopped on the chrome plated Schwinn bike his neighbor let him borrow, peddling fast in the crisp Sunday morning air.

Begging for bread during the Depression fell to the second son of the Parkers. People could not resist his angelic look with sad blue eyes. This day, Andy stood vigilant in the alley keeping a watchful eye out for Officer Murphy. He needed the ration of day old, stale bread for the family or they would go hungry for a second day. The Jewish owner closed the bakery Friday evening before sunset and all-day Saturday for Sabbath. As Andy heard the metal door safety bar pull back he stepped to the side.

"Morning Andy. How's your mom's lumbago?" Baker Goldstein inquired as he swept away the leaves around the backdoor.

Looking down at his feet, embarrassed, Andy responded, "Fine, sir. Ma thanks you for asking."

Mr. Goldstein stopped sweeping and looked at the frail lad. "You know Andy, in a few years you'll be old enough to work full-time, but until then, why don't you come help out at the bakery a couple of mornings a week before school? You can sweep and mop the floors and empty the trash. My ole' aching body can hardly lift a tray of cookies these days," he said rubbing his lower back. "I can pay you twenty-five cents a day and a fresh loaf of bread. How does that sound?"

Kicking the dirt, he answered his new employer,

"Oh, gosh, Mr. Goldstein, that'd be swell. What time do ya need me?" Andy asked breathlessly.

Handing him two loaves instead of the usual one loaf of day-old bread, the baker said with a wink, "Be here at 6:30 sharp tomorrow morning and I'll show you what to do, okay?"

"Yes, sir, Mr. G. You can count on me," he said shaking his head up and down.

On this day of rampant hunger, October 23, 1932, in Boston at Kenmore Square Station, a dual island rapid transit, the Green bus line opened. This development gave hope that the Great Depression would soon end.

Andy was the second of two sons born to Russell and Winifred Parker. Siblings agree that he was mom's favorite. He would one day tell his own children about his family's frequent moves due to non-payment of rent and how he was the designated beggar during the Depression. Andy often sang a cute childhood ditty in a false Italian accent to his family: "Winnie take down the wallpaper we're going to move."

Elbows under his chin, resting on the chrome tabletop, Andy sat cross-legged in the creaky wooden kitchen chair while his mom shucked corn across from him.

"Ma, tell me about my Canadian relatives. I don't think I'll ever get to go there to see 'um."

"You, never know. You might go someday," Winnie Parker said, smiling at her son. "What do you want to know that I haven't already told you a hundred times?" she said chuckling.

"All of it. It makes me feel close to them the way you tell it," he said settling in.

Sighing she said, "Okay, here goes," using her fingers to mark each relative. "My mother's parents, Susan Baron Lam and George Lam, immigrated from Nova Scotia, Canada in the spring of 1873 after the November 9th, 1872 Boston Fire. My grandfather Lam, was a popular volunteer firefighter in Hants County, Nova Scotia. His friend, Sam, showed him a newspaper article about the fire that said it was as bad as the Chicago one, the year before.

Sam told Grandpa Lam, 'You're as strong as an ox.

If you'd been there, it wouldn't be such a mess. Why, you can hold leather hoses twice your size! Now they need strong backs to rebuild Boston. You said you wanted an adventure, so go.'

"They went, but my great uncle, John Baron, Grandma Susan's brother stayed behind with his wife Ruth to tend the five-generational farm in Scotch Village. It's a hundred and fourteen miles from the Bay of Fundy. You can look it up on a map, later. Great Uncle John's daughter, Beatrice, married Otto Brown in 1898. Uncle Otto helped his father-in-law farm the homestead until 1900 when Great Uncle John, bored with farming, followed with Great Aunt Ruth, my Grandma Susan, and Grandpa George down to the lower 48. My second cousin, Nellie was born to Beatrice and Otto in 1903, but unfortunately Beatrice died when Nellie was born.

"Grandma Susan and Grandpa George had my mother Harriet in 1872, before they left Canada. My mom grew up here in Boston," she said pointing toward the floor. "My mom met Harold Lee, my dad, a native Bostonian horse drawn carriage driver in 1893 and married him in a proper Episcopal church ceremony in 1894. Then after two miscarriages, I was born in 1896."

"So, how did you first meet your cousin, Nellie?" Andy asked intrigued to learn about his ancestral roots.

Tossing the husks into the large paper sack, Winnie said, "Well, I first met my second cousin, when I was seven and she was just a baby," eyes looking to the right. "Grandmother Susan and Grandfather George took me there for a family reunion shortly after Cousin Beatrice died. I remember the sweet smell of the white clover in the meadow and the overpowering odor of the hay in the barn. My cousin Doris, younger than her sister Beatrice, cared for Nellie, after Beatrice died. Doris wore a flowered full apron with her hair in a tight bun. Flour tickled her nose as she rolled out the dough with her glass rolling pin filled with cold water to make biscuits," Winnie said, motioning her hands like she was rolling out the dough. "I can still see her putting wood into the stove to get just the right temperature to make the biscuits turn golden brown. They were so flaky they melted in my mouth swimming with butter and honey," she said drooling.

Andy licked his lips and fingers pretending to eat the biscuits his mom described and then asked, "So, have I ever met any of my Canadian cousins?"

Winnie put down the last ear of corn into the steel pot on the table and said, "Don't you remember my cousin Nellie and her daughter Sarah stayed with us about a month back when you were six?"

Andy scrunched up his face trying to remember. "Naw, I don't. Whatever happened to Nellie after she lived with us for a while?"

"I'm not sure. I've lost track of her. I heard she went back to Scotch Village. I'd forgotten all about her after my one visit to the farm until she started writing to me when you were about two. She was teaching, but I was too busy with your brother Sam and you on the way to write back much. I was surprised when she asked to stay awhile with us. Pop had no problem with it. So, they came."

"Okay, Ma, Now, tell me again how you met, Pop."

She chuckled. "Andy, I've told you that story at least a hundred and fifty times." "I know, but I want to hear it again, please?" he said with his palms turned upward.

"Okay. I was sitting in the balcony at First Baptist church and something wet, kept hitting my neck. I put my hand under my hair to see if it was a bug or something. It was a spit ball! Then I heard snickering behind me. Your dad was being teased by the guys beside him for trying to get my attention."

"And then what did you do?" Andy asked, as if it was a never-told tale.

"Andrew Parker, you could tell the story yourself," she said as she swatted him with her tea towel thrown over her shoulder.

"C'mon, Ma. Finish the story."

"All right, already. I turned to face your dad and said, frowning, 'Hey, cut it out!' He said, 'I will if you go out with me.' I told him, 'not 'til you walk me home.' He did and the rest you know."

Andy loved to chat with his mom in between working at the bakery and going to school. Mr. Goldstein kept Andy on at the bakery until he retired at the end of 1935. Suffering from dyslexia and wanting to lighten the financial burden on his family, Andy dropped out of high school in the ninth grade to work odd jobs. At seventeen he entered the Civilian Conservation Corps (CCC). Working outdoors, he planted trees. In remote areas, his unit cleared land in preparation to build roads and stone safety walls along highways. CCC, a civilian "tree army" project for unemployed, single men whose families were on governmental relief, was part of Franklin D. Roosevelt's New Deal program. Participants were fed, clothed, and housed. Of the $30 laborers earned each month, $25 was sent home to the family. After Andy completed the program and being well-disciplined from the experience, he enlisted in the Army. He followed the path of older brother Sam.

Andy, now serving his country, missed his kitchen table chats with his mom. Winnie missed them too. Her sparse knowledge of her Canadian roots stopped after she lost track of Nellie and Sarah. Nellie did not reveal details of her life during the brief interlude when she and Sarah lived with the Parkers. Had she divulged the information then Andy's future path might have been different.

Nellie suffered from the "Cinderella" complex.

Nellie's father, Otto, remarried when his daughter was six. Her stepmother, Ms. Lois, treated her like the redheaded stepchild that she literally was. Nellie stayed to herself between chores, locked in her upstairs bedroom, talking to her imaginary friends that only she could see. At night ghosts haunted her. Fearful of harm, Nellie slept with a hammer under her pillow and a clove of garlic fastened around her neck.

Nellie awoke in a cold sweat. She felt an eerie presence in her room. Barely opening her clenched eyelids, she peered into the darkness, whispering. "Who are you? What do you want?" she asked trembling. She leaned over to push back the curtain to let the moon rays illuminate the room. As she did, she caught a glimpse of an apparition standing by her closet. Fear gripped her as she stared, noticing a familiarity about the ghost who then spoke.

"I am the mom, you never knew, Nellie. My heart longs to hold you. I come when you are asleep to watch over you. I protect you."

Unconvinced, Nellie said, "Um, how do I know that you are real and not of the devil?"

"Remember, the day you fell into the pond swinging from the tree limb and almost drowned? Do you recall how something lifted you out of the water and onto the bank?"

Nellie's eyes grew wide as she asked, "How do you know about that?"

"Because, my dear child I brought you up out of that water."

"Oh, I always wondered how that happened."

"I can't stay now, but remember. I'm always here for you. I love you, Nellie."

Beatrice's spirit disappeared, but Nellie never forgot that night nor told anyone about it. From then on, she slept peacefully, even though the daytime was not so pleasant.

Stepmother Lois often berated her, "Nellie, you're plumb crazy, talking to spirits that don't exist. No man will ever want to marry you. You're so homely."

Nellie kept quiet and hid in her room reading books by the light of the fire. When her lumberjack dad came home each evening, Stepmother Lois pretended to fuss over his daughter.

"Nellie," Lois said passing the plate to her, "dear, have another biscuit with gravy. You're wasting away to nothing."

"No, thank you, Ms. Lois. I'm not hungry. May I be excused?" she said with eyes downcast so not to tip off her overworked dad. Sarah left the table without speaking to her five-year-old half-brother, George, or her three-year old half-sister, Maude, who stared curiously at their older sister.

That night after checking on George and Maude, Lois kissed them on the forehead and tucked the covers snug under their chins in the chilly unheated air. Quietly tiptoeing, backing out of the room, Lois suddenly jumped.

Nellie stood in the hallway peering into the room. Raising her voice in a loud whisper, Lois asked,

"What are you gawking at, Nellie? Can't a mother tuck her children in for the night without you lurking about?" Shaking her finger and poking it into her stepdaughter's chest, Lois said, "I saw you staring at George and Maude. Now don't you go filling my children's brains with your nonsense of spirits and bewitching ways. I don't even want you to touch or even look at them. Do you understand me?" Her voice rose. "Why, I wouldn't put it past you to put a curse on those sweet youngins," she bellowed, waking George and Maude out of their innocent slumbers.

Nellie's eyes glared right through her evil stepmother as she answered, "Sure, I understand."

With that, Nellie turned, muttered a curse under her breath, then slammed and locked her door.

After Lois calmed the frightened children, she marched downstairs to find Otto reading the newspaper sitting at the dining room table. "You have to do something about Nellie," she said hands on her hips, lips pursed.

"Now, Lois," Otto said looking over his spectacles, lowering the newspaper. "You know, I'm all thumbs when it comes to raising kids. That's women's work. Nellie will be old enough to move out in a year or so. Just make it work okay?"

Lois swung the dining room door to the kitchen hard and made herself busy slamming cupboard doors as she put away the supper dishes. Otto ignored her as he continued to read the paper.

All that winter Nellie obeyed Lois' order to stay clear of her half-siblings whenever her father was out of the house. She shivered as she huddled under her covers reading, emerging only long enough to pee into the chamber pot, avoiding her stepmother's wrath. She too counted the days until she was old enough to move out on her own.

By June, the metallic smell of fresh rain at dusk coaxed Nellie to carry her patchwork quilt down to the porch glider and finish reading *Anne of Green Gables* until the fireflies came out. She spent the remainder of the lazy summer days reading whatever she could borrow from the town library unless her "wicked" stepmother had ironing for her to do.

One warm, clear, starry night in mid-August, the family fretted when Otto failed to return home by dark.

Farmhand Amos rode out on his mare in the morning to hunt for him. Otto lay under a tall cut pine tree with a cracked skull. Chopping down the tree, he miscalculated which way it would fall. He had been dead for many hours. After the funeral, Nellie only came downstairs to scavenge for food at night in the kitchen. Being a girl with nothing to inherit, there was no sense hanging out any longer at the farm. She walked the half-mile to the village store and asked the shopkeeper, Mr. Max, in a hushed voice, "Are there any jobs I can do around town?" She shuffled from one foot to the other furtively glancing at the men playing checkers on top of the cheese barrel.

Mr. Max looked up from tallying a column of numbers and put his pencil behind his ear. He said, "Ms. Nellie, the school house is looking for a teacher. You get room and board and $25 a month. Will that do?" He asked, certain she would accept.

She began the next week without even so much as a farewell to her step-family. After two years, she met Peter Summer when he came to build some new desks for the one-room school house. Nellie hid her delusions during the courtship. Since teachers were not allowed to be married, she resigned her position when she agreed to marry Peter and move into his mother's house. It was a good thing for her to leave teaching. The parents were about to ask her to resign because she did not communicate well with them. Plus, the students reported to their parents that Ms. Brown often talked as if to some invisible person.

Throughout the brief marriage, paranoid Nellie always believed people were talking about her behind her back. She wore a money belt around her waist under a snug girdle hiding the money she saved from teaching.

Never properly diagnosed, she suffered from Schizoaffective Disorder. People talked about her eccentric ways. She always muttered to herself, looked anxiously around as she hurried into the post office to mail a weekly letter to her second cousins in Boston whom she had been corresponding with since teaching, but avoided eye contact with anyone. She kept her wedding presents in their original boxes in the back of the closet for the time when she and Peter could move out from his mother's sprawling farmhouse and into their own little bungalow. In October, Sarah, a perfectly healthy daughter, was born to Peter and Nellie, Andy Parker's third cousin. Peter's mom, Jeanette, ran the household by strict rules. The baby could only be fed on a schedule. She could only be picked up at certain times. Often baby Sarah had to learn to cry herself to sleep. Peter began siding with his mom about how things should be handled. Nellie, in a fragile mental state, was about to break.

As Nellie lay awake long after Peter began snoring, she looked over at three-year-old Sarah asleep on the pallet on the floor. Her brown curls lay sprawled onto the floor beyond her pillow. The voices in Nellie's head pleaded with her, "You can't stay here. He'll kill you and Sarah.

You must run."

The next morning, she planned her escape, hurriedly packing a duffle bag and shoving it under the bed while Jeanette walked down to Hants General Store to get the mail. After supper Peter returned to his woodworking shop three blocks from the farmhouse to finish sanding a table he was crafting. Jeannette went out after him to feed the chickens at dusk, locking the door from the outside. She sneered, patting the key resting securely in her apron pocket. Nellie knew it was her only chance to get away. Quietly she picked up Sarah and put her finger to her lips to tell her not to make a sound. She sneakily opened the bathroom window on the opposite side of the house from the chicken coop, the only one that had not been nailed shut. She hurriedly squeezed through it with malnourished Sarah and ran as fast as she could through the knee deep powdery snow to her maternal Aunt Doris' house down the hill, in the opposite direction from the woodworking shop. Too late and too dark to begin a search for his wife and daughter, Peter waited until morning believing Nellie would return, having no place else to go.

Before dawn the next morning, Nellie fearful of Peter's wrath, boarded a bus with Sarah headed for Boston while Aunt Doris kept her secret. Neighbors said Nellie was always strange, but also true, Peter had an unhealthy relationship with his mother that favored her over his wife and daughter.

Nellie and Sarah went to live briefly with cousins, the Parkers in Boston, the ones she had written to for years. Nellie left the Parkers' abode after about a month to cook and clean for the wealthy Bostonian MacDonald family. Fortunately, Sarah was welcomed by the MacDonald's to mingle with their children, but Nellie's culinary skills lacked finesse. After sixteen months, the family let Nellie go. By then, Sarah was five and ready to start kindergarten.

No longer fearing Peter's temper, Nellie contacted Aunt Doris to ask if they could stay with her. She agreed. They returned to Nova Scotia traveling again by bus. Peter's friend Oscar advised him that Nellie and Sarah were coming as the two buddies sipped their scalding coffee and dunking their Saskatoon Berry muffins in the creamy brew laden with sugar. Licking his fingers first, Peter then picked up his stack of invoices, bid Oscar adieu and headed over to the Hants Corner General Store and Post Office. "Max," Peter said as he handed the shopkeeper/postmaster his woodworking customer's bills to mail out. "I hear Nellie's coming back. Is, that, right?"

"Yup, it sure is, Peter," said Max as he licked the 1cent stamps and secured them in place with his index finger.

"Well, when you see Nellie, would you tell her I'd like to see Sarah?"

Holding out his hand to receive the twenty-five-cent payment, Max said, "Sure, Peter, I'll do that when she comes to get some books I saved for her when the library closed."

Max delivered the message and a visit was arranged. Nellie again stayed with her Aunt Doris. She had no intention of visiting her step-family. She had no desire to see Peter either. Oscar agreed to meet Nellie and Sarah at the store Saturday at 1p.m.

Arriving one minute before 1:00 p.m., Nellie greeted Oscar whom she knew from high school. They exchanged pleasantries and Oscar agreed to return Sarah by 4:00 p.m.

Sarah had no recollection of her father, but eager to connect with him, she trustingly went with Oscar to meet up with her dad for a boat ride.

Oscar held Sarah's hand as they walked the three blocks down to the lake. Peter waved to them as they approached. Oscar lifted Sarah onto the dock where Peter was waiting.

"Sarah," said Peter reaching his outstretched hand to her, "come get in the boat with daddy and Mr. Oscar."

Holding back Sarah answered, "I'm scared, Daddy.

I've never been in a boat."

He grabbed her by the arm and pulled her off the dock onto the floor of the hull of the tiny, blue wooden red trimmed row boat, laughing in a sinister tone.

Oscar said to Peter, "Be gentle with her, she's scared."

Peter angrily rowed to the middle of Nelson Lake as wide-eyed Sarah sat frozen, too afraid to move from where she was placed. Peter glared at Oscar as he laid his oar down next to Sarah and said, "I'll show her what real fear is, and be done with it." He picked Sarah up by her shoulders and dangled her overboard. He laughed as Sarah, who had not been taught how to swim, shrieked in fear and violently kicked her legs as she tried to get back into the boat.

"Peter, stop it!" Oscar reached over, carefully to not rock the boat, and grabbed Sarah out of Peter's grasp, cradling her in his arms. As he slowly sat down he said, "Are you out of your ever-loving mind, Peter? She could have easily slipped from your fingers and drowned."

Peter picked up his oar and said, "I was just fooling with her."

"That's sick." Pointing toward shore Oscar said,

"Row us back now!"

Thrusting his paddle in rapid succession on either side of the boat he said, "Ya know Oscar, you're a real killjoy. A guy can't even have fun with his own daughter."

"This is not fun. It's no wonder Nellie left you."

"Well, her crazy ass thinking was no picnic either," Peter said as they neared the shore.

"Peter, don't say all this in front of Sarah."

Sarah calmed, secure on Oscar's lap. As Peter tethered the boat, Oscar waded in the knee deep, frigid water carrying Sarah while telling her that he would not allow her father to grab her again. Oscar escorted Sarah the half mile to Doris' house and revealed the frightening details of the aborted outing.

Although never verified, village folk rumored that Peter was arrested after hearing Oscar tell the story to the men gathered around the checkerboard at Hants. Since Nellie's delusions were well known, people gossiped that she had probably fabricated some of the details to authorities to make it appear even worse than Oscar's version. Regardless of which version shared was fact or fiction, Sarah never saw her father again.

Nellie returned to Boston as a private duty nurse after Sarah finished kindergarten. Nellie lived on her patient's premises. When a single mom had to work in the 1930s, there were few childcare options. Throughout the years, Nellie placed her daughter with strangers in boarding homes.

"Mrs. Summer, you have tomorrow off. Do you want our driver to take you into the city to see some family or something?" asked Mrs. Roberts, the patient's wife, standing in the doorway of her husband's room.

Meekly, Nellie turned her head away from Mrs. Roberts and answered, "Ah, no thank you. If it's all right with you and Mr. Roberts, I'll just stay in my room and catch up on some writing."

Once a month Nellie visited Sarah on her day off, but most of the time she wrote stories in her spare time. She often muttered under her breath about UFOs and little green Martian men communicating with her. Some of her literary work was published in the Boston Globe under the pen name of Francis Summer. To open more doors for herself, she used a male pen name.

Meanwhile, nine-year-old Sarah tried to earn her keep at the boarding house sweeping floors, beating rugs and clearing the dinner table.

One day, Mrs. Weston, the boarding house owner, said, "Sarah, come here."

Timid Sarah quickly put down the wooden clothes pin she was pretending to be a doll and entered the kitchen. "Yes, ma'am. What do you want?" she asked staring at the floor.

"Go get your sweater and put your shoes on. Mr. Weston is taking you for a ride."

Perplexed Sarah tried to understand where he might be taking her. She did not have time to get her toothbrush or the ring trinket she got out of a box of Cracker Jacks. Her green wool sweater, her only coat, had a hole in the side where a pocket used to be.

The car ride was short to Beacon Hill where boarding houses were common. As they pulled up to a three-story, yellow wood-framed house, Mr. Weston said,

"Okay, Sarah, this is where you're going to stay now."

He got out of the car and waited on the sidewalk for her. Obediently she opened the car door and followed him, biting her bottom lip. This was her third such place in the last six months. Mr. Weston handed Mrs. Jackson $5.00 and said, "I'll have her mother send the rest," knowing full well there would be no more money. No one knew where Nellie Summer lived or worked as she frequently changed assignments and left no forwarding address.

Abused first by her father and then abandoned her mother, Sarah trusted no one. At night as she curled up in a fetal position, she clutched the tattered sweater, her only remaining possession from her last three boarding homes. Throughout her life, Sarah learned to hold onto any possession she could, knowing it may be left behind at any moment.

At the end of one month and no further payment, the Jacksons put the word out that a young girl was available for work. The day after her unacknowledged tenth birthday, Sarah ate her oatmeal at the dining room table surrounded by other boarders and day laborers.

Mrs. Jackson stood behind Sarah's chair. She reached around Sarah's left arm to lift the unfinished bowl of oatmeal from the table while Sarah spooned a mouthful of the rubbery texture smothered in brown sugar into her mouth. Mrs. Jackson said, "Sarah, you will be going to help a family today. Go brush your hair. You don't want to be unpresentable to the new folks."

Fighting back the tears, she sighed, mumbled, "Yes, ma'am."

The address was written on an old envelope. It was just two blocks away uphill. Sarah, too afraid to ask, did not know if she should take her hairbrush and toothbrush with her or not. As Sarah walked she pulled her sweater tighter around her chest. She braced against the wind blowing off the Charles River. Looking down at her feet she noticed some ants marching across her path.

"Hey, Mr. Ant. Where you going today? Wanna know where I'm going? I got no idea. At least you got your family trailing along. Wish I had some with me."

Looking at the faded envelope in her hand the address matched the nondescript brownstone numbers, so she rang the doorbell. She could hear people inside crying. Perplexed she waited for the door to open.

"You must be Sarah," the pale woman dressed in a black velvet dress with a tight gray bun said as she opened the heavy oak door. "Come in. I'm Grandma Smith. You look about the same age as my granddaughter Pamela," she said with her damp handkerchief blotting her eyes.

Sarah timidly inched into the hallway behind Mrs. Smith, hesitant to approach the wailing sounds coming from the parlor. Holding back, Sarah was unsure of her task. Mrs. Smith coaxed her into the room. The Smith family's ten-year-old daughter, Pamela, dressed in a perfectly ironed, pale blue dress with a white Peter Pan collar, was laid out in a coffin in the living room, having died from pneumonia.

Standing next to the casket was a woman similar in pale features leaning over the coffin combing Pamela's locks, her tears dropping onto the starched collar of the dress. The grandmother touched the arm of her daughter-in-law and pointed toward Sarah. "This is Sarah, the girl the Jacksons sent over."

Pulling herself away from her deceased daughter, the younger Mrs. Smith said, "Mr. Smith and I need to talk to Father Monahan about Pamela's funeral mass. You need to sit here in the parlor until we get back. Do you understand?"

Fear gripped Sarah's body, evident in her wide-eyed stare, but she was more afraid to not answer so shaking her head vertically, replied, "Yes, Ma'am."

When Mr. and Mrs. Smith, along with Grandma Smith, departed the house, it was eerily quiet after the loud wailing. Sarah sat frozen, petrified in the straight back, dining room chair closest to the front door. She shut her eyes tight, afraid to look at Pamela. As the sun shone through the sheer curtains of the bay window, the room heated up. Sarah's chest felt tight. Her breath came in short bursts. She gripped the seat of the chair afraid to move, her knuckles white.

She whispered, "Please God, don't let her wake up and make me dead too. What's it like to not breathe, I wonder?"

She held her breath, heart pounding, until, as if hit in the chest with a sucker punch, she exhaled with her eyes still tightly clenched. Sarah remained glued to that chair until the Smiths returned.

After the funeral, the Smiths started packing suitcases. Sarah, silent, wondered if it meant she had to leave again, but if so, where would she go? If she did stay, what would she do?

Tears stained Mrs. Smith's cheeks as she spoke haltingly to Sarah, "In the morning we are catching the train to Maine for two weeks. You can stay here. There's some food in the icebox and some canned goods in the cupboard.

Don't you go snooping or mess up the place. I expect it to be spotless when we get back."

Hands clasped behind her, staring at the floor, Sarah answered, "Yes, Mrs. Smith."

The next morning Sarah rose from the parlor couch where she fitfully slept the night before, afraid that Pamela would show up as a ghost and take her away. The Smiths called Sarah into the kitchen.

"We're leaving now," Pamela's mother said, placing a hairpin in her hat. "Remember don't go snooping, 'cause I'll know."

"Yes, Ma'am."

The blast of cold air left as they shut the backdoor and Sarah thought to herself, w*ell, at least there isn't a dead girl here now. Boy, it's spooky. I'm glad I can still go to my school. I've never slept alone in a house, but I don't have to cook for anyone. I think the leftover sandwiches will last me a few days.* At night after she finished her homework, she nibbled on stale sandwiches, rationing them. The black wool blanket scratched her skin as she tried to get comfortable on the parlor couch and the upholstered throw pillow.

When the Smiths returned in a fortnight, they told Sarah to continue to sleep on the parlor couch instead of in the undisturbed room of their deceased daughter. Even just one item of clothing from the dead child's full closet could have helped Sarah not feel so out of place at school when she wore her tattered and faded short-sleeved white blouse and plaid skirt two sizes too small for her. The family could not bear to part with any of Pamela's clothing yet. They expected Sarah to cook and clean in exchange for a place to live. Because ten-year-old Sarah reminded them too much of what they lost, they soon shipped her off to another boarding home.

The next home was better, and Sarah lived there for eight years. Mrs. Van Doran was a kind woman who taught her many useful skills. The only drawback to the living arrangement was Mr. Van Doran's alcoholism. Sitting at the chrome kitchen table with yellow formica top in the breakfast nook as the late afternoon shadows danced on the floor, Mrs. Van Doran said to her husband sitting across from her, "Mickey, you really need to stop drinking. These spirits are killing you," as she handed him his whiskey glass into which she had just placed four drops of formaldehyde before she sat down. Looking up, blurry-eyed Mickey answered,

"Woman, if you stopped nagging, I wouldn't need to drink," he said sloshing the contents of the shot glass as he downed the shot.

"One day," she said, as she shook her finger at him.

"You'll regret ruining your life with this rotgut."

"Maybe if I'm lucky and I drink enough, it'll drown out your bitching at me," he said shaking his head from side to side.

"Mark my words, you'll pay for this," she said as she got up and headed to the kitchen sink out of Mickey's line of sight. She carefully lifted the poison bottle from her apron pocket and gingerly placed it on the top shelf of the cupboard.

Mrs. Van Doran put her finger to her lips as she turned toward Sarah standing in the kitchen doorway and whispered, "This is our little secret, okay? You don't want me to go to jail, do you?"

Sarah whispered back, "Yes, our secret. I don't want to have to leave here. If you went to jail, they'd probably take me too."

When Mr. Van Doran later died from apparent complications of his drinking, the cause of death was ruled alcohol-related, an indirect truth.

Mrs. Van Doran taught Sarah to cook and to care for a home. The two women bonded washing dishes as they laughed and sang along with the radio. When Sarah graduated high school, Mrs. Van Doran bought her a broom and dustpan and a few other household items.

Sarah hugged her foster mom with tears glistening in her eyes as she closed the latch on her suitcase. "Mrs. Van Doran, how can I ever repay you for all you taught me? Please, promise me that you will come visit me once I get settled in my efficiency apartment. I start my job next Monday. I'm not sure how I'm going to handle it all on my own."

Mrs. Van Doran looked lovingly at the girl she raised and guided. As she stroked Sarah's hair she said, "Dear, you'll do just fine. You have worked hard to be out on your own. You're pretty and smart and some guy will snatch you up before too long."

Sarah went to work on the third floor of Gilchrist's department store in downtown Boston selling dresses to pampered and privileged women of upper-class Boston. Her first week on the job a woman wearing cat-eye brown glasses and permed short reddish-brown hair approached her.

"Miss, can you help me? I'm looking for a dress for my son's wedding?"

Sarah smiled and replied, "Yes I can. What size do you wear?"

The woman stared at Sarah's name tag. "Do, I know you? You look familiar." She asked, "Do you have relatives around here?"

Perplexed, Sarah hesitantly said, "Well, my mom, Nellie Summers works somewhere in town, I think. I haven't seen her in years."

"Did you say, Nellie Summers?"

"Yes, ah, why?"

Smiling Winnie said, "She's my second cousin. You two stayed with us when you were three. I'm Winnie Parker," extending her hand.

Sarah laughed and said, "Oh, I don't remember, but I'm glad to see you again."

"Where are you staying?"

"I'm staying at the McFarland's Boarding House at Beacon Hill."

"Good for you. How 'bout you come for dinner Sunday?" she said writing the address on a yellowed envelope from her purse.

"Thank you, I will. Now let's find you that dress," Sarah said, steering Winnie toward the size 12 rack.

Sarah settled into a comfortable routine and looked forward to Sunday. Each evening as she walked home she proudly reviewed her life. After cooking some potato soup on her hot plate, she sat down on her daybed to eat and listen to the radio. A knock at the door surprised her. She was not expecting any one.

She asked, "Who is it?"

A familiar voice simply said, "Mom."

She left the chain lock on as she opened the door a crack "Mom? What are you doing here?"

"Can't a mother come visit her daughter and stay for a while?" Nellie asked pushing on the door.

Sarah opened it as she commented, "I haven't seen you in seven years. What brings you here now?"

"Oh, I got bored with nursing, so I got a job at the Shop Rite Supermarket down the street in their accounting department. I saw Winnie in the produce aisle the other day and she told me you moved into your own place. So, I decided we could save money and live together," she said edging her way into the room.

Sarah did not know what to say. "Oh," is all she could muster.

"Winnie and Russell invited us over Friday night for a party. You can get reacquainted with them, then." Nellie said surveying the layout. She eyed the hot plate sitting on the counter next to the Norge yellow refrigerator. She brazenly opened the icebox and commented, "I wonder how many of those ice tray contraptions will fit into this compartment?" Turning back to face Sarah she said, "This place will work just fine."

Sarah did not reveal she already had an invitation to Sunday dinner. Although Sarah was angry with her mom whom she barely knew for abandoning her, she was also curious to acquaint herself with her long-lost relatives. They settled in together.

"Mom, would you please wash up your dinner plate? It's been in the sink for two days," Sarah asked while Nellie sat at the kitchenette table, her head buried in a book.

Sarah sighed and noisily slammed the icebox door getting two metal ice cube trays out, hoping the noise would prompt a response. Nellie continued to ignore her. The next day Nellie brought home her paycheck and set it on the table.

"Oh, good Mom, you got paid. It's time to pay the rent. I need ten bucks."

Nellie unzipped her money belt to insert the check. She just stared at Sarah and said nothing, walked over to her cot in the corner and curled up in a fetal position to go to sleep.

Sarah knew the only way to pry any money from her mother's hands was to get it while she slept. After she was sure Nellie was fast asleep, she tiptoed over to her mother's purse lying under the bed and carried it into the hall communal bathroom. She did not even bother to turn on the light in the efficiency. The full moon shining in through the window made her theft easy. Lifting two fives from the purse's secret inside zipper compartment, Sarah saw the wad that remained. She was careful to re-position the purse in the exact position she found it. Nellie, none the wiser, continued to snore with her full money belt still snug around her waist.

Each morning as Sarah entered the Gilchrist Building at the Winter Street bakery entrance, her mouth watered as the aroma of the famous, freshly baked, almond macaroons drifted into her nostrils. She resisted the temptation to give in to the luxury. She had a goal to achieve that even two cents for a cookie would delay. Ashamed of her Rickets-damaged teeth, Sarah hid her face when she spoke. She squirreled away enough money to have her teeth removed and dentures made, all at the young age of eighteen.

Even with her improved smile, dates were not plentiful. Sarah did not seek a boyfriend because there was no money to buy clothes even with the ten percent employee discount and no private place to entertain suitors. Sarah felt certain Nellie's actions would embarrass her in front of company.

For fun and because it was free, Sarah and Nellie went to the Parkers' house to drink and dance. Partying and laughter with her cousins eased the poverty in Sarah's life. With coffee, sugar, milk, meats, cheese, and canned goods, all rationed during this time of World War II, it felt good to unwind with family, plus it did not require a lot of money or expensive clothes.

The Parkers' extended family stuck together and welcomed all who entered their abode. Russell Parker, the patriarch of the family, was a jovial man. He leaned his cane, straight back chair against the house as he sat on his front porch sipping on an American Brewery long-neck beer. He spied his neighbor George walk up the street from the bus stop. "Hey, George, come sit awhile," he said, reaching out a bottle to him.

George sat on the step and wiped his brow. "Don't mind if I do, Russ. Thanks. It's been a hell of a day with Foreman Peabody on my back pushing me to work faster. Like I have control of that dang shipyard. My fingers are so numb I can hardly hold this cold one," he said barely raising up.

Russ looked at George's sweat caked, tired face and remarked, "Ya know George, the best job I ever had was night watchman at Wesley. Why, one night making my rounds, I stumbled across six women all swimming naked as a j-bird in the pool. I hid behind the pillar, all googly-eyed and got so hot I had to take care of myself. Too bad they caught me drinking on the job or I'd still be drooling over those broads."

"Yup," said George. "I can just picture it. Well, thanks for the cold one, but I better go wash up before my ole lady starts hollering for me."

"Anytime, George, anytime," Russ said patting George's shoulder as he walked past Russ down the porch steps.

Cement covered the yards of the low-income Cambridge neighborhood where the Parkers lived. Home exteriors were made of wooden clapboard and the family rental units were crowded together. The paint, once a bright white, had long ago faded. Curb appeal was not a high priority during a war. What mattered was being safe. "Loose lips sink ships," was a familiar phrase. In fact, at dusk, the venetian blinds were ritualistically drawn to ensure German submarines could not see house lights which might direct them to the Boston Harbor where they would sink ships. People worked together as they shared the juicy red tomatoes, crunchy carrots, crisp lettuce, pungent smelling beets, and English peas from their Victory gardens; they patriotically supported the war effort by sacrificing their luxuries of sugar and coffee, and volunteered their time at the local USO to boost the morale of the troops that were home on leave. Many bought war bonds to help fund the cost of the war. Amid angst, people found ways to laugh and ease the tension.

Russ stepped outside to cool off, holding a beer in his hand. Once again George was coming home from another long day at the shipyard.

Russ raised his bottle and said, "Hey, George we're having a gas at the house tonight. Bring your dance stompers. You know the usual Friday night get together with a little whiskey, a few dirty jokes, and a lot of looking at the pretty women while we dance the night away." Climbing the steps to his own porch, George waved his arm toward his neighbor as he said, "Russ, I can't. My ole lady said I get too drunk, doll dizzy and forget to come home." Then George paused and turned toward his neighbor and said, "Ya know with all this partying, Winnie's going to snap your cap and you'll be sleeping in the street."

Russ raised his arm as if to push back the comment and said, "Naw, she knows I always come home to her." "Be careful, man. Sometime a husband may not fancy you pinching his wife's ass."

"Ha Ha, good one, George. As our Ducky shincracker, you'll be missed tonight."

George opened his screen door and hollered over,

"Maybe next time Russ, maybe next time."

As Russ reentered his shotgun-style apartment, he playfully grabbed his wife's arm, twirled her around and said, "Hey Winnie, you ready to cut a rug?"

Winifred laughed at him as they did the jitterbug to the sound of Benny Goodman playing his clarinet. As she pulled away she said, "Russ, I gotta finish frosting the cupcakes or our guests won't have anything to go with their watered-down liquor and coffee."

Russ teasingly said, "Aw, Winnie, it'll wait til the song's over, c'mere."

Sighing she let her apron fly as she kicked up her heels and giggled in delight, her lumbago in remission. Once the song ended she returned to the stove to stir her now boiling chocolate icing. It was such a rare treat to have chocolate that she did not want it to burn.

When Nellie and Sarah arrived, Russ gave them a welcoming bear hug. "Hey ladies, you ready for a good time tonight?"

Nellie muttered something unintelligible to herself, crossed her arms and then asked, "So who all is coming to this shindig?"

The gracious host replied, "I dunno, whoever's ready to have some fun, I guess."

Pointing to the new phonograph in the corner, Sarah asked, "When'd you get that?"

Winifred responded from the kitchen, "Sammy sent the money home, so we went to Gilchrist Basement Sale and bought it. We were going to come up and see you, but I had to get home to fix supper."

Intrigued, Sarah asked, "So didja get some new records?"

Russ beckoned Sarah over to the player as he said,

"Let me show ya. I got a pile of 78s: The Andrew Sisters singing "Shoo Shoo Baby," Bing Crosby singing "I Love You," and Perry Como singing "Long Ago." What d'ya wanna hear first?"

"I don't care. Surprise me, I like 'em all." Russ carefully placed the phonograph needle on the record as he announced, "It's gonna be a real killer-diller tonight."

The final partiers arrived, two fellow security guards from Wellesley College and two soldiers, Walter and Richard, on leave. As the soldiers placed their olive green envelope military caps on the side table next to the stairs, the Parker's two teenage daughters, Eleanor and Wanda appeared on the up-stairs landing with perfectly coiffed shoulder-length curls created by hours of sleeping on twisted hair held uncomfortably in place by bobby pins. The girls pranced down the steps swishing their identical knee-length, red cotton, gingham dresses. They thrust out their chests accentuating the dress's squared shoulders and their narrow waistlines. The two GIs whistled. Russ laughed, pleased the men found his eligible daughters desirable.

They danced the night away playing the tunes over and over until everyone tired of the selections. Then they turned on the Philco Tube console radio to listen to the news. A radio was a household necessity. Everyone had listened to FDR's Fireside Chat that past Monday. They heard Roosevelt say, "Yesterday, on June 4, 1944, Rome fell to American and Allied troops. The first of the Axis capitals is now in our hands. One up and two to go!" Optimistically, the whole nation felt that the war's end was in sight, so it lightened the mood at the party. High spirits in the wee hours of the morning signaled the end of the merrymaking. All the liquor bottles were empty, the shades were drawn, and stragglers lay crashed on the sofa adjacent to the dance floor (living room floor minus the rolled-up rug).

At the next Friday night get together, Winnie sat at the kitchen table shell-ing peas. Sarah came in and sat down to assist her. Winnie stared off into space.

"Winnie, what's wrong? Your lumbago bothering you or something?" she said, concerned.

Sighing Winnie answered, what Sarah already intuitively knew, but did not reveal, "No, I just got word that Andy's being shipped home early. He got ma-laria fever and a black widow bite. They say he's got shell shock. I don't know how bad he really is. A mamma worries about her kids no matter how old they get, but especially when they're off fighting in the war."

"Oh, dear. I hope he's okay. How can I help?" Sarah asked placing her hand on top of Winnie's. "Not only does he need to heal his body, but he'll be sad too. His girl went off and got married and he doesn't know. Can you maybe be sweet to him til he gets over it?" Winnie asked apprehensively.

"I'd be happy to do that for him and you. After all you've done for me and my mom, of course I will."

Wally, a fellow vet, with less injuries, escorted Andy home and helped him up the stairs straight to bed. Andy thrashed around in his bed for two days with high fevers and delusions, placing him smack dab back in the New Guinea jungle. Snatches of his war memories were heard throughout the house. He sweated profusely as his vibrating tremors shook the bed. He called out for the nonexistent Army Hospital nurse to cool his fevered brow and quench his parched throat. His family tiptoed around him, afraid that he'd think them the enemy. The family kept things low key for a couple of weeks until the malaria attack passed. Then the Friday night shindigs resumed.

Like many vets, Andy did not talk about his Army days. Relatives were instructed to be silent about the matter, thereby avoiding any stress the topic might invite.

Andrew, three years older than Sarah, had not seen her since she lived with them briefly as a small child. As was now typical, the next Friday night Sarah stopped by the Parkers' for entertainment rather than to return to her one burner hot plate and her mother's delusions. She was surprised to see Andy standing by the front door. His chalky complexion startled her. His flesh hung in loose rolls under his arms. His glassy eyes seemed to be focused in some faraway place. She did not know whether to hug him or offer her arm to support him to the couch. Fulfilling her promise to Winnie, she stuck by his side throughout the festivities of the evening.

As the final partygoers trickled out the door, Sarah and Andy continued to sit on the parlor sofa, adjusting to the absence of vibrating music and drunken guests.

Andy, uncomfortable in the silence, turned to Sarah and asked, "Hey, what's buzzin', cousin? Are you rationed?"

She kept her gaze to the floor as she answered, "No, Andy, I'm not. Since mom moved in with me, my life revolves around work at Gilchrist's and Friday nights here for fun. Listen, I just want to say that I'm really sorry Mary ran off and married Jack without a word to you." Sighing, Andy said, "I wish her the best, but I'm ready to move on. You wanna go to the picture show with me tomorrow night?"

"Sure, that'd be fun," she said, looking over at Winnie smiling, working at the kitchen table behind Andy.

Sarah, eager to get out of her small apartment and away from her mother, began to regularly spend time with Andy. She felt good about fulfilling her promise to Winnie. After one week of going out, Andy slid his hand into hers as they sat on the front stoop watching the neighbors stroll by in the warm summer heat. Her heart quickened. No longer was this an obligation to fulfill, but a desire to spend time with him. As she smiled, she turned to face him and they both let out a big contented sigh. Each night after work Sarah ate supper with the Parkers. When the news finished on the radio, Andy escorted her the four blocks home and passionately kissed her good night below her second-floor window. Nellie saw what was transpiring but said nothing -- good or bad about the blossoming relationship. In those days, to marry a third cousin was not unheard of, so no one thought anything unusual when Andy and Sarah announced their intention to get married. The wedding was planned for March of the following year. As newlyweds, they joined the household of Winnifred and Russ, Andy's three siblings, and his paternal Aunt Sadie. The Parker red brick row house had three dwellings attached on either side of it. Each unit had a front porch with white spindly waist-high wood posts. Inside the front door was the staircase to the three-equal sized upstairs bedrooms. The downstairs master bedroom was just off the parlor where the Friday night gatherings centered around the mahogany-mantled wood fireplace. The canary yellow kitchen was only large enough for a small round table. The back door led to the communal outdoor space with a patch of grass and a cement patio. Purple lilac wallpaper adorned the living room and staircase. The one bathroom with claw tub was upstairs at the end of the hall. Everyone living in the household shared the same war rations until the war's end. Three months after the nuptials the New England Confectionary Company in Cambridge which packaged Necco wafers hired Andy for a temporary nightshift job.

On Saturday, August 4, 1945, Sarah had to work, so Andy hiked the three miles to Fenway Park. The tolling bells at 193 Salem Street at Old North

Church rang out as Andy scurried by the church on his way to the Red Sox game. Even though his home team was in seventh place that season, he was an avid fan. He never forgot seeing Tom McBride tie a major league record that day with 6 RBIs in the 4th inning against the Washington Senators. It was worth it to spend his last buck and two bits to be part of the historical event. His lingering depression and anxiety briefly lifted as he rooted for the home team. He slowly sucked his Camel down to the filter trying to make it last on the walk home. Then he would bum more smokes from his brother.

On the first Friday in October, Andy walked home from the factory which took about fifty minutes if the traffic on Massachusetts Ave was not too heavy. Hurrying along in the coolness of the early dawn light, he puffed on his cigarette while intermittently chewing broken pieces of Necco wafers, factory rejects he cradled in wax paper in his left hand. As he entered the kitchen through the backdoor Eleanor and Wanda, munched on hen fruit and toast smothered in apple marmalade, careful not to touch Andy with their sticky fingers as they said, "Hi-de- Ho, Andy."

Sleepy Andy responded, "Hi-de-Ho, to you."

Eleanor picked up on his down mood and asked, "Brother, what's wrong? You look so sad."

Sighing, he said, "The factory laid me off this morning. Said there just wasn't enough work for the regulars let alone the temps. I don't know how I'm gonna tell Sarah. I've only been there six months."

Both sisters felt bad for him. Wanda said, "Maybe you'll find a better job. She must understand that you're doing the best you can. At least she still has her job at Gilchrist's for a few more weeks until she starts showing." He inhaled deeply as he said, "I hope you're right. We've saved for months to get our own place. I want her to be in it before the baby comes." Shooing his sisters with his outstretched hands he said, "Now you girls better hightail it to school before the attendance officer comes to look for you."

He tiptoed into the bedroom to gingerly wake Sarah, hoping to avoid triggering morning sickness. Kissing her lightly on the forehead he said, "Good morning, Duchess."

Sarah, yawned, stretched her arms and responded,

"Good morning, Duke. How come you're home so early?"

He ignored her question as he handed her the few chalky bits left of the Necco wafers he cradled in his hand.

"Here you go. I'm sorry I ate most on the walk home."

She set the remaining wafers on the bed frowning as she asked, "Andy, is everything all right?"

He paused. He cautiously sat on the bed to avoid spilling the crumbs on the floor and said, "Ah, not really. I got laid off this morning. They said all the temps had to go, to give enough work to the regulars. I'm sorry Sarah. I really tried to keep this job, but it's not my fault."

Drawing in her breath, Sarah sat up, quietly pondering their next step. Reaching out to grasp Andy's hand in hers she said, "I think we saved enough money to make it for a couple of months, so I'm sure you will find something before the baby comes in March. I'm so ready to be in our own place."

Letting go of his wife's hand, he stood up and said,

"Thanks, Sarah, for understanding. I'll start to look once I get some shut eye after you go to work. Do you want me to bring you some hen fruit on toast?" Nausea washed over her as she said, "I think I better wait a bit till this queasiness passes."

So, Andy dumped the leftover wafers in the trashcan beside the door.

Session Two

"Welcome back, Marion. How did you feel now having shared the start of your family history in our first session?"

"You know what, Dr. Weinstein? I feel a little lighter. The stories I shared with you last week I have been told my whole life. It is different when I tell them. It helps me see how it all fits together. It kind of gives me an insight into what my parents had to deal with. I have an urge to tell you more, so I can feel even better. I just don't like that I have to go for a whole week in-between."

"Marion, sometimes we need that pause in between to process what it all means. I'm ready when you are to tell me more."

"Okay, Dr. Weinstein, Chapter Two.

Alcohol Seals the Deal

GRETCHEN PARKER, NINETEEN inches long and just shy of five pounds, was born a year after the wedding. Her fine blonde hair reminded Sarah eerily of Pam's locks cascaded on the coffin pillow years earlier. Times were tough. Andy competed for jobs with all the other WWII returning soldiers. By now living in their own apartment, Sarah washed diapers by hand. Their malfunctioning, toxic-fume producing coal furnace was trouble enough, but the meager money they acquired, Andy spent when he met with his old Army buddies. Often their outings began with a few beers that mushroomed into an all-nighter. He staggered home with no remembrance of where he had been or what he had done with the money. Accusations of infidelity never surfaced, but where all the money went was a mystery to Sarah.

Winky, who served in the same unit as Andy, grabbed Andy by the shoulder and turned to his buddy with slurred speech, saliva drooling on his chin and asked, "Hey Andy, you buying another round? I'm fresh out of dough," turning his pockets inside out. "My ol' lady said I'd better leave her some grocery money or I'd be coming home to an empty house."

Even though Andy pilfered the rent money from the cookie jar, he hesitated to spend the last five bucks. But, as he released the Ben Franklin into the bartender's hand he said, "Nothing's too good for my buddies who kept me alive in them fox holes."

"You're damn right we did. No Jap or Kraut was going to break up our gang."

Winky, too drunk to stand up straight, said, "Hey, let's get this doll to snap our picture." The bleary-eyed smiling vets drew in close to capture the moment on film. Food scraps were evident on everyone's plate except Andy's. Only empty beer bottles graced his unused place setting.

As Sarah grew tired of the partying scene, she knew something had to be done about all these alcohol-related negative influences. Walking into the kitchen the morning after the picture taking, she opened the cookie jar to extract the saved rent money. The jar only held a few stale cookie crumbs.

Hands on her hips she marched into the bedroom where Andy was deeply snoring. She shook him awake.

"Where were you last night?"

Groggy he simply responded, "Out with my buddies."

Angrily she demanded, "Where's the money I had in the cookie jar saved to pay our rent?"

She stomped her foot and balled up her fists shaking them at him. "It's our rent money, Andy."

He averted his eyes downward and said, "I borrowed it, but I think I lost it."

She grabbed Andy by the arm and he looked up as she bent close. "Don't give me all this gobbledygook. You just grandstand to your buddies."

She righted herself. "Where are we going to get money now?"

Turning away he said, "Don't flip your wig. I'll borrow some from my brother."

She retorted, "But, we can't pay it back."

"I'll figure it out."

Hands back on her hips, her voice ever rising she announced, "Every time you go out with your buddies, you come home plastered and forgetful. I want us to move. Away from your drunken Army buddies."

Resigned, Andy, slunk out of bed into his overstuffed chair, lit up a Camel, and said "Sure, whatever you want, Sarah."

Fuel added to Sarah's rising fire at one of the Parker family gatherings and completely blew her over the edge. At a typical Friday night Parker house party, Sarah went into the bathroom to use the facilities. The lock was broken so she quickly tried to relieve herself. As she was pulling down her skirt and re-positioning her slip, Russell walked in without knocking, drunk as usual. With nauseating whiskey breath, he leaned over and grabbed Sarah's breast and breathed into her face. "If you ever want a little variety, let me know. You've really got a nice piece of ass that I bet Andy doesn't appreciate like I do."

She pushed him off her and left the bathroom without even washing her hands. She went downstairs to find Andy and told him, "I'm ready to go home, NOW."

Andy was not ready. He continued to drink two more beers and finish his game of Hearts at the kitchen table with his brother. Sarah, angrier than scared, stormed back upstairs to the room where Gretchen lay asleep on Wanda's bed, locked the door and laid beside her child.

When they finally went home, Sarah carried Gretchen to her junior bed and returned to the living room.

Andy observed her tears flowing freely as he puffed on his Camel and asked, "Duchess, what's wrong? Why are you crying?"

Sarah tearfully raised her voice while angrily pointing her finger at Andy and said, "Your dad, drunk out of his mind, grabbed my breast and told me he wanted to screw me. I pushed him away. I'm so hurt and angry. You were in the kitchen just laughing, drinking and playing cards. Something needs to be done about your dad. I'm not going to stand for it."

Andy sheepishly and quietly responded as he pulled her onto his lap, "You know Sarah, my dad means nothing by it. It's just 'whiskey talk'. He won't even remember it tomorrow. Just forget about it."

Tears streamed down her face. "I can't. Every time I close my eyes I can smell his whiskey and feel his fingers on my breasts. I get sick to my stomach. Please do something."

"It'll be okay. Just don't be alone with him again and it'll be all right," Andy said, hoping to reassure her.

"I doubt that'll work, but I'll try," she murmured.

Sarah's way to deal with it was to avoid the Parkers' parties as much as she could to avoid being cornered by Russell again. At first the family assumed since she became a mother she did not want to bring the baby out into all that partying scene.

Andy's brother Sam asked him as they played Gin Rummy at their parents' kitchen table, "Where's Sarah? We haven't seen her in weeks. She's not becoming weird like her mom Nellie is she, speaking to spirits and such?"

Andy, sighed and brushed it off with a hand gesture.

"Naw, nothing like that. She wants Gretchen to get to bed at a decent hour, that's all."

"We thought maybe now that she's a mom she thinks she's too highfalutin for the ol' gang."

Andy, defensive, tried to change the topic, "Sammy, are we going to play this game or not," he asked as he laid his winning hand down on the table.

Sarah had taught herself to not speak in a crude manner, to act like a lady, and to not laugh at dirty jokes. Did that put her in a higher social class? She did not think so.

Andy went to his parents' house usually by himself, a pattern set from then on throughout their marriage. As time went by, and without evidence to the contrary, the Parkers began to believe that Sarah inherited Nellie's ways of being – different, odd, unable to fit in, or have fun. Andy did not reveal the true reason she avoided them. The family felt sorry for Andy, but never asked Sarah directly why she stopped coming to the house.

Sarah felt Andy took the side of his family and did not stand up for her. Her trust in him eroded further. The matter was not brought up again until years later.

Andy, on the other hand, sitting at Winnie's kitchen table did think about it. Unknown to Sarah, he tried to discuss it with his mother when they were alone.

"Ma, do you ever wonder about Pop cheating on you?" he gingerly asked as they shared a cup of joe at the kitchen table while the rest of the family listened to the Philco in the living room.

Winnie set down her coffee cup and looked her son in the eye. "Andy, your dad has always worked hard to care for you kids. If he drinks or flirts a little too much, I always remind myself that he comes home to me. Now if you got something to say, say it."

"Naw, Ma you're right," Andy said as he got up and rinsed his cup in the sink.

He knew that his mom's real reason to not want to broach the subject was the fear of what would she do if she found out the truth she already knew in her heart. Where could a single mom with two girls still at home and no job skills get hired in the 1940s? If a factory hired her, it would be considered unpatriotic give a job to a woman instead of a deserving WWII vet. Denial was easier. Andy did not tell Sarah of his conversation because he knew she'd call him a coward for not confronting his father directly. Unconsciously, Andy just mulled it over, eager for a simple resolution, not connecting the heartburn he felt whenever he went to his parents' house alone, to the angst he felt about the situation.

Baby Gretchen captured her parent's full attention, rarely leaving time for any passion between them.

When Gretchen was four, she often played ball with her neighbor friends outside the apartment on Clifford Street while Sarah prepared supper inside listening to the children's activities. Although the view was obstructed by the porch columns, she could visualize their play by the sounds she heard. One, cloudy, early evening, Gretchen's friend Veronica, invited Gretchen outside to play ball. As Sarah washed dishes in the kitchen sink, she suddenly heard a squeal of tires and the children's screams. She ran into the street, dishwater still dripping from her wet hands, horrified to see Gretchen pinned under the wheel of a 1950 midnight blue Ford truck with wooden slats whose load of tires ejected upon impact, bounced and rolled down the sidewalk. The unsuspecting four-year-old had slipped into the street to retrieve the ball her playmates had not dared to fetch.

Sarah nearly fainted as her unconscious daughter lay helpless under the truck's wheel. The driver, shaken to the core, hopped out of the truck with the stalled engine. A neighbor, Mr. Adams, reading the evening newspaper on his porch, witnessed the whole event. He ran into the street. Veronica and the other children scattered quickly to their homes believing their playmate was dead. Mr. Adams organized the men gathering around the scene.

"Come on men, we can lift it off her. You, in the gray shirt, take the left side. You in the plaid shirt take the right side. All the rest of you gawkers get over here!"

As if unfrozen, they all took a piece of the truck while Sarah lay on the ground stroking her daughter's brow, while gut wrenching tears shook her body. The twenty men managed to lift the front end enough to have a policeman gingerly pull Gretchen out from under and place her in the blanket Mrs. Adams grabbed off her sofa. It seemed to take an eternity for the ambulance to arrive. The Adams informed Andy when he returned from job hunting.

He ran the 2.2 miles from Clifford Street to the Boston's Children's Hospital.

The surgery on her hip to place a pin, and then weeks in traction, fatigued Gretchen. Typically, Andy and Sarah were not encouraged by hospital staff to visit often as kids were to learn to be tough. Scared and alone, Gretchen felt abandoned and the separation took a toll on everyone. One long month in the hospital was worth the hardship to save her life, but poor Gretchen thereafter always had jaw and pelvic difficulties, which prevented her from ever being able to carry a child. The night before they could bring their precious daughter home, Sarah sobbed as they lay in the dark talking to each other. In a rare move, Sarah allowed Andy to cradle her in his arms. They found comfort in one another.

Exiting the elevator on the fifth floor of the Children's Hospital the next morning, Andy, delighted to take his baby girl home said to the nurses, "Where's my Greta? I'll bet she's ready to leave this joint."

As Andy appeared in the doorway, Gretchen lit up, "Daddy, you finally came. I thought you were never coming back."

"Not on your life, you're my favorite little Missy Muffet. You ready t' go home?"

She looked around the room and into the hallway, "Where's mommy? She's coming too, isn't she?"

He covered for his wife. "Oh, not to worry. Mommy's probably down the hall signing the forms to get you out of here. I'll go look for her. Get your sweater and hairbrush. I'll be right back."

As Andy went into the hall, he saw Sarah walking toward him, her lips tightly clenched. Frowning, he braced himself for whatever was about to be said.

She said loud enough for the whole nurses' station to hear, "I don't know why they have to treat me so badly.

It's not my fault that the truck hit her. It's not my fault that you're out of work again and we can't pay the bill."

Andy, responding to the nurses' frozen stares quipped, "Hey, did ya hear the joke about the priest, the monkey, and the rabbi? They were all in a rowboat…." Embarrassed by his actions, Sarah walked off to Gretchen's room and matter-of-factly said to her young and infirm daughter, "Get your shoes on so we can get out of here before your dad embarrasses us anymore."

She tried, but winced in pain, so Andy, re-entering the hospital room said, "Come on Missy Muffet, Daddy'll help you."

Andy carried Gretchen out of the hospital all the way to the bus stop fearful that she would fall and re-injure herself. Sarah, hung back, uncomfortable, resentful, her own emotional needs unmet. She could not get past the memories that she suffered and survived, so her daughter would have to learn to survive also. To bring her soup and crackers on the couch was fine, but to hug her was not.

During the long recovery at home, Gretchen became reluctant and fearful. She stopped going outside to play. Her friends stopped by to say hi, but no amount of coaxing could get her to venture outdoors. Drawing figurines on butcher paper left over from the meat market kept her occupied.

"Mom, can I have a drink of milk please?" Gretchen asked propped up by pillows on the couch.

Sarah harshly said, "No, cause your dad didn't make enough money last week and won't bring home his paycheck from his job at the Rubber Company till tomorrow. Go get some water from the bathroom sink, if you're thirsty.

Gretchen said, "Okay." It took her fifteen painful minutes to work up the courage to delicately lift herself off the sofa and dash as fast as she could to the toilet so not to wet her pants. Sarah just continued to sit at the kitchen table, her back turned, listening to the radio.

The hospital could have released Gretchen sooner if Andy and Sarah had the money to pay the bill. Andy had been out of work during her hospitalization and only hired on at the Cambridge Rubber Company which began three days after Gretchen's discharge. The couple signed an agreement for the truck driver's insurance company to pay the hospital directly.

Six months after Gretchen's discharge, the insurance company paid the hospital bill. The remainder of the settlement money was placed in the bank to fund a fresh start.

Eight and a half months after Gretchen's hospital release, the three enjoyed a family outing. The sound of patent leather shoes grinding the loose sand into the cracks in the sidewalk could be heard across the cemetery as five-year-old Gretchen Parker loudly pleaded with her parents Andy and Sarah, "Swing me, swing me."

Sarah, thirty-eight weeks pregnant, waddled behind her daughter and husband all the way from the bus stop to the grassy knoll where a bench awaited her swollen feet.

"Gretchen, mommy can't. Daddy will have to do it," she said as she plunked down on the curved cement bench, out of breath. "This baby sure is active today." Andy put Gretchen on his shoulders and danced around with her as he gleefully sang, "Greta's going to have a new baby brother or sister in just a couple of weeks.

Won't that be grand?"

Sarah smiled as her belly moved in time with Andy's singing. "I think the baby likes your song," she said patting her hand over the foot she felt poking the wall of her abdomen. "We better get moving. Lots of graves to decorate on this Memorial Day before this baby decides to come out and join us." Slowly, painfully she rose to join them already one row of headstones over from her. "Wait up, you two. I can't go very fast."

"Mommy, here's a flag for you," Gretchen said handing it to her. "I already put one in Great Grandpa Parker's holder. How many dead people do we have to do this for? I don't like it here."

Andy put his hand on her shoulder. "We do this Greta to show that we are glad for the men who fought in the wars for us so we can be safe and free."

Gretchen turned around and asked, "Why are there wars, Mommy?"

Sarah looked over at Andy and smiled. "You can answer that one."

"Well, Gretchen it's like this," her daddy started with outstretched hands. "People both want something that the other one has, and they get so mad over it that they start to fight," motioning his hands like a tug of war. "And someone gets hurt."

Grabbing Andy's hand in hers, Gretchen responded,

"I hope you don't have to go to war again, Daddy." Looking off into space Andy responded, "Me too, Pumpkin, me too."

As Sarah leaned over to remove a dandelion from her husband's family plot she felt a sharp twinge in her abdomen and remarked, "Ow, that hurt. I guess I shouldn't bend over that way.

"You okay?" Andy asked with a furrowed brow, coming over to help her up.

"I think so, but maybe I better sit down for a bit.

You keep Gretchen occupied and I'll rest."

As she sunk into the dewy grass she felt the urge to pee, but cemeteries do not have public restrooms. She knew the bus station had one, just down the hill. She motioned over to Andy. "I gotta pee. Can you help me get down to the Greyhound Station, so I can use their bathroom?"

"Greta, come on. We're going down to the bus terminal. Daddy will buy you a Milky Way, if you're good."

Gretchen skipped across the grass, accident injuries still mending, eager to earn her reward. Painfully they made it down the hill to the toilet in time. Sarah, wiping herself, saw a tinge of blood on the toilet paper.

"*Uh oh. I know what that means. This baby is about to make its entrance.* Knowing she may have twenty-four hours or more until delivery, she casually mentioned it to Andy as they trudged back up the hill to finish their task before the next across town bus came in one hour.

"Sarah, are you going to make it?" he said, nervously wringing his hands. "I don't like being so far from the hospital. Do you want me to find a phone and call my brother to come get us?"

Knowing there was no money to pay for a hospital bill she told him, "Andy, don't worry about it. When my contractions start, I'll keep track of 'em and then we'll have plenty of time to get to the hospital. You got your watch, right?"

Anxiously, Andy unzipped his red light-weight jacket and pulled his pocket watch out of his shirt pocket. Even though the temperature was in the mid-sixties it was still damp in the cemetery. He opened the cover, and shook it to make certain it was ticking. "Ya, it's working."

"Good, because I think this bundle of joy is tired of being inside of me."

Sitting down at the top of the knoll, she felt some wetness in her underwear, *I guess I didn't wipe good enough when I peed. It's so hard to reach.*

Before she could grasp the enormity of what was happening, a gush of liquid poured out and drenched her skirt and the ground beneath her.

"Andy," she screeched as he was putting the last flag in the vase above his great uncle's headstone.

He knew by her tone that whatever came next was very urgent. He ran to the spot where Sarah had been, but she rolled above the knoll and laid with knees drawn into her chest, writhing in pain. The pungent odor of newly mown grass provided a brief distraction between the piercing labor pains that came so swiftly.

Leaning over her, Andy felt scared to breathe.

Frantically he asked, "What's wrong? What am I supposed to do?"

Sarah half smiled between contractions, "The baby's coming."

"**HERE? HOW?** I thought you said we had time to get to the hospital."

Gritting her teeth, she answered, "I thought we did."

Andy looked around for a person who could run for help. Unaware of the situation, Gretchen, in her blue wool sweater, played hopscotch on the sidewalk, ten feet away from her birthing mother. Andy started to shout, looking left and right, "Help, help. Anyone, come quick!"

Nearby, Mrs. Bartoni, an Italian Catholic widow, who was revisiting the grave of her recently deceased husband Alberto a few yards to the left of the Parkers' plot, looked up.

She heard the call for help and came running over.

"What's wrong? I heard you calling for help." Looking down at Sarah she knew the answer to the question. "When are you due dear?"

Between panting breaths Sarah said, "In a week."

This angel midwife did not wait to be introduced.

She motioned to Andy, "Go get the tarp over there next to the little shovel. I'll need it."

Just then Gretchen appeared, perplexed. "What're you doing Mommy? Aren't we supposed to ride the bus soon?"

Back with the canvas sheet, Andy dropped it and steered Gretchen away from the scene. He announced,

"We'll be over by the mausoleum, if you need us. Do you want me to call somebody, ah whatever your name is?"

"My name's Bartoni, but there's no time for such pleasantries or getting help. I birthed six young'uns at home with the good help of the Virgin Mother. Now skedaddle. I'll call ya when I need ya."

Andy shielded Gretchen's eyes, pulling her away. Mrs. Bartoni placed the canvas sheet under Sarah's hips.

"What's your name, by the way?" the makeshift midwife asked.

"Sarah," she said. Her face reddened as she began to push.

"Sarah sweetie, your baby's crowning, keep pushing. Another push and the baby will plop into this shawl. That's it." The widow's multi-colored hand-knitted shawl caught the five and half pound baby girl as she emerged with one last hard push.

Marion Anne Parker chose to make her grand entrance beside the gray speckled granite headstone of her paternal great-grandfather Samuel Parker.

Andy came running back over, Gretchen in tow, when he saw his new baby cradled in Sarah's arms. Andy stammered, "Ah, Mrs. Bartoni. I can't afford to pay you anything."

"Child, don't worry about it. Just promise me that you'll get this precious bundle properly baptized and we'll call it even, okay?"

"Um, sure thing. We can do that. Thank you so much. Where should I return your afghan?" he asked as it swaddled tiny Marion.

"Just keep it as a gift."

"God bless you, Mrs. Bartoni and thanks again."

Pleased with herself, she gathered up her tarp now holding the afterbirth and walked, smiling, to her 1950 canary yellow Plymouth Coupe parked at the bottom of the hill. *Won't the caretaker be surprised to see this in the trash?*

Andy ran down the hill to the bus station to call his brother Sam with the news and to have him bring the car. Gretchen waited with Sarah and her new sister while Andy hurried to accomplish his task.

Gretchen asked, touching the crocheted swaddling cloth, "Mommy, what's her name?"

Sarah looked up from stroking her bundle of joy and remarked, "I think we'll call her Marion."

Gretchen said, "That's a nice name."

Andy returned to announce Sam was on his way. He sat down beside Sarah and his new daughter. Gretchen looked over at her dad and said, "Daddy, can you guess the baby's name? I know what it is."

Andy took hold of his newborn daughter and peeked into the shawl and said, "Let's see, is her name Pumpkin?"

Gretchen laughed, "No, Daddy. Her name is Marion."

"Oh," said Andy, "What a nice name."

Gretchen returned to her hopscotch game licking the Milky Way moustache off her face, tired of waiting on her uncle. As she played within eyesight of her parents, Sarah remarked, "You know Andy, I'm so surprised."

"You mean about this darling baby girl coming now?" he said smiling.

"No, that a Catholic helped us. I was always taught they couldn't associate with us, cause we were not in their faith."

"Hmm. I guess whoever taught us that did not know everything," Andy said. "I'm so glad she was here and knew what to do."

"Me, too," said Sarah, "Me too."

Session Three

"Hello, Marion. What insights have you gained from our last session?" Dr. Weinstein asked as Marion comfortably sat back in the leather swivel chair.

"It's strange," she said cocking her head to one side, lifting her finger. "You're right. Acting as the narrator gives me such freedom to tell my family history from my perspective. I can see how the events of my parents' lives shaped how they raised me. I bet they did not know they had other choices available to them, just as I did not know."

Dr. Weinstein nodded and waited for Marion to begin Chapter Three.

Geographical Cure
Number One

"Hey, Sarah. Guess what?" Andy said as he opened the door to their tiny duplex apartment, face red from the cold brisk walk from the Rubber Plant.

"Hi, Andy. What's up?" she asked, chasing seventeen-month-old Marion down the hall to change her wet diaper while Gretchen sat staring out the front window watching other kids play.

"My sister Eleanor called from Wisconsin when I stopped at Mom and Dad's on my way home. She says they're hiring in a few months at Seroogys candy company in De Pere. She thinks I can get on there."

Smiling as she grabbed the squirming toddler, Sarah said, "Oh, Andy that'd be great, to get out of the big city to lush green grass and no neighbors' radios blasting the Mass on Saturday evenings."

"Both my sisters are coming home for Thanksgiving next week. Will you go to my parents' house, just this once please?" he asked with outstretched hands.

"I guess, if you keep your father away from me." "Sarah, I will, I will!" He picked up Gretchen suddenly full of smiles and swung her around to celebrate.

"Andy, stop that," said Sarah as she pointed her finger at Andy. "You know she's still fragile."

Gingerly he put her down on the sofa noticing her face returning to submission and went to wash up for supper. Andy internally smiled counting the days until whole family would gather.

Stuffed after the turkey, dressing and cranberry sauce, the Parker family lingered around the dining room table. Sarah took sleepy Marion to Russell and Winfred's master bedroom to have a nap. With her baby secured by the row of pillows, Sarah tiptoed out, back to the festivities, certain that Marion was safe. She had no forewarning of the danger that lurked for her innocent daughter. Forty-five minutes later, Grandpa, too drunk to continue shuffling the Pinochle deck of cards, left the table and retreated to the bedroom to sleep it off. Awaking next to her grandpa, Marion playfully crawled up on his chest as he masturbated with his left hand. Russell took advantage of the available oral cavity and thrust Marion's head down on his penis and promptly ejaculated into her gagging mouth. He promptly fell asleep. Marion toddled out to the kitchen, the family oblivious. Why did no one notice the smell on her breath? Signs of trauma followed in the months after Thanksgiving. Marion panicked whenever her head was held down. It was odd to the family, but no one knew about the unknown incident. Even Grandpa Russell, in a blackout, recalled nothing of his incestuous act. Luckily for Marion, Grandpa had no time alone with her to inflict more harm because Sarah resumed her avoidance of the in-laws up to the day they moved in July.

Eager for the transition, Sarah scoured the library for information about their future home. She learned all that she could from the World Book encyclopedia that her sister-in-laws had not told her when they came for Thanksgiving.

Lodge, Wisconsin was 1200 miles away from Boston. This former Native American settlement's main street, fashioned from faded, smoothed, red cobblestones and bordering dirt side streets with worn grassy walkways, drew tourists to the annual free ox roast held each July. The festival commemorated their Indian roots. The two-lane 750-foot cement bridge, high over the East River, yoked the East and West ends of town. Due to lack of public transportation, the population of Lodge, officially a De Pere suburb, still hovers around 7000.

Andy's two sisters, Eleanor seventeen, and Wanda eighteen, settled there a year earlier with their new husbands Walter and Richard. The couples' first date was at the USO club. Soldiers were stationed in Boston and they often attended the Parkers' shindigs. The brothers-in-law, lifelong friends, enlisted in the Army after graduation from Lodge High School. Upon discharge, the Seroogy's Confectionary plant hired them where Andy planned to also work.

Marion, her tender ears impacted, let out a high-pitched squeal as the cabin pressure in the airplane equalized. Gretchen vomited into a waxed bag as the plane ascended on the family's first ride on a turbo-propeller airplane together. As anticipated, the breathtaking view from the air painted a drastic contrast to the crowded city of Boston.

Approaching the Green Bay airport, tugging on Sarah's elbow, Gretchen pointed out the window. "Mommy, look at all the green down there. I don't see any cement like back home in Boston."

"No, Greta. It's not a big city. There're farms and lots of grass to play on. You're going to like it. You'll see."

Andy cradled sleeping Marion in his arms afraid to move for fear she would scream again.

Andy's sister, Eleanor, met them at the airport and housed them for a couple of months in her small Lodge bungalow while Andy and Sarah house hunted. The GI bill allowed for zero down payment and low interest on new construction homes in the 1950's. The Parkers bought a brand new two-bedroom white cinder block house with green wood trim just a mile from Eleanor's.

"Duchess, you ready?" Andy asked hoisting ninety-five-pound Sarah over his shoulder across the threshold of their new home while Gretchen and Marion giggled.

Sarah laughed. "Duke, put me down before the neighbors see my underpants."

Inhaling the living room fresh maroon, swirled paint job, Sarah said, "I think our move west is going to be good."

Andy squeezed her arm, mutually proud of their accomplishment of the American Dream: two children, a white picket fence, and new house. He was hired in July as a temp at Seroogy's Confectionary plant to prepare for the Halloween and Christmas rush.

As Sarah sat at the breakfast built-in nook the beginning of November she studied their savings account passbook balance. *What had gobbled up all their savings?*

Frazzled she jumped when she heard the screen door open to the house. Looking up at Andy she said, "Any luck hunting for a job today?"

He plunked down in the overstuffed chair staring at the floor. Then looking up at his anxious wife he said,

"Sarah, I just don't get it. I work hard, if anyone will give me a chance. I don't lay out sick. I don't even take a smoke break, but will they give me chance? No. They say:

'Mr. Parker where'd you graduate from?' My family had to eat, school got me nothing. You'd think being in the Army was good enough."

"Maybe Seroogy's will hire you back to make the Easter candy after the new year," Sarah said handing Andy a glass of tart lemonade minus the sugar.

"Sure," Andy said, puckering his lips at the sourness, "when all the working guys can afford to buy their family a new car, but not me," he said turning his head toward the wall after handing back the empty glass.

As the days turned into weeks of unemployment Sarah tossed and turned at night worrying how she would feed her girls while Andy fitfully slept. Andy dreamed of getting a steady job with no possibility of a layoff.

One blistery cold, winter day when the "new start fund" was depleted and the cupboards were bare, Andy hitchhiked into Green Bay to try to find some day work and come home with at least something to feed his hungry family. It reminded him of begging Baker Goldstein for day old bread. Trudging with nearly frozen feet in his thin-soled oxfords, his head bent against the wind, Andy pulled his Army peacoat collar up toward his ears. He could barely feel his fingers. Six miles from home, his head throbbed from hunger. Heading west on the edge of Highway 32 Andy heard a car ease up behind him. He turned around surprised to see the red flashing lights of a police vehicle. He stopped and waited.

The officer stepped out of the patrol car and Andy nodded toward the authority figure. "Mister, you mind stepping into the squad car for a minute?"

Eager to feel the warmth of the car's heater Andy responded, "Sure."

Officer Jeff opened the back door and Andy slid in not caring that the space lacked an exit handle.

"You got any ID on you fella?"

Pulling out his wallet, his military ID fell on the floor. He picked it up and handed it to the officer. The deputy studied it carefully and handed it back comparing the picture to the man in his car.

Smiling, Mr. Jeff let out a frosty exhale. "Mr. Parker. I thought you were a fugitive. There's this guy that fits your description on the loose from a bank robbery this afternoon. You gave me quite a scare. I thought you were him!"

"No, sir. I was hitchhiking to try to get some day work to feed my family. No one wants to hire me and now I don't have anything to bring home to my wife and kids.

You'd think a guy who served in the Army would get more respect, but no sir. Nobody's hiring," he said shaking his head.

"Tell you what, Mr. Parker. Let's stop here at Oakley's Farm Market and get you at least a sack of taters to bring home. Will that work for ya?"

"Man, that'd be great, but I ain't got no money for that," he said turning his pockets inside out.

"No worries, man. I got this."

Perplexed, the family peered out of the sheer, white starched curtains as the police car eased into the driveway and assumed the neighbors did the same.

The kind officer drove Andy home. Sarah did not know until the children were fast asleep what happened. The neighbors may have gossiped about the situation, but if they did, neither Gretchen nor Marion ever heard a word. Both Sarah and Andy were too ashamed of their circumstances to discuss it with anyone.

The neighborhood of a burgeoning baby boom generation where the Parker family lived, was the epitome of the times. New babies in blue plaid patterned carriages with collapsible hoods and metal frames paraded up and down the street by moms wearing their angora sweaters, a clip across the neckline. Pre-baby boomer generation boys hung out, swaying to the sounds of the Rock and Roll King, Elvis Presley. Seemed every male wore duck tail haircuts and sported two-toned brown and white saddle shoes with Bobby socks.

One day four-year-old Marion played in the baseball field next to her house; adults tucked away in their homes. Kevin, her sixteen-year-old back door neighbor, came up on her while she picked dandelions and asked,

"Hey little girl, do you want me to swing you around?"

"Sure," she said.

He swung her by the head. The breeze felt good as she circled around, but then her neck began to ache. "Stop. It hurts!" she cried. "Stop!"

He did one last twirl and flung her hurling to the ground. She landed six feet away from him.

"Ow," Marion said rubbing her knee.

"Aw, don't be a baby. You know you liked it," Kevin said laughing, standing over her.

Another day he coerced Marion to slide down a wooden board he fashioned leaning against the white wooden fence. Although, warped by the weather, it still worked fine the first two times.

The third trip down she stopped midway.

"Ouch!" she said, looking down at the rusty nail embedded in her labia. She grabbed her crotch and began to holler.

"Hey Red, come on into the shed. I've got something to show you, so you'll forget all that bellyaching."

She sucked in her breath, hopped off the board, sniffing with her hurt. Naively, she painfully entered the dilapidated old shed. She just knew Kevin would remove the nail. As she crossed the threshold, he balled up his left fist and punched her in the genital area. She raced home, crying uncontrollably.

Opening the wooden screen front door, she bounded into the kitchen screeching, "OUCH! Mommy, look what he did to me. Get it out of me now!"

"Who, Marion? I don't see anyone," said Sarah looking out the kitchen window adjacent the baseball field.

Turning back to her sobbing daughter, Sarah said, "What am I going to do with you? You're always getting hurt, creating more work for me. How did you manage this?"

Marion just made loud blubbering noises holding herself instead of responding. Marion did not know Kevin's name at that point. Tending to her physical hurt, they took her to Doctor Morgan's office. Marion sat nestled between her two parents on the front seat and smiled. She thought, *I like having mommy and daddy all to myself. I'm glad Gretchen had to stay with the neighbors. Maybe mommy and daddy will take me for ice cream after the doctor gets this hurting thing out of me*!

Sarah and Andy silently stared ahead, each lost in thought about how to pay for the unbudgeted office visit.

Grinning wide, Marion looked up at Sarah and asked, "Can we stop for ice cream, Mommy?"

Sarah, instead of answering, grit her teeth and questioned her downcast daughter, "Who did you say told you to slide down that board?"

Marion folded her arms onto her chest, "I told you.

The neighbor boy who lives behind us, Mommy."

Sternly, Sarah said to her, "We're not always going to be around to fight your battles for you, Marion! Nobody's going to help you. You need to learn to stand up for yourself or stay away from such people."

Dejectedly, four-year-old Marion sucked the pain and a flood of disappointment. She whispered to herself, "Nobody's ever going to help me."

That night Marion woke up around midnight. No one was moving about. The moon shone brightly in through her bedroom window. She turned to look at the moon illuminating her room. As she did, a face appeared, peering in through the glass. It was an angry man about fifty years old. He had a scowl on his face and he pointed at Marion. She tried to scream but nothing came out of her mouth. She hid under her covers praying that her full bladder would not leak before dawn. Upon rising six hours later, she slid out from her side rails of her junior bed and scampered into her parents' bedroom hollering.

"Mommy, Daddy, wake up! A man is bothering me!"

Sarah slowly opened one eye then the other, looking up at her trembling daughter. "Marion, you probably just had a nightmare. Go back to bed. No one is bothering you." Sarah rolled back over.

Andy roused, asked, "What's the matter, Pumpkin?"

"Daddy, some man is trying to get me through the window," she answered sobbing clutching her arms around her middle.

Andy got up and followed her into her room. By now the dawn light peered in through the window.

Looking in the closet and under her bed he said tucking the covers around his frightened daughter's chin, "The bad man is gone now. Go to sleep. If he comes again, call me and I'll come in."

"Daddy, I have to go to the bathroom, but I'm scared. Will you take me?"

Sarah did not allow Andy to see the girls without clothes, so he closed his eyes as he pulled back her covers and she dashed to the bathroom. He stood with the bathroom door cracked as Marion emptied her bladder.

Once the crisis ended, Andy crawled back in bed. Sarah chided him, "You know, if you give in to her craziness it will get worse. She needs to learn to get over these imaginary things or she'll be labeled off her rocker, like my mom. You don't want that, do you?"

Caught between keeping peace with his wife and comforting his daughter, Andy prayed there would be no further issues needing resolution.

The Seroogy's Confectionary Plant hired him back periodically for the various candy-related holidays. In between he collected unemployment or worked other temporary jobs. The family scrimped to have enough money to purchase a used white 1950 two-door Ford Custom Deluxe Coupe. The brakes had to be pumped to get them to work, but it was better than to walk in the bitter cold of winter. The Plant had a Christmas party for the workers' children, each youngster received a gift.

Christmas morning Marion woke up before dawn. Her feet barely touched the cold tile bedroom floor as she climbed out of her bed and quickly bounded over to her sister's bed. "Gretchen, wake up. It's Christmas. Let's go out to the living room and see what Santa brought us." Rubbing her eyes, Gretchen yawned and asked,

"What time is it?"

Marion could not read a clock and did not waste time reminding her sister of that fact. Donning her pink chenille bathrobe and fuzzy Mickey Mouse slippers Marion tiptoed like a cat into the living room exclaiming with a loud shriek, "Oh, my! Look at all the stuff under the tree.

Gretchen come quick."

Candy canes and oranges fell out of her stocking as Marion turned it upside down. A ring toss game and a box of unopened modeling clay soon to be fashioned into the shape of some animal lay close by. So many toys and gifts to enjoy. Andy and Sarah soon joined in the gaiety, laughing. Andy made up a new song. "This is our best Christmas ever." The girls chimed in "And we want it to last forever."

Each family member anxiously held their breath, savoring this unusual stroke of good luck. Silently, they individually expected the good times to leave as quickly as they came, the well-established pattern of doing without they knew only too well. Maybe, hopefully, like the shimmering tinsel on tree, a brighter future could take root. Hopes were dashed by the end of April when Andy was laid off again.

One Saturday evening in late summer as Sarah placed the palm of her left hand on the top of Marion's head, gently pushing it over the edge of the porcelain claw tub to prepare to wash her hair, Marion panicked.

Anxiety raised to the hilt, Marion screamed, "Stop it! You're drowning me."

Impatient, Sarah chastised her, "What's wrong with you? I'm only washing your hair. You are NOT drowning."

As she forced her head away from her mother's grasp she cried hysterically saying, "Mommy please don't wash my hair. I'm scared and my tummy hurts. I feel like I'm going to throw up."

Without compassion, Sarah, ever the task master told her, "Fine wash your own hair, but get it done. I don't want anyone to think I have dirty children." As Sarah marched out of the tiny bathroom, her feet stomped loudly across the living room tile floor, and Marion, only five, attempted to wash her own hair as best she could. A few suds left here and there was better than the panic of someone holding her head down. Marion did not know why she reacted that way, when Sarah dunked her head under the faucet, but she avoided that scenario at all costs. Sarah later found a plastic halo that that fit over Marion's head below her hairline above her eyes on her forehead to keep the water out of her face so she could allow her mom to shampoo her hair without panic.

Gretchen shared stories of how much fun kindergarten would be for Marion to distract her from the gloomy air in the home and lessen Marion's evident anxiety. The five-year-old could hardly wait to begin the afternoon sessions. Two weeks into the school year Marion complained her stomach hurt. As Gretchen departed to walk the four blocks to school, Marion shuffled into her parents' bedroom, arms laced over her abdomen and announced, "Mommy, my tummy hurts. I think I'm gonna throw up."

Sarah sighed to reach the moon, "Marion, you tell me that every morning. You can't be sick every day. If you are really sick, go back to bed."

Marion went into their only bathroom to retrieve the dented metal vomit pan kept under the claw tub. She placed a little bit of water in the bottom so the throw up would not stick to the sides as she walked across the floor careful not to spill the contents of the pan. She climbed back into her bed. As she lay on top of her sheets with waves of nausea rising and falling she wondered why Sarah did not come to check on her. As the heaving started, she knew to put her head over the edge of the bed to puke into the pan and not mess up her only set of sheets. Mom only did laundry on Saturdays. It was a day long procedure with the wringer washer water lines attached to the farm house kitchen sink. If she threw up on her sheets on Monday, mom would be mad.

After she emptied the contents of her stomach - the hotdog and peas from last night's supper, she called out,

"Mom, can you please come empty the pan? I'm still sick."

It took a while for Sarah to come into the room. "Marion, what am I going to do with you?" she said, exasperated, hands on her hips.

Marion apologized. "Mom, I'm sorry. I'm sick," she said with chalky pallor. "I can't help it."

Sarah stared straight ahead, back arched, arm stiff as she patted Marion on the head, "You'll be okay, it's probably just your nerves. When you go to school tomorrow, you'll feel better."

She stayed in bed until Gretchen came home. A cup of water minus a few sips sat beside the multi-colored rag rug on her floor. She had been too nauseated to ingest much of the liquid.

Gretchen entered the bedroom and sneered, "What's wrong with you? You're always sick. You're no fun to play with. Mom and Dad don't have the money to take you to a doctor, so you better get over this and go to school."

Fatigued, guilt-ridden, and scared, Marion felt all of her five years. She just knew that she caused her illness and had better stop it. But she did not know how.

When Andy returned from job hunting, he came into the house and asked, "Where's Marion?" Sarah just pointed to the bedroom.

Cheerfully he entered her room, sat down on the edge of her bed and asked her, "So how's my Pumpkin doing?

Marion sat up in bed, tears streamed down her face.

"Daddy, my tummy still hurts and my throat too." Reassuring, he said, patting her on the top of her head, "If you're not better by tomorrow, we'll take you to Dr. Morgan and he'll make you all better, okay?"

Trusting he was right she said, "Okay, Daddy."

Marion could hear her parents hushed argument across the hall in the master bedroom.

"Why did you tell her that? You know we don't have money for a doctor. She just doesn't want to go to school. If she goes, she'll be all right. No one took care of me when I was sick growing up. She just needs to suck it up, get up and move on."

He took up for his ailing daughter when he said,

"Sarah, I'll find the money to take her to the doctors. I think she's really sick."

"Well, Mr. Big Shot, where you gonna get the money to pay the house note that's due? Doctors are a luxury we can't afford," she said poking her finger into his chest.

Silently, Andy walked out to the backyard breaking up big clods of dirt with the hoe as he tried to think how he could take care of his sick daughter and get a job, so they did not lose their house.

Gretchen sat drawing at the built-in breakfast nook blocking out the argument and subsequent silence between her parents. To do something was better than to be in the bedroom where the stale vomit odor still hung in the air.

Andy borrowed money from his sister Eleanor, who, because she could not stand to see her niece sick, said, "I don't care if you can't pay it back. Just take her to Dr. Morgan."

Dr. Morgan, stumped, referred her to a child psychiatrist who diagnosed Marion with separation anxiety.

"If she gets more love, she'll be fine."

Andy and Sarah just looked at one another when he said that, confused. Sarah had no such role-modeling to know how to carry out that suggestion. Both Andy and Sarah sat silent on the ride home pondering the "how" to do as suggested. They did not even know what separation anxiety meant and were too afraid to ask. Andy was too afraid of Sarah's wrath to initiate any action or even suggest something.

While Marion soaked up some much-coveted time alone with her parents to and from the doctor visits, she did not feel satisfied. One day Sarah asked Marion a question while they rode home from the grocery store.

"What present would you like, Marion? (thinking that would show love to her daughter)."

Marion hesitated. Even at five, she remembered the conversations she overheard and felt guilty to express her desire but decided upon a doctor kit. She saw so many doctors, it seemed like the right gift to choose.

Andy and Sarah followed the doctor's orders as best they could, but Marion's stomach aches, sore throats, fevers, and fatigue persisted. The metal pan emptied by a silent, resentful Sarah many times over the next several weeks became a permanent fixture on Marion's bedside rug. Sarah ordered Marion to stay in bed, which she did, too fatigued to argue. No energy to gather any of her meager toys from the corner shelf in her room, she created her own entertainment.

"Hey, Fairy. I see you dancing in the sunlight on my rug," she said pointing at the wisp of movement.

"How come nobody else can see you?"

The response was straightforward, "Because you believe in us."

Marion smiled.

"Robbie, are you still here?" Marion asked looking around the room. "I haven't seen you in a while."

"My dear child, of course I'm here," said the three-foot blue silvery apparition standing next to her bed on the rag rug. "You haven't seen me much because you're going to school now," he said gently.

"Robbie, how come you don't go to school with me so we can play like we always do?" she asked, perplexed, laying on her side facing her window.

"Marion, your teacher would not want me to come to school with you. She and your friends can't see me, only you can. She wouldn't understand you talking to me. She'd think you were strange," said her constant companion since she was an infant.

Tears welling up, Marion reached out for him and asked, "So you're going away?"

"Sweetie, no, but you won't be able to see me anymore, but I'll still be around," Robbie reassured her. "After a while you will forget about me, but I'll come back from time to time as you grow up, but I'll look different.

It'll be okay, I promise."

"Who were you talking to, Marion? Just now? Was someone in your room?" Sarah asked, curious, peeking her head in the doorway as she exited the bathroom.

"Mommy, I was just talking to the fairies playing on my rug," she said, earnestly pointing to her rug and her friend Robbie. "He says he can't go to school with me."

"Now Marion you know all that is not true. You better not talk to anyone about that or they'll call you crazy like Grannie Nellie. Do you understand?" Sarah said with a harsh tone.

"But why Mommy? Does Grannie see fairies and Robbie too? Robbie says only I can see him."

"Okay, Marion. That's enough questions," she said, coming in and pulling back her bedcovers. "I think you can get up now. Come on in the living room and I'll let you watch a little television. Tomorrow you'll go back to school."

Robbie left, and she missed him, but eventually the memory of him faded. With no physical relief in many months, a local osteopath recommended Andy and Sarah take Marion to an ear nose and throat specialist since her throat appeared red and swollen. With fear and trepidation, the parents did so. Sarah was concerned about the cost and Andy more concerned about the diagnosis. The diagnosis was tonsillitis. Grannie Nellie loaned them the money for the $75 surgery, and knew she would not be repaid. Improperly diagnosed, Marion missed half of the school year, but still, she managed to pass kindergarten.

On the day of the celebratory end-of-the-schoolyear-picnic, she entered Wisconsin's Children's Hospital to have her tonsils and adenoids removed.

Marion was in a grumpy mood. She could only have liquids in preparation to have her tonsillectomy.

On the ride to the hospital Marion sat between her mom and dad in the front seat. Gretchen sat in the back reading a Nancy Drew book. Marion angrily pointed to the backseat, "Mommy, why does she have to get her tonsils out too? I thought it was gonna be just me."

Pulling Marion's hand down, Sarah said, "Now Marion don't start something. Your sister had hers out when she was your age, but your doctor looked in her throat and said they grew back so she has to have them out now, like you."

Marion was put on the children's ward in an oversized crib with safety rails that locked in place. The other six children in the room were excitedly talking about the gifts their parents were going to bring them after surgery. As Marion's parents kissed her on the forehead before they headed home, she hesitantly asked her daddy,

"Can I have a gift too, like all the other kids?"

Andy, not willing to disappoint his daughter, turned first to get Sarah's approval. Sarah shrugged her shoulders.

"Well, Missy Muffet. It depends on what gift you want."

"I want a camera, so I can take pictures, pleaseeeeeee?"

Kissing his daughter on the top of his head, Andy said, "Go to sleep now, Marion and Daddy will see what he can do about that."

Marion smiled and curled up in a fetal position under the starched sheet as her parents went across the hall to say good night to Gretchen.

Driving home from the hospital, Sarah remarked, nodding her head to the empty backseat, "Andy, it's so quiet without the girls. We better enjoy it before they come home throwing up with sore throats and grumpy moods." "I know

Sarah. I'm glad I don't start back at the Plant til next week, so I could be with you and the girls. How about we stop at the Blue Bird Café for some pie and coffee to celebrate our brief time alone before we go home?" he said with a wink.

The next morning the orderlies lined up the dozen children on stretchers in the hallway each awaiting their turn to be anesthetized. The ether given for sedation smelled horrible and created nightmares. Marion woke up back in the oversized crib with her dad standing over her. As soon as she opened her eyes, she threw up into the vomit pan Andy quickly put under her chin.

"How you feeling, Missy Muffet? Your throat hurt?" Andy said stroking her forehead.

All she could do was nod her head up and down with hot tears streaking her cheeks. Sarah was tending to Gretchen across the hall.

Daddy whispered to his beloved daughter, "I love you, Marion. I brought you what you wanted. Can you sit up?"

As Marion sat up, the room spun around like a merry-go-around, but she was determined to receive her gift. Andy handed her a little box. She looked at him with questioning eyes.

"Go ahead, open it. You'll see," he said.

He helped her shaking hands to open the lid. Inside was a miniature store display model camera in a camel color leather case. It housed a roll of film.

Marion hoarsely whispered, "Thank you, Daddy."

She laid back down and promptly went back to sleep. Film development was considered an unnecessary expense, so the film lay unexposed inside the camera. Since no company manufactured replacement film for these models, it thereafter sat on her toy shelf. So even though the camera did not function as requested, nonetheless it was a gift from her parents that was a solace for the traumatic hospital experience.

She and Gretchen came home on Marion's sixth birthday. Only allowed red popsicles and chicken broth to ease her stinging throat, it did not suffice for the desired luscious, birthday cake.

Marion finally felt better as the summer took over. Andy, with Sarah's permission of course, helped Marion learn to ride her two-wheeler without her training wheels.

"Daddy, watch me. I'm riding like a big girl," Marion proudly announced.

"That's my little Pumpkin. I knew you could do it. Now ride it on home. I'll run along beside you."

Sarah stopped planting her white, pink, and orange bachelor buttons in her flowerbed and looked up. She laughed, "Marion, you're doing a great job. Keep it up. Mommy's proud of you."

Andy swatted his wife on the backside in a love pat and then wheeled the bike toward the garage. Sarah smiled, her hips revealing the weight gain. Since there was enough food to go around, she did not have to falsely claim lack of hunger. That night for the first time in a year Sarah and Andy had sixteen-year-old neighbor, Linda babysit while they went to the drag races. The next Saturday before Andy left to pick up the babysitter, he kissed Sarah in front of the girls as he headed out the door. The girls giggled. Sarah and Andy went to watch the Harlem Globe Trotters play at the Green Bay Civic Center. In a rare family outing, they went to the Brown County Fair. Marion overheard her parents' discussion of limited funds, so she decided she would not eat to save money. Sarah, Andy, and Gretchen sat on stools to enjoy stacks of flapjacks smothered in melted butter and swimming in pure maple syrup. Sarah turned to Marion standing behind her, offered her a forkful and said, "Here, try a bite." She did enjoy a few more small morsels as the syrup dripped off her chin.

The proprietor, a large burly unshaven guy wearing a white tee shirt with a grimy white apron tied around his waist, came over to them, pointed his finger and yelled,

"No sharing of food. If she eats, you pay for it!"

Marion, shamed, stepped back and immediately spit out the contents in her mouth. She said, "It's okay, Mom. I'm not hungry anymore." For the remainder of the meal she hid behind Sarah, her face nestled close to her mom's shoulder-length hair. Like she had seen her mom do many times, she pretended to not be hungry.

Gretchen remained a very quiet girl, but she spent many hours over the course of that summer creating a fair in the backyard complete with a fish-pond, ring toss, and yummy oatmeal raisin cookies she made herself. For prizes, she raided Marion's bottom dresser drawer and took her cherished pristine possessions without permission.

Marion entered the shared bedroom to get her musketeer ears. Angrily and loudly Marion asked, grabbing her belongings off Gretchen's bed, "Gretchen, what are you doing taking my things? You have my camera, make up kit, and there's my paint set (pointing at the items) and play money from my bottom drawer." Holding onto to some of them, Gretchen said,

"You're not using them, so I'm going to use them for prizes for my fair. I'll give you some of the money if you help me."

"No!" reaching for the rest of her items, Marion said, "I'm putting my stuff back. Use your own stuff."

"Fine. I'll keep all the money for myself."

Yelling out to Sarah in the kitchen Marion hollered,

"Mom! Gretchen took my stuff without asking."

Sarah sat drooped, palm on her chin, elbow resting on the breakfast nook tabletop, but now snapped to attention. Hollering back two rooms away, she said, "You two stop fighting. I have to figure out what to fix for supper."

She called them to her. Marion came, clutching her prized possessions all except the camera that Gretchen hid behind her back. "Gretchen, give her back her camera. Marion will help with the games. You'll give her a portion of the profits. I'll decide the amount after the fair. Now go play and let me be."

Marion triumphantly whispered as she scampered back to her room to put the items safely back in her bottom drawer, "Told ya, ha ha."

Gretchen just flopped onto her bed and started drawing designs on a sketch pad and making a list of what she needed. Marion took her crayons out and began coloring in her Mickey Mouse coloring book. Gretchen probably made only a dollar for her efforts as she fashioned homemade prizes since her initial plan was foiled. Yet, a whole dollar could buy twenty fudgsicles or a hundred packs of penny chum gum. After she gave Marion ten cents of the proceeds, there was enough profit to make it worthwhile, and thus the fairs became a regular event.

When it was too cold to venture outside and while Andy and Sarah bickered as they did, Gretchen, inwardly drawn, sketched people free hand from family photographs or created ink drawings from memory of mom's multicolored roses.

Sarah turned from the kitchen sink and said,

"Gretchen, those are beautiful drawings. You'll go far with your art, but we need to put your supplies away now, so I can set the table for supper." Gretchen smiled as she packed up her sketch pad and colored pencils. Marion wanted her mom's praise. She felt ignored. Marion was jealous of the attention Gretchen got and with a five-and-a- half-year gap between their ages, they mostly bickered with each other.

The Seroogy's Confectionary Plant once again laid off workers in December after all the Christmas candy was distributed to stores.

Sarah, with hands on her hips, stood over Andy as he sat, shoulders slumped, eyes downcast the next morning.

"When are you going to get another job? Christmas will be here in a couple of weeks. How we gonna get the kids' presents? Huh, huh? (she nudged his shoulder). If you had stayed in high school, we wouldn't be in this mess."

Sulking in the overstuffed prickly, gray upholstered chair, first sighing, he then said looking up at her, "Sarah, what do you want me to do?"

"I want you to get and keep a job like other husbands. I want you to stop making jokes over serious situations," she said gesturing with open arms.

In his most earnest face he said, "Sarah, look at the good part. I am here to give you a break with the girls and to fix you my famous mustard omelet."

"That's what I mean. This is not funny. We don't even have enough eggs to make one omelet. I'm going for a walk. You watch the girls."

Andy, sullen and unable to think of a solution, got in the car, the gas gauge near empty and took the girls to Eleanor's. Aunt Eleanor fed the girls bologna and cheese sandwiches before they played with their cousins, oblivious to the magnitude of the dire straits.

During these unemployment times, Marion learned to not ask for things and to tip toe around when her mother was ranting. She noticed her mom pulled out the vomit pan a couple of evenings in a row and her tummy was bigger.

Andy's month-long temporary job with the town's garbage pickup ended Friday, January 31st. Sarah knew the scenario only too well and she had learned to be very frugal. She could pressure cook a poor cut of government supplied meat to make it almost palatable. She usually skipped meals during this time, but now Marion watched her father scoop an extra spoonful of mashed potatoes on Sarah's plate.

Sarah tried to put her hand out to refuse, but Andy said, "Come on you gotta eat. It's not just for you." She reluctantly forced herself to ingest the increased calories.

Marion just watched, but said nothing.

The next night, Andy, with no money or gasoline to go anywhere, made his mustard egg concoctions and fried potatoes for supper. He robbed Gretchen's piggy bank of some of the fair proceeds (she was saving up to buy more art supplies) to scrounge up 25 cents so Sarah could purchase a tube of lipstick or walk the mile to the picture show to give her time to herself.

The first of February Marion heard the announcement over the intercom, "Lodge Elementary School will have its annual Spring Talent Show on March 4th. Sign up in the lunch room."

Wow, I could do that. Hmm. Wonder what talent I have. Oh, yah. I've watched Pam practice her lessons twirling her baton and marching to the music. I bet I can do that. Then everybody will clap, and Mom and Dad will be so proud of me, she thought with a big grin on her face. Marion asked Pam if she could borrow her polished white boots with yellow floppy tassels. Marion didn't need a baton because she had her own as all girls did in 1958. Luckily, Pam and Marion wore the same size clothes, so the borrowed majorette costume of a red felt short skirt and white blouse with shiny pearl buttons fit perfectly. She chose *Stars and Stripes Forever* music for her made-up routine. Her first grade teacher, Mrs. Barclay, loaned her the record when Marion promised not to break or scratch it.

Nine months to the day after the girls' hospitalizations, Andy sat the girls down on the couch after school.

"Aunt Eleanor's coming to drive Mom to the hospital." "Huh, why is she sick, Daddy?" Marion asked wide-eyed.

"No, Missy Muffet. Mommy's going to have a baby and it's time to go to the hospital for her to have it." Andy said tenderly.

Gretchen already knew, but did not let on. Prearranged, Gretchen walked Marion down to Pam's house, whose mom greeted her at the door, smiling.

"Come on in, Marion. Pam is playing in her room." Andy returned later that evening to Pam's house, smiling. He stood in the entryway as Marion came running out.

He picked up six-and-a-half-year-old Marion and swung her around. "You have a brand-new baby sister named Rhonda."

Marion announced, "But Daddy, I wanted a baby brother, not another girl in the family."

Laughing, Andy responded, "It'll be okay, Marion. You'll see. Daddy's going back to the hospital, so be good now for Pam's family, okay?" He said kissing her on the top of her head.

"I miss Mommy. When is she coming home?"

"In a few days, don't worry. It won't be long. Bye now."

Marion returned to playing dolls with Pam.

The next day after the last class bell rang, Marion and the other performers practiced their routines in the gym. When it was time to take her turn on stage, she marched to her music and twirled her baton, threaded it around her legs, tossed it high into the air and made figure eights just like Pam. All the while Marion envisioned the audience, who were amazed at her natural talent to twirl. She did not need any lessons. The walk home alone after practice was not too scary for this almost seven-year-old. She could have asked one of the other kid's parents to give her a ride, but didn't, too embarrassed to have them see where she lived in the industrial section and to know her family had an old broken-down jalopy. Since she only lived four city blocks away from the school, she scurried home, not talking to any strangers along the way. Her parents warned her not to accept rides or even talk to people she did not know, so she avoided eye contact with anyone she met on the quick jaunt home. Yet Marion turned the lonely walk into an adventure. In her daydreams, she was invincible. People noticed her and discovered her likeability. Determined to be in the talent show to prove to the world she could and was worth being noticed, Marion felt her confidence rise. She felt the familiar, heartfelt desire to be noticed, to be the center.

Baby Rhonda arrived a week before the talent show, right during the final week of practice. Staying at Pam's house, Pam's mom, Mrs. Boomer asked, "Marion, Mr. Boomer will be coming home about the time you finish practice. Watch for him as you walk home, and he'll pick you up, okay?"

"Yes, Mrs. Boomer, I will." She had no intention of getting a ride from him, but would instead take the shortcut through the empty field so not to have to ride with Mr. Boomer who always felt creepy to her.

As was standard in the 1950's, Sarah remained in the hospital five days after Rhonda's birth. Sarah turned 32, the day she brought Rhonda home.

Marion played the scenario over and over in her head as she walked to the Boomers. "If mom comes to the talent show, she'll be so proud of me. If she doesn't, I don't know what I'll do. I just want mom to say I'm good at something like she does Gretchen with her art stuff. I'm going to do this no matter what! People will notice and tell me I did good; I just know it. Then mom will too."

When Marion got to the Boomers that afternoon Mrs. Boomer excitedly told her, "Your mom just called. She said you can come home now. I'll bring your clothes over later and meet your new sister."

Marion ran as fast as she could the three doors down to her house. She quietly opened the front door unsure what to expect. Sarah heard her and beckoned her into the master bedroom as mom cradled baby Rhonda in her arms dressed in a Japanese style kimono bed jacket. "So, what'd ya think of your new baby sister, Marion?" Sarah asked pulling back the flap of the baby blanket for Marion to get a good look.

"Why is she crying?" Marion said standing back. Matter-of-factly Sarah said, "You did that too. She'll stop when she goes to sleep."

Interrupting Sarah, "Mom, you remember my talent show's tomorrow night. You're coming, right?" she asked kneeling on the floor beside the bed.

Looking down at her begging daughter, Sarah paused, "I don't know Marion. It depends on Rhonda. If she's fussy, your dad may not be able to handle her."

Disappointed Marion hung her head and whispered, "Okay."

Marion already knew she was not going to like the baby, another competitor vying for her parents' attention. She backed out of the bedroom and donned her musketeer ears in time to watch Mickey Mouse Club on their 1956 GE blonde wooden 21" black and white floor model television with a rectangular screen.

The next night the Spring Talent Show curtain rose. Faking confidence, Marion stepped out onto the stage into the spotlight, her whole slight body trembling with anticipation. Mom sat in the second row, beaming from ear-to-ear. Marion overflowed with joy. Andy stayed home with Gretchen to watch new baby sister Rhonda which did not dissuade Marion's excitement. It was too cold and too soon to bring out the newborn around crowds. Anyway, this was Marion's night to shine and drink in her desired attention.

After all the performers took their final bow, Marion jumped off the stage and headed for her mom. Beaming with excitement, proudly displaying the majorette costume spinning around Marion asked, "Momma, did you see me? How'd I do?"

Sarah ignored her question as she gathered up the program and her purse. A hint of bitterness dripped in her voice as she said, staring off into space, "I wanted to be a ballerina when I grew up, but my mother said no. It's not fair that I couldn't do as I wanted."

Marion tugged on her mom's blouse with expectant eyes to force her back to the question at hand.

Sarah tilted her head back and forth as she said, "Oh, you, you did all right. Your steps were a bit off with the music, but be thankful you got to do it. I never got to."

Marion's heart fell heavy. *Mom tells Gretchen she does good at art. She hugs baby Rhonda and kisses her.*

She never hugs me or tells me I'm good at anything. I just want Mommy to say she's proud of me and that I'm special in some way too. She dejectedly sighed as they began the walk home in silence.

As they walked, their feet crunched on the hardpacked snow, breaking the silence. Sarah was unsteady, having given birth eight days earlier. Looking down at Marion, Sarah contemplated, *where does she get the confidence to perform in front of all those strangers? Not from me. That's for sure. I better not fill her head with high hopes or they'll get dashed just like mine did.* Sighing, she finished her thought. *After all, she should appreciate that I came. No one ever came to any of my school activities.*

Session Four

"Hello, Dr. Weinstein," Marion said extending her hand to shake his. Tears glistened in her eyes as a smile spread across her face.

Raising an eyebrow Dr. Weinstein asked, "So, I assume those are happy tears, right?"

"Yes," Marion answered. Before I met you, Dr. Weinstein I always thought I had to keep my secrets well-hidden, so they would not be used against me. I see now as I unfold my story, my stress so tightly wound is unraveling and my trust is building. Being the story teller helps me be objective and not take everything so personally. But I do wonder where I would be today had my parents not squelched my psychic gifts."

Dr. Weinstein nodded and said, "Well, you can't go back and change what has happened, but you can learn from the circumstances of your past and make better informed decisions from here on. Let's see what you learn from sharing Chapter Four."

Elementary Years

THE FAMILY SUFFERED once more through Andy's unemployment until a turn for the better finally came in 1959. The local paper factory hired Andy to work on the assembly line. He monitored a moving wire mesh screen that allowed the water to drain from the slurry (tree fibers that contained water and caustic chemicals) before it went to the press step in the process.

As "better times" flourished, the family moved from the two-bedroom cinderblock house into a white, wood framed two-story century old home with a gray painted slanting front porch, three bedrooms and one bath. This house was formerly a doctor's office.

Marion's bedroom floor shook when anyone climbed the varnished mahogany stairs to the second floor. The rubber runners did not soften the squeak as each step sounded out its age when a foot contacted it. Marion's bedroom above the living room had two windows symmetrically placed on the east side of the room. Her junior bed minus the bedrails straddled the windows. Each morning the rising sun swept across Marion's brow gently waking her. Marion's bedroom gray and pink linoleum with a metal strip down the middle did not provide any warmth in the drafty house. The walls, painted a pink bubble gum color looked much better than the dingy flower wallpaper that Sarah meticulously stripped while the older girls were in school. When Rhonda slept in her crib flush with the wall between the closet and the bedroom door, Marion felt less afraid of what lurked in the shadows of her room. Due to a sloped floor the cedar wardrobe, five and a half feet tall leaned against the north wall. It held winter coats, Andy's army uniform, an Indian blanket, and one more unusual item.

On the west side of the room was a door to a storage closet with shelves behind the door. As you entered the room on the right was an attic space absent of any electrical outlet to plug in a lamp to pierce the darkness. Sarah stored their few Christmas decorations on the shelves in cardboard boxes with see-through cellophane tops. On the floor across from the shelves a gray vinyl rectangle chest stored the winter hats, scarves and mittens wrapped in moth balls. The acrid odor of the moth balls overpowered anyone who raised the lid. The room was spooky and avoided by all the children.

Marion enjoyed watching Andy draw farm scenes at the dining room table in their new house with an artistic style that people said reminded them of Grandma Moses' paintings. Marion envied Gretchen's ability to create a circus out of modeling clay. Marion was art-challenged. She had ideas, but did not know how to develop them. One rainy spring afternoon Marion and Gretchen, bored playing Monopoly brainstormed some inventive ideas.

Sitting on the bottom landing of the steps to the second-floor, Marion verbalized her list of inventions she would design to make life easier. She was nine and Gretchen was fourteen. "I know what I would make," said Marion as she stared out the window.

"What silly invention would you create?" said Gretchen while mocking her sitting cross-legged in the middle of the living room floor.

"I'd make a way to carry the trash from the house to the barrel without having to go outside in the cold or rain.

I'd also make a box of Kleenex that would pop up the next one so you wouldn't have to use snotty fingers to pull up it up." "Ooh, yuck!" exclaimed Gretchen shaking her head. As she did she started fashioning her erector set like a crane.

"What'cha doing, Gretchen?" Marion asked bounding over from the landing.

"I'm not dreaming my invention. I'm making it now," she said smugly.

Captivated Marion sat down across from Gretchen and watched. "What's it 'posed to do?"

"Wait, watch, and you'll see. Got any bubble gum?" Gretchen asked, intent on her work.

Marion raced upstairs to her dresser before she changed her mind about sharing her stash. Hidden in the bottom drawer underneath her miniature camera were five bubble gum pieces still in their wrappers. She snatched them up clutching them in her hand. Once downstairs Gretchen had to pry them out of her palm.

Gretchen dumped shredded newspapers in the bottom of a cardboard box. She fastened string to her crane handle to hoist the apparatus. She buried the gum in the bottom of the box under the newspapers. Gretchen delighted Marion as she lowered the crane and retrieved the bubble gum picking it up with the bucket of the crane.

"Do it again, Gretchen! Do it again. Can I try it?" Marion asked reaching out for the crank handle.

Gretchen pushed her hand away. "No, you might break it."

Marion pouted but watched fascinated as her sister extracted another piece of gum from the bucket. They each unwrapped a piece of the stale gum and chewed it seeing who could blow the biggest bubble. The rainy afternoon ended with giggles.

Marion wanted a talent that her mom would favorably notice, something to set her apart from her dad and sister's artistic skills. Sarah often told Marion,

"Gretchen has the gift of art, not you Marion."

Feelings hurt, she refused to accept such declaration. She wanted to explore to see what she could do, so she wrote poetry. She penned this:

Day or night when I turn on a light
It casts a shadow and makes me fright
So, I run and run til I'm out of its sight.

At school, left-handed Marion experienced frustration in trying to use the only available scissors in her classroom, which were made for righthanded people. One day while she was trying to cut out mimeographed shapes to create a collage, she failed. The result was a crumpled mess. Feeling incapable of ever mastering scissors, she got the bright idea to see what the shears could cut.

Reaching down, she made a cut on her seatmate Holly's sock. It worked, but boy was Mrs. Peake mad. Marion was not allowed to use scissors for the rest of the school year, a heavy price to pay for exploration of her creative abilities. Marion learned thereafter to cut with her right hand.

Marion's clothes, Gretchen's hand-me-downs five years out of style, would be gifted to her each school year. Marion tried her best to wear them out so she could have new ones, but Sarah just patched the knees on her dungarees and chided her to be more careful.

Every Wednesday was Andy's payday. Gretchen's thirteenth birthday fell a Wednesday, sixteen days before Marion's birthday. Gretchen had the usual cake and ice cream and presents. Marion's birthday fell on a Friday, two days after payday. Marion asked for a new bike for her birthday since she had outgrown her old one. Gretchen asked for a new bike for her birthday. She got a red Schwinn beach cruiser with silver fenders, a chrome bell on the handlebars and a black wire basket on the back on her birthday. All excited, Marion dreamed what her own new bike would look like. She woke up before everyone, searching the garage, basement, and even the scary storage room for her anticipated new wheels. Finally, Sarah awoke as Marion excitedly stood over her.

"Mom, where is it? I can't find it," Marion said her voice loud and hands moving up and down.

"Find what, Marion?" Sarah said as she rubbed her eyes and sat up in bed.

"My new bike. For my birthday. That I asked for," Marion said as she stood erect waiting for Sarah's response.

"Oh, that," Sarah said as she rolled away from Marion. "Well, your dad doesn't get paid again until next Wednesday so we'll have your cake, ice cream, and presents then. We decided we will let you have Gretchen's old bike and you can decorate it or paint it whatever color you want," she said, not looking as Marion's face crumpled.

Tears welled up in Marion's eyes as she turned from her mom and dashed out to the garage to sob in a cobwebby corner. "I never get what I ask for. Gretchen always gets what she wants first. It's not fair," she said sitting Indian style with crossed arms.

Sarah shook Andy awake beside her and said, "Why didn't you tell her? The fact that you don't make enough money is the reason why she can't have a new bike, so it should be up to <u>you</u> to tell her!"

Andy sleepily answered, "Sarah, things are getting better. I'll make it up to her."

Stiffening, Sarah abruptly sat up, slid her feet into her fuzzy blue slippers and said as she walked out of the bedroom, "Well, I never had a bike growing up, so she'll have to learn you can't always get what you want."

Neither parent ever came to comfort Marion, as was the custom, leaving a lasting impression that she did not deserve to receive what she wanted or asked for, and that she was second best. Like Sarah's own experience growing up, Marion learned to depend only on herself, never to trust that anyone really cared about her. From then on, she did not reveal her wants to avoid further disappointment. Her lifelong motto became: "Expect nothing, regret nothing."

Marion began to spend more and more time alone talking to herself, swinging on the swing set imagining her life when she was old enough to leave home and do what she wanted to do.

During a commercial break while watching television as she sat on the couch Marion turned to her mother and said, "Mom, someday I'm gonna leave Lodge and never come back. I'm gonna go work for the FBI and figure out who killed people just like Perry Mason does."

"Now, Marion don't you get any highfalutin ideas," Sarah admonished shaking her finger at her daughter.

"You know that takes a lot of schooling to do that kinda work. You'll have ta' get a scholarship to afford college cause your dad doesn't make the kinda money that the Armstrongs do next door."

"I know, Mom. You tell me that all the time, and I'm studying hard."

Patting her daughter's head Sarah replied, "Good, 'cause I wanted to be a ballerina or go to college, but my mom said no. Why don't you go upstairs and get your pajamas on before the next show?"

"I can't, mom. It's too scary up there. Will you go with me, please?"

"I don't understand what you're so afraid of Marion. It's just an ol' creaky house," said Sarah attempting to discount her daughter's fears.

"Mom, there's someone in my wardrobe," Marion said with fear rising in her voice. "He stares at me when I'm trying to go to sleep. He has huge blue eyes and he's tall and he's wearing feathers like on that Indian pillow that was Grandma Parker's. He scares me. He tries to talk to me, but I tell him to go away."

Sarah anxiously looked at Marion and said, "Maybe you are just imagining this. Maybe you ate some food that made you have bad dreams or something. If you keep talking about this, people are going to think you are just like Grannie Nellie, weird and crazy."

Marion took it all in and from then on held her fears inside. Sarah stood halfway up the stairway as her psychic daughter quickly ran two steps at a time and retrieved her nightgown before Sarah retreated to the last step.

At this point, Sarah still denied her own "sixth sense," afraid she too would be labeled a mental case like her mom.

Only Marion could see the spirit of a very sad and scared seven-year-old boy who sat outside the storage room window on the slant of the roof by the chimney. She was too petrified to talk to him so she avoided going in the room even in the light of day when she and Gretchen would play hide 'n go seek. Gretchen knew if she hid in the storage room that Marion would not come look for her.

After many nights of quaking under her covers, Marion decided to be brave and figure out why a Native American chief spirit lived in the bedroom wardrobe. She spoke in her head without uttering a sound so that her parents wouldn't overhear and wonder to whom she was speaking.

"Why are you in my wardrobe?"

"To guide you."

"But I am only a child. Why do I need guiding?" "There are things I will help you do as you get older. Remember Robbie when you were little? Just like that time you will forget this conversation for many years. Just know I am always here."

"Robby was fun. I forgot about him, but you scare me. Please go away."

"I will now, but later you will understand and remember. Sleep now."

As foretold, she did forget until almost a decade later. Every night she hid under the covers afraid, if she was exposed, the spirits would take her away into their world. After this encounter, the family, unaware of Marion's "visit," discovered the doctor who previously owned the house had performed surgeries in what was now Marion's bedroom and more than likely some patients even died in that bedroom.

Marion learned it was not wise to share her "gift" or talent of seeing spirits with others who only made fun of her. Certainly, such a skill could not successfully be displayed in the school talent show.

Marion pondered her abilities as she tried to block them out and live a normal life. She was contemplating all this one evening when her dad made an announcement at the supper table.

"Well girls, I have a surprise for you," Andy said as they sat down for supper. Rhonda just two and a half, sat in her booster seat munching on carrots while Gretchen and Marion stared at their dad waiting for him to reveal what he had to say.

"Grandma and Grandpa Parker are coming for a visit. Aren't you excited?" Andy exclaimed as he began to dive into his mashed potato mound.

Gretchen asked, "How long can they stay? Will they sleep here? I guess I could share a bed with Marion, if I have too," she said frowning.

Marion's stomach felt funny. She had a choking feeling in her throat. She lost her appetite. She asked to be excused. She went to her safe place on her swing set and just got lost in the breeze as she pumped her foot to go higher and higher. Sarah and Andy did not ask the reason for her lost appetite. Marion would not have been able to give them an answer any way. It was the first-time Russell and Winifred came to visit after their son's move to Lodge, Wisconsin.

When they arrived the next week, Sarah did not hug Russell. She had her hands nestled deep in her apron pockets. She excused herself to prepare food in the kitchen. Winnie followed her. Grandpa Russell said to Marion, "Let's go out in the yard and play."

"Okay, Grandpa," she said while Andy and Gretchen set the dining room table for the meal. Rhonda was napping.

"You two have fun," Andy said.

The screen door slammed shut and they ran off the porch into the front yard. Grandpa started chasing Marion around in circles. Each time he caught her he would tickle her under her arms and on her stomach until she could wiggle her way out of his grasp. Out of breath, Marion could not escape fast enough. It felt like the same fun when Kevin first swung her around in the baseball field, but then, like the previous incident, it became uncomfortable.

In between gasps of laughing and catching her breath Marion yelled, "Grandpa, stop!" He did not.

"Stop Grandpa or I'll pee my pants."

He did not stop. Andy came out because he heard her pleading.

Authoritatively Andy said, standing on the porch's top step with hands on his hips, "Dad, stop. She's had enough."

Grandpa defensively replied as he let go of Marion's waist, "I was just playing with her."

"But Dad, she asked you to stop," Andy said walking towards Marion.

Russell silently went back in the house. Marion thankfully hugged her dad for rescuing her.

Sarah did not witness the rescue as she prepared the meal in the kitchen. It was a triumph for Andy to speak up to his dad in the moment and to protect his daughter. If he ever doubted it before, he knew now that the move to Wisconsin was the right decision. He thought it best to not share the details of the tickling with Sarah who already had an unsavory opinion of Russell.

A few days later, Gretchen, now fourteen, babysat the cousins at Aunt Eleanor's house while all the adults went out to a club. As usual, Grandpa Russell got drunk. When they came home, Grandpa, on the way to the bathroom, stumbled on the slippery, uneven hardwood floor and bumped into Gretchen, asleep on the rollaway bed in the hallway. He laid down on top of her, unzipped his trousers, and began to stroke his penis on her leg.

Frightened, she awoke as her Uncle Richard pulled Grandpa off her, and directed him to the bathroom.

Gretchen, traumatized, went out to the couch and curled up in a ball in a blanket until her mom and dad told her to get in the car. She wondered to herself, *why did Grandpa do that? I feel so yucky. How come Mom and Dad aren't saying anything? How come no one is asking me if I am okay?*

The silence on the mile ride home was deafening. Gretchen stared straight ahead replaying the scene over and over in her head. Rhonda lay asleep on Gretchen's lap and Marion was positioned in the opposite corner with a pillow cushioning her head. Sarah carried Rhonda to her crib once the car was in the driveway. Andy carried Marion to her bed. Gretchen slowly exited the car in a daze. She very quickly fell asleep hoping to awaken from the living nightmare. Safely in their own bedroom, Sarah cornered Andy by the closet as he hung his pants on the door hook. Sarah glared at him as she said, "I told you, your dad is a pervert. Now the family will talk about what he did to Gretchen. She'll get blamed, you'll see. I want to puke as I relive him, pawing me, wanting to screw me years ago. I'm glad they're going home tomorrow."

"Sarah," Andy said gently touching her arm. "I'm sorry my dad is such a dirty old man. I could have said something to him, but as usual he's so drunk he will not remember any of it tomorrow. I think it best we just forget it and when they go home tomorrow, we can put it all behind us, okay?"

Andy then surprised Sarah saying, "I'm so glad we moved here away from him."

She let out a sigh of relief as she said, "Me too."

Tension somewhat lessened in the Parker household when the grandparents returned to Massachusetts, but Marion's health was an on-going stressor. Throughout her young life ailments plagued her. In fifth grade, she came home from school each afternoon so fatigued that she did not even watch cartoons on television.

"Mom, can I lay down on your bed?" she asked cautiously.

Sarah touched her daughter's forehead. It did feel warm. "Marion, what is wrong with you? You can't be sick again. Your dad doesn't get paid til next week and Dr. Morgan won't see us without paying. Maybe it's just your nerves. Lie down and see how you feel at suppertime." "Okay, Mom," she answered wearily.

I don't know why I feel so weak. I really want some chocolate. I know Mom keeps her stash in the top dresser drawer, but if I took some she'd get really, really mad.

Sarah tiptoed back into the room to put away some laundry now that she could wash clothes any time with a regular washing machine hooked up on the back porch. She saw Marion resting peacefully with her eyes closed so she set the clothes down on the cedar chest and backed out slowly.

A year later when insurance kicked in, lab work revealed the cause of Marion's fatigue: anemia and magnesium deficiency. To this day as she still struggles to maintain proper nutrients, Marion rationalizes her chocolate habit as a nutritional necessity because it contains magnesium.

Although sick, she never missed a day of fifth grade. School was her place to escape from the spirits in her bedroom and her parents' constant bickering. Based on experience, she never knew if there would be enough money for food, clothing, birthdays, or Christmas. At school, such worries were forgotten.

Marion created an act for classmates to march to the song *The Ants go Marching One by One* for the annual Spring talent show. The teacher, Mrs. Smith was pleased, but two days before the performance was to take place, she made an executive decision. One student, Julie, a Native American with jet black straight hair, and an apple-shaped body and horned-rimmed glasses, a recent transfer to the school, would perform in Marion's place. Julie was often ridiculed due to a lack of everyday resources like pencils and paper. Kids teased her when she used her notebook paper as a Kleenex. The classmates singled her out because her skin had a different hue than theirs and she dressed poorly. No blacks were allowed in the town so Julie was the only ethically different person they ever met. Marion did not reveal that a Native American spirit lived in her wardrobe. No black people were allowed in Lodge after sundown so Julie was the obvious minority choice to harass. The teacher explained to Marion, of all the students, she could handle the shift. Mrs. Smith told her how proud she was of all Marion's efforts to prepare the act and then to allow Julie to assume her role. The praise eased Marion's disappointment just a bit.

Years later Julie told Marion how her kindness had made a big impression on her. In response Marion smiled, glad she had not taken out her anger on Julie about the switch. In hindsight, Marion wondered if Mrs. Smith, aware of

Marion's lack of musical ability, as well as her kindness, decided to offer Julie a chance to develop her budding vocal talent.

November of 1962 the family discussed purchasing a new Ford Fairlane. They unanimously voted in favor of it, but they had to tighten their belts to afford the $60 a month car payment. After all, the car note was almost as much as the $65 mortgage payment, and became a luxury easily afforded for only two months.

On January 13, 1963, at thirteen degrees above zero, Paper Products Company owner, John called Sarah because Andy had collapsed at work. Thought to be a "normal" attack of malaria, Marion, who was home from school at lunchtime, turned down his bedcovers and set out his pajamas. Normally, Gretchen arrived home from school around 4:00 p.m. Marion was surprised to see her when she came home from school at 3:15.

Looking in the bedroom and not seeing her father,

Marion asked, "Where's dad?"

Trying to relay the facts without inducing fear Gretchen said, "He's in the hospital."

Marion asked, "Is it his malaria? Will he be okay?" Gretchen simply answered, "They don't know yet.

Mom is with him and Rhonda is at the neighbor's house. I need to go get her."

Andy, only 42 years old, was in the hospital with a heart attack. How would the family ever manage was the question on Sarah and Andy's sisters' minds.

In the 1960's doctors treated heart attacks differently than today. Andy was ordered to stay in the hospital room bed. Children were not allowed to visit, the medical staff afraid disruption of the needed quiet would worsen his condition and that exposure to unwanted germs would make him sicker. Andy was hospitalized for six weeks. One night while Sarah and the girls were upstairs in Gretchen's room, they heard their dad's footsteps walking downstairs across the dining room floor. Excitedly, they all ran downstairs, but no one was there. Later they found out the time they heard his footsteps was the same exact moment he had a "spell" of arrhythmia in the hospital and they almost lost him.

To keep the house, the new car, and food in the children's stomachs, Sarah became creative. She borrowed money from Andy's life insurance policy and the Lodge Methodist church helped pay for some necessities. People invited them over for dinner, but strangely at every single house they were served pork n' beans. Was this supposed to be a sign of support or was it just inexpensive and plentiful? The family did not complain. They graciously received all gifts.

Sixth grade, the year of Andy's heart attack, had been an intense one for Marion. This boy, Jerry Rark, sat behind her in alphabetical order since first grade. He pinched her, teased her, and called her names like "Red" due to her red hair or "Shorty" due to her short stature. She finally had enough. All these years, she never tattled on him because she remembered what her mother told her at age four, "You have to fight your own battles."

This year, this time, Marion with a sly smile said,

"Jerry, you can go in front of me at the drinking fountain line."

Jerry cocked his head to the side and looked her dead in the eye. "I can? You're sure being nice today."

As he approached the faucet, she pushed his head down, intending to immerse it in water. Instead, his nose hit the faucet and blood gushed out. The teacher, Mrs. Angelo scolded Marion shaking her finger at her and said,

"Marion, I'm very disappointed in you for such behavior unbecoming a young lady. You're not allowed to get a drink from this fountain for the rest of the school year."

The class, in shock, just stared at Marion as she quietly retook her seat, stifling the sobs welling up in her chest. Luckily for Marion, Mrs. Angelo, did not call her already stressed out mom. Reminiscent of the scissors event in second grade, Marion helplessly complied, offering no explanation for her behavior and no one asked.

Maybe the drinking fountain fiasco bombed, but clever Marion learned to get what she wanted using words. In Mrs. Angelo's sixth grade class all the students went to camp over spring break. With her dad out of work and still in the hospital how could she convince her mom to let her go? The determined Marion believed in the adage, "if there's a will there's a way."

"Mom, do you know how much it costs to feed me for a week?" Marion asked her mother as Marion shoveled Spanish rice into her mouth while sitting at the dinner table.

Absentmindedly Sarah responded, "Yes, about five dollars, why?"

"Well, you know my whole school class (slight lie) is going to Green Springs Campground on their Spring Break trip," Marion said in a rush. "I know it costs $15 to go, but with me at camp it will save you some grocery money. I'll eat less when I return (using food to grease the plea was deliberate) and I am sure Lodge Methodist Church who gave us some money, would approve of me going and Dad would want me to go. Can I go? Huh? Please?"

Exhausted with no defense, Sarah agreed. Marion was triumphant harnessing the power of persuasive words to get what she wanted.

When Andy returned home, the whole routine was different than before. No more coffee and doughnuts for dad at breakfast. All meats were either pressure-cooked or broiled. Voices were hushed inside so not to create stress and another heart attack for Andy.

It was June, six months after his heart attack, before Andy was released to return to work. Praise went to Sarah, who creatively used her adaptation skills to make the money stretch during the long recuperation period. Andy returned to the plant working away from the strong chemicals believed to have induced his heart attack.

As soon as Andy was safely able to physically handle the work at the paper plant again, Sarah sought employment briefly at the local five and dime store. Unreliable babysitters and children showing up uninvited to the store impeded her ability to be a dependable and dedicated employee. A more practical solution was for Sarah to clean houses. She could drop Andy off at work, take Rhonda to a babysitter, and have the cleaning done at her own pace before the kids returned from school and Andy could ride home with a co-worker. Sarah's financial skills increased as she earned more money to manage.

Session Five

Marion entered the therapy office with her shoulders straight and her head held high.

"I really am getting so much out of telling my story. I wish I had done this years ago. From the last session I learned if teachers had the training and time to explore the meaning behind behavior problems in the classroom a bunch more kids would get help early. Then they would not have to have intensive therapy like me when they get older."

Dr. Weinstein nodded his head and simply said, "Yes, but many are not ready at a young age. They need time to be able to process it all. You are ready. Some people never are. I get the joy of watching you heal week by week just by opening the door to your pain. Ready to heal some more?"

Change is Coming

As Sarah contributed to the household income, she became even less tolerant of Andy's perceived carefree attitude. Before his hospitalization, Andy simultaneously held down three jobs: Paper company assembly line employee, repairman at the local appliance store, and house painter. The multiple jobs necessary to meet financial obligations led to lessened sleep, improper eating habits, no off time. All these combined probably contributed to his heart attack.

Andy still loved drawing those farm scenes at the dining room table and making wooden doll furniture pieces by hand at his workbench in the basement. It lowered his stress level, but there was no time for such frivolity with monetary woes. Sarah believed if there were bills to be paid, someone must create income to cover them. Artistic endeavors did not create income, so they must be abandoned. Andy did not have the stamina to work more than one job after his heart attack so the tension between the couple increased. Sarah criticized any handiwork he created.

Sarah leaned over Andy at his workbench breathing hot air on his neck. "Andy, why are you wasting your time making this ridiculous doll furniture? Why don't you go out and find a part time job so we can afford to pay your hospital bills?"

He interrupted his tedious task of gluing toothpicks together to make a dollhouse tabletop. Looking up at his irritated wife he said with sad eyes, "Sarah, I'm sorry. I'm doing the best I can, but I'm exhausted when I get off work and it's too late in the day to look for a part time job."

She said, "Humph," as she turned to ascend the stairs. Halfway up she muttered under her breath, "If you weren't a high school dropout, we would not be in this financial mess."

Andy silently slunk back upstairs to the bedroom. Sarah, exasperated, slammed cupboard doors and muttered loud enough for everyone to hear, "I don't know what I ever did to deserve such a poor life. If it wasn't for my girls, I wouldn't be here."

Anxious, devastated and depressed Andy put the covers over his head to drown out her bitching.

The smell of pressured cooked liver filled the air as Sarah called the family to supper the next night. Each one sat at their designated place not quibbling when the meat and instant mashed potatoes were rationed to each plate. Andy tried to break up the tension, "Guess what girls? There's strawberry ice milk for dessert tonight. Your dear ol' dad picked it up at the IGA on my way home."

Marion looked down at her liver on her plate and then up at her dad, and then her mom. "How many more bites until I can have dessert?" she asked expectantly.

"All of it," Sarah said looking sternly at her frail daughter. "You need it to build up your blood."

Sighing, "Okay. Since I have to, would you please pass the mayonnaise? If I smother it on these pieces, it won't taste so horrible."

After Gretchen silently swallowed the last forkful of liver she asked to be excused to go study for her English test. As soon as Gretchen left Andy started joking with Rhonda to get her to eat the five bites on her plate. Sarah frowned at Andy and said to Rhonda in a disapproving tone. "Rhonda, if you're not going to eat your supper you can go sit in the chair in the living room, but no ice cream and no T.V. If you get hungry later, you can come and finish it."

Sniffling, she left the table with Andy not far behind.

"And just where are you going, Mister?"

"I'm not in the mood for ice milk."

He sat in the living room with Rhonda until Marion finished her one scoop of strawberry ice milk and then he retreated to his workbench.

The girls were not permitted in his workbench area because Sarah feared they would suffer some sort of harm from a stray tool-or worse, see the bad example that Andy was setting by failing to meet his family's financial needs.

One evening weeks later after supper, Sarah reached across the kitchen table and snatched the newspaper out of Andy's hands. "What the hell are you doing buying a newspaper when the girls need new shoes?"

He defensively but very softly answered, "I'm looking for a part-time job so I can make the extra money you want to pay for the girls' shoes."

Her enraged voice escalated as she spat, "You always have money in your pocket for pie and coffee for your breaks and cigars, and what do I have? No money in my purse to even buy a stick of gum. I don't know what has happened to you. You just sit for hours staring at the television. You haven't even worked in the basement for weeks, which I hated anyway."

Carefully he chose his words, "I dunno, since my heart attack, I just don't have the energy to do those things or want to do 'em."

Wagging her finger at him Sarah angrily retorted, "Well, you better find a way, cause the bills gotta get paid. We got a daughter going off to college in less than two years, so figure it out."

Without another sound, Andy slumped over and slid onto the cold linoleum floor.

Sarah announced, "Just ignore your dad. He's only faking it to get attention."

Eventually, he came to, got up, and quietly retreated to the master bedroom. It was not common knowledge in the 1960s that heart attacks could bring on depression and fatigue. His collapse may have been due to possible heart arrhythmia or just the stress of everything.

His sullenness increased, his lack of desire to do anything with the family intensified, and every answer he gave seemed to take a huge amount of effort.

Angry and impatient Sarah stood, with hands on her hips, leaning over their bed, "Andy you can't go on like this. You must pull yourself together. If you can't do that, then you'd better go to the VA so they can help you, cause I can't stand it anymore."

Mustering up every ounce of energy Andy could, he tried to sit up and said, "Sarah, I can't shake this. I'm too exhausted."

So she asked him. "So, you'll call your VA rep and go in the hospital?"

With no fight left in him he said, "Ya sure."

Afraid of public embarrassment Sarah said, "We'll just tell people you're sick, 'cause we don't want people to think you're crazy."

Defeated, he answered, "Do whatever you want."

The VA rep gave Andy a pass to go to the Green Bay VA hospital. The facility was a multi-story brick building with wrought iron bars on the windows. The sixth floor housed the locked Behavioral Health Unit. People wore a badge that simply said "visitor" when they came to see loved ones. Morning and afternoon group therapy sessions centered on readjusting the soldier's thoughts so they could function back out in the world. A fifteen-minute session a week with the psychiatrist yielded nothing more than additional drugs or a patient discharge form. The longer a patient stayed, the higher the disability score which added to their monthly government check. The Vets spent waking hours lounging in the sunny dayroom that overlooked the city. They chain-smoked unfiltered Camels, and drank cup after cup of strong coffee in porcelain mugs clinking their spoons to dissolve the mound of sugar while absentmindedly playing Solitaire. The patients realistically believed medication was put into the coffee to make everyone behave appropriately.

No one informed Andy when he entered treatment that he had signed himself in and thus he could also sign himself out. He was under the false assumption that only Sarah or the psychiatrist had the power to say when he could leave.

A few weeks into his in-patient stay, the psychiatrist asked Andy, "Soldier, why are you here?"

Snapping to attention he replied, "Because my wife said I needed to be here sir, because I was depressed." "Soldier, do you think you need to be here now?"

Hesitantly he responded, "No sir."

Probing, the psychiatrist wanted to see if Andy knew how bad his depression was, so he asked, "Mr. Parker, when you came in three weeks ago, you were not sleeping well, not eating, and just stared off into space. Do you know the reason?"

He delayed his answer hoping to think of the right one. He finally responded. "I had a heart attack this last year and I don't have the energy I used to when I worked three jobs. My wife gets mad at me 'cause I do not make enough money. I want to, I try to, but I can't do it. I'm afraid I'm gonna have another heart attack and not be able to work at all. What'll my family do then?"

Looking him straight in the eye, Major Whitaker, the psychiatrist got up close and personal as he said, "Andy, I think your wife is putting too much pressure on you. You were depressed when you came here, but I don't see it now. You've had a lot happen to you: the shock from combat in the War, malaria, the black widow spider bite, and now a heart attack. I'm going to write a letter to get the government to up your service-connected disability.

Will that help?"

Andy almost saluted and with a wide grin, said, "Oh, yes sir, thank you sir."

"By the way Mr. Parker, did you know since you signed yourself in that you can also sign yourself out?"

Letting out a sigh of relief, he said, "No, sir. I didn't know."

"You only need to be here now if you think it is needed. It's not your wife's decision." "So, I can go home and go back to work?" Andy said standing up from his chair.

"Yes, whenever you are ready."

Skeptically he asked, "Now?"

"I'll fill out the paperwork for you to sign."

So, Andy signed himself out and was on a bus headed home within two hours. Ironically, he did not appear as depressed when he was away from Sarah's nagging. Andy was driven to get home and back to work no matter how he felt. He hoped Sarah would be glad to see him, appreciative of him returning to work to care for the family.

If Andy had stayed a few weeks longer, his disability VA benefits would have increased to 100 %, enough to meet their financial obligations which explained why Sarah was visibly upset when he walked through the door.

The responsibility of figuring out how to cover their expenses, she believed, was once again up to her. He wanted to tell her about the raise from 10 % to 50 % in his government disability check, but her tirade did not give him an opportunity do so. Andy, perplexed, expected her to be happy to see him. Since neither of them communicated clearly their thoughts or how they felt before or after his inpatient mental health stay, their marriage increasingly unraveled.

After Andy's return, the mounting parental tension affected Gretchen physically. One bleak winter day as she sat at her turquoise steel and chrome desk in her senior homeroom class in Lodge High School, she felt her heart racing. Gretchen anxiously raised her hand and said, "Mr. Turnbull may I please go to the school nurse? I don't feel well."

The ashen look on Gretchen's face prompted the teacher to send classmate Joyce with her. Gretchen leaned against the cement block wall with her right shoulder while Joyce supported her left side. Together they managed to navigate the fifty yards to the nurse's office, cattycorner from the front office housed between the janitor closet and the teacher's lounge. The smell of floral scented sawdust kept in the janitor's room next door to absorb vomit was overpowering, but she fought back the gag reflex. Nurse Snyder, fiftyish with her wiry gray hair knotted in a bun was matronly dressed in a simple brown pleated knee length skirt and a dusty blue turtle neck sweater absent of any jewelry or makeup. Mrs. Snyder looked up from her paperwork on her desk to see Gretchen painstakingly making her way toward her and rushed into the hall to guide her to the examining table. Cotton swabs and tongue depressors sat neatly in glass jars with chrome lids symmetrically lined up on her knotty pine wooden desk. The stethoscope hung on a hook above the porcelain round sink with separate hot and cold knobs and three overflow drain slots below the faucet. A rubber stopper attached to a metal chain lay on the sink's rim. Nurse Snyder calmly took Gretchen's pulse, but her furrowed brow revealed her concern. The mercury thermometer was wrist-shaken and placed back in the alcohol solution after Gretchen showed no temperature.

She let out a long breath as she asked, "Gretchen did anything happen to cause your heart rate to be so fast?" Breathlessly Gretchen spoke, feeling like her heart was going to explode in her chest. "No. It started in homeroom. I'm scared. What's wrong?"

Panic mounted as Nurse Snyder said, "I need for you to go to the hospital to get checked out. Your pulse is 160 and your blood pressure is 200 over 100. Something's wrong."

Anxiety rising, Gretchen said, "My dad's at work and can't leave. He has our only car. I'll have to wait until he gets off to go get it checked out."

With sternness in her voice Nurse Snyder placed her left hand on Gretchen's right shoulder and said, "Gretchen this can't wait. I'm going to call for an ambulance to come take you now."

Eyes widened as Gretchen's tears freely flowed while her hands and body shook uncontrollably. Patting her on the shoulder Mrs. Snyder said, "I'll call your mom and drive her in my car. (Feigning assurance) she said, "You'll be okay."

The students in classrooms on the Reynolds Street side heard the siren of the approaching ambulance; they wanted to see what all the commotion was about. The thoughts that ran through their heads were, *is someone dying? Is it a teacher or a student?*

As Principal Jones escorted the paramedics into the nurses' office he saw teachers and students peering into the hallways outside their classrooms. To control pandemonium, he walked back into front office, grabbed the microphone and announced over the PA system, "Go back into your classrooms. A student is only going to be checked out at the hospital."

It was not the kind of attention that Gretchen ever wanted or needed. She was admitted to Green Bay Hospital's cardiac unit, the same floor where Andy had recovered from his heart attack. Cardiologists suspected a heart malfunction, perhaps a genetic factor, but no cause was detected. While there, she confided in the social worker how stressful it was to be around her parents. She had no desire to return home.

The next morning as Sarah swept the thirty-year-old dingy yellow and brown zig zag patterned linoleum kitchen floor she was surprised to hear the black, rotary dial, table top phone ring in the dining room a few steps away. She was not expecting any calls. It was the hospital social worker.

"Mrs. Parker?"

With a quizzical expression on her face she said,

"Yes, this is she."

"This is Wanda Moyer, social worker from Green Bay Hospital. Do you have a minute to talk?"

Inhaling, with fear rising inside of her, Sarah braced her left palm against the upright Wurlitzer Spinet piano and said, "Yes, I do. What's this about?"

Ms. Moyer paused to carefully choose her words.

"Your daughter Gretchen and I had a talk. She knows I'm calling you."

Guardedly, Sarah asked, "What did Gretchen tell you?"

Authoritatively, speaking as the person who could decide where Gretchen would live, she said, "She revealed the tension between you and Mr. Parker and how the arguing is too stressful for her. I believe her blood pressure is affected by it. I have consulted with Children Protective Services….."

Defensively, Sarah interrupted, "Why did you do that? Gretchen is not abused or neglected. "I didn't say she was. We're just investigating this. After a consultation with CPS we think it would be wise to see if maybe a different environment could help lower her blood pressure. You do want her to be okay, don't you?" she asked, certain Sarah would comply.

"Of course, I do," inside Sarah's mind raced, *how come no one cared about my well-being when I grew up*?

Emphasizing a short duration Mrs. Moyer asked, "Is there someone she could stay with for a *while*, like a relative or a friend?"

Sarah thought out loud as she answered, "My mother lives too far from Gretchen's school to stay with her. I'll have to think about it. Can I call you back later today?"

"Yes, but we need to make arrangements today because Gretchen will be discharged tomorrow and if you cannot find her a suitable place, she will go into a CPS foster home."

Compliant, Sarah answered, "Okay, I'll work on it.

Good bye."

As she placed the phone back in the cradle she just sat motionless, her tears dropped on the notepad smearing the phone number Mrs. Moyer had given her to call back. The droplets were more from anger than sadness.

Sarah's temper flared as she slammed her fist down on the phonebook and cursed, "Damn Andy. This is his fault. If he provided better for the family, we wouldn't argue so much."

Not knowing with whom she could share the embarrassing details, Sarah just reflected on her own history. "I survived much worse than Gretchen ever has. She has no idea what real stress is. What if people find out she does not want to come home? What will they think of me?"

Contemplating her options, she decided the Methodist pastor could be trusted. He arranged for the youth group leader's family to take her in. Marion and Rhonda knew their sister was gone and they could not visit her, but no one explained why.

Life appeared to be a safe and secure environment in one moment and then, in the next moment, it evaporated, a pattern that was repeated from generation to generation. Sarah, living with her mom Nellie and dad Peter one minute, was whisked away in the night the next. Sarah living in one boarding home then moving to another with no notice, no time to collect thoughts, or even pack treasured belongings. Andy's hospitalizations first for the heart attack and then for the depression re-impressed upon Sarah and Marion how something can suddenly disappear or re-appear with no warning. Gretchen's subsequent departure left Marion confused, off balance, and feeling like she teetered on the edge of one day being sucked away too.

Two days later as Andy stood next to the mahogany drop leaf dining room table with the cream-colored plastic embossed tablecloth as he sorted the pile of mail when Sarah standing in the dining room doorway drying her hands on her apron launched into her tirade.

"This is your fault. If you were a better provider, she would still be here."

Andy, secretly grieving inside, deflected her hurtful remarks with humor. "I guess Gretchen got tired of dad's ol' mustard-egg concoctions."

Sarah just glared at him and walked away. Andy's only way to cope was to live in a state of denial, acting as if like nothing was out of the ordinary. He'd hide in the basement after supper until bedtime to once again make doll furniture unconcerned with whether Sarah liked it or not.

Late one afternoon before Andy got home from work Sarah told Marion, "I want you to watch Rhonda while I go outside to shovel the walk."

Marion, engrossed in her *Tom and Jerry* cartoon, absentmindedly responded, "Okay," as she turned back to her program.

Rhonda wandered into Sarah's room and began to experiment with mom's make-up. Sarah reentered the house shook off the snow and stomped her feet to get warm.

"Marion, where's Rhonda?"

"Ah, I don't know."

"You said you'd watch her."

Fear welled up in Marion as she jumped off the couch to go look for her sister. Horrified, she found Rhonda in her parent's bedroom, proudly modeling the shiny bright cherry red lipstick smeared across her lips and cheeks while the new tube lay broken on the dresser. "Oh, Lord Rhonda, what've you done? Momma's gonna kill me and send me away like Gretchen and then who will look after you?"

Out of earshot, Sarah shouted, "Have you found your sister yet?"

"Yes," Marion answered as she shuffled into the kitchen showing the broken tube of lipstick. "I'm sorry. I'll buy you a new one," hoping it did not cost too much to replace.

"I don't have time to worry about it right now. Go set the table for supper after you wash your hands and turn off the television."

"Yes, momma. Come on Rhonda. I don't want you out of my sight again or I'll get into more trouble."

As abruptly as she left, Gretchen returned home six weeks later as if nothing had happened. Her absence and return were not discussed. The unacknowledged "elephant in the room" was very baffling to Marion.

Marion climbed the stairs and cautiously stood at the threshold of Gretchen's bedroom. The room untouched and not entered in her six-week absence with colonial orange and brown print wallpaper and a rust colored area rug hugging the floor. An oval mirror with a silver etched border used to check appearance before departing the house hung on the wall adjacent the window that faced the side yard. Marion dreamed of the day when the room would be hers and she could be away from the spooky wardrobe in her own room. She said to Gretchen, "I'm glad you're home. I missed picking on you."

Gretchen, reticent to reveal the truth responded,

"Yeah, Marion, you always did like to tease me. Who'll you pick on when I'm gone, little Rhonda?" she asked folding clothes on her bed.

"No, she's too little. She cries too easy. Besides I'm more a mom to her than mom is."

"Well that may be true, but you gotta get out of here when you can."

Marion tilted her head in a questioning way as she asked, "Whatcha mean?"

Gretchen motioned Marion to sit in the chair inside the door. Then she revealed, "I really don't want to be here, but I gotta til I finish school in two months. I'm going away to college and I don't ever plan to come back. Mom and dad's arguing gets on my nerves and the sooner I get away from it the better." Additionally, Gretchen thought to herself, "*No one really cares about me anyway.*" Hearing that, Marion felt an overwhelming sadness.

She said, "Gretchen, will you write when you leave?"

"Maybe. It depends on how busy I am with college stuff."

Marion implored her big sister, "Can we not talk about this anymore right now, cause it's making me sad?"

"Okay, let's go watch *Bonanza*.

Once a week Gretchen left high school early and rode a bus into Green Bay, to see the social worker, Mrs. Wilson. Classically, there was no mention of this in the Parker household. Marion only found out about it a year later at the age of fourteen when her mother dragged her to the same social worker when she experienced daily headaches.

"So, I understand you have daily headaches, Marion."

Flippantly, Marion responded, "Yeah, so? I don't want to be here."

"Can you draw me a picture of your family?"

Matter-of-factly, "No, I'm not the artist, Gretchen is."

"Okay, you don't have to if you don't want to."

Seeking Mrs. Wilson's approval, Marion asked, "I could draw you stick figures, if you want, will that work?"

"Yes, great. Here are the colored pencils."

Mrs. Wilson commented on her artwork, "I see you like to draw with a lot of black colors."

Engaged in the process, Marion answered, "Yup. I do."

"What do you think is the cause of your headaches?"

Definitively Marion announced, "My parents arguing. You need to fix them or they need to get a divorce. There's nothing wrong with me."

Nodding Mrs. Wilson said, "Oh, I see. Well, if you want to come back and talk more about it, I'll be here for you."

Emphatically the defiant teenager said, "No, I don't want to."

"Okay, then you don't have to."

Tension in the Parker household continued to mount. By 1964 Andy's mother-in-law, Nellie, who had lived and worked in Wisconsin for about eight years, encouraged him to apply for a state job as she had done. He did and was hired on as a state highway clean-up crewmember picking up trash and road kill along the highway. It reminded him of his CCC work back in the 1930s. Now he had benefits and a regular salary, but even the financial reprieve did not heal the growing rift between he and Sarah. In fact, the gap between them widened after Gretchen graduated from high school. Together Andy and Sarah drove her to Monroe Conservative Christian College in Tennessee, but after dropping her off, they barely spoke on the route home.

One month after Gretchen left for college, Sarah decided she wanted to separate from Andy. She took the younger two girls to Nellie's one-bedroom apartment. Andy was distraught, thinking she must have found someone else. He called her repeatedly. After staying only two days Sarah dejectedly returned home with Marion and Rhonda. She had not thought through her departure plan. She had no money saved to afford an apartment or buy a second car. Depressed and defeated, it was obvious she didn't want to be in the marriage any more. She too applied for a state job and was hired to work in the driver's license processing department. She started to sleep in the upstairs guest bed.

No sooner did Sarah get the state job than Marion developed health issues. In the first few weeks of school her period arrived but was different this time. She had blood clots before but now also had excruciating pain. Even the paregoric drops did not abate the menstrual cramps. Her mom could not take time off from her new job so their neighbor, Marilyn, took

Marion to the gynecologist. In the mid-1960s, birth control pills were the new form of treatment for vaginal hemorrhaging. Four pills a day seems excessive now, but not so back then. The side effect was an immediate thirty-pound weight gain, weird food cravings, and a deepening of her voice. Classmates teased her saying she was pregnant due to her thickening belly. She did not know which was worse the side effects or the previous constant bleeding.

Prior to the medication intervention, she had a period that lasted six months. She could not participate in gym class due to the heavy blood flow which caused her to become anemia. She often berated herself, mistakenly believing she somehow caused the menstrual hemorrhaging. One day as she sat off in the corner of the gym she had this conversation with herself.

"I'm so embarrassed. I leaked through my sanitary napkin again onto my skirt. I know everyone is looking at me and knows I am bleeding. The smell is retched. I can't even do gym class calisthenics. I'm so weak. The blood clots keep coming. If I stayed home, how would I answer people's questions about what was wrong with me?"

Three months after the start of the medication intervention, muscle spasms daily plagued her along with high blood pressure and visual disturbances.

The gynecologist, Dr. Carson sat behind his large cherry wood desk with folded hands, and spoke in a very serious tone. "Marion, I am extremely concerned about these side effects. We must immediately discontinue the hormone therapy. At least your Menorrhagia has stopped." Sighing heavily, he added, "I had hoped that the pills would reset your cycles so that by the time you marry and have intercourse, your periods would be normal. Unfortunately, from the graphed temperature charts you kept, you do not ovulate. That means you most likely will not be able to conceive. Maybe your menstruation will normalize when you marry and have regular intercourse. I just don't know. I'm sorry," he said as he reached across the expanse of the desk and patted the back of her hand. The immensity of his words did not sink in her brain at that time.

Dr. Carson followed up the visit with a letter to Sarah to punctuate the seriousness of Marion's condition since Sarah was unable to attend the appointment. Sarah never told Marion about the letter.

Dear Mrs. Parker:

This is a note attesting to the necessity of continued observation concerning your daughter's (Marion) Hormonal Imbalance.

A careful study and appropriately indicated treatment are essential not only to prevent possible uterine hemorrhage, but also to assure the future integrity of her reproductive capacities.

Sincerely,

J. A. Carson, M.D.

The idea of Marion becoming a mom was the least of her worries at fourteen, but her classmates thought otherwise. Within ten days Marion lost the thirty pounds. Again, her classmates teased her.

Her biggest tormenter was Dale, a scrawny freckle faced red-haired adolescent with an IQ of a rock. His only skill was bullying. Loitering in the school hallway he taunted her as she walked past him. He jabbed his elbow into his crony John's rib before launching into his tirade. Dale said, "Marion, fess up. You were pregnant, weren't you? That's how come you got fat and lost it so quick, right? You can't hide the truth 'cause we know. We can tell. So, where's your baby? Who's the daddy?"

Hoping the Earth would open up and swallow her, Marion tried to walk away, cheeks flaming but the boys followed and relentlessly plummeted her with the same questions as they entered their homeroom class. Like every fourteen-year-old all she ever wanted was to be positively noticed and approved by people. For years she could not look at herself in the mirror without feeling the pain of those taunting flashbacks. As a result, she lost all interest in the one things most teenaged girls are obsessed with: their appearance. Marion no longer cared about wearing stylish clothes, or fixing her hair. There was no incentive to improve her appearance. A After losing the weight she took a day trip to Ashwabomay Lake with her church youth group to enjoy the sun and water. Lazily sprawled on her Beatles beach towel on top of the wet sand at the edge of the water Marion relaxed. The sun shone warmly on her back while she proudly wore her new brown and yellow polka-dotted swim suit with the white patent leather belt. Lucy spread her towel beside her and sat down to her left. Pointing at Marion's thighs Lucy asked, "What are all those ugly purple marks on your legs?"

Humiliated, Marion said nothing and tried to cover her legs only to have Julie, another youth group member basking in the sun on Marion's right asked, "Why is your stomach so fat?"

Feeling her body too hideous to look at she avoided future lake outings. Convinced she was homely and lacking the funds to do anything to improve her image, she just cloistered herself in her room and devoted her time to her studies.

Around this same time, classmate Patty pulled her aside and said, "You know with your buck teeth no man is ever going to want to marry you." They had been discussing their future dreams of a big church wedding with all the family in attendance, a beautiful gown, and a handsome groom.

Shocked, to be bluntly told how noticeable her protruding teeth were from years of thumb sucking, Marion was unable to respond. She wrote on a piece of paper what Patty had said and slid it under her bed. Sarah found it one day while mopping.

Interested, Sarah asked Marion, "What is this I found under your bed?"

Surprised her mom had not only found the note, but also read it and wanted to discuss it. Marion answered, "That's what Patty told me. Is it true?"

Sternly, Sarah replied, "You can't believe what other kids tell you. When you get out on your own, if you want, you can have your teeth straightened."

Marion looked questioningly at her mom and asked,

"How much does that cost? I want to do it before I ever get married."

"It costs a lot of money. When I had my dentures made I had to pay for it myself."

Persistent, Marion pushed her mother for more information. "Okay, mom, I know you told me that many times, but what do braces cost?"

"I don't know, but a lot, maybe $1000!

"Wow, I don't have that kind of money."

"Maybe you can save up your money. Let's not worry about that right now. It's time to wash up for supper.

We're having your favorite, sloppy joes."

It was one of the rare moments Sarah showed any smidgen of concern for Marion's feelings.

Marion smiled and said, "Great, I'll be there in a minute."

That conversation sparked something in Marion which set into motion the idea that maybe she could do some sort of work to obtain the things she wanted, instead of being locked into poverty. She distributed a flyer to the neighbors asking for work. Marilyn, her next-door neighbor paid her 10 cents to wash dishes, 15 cents per hour to babysit, and a $1 a week to clean her house. Not surprisingly, Marion, learned she could manage her own money, saving most of it, but occasionally splurged a quarter to go to the movies, and spent a nickel for a bag of popcorn. She felt better about herself when she had money to buy clothes to enhance her appearance.

Her first summer home from college Marion's sister Gretchen began proselytizing to anyone unfortunate enough to cross her path. At her conservative college, conformity to their rules was not only expected, but punished if not obeyed. Females could not date upper classmen unless a committee approved. Actual physical distance between couples was measured with a ruler. If less than six inches apart, the school-imposed restrictions on the suffering couple, barring all contact in person, by phone, or letter, for a period of six weeks. Feeling structure was missing in her early life Gretchen thrived on the false sense of safety and security the rules provided her. The college's administration convinced her that everyone in her family was going to Hell unless they personally invited Christ into their hearts. She had to save her family so they would not burn eternally.

One day in early June, Gretchen invited Marion into her bedroom.

"Hey Marion, c'mere a minute. I wanna to tell you about something."

Always eager to spend time with her older sister Marion asked, "What is it?"

"Sit down in the chair right there and I'll show you this book I want to read you. It's called *The Four Spiritual Laws.*"

The little booklet was the size of a postcard and looked like it might be interesting.

Gretchen pointed to the first page as she read, "Did you know that God loves you? All of us have fallen short of the things God wants us to do. That is why God sent Jesus to tell us he loves us and to save us so we can go to heaven when we die. You do want to Heaven don't you? (Not waiting for a response, from Marion, she continued.) "He wants us to be his children. To do that, we have to confess that we are sinners."

Gretchen told Marion those words came from the Bible in the third chapter of the book of John verse sixteen. Gretchen instructed her that she must believe that Jesus died for her sins and ask Him to forgive her sins to be saved. Dutifully, Marion recited the sinners' prayer. Because knowledge of the exact date of one's conversion is imperative in Baptist circles, Marion recorded June 8th, 1965 inside the booklet Gretchen handed her. She did not know until then what a sinner she was. Once salvation was secured, the next step was to get into a Bible-believing church and read the Bible daily. Gretchen and Marion left Lodge Methodist Church and literally walked across the street to the Independent Baptist Church. Baptism by immersion was the next requirement. Even though she had been sprinkled as an infant, it did not count in Baptist circles They believed a person must wait to make the decision when they reached the age of accountability, twelve or older. No one had given such structure to Marion before and like Gretchen, she thrived on it. Sarah felt guilty leaving the Methodists who had helped the family in their many times of need, but eventually she and Andy followed the path of their daughters. The Parker family continued to attend Lodge Baptist Church even after Gretchen returned to college.

The Lodge Independent Baptist Church worship service was different from the services at the United Methodist one. Everyone brought their King James Bible to church with them. Most attendees went to Sunday school prior to worship. As they entered the sanctuary voices were hushed to not interrupt those praying for a blessed service where lost souls would be brought into the Kingdom. The cross hung over the choir loft, securely fastened with cable wire. Unlike a high church service there was no pipe organ prelude, procession-al, and recessional. The pianist and organist sat in full view of the congregation on opposite sides of the chancel. The pulpit raised above the congregation was made from oak and engraved on it were the symbols *ihs* the same as on the communion table. The color of the tapestry behind the choir area and above the baptistery was a deep wine color and made of velvet fabric. Six stained glass windows adorned the wall; three on the east and three on the west pictorially each depicting a Bible story. They included: Jesus allowing the children to come to Him; the disciples leaving their fishing nets to follow Him; the Garden of Gethsemane; the Flood; the manger scene; and Adam and Eve in the Garden of Eden. The center aisle had a carpet runner in the same deep rich wine tone as the drapery. The oak floor and pews weathered over decades by the soles and seats of repentant sinners stood the test of time. The clock on the back wall could be heard ticking as congregants prayed silently for a sick member. Time in this place of worship was irrelevant, because when the spirit moved the preacher to spew forth his weekly message, no one dared turn to look at the clock lest they be identified as the sinner to whom God was directing the sermon that day.

Pastor Gates spoke loudly and pointed at the congregation. "Church do you know where you will be tonight if you die? Do you want to burn in the eternal fire of damnation because you refused to accept Jesus Christ as your personal Savior? I'm gonna have the organist play *Just As I Am* verses one through four again until someone comes forward. God has laid on my heart that there is someone here who is reluctant to come forward. With every head bowed and every eye closed raise your hand if you don't know Jesus. That's it. Now come into the center aisle and walk down here to the front. Our deacons will direct you to pray the sinner's prayer. Come. Jesus is coming maybe morning, maybe noon, but surely soon. You don't want to be found in a place of immorality like a movie, or at a dance, or playing cards when our Savior comes and be passed by. I preach this to keep you safe from all the world's evils. Someday when you are tempted, you will remember these words and appreciate what I tell you."

It could go on for fifteen minutes. If no one came, one of the deacons would come to the altar to be prayed over so the invitation could finally end.

The Parkers sat together in worship, for all intents and purposes, as a well-adjusted and happy family. Gretchen, while away at college, prayed that the church's spiritual influence would heal the marital discord between her parents.

Session Six

"Dr. Weinstein, you know what I am learning?" Marian asked as she settled into the therapy chair.

Tapping his pen on his notepad he smiled and offered, "Let's see. Is it that we are all shaped by our perception of our experiences, that everyone makes decisions that impact others, that most people do not usually intentionally choose to behave to hurt others, or that everyone thinks their behavior is justifiable?"

"All that and more," said Marion. She took a breath and asked, "Dr. Weinstein, do you think that we can change how we respond in certain situations?"

Dr. Weinstein took off his glasses and looked directly at Marion as he said with the most intense stare, "Marion, if I did not think that was possible I would not be a therapist. I know you can change how you respond in situations and I plan to be here to guide you through that process for as long as it takes. Will you commit to that agreement too?"

"I want to and plan to, but right now it is so difficult to open up about all the pain in my life that I cannot sincerely say I will stay for the duration. Is that fair enough, Dr. Weinstein?"

"Yes, Marion, it is more than reasonable. Shall we begin?"

"Today I will describe how my family began to fall apart," Marion said.

The Unraveling

IN THE LATE fall after Gretchen had returned to college, Andy said to Sarah, "How 'bout I treat the family to the Svenden House Buffet for supper tonight?"

Wagging her finger at him in front of Marion and Rhonda, Sarah answered, "You know Gretchen's college tuition is due again in two weeks. We can't waste money on such luxuries."

Silent, Andy sat down in the living room wooden rocker and leaned hard against the chair's decorative metal upholstery tacks while he held back his anger.

Andy tried all he knew to do to make his wife happy, to no avail. The harder he tried the more Sarah harped on what he did wrong.

He descended the basement stairs to his safe haven out of earshot of Sarah's screeching criticisms. Andy put his head down on the wooden plank workbench and cried out softly so the family would not overhear through the floor registers, "God, I don't know how to make Sarah happy. I can't ever do enough. I don't want to live like this anymore. I'm too embarrassed to tell anyone. I'm ready to say good bye to this old world."

For the first time, he left the house without a word and drove off in the car. Sarah told Marion and Rhonda, "Your dad's crazy. I don't know where he's headed or what he's about to do, but I do know he's an embarrassment to us all."

Sarah shut herself in her room and Marion, lacking an appetite, fixed Rhonda a peanut butter and jelly sandwich for supper. An hour later when Andy was still not home, Sarah called Andy's sister Eleanor.

"Hey, Eleanor, is Andy there? I need him to get some milk on his way home."

Perplexed Eleanor said, "No Sarah he's not here. I haven't seen him since Wednesday night.

After mulling it over for another hour Sarah called the police. She did not want the shame of him publicly killing himself for the whole town to know about. When Officer Jeff came to the house to get the details to file a report she told him about Andy's depression and suspicion of his suicidal condition.

Despondent and alone, Andy drove around town for an hour and finally ended up down at Hamilton Park, a wooded area popular with hikers during the day, but fairly secluded at night. It was dusk by this time, and he left the car in the parking lot and entered the hiking path. As the last remnants of daylight filtered through the trees, Andy finally stopped walking and sat down on the railroad tracks at the edge of the train trestle built high over the East River. With his pocket knife poised in his shaking left hand he opened the blade and hovered it above his right wrist - "*What am I waiting for? No one cares if I live or die. If I slice my wrist it will be messy and slow. If I wait for the next train, it might take too long to get here. God, why don't you help me? I really don't wanna die, but I don't know of any other option.* Andy sighed deeply. "Ok, maybe if I try one more time to talk to Sarah she'll understand. Ok, God one more time and then I'm done."

Andy trudged back to his car and drove home, slinking back into the house. The silence was deafening.

The cold stare from Sarah pierced his soul.

Tearfully he sat back down in the same rocker he was sitting in before he left, and told his family, "Your ol' dad almost did himself in tonight sitting on the railroad track, but I couldn't do it. I want life to be better for you girls and for your mom to be happy. I just don't know how to do it."

Marion and Rhonda did not fully comprehend the enormity of what they just heard, so they awaited Sarah's response as their lead.

Sarah, with hands on her hips, stood over Andy as she berated him. "That'd be all I need the disgrace of you killing yourself leaving me with three kids to support. Did you think about that? Huh, did you? No, you only think about yourself and having a good time while I'm stuck always trying to make ends meet. I'm sick of it, you, and everything," she said as she slammed the door to the master bedroom. From the other side of the door Marion heard her mother yell, "Marion go call the police back and tell them that your good-for-nothing father is home."

Sarah's response told Marion she better do as she was told and then keep quiet. Andy interpreted the family's response as verification of his belief that no one cared or understood his feelings.

Officer Jeff came back to interview Andy since the family had reported him missing and suicidal. Filled with trepidation and dread Marion went to school the following morning certain that the whole town knew of her father's attempt to end it all. Thankfully, no one did.

The next Sunday Andy went forward during the altar call. Sobbing, Andy threw the knife on the altar, the one he lacked the courage to plunge into his wrist.

"Pastor, I have sinned," admitted Andy, in a voice loud enough for all the congregants to lean forward in their seats eager to hear his confession. I tried to kill myself the other night, but didn't have the courage to do it. I'm so ashamed and don't know what to do. I can't go on like this."

Marion slid down in her seat, embarrassed to have her family's turbulent life on display. What if people felt sorry for her? What if people stopped being her friend? What if the minister said they could not come back to the Baptist church anymore?

Pastor Gates whispered, "Andy, why don't you and Sarah come to my office after the service and we'll talk." The minister's counsel was direct and without emotion. Neither divorce nor suicide were options in God's plan.

No one knew the deep cavern of depression filling the inside of the Parker home. Becoming born-again Christians did not solve the problem. The distance, so vast between Sarah and Andy, weighed heavily on anyone who ventured into the house. Few outsiders were allowed in. Fearful of her mother's wrath, Marion sided with her mom that dad was, in fact, crazy. Marion became mom's confidant.

A confidant had privileges. One night after Andy had long gone to bed, Marion came downstairs to get a glass of cold milk after she finished studying. Sarah sat in the red vinyl chair at the kitchen table staring off into space.

Unconsciously Marion knew she was opening a door she could not ever close when she asked, "Mom what are you doing up at this late hour?"

As Sarah shoved a Hersey's square from her precious chocolate stash toward Marion she answered,

"Just thinking."

Unable to resist that invitation Marion said, "About what?"

"Do you think your dad forgets things on purpose and really doesn't understand what I ask him to do?"

Feeling empowered, siding with Sarah, "I dunno Mom, but whatever you think, it's probably right."

Sarah slammed her first down on the tabletop making Marion jump.

"I knew I was right. If he is pretending to be dumb, then I don't have to put up with it."

Marion, egging her on, "So what are you going to do, Mom?"

"I'm not going to stand for it. This group counseling, I just started on my lunch hour helps women like me make decisions about what to do."

Fearful of another unplanned disappearing act, she requested, "Mom, if you decide to not be married any more, let me know, okay?"

Preoccupied, Sarah unconsciously said, "Sure." Still, Marion knew her mother would blindside her like with other events of the past.

Despite the church's edict and with the therapy group's support, Sarah decided enough was enough. In 1966, she drew up papers for legal separation. With no notice, the police showed up at the house.

Officer Jeff knocked on the wooden screen door that was open on the front porch, "Mr. Parker?"

"Yes?" Surprised to see the police, Andy opened the door and invited Officer Jeff to come in.

Standing at the kitchen sink, Sarah, froze, holding her breath. Eight-year-old Rhonda, sat spellbound at the dining room table with an orange crayon midair above her coloring book, while Marion, shocked to hear Officer Jeff's voice in the living room stopped placing the silverware on the kitchen table and waited, her stomach knotting into a tight ball of fear.

Reluctantly, Officer Jeff handed Andy some paperwork.

Andy stared quizzically at the documents in his hand and asked, "What's this?"

With a deep sigh, Officer Jeff said, "Andy, it is an order to have you removed from the home."

Incredulously Andy stepped back, "Why, what for?"

Officer Jeff saw Sarah now, as she stood in the doorway of the dining room, wiping her hands on her paisley deep-pocket apron and nodding her head toward him.

Officer Jeff said reluctantly, "It's separation papers."

Trembling all over Andy raised his quavering voice as he turned to address Sarah who smugly stood in the doorway as he said, "Separation papers? Are you saying you want a divorce? Where'll I go? What about the car?

What about my girls?"

Before Sarah could answer Officer Jeff said, "Mr. Parker. I'm sorry. You can get an attorney to work all that out. Right now, you have thirty minutes to pack a suitcase and I'll escort you out."

Tears welled up, "Where are you going to take me? I haven't even had supper yet."

"I'll fix him a plate to take with him," Sarah said coldly.

For the first-time Andy fired back. "That's it after twenty-one years of marriage? I get thirty minutes and a plate of food to go?"

In an effort to defuse Andy's rising anger, Officer Jeff said, "Come on Andy, I have a place to take you where you can calm down and think all this through, okay buddy?"

"I guess I don't have a choice," Andy said shrugging his shoulders.

As he assembled what he could gather in less than thirty minutes Andy departed kissing Marion and Rhonda on the top of their heads. He thought, *Sarah can't stop me now from kissing my girls with Officer Jeff present.*

Officer Jeff was a familiar face to the family from previous crises. He had driven Andy home in 1954 after he was falsely accused of being a felon. He was also the officer who came to the house to assess Andy's mental state after Andy contemplated suicide at Hamilton Park. Now instead of making certain all was calm within the household Officer Jeff was escorting Andy out to a world of unknowns.

After he left the house it was deadly quiet. Sarah jubilantly felt the cause of her depression and lot in life had been ordered out and driven away. She had the law involved because she was unsure of the outcome if she presented the separation papers herself. Would he refuse to leave, destroy things or kill himself in front of the children? With anticipation, and with Andy now gone, she believed a flourishing life was possible.

The supper Andy refused, turned out to be Sarah's victory dinner. She sat down at the kitchen table in a giddy mood as if the "wicked witch was dead."

"Come on girls, let's eat. Ya know what? We're gonna be fine. We'll no longer have to put up with your dad's craziness. We'll be just the Parker girls."

In spite of Sarah's reassurance Marion and Rhonda felt extreme uneasiness. A life-changing traumatic event just took place and there was no one to discuss it with, certainly not Mom.

Andy rented a room from Kent, a man across town. He called regularly to check on his daughters, but Sarah thought it best if the girls cut off all contact with him so she found excuses for them to not visit or talk to him. Through it all Andy found his footing. His two sisters and their families who lived in the area embraced him. His parents and other siblings back in Massachusetts said, "Come home."

Andy's prayer to God, "I'll try one more time," in a way was answered. The trial was over. The inevitable dissolution of the marriage had come to a head.

Like Gretchen, Rhonda did not openly express her feelings. Rather, they showed up in physical symptoms of stomachaches and constipation.

Sarah attempted to coax Rhonda into eating, as she lay on the floor watching a cartoon on television, "The Jetsons."

"You need to eat something so you can go to the bathroom. I bought you this new cereal called "Apple Jacks." Try it."

"I'm not hungry Mommy. I'll try 'em later." Rhonda only wanted to eat macaroni and cheese and peanut butter and jelly sandwiches, adding to her constipation. She sucked her left forefinger to self-soothe. Gretchen, away at school, was uninformed of the change until the approaching Christmas holiday.

Sarah, on a rare occasion, spent limited funds on a long-distance phone call to Gretchen at her college dorm. As she sat down at the dining room telephone table she rehearsed in her mind what she would say to Gretchen. Sarah figured a "just the facts ma'am" approach was the best way to break the news. As the red felt Christmas bell with the gold chain chimed out Silent Night in the background she dialed the number. It was the first Saturday in December. When another student answered, Sarah asked, "May I speak with Gretchen Parker please?"

"Sure, it'll take me a minute to go get her."

Gretchen was down the hall folding her weekly laundry on the metal shelf above the quarter slot on the washing machine. Figuring something must be wrong if her mother was spending money on a long-distance call, Gretchen dropped her white wicker laundry basket and hurried to the phone.

"Hi, mom, what's up? You never call," Gretchen said holding her breath.

Sarah ignored the criticism. "I thought you ought to know before you come home for Christmas that your dad and I are separated."

In disbelief, Gretchen let out her breath and asked,

"What? When did this happen?"

Without missing a beat Sarah responded, "In September, the month after you left."

"Mom, where's Dad?" Gretchen anxiously asked.

Sarah curtly answered, "He's staying with a guy across town."

Gretchen paused then said, "Oh, okay," unsure what she was supposed to say at this point.

"Well, that's it. I just wanted you to know. When are you coming home?" Sarah asked.

Still in shock, Gretchen responded, "I'm catching a ride with a guy from Neenah. I should be home by December 20th."

"Okay, good. See you then. Bye."

"Bye."

No warmth, no "I love you," no "How are you," or "The reason I have not called you before now is"….nothing, Sarah just left Gretchen with that news two days before final exams.

Marion's method of coping with this family status change was to immerse herself in church activities so as not to think about *any* of it. The Lodge Independent Baptist Church had a scriptural answer for every question. She had lots of questions, but, embarrassed by the family drama, kept her queries to herself. Her Sunday school teacher, Dr. Boyston, was also her optometrist. Because Dr. Boyston knew about the family's financial struggle, he quietly paid for Marion's summer camp fees and other church expenses which helped her to stay connected. To not lose the support of her church, which by now had become her refuge, Marion signed up to participate in every function she could, often four days a week involved in church activities. As a model Christian, she prayed God would bless her with happiness and a good life. She believed the church's hierarchy were God's direct representatives and if they disapproved of her, she would be cast out and God would turn his back on her and she would have no one.

Attending church camp was the highlight of her summer, to be away from the constant tension in her household.

Thank you, Dr. Boyston for paying my way to camp. God really blessed me to meet with such fine Christian young people and to speak to me in my devotional time about his will for my life.

Sincerely,
Marion Parker

Pastor Gates delivered a sermon directed toward the church youth, cautioning them about the pitfalls of dating to illuminate the way for Marion and all young people to be in God's favor.

"Do not give in to the sin of immortality. Entering the den of iniquity is only the beginning of your downfall. The Devil will delight in tempting you to drink the libations that only lead to moral destruction. All those gyrating sexual moves on the dance floor will end with you burning in Hell. Pray sinner for God to keep you pure. If you pray earnestly and keep chaste until your wedding night, God will bless your union."

Marion was frightened by the possibility of eternity spent in Hell. She was determined to be the obedient child of God. She began to witness to her classmates, and to carry her Bible to church and school. On Friday nights during football season, the church youth group had 5th quarter parties so the teenagers would not be tempted to go to the school dances. She even endured the cackling of the hoodlums who hung out on the bridge as she walked the half mile to church on Wednesday nights.

"Hey, look at Red carrying her Bible there. You gonna preach to us and tell us we're going to Hell?"

She looked straight ahead and prayed for protection that one of them would not toss her off the bridge since she could not swim.

While the death of her parents' marriage processed slowly, Marion's haven was the church. Gretchen, on the other hand, found college classmate Tim to take her away from all the family chaos. They planned a wedding in elaborate detail. Her major had been art and her dad was so proud of her, but Sarah didn't think she could make a living at it. At the end of her sophomore year, the oversight committee that reviewed students' goals called her in.

Gretchen anticipated a perfunctory agenda so she had no apprehension about the meeting. She would complete her two final years, marry Tim and live happily ever after.

But the Committee had a different agenda.

Sternly, Mr. Sharp addressed her with his glasses cradled on the bridge of his nose, "Miss Parker, we have reviewed your grades and your class evaluations. We have made a decision about the future direction of your studies."

Perplexed, Gretchen moved to the edge of her seat as she held her breath. She finally asked when there was a pause, "What direction do you recommend for me?" "Well, your artistic skills are not sufficient for you to continue as an art major. We are switching you to a career in early childhood education. You'll be able to work in a church as an education director."

She did not hear anything else they said after their declaration. After what seemed like an eternity, she was dismissed. After departing, she immediately sent a message to Tim through a fellow classmate to meet her in the library.

Tim got to their private corner behind the Bible commentary reference shelf, first.

"What's so urgent?" Tim asked cautiously as he looked around so not to be seen touching her hand.

Through gut-wrenching sobs, she told the details. "My whole life has been preparing to be an artist.

My advisor set up my course of study. No one told me they could take that away. Every time I get someplace good in my life, it's taken away."

Unafraid now for someone to see them, Tim turned her chin toward him and looked into her hazel eyes to reassure her.

"It'll be okay. We can get married sooner and you can finish your degree somewhere else. I graduate at the end of next year. If you stay until the end of next year, you'll only have a year to go somewhere else. The Committee doesn't know your talent like I do. We'll find a way for you to use it. I promise. Besides with me as a pastor somewhere you can use the Christian Education stuff they want you to learn to help wherever we are hired."

So, Gretchen did as he suggested. She moved back home after her third year of college and worked to pay for the wedding. Fiancé Tim graduated before she went home returning to his parents' home in New York State to save enough money to fund his and Gretchen's future. Neither Sarah nor Andy could afford to pay for their share of the wedding costs. Gretchen and Tim were in love and did not want to depend on anyone but each other. They also wanted no part of a divorce process, because to them it was against God's Divine plan.

Tim worked for a printing company in Ithaca and Gretchen, working as a clerk at the local hospital. During that year, Gretchen seldom interacted with Marion, Rhonda, or Sarah, and rarely spoke to her father. Every sixty days Gretchen rode a Greyhound bus to New York spend time with her betrothed and to further plan their wedding. In between, she talked on Wednesday nights privately to Tim, shutting herself in the kitchen with the only phone in the house, the cord stuffed under the dining room swinging door. She daily wrote Tim letters in between the phone calls.

My Dearly Beloved Tim,

In only 170 days we will be forever united. I can't wait to see you on January 4th. I may arrive before this letter does. My dad called yesterday to ask me to meet him in downtown Green Bay on my lunch hour. He wanted to give me my Christmas present. I told him, no. I know he is my dad, but like we learned in school we cannot agree with this whole divorce process. I pray for my dad and mom every morning for them to get right with God so their marriage can be restored. Very soon I will leave all this chaos behind me, thankfully. This is all for today's letter. Love, your future wife, Gretchen.

One weekend in March when Gretchen planned for her mom and sisters to meet her future in-laws, Marion developed a fever and did not feel well enough to make the trip. She convinced Sarah that she would be fine at home by herself and would call her friend Diane's mom, if she needed anything. Sarah allowed her to stay at home. The previous Sunday Marion brought home her Sunday school handout paper which contained an article about missionaries' dealings with evil spirits in Africa. Those entities were demonic and she wanted no part of them. Just reading about them gave her the jitters. While her family packed the car, she took the paper out to the burn barrel, confident it would no longer plague her mind.

As Marion prepared for bed that evening she walked into her closet to get her night clothes. There on the floor was the article she had placed in the burn barrel. Frozen, she believed evil had invaded the house. It took her about sixty seconds before she could move and grab her flannel nightgown and hide under her bedcovers with her Bible firmly in her grasp. The next morning too petrified to know what to do, she sat for hours by the front door in the green striped upholstered chair with dark walnut arms and legs. She prayed for protection and peace. When the family returned, she personally carried the paper to the barrel again and lit a match as she watched, to make certain it totally burned. She had not experienced such fear from an evil influence until then. The bad man she saw in the window at the previous house was not as scary.

Her evil entity experience was contrasted by a good spiritual experience in April of 1968.

As the organist played the third verse of "Just As I Am", Marion felt the nudge of the Holy Spirit. The ignored clock with hands already past noon, ticked away while the parishioners growling stomachs gurgled, anxious for the service to finish so the simmering pot roast could be devoured.

She could wait no longer. Heads turned as she stepped into the aisle to meet the minister. Proudly she announced, "Pastor Gates, I've come forward because God is calling me into the ministry (to become a preacher)." Pastor Gates corrected her as he said, "My dear Christian young lady. It's remarkable you wish to enter God's service. You will do well as a missionary or a faithful pastor's wife."

Because of the flurry of activities surrounding Gretchen's upcoming nuptials and the family's lack of comprehension of the seriousness of her call, it was all but forgotten except by Marion. It was indelibly etched in her mind.

About the same time that Gretchen and Tim got together, Andy's mom, Winifred, concocted a plan. His childhood sweetheart Mary was now divorced from her alcoholic husband. Winifred arranged for the two of them to reconnect like she had for Sarah and Andy twenty-five years earlier. Mary and Andy began courting. Years of no contact quickly faded as they re-kindled the old flame. Sharing their similar heartaches bonded them to one another. Once a month he made the drive to Boston to spend a weekend to make plans for their future life together. Had he and Gretchen been communicating; their paths might have crossed as they both periodically traveled east. Andy and Mary's wedding date was set for the fall after Gretchen and Tim's.

When Sarah heard about Andy's upcoming nuptials, she was sad. She did not know how to think about him remarrying.

"I have no man in my life. Andy was always the problem in our marriage, not me. Now he and Mary are getting back together. How can it be? How can he have someone, and I don't? Did they hook up while we were married? No, it's not possible. We lived 1200 miles apart these last fifteen years. Maybe he's changed. Maybe he's not as bad as I thought."

She had not completed the divorce process because there had been no hurry. Now unsure, she did not know if she wanted to continue the process since Andy had someone who wanted him. Maybe she still wanted him. Amid joy that her oldest was to be married off, she questioned if she should reconcile with her soon-to-be ex. A meeting was arranged. Leaning on the upstairs railing, Marion announced, "If you two get back together, I'll move out. Even though I am only sixteen, I will go find somewhere else to live. You two are horrible together," then she ran up to her room no longer afraid to be upstairs alone.

After Andy left, Sarah sat Marion down at the kitchen table and defended her actions looking her daughter square in the eye, "I can't divorce your father. The church said divorced people go to Hell."

"Well, Mom, tell God it was my idea and to blame me," Marion said as she pushed her chair back and retreated up to her room.

Marion was not the instrumental force in thwarting the reconciliation plans, but luckily, they did not reunite, so Andy's plan to wed Mary moved forward. Until Sarah's death, the daughters did not know it was Andy who filed the final divorce paperwork. On June 7th, the divorce between Andy and Sarah was finalized.

Just eight days after the divorce Gretchen and Tim took their vows. As Sarah and Andy posed next to one another in the wedding photos their grins belied their frozen Cold War relationship. Mary, the soon-to-be stepmother, was not invited to the event.

Mary and Andy tied the knot three months later in Boston and promptly moved all Mary's possessions to Wisconsin. Mary's three adult children: Richard, Ellen, and Stephen all remained behind in Massachusetts. Andy, promoted from the road kill cleaner position to a better job in the mailroom for the State of Wisconsin, had enough salary to pay child support and take care of his new wife.

Session Seven

Dr. Weinstein greeted Marion at the door. "Welcome back. Did you enjoy your vacation?"

"It was so different visiting my family. I didn't feel as anxious. I wasn't trying to fix everyone or make everyone be happy. Of course, I did not tell them I am in therapy. I know now, it is not their business, but only mine. Some noticed my change of behavior and tried to invite me back into old ways, but thanks to your help I was able to stay on my new path."

"Good for you, Marion. Now let's get some more healing started. Where do we begin this Chapter of your life?"

Marion's Escape

ON THE DAY of Gretchen and Tim's wedding Marion had an escape plan to leave right after the reception with her friend Diane to go work for the summer on Mackinac Island, a popular resort destination in the Upper Peninsula of Michigan. Marion had already experienced a taste of the Island life the summer before when Diane invited her up for a weekend. Two of Diane's male friends from her church worked for her cousin shoveling manure and guiding tourists on horseback around the Island. Diane had a crush on one of the boys, Mark. Marion was thrilled to be paired with Craig, blonde-haired and with a slender build, he was 5'7" and cute. The guys offered to take them on a tour of the Island. Marion was excited to think she was going on a date with a "hunk" of a man. As soon as they were all seated in the carriage Craig bluntly announced, "I have a girlfriend back in Green Bay, so this is not a date." Totally crushed, Marion kept her composure while Mark and Diane cuddled in the horse drawn carriage and "sweet talked" to one another on the front seat. The ride was unbearably tense as Marion sat next to Craig who obviously would rather be with someone else.

The whole scenario reminded her of her freshman year when she asked one of the boys from church named Stanley to escort her to the Youth for Christ banquet. None of her friends could believe she did such a brave thing. Stanley was popular, having just been elected as the rising class president for his junior year. Marion primped, and starved herself down 110 lbs., but her anxiety soared as the day approached. She had not ever been on a date and did not know what was proper. Her friends old enough to drive and experienced daters prepped her all along the way. As Stanley met Sarah, now a single parent, he cautiously, appropriately asked, "What time should I have Marion home?"

Sarah, embarrassed Marion saying, "I'll let you use your own good judgment on that."

Marion wanted her mom to set a limit to show she was in charge. Instead, Marion felt like Stanley pitied her for living in a broken home with no parent responsibly in charge.

For weeks, she envisioned what this night would be like and memorized what she should say and do. Her heart pounded as she casually moved her hand onto the car seat hoping he would hold it or at least touch it. But he did not. Attentive, but obviously not feeling any spark went through the motions while Marion sucked in her hurt and prayed for a miracle, at least a kiss good night.

Stanley's undemonstrative farewell was simply, "I had a good time."

Marion's dream dashed, she replied, "Thank you for taking me. I had a good time too."

That was it, no second date or even any conversation at school. With a heavy heart, she greeted him when she passed him in the hall or saw him at church. To her she surmised that she was not worthy of someone like him. Her family was second best and she had better just accept it, but she was reluctant to do so.

As she returned to Mackinac Island she was determined to have a wonderful summer. The Island, located 7.9 miles from the mainland of Mackinaw City, Michigan, accessible exclusively by boat or airplane, and had only horses, bicycles, or walking as the means of transportation. The nineteenth century tall wooden structures stood firm, weathered by rain, snow, and ice. They greeted the visitors as the fog cleared during the thirty-minute ferry ride. One's first whiff of Island air stepping onto the gangway was the putrid overpowering smell of horse manure. To quickly divert their attention to something more aromatically pleasing, tourists peered in shop windows enjoying the sweet smell of hot fudge concoctions poured onto marble slabs, and caramel being stirred into freshly popped popcorn. To work on Mackinac Island was a privilege usually awarded to aspiring college students who applied in February. Marion, at seventeen, was lucky that Diane's relatives, Island business owners, had connections to get them both a job at the Price Gift Shop.

Marion had mixed feelings leaving for the summer. She feared that she was abandoning Rhonda, believing that she was the stabilizing force in her little sister's life - the one who took her to church, made sure she brushed her teeth, and told her she was loved. Sarah did not do those things, but Marion knew if she did not get away, she might never be able to leave.

On a Tuesday night around dusk, against the backdrop of a blood red sky, the harbor was dotted with yachts drying their multi-colored sails on their decks. The largest fresh water 333-mile world class yacht race from Chicago to Mackinac Island was in full swing, an annual event that attracted yachts of every size and color and sailors from as far away as Australia and Japan.

Hank, a roomer at the Miller Boarding house where Marion and her friend Diane stayed suggested all the workers go to Fort Mackinac to get a view of the yachts with their sails in the harbor. Upon finding the Fort gate locked, Kevin, also a roomer, suggested they climb over it. Kyle, another roomer, said, "No one's here and it's not like we're breaking in. We just want to see the yachts.

There's only two policemen on the whole Island. Do ya think they're gonna care or even see us?"

That was all the convincing the novice hoodlums needed. As they climbed over the fence they oohed and aahed the array of colored sails lying on the decks to dry. As they tired quickly of that activity Kevin suggested,

"Let's hole down the rills in Parkquette Mark."

He meant "Let's roll down the hills in Marquette Park." A weekly sketch on the show Hee Haw involved Archie Campbell spinning a tale mixing up the letters to words (spoonerism) liken to "Pig Latin." Kevin was copying that style.

Oh, what fun they had as they laughed hysterically while dizzily they tumbled down the hill, afraid of rolling onto Main Street in the path of a horse drawn carriage.

While they took one last view of the harbor from the top, Marion was surprised when middle school teacher Hank, leaning against the Fort wall also viewing the yachts below, introduced himself. His five-foot-five frame fit nicely into his worn blue jeans with a tear on the left back pocket. His leather belt fit him snuggly due to the culinary skills of the Miller Boarding house cook, Agnes, Diane's mom. He wore a red and blue checked flannel shirt and scuffed brown work boots that reeked of horse manure.

Boldly, Hank approached Marion moving his right arm in a sweeping motion, "Hey what do you think of all this?"

Quizzically she answered, "All what?" Hank authoritatively responded, "You know, living away from home with no curfews or rules."

She wondered why an older guy was talking to her.

She appropriately answered looking down at her shoes, "It's nice. I'm having a good time."

"Good. You need to," he said offering his hand to help her climb back over the fort fence.

He began to seek her out. They developed a friendship. Marion sat on the steps of the front porch of the boarding house as she anxiously waited for Hank to appear. Every Tuesday night he would come to the porch to socialize with the boarders and eventually ask shy Marion,

"Would you like to go for a walk?" Blushing, she said, "Sure."

First closing the picket fence gate, they would walk north toward the Grand Hotel. Passing tourists who savored the last glimpse of daylight squeezing every minute of enjoyment from the Island life, would invariably ask them questions.

"Do you live here? Where is the Pink Pony Bar and Restaurant? How do I get to the Fort?"

Each time they patiently and gladly answered as if the Island was theirs to dole out in tidbits to people who could appreciate its charms. Gently touching Marion's arm, he held her back from entering the crosswalk as a manure wagon turned into their path. It felt good, albeit strange, to have someone look out for her. They walked the one block down to the schoolhouse and sat on the playground swings discussing what she wanted to do with her life. He suggested they walk to the other side of the boardwalk to the cement benches down by the water. As Lake Superior's frigid waters lapped against the shore they watched as the lights on the Mackinac Island Bridge blinked out for the night.

"So how was your day at the gift shop?" Hank asked.

Marion answered, "Interesting, but my boss sure was grumpy."

Curious about his life, Marion asked, "Working away from your family, do you miss them?"

Hank nodded. "Of course," he said. "But as a school employee, I need summer work and since I'm friends with Jim here at the stables, he hired me.

"So, what are you good at in school?" His smile warmed her all over. "What have you wanted to do, but have been afraid to try?"

Focused on the second question she sighed and said,

"I want to be in the school Junior Miss Pageant, but I don't have any talent to perform."

"I'll bet you can do anything you set your mind to do," he said as he patted her shoulder.

"Do you really think so?" she asked, wrinkling her nose.

Flattering her, he said, "Of course! You're pretty, smart, and a woman who takes risks like riding on the maiden voyage of the ferry boat when you were scared it would sink."

"No one has ever said I was pretty, or smart, or had any talent," she whispered.

Hank softly said, "Look at me."

With downcast eyes, she said, "I'm afraid to look at you."

"Why?"

"Because I'm afraid you will look at me and see I'm not really the things you say I am and then you will laugh at me."

"Look at me and take a chance," he spoke softly.

She gazed into his clear, cobalt-blue, glistening eyes. They were warm, inviting, and a big smile spread across his face. Inside and outside she was visibly trembling. No one had ever told her the things he said. She wondered if they were true or just some line to mess with her head.

"See, I'm not laughing and I have not changed my mind about you. Maybe one day you'll believe those things about yourself or be mad at me."

In the process of trusting Hank, she took risks like going out to eat with him along with the rest of the boarding house crew. She overcame her fear that she would miss the Second Coming when she went to the movie *Camelot* with Hank and Diane. As her confidence soared, she began to have sexual feelings for him, a man ten years her senior and married.

On Tuesday night, August 13th, as they returned to the boarding house after their walk, Hank turned toward her just inside the door. His tone got serious.

He locked eyes with her and said, "You'll be headed back to school in a few weeks and I'll leave soon to go to a new school position in Ithaca, New York. I wanted you to know."

The silence was deafening. "Oh, (was all Marion could say her heart beating so loudly she thought he could hear it). "My sister and her new husband live there," she said looking away from him.

"Come here." He cupped her chin with his hands, drew her to him and kissed her lips, breathing heavily and without a word uttered. As quickly as he caressed her inviting mouth, he pulled back and walked away.

She stood in the hallway pondering what just happened outside the room she shared with her best friend Diane, afraid to enter, fearful Diane may have overheard what had just happened. Hank was about to leave, but he kissed her just in the same way that she had fantasized and now Marion had to figure out what his actions meant. Was it an affair that finished it ever started? Perplexed, but too afraid to call him back to ask, and by now, too aroused to just go to sleep, Marion tiptoed into her room, slid under the covers and prayed for forgiveness for her lustful thoughts. Eventually, from pure mental exhaustion, she fell asleep.

Marion knew it was morally wrong to kiss someone else's husband. Still reeling from mixed emotions, she awoke in the morning devastated to find he was already gone. Finally, someone had been there for her and now he was gone. He offered no apologies, no promises of a return, he was just gone. The emptiness was unlike anything she ever experienced., leaving her with an unrelenting, aching hollowness. Alone with her thoughts and overwhelming grief, Marion could not reveal her feelings to anyone for fear of condemnation.

That evening after work, magnetically drawn to the water, the air a chilly fifty degrees with a wind blowing off Lake Superior, she sat huddled on the boardwalk dangling her legs contemplating how long it would take to drown herself in the freezing water.

A policeman approached her and pointedly asked,

"Miss, what's your name?"

"Marion Parker."

Firmly, but compassionately he asked, "Where do you work?"

Looking up at him she said in a monotone, "The Price Gift Shop on Main Street."

Eyes intent on hers asked, "Miss Parker where do you stay?"

Snapping back to reality she answered truthfully, "At the Miller boarding house down from the Grand Hotel."

"I'm concerned about you Marion. You're not suicidal, are you?"

Thankful now for a human presence she answered,

"No sir, officer. I'm just thinking."

Encouraging her he said, "Go back to your boarding house. This is no place for a young girl to be out alone at this time of night."

"Okay," she said as she arose and began walking back to the boarding house.

Convinced that she was walking in the right direction, the officer continued his beat but circled back in an hour to make sure she had not returned.

A week later with the summer over Marion was back home preparing for her senior year - older, wiser, but depressed.

Once home, Marion told Pastor Gates about Hank, how he listened to her and helped her, but deliberately omitted any mention of the kiss she and Hank shared. Aware of the extreme dysfunctionality of Marion's home life, Pastor Gates told her he believed her friendship with a middle school teacher was good for her. Marion knew had she shared the intimate details of that friendship her pastor would have condemned them both to Hell.

Rhonda and Marion had not been told about their father's marriage to Mary. Perhaps Andy knew Sarah would not have permitted the girls to attend the wedding ceremony. In October, a month after the wedding, Andy called the girls. When Marion answered, he began the conversation with, "Guess what?"

"I don't know, what?" Marion said, covering the receiver so her mom would not hear.

"I got married." Incredulously, "You did? Who is she?" Marion said forgetting to hush.

"Someone I knew before I married your mom. Her name is Mary and I want you to meet her. Will you do that for your dear old dad?"

"I don't know, dad. Mom might get mad," Marion said honestly, looking around to see if Sarah was eavesdropping.

"It's okay. You can decide if you want to tell your mom after you meet Mary," Andy said.

"Okay, I guess so," Marion agreed, cautiously.

Sarah knew Andy got married, and it was inevitable that her daughters would at some point meet the woman, but she was unaware that a plan was already in the works. Marion pulled her mom's two-door Chevy beside her dad's light blue four-door Cutlass at the Green Bay K-Mark Store Parking Lot. Andy and Mary got out of their car and walked to the driver's side window where Marion sat with Rhonda beside her in the front seat. Mary wore a blue polyester dress with gold buttons on the bodice. Black tights covered her varicose veins and curly dark hair covered her head. Her appearance so was totally unlike Sarah that Marion and Rhonda just stared. When Mary laughed at Andy's attempt to engage the girls, they sat frozen unsure what they were supposed to do next.

Andy turned toward his car and held open the back door of his passenger seat as he said motioning, "Come on, girls. Let's go get some ice cream." Marion and Rhonda obediently piled into the backseat.

As they did Marion turned toward Marion and Rhonda and smiled at her stepdaughters as she said, "Nice to meet you girls."

Shyly, Marion and Rhonda simultaneously mumbled said, "Nice to meet you too." They did not know how to address her. Sarah wanted them to hate this woman, but she was likeable.

Mary was forty-six, two years younger than Andy, and spoke with a heavy Bostonian accent. The first outing was just for ice cream to help Marion and Rhonda get introduced and accustomed to their new stepmother. As Marion drove Rhonda home afterward she said, "Hey, Rhonda. I think it best that we don't mention to Mom the details of our time with Dad and Mary, okay?"

Rhonda slunk down in her seat and sighed, "Yah, okay. I get it. Mom couldn't handle knowing Mary's nice."

"That's right, Sis."

In direct contrast to their mom, Mary was publicly demonstrative with her affection toward Andy. She encouraged Andy to spend time with his daughters, to hug them, and for them to call him whenever they wished. Mary, a great cook, also liked to bake cookies and crochet. On their next visit Mary gave the girls their first delicious taste of lasagna.

The table was set with a starched white crocheted tablecloth and napkins that Mary had made. The shiny stainless-steel silverware reflected the light off the brown faux Tiffany lamp overhead fixture. The plates were made of Melamine of various hues of orange, aqua, and yellow. Andy put a pea on his spoon and flung it into the air. Both Marion and Rhonda gasped. Such frivolity was never allowed at their mom's dinner table. They sat with bated breath to see how Mary reacted, forks midair. Mary laughed and flung one herself. It did not take long for the wall between Marion and Rhonda and Mary to break down. The girls eagerly learned it was okay to have fun. As they gathered on future occasions Marion and Rhonda teased Mary about her accent. To playfully mimic their new stepmother, they asked her, "Did you pauk your ca in Havad yad, Mary?"

She would laughingly go along with their game and respond, "Yes, and I put my groceries in a sack, too."

In November, with Hank's encouragement from the previous summer and the nudging of her father and stepmother Mary, Marion entered the school's Junior Miss Pageant. The boost to her esteem was nothing short of remarkable. Inspired by Rod McKuen's album *The Sea*, Marion wrote a piece about her summer work experience on Mackinac Island and performed it as a dramatic reading. The content was based on meeting someone on a walking path, joining in silence with the person and then each parting in their own direction, both wiser and enriched by the encounter. Symbolically, she described her "affair" with Hank, but did not tell anyone. Although she did not place in the competition, she felt like she won.

Confidently, she performed the piece again at the school's talent show. Photographs still capture the crowning moment of both performances caught on film and displayed in her high school yearbook.

Despite Hank's "abandonment," Marion flourished in her senior year. She saved enough money over the summer working on Mackinac Island to afford nice clothes and to pay for her senior expenses. Money in her pocket boosted her confidence and talking to popular classmates no longer frightened her. Her self-image was not diminished like it had been in eighth grade when Dr. Carson put her back on birth control pills to regulate her menses. This time there was no weight gain because he prescribed only one tablet daily instead of four. With her pumped-up self-confidence, she filled out the application for Philadelphia College of the Bible to be trained as the missionary she felt called to be. The school newspaper even did an article about her summer on Mackinac Island.

Marion Parker Beats the Mackinac Island Record

Marion Parker, summer employee at the Price Gift Shop on Mackinac Island set a new record. MSU college student Avery Winters set the record of bicycling around the nine-mile Island in 40 minutes and 3 seconds in the summer of 1966. This past summer Marion, clocked by friends, succeeded Avery's time by twenty-seven seconds on June 29th. She attributed her speed to riding one of the Miller Boarding house mountain bikes and bike racing since age five when her training wheels were removed. Armed with this success she hopes to win the Junior Miss Pageant performing a piece written about her summer work and life on Mackinac Island. Upon acceptance, after graduation she will enter Philadelphia College of the Bible to be trained as a missionary serving overseas."

Peers, once avoided due to anxiety, now commented and congratulated her. Others chided the school newspaper for publishing a story about a "Nobody." She overheard them and vowed she would show them that she was a "Somebody." Her senior year was going splendidly, so different compared to earlier school years.

In early March while in her room studying for an English Composition test, Marion heard Sarah calling up the stairs.

"Marion, come down quickly. There's a man on the phone from that college you applied to," Sarah said breathlessly.

Marion skipped down the steps two at a time as she raced to the phone composing her voice before she picked up the receiver.

"Hello, this is Marion."

"Hello, Marion. I'm Todd Becker the Director of Admissions at Philadelphia College of the Bible," he said announcing himself.

Remembering her manners, she replied, "Oh, it's a pleasure to speak with you, Mr. Becker."

"I have good news for you, Marion."

Joyfully she said, "You do?"

"We are granting you a partial scholarship for $500 to cover one third of your tuition. You will need to come up with the remainder. Are you interested?"

Trying to contain her excitement, "Oh yes, Mr.

Becker I'm very interested. Thank you so much."

"I'll mail you the paperwork for your parents to fill out, okay?"

"I understand. Yes, I'll have them fill them out.

Thank you, again."

"It is my pleasure and may God grant you his blessing as you pursue God's will for your life," he said in parting.

"Good-bye, Mr. Becker."

Marion hung up the receiver and burst into tears while sitting there at the telephone table, something she had not done in front of her mom since she was ten years old.

Sarah, looked back at Marion from the kitchen sink where she was washing dishes and asked, "Why are you crying?"

"Mom, I got accepted to college with a partial scholarship. All I have to do is have you and dad come up with the rest of it," she announced.

"Just where do you think I can get that kind of money?" Sarah bellowed. "I never got to go to college. No one helped me," she complained making loud splashing noises with the water in the dishpan.

Marion stood up and pleaded, "Can you please talk to dad and see if there is a way to make this happen for me?"

Extracting herself from the quicksand of her family existence was in her grasp; all she had to do was come up with the other $1000 a year. A large amount, but certainly her parents could for once, come through for her. They did it for Gretchen somehow so surely, they would for her. She did not discuss it with her mother again until the papers arrived. She handed them over trusting that her mom would find a way.

With spring break approaching, Sarah suggested they visit Gretchen and Tim in New York. Hibernating as newly married couples often do, no one thought it odd that communication from Gretchen and Tim was sparse. Since Gretchen had gradually pulled away from the family when she first entered college, Marion did not question it. Marion's thoughts were not about her sister anyway, but about Hank. She casually mentioned to her mom that her friend Hank lived there saying she wanted to look up a fellow summer employee who had moved there. Honestly, her thoughts were not centered on Gretchen at all because Marion had become used to Gretchen being gone and there was little interaction since she married. The excitement of a trip to Ithaca was with the hope she would be able to see Hank.

Expectantly, upon arriving in Ithaca Marion opened the newly delivered Ithaca, New York telephone book.

There was Hank's name and phone number in black and white. With trembling fingers, she dialed the number. Her heart pounding, she wondered what to say when someone answered.

"Hello," said Hank's wife.

'Um this is Marion Parker. I worked with Hank on the Island and I'm in town for a visit. May I speak with him please?" squeaked Marion.

"Sure."

"Hello, this is Hank," he said cheerfully.

Marion hesitantly managed to say, "Hank it's Marion. I hope this is okay. I'm in town visiting my sister and thought maybe I could meet your family, if you and your wife don't mind,"

"Sure," he said excitedly. "I can come tomorrow after school around 4:30, pick you up and bring you home for dinner."

With a sigh of relief and anticipation, she said,

"Okay, thanks. The address is Elderberry Apartments off Dorchester Road, Apartment 206."

"Great. See you tomorrow," Hank quickly said.

"Yes, I am looking forward to it," Marion replied. She spent a sleepless night. What if his wife figured out she had feelings for him? What if he made a pass at her? What if her family figured it out? Her reason for meeting his family was to observe how he acted around his wife and children. Was his wife a "bitch"? If she was mean, it could justify Hank's actions toward Marion. If she was pretty and nice, she did not know what she would do. The Baptist part of her hoped she would find him happily married and their friendship was all just a figment of her imagination so she could end her crush on him.

When he came to pick her up, she introduced him to Sarah, Rhonda, Gretchen and Tim. No one addressed the question that was on all their minds, *Who is this guy and what's his relationship to Marion?*

Nervously, Marion rapidly talked about anything she could think of as she rode in Hank's car on the way to his house. She feared what would happen if there were silence. She felt a swarm of butterflies fluttering in the pit of her stomach. Hank listened without interruption and smiled. He patted her hand when she finally took a breath.

"We're here, Marion. You can relax now," said Hank.

Marion let out a big breath and said shakily, "Okay."

Hank's wife served baked chicken with white milk gravy, creamy mashed potatoes, and green beans dripping with butter. Dessert was a warm tart cherry pie with a scoop of vanilla ice cream on top. Marion barely nibbled on her food. She was still so nervous her stomach did flip flops. Hank's wife, Sally, asked many engaging questions and was very cordial. If Sally suspected anything, she hid it well. Marion was a good guest. She played with Hank's two sons and complimented the hostess.

On the ride back to Gretchen and Tim's apartment, Hank joked about pulling off to go parking. Marion was shocked at how he could just leave his family not five minutes before and now he was talking about making out with her. Although her body wanted to, she resisted. She dutifully took him back upstairs to her see her family before he departed. She told them she was going to walk him back down to the street exit. When Marion and Hank got in the doorway and before she could resist, he cupped her chin again in his hands and kissed her passionately for the second time in seven months.

She pulled away and said, "Go home to your wife and kids." It was not really what she wanted, but her religious convictions were inwardly screaming at her to behave properly.

Marion's visit with her sister and husband was strained. The couple had only been married for nine months and lived in a one-bedroom apartment. Having Gretchen's family inviting themselves for a visit was awkward. Gretchen and Tim relished their privacy, so Sarah and her daughters stayed at the Ramada Hotel downtown. Marion was in her own world replaying her time with Hank and his family, reliving every scene, every word over and over in her head. Did he care for her? What about his wife and children? What about her religious upbringing denouncing her actions?

Life's rules dictated by Independent Baptist interpretation were a bunch of "Don'ts" to ensure God's approval. They included: do not drink, do not dance, do not play cards, do not go to movies, do not have sex before marriage, do not be angry, do not utter curse words, and of course, do not have an affair with a married man. If, God forbid, someone violated these sacred tenets, the punishment would potentially be God's wrath, or worse yet being left behind when the Second Coming of Christ took place which was always preached to be imminent. These instructions dictated every move of the Church's dedicated followers. There were no gray areas, members of the congregation either obeyed or fell outside of God's favor. If Marion violated these tenets, she feared being totally alone with no guidance, no support, no God in her life. The panic she felt every time she behaved in a manner that would not be approved by the elders of her church, produced such anxiety she withdrew and told no one. She harbored the guilt and shame for her actions with Hank and her feelings toward him.

To try to avoid this sinful behavior, she had no other contact with Hank from that visit in March until she returned to Mackinac Island for the summer after graduating high school. She had been too afraid to ask him if he was coming back. She did not want to hear him say no. She secretly wished on the one hand that someone else could be there for her and her alone, but on the other hand the physical lust for Hank was so intense she could not wait to see him.

Freshly ferried over from the mainland, and even before the boat was tethered, the familiar pungent smell of horse manure wafted into her nostrils, but did not deter her excitement to settle back into Mackinac Island's unique way of life. The summer workers met up at the gym in the local schoolhouse to reconnect with old friends and to begin making new ones. To her sheer delight, Hank was there playing basketball with other workers. Her heart was about to burst, yet her religious convictions were strongly beseeching her to avoid any improper behavior. She made a vow to herself not to do anything regrettable. The thought that maybe his wife had come with him, abated her temptations.

Within a week, they were regularly meeting again on Tuesday evenings. Sitting once more at "their" place down by the water's edge they talked about life, relationships, and the future.

Hank complimented her saying, "Marion, you are so mature now that you have graduated high school."

Throwing it back at him, "Thanks, but it was your help that made it all possible. Encouraging me to enter the Junior Miss Pageant was such a thrill. I never believed I could do it."

Affirming he said, "I told you that you are smart and pretty."

Ignoring his compliment, she said, "Yah, entering the Junior Miss Pageant was so much fun. Having an article about me in the school newspaper was so unexpected. Oh, you didn't know that I wrote a book about Mackinac Island which is now in the Island library and one is housed at the State of Michigan Library. My composition teacher helped me do that. I'm so excited about the possibilities of what I can do. Thank you for helping me."

Hank smiled as he looked directly into her eyes and said, "The first time I saw you there up at the Fort, I knew you were special. You had a shy quality about you, but you just needed someone to help you blossom."

Checking her watch, Marion gasped. "Oh my, it's 2:00 a.m. and I have to be up in a few hours to go to work."

Hank offered his hand to help her stiff body up off the worn boardwalk planks where they had sat talking for hours.

As they walked back to the Miller Boarding house, an acquaintance of Hank's passed them and commented,

"Don't let your meat loaf."

Hank asked Marion, "Do you know what that comment meant?"

"Not really," Marion said.

Smiling he said with a wink, "It means if you are going to get aroused by someone, don't waste it, have sex with the person."

Blushing in the moonlight she responded, "Oh."

End of the discussion. The implication was they both knew they wanted to have sex, but avoided the reality.

One night Hank offered to show Marion where he stayed, having moved from the second-floor boarding house with all the other stable hands to his own efficiency next to the barn. Consciously anticipating some physical involvement, she accepted his invitation, trying to ignore her guilty conscience as it implored her to stay away.

"Are you sure you want to see where I sleep?" Hank asked letting her inside.

Breathlessly, "Yes, but I need to make sure no one sees me going in," she replied.

"Why?" he inquired.

"Because Diane and her mom already think I am doing things I shouldn't with you and I don't want to be thrown out of the boarding house."

"Okay, we won't stay long."

One room, the size of a large closet, adjacent to the stable, reeked of horse manure and leather from the saddles lined up outside the door of the dwelling. Inside was a wrought iron single bed with a flannel blanket to protect Hank from the cool Michigan nights and a brown wooden slated straight back chair where he hung his stable hand clothes. Entering the abode felt very wrong, yet also very tantalizing. He invited her to sit on the bed. Gingerly, she lowered her buttocks to meet the mattress so as not to have the spring coils squeak. She looked at him standing still in the doorway and knew; they both knew that they would not consummate their relationship this night. She left the unused love nest and sneaked back into the boarding house. In the morning, paranoid, she believed all eyes were staring at her chest envisioning a big red A stitched across it, so she quietly ate her breakfast and left for work.

Even though the sexual revolution was going on in Woodstock, New York in 1969, in northern Michigan, proper behavior for women still included wearing skirts or dresses to work and not being seen in compromising situations. Marion's boss started grilling her about her off-hours activities. Increasingly Marion appeared preoccupied. When questioned, she made up stories to try to divert the interrogation. It only intensified Marion's guilt. The result was that her boss fired her, suspecting something "fishy" was going on between Marion and some mystery person.

In tears, Marion called up to the second floor of the boarding house where Hank and the other male stable hands hung out after work. She asked him to come talk to her. He took her down by the Grand Hotel's pool while she relayed the details of her firing.

"Marion, you know your boss is a very strict, judgmental, alcoholic woman, but you can do any job you decide you want to on the Island. Jobs are plentiful. I'll bet you can get one today, if you try."

"I don't wanna have to go home." Sobbing, speaking haltingly between sniffles she got the words out.

"I tried. I really did try to please her just like I do my mom.

It's never enough."

"Marion, you don't have to cry." He put his arms around her and hugged her tight to his body and then his hands moved to her derriere and began to caress it. He kissed her on the lips and she just sunk into his arms and this time did not stop him. After a couple of minutes, he pulled away and looked at her. "You're going to be okay. Go talk to Mr. Waterman about a job at one of his hotels or restaurants. I have to go bed the horses down for the night now. We will talk tomorrow, okay?"

"Okay."

Even though his physical touch felt good, it was not the response she needed to feel reassured. She was confused. She asked for help and he sort of gave it, but it really felt like he took advantage of her while she was vulnerable.

Hank was right about plentiful jobs. She acquired one right away, employed as a maid in a local hotel. She moved into the dorm with the rest of the female summer help, away from the stares and whispers of the Miller Boarding house residents.

As Marion was packing up her clothes into her big suitcase, her friend and roommate Diane laid on her bunk and said, "Marion, don't you see what Hank is doing to you? You know he's married and he's leading you on.

He's not going to leave his wife. He's a sleaze-ball and I'm angry with him. My cousin Jim has talked to him and told him he has to stop this 'relationship' with you or he will be fired."

"Diane, all I am doing is talking to him. I have never had anyone treat me like he does, or explain things to me like he has. He has not led me on or lied to me."

"Why don't you find a boyfriend your own age who is not married? This is not God's will for you and you will be punished if you continue this relationship," Diane argued.

Turning around to face Diane, Marion said, "I'm open to a boyfriend. I've just not found one. I'll pray about this."

Marion tried to immerse herself in the new hotel maid job to keep her mind off Hank. She and Diane spent little time together as Marion mingled with the other young people living in the dorm. She was open to finding a boyfriend, but knew it was not feasible since she was leaving at the end of the summer to enter Philadelphia Bible College to hopefully become a missionary and leave her sinful life behind her.

When Diane left the Island to begin nursing school, she cut off all communication with Marion, ending their five-year friendship. Marion believed her sinful actions caused the breakup. Sad, angry, and confused, she mourned the loss of Diane in her life. She also grieved Hank's departure, and wondered all the while why she could not have a real boyfriend like her friends did. No time to wallow in her sorrow, she was leaving Hank behind, or so she thought.

Session Eight

"Dr. Weinstein, it's hard to believe that I've only been coming to see you for a couple of months. How come no one tells people growing up that it's okay to go to therapy to process your life, to make sense of how it is all woven together?" Marion asked.

"Sometimes, therapy exponentially moves people along at an accelerated pace the further they get into it. Just think, we've covered a hundred years of family history, and eighteen years of your life, in two months. That is a great deal of territory. You cannot even fathom where you are going to be by the time all this is finished, but I can because I have witnessed it in so many. Marion, maybe one day you can write about it and people will read your book and know it is okay to enter therapy."

"I like that idea, but I have to finish telling my story, before I can ever write it. So onward and upward," Marion said gesturing with her hands.

New Path

THROUGHOUT THE SUMMER, Marion rarely heard from Sarah. She dutifully wrote letters home once a week excluding any mention of Hank, her sadness, or disappointment. Mom and Rhonda came for a short visit the end of July staying at the Island's Smith Bed and Breakfast Inn. The visit only intensified Marion's desperation to leave behind her enmeshment in serving as a de facto confidante and surrogate spouse for her mother. Sarah shared too many details about the perils of being a single parent, thereby overburdening an already confused Marion. Thinking it must be her job to solve her mother's dilemmas to prevent her mother from rejecting her too, Marion complied.

Sarah routinely sought Marion's advice on personal issues. One day she asked, "Do you think I should date Bud, Mildred's ex-husband? I like him as a friend, but dating him seems odd."

Exasperated, Marion harshly replied, "Mom, I don't know. If you like him go to a movie, or tell him you just want to be friends."

Raising her voice, Sarah shot back, "Marion, you don't have to get snippy with me. I just asked your opinion."

More calmly, Marion replied, "Mom I'm sorry, but I don't have any dating experience. I don't know what to tell you."

"Fine. I won't ask your advice ever again," Sarah retorted, storming out of the room to go look for ice.

Rhonda, who was now eleven years old, just sat on the bed staring out the window hoping Marion and Sarah would stop bickering.

"Rhonda, I'm sorry mom and I fought. I don't know what to tell her and I hate that you are with her all alone," she guiltily admitted.

"It's okay, Marion. I stay at my babysitter's most of the time and even some weekends unless mom lets me go visit Dad and Mary. Mrs. McMillan has cats and plays games with me and her kids treat me like their sister. I'd rather be there anyway," revealed Rhonda.

"Remember, I love you and I'm always there for you when I can be and I'll take you wherever I am when I can," Marion promised.

"Good, but I'd better get my things packed up before mom gets mad at me," said Rhonda.

Silence reigned over the remainder of the afternoon after Sarah returned, until she and Rhonda finally embarked on the ferry headed for the mainland and their drive home. Two weeks after the visit and two weeks before Marion's scheduled departure for college, she received this note from Sarah.

Dear Marion,

I'm writing you because I could not reach you at your Island dorm. I'm sorry, but as I told you back in March your dad and I do not have the money to pay the difference between your scholarship and the remaining tuition balance for Philadelphia College of the Bible. We will talk when you come home.

Mom

How could her mother let her down like this? College was her one and only escape hatch from the quicksand of her existence? Why couldn't Sarah have mentioned this during her visit to the Island? With no alternative plan, Marion's hopes fizzled like air being squeezed out of an untied balloon. Going to Bible College to be trained as a missionary was to be her redemption from her wayward path, but the rug was suddenly yanked out from under her due to lack of funds. She contemplated her options while sitting down at the water's edge at her and Hank's special spot. She remembered contemplating suicide here at one point during the former year, but this time, instead of suicidal thoughts she was now determined to find a new path. She decided to work until the end of the season then going back to Lodge to attend Green Bay Community College while she revised her plans. Before she left the Island, an event occurred which forever changed how she viewed her abilities to be persuasive. On September 5[th,] Marion, with some of her dorm mates, decided to ride down their bicycles down the steep Grand Hotel hill. One of the women, Debbie, hesitated to join in, but with Marion's urging and teasing, she reluctantly consented. Halfway down the hill, Debbie, who was unfamiliar with navigating such terrain, slammed on her brakes. As a result, she flew over the handlebars and hit her head on the curb. Looking cautiously back, and wondering why Debbie was not beside her, Marion gasped in horror seeing Debbie lying unconscious on the grass, thinking she caused her friend's death.

Once by her side, Marion rapidly slipped into crisis management mode. Although she thought, *Where do I go? There are no phones nearby and no cars on the Island.*

As a crowd gathered, Marion's heart was beating so fast she could barely talk. "You, guy in the khaki shorts, stay with her while I run to the golf course pro shop to call for help." Dumbfounded and frozen, the dorm mates just stared at the scene in disbelief.

Marion's only thought as she ran across the golf course was, "*I have to get her help fast.*" With everything appearing in slow motion, Marion sprinted in front of the foursome hurrying to finish up the 18th hole at dusk. Wasting no time to apologize, she dashed uphill the last ¼ mile to the pro shop.

Once inside she breathlessly said, "There has been a bicycle accident on the Grand Hill. My friend needs help now. Please send the emergency people quickly. I'll be there waiting."

In what was probably less than a total of ten minutes she was back at unconscious Debbie's side talking to her softly, "I'm so sorry I made you ride down the hill. Please forgive me. Please, God make her be okay."

The only Island emergency vehicle, a decade old Ford station wagon with white painted side panels and red paint peeling off the "b" and "c" of the word "Ambulance," rolled up to the scene. "What happened?" the paramedics asked. Marion relayed the story, the words spilling out rapidly, steeped in guilt. Debbie urgently needed to get to the hospital in Sault Ste. Marie, fifty miles away *after* a thirty-minute high-speed boat ride to the mainland.

Marion's boss, Mr. Waterman, owner of the Lake Michigan Hotel, met her at the dock and handed her a $50 bill equivalent to three times that amount in today's economy. Loading the still-unconscious Debbie into the speedboat took precedence over Marion's fear of the water. If anything happened to Debbie, it was Marion's fault, an unfathomable possibility. On the way to the hospital the paramedics asked Marion several questions, oddest of all,

"Does Debbie smoke? We could give her a cigarette, if it would help calm her."

Marion knew smoking was not right for someone unconscious hooked up to oxygen, but things were done differently in 1969.

Once Debbie was triaged, Marion had the formidable task of notifying her parents and acquiring the insurance information. What do you say when waking someone up at 3:00 a.m.? They soon began the eight-hour drive to tend to their daughter.

Debbie was unable to return to college for the Fall semester due to the need for extensive dental work to repair her broken teeth. Fortunately, she did not recall anything after initially getting on the bike. Marion and Debbie remained friends for over four and a half decades even though they lived a thousand miles apart.

Within a week of Debbie's accident, it was time to return to the haunted house of Marion's childhood. The half hour ferry ride to the mainland and ten-hour bus ride back to Lodge was not long enough for her to transition from her morose mood into a hopeful one.

Stepping back into her pre-graduation life was knowingly walking into quicksand with no life line. The home environment was tense, attributable partly due to Marion, who was unemployed, enrolled part time in Green Bay Community College. Marion longed to flee the nest but Sarah, who received no child support from Andy for eighteen-year-old Marion, was determined that Marion must pay her own way. Before graduating high school, Marion had cleaned the house and cooked supper, but now all she wanted was a fresh start, hopefully with no more disappointments, dashed dreams, or people abandoning her or telling her what she *should* do.

Marion's family geographical cure was to move to Wisconsin. Marion's own first geographical cure started with a 3a.m. visit from a spirit. Marion, rubbed her eyes and got adjusted to the brightness illuminating her room coming from the opaque shimmering figure standing at the end of her bed. Even though she and the apparition did not have to utter an audible word, it was a very precise conversation, nonetheless. Marion, did not fear this entity like the man in her window, the boy on the roof, or the spirit invading her house related to the Sunday school paper. The God-connected ones were more familiar because she had been experiencing them since she was a small child. It was strangely reminiscent of her bedroom exchange years earlier. "Go to Ithaca," the Light entity told her in her head in an echoing voice.

Sitting up in bed she protested, "No, Hank lives there and I'm starting a new life and staying away from him. I'm taking college classes here. I can't go there. It's wrong!"

Commanding, he extended his right arm in the direction of her east window and said, "Go! I told you years ago, I am your guide, remember now?"

Relaxing, recognizing him now, she said, "Oh, it's you again. I just don't understand why I should go to the place I'm trying to avoid." "When you go, you'll understand," said the disappearing Indian Chief.

In her prayer time, a few hours later she sought God's direction asking, "Do I move to Ithaca as the Spirit said or not?" After contemplating the possibility, she decided to go for a visit and then decide. She called Gretchen and Tim to ask if it was okay for her to visit. They agreed. She obtained her college assignments for the week, called a travel agent, extracted money from savings, and within twenty-four hours was on a plane headed for Ithaca, uncertain where this journey was leading.

Without Sarah present, Gretchen and Tim were encouraging and more hospitable. They suggested Marion temporarily move in with them, get a job where Gretchen worked, and figure out what she wanted to do with the rest of her life. Marion did not inform them the role Hank played in her decisions or of her noticeable depression.

Before flying back to Green Bay to potentially withdraw from college and arrange to move to Ithaca, Marion called Pastor Gates to inquire of a place she could go to prayerfully consider her options. The woman, Maude Griswold, widowed for fifteen years, lived next to the Green Bay Baptist Church. Her ministry was to provide a haven for those who were in the cross roads of life, unsure which fork to take.

Timidly, "Mrs. Griswold, thank you for opening your home to me. In the last forty-eight hours after much prayer and consternation, I made my decision. I'm dropping out of Green Bay Community College, and moving to Ithaca, New York to start a new life."

Marion's only regret was leaving Rhonda behind again, to fend for herself. Sarah was preoccupied with finding her own way in the world, exploring what it meant to be a divorcee in the 1960's. The community shunned divorce fearing it might be contagious. Thus, people avoided the Parker house. Marion knew she somehow had to set the example, modeling for Rhonda how to escape from the family pattern of being stuck in poverty, suppression, and depression.

As nurturing as possible, Marion sat Rhonda down for a talk in the same chair in the bedroom where Gretchen had introduced her to the plan of salvation. "Rhonda, you know I love you, right?"

With a questioning look, Rhonda asked, "Yeah, but why are you telling me this?"

Taking in a deep breath Marion gingerly said, "Because I'm going to Ithaca to temporarily live with Gretchen and Tim until I can afford my own place. I'll bring you there when I can. I want you to still brush your teeth, go to church, and don't let mom's ways get to you, okay?"

With tears streaming down her face, Rhonda bravely answered, "Okay, but you promise you'll come get me when you can."

Pledging while making an imaginary X across her chest, "Cross my heart and hope to die, I will." "When are you leaving?" Rhonda inquired.

Sighing Marion reluctantly said, "Unfortunately, two days from now."

Sad, Rhonda asked, "So soon? Does Mom know?"

"Not yet. I'll tell her tonight when she gets home from work," she said leaving that the last item on her "to do" list.

Little sister revealed what Marion already knew.

"Mom's going to be mad that you're leaving."

"Maybe, but I was supposed to go off to college, so maybe she'll be okay with it," knowing it would not be that simple.

Later that evening Marion cooked Spanish rice for supper, something she had not done in four months which alerted Sarah that something was up.

As anticipated when the plates were cleared Marion said, "Mom, I have something to tell you."

Sitting back down at the same kitchen table where a divorce was planned as well as Gretchen's wedding now Marion announced, "Mom, I'm moving to Ithaca to live with Gretchen and Tim and work at the same hospital that Gretchen does."

With a look of sadness mixed with concern, Sarah said, "Did Gretchen and Tim really say you can stay with them?"

Taking on the reassuring parent role, Marion said,

"Mom, you gave me all the ingredients. I need to be an adult and now it is time to go put all that together."

Sarah, feeling more the abandonment than the apprehension that her strong-willed daughter would succeed, sighed, wringing her hands and said, "I thought you would get a job here and help out financially."

Not realizing the weight of her words Marion said, "Mom, I need to leave Lodge and make a new name for myself out in the world with a clean slate where no one knows me or judges me by my actions."

Perplexed, "What actions?"

"Mom, you know by the choices I make, who I hang around with, where I go, stuff like that."

Surprised Sarah said, "Oh, I didn't know anyone was judging you."

Trying to put her off Marion said, "It's no big deal, just forget it."

Back on topic Sarah asked, "So when are you going?"

Answering confidently, "The day after tomorrow." "I see. Well what will you do with all your stuff?"

Sarah asked.

"When I get settled I'll have you ship to me what I want."

With furrowed brow Sarah answered, "That's fine, but I don't have extra money to send them."

Reassuringly Marion affirmed, "I'll pay for it." Nothing more was said that night as each let the news settle into their brains.

By November of 1969, Marion, working for Ithaca Hospital, the same as Gretchen, moved in with a neighbor named Shirley, thus taking one step closer to total independence. One evening Shirley invited her former boyfriend Mike and his cousin Rick over. Rick, just back from Vietnam, insisted the country owed him big time for his service.

He told Marion while they were sitting on the couch, "You are the first girl I've been out with since I got back from Nam."

As if his service awarded him free privileges, he proceeded to make unwelcomed advances toward Marion. She did not even know his last name.

"Rick, stop! I don't like what you are doing," she said pushing him away.

"Aw, come on. You know you like it," he said tightening his hold around her waist.

"No, I don't." As his grip tightened, she became more frightened.

Shirley, making out with Mike in the bedroom, laughingly shouted, "Relax, you might enjoy it." Marion wondered what was wrong with her. Was she supposed to enjoy someone touching her without her permission in a physically unpleasant way?

During the encounter, images of Kevin in the toolshed resurfaced and she had the uncanny feeling that this action was not new in her life. Feigning a full bladder, she managed to lock herself in the bathroom.

Rick left cursing under his breath, "Ungrateful American girls. After I fought for this country, unbelievable!"

She wore long sleeves for weeks until the bruises on her arms faded. She never saw or heard from him again.

Six weeks after she moved to Ithaca, Marion hesitantly, finally contacted Hank to invite his family over for dinner.

Shirley, told Marion, "You're not over Hank, so you'd better be careful."

Hank, Sally, and sons Hank Jr and Matthew came for dinner. Novice cook, she made roasted chicken like Sally fixed for her eight months earlier along with lumpy mashed potatoes, lumpy gravy, green beans, and brownies. Laughingly, they all ate the flawed food watching the boy's antics aged eighteen months and four years old.

"Sally, why don't we help Marion get settled in her new apartment when she gets the keys?" Hank asked turning to Sally sitting across from him at the kitchen table.

"Hank," she said half-smiling, "Remember, we have multiple Christmas obligations over the next few weeks. I'll collect a few items from our house to help her get started."

"Thanks, I'll let you know when I get the keys," said Marion smiling.

By January she was in her own efficiency apartment in the same complex as Shirley and Gretchen. Hank and Sally did give her some things for her apartment, but did not pursue a regular ongoing relationship. Marion managed to go to work, buy a single bed, a used table, a radio, a phone, and put money in savings. Life was certainly better than living back home.

Session Nine

Marion inquired, "Dr. Weinstein, you're Jewish, right?"

"Yes. Why? Does that matter?" he asked. "No, I'm just curious. Does the Jewish faith use guilt to control people as much as I believe some Christian churches do?"

He laughed, "No one faith has a monopoly on inflicting guilt. It is universal in hopes that we will escape God's wrath."

"I can see how guilt and shame have shaped my life," Marion said as she unfolded her hands, ready to share the next chapter of her life.

Caught Unaware

JUST FOUR MONTHS away from her nineteenth birthday, Marion felt proud to be living on her own in her brick 1930's era third floor walk-up efficiency apartment even if the hand-cranked windows did not open fully. On Saturday evening, she pulled up her T.V. tray beside her single bed/couch and lifted her bowl of chicken noodle soup with mushed saltine crackers onto her lap. As her cup of Lipton's pekoe tea cooled on the table she wondered what Hank was doing with his family on this night. Would there ever be someone she would share her life with? Her only social contact outside of her Ithaca Hospital's accounting department job was to grab a quick cheeseburger with Gretchen on payday.

"Boy, Kroll's is so crowded today. Do you think we'll find a seat in time to get back to work by 1:00 p.m.?" Marion anxiously asked Gretchen.

"Don't worry about it, Marion. If we're a few minutes late, we can make it up. Relax."

"I wish I could relax. Tell me something good about being married."

"Well, Tim is a good listener. He is very protective. He loves me and is very gentle. That about sums it up, don't ya think?"

"Yup, you're right. Here comes our food. We'd better hustle. I see hungry people standing in line waiting, drooling, eyeing our meal."

Smiling Gretchen said, "Marion, you have mustard on your chin. That is probably why they are staring at us."

Both laughing, they chatted on, heedless of the hungry vultures waiting for their booth.

In addition, to hear a friendly voice in between paydays, Marion began calling Gretchen on Tuesday nights, but sensed she was interrupting their privacy so she always kept the conversation short.

While trudging the two blocks through the hardpacked snow to the bus stop each morning, Marion dreamed of her future husband and how great her life would be when she could fulfill her call to do missionary work. As she shivered, she prayed the bus would be on time on that cold January morning in 1970.

While she impatiently waited for the bus, she was approached by a petite young lady with shoulder-length blonde hair wearing a blue polyester pantsuit visible from her open brown-wool car coat. The woman blew on her chapped, ungloved red hands to keep them warm.

Marion wondered why she did not button up her coat or wear gloves in the nippy air.

Reaching the end of the sidewalk at the bus stop sign, the young woman introduced herself to Marion, "Hi, my name's Betty. I've seen you in our building. I live below you in 409 with Fred and Eileen. I'm a freshman at Ithaca Community College." Beckoning she said, "Come wait in this building's entryway. It'll shield us from this nasty wind and we'll see the bus coming long before it gets here."

Teeth chattering Marion replied, "Thanks, I'm Marion. I moved here in October from Wisconsin and I'm still learning the ropes. Aren't you cold with an open coat and no gloves? Oh, here comes the bus now."

As they boarded the bus Betty answered, "I woke up late and had no time to button up or find my gloves. Another minute and I would have missed the bus and my first class."

Each weekday morning thereafter, Marion and Betty met at the bus stop and chatted as they shared a seat on the jostling express bus. Marion asked Betty, "Do you think we'll make it to Midtown Center by 7:30? I have a meeting with my supervisor at 7:45. I dread that walk through the plaza with that cold wind blowing."

Betty responded, "I know. After the bus lets me off, I carefully step over the slippery gravel, in the parking lot on the way to my classroom building while the wind whips through my wool coat and numbs my legs. I'll be so glad when I get married and can have a car to drive to school."

"At least you can wear slacks. We can't at work.

When are you getting married?"

"We're thinking about doing it on Ronnie's birthday in March."

As she smiled Marion said, "Oh, that's nice."

Sighing, she quietly added, "I hope to marry someday."

With glazed eyes, she silently just hoped for a boyfriend for herself.

"You know Marion? I was just thinking – Ronnie's got a brother who is not seeing anyone that I know of.

Maybe we could double-date sometime."

Marion did not respond as they pulled into the bus hub. "Have a great day, Betty. See ya." "Bye Marion. Don't freeze to death."

On the first Monday morning in February, winter was in full force at only ten degrees above zero. Marion's breath hung in the air as she blew warm air through her olive green thick mittens in an attempt to keep her hands from stinging. Cayuga Lake's warm moist air mingled with Ithaca's dry cold air creating a condition called "Lake Effect." It made the air feel colder and wetter than the Wisconsin winter to which Marion was accustomed. She trudged to the bus stop, legs covered by tights under her green and blue plaid woolen jumper but still burning in the frigid air. Underneath the un-shoveled sidewalk lurked patches of ice. She slipped on one, but managed to stay upright thanks to her rubber soled black suede snow boots. With her lunch bag in one hand and shoe bag in the other she maneuvered her frozen hands inside her mittens adjusting her black woolen scarf to keep her mouth covered. Her ears were concealed inside her knitted variegated cap, but she could still feel the stinging of the cold air penetrating the fabric. Just as she reached the steps of the waiting bus, Betty dashed up behind her sliding all the way until she grabbed the step's railings.

Stomping their feet to remove the snow and start the warming process, they laughed and found a seat close to the front heater. They caught up on the weekend's activities. Marion had none to report. Her weekend consisted of staying inside and reading since she had no television, no car, no money for socializing, and so far, no friends to hang out with.

Betty exuberantly said, "You should have been with us. Ronnie and I had a blast ice skating down at Midtown and warmed up after with a cup of hot chocolate. We slipped and slid all over the ice, but we laughed the whole time. You should go with us sometime.

"Oh, by the way, did I tell you about Ronnie's brother, Frankie?"

Smiling, repeating what she had heard multiple times, Marion said, "Yes, he's about thirty, has a kid, is divorced, a $1000 in debt, and was called into the ministry.

Did I get it right?

Interrupting and before Marion could say another word, "Yeah but you forgot the part about he's a nice guy."

Impatient Marion said, "So? Why are you telling me this?"

Pausing, "Well......Wednesday is his birthday."

Marion, shook her head and turned toward Betty, who was sitting beside her on the brittle camel-colored bus seat. With blazing blue eyes Marion said, "I know what you're going to ask and the answer's no!"

Coaxing, Betty said, "Aw come on. It's the guy's birthday. It's only one date. If you don't like him, don't go out with him again."

Emphatically Marion stated, "I told you my last blind date was a disaster and I'm still trying to recover from that."

Betty tilted her head to the right and teasingly said, "Yeah, but Frankie maybe can help you get over that."

Marion puffed her cheeks and then let out a slow deep breath as she turned toward the window fogging the glass. Her shoulder muscles relaxed while her eyes moved downward in a thoughtful pose. Softening a little she said,

"I don't know."

Gesturing with her open palms, Betty pleaded, "Come on. Give it a try for me. Pleeeeeease?"

Pointing her finger at Betty, Marion said, "Just once. You owe me big time. If this doesn't work out, it's your fault." "You'll have fun and thank me later," Betty predicted.

Resigned Marion said, "Okay, but you'd better be right."

"Trust me, it'll be fine," Betty reassured her.

Marion began to absentmindedly fiddle with the strings on her coat while reminiscing about her time with Hank on the bench by the Island boardwalk. Their deep discussions shaped her life and she felt now like she was betraying him if she dated someone, even though he was married.

Around six p.m., before Marion was to meet up with Betty, Ronnie, and Frankie for the blind date, she went downstairs to finish her weekly laundry. With curlers in her hair the size of orange juice cans, wearing bright blue slacks with huge multi-colored flowers imprinted on them, and a white blouse with a notched collar, Marion descended the stairs to the laundry room. Almost colliding with this guy coming up. Dressed in a bleached white cotton button down shirt with black pleated cuffed trousers and scuffed black wing tip shoes, wearing a black knee-length trench coat reeking of cigarette smoke, he exchanged mumbled excuses with Marion for their near collision as they moved past one another.

Two hours later she went down to the apartment where Betty boarded with Fred and Eileen. She greeted her blind date when the door opened, thinking to herself, "*Oh it's him, the guy on the stairs. He doesn't look thirty. He's rather large, but good-looking, has a nice smile, and makes good eye contact. Hmm, is he too good to be true, I wonder?*"

Attempting to appease her awkwardness while looking at Fred and Eileen's maple bookshelf, Marion asked Betty, "Got any good bedtime reading material?"

Frankie grinned at Marion as he sat on the armless aqua upholstered sofa saying, "I could tell you a good bedtime story."

Blushing, Marion immediately felt uncomfortable, yet she was intrigued with his Frankie forwardness. Being an inexperienced dater, Marion allowed the other three to choose the group's destination. Sitting around Fred and Eileen's drop leaf dining room table, the other three debated the pros and cons of each night spot. Finally reaching a consensus, they all piled in the car, stopping first at the *Penny Arcade Nightclub* to listen to a local band called "*Old Salt*" play loud rock music. Frankie chugged down three Utica Club beers in less than an hour.

Marion heard Pastor Gates' voice in her head: "Do not give in to the sin of immorality…" She felt extremely uncomfortable being around drinkers and smokers. Would God punish her as her pastor warned for being with someone who had such ungodly habits? Dancing with him was worse, the work of the Devil, and it could only lead to immoral behavior and away from God. As much as she wanted to fit in, she felt like a fish out of water. Declining alcohol was not a problem, but standing on the dance floor with a man gyrating in front of her while she moved like a robot embarrassed her.

Marion felt dizzy as the dance floor strobe light revolved and made freakish shadows on the walls. Frankie noticed she was not having any fun. He shouted over the blaring music to his brother, "Hey Ronnie, let's make like a hockey player and get the puck out of here. I can see that Marion isn't having a good time and the music's too loud.

How 'bout we go to Star Bowling Lanes?"

"What? I can't hear you. The music's too loud," said Ronnie while motioning for them to leave.

Outside everyone's ears rung as they stomped through the snow to the car with their breath visible in the frosty air.

Once inside the bowling alley, they warmed up a bit. Frankie, very affectionately, teased Marion. With a wink he said, "If you get a strike, I'll kiss you on the lips." Marion, eyes downcast and with a voice barely audible, said, "I've never gotten a strike so I doubt that'll happen." Before the words were cold she rolled a strike.

Smiling Frankie said, "Way to go! Now come over here and let me kiss you."

Ill-prepared, Marion, had always been an obedient child so did not know she could resist. Her father was never forceful or commanding so Frankie's behavior was different than any man in her life. She did as she was told all the while a knot formed in her stomach. Pastor Gates had warned against immoral behavior, but had not defined the particulars. Kissing someone two hours into knowing them did not feel right, but she could not put her finger on why she felt so uncomfortable. He drew her to his lap and kissed her with a full open mouth. Was she supposed to resist? Having only kissed Hank, the married man, on two occasions, she did not know what was normal to do on a first date. She was embarrassed and very cognizant of her lack of finesse in this dating situation. She had no clue how to act. Preoccupation with her own behavior consumed her thoughts.

The New York state legal age to drink age was eighteen in 1970.

Grabbing a beer from the concession counter Ronnie brought it over to Betty, the scorekeeper, careful not to spill it on the way as a Camel cigarette dangled from his mouth. "Here ya go, Sweetie, a beer for us to share," he said as he placed it in the beverage holder beside the bright blue plastic molded seat she sat in.

"Thanks, honey," as she sipped the foam off the top of the mug.

Marion vicariously enjoyed watching Ronnie and Betty interact in sync like the internal mechanism in a clock, each responding to the other with the right words, at the proper time, and what appeared to be effortless affection. Secretly, Marion wished she could feel comfortable enough with male relationships to replicate those behaviors, which looked like fun, but she equated fun with sin.

Betty looked over to see Marion on Frankie's lap and smiled and said, "I told 'ja you'd have a good time." Marion excused herself to go to the restroom and Betty followed. Betty sensed her uncomfortableness and encouraged her, "Marion, you need to relax. Frankie's a nice guy. Enjoy yourself."

Marion let out a deep sigh and said, "I'm trying to. I haven't had much dating experience so I'm not sure what to do."

"Don't worry about it, honey. You're doing fine," said Betty reassuring Marion.

Going back out to the lanes, Ronnie asked the girls,

"Had enough?"

Looking at each other Betty and Marion chimed in unison, "We have."

"Ok, let's head back to the apartment," said Frankie, the driver.

Driving home was tricky on the ice which had formed under the new fallen snow. Back at the apartment building, Frankie, manners intact, opened her car door and offered his hand so Marion would not slip on the snowy sidewalk. She expected Frankie to walk her to her door, make some excuse to leave, and the date to be over. He surprised her.

Walking up the three flights of stairs to her efficiency, Marion paused, leaned against her solid brown metal door and turned to say good night.

Frankie towering ten inches above her smiled and asked, "So, Marion may I come in?"

Marion's body stiffened and she put her left hand on her doorknob as she said, "No, I gotta work in a few hours and my mom always taught me (she really had not) to not let boys in on the first date."

Dejectedly, Frankie stepped back a couple of inches, lowered his voice and said, "Okay, when can I see you again?"

Puzzled she responded, avoiding his gaze,

"You…want a second date with me?"

Surprised, with his hands outstretched, he said,

"Yah, why not?"

Speaking softly with regret in her voice she said, "I thought because I don't drink, or smoke, know how to dance or bowl, or even say much, you wouldn't want a second date."

Demonstrating a little foot maneuver, he said, "Naw, I dance like a fool when I'm drinking, but I'm really shy, an introvert. I talk a lot cause I'm nervous. Let me come back tomorrow night and we can get to know each other better, okay?"

Unsure, if he was weaseling his way in, she haltingly said, "I guess so."

Pleased with himself he said, "Okay, I'll be here after I get off work around eight."

As a parting reminder, she raised her left index finger, as if issuing a parental warning and said, "I have to get up for work around six so you can't stay late."

His challenging response, "Is that, right?" was met with a slight body dip to the right and a perplexed look on her face. Frankie knew he had her then so he said with a gleam in his eye, "Okay."

Having only three first dates in her life, she was unsure what the proper etiquette was for the very important second date. Dashing home from the bus stop, her thoughts raced, *Should I curl my hair, put on fresh makeup, change out of my work clothes? I'm so nervous I'm afraid to eat 'cause it'll upset my stomach. What should I talk about? How late will he stay? What if he decides to not come?*

Before she got too excited anticipating the evening's activities and almost as an unwelcomed afterthought that put a damper on her plans, she remembered, *Oh and I gotta do what my pastor says is right and proper.*

Impressively, Frankie returned as promised, without Ronnie and Betty, at exactly 8p.m.

Embarrassed at only having a single bed and a used 2x6 foot chocolate brown Formica fold-out table with two mismatched chairs in her apartment she welcomed him in. The dark brown tile floor covered with a 6x9 foot orange and brown shag area rug helped cushion the sound to floors below but only minimally took the bite out of the cold permeating the air. The orange, yellow, and chocolate brown nylon curtains did not block the cold air from blowing in at the window sills either. In the background, playing on the Zenith table top stereo was the catchy hit tune "Raindrops Keep Falling on my Head" as they greeted one another with a brief hug. Lacking a television to entertain them, they resorted to conversing about each other's lives leaning against the wall, both initially sitting on the bed until the wee hours of the morning. Marion, only five foot-one and 119 pounds, was dwarfed by Frankie's five feet eleven 200-pound frame.

Frankie, an attractive fellow, who was a college graduate, managed a produce section of Shumans grocery store. Pursuing the validity of what Betty had said about Frankie, Marion slid onto the floor and looking up at him inquired cautiously, "I want to go to college, but it's expensive. How'd you afford it, Frankie?"

"Oh, New York State helps with tuition and I took out some student loans to help cover my books. I still owe $1000 bucks, but I'll have that paid off in two years." She was relieved and prodded a bit further. "My parents got divorced two years ago. Divorce is hard on everyone. Any divorce in your family?"

"Nope, my folks have been married for twenty-five years and I don't plan on ever getting divorced," he said lighting up a cigarette.

"So, Frankie, what do you want to do when you grow up?" she said hugging her knees.

"Funny you should ask that, Marion. I got called, believe it or not, to be a preacher, but I told God, 'you got the wrong guy.' I like my evil ways too much to give 'em up."

"That's very interesting. I was called to be a missionary, but can't afford to go to Bible College to prepare," sigh.

She continued, "Do you ever want kids, Frankie?"

"Naw I don't think I can. I sowed my wild oats plenty and prayed for crop failure. Of all the women I've been with, no basket has been left on my doorstep with a note that said, 'this baby is yours'. I think I'm sterile. You got an ashtray?" he said flicking the ashes into his hand.

"Yah, my doctor said I can't have kids," Marion said softly, handing him the wastepaper basket on the floor.

Frankie either did not hear it or ignored it. She did not pursue it further.

Betty's description of him being divorced was inaccurate, a characteristic her Baptist background would have frowned upon. So maybe she could relax a bit, find out more about him to see if he had redeeming qualities. His sexual history did not deter her curiosity about whether his days of philandering were over.

Frankie leaned against the wall with Marion's foam rubber pillow behind his head with his legs dangling over the side of the single bed as he said, "Marion, you're so easy to talk to. I can't believe I'm telling you all these things."

Marion, not ready to be too close physically, continued sitting on the floor hugging her other pillow between her bent knees and chest while sitting on the thin rug that barely cushioned her behind from the cold emanating from the tile floor. As she shook her head affirmatively she said, "Yeah, most people tell me their secrets including my Composition teacher last year revealing the details of his wife's affair. I'm a big sister to all my guy friends." She paused. "Funny, but there's not one of my guy friends that I could call my big brother," she sighed.

Nodding his head, Frankie said, "Wow that's pretty intense having your teacher tell you that stuff. He must've really trusted you."

Fearing she had revealed too much, Marion lowered her eyes, diverting his attention away from that topic. She asked him, "Would ya like some Seven-Up? I don't have much in the way of drinks to offer you."

"Sure, that'd be nice," he said as she took the ten steps to her mini fridge, pulled out the soda bottle, and poured an equal amount into two plastic tumblers, before sitting down beside him.

Frankie kept on talking, "I'm a big ol' teddy bear to lots of my female friends, but I've dated a bunch too. That one special woman hasn't shown up yet, even though I'm now twenty-three and one day old!"

Ever the Romeo, he opened up further. "Yeah, when I was engaged to Michelle from Albany I'd hitchhike up there for the weekend while she was in high school. When she went off to Minnesota to college she found some other guy. She broke up with me during finals week. That really threw me into a tailspin," Frankie said sighing.

"Oh, I'm sorry. I'm sure that hurt," Marion said patting him on the arm. "Did you date anyone else since then?" "Nothing serious, but I had a standby gal in Cortland through the whole relationship. All I had to do was prime her with a beer and she'd do whatever I wanted."

"Oh, I'll bet Michelle didn't approve of that," Marion said frowning.

"No, need to tell her. A guy has needs. If you can't be with the one you love, love the one you're with, right?" Frankie said nonchalantly.

She did not know how to respond. She was startled by his confession, but did not take it personally, believing he, like other guys, would just share his secrets, needing a sister, and move on. She dared not think he might be desirous her.

Finally, around 2:30 a.m. and proud of herself for setting a limit, she told Frankie, "I have to get up for work in three hours. You need to go."

Suggestively he said, "I could just sleep here."

Firmly she responded, "No, my sister and her husband live down the street and I don't want them to think I'm entertaining men overnight. After all, I don't want the neighbors to talk."

"Who cares what the neighbors think?" with hands outstretched, he asked. Then lowering his hands to his side, he said with a smile, "But since you nicely asked me to go, I will. Good night Marion Parker. I had a nice time."

"Thanks Frankie, so did I."

Walking toward the door, he stopped, turned his head to look over his left shoulder while his right hand rested on the doorknob and said, "How 'bout I take you out to dinner Saturday evening?"

Pleased, with a wide grin, she said, "Okay that would be nice."

Beaming, Frankie nodded and said, "I'll call you tomorrow night and we can discuss where you want to go eat."

She shifted her weight from one foot to the other and said with a deep sigh, "All right, but remember I need to get some sleep so please don't make it too late."

He asked, "How 'bout nine?"

She agreed, "Yes, nine's fine."

She walked toward the door preparing to secure the safety chain once he exited. Lingering at the door, like a child finding every reason to delay bedtime, Frankie boldly asked, "Can I have a kiss good night?

Her heart beat so loudly she believed he could hear it as he gazed down into her clear, wide, blue, uplifted eyes.

"Ah… yes," she breathlessly said.

As their expectant mouths met, he tried to slide his tongue into the kiss, but she resisted. He leaned back against the door with a disappointed grin, "What, no tongue?"

Defensively she retorted, "No, I don't do that." In truth, she had never experienced it and was caught off guard.

Sigh, "Okay, see ya later. Good night."

"Good night."

Marion crawled into bed, exhausted but exhilarated because someone so handsome, and who was not married, paid her attention, wanted to spend time with her and spend money on her. Was he too good to be true or a wolf in sheep's clothing? She did not know, but believed she would find out eventually.

On day three he called surprisingly early, around 6:30 p.m., and asked if he could come over. She did not have any other plans so she agreed.

Sitting down beside her he said, "So Marion Parker, how was your day?"

Pleased, that he was interested she answered,

"Good, I got the daily totals to balance at the hospital accounting office where I work. How was your day at the grocery store?"

He absentmindedly answered, "Oh, the same as every day. Angry, impatient, complaining customers. I don't want to talk about work right now. I want to kiss your inviting lips. Is that okay with you?"

Bashfully, blushing, she said, "I guess so."

He tilted her chin toward him as he closed his eyes and enveloped her receptive mouth. As she closed her eyes she felt butterflies in her stomach, but her conscience set off warning bells. *"Danger Will Robinson, Danger!"*

As she welcomed his kiss, she could hear the echo of Pastor Gates' words in her head, "Do not give in to immorality, but let your bodies be a temple for Christ." She got that, but no mom, sister, friend, or church leader had instructed her as to what the actual definition of immorality was and where to draw the line. To Marion, prolonged kissing equaled intimacy and that posed a dilemma for her. According to how she interpreted the sermons, intimacy was to be shared with the one and only person she would unite with for the rest of her life in marriage. She wanted that promise of a happy blessed marriage, but not yet. She was only eighteen! Marion had no plan for making this a permanent relationship because she wanted to travel and to fulfill her missionary call to work with teenagers in Australia of all places. Marion feared that if she ever gave into her emotions before marriage, they would drown out her conscience and thus provoke God's wrath.

When Marion opened the door to Frankie's arrival on day four of their relationship, he briefly kissed her on the lips and said, "Hey beautiful. Are you ready to go to the Brass Rail for dinner?

Marion smiled, feeling grown-up and flattered by his words. She said, "Ya, just let me get my coat," but inside she felt anxious due to lack of experience.

The Brass Rail was a fine restaurant that served alcohol. Frankie had a medium rare juicy sirloin steak, a salted baked potato dripping with butter and sour cream, steamed green beans, and three Pilsners. Frankie's size intimidated Marion. Although she felt protected around him, she also felt that his looming stature afforded him power over her. Marion felt as nervous as a teenager taking the road test to get her driver's license, and so had little appetite. While she nibbled on a lettuce and tomato salad and intermittently sipped on a Coke, Frankie said, "You're certainly a cheap date."

Returning to her apartment, she used the restroom while he lit up a Marlboro.

When Marion re-entered the front room, Frankie puffed on the cigarette, patted the spot beside him on the bed and said, "C'mere," which meant he wanted to make out.

She wanted to do other things like talk, yet she was lonely, enjoying his compliments and being taken to dinner, so she remained silent. She feared if she stated her wants, he would believe she was ungrateful and leave, never to return.

Sitting next to Marion on her bed, Frankie said,

"Guys in my hometown like to date the girls from the Baptist Bible College because they don't go to movies, or dance, but boy can they make out!"

A smooth talker, Frankie convinced Marion to cuddle with him on the bed. She kept pulling away, trying to talk to him and to find something to do other than heavy petting. Frankie became whiny, accusatory, and pleading. "My balls are blue cause you got me all excited.

It's painful. Now you need to do something about it." Marion was a bundle of confusion, so uncertain. She recalled Pastor Gates' sermon about sinful Eve tempting Adam in the garden and her punishment was childbirth pain, a consequence for all women, thereafter. Marion, so naïve, had now unknowingly sinned like Eve, by tempting Frankie, and she now felt shame, fear, and anxiety. What Marion wanted was a relationship, to be treated with respect, and to have a guy all to herself, not shared with someone else. Conversely, Frankie's words were neither loving nor sweet to her, and were instead raunchy, not romantic like she imagined a boyfriend would be. His words were commanding and reminiscent of Kevin beckoning her into the shed only to discover he meant harm, not good.

Inside she did feel responsible for Frankie's "blue" condition, but did not know what she was supposed to do about it. She felt guilt, torn between doing what Frankie -- and, as she herself discovered, desired, or following what the church taught her. Like the apostle Paul, she felt cognitive dissonance as her actions clashed with her faith. She identified with the passage: "That which I said I would do, I do not and that which I said I would not do, I am doing." Confusion reigned.

Sitting upright, Marion emphatically said, "Frankie, I'm a virgin and plan to stay one until I marry the person God has for me."

"I get that, but there are things we could do, making out, that do not take away your virginity," Frankie said holding onto her wrists.

Marion had never in her sheltered life heard of anything other than inter-course, and she did not even know how that officially, mechanically, worked. She was too embarrassed to read about it in the library and such things were never discussed in her family's household.

As Frankie guided her to lie back down on the bed he talked softly to her, "Marion, I think I'm falling for you."

As he breathed into her ear and gently nibbled on her neck, she involun-tarily moaned in a heavy whisper, "Oh," and unconvincingly said, "Pleeeease stop." As she did so, he hastily, inconspicuously, unzipped his pants exposing his penis.

As Frankie slowly moved away from her ear he firmly grasped her head as he forced it down on his penis securely holding it in place, just like her grand-father had done. Frankie said, "Oh, Marion that feels so good. Suck it hard." It did not take long for him to ejaculate a thick clump of a white liquid tasting like bitter green leaves, into her mouth.

Marion's mind, reeling in disbelief, did not quite understand what had happened. It felt vaguely familiar, but hazy. She promptly ran to the bathroom and threw up, including the Three Musketeers bar she had just eaten on the way home from dinner.

After flushing the vomit, she sat on the bathroom floor and leaned against the tub, in shock.

"Oh, God no! What did I do? I don't understand what happened. How could I allow such a thing? I'm so sorry. Please forgive me."

She was so confused. Prior to him holding her head she was aroused, but felt what he just did was not right. She could not stay in the bathroom and thankfully Frankie did not come after her. She stood up not to drown in her guilt. She re-entered the living area and found Frankie reclining on the bed, smoking a cigarette, and appearing very relaxed.

She thought, "*Okay, I don't understand what just happened but I'm not doing that again.*"

Standing on the cold dark tile floor a foot from the bed, Marion looked at him with an expression of anger, fear, and mystery all rolled into one.

Shaking she asked, "Frankie, why did you do that?" He leaned back against the wall, propped up on his left arm, smiled and jokingly teased, "Bet you never had that happen before did ya?"

Her voice quavering, she tried to make it sound strong and firm, "I didn't like it at all."

Sitting up, he leaned over and started to put his shoes on and said, "Well, I've got a way to make you forget all about it."

Keeping him at arm's length, she raised her eyebrows, tilted her head to the side and asked, "Watcha mean?"

Deliberately putting her off he said, "That I'll explain tomorrow. I gotta get up at six for the early shift at the store."

After he left, she plunked down on the unmade bed, sheets and blanket strewn every which way, the same bed where the carnal act took place. Sinking into despair, despite her vow to not allow it to happen, guilt consumed her. What he did, caressing and kissing her, felt good, but was it wrong? How far was too far? Where should she cut it off? Even though Marion was aroused by what Frankie was doing, secretly, guiltily she wished it was possible to enjoy such intimacy with Hank as a single, available man.

"God, I know I shouldn't have let him do that. I know you're mad at me. I'm sorry. No one ever told me about such things and I didn't see it coming."

She was curious, hurt, ashamed, angry, and bewildered all at once. She did not know what to do, but felt she had crossed a line. Whether ignorant of his approach or not, she was now damaged goods. Damaged goods were second helpings that no one wanted. The big red-letter A she believed visible to all when she kissed Hank, a married man, now paled in comparison to the fornication she had unwillingly committed with Frankie. Such behavior was an abomination to God. What recourse did she have? Typically, she plotted her course. She thought perhaps she could create a relationship with Frankie which was respectable and acceptable and that would be approved by her family and church, but only if they avoided any further heavy petting with climactic outcomes. Hoping she could remedy the situation, she allowed him back.

When he returned on day five, she was determined to do something other than make out, to talk about their day, discuss their individual future dreams, their connection to God, etc., but Frankie had a different plan.

As Frankie knocked on Marion's apartment door she drew in her breath with a resolve to behave as a proper Baptist girl should on this night. "It's open, come on in."

Frankie waltzed into the efficiency uncharacteristically locking the bolt and chain as he entered. He announced, "Don't want any nosy neighbors or uninvited guests coming in on our time together, do we?"

Puzzled by his actions, Marion said, "I don't give much thought to locking the door. I only know Betty, Fred, and Eileen in the building, and they never come up 'cause there's no place to sit. My sister's the only one who visits, but calls first. It's okay with me if locking the door makes you feel better. Come sit down here at the table. Supper's ready."

"Let me get my coat off, and go pee first."

They savored the quiet as they sat across from one another gazing into each other's eyes as bits of crumbled meatloaf fell off their forks and tumbled back onto their plates. Frankie was complimentary, "Thanks for the great meatloaf and smashed taters."

"You're welcome, Frankie. I'm glad you liked supper, but next time I won't add so much water to the potato flakes so they won't be so runny."

Quickly, she opened her mouth to voice her wants for the evening, but Frankie interrupted saying, "Remember our conversation last night that I said I had a way to make you forget throwing up and all that?"

"Of course, I do. What'd you have in mind?" thinking he meant taking her out someplace, she listened intently.

"Well, I want to explain what it's like for a woman to have an orgasm."

Perplexed she said, "A what?"

He answered, "Boy you're really naïve and Baptist indoctrinated."

Genuinely curious she said, "I don't know what're talking about." "Never mind," he said, temporarily getting off track from his plan.

"I'm sorry Frankie. I haven't been on many dates,

I'm only eighteen and my friends haven't either. We don't know about this dating stuff."

He said patiently, "It's okay." Putting his right forearm on the table, he said, "let me explain it to you."

Still curious, but now more nervous, Marion sat up straight in her chair and said, "Go ahead."

Like a teacher, he explained the female anatomy and how an orgasm was achieved. Eyes wide, she leaned closer to hear the details as he vividly described the process, which now was forever etched in her mind.

Pausing for dramatic effect, Frankie said, "The best part is, it's not really sex because it's not intercourse, so eatin' ain't cheating."

Incredulously, she asked, "So how come no one ever explained this to me in my church?"

Frankie said, "Maybe because they didn't want you to enjoy yourself."

"What does this orga…thing feel like?" she asked. "That's a good question. The best way I can explain it is, ya know the good feeling you get when you have a healthy dump?"

Snickering she said, "Yeah."

"Well it's kind of like that."

Her naivete showing she asked, "Does it hurt?" "Heck no, it feels good and after you wanna go to sleep. Like when you got me all hot last night. But it hurts, if the pressure's not released til I cum," he convincingly said.

Unsure if what he told her was truthful, she said, "Ohhhh, okay. Thanks for explaining it to me."

Preparing her, he answered, "You're welcome. Sometime I'll show you, if you want."

Hesitating, "I don't know. I'll have to think about it."

"Okay, but I promise ya, you'll like it and beg for more."

After they chatted for a while, he leaned over and started kissing her on the lips. He guided her by the hand to the bed. Aroused, she followed, but once reclining she tried to push him away. As she held him back, he ignored her resistance as he moved his face all the way down her torso. Curious and aroused, Marion did not resist, enjoying it blissfully until she reached orgasm. Then, anticlimactically, the guilt set in. It overwhelmed her, since technically, she was no longer a virgin. She was truly damaged goods now. As Frankie closed his eyes, she quietly slipped into the bathroom and cried. How could such pleasure be so wrong? She wondered what else her church did not tell her, and who was she to trust to tell her the truth? A disconnect developed between what she had been taught and her new experience. Ashamed and unsure with whom to discuss it, she kept it all inside.

She had many discussions with God over the next few days. She thought and felt her emotions intensely.

"God, what am I supposed to do now? I can't go back and become a virgin again."

On day six of their relationship, Frankie arrived after work around seven. Gently turning the knob, finding it unlocked, he announced as his snowy wet wingtips squeaked as he crossed the threshold, "Honey, I'm home." He added with a wink seeing her peek out from around the kitchen doorway, "You should be careful who you let in your open door." Then he said, "Mm, mm, what smells so good?" when the aroma of the spaghetti and meatballs with garlic toast hit him.

Feeling hopeful about this night, behaving as a proper Christian woman should, she chuckled and asked him as she held up the metal pot, "Do you think you can drain this pasta without a colander? I can't. I already lost the first batch in the sink."

"Let's see," as the slippery spaghetti slid into the aluminum sink basin. Rinsing it off, they salvaged enough to satisfy themselves. He sat at the table, on the bronze vinyl chair while Marion sat across from him smiling while he ate.

"Thank you for fixing another fine dinner," Frankie said.

"Do you want some more? You ate that like you were starving."

"I was. Know what I need now?"

Brow furrowed trying to figure it out she said, "No, what?"

"Got any coffee?"

"No, sorry. I don't drink it."

"The best finish to a meal is a cup of coffee with a cigarette. Maybe I can get a coffee pot and keep it here. Would that be okay?"

"Sure, but I don't know if I'll drink any of it."

Walking over to his coat pocket he pulled out his box of Marlboros and his Zippo lighter. Sitting back down at the table, he lit his cigarette and took a long slow drag staring off into space. He flicked his ashes into the new ashtray he bought.

He finally spoke, "Marion I have something I want to ask you, but I know it's too soon."

Marion had no inkling of what he was about to ask her – was he leaving, was he married, was he dying? She waited, holding her breath for the question.

He got up from the chair and anxiously started pacing. Finally, he asked, "I know I have only known you for six days, but will you marry me?"

Questioning with wide eyes she screeched, "What? Marry you, no. I can't. I wanna travel, to be a missionary, and to get a college degree. How could I do those things if I married you?"

Overcoming her objection, he said, "You could still do all those things with me."

Still in shock, unsure how to answer, Marion said, "I'll think about it."

Frankie looked dejected. Grabbing his overcoat, he said, "I'll be up on the roof."

Marion, once again caught off guard, knew intuitively that the proposal was probably just manipulation for more sex, but she was too bewildered by the speed at which this whole relationship was developing to know how to respond. Eventually, she climbed the steps to the flat roof top overlooking the City of Ithaca.

A cold rush of air enveloped her as she opened the heavy metal door to the rooftop. Eyeing Frankie off to her right, who was leaning against the gray cement wall and smoking a cigarette, shivering, Marion gathered her arms close into her chest and asked, "Frankie, other than having a smoke, why are you up here?"

With his bottom lip poked out, he answered quietly like a disciplined ten-year-old as he flicked his cigarette ashes into the wind, "I got my feelings hurt. I don't ask just anybody to marry me and you shot me down."

Gingerly, like a caring parent, she walked across the asbestos covered roof floor, avoiding puddles of half-frozen ice, and touched him on his left shoulder as she soothingly said, "You're a great guy and all, but I don't even know you. We've only been going out for six days. I'm just eighteen and I have many things I want to do with my life. I'm just starting out. But I'll tell you what…I'll think about it. Okay?"

Sighing he said, "Yeah, I guess. Let's go back down inside. It's freezing up here."

Laughing she said, "Okay, last one down's a rotten egg."

She thought about the marriage proposal continuously over the next week. No one ever proposed to her before. She was flattered on one level, but intuitively she believed he had ulterior motives. Too afraid to confront him, for fear he would leave as other men had in her life, she kept quiet.

She had not told anyone, including Gretchen that she was seeing him, because she was embarrassed at how quickly their romance had progressed. She could not tell people she was "dating" someone because to her that meant going out to do things. To Marion they only had two dates – the first was their blind date, and the second date was dinner at the Brass Rail. Now all he ever wanted to do was come over, eat the meal she prepared, and make out. She did not even tell Betty. Marion judged herself harshly, as she believed the church elders would, the very men who had been her savior from the chaos of her home life while growing up. She was "less than" desirable since she began fooling around with Frankie. She felt shame and disgust for herself, a secret she did not wish to disclose to anyone. She contemplated the options of how to turn herself into something respectable.

Naïve Marion knew only what "good" Christian women were *not* supposed to do. She had no "after the first date" experience and no healthy role modeling about how to develop a relationship. She did not even know what was normal or proper.

Realistically, even if she had wanted to marry Frankie, neither of them could afford a wedding at this point in time, or even in the near future. That would mean her dream wedding was in the toilet. Since Frankie's brother, Ronnie, was getting married soon, his parents could not afford to pay for two weddings. And, it was only just six months ago that Marion's parents said they could not afford her college tuition, so obviously, they could not afford a wedding either. Grannie Nellie had given her $500, to be set aside for college, but allowed Marion to use it to set up housekeeping, and now that money was almost gone. A wedding was just not financially feasible. "*Why am I even considering his proposal?*" she asked herself as she stared blankly out her apartment window.

On the other hand - she did have sex with him, not intercourse, but other climactic methods that brought as much pleasure as an inexperienced naïve eighteen-year-old Baptist girl could enjoy. No longer a virgin by her own definition, Marion now understood an orgasm should have happened first on her wedding night. Ashamed, she took to the notion that no Bible believing male would now want her. Giving into her lust, her temptation, sealed her fate to be yoked to Frankie for the rest of her life. If she married him, it would make an honest woman out of her. And she thought, she could have sex without guilt. Because she experienced the pleasure of a climax, she did not want to fathom sending Frankie away only to end up an old maid for the rest of her life.

By her church standards, marriage to Frankie was an unequal yoking talked about in the King James version of the Bible in II Corinthians 6:14 which says, "Be ye not unequally yoked together with unbelievers: for what fellowship hath righteousness with unrighteousness?" Because Frankie was Lutheran, by the Baptist standards he was unrighteous. Perhaps he was not even a believer at all, as evidenced by his sinful sexual behavior. Only a man and woman of the same, one-true faith, meaning Independent Baptist or some other approved church could be guaranteed God's blessing in marriage. Lutherans, she had been coached, did not believe in an individual relationship with God, which was commenced by asking Jesus into the heart to forgive the sins as did the Baptists. If someone married a person unsaved in the Baptist way, the marriage was doomed to fail. Maybe Frankie wasn't even saved, which meant he would not go to Heaven. The thought of him burning in the eternal fire of damnation frightened her.

She attempted to mentally block those religious teachings because she secretly enjoyed the intimacy she shared with Frankie. She wondered what actual intercourse would be like. Determined, she vowed to herself not to have intercourse until a wedding ring was on her finger. That pledge to herself did not stop her from accepting the daily oral pleasure Frankie offered which she guiltily enjoyed.

If Marion consulted with her pastor back home about her sinful behavior, she believed he would tell her she had to marry Frankie since "she made her bed, so she had to lie in it." It became settled in her mind. She had to marry him. Since she was no longer a virgin, and did not want to be an old maid, she felt there was no other option.

Instead of joy, she felt empty, sinking into quicksand sadness. Instead of anticipation of her distant future ideal wedding day, she felt anxiety and dread because the path that she charted had been abruptly altered because she gave into sin. Prior to meeting Frankie, Marion believed she was a dedicated, religious zealot judging others for doing what she was now engaged in. Her dream of traveling, going to college, and one day going to Australia as a missionary, were now only a wisp of a memory. Instead, she vowed to make the best of this altered plan, just like she had with other situations in her past.

On Valentine's Day, just ten days after she met Frankie, they sat on Bluff Road in Cortland, New York, in his 1963 light blue Ford Galaxy awaiting the tow truck to pull them out of the snow bank. He had brought her home to meet his family.

Huddling on the front blue vinyl bench seat, Frankie leaned over to Marion and said with a wink, "It's colder than a witch's tit out here. Got any ideas of how to keep warm?"

Marion believed "French" kissing demonstrated commitment. Turning her face toward Frankie she smiled and said, "I think I do."

She opened her mouth and slid her tongue into his inviting mouth.

Frankie, at first pleased then shocked said, "Is the cold making you behave like a slut or are you giving in?" Her voice shook along with the rest of her shivering body as she simply said, "Yes." Perplexed Frankie asked, "Yes, what?" "Yes, I'll marry you."

"Huh? What did you say?"

"I told you I would think about it and I did. Today is Valentine's Day and it is a good day to get engaged."

Frankie was speechless. With some hesitation, he finally spoke. "Uh, wonderful. When?"

"We can figure that out later. Oh, and I don't need an engagement ring. A simple ceremony will do."

When they returned to Frankie's house and told his parents of their intention to marry, all they said was,

"That's nice."

When she and Frankie prepared to head back to Ithaca, Frankie's mom came out to the car.

"Frankie, here're your favorites, a triple-decker peanut butter and jelly sandwich and some cold pork chops.

Marion, it was nice meeting you. I hope you'll come back and visit again."

"Thank you, Mrs. Finch."

"Please, call me Barbara."

Good-byes were said and as they were driving away Marion asked. "Did I make a bad impression? Did your mom not like me? All she said was, 'Come back again.' What does that mean?"

"Don't worry about it. It's the first time they met ya. Give 'em a chance."

Marion did not know Frankie had previously brought home more than one fiancé.

Back home the next day Marion asked, "Frankie, do you have some nail clippers I can borrow? I have this hang nail."

"Yeah, my toiletry kit is still in my car from our trip yesterday. You can go get 'em. Here's the keys."

"Thanks, Frankie."

Unlocking the car, she saw his diary open on the front seat. He had written, "I asked Marion Parker to marry me. She said yes, God help me."

Nervously moving the journal aside, she removed the clippers from the toiletry kit and absentmindedly removed the hangnail while contemplating what to say about the entry. She had not snooped and if he did not want it seen why leave it in the open?

Gathering her courage, she asked, "Frankie, what'd you mean when you wrote in your diary about asking me to marry you?"

Surprised, he quickly answered, "That I've never been married before and have no clue what I'm supposed to do."

Marion supportively said, "I'm sure you'll be a great husband." But inside she thought, *"I wish I had more than lustful feelings for you or that my feelings for Hank would go away, but I've made my decision and I best accept that I am marrying you, Frankie."*

Session Ten

Dr. Weinstein put his feet up on the foot stool and laced his fingers together. "So, what wisdom have you gained this week, Marion?"

Marion answered, "I made past decisions based on what I knew at the time. I know things differently now. I need to stop guilt-tripping myself over those choices."

"Very wise, indeed, Marion. Are you ready to move on to the next chapter?"

"Yes, sir."

The Engagement

MARION FELT SHE should break the news to her sister who lived two buildings away. She took in a deep breath before dialing the number. Twisting the telephone cord on her aqua princess style handset she waited for Gretchen to answer.

Gretchen answered on the second ring cradling the phone under her chin while drying her hands on the dish towel.

Surprised Gretchen said, "It's Monday. You usually call on Tuesday. What's up? Are we still meeting Wednesday at 11:45 in the lobby to go to lunch?"

Pausing Marion gathered her courage. "Ya, sure, but I have something to tell you first. I want to let you be the first to know I'm engaged."

Completely stunned, Gretchen dropped into a chair at her kitchen table, saying, "What? You never mentioned anyone when we had lunch the last few times."

Smiling as she relayed it now, the cat out of the bag, Marion answered, "I know I was keeping it private. His name is Frankie Finch. He's twenty-three and manages the produce department at Shumans."

Marion could hear Gretchen relay the details to Tim in the background, even though Gretchen had covered the receiver. Tim was listening to the BBC on the radio as he did every evening sitting in his winged back gray chair wearing his favorite blue-green plaid flannel shirt. Marion could hear muffled sounds of him instructing Gretchen about what to say.

Uncovering the receiver Gretchen asked, "How long have you known him?

Where did you meet him? Is he a born-again believer?"

Avoiding most of the quizzing, Marion answered only the first question - "Awhile."

Delving further to get a straight answer, Gretchen said, "You've only been in your apartment for six weeks so it couldn't have been very long."

"I know, but he's nice and has a college education. You'll like him."

"Does mom know?"

"Not yet. I'll write her a letter." Not wanting Mom's judgment or questions, Marion had avoided writing the letter or calling. The excuse she made to herself was that the cost of a long-distance phone call did not fit into her budget so she just kept delaying the inevitable. In truth, she was embarrassed and did not want to have to explain her reasons for marrying him so soon.

Gretchen asserted herself and said, "How 'bout we come over Friday evening and meet this man?"

Apprehensively Marion said, "Okay, let me ask what time he gets off work."

"Let us know," Gretchen commanded.

Compliant, she answered, "Okay," and hung up the receiver.

Friday night, Gretchen and Tim walked over to Marion's apartment, carrying two folding chairs up the three flights of stairs so that they would have a place to sit. Upon arrival, Frankie shook their hands and was cordial enough to his future sister and brother-in-law. Marion and Frankie held hands as they sat on the bed, instead of in the vinyl kitchen chairs.

Tim brought his Eastman Kodak projector with slides of their latest trip to the Iroquois Wildlife Center which consisted of hundreds of pictures of geese and goslings. Marion served Kuchen, a German pound cake, and coffee, her newly acquired taste with Half and Half and sugar added.

Tim, looking Frankie straight in the eye, said,

"Young man, I expect you to treat my sister (meaning sister-in-law) with respect and great care. Can you do that?"

Nervously fidgeting, Frankie averted his gaze but said, "Yes, sir, I intend to do so. I love Marion."

The inquisition continued. "How long have you known Marion?"

With hesitation, but conviction, he said, "Long enough to know she is the woman I want."

Gretchen and Tim had discussed prior to coming what to say to the newly engaged couple.

Tim placed his hand on Frankie's shoulder while locking eyes with him said, "You two are so early in your relationship. You need to get to know one another and to save up some money for a wedding. Marion's sister and I dated for a couple of years. We waited for our honeymoon to consummate the marriage. That's God's plan. You say you want to get married in September. That is only six months from now. I strongly suggest you wait a year."

Frankie, not wanting to be disrespectful, responded,

"Thank you for your advice. We will consider it."

Marion sat quietly observing how her sister, brother-in-law and Frankie interacted. She wondered if Gretchen and Tim could tell that their advice to wait for the wedding night to consummate the relationship fell on deaf ears. Fearing Frankie might reveal too much, she feigned sleepiness, yawning frequently. Her sister took the hint. Tim shook Frankie's hand and dubbed him as a predator. Tim said, "Come on Frankie, we'll walk you to your car. Marion needs to get some rest now."

Frankie looked at Marion and back to his future in-laws and said, "Okay, let me say good night to my fiancé first."

They walked out into the hallway pretending to say good night. Frankie whispered to her, "I can circle around the block and come back if you want me to. A little fooling around would be nice."

Speaking in a hushed voice she said, "I think you better go in case they decide to come back and check."

Perplexed, Frankie incorrectly thought that he held more sway over her choices at this point and thus did not quite comprehend the reason she cared about their opinion. Disappointed that he was not going to get "a little," he reluctantly left.

Marion thought about what Tim had suggested – waiting a year to get married. She reasoned in her head, *I don't think Frankie will wait for me for a year. Besides, I don't want to wait a year to have intercourse, six months is even too long. If he doesn't wait, then where will I be?* The plan was to marry in September on his parent's anniversary, giving them time to maybe save up some money. No location

169

was chosen because Marion's family could not afford to come to New York State and Frankie's family could not afford to go to Wisconsin.

The engaged couple soon spent another weekend visiting Marion's future in-laws, with the intent to broach the subject of wedding plans. Frankie, not thinking, took Marion into O'Malley's Bar. On a barstool sat Gigi, a woman Marion knew nothing about. Frankie quietly whispered to Marion, "Put down your drink. Don't look to either side and walk out with me right now."

Perplexed she asked, "Why? What are we doing?"

As they sat outside the bar in the car Frankie explained. "Did you see the blonde woman sitting at the bar?"

"I did. She looked so angry. Do you know her?"

Inhaling deeply, Frankie wrung his hands as he said, "When I met you, I was dating her."

"Oh, my! Why didn't you tell me?" Marion said as she glared at him. "Does she know who I am?" Unfortunately, sort of. Let me explain." "Go ahead," Marion said fearfully.

"Her name is Gigi. She is an EMT. I was seeing her when I was in Cortland. When you and I started going out, I called her and told her that I was breaking up with her and going to marry you."

"Wow, that poor woman. I want to go in and talk to her, to tell her I did not know."

"Hell no. That would only make it worse," he said as he put the key in the ignition and sped off down the street.

How he handled the situation should have been an eye opener for Marion, but in retrospect, it took many years for his callous nature to finally sink in.

That weekend became additionally stressful as they rounded the icy curve leading to Marion's apartment. A 1968 black two-door Buick Skylark approached from the opposite direction.

Frankie calmly said, "We're gonna hit him."

As he applied the brakes Marion anxiously anticipating the impact, put both palms on the dash board and braced her feet. As they hit the Buick squarely in the radiator, Marion let out a moan. "Ow, that smarts."

"What happened?" Frankie asked as he looked at her with his hands trembling and sweat pouring off his brow.

"I twisted my right ankle when we hit him. I guess I was tensing up preparing for impact."

Frankie put his head on the steering wheel and cussed, "God Damn... Now how am I gonna get to work?

Why did this have to happen to me?"

As he opened the car door he told Marion, "Get out so we don't get hit again. As she tried to exit out the passenger side door she winced in pain.

"My ankle's so painful and swollen already that I don't think I can walk on it." Pointing to the apartment building on the left side of the car she said, "That's Gretchen and Tim' building. Maybe they'll let us use their phone to call the cops."

With steam spewing out of both car's radiators Frankie and the Buick driver exchanged car insurance information. Afterwards Marion leaned on Frankie as she hopped on her left foot up to her sister's second floor apartment.

Transported by ambulance to the emergency room, Marion was given the bad news that her severe ankle sprain was worse than a break, requiring her to learn to walk again once it healed. In between physical therapy, she hobbled on crutches and crawled up the three flights of stairs to her apartment. The pain was so unbearable that she became immobile.

Melancholy set in after hours of elevating her right foot. She brooded over how long it would take to get back to her normal routine. She feared Frankie would get impatient with her inability to wait on him and leave. He was not the type to wait on her so she managed to hobble to the bathroom and in the era pre-dating microwave ovens, heated up a can of cream of potato soup on the stove while leaning on one crutch. Her morose mood was interrupted when Gretchen called the following Sunday after the accident as Marion and Frankie were listening to the new hit song "Bridge Over Troubled Water" on the radio.

"Marion, this is Gretchen. Tim and I want to talk to you about something."

Drawing in her breath, Marion waited to hear the details as she responded, "What about?" "Tim and I are your self-appointed guardians because you are so inexperienced being out on your own. We have concerns about Frankie. He talked about getting drunk when we met him. As you know, drinking is a sin. I think he is going to become an alcoholic."

Defensively supporting Frankie, Marion angrily retorted, "You don't know him. How can you say that about him? Just because someone drinks, does not mean they are or are going to be an alcoholic. I don't need guardians. I am an adult and I can make my own decisions."

Sighing, Gretchen sadly said, "Okay, but what about your rent?"

What'd ya mean?" Marion inquired.

"Well, you have been out of work for a week so you won't get paid. How you gonna afford the rent that is due in two weeks?"

"I can't work right now 'cause I'm going through physical therapy. I'll go back to work as soon as I can. I'll figure something out like I always do, but why is that a problem to you?"

Sounding parental, Gretchen answered with her voice rising, "Because Tim and I co-signed on your lease for you to get the apartment. If you can't pay it, then we have to and we are not going to. I suggest since you've obviously chosen Frankie over the advice of your family that you ask him to put his name on the lease and take ours off."

"I can't ask him to do that. We aren't married yet. He has his own place to pay for."

"Fine, but figure it out," Gretchen said and hung up.

Marion knew, as always, she could and would find a way to take care of her financial obligations, but she did not yet know how.

Frankie, sipping a cup of coffee, looked at her and asked, "What was that all about?"

She told him and his only response was, "That sure doesn't show concern. She didn't even ask how you were."

"I know. I have never been able to count on my family. As always, I gotta figure out my own problems," she said as she paced the floor on her crutches, wringing her hands.

Frankie, continuing to drink his coffee said, "Ya know Marion, I got problems too. I got fired from Shuman's 'cause I had no transportation to get to work. I couldn't afford my apartment so I had to move in here.

Don't worry about your family. We'll figure it out." Marion stood still. For the first time in her life someone said, "**We**'ll figure it out." It gave her hope and reassurance that maybe she and Frankie could be okay together.

Even though "shacking up" was frowned upon then, Marion felt justified for their actions. Since they were betrothed, marriage was pending, and no other option was affordable, they were allowed to make the best of it. She told none of her Wisconsin Baptist friends, co-workers, or family about Frankie, her living situation, or her activities. Gretchen rescinded the payday lunches, a relief, so Marion did not have to report her activities to her now removed self-appointed guardian sister.

Marion suffered another loss, as Betty moved home to prepare for her upcoming wedding their communication ended. In an era before the Internet and cell phones, long distance communication was sparse, due to the price of a phone call. A call, if made during certain hours on a Sunday, would cost seventy cents a minute, plus tax. The minimum wage was only $1.45. That meant to call long distance to talk to anyone for twenty minutes would cost a whole day's salary. Since it only cost six cents for first class postage, Marion preferred this method of communication. But Marion had stopped writing letters to her family and friends due to her shameful behavior. She just hung out with Frankie. He shared slides of his trip to Italy, an award he won as a paper route carrier, signing up the highest number of new customers. He excitedly outlined what he would show her when he could afford to take her there.

Marion needed fresh scenery to ease her boredom from being cooped up in the efficiency all day with her bum ankle. She hobbled down to the lobby to get her mail. She happily tossed the junk in the trashcan, but was disappointed that there were no letters from home to carry upstairs in her green sweater pocket. At least there were no bills. As she turned to make her ascent to the third floor, Eileen entered the building with snowflakes melting on the collar of her black car coat.

"Hi, Marion. I'm Eileen, remember? Betty roomed with us. Do you miss her?"

"Oh, hi. I sure do. Riding the bus to work wasn't the same without her."

"Wasn't? What'd ya mean? What happened to your foot?"

"Oh, two Sundays ago Frankie and I were in a car accident and I sprained my ankle so badly I can't walk on it or work right now. I'm getting physical therapy for it." "I'm sorry to hear that. How is that nice young man, Frankie? You went on the blind date with him last month, right?"

"Yes, I did. He's fine. He's up in my apartment right now."

"Do you need some help maneuvering up those stairs? You can lean on me as you hop up." As an afterthought she said, "Hey, why don't you two come down for a drink around 8:00?"

Hesitantly, Marion responded, "I think I can make it, thanks. Let me check with Frankie first, about the drink."

They called down to accept the invitation. Frankie held her arm as she hopped down the stairs a step at a time.

"This sure is exhausting," Marion said.

"I'll be glad when you're off crutches and can make playtime more fun. It's hard for me to listen to you wince when I'm enjoying my pleasure."

As Fred opened the door he whistled: "Wow, Marion. What happened to you? Did Frankie trip you or somethin'?"

"Nah, we were in a car accident right here in front of the building. I braced my feet against the floor boards. When we hit the other car my ankle twisted and is badly sprained."

"So Frankie, you didn't abandon her. That's good." Frankie joked, "No, I couldn't. I have no car. It's in the shop, but if she doesn't get better soon, I might have to find a replacement to take care of me. It's hard to serve me coffee hopping across the floor on crutches."

Eileen, pushed Fred aside and said, "You men are all like. It's always, what's in it for me! Marion sit down on the couch and elevate your ankle. Fred, get her a drink. Ya want a Bloody Mary, Marion?"

Marion nervously entered this new world. She was a novice drinker of libations. Never having had alcohol since she accidently drank the wrong punch at her aunt's house at age five, she was unsure what to do. When Eileen handed her the glass she sipped the concoction feeling a little light-headed. Not tasting the alcohol, she gulped the rest like tomato juice.

"Say there missy – you might not want to chug that so fast. It'll knock you flat," said Fred.

Too late, the alcohol hit and she got very sleepy. Frankie sent her up to bed while he stayed to watch a basketball game with Fred. She discovered that she liked alcohol. The buzz temporarily shut out the judgmental voices in her head. It was another new behavior she tried that was against "God's rules for living."

As she sat on the commode experiencing "the morning after the night before," hangover from just one drink, her racing, judgmental thoughts began admonishing her again.

How can you call yourself a Christian? You are unworthy to be God's child engaging in such sinful behavior as drinking alcohol. How do you expect God to bless your relationship with Frankie when you stray further and further into immorality?

The inward monologue only exacerbated her feelings of alienation and unworthiness to be loved by God or anyone.

Her 'living in sin' behavior prompted a decision about whether to stay or move out of the efficiency. The lease allowed only one occupant per efficiency apartment, but no one-bedrooms were available. Thank goodness since they were both out of work and could not afford to pay additional rent. They managed to cover the cost of the rent from Frankie's final paycheck which bought them another month to figure out where to find the next month's rent.

Each morning while her injury healed, Marion stiffly rolled out of the single bed they shared, her ankle throbbing. She fixed Frankie's coffee as he slept in. She felt resentment towards him, because of his apparent lack of concern about being unemployed. Around eleven a.m. Frankie strolled down to the corner newspaper box and placed a dime in the slot to retrieve the daily want ads. He smoked his Marlboros continuously, never emptying the ashtray, while he read Robert Heinlein science fiction novels. Each afternoon before he took a nap he convinced Marion to give him a "blow job" and one before bed to help him de-stress over his lack of employment. Marion reasoned that she was already in over her head and had no one else in her life now so she complied. Once a week he checked into the unemployment office to see if there were any openings that fit his qualifications. His B.A. degree in history did not lend itself to plentiful jobs. The fact that he was fired from Shuman's did not help his case either.

Marion, on the other hand, driven to improve her health situation, hobbled to the corner to ride the bus to physical therapy Monday through Friday. She worried that the rubber grippers on her crutches would slip on the sidewalk's slushy melting snow and that she would fall, unable to raise herself up again. Her bruised underarms ached from the friction of the crutches rubbing on her clothing against her flesh. Fatigue increased as she daily struggled to be released to return to work.

While riding the metro bus, she created a workable plan to rid herself of the guilt of being sexually active, a way to make their relationship openly respectable, and for God to hopefully bless it.

She inwardly resigned herself to accept her fate that she would never have the big church wedding she had envisioned since fourth grade with the family all joyfully participating, friends congratulating her, and a gown people would rave about for weeks after. She threw all that away because she did not wait to have sex on her wedding night. As damaged goods, she did not deserve that dream. Marion convinced herself that when she had an orgasm with Frankie, it sealed their relationship for eternity. She was ready to move forward with her consequences for disobeying the way the church taught to have a blessed marriage. She was going to make the best of it. After all, she would need him to help financially once he got a job or she would end up on the street.

Her conscience steadily, increasingly objected to her new worldly behaviors so much she ended up with pelvic pain and an infection. She went to the emergency room.

"Ms. Parker, you have a floating uterus. Your abdomen is as tight as a drum. You need to find a way to relax. Do these exercises and it might help your uterus stay in place."

When the pain did not abate, she saw her sister's female gynecologist, Dr. Carol.

After the exam she told Marion, "Get dressed and come into my office across the hall." The office was stark with a wide oak desk, a few diplomas on the wall, and a metal Army green trashcan beside the maroon leather chair reserved for patients.

Timidly, she entered the gynecologist's office while favoring her still swollen ankle and holding her bloated abdomen. She told the doctor about the trip to the Emergency Room and the exercises she tried to no avail.

"Sit down, Miss Parker." Looking over her glasses resting on her nose, Dr. Carol said matter-of-factly, "You have an infection in your fallopian tubes called Chlamydia Trachomatis. The only way you get that is through intercourse. Who are you having sex with? We need to treat your partner too."

Marion crossed her arms defiantly and stated loudly, "I'm not having intercourse with anyone."

"Then how did you get a sexually transmitted disease?" Doctor Carol said pointedly, her pen in midair. Feeling judged, Marion fought to hold back her tears while she barely audibly said, "I don't know. Maybe from a toilet seat or from a tampon."

Dr. Carol insisted, "Marion Parker that is not possible!"

Eyes downcast, Marion felt God was punishing her as she asked, "Can you please just give me medicine to make it go away?"

Sternly, Dr. Carol replied, "I'm going to do that, but if you sleep with this guy again, it can come back and be worse. Gretchen told me about your fiancé. I'm not as puritanical as your sister is. What I bet is, whatever you are doing with your fiancé, is emotionally causing you to feel physical pain."

Chagrined that a doctor could see right through her emotional pain, she accepted the Vibramycin prescription and promised to take it as prescribed.

She came home muttering. "That doctor was so rude. She said I was having intercourse. We aren't. I don't know what my sister told her, but I'm not going back there again. I just hope this medicine makes the pain go away."

Frankie, genuinely concerned about her pain said,

"Marion, we'll find another doctor to see you, if you don't get better."

She did not mention that she had a sexually transmitted disease because she genuinely believed since she was not having intercourse she could not have gotten it from Frankie. She did not know it could be transmitted through oral sex, as well.

Inwardly, she reasoned, "*All I need is to be restored to God's graces. When we are married and I'm able to have intercourse, Frankie will be happy and God will hopefully forgive me. Until then this pain is my punishment. I must endure it. Hmm…maybe there is a way to make the pain go away before our planned wedding day."*

Confident of her plan, Marion announced to Frankie as he surveyed the want ads sitting at the table, "Frankie I have an idea how to solve our problem."

Quizzically, "Which problem?" he asked without looking up.

"Ah, affording a wedding."

"Getting married is the least of my worries right now. I need my car fixed so I can find a job," he said, speaking pragmatically, yet not understanding how crucial it was to her to make herself acceptable in God's eyes.

Crushed, unable to contain her disappointment over his callous response, tears slid down her cheeks.

Frankie looked up with a furrowed brow and put down his newspaper as he said, "I'm sorry, Marion. Tell me your plan."

Wiping her nose on a tissue she responded, "Well, ya know Ronnie and Betty are getting married next week…"

"Yeah, so?"

Loudly inhaling she said, "What if we get married right after them?"

Perplexed as to where this conversation was going,

Frankie said, "I'm trying to follow, but you gotta fill in the blanks."

"We don't want to take away from the big wedding they planned, but we can do it quietly here in town after it's over. That way we don't have to wait until August to have intercourse." And, thought Marion, *"so my conscience will be clean and my pelvic pain will be gone."*. "What'd ya think?"

"If you wanna do that, we can, but you know I could've had you at any time, but I haven't cause you wanted to wait."

Smiling and nodding she said, "I know, but now we won't have ta wait."

The thought that Frankie might penetrate her without her consent before nuptials scared her. She wanted to save at least something for her wedding night. She believed the oral sex would have to suffice until they married, but she was unsure how long he would go before he insisted on intercourse. She naively believed that, once married, intercourse would be the only kind of sex they had. She deceived herself into thinking that oral sex was reserved exclusively for pre-marital use, even though Frankie told her he preferred it over intercourse. To Marion, intimacy in marriage equaled intercourse in the missionary position.

"Frankie, I'll call the local independent Baptist minister to see if he'll marry us. We can take the rest of my savings to buy our rings and a dress for me, okay?"

Without enthusiasm he responded, "If you want to do it, fine."

Marion assertively announced to Frankie, "I only plan to get married once. If I can't have the traditional wedding, I at least want a wedding dress, veil and some wedding cake."

"Fine, but how are you going to pay for it?"

"I'm going to use the last of Grannie Nellie's money since I'm not going to college now."

"Okay, it's your money."

They spent fifty dollars for two white gold engraveable wedding bands, $100 for an above the knee length white wedding dress and veil, and $5 for the marriage license. Marion decided Easter Sunday afternoon, the day after his brother Ronnie's wedding, would be a good day to get married.

Marion said, "It'll make our relationship unique and memorable. I met you on your birthday, we got engaged on Valentine's Day, and we married on Easter Sunday.

It's so you won't forget the dates like many husbands do."

Not seeing the wit in her comment, he said, "Very funny, Marion."

Thursday, Marion called the pastor and he agreed to meet them the next day, Good Friday afternoon.

Marion was on a mission to turn her life into something that could be seen in public. She planned her strategy carefully. After giving Frankie his "afternoon delight" and allowing him to nap for an extra thirty minutes, she woke him up with a kiss.

"Hey, Frankie I made some chocolate chip cookies and I got some milk to wash them down with."

As the aroma wafted into his nostrils he sleepily sat up and looked quizzically across the sleeping area over to the kitchen table where Marion already seated, with a smile on her face.

"Come on over," as she patted the chair beside her.

"I got something to tell ya."

"Am I gonna like it or not?"

"You'll appreciate it when we go talk to the preacher about getting married."

"Is that right? Is it a test or something?"

"Yeah, sort of."

He complied, quickly gulping down two warm cookies with an eight-ounce glass of whole milk, licking the melted chips off his fingers.

She prepped Frankie for their premarital counseling session knowing the questions that would be asked.

"Frankie, to make sure we are equally yoked (both born-again Christians), the pastor will ask you the exact date you were saved."

Defensively, he answered as he lit up a cigarette,

"But I don't know an exact date. It was sometime around my 12th birthday."

Coaching further she said as she munched on a cookie freshly dunked in milk, "Okay, just make up a date so he will marry us, okay?"

Questioning her motive, "I don't see what this has to do with us getting married, but okay. I'll say January 8th, 1959."

Growing more confident in her plan, she patiently answered all his queries.

"Good, now when he asks us if we are having sex, what will you say?"

Semantically and justifying his answer he sighed as he said, "No, because to Baptists sex equals missionary position and we aren't doing that."

Nodding, grinning, she said, "Oh, that's a good answer, but leave out the because part."

Not wanting to admit it, she knew consciously that saying they were not sexually active was a lie, but she accepted his definition/perspective to accomplish her mission to get married.

"One last question. He'll want to know your address. If we say you're living here, he'll not marry us."

"Oh, I got that figured out. We will use Fred and Eileen's address for mine."

Smiling, pleased with her coaching session, Marion felt they were ready for the pre-marital counseling appointment.

In the 1970s, Baptist circles believed if a couple had premarital sex, the minister should not perform their wedding ceremony, unless of course the woman was pregnant. Getting married by a minister from a different denomination was judged as unacceptable, an action that could get a member to appear before the elders, risking possible expulsion from church membership and barred from taking communion. Repentance might get absolution, but the couple would forever be under the watchful eye of the church authorities labeling them as backslidden sinners. The only other alternative, getting married at a courthouse, was not recognizable in the eyes of God according to the church edict. Once given into the sin of fornication, the man or woman was condemned to forever being labeled a person outside God's favor. Thus, Marion felt that she and Frankie had to be very careful how much they told the minister when they met with him.

As Frankie and Marion entered the minister's office she introduced herself extending her right hand. "Hello, Pastor Herbert. I'm Marion Parker and this is my fiancé, Frankie Finch.

"Welcome. Have a seat on the sofa right there," pointing to the black leather settee. Marion, jittery, sat down next to Frankie while he nervously fidgeted beside her, chewing the nail of his left index finger. The yellow and white flowered shift dress Marion wore rose up as she crossed her legs, her thigh revealed.

"Miss Parker, after you're married you will have to learn to sit like a lady. I can see all the way up your dress."

Face flushed, Marion did not know what to say. She felt embarrassed and fearful that he could read her mind so she quickly put her feet on the floor.

Marion's rehearsal for the premarital counseling session paid off.

Pastor Herbert said, "I perform marriage ceremonies for people your age all the time, but usually the parents are involved. Do your parents know you two are getting married?"

Frankie answered firmly, "My parents were told last month. They're okay with it."

Marion, averted eyes and said simply, "Yes."

"How old are you two anyway?"

Proudly, Marion answered, "I'll be nineteen in six weeks, sir."

Frankie maturely answered, "I turned twenty-three last month and I am a college graduate."

Pastor Herbert moved onto more important spiritual matters. "You know if you are not of the same beliefs, you will not have a blessed marriage. Do each of you personally know Jesus, and if so when did you accept Him as your Savior?"

"I prayed the sinner's prayer on June 8th, 1965," Marion proudly replied.

Frankie rattled off what he rehearsed. "Pastor Herbert, I went down the aisle on January 8, 1959. I was baptized afterward."

"That is all well and good, young people, but now we get to the crux of this session. Are you two fornicating? If you are, I will not marry you. You know it is against God's plan to give into the temptations of the flesh before you marry."

Afraid to look him in the eye they said simultaneously, "No sir."

"Well, it is good then to make it legal in God's eyes before you sin."

"Yes, sir," they both responded.

He agreed to marry them on one condition, and one request.

"I will marry you two, if you do not have sex between now (Good Friday) and Sunday at 4p.m. (Easter Sunday)."

"Yes, sir," they both agreed.

"I also strongly recommend that you attend services here or somewhere that is biblical sound to ensure your marriage is blessed by God. Will you agree to do that?"

Marion was glad to hear Pastor Herbert ask that, but Frankie's less than enthusiastic response worried her. Frankie said, "Sure, we'll try."

Pastor Herbert caught on. "Young man, it is your responsibility to be the spiritual head of this woman. Are you ready to take on that task?"

Now Frankie just wanted to escape so he answered,

"Yes, sir."

Satisfied that he had sufficiently chastised Frankie, Pastor Herbert let them leave.

Frankie's parents knew the wedding was happening, but not when. Marion was afraid to tell her parents for fear they would talk her out of marrying him at eighteen after only knowing him for a total of seven and a half weeks. If she told them it was because she had sex with him, they would be disappointed in their "good girl." She could not handle that. In her mind, she justified her answer to Pastor Herbert. Since her sister knew (they said themselves they were her *past* resident guardians), it was like telling the parents. Gretchen and Tim still did not know they were marrying immediately. Perhaps Gretchen had told Sarah and Andy, but it was highly unlikely because she was not communicating with any of her family. In Marion's mind, she was making the best decision to make an honest woman out of herself. She put on a smile that was convincing to those around her.

Marion's strained relationship with Gretchen and Tim weighed heavy on her heart. She was not close to her father. She did not really know him since she had only begun to see him in a new light a year earlier when he married Mary, but then Marion moved away. She wanted someone to be there for her, to care about what she wanted and needed. Frankie appeared to be the only person presently to do some of that. She feared her mother's wrath; perhaps she would be cut off from her if she showed too much attention to her father. If she involved herself much with her mom, then Gretchen backed away. Tim and Gretchen did not appear to approve of Frankie. The unrealistic fantasy of a dream wedding with an amicable family died when she realized it could never happen as she envisioned all because she committed fornication. She began to see for herself that not everything her mother told her about her father, or everything the church had told her about life was exactly accurate. She had to grow up and face reality. The plan she had for her ideal future no longer existed because she gave into lust. She better swallow her pride, accept her punishment, make the best of it, and get on with her wedding.

Friday, the soon-to-be newlywed couple rode with Fred and Eileen headed to Ronnie and Betty's wedding with Marion limping, fresh off crutches. The wedding, a formal affair held in a Lutheran church overflowed with a hundred guests from both the bride and groom's family and their friends. Betty's father, Wayne, escorted his oldest daughter down the aisle to the traditional bridal march, *Here Comes the Bride*. Betty wore a long-sleeved antique white lace gown adorned with pearls. Ronnie dressed in a black, satin accented, tuxedo with a matching symmetrically tied bowtie. He anxiously grinned as he captured the first glimpse of his bride gliding down the aisle to join with him in holy matrimony. It would be easy to remember their anniversary as it was Ronnie's 21st birthday.

Marion watched in raptured silence as she took everything in. All that she had wanted since a child was passing in front of her eyes, so close. She put on a smile, feigned her happiness for the marrying couple realizing in just twenty-six hours she would be reciting her own vows but in a much different environment. Her heart ached because there would be no bridesmaids tending to her every need, no guests congratulating her, no music to march to down the aisle, and no family in attendance.

Marion carefully favored her right ankle as she descended the stairs to the fellowship hall for the reception. Neither she nor Frankie were invited to participate in the wedding since they could not afford to do so and Betty already had her attendants selected before she met Marion.

With no responsibilities, they were free to mingle. Gingerly holding a cup of red punch, Marion looked for a place to sit while Frankie went outside to smoke. Feeling the outsider, she sat in the corner and quietly awaited Frankie's return. She felt safe away from the crowd because she was still unsteady on her feet and dared not try to walk around holding onto any food.

"Mind if I sit next to you, here all alone in the corner?"

Smiling, "No, have a seat. I'm Marion, Frankie's fiancé."

"Hi, I'm Rachel, Frankie's old college friend and sister to Michelle, Frankie's former fiancé from Albany."

"Oh, yes. Frankie has told me about you."

They chatted for a bit about the wedding and the weather.

Rachel wanted to make certain she dropped her bombshell before Frankie returned.

"You know my sister broke up with him right before his college finals. He never got over it or her."

Trying to sound convincing, "Yes, Rachel, Frankie told me all about it. We're good. We'll be fine."

In truth Marion knew very little about it and felt fearful. If given the chance, would Frankie leave her for Michelle?

Frankie reappeared searching for Marion among the guests all mingling over punch and munching on Golabkis (pigs in a blanket). He eyed her in the corner. His brow furrowed as he crossed the room. Marion did not know what that expression meant. Was he mad that he could not find her, was he worried what Rachel had said to her, or did it not mean anything?

As he approached and placed his hand on Rachel's back, she turned around as he said, "Hi, Rachel, how the hell are you? You look as sexy as ever."

Batting her eyelashes, moving her hair behind her ear with her right forefinger while blushing Rachel answered, "Aw Frankie you always say that. You know we never were single at the same time. If we had, maybe we would have gotten together."

Glancing over at Marion, Frankie ignored her statement. Marion felt uneasy about Rachel's flirtatiousness, sensed a chemistry between them, but Frankie quickly whisked her away saying, "Rachel, it was good to see ya, but we gotta go find the bride and groom before they take off on their honeymoon."

On the way to find Ronnie and Betty, they got stopped.

"So, Frankie give your old Aunt Bess a hug. Who is this redheaded cutie on your arm?"

"Marion, this is my Aunt Bess and Uncle Charles. Aunt Bess and Uncle Charles this is my fiancé, Marion Parker.

Uncle Charles said smiling, "Nice to meet ya.

When are you two getting hitched?"

Shyly, looking at the floor, Marion responded,

"Tomorrow."

Disbelieving, Aunt Bess, like Barbara, said, "Well, that's nice. Hope to see you at the next family celebration.

Time to go to that scrumptious buffet."

Eventually, they found the couple as they finished with the photography. Marion thought it odd that not one picture was taken of the two brothers, Ronnie and Frankie, but she did not pry.

"So, bro how's it feel to get married on your 21st birthday?"

"Ah, I don't rightly know. I've been so busy doing what everyone directed me to do I haven't had time to think about it," Ronnie said cleaning his glasses.

"Well, you better get downstairs before all the food is gone. You know dad's relatives know how to chow down."

Marion said to Betty, "You look very pretty. I hope you will have a long and happy marriage." "Thanks, honey," Betty said hugging Marion.

"Frankie told Ronnie that you're getting hitched tomorrow.

That's great. Aren't you excited?"

"Not yet."

Ronnie grabbed Betty by the hand and said, "Come on Wench, as your husband I'm telling you it's time to go eat and then off to the honeymoon to screw your brains out."

Laughing Marion said, "You better go do what your husband says."

The celebrating continued until supper time when Marion and Frankie went back to his parents' house to spend the night. Marion's ankle was throbbing and she just wanted to go to bed to be fresh for her own wedding day. Frankie had other plans.

"No one's in the house, we could fool around and no one has to know."

Firmly she said, "No, I promised Pastor Herbert we wouldn't and I'm keeping that vow."

"What difference does one day make anyway?" implored Frankie.

"It makes a great difference to me. We can cuddle, but that's it."

Pouting, he crawled in bed beside her and quickly fell asleep.

Early Easter morning, Marion and Frankie greeted Fred and Eileen, their wedding witnesses at the downtown hotel. Together they drove back to Ithaca. On the ride home Fred criticized Eileen's lack of cooking skills, said her laugh was too loud, and explicitly asked Frankie about his sex life with Marion.

"So, Frankie, did Marion put out for you on your last night as a free man? Eileen put out for me when we were dating, like a rabbit in heat."

Frankie answered Fred, "Naw, she said something stupid like, 'I told the preacher I'd wait.' I told her one day didn't matter, but to her it did."

Fred spoke up, "Well, buddy roe, tonight's the night you'll get laid for sure, so enjoy it. I used to."

Eileen sat silent in the front seat while Marion, uneasy with such talk, sat quietly in the backseat behind Fred. She did not know what to say, so she just thought about her wedding in a few hours. It would be so different than she imagined. She felt sad. She just wanted it over with so she could have a clean slate with her sinful life behind her.

Session Eleven

"You know what, Dr. Weinstein?" Marion asked as she sat down.

"No, but I'll bet you'll tell me," he said smiling.

"I learned this week that the fantasies of a twelve-year-old are not always possible, but it is normal to have them. I also now know that being naïve can be dangerous. Churches try to prevent people from engaging in immoral behavior by declaring God's judgment against such activities. The church institution is ineffective in this endeavor and they offer no grace. The result is people feel unredeemable and therefore pull away from the judging eyes of the church hierarchy. This is so opposite my experience now with the God of my understanding," she said.

"Ah, that is good to hear that you see yourself as having normal behaviors," Dr. Weinstein said, reaching over and patting the back of her hand. "Let's see what else you can learn from sharing the next chapter."

The Wedding

BACK IN ITHACA Marion sent Frankie down to Fred and Eileen's to get dressed. It did not take much as he wore the same outfit he had worn to Ronnie's wedding, but with a freshly laundered shirt.

Marion dressed herself upstairs. Sadly, she wished at least one of her female friends could have been present to help her or at least wish her well. Sighing deeply, she said to herself, "Suck it up girl. You did this. Now you are making it right. Smile and get on with it."

She unrolled her white satin hose and gingerly inserted her toes carefully pulling the stockings up to attach to her white garter belt with a blue border. Her open-toed sandals might run the hose, but she could keep them pristine for a couple of hours. Her knee-length white chiffon dress had scratchy nylon sleeves with three satin colored buttons on the outer edge. It took her a few minutes to gently push each button through its corresponding hole. Miscalculating, she had to redo her left sleeve twice. The waist bow fit snugly as she fiddled to fasten the eye hooks after reaching to zip up the dress. Looking in the mirror at her auburn hair coiffed flip she shellacked the do in place by Aqua Net hairspray. Once the spray dried she placed her two-tiered blusher veil on her head with the netting covering her face and secured it with three brown bobbi pins.

Not wanting Frankie to see her before arrival at the church, she called downstairs to say she was ready. Fred came up and knocked on the door. Opening it he whistled,

"Wow, you are a beautiful bride, Marion."

Blushing, she thanked him as he placed the white orchid corsage on her right wrist. At least she could have some of the traditions even if she could not have all of them. "Something old, (the necklace her mom got her years ago), something new (the 1970 penny securely deposited in her bra cup), something borrowed (Eileen's hairspray), and something blue (the border on her garter belt).

Fred, behaving appropriately, drove Marion in his car and Frankie drove Eileen in his newly repaired blue Ford Galaxy, now sporting a red hood, to the church.

Frankie entered the expressway going east instead of west. Whether the wrong turn was stress induced or cold feet Marion did not know. Regardless, he arrived at the Ithaca Independent Baptist Church on the dot of 4:00 p.m.

Wobbly, with a stomach full of butterflies, Marion walked into the church on her second day off crutches. Frankie wore his brown tweed sports coat with his brown pleated hemmed trousers, his white oxford shirt, and his newly polished black wingtip shoes. Pinned on his left lapel was a white carnation.

Frankie stood to Marion's right in front of the Reverend Herbert in the pastor's study. Fred was Catholic, Eileen was Jewish, Frankie Lutheran, and Marion, a former Methodist turned Baptist. Marion believed it was an ecumenical wedding, and therefore somehow should magically be a successful marriage. Officiating the ceremony, Rev. Herbert could not remember Frankie's name.

"Ah….do you, Tiger, take Marion to be your lawfully wedded wife?"

With both bride and groom snickering, Frankie said,

"I do."

"Do you Marion promise to love, honor, and cherish, Tiger here?"

Chuckling, she responded, "I do."

"I told you I was going to ask you this. In the eyes of God and in front of these witnesses, truthfully answer.

Have you had sex together since Friday?"

Not having to worry about God striking them dead they honestly said together, "No."

"That being the case. By the power of God invested in me and the authority of the State of New York, I now pronounce you husband and wife. You may now kiss your bride."

Smiles all around, they gently kissed on the lips, a respectful public display of their union.

Without a musical procession, or family to congratulate her, her nuptials were completed. She signed the marriage license and officially became Marion Finch. Fred and Eileen signed as witnesses and handed the preacher a $10 bill, not bad for ten minutes of work in 1970.

Out to the cars they went. Blowing the horn on the way back to the apartment, they took turns throwing rice on each other. Instead of being jubilant, Marion was sad as the perfect wedding imagined in childhood turned out nothing like she envisioned all because she gave into lust. Additionally, as hard as she tried to deny her emotions, inwardly she knew she still had feelings for Hank. Frankie nervously laughed as he blew the horn and threw rice on Marion.

"Wow, who would 'a thought I'd be married and to a short red-headed Baptist. I always figured I'd marry a tall blonde."

That hurt. She wondered if did he really meant Rachel. She did not ask nor comment.

The whole event was surreal. She carefully favored her still weak right ankle up the two floors to Fred and Eileen's apartment.

"Fred, honey, would you please get the bottle of champagne out of the frig?"

Fred acting more civil toward Eileen said, "Sure, you want the cake out too?"

Turning to Marion, Eileen asked, "So how does it feel to be an ole married lady now, Mrs. Finch?"

"I don't know, never been one before."

Frankie lit up a Marlboro, took a long drag, and stared off into space.

"Frankie, do you think we should call your parents and tell 'em we got hitched?"

"No, they knew we were gonna and they're still recovering from Ronnie's wedding yesterday. We'll just take some pictures and send a copy."

Eileen got out the camera and the cake knife. "Are you two ready to slice this tasty mound? This cream icing sure is good," she said as she licked her finger.

Fred, acting more celebratory, told Marion and Frankie, "Stand on the other side of the table and let me snap this Polaroid as you stuff cake into each other's mouth."

As they washed down cake with the champagne,

Eileen made a toast. "May your marriage be long and happy," as she muttered under her breath, "unlike mine these last ten years."

They all clicked the glasses and said, "Here, here."

Marion gulped down the contents of her glass of bubbly. As an inexperienced drinker and as a way to cope, she rapidly swallowed as much pink champagne as she could to prepare for the full consummation of the marriage.

When she was visibly tipsy, Frankie asked, "So, you ready to go upstairs and finally let me have my way with you?"

Unsure what sentence she had signed on for the remainder of her life, she said, "Let's go."

She barely remembered Frankie carrying her over the threshold and plopping her on the bed. The wedding dress laid in a clump on the floor. The long-awaited penetration was over before the champagne reached its full effect.

After a short nap, the reception continued at Frankie's friend's Firehouse restaurant. Since consummation, re-donning the wedding dress felt anticlimactic, but she bought no "after" dress. Free drinks flowed to honor the newly wedded couple. More bubbly was imbibed, along with a bloody Mary or two that created only a hazy memory of the whole affair. Too drunk to walk, Marion was carried out to the car, off to start her new life as a married woman.

Session Twelve

Dr. Weinstein held open his office door as Marion confidently met his eyes and smiled.

"Are we feeling good, today, Marion?"

"Yes, sir I am. The eighteen-year-old part of me was doing the best she knew how. I can admire her spirit and courage in the face of such a conundrum with respect to how to align her faith to her present life circumstances."

"We find our resiliency can surprise even us in hindsight, but not in the moment. You are a strong woman, Marion, who has overcome many odds. I am certain you have not even touched on all of them yet. I have great respect for your journey and bravery to reach out and ask for my help," Dr. Weinstein said.

"Thank you, Dr. Weinstein. That means a lot to me. Time to move on now."

Married Life

BOTH BEING UNEMPLOYED was not the best start for a marriage, but Marion had lived through much worse and so had Frankie. The unfilled dream wedding did not prevent her from mailing out announcements of their marriage. On the congratulatory cards, Frankie's friends and relatives expressed their surprise that the overheard casual comment made at Ronnie's wedding about when Marion and Frankie were getting married was, in fact, true.

Financially creative like Sarah, Marion used the wedding gift money to cover their living expenses until they both returned to work.

Marion's doctor declared her ankle well enough for her to complete physical therapy and return to her job. On April Fools' Day as she kissed her unemployed sleeping new husband good bye, Marion cautiously navigated the three flights of stairs to prevent further slippage. She wondered, *Will Frankie get another job? Will I become the sole provider for us? What have I gotten myself into? Oh well, no turning back. I must put a smile on my face and move ahead. I will concentrate now on what to say to my co-workers.*

The black sooty melting snow darkened by vehicles' exhausts made sloshing through the semi-liquid squishy. Her ankle throbbed in the chilly 40-degree weather.

With trepidation after a three-week absence she reentered Ithaca Hospital accounting division. The scene had not changed. The brown asbestos tile squares still echoed her now unsteady footsteps and the silver metal-framed windows bordering the green cement block walls on the north side of the room were foggy. Co-worker Jean looking up from a stack of payments she was tallying said,

"Welcome back. What did you do for Easter?"

Sheepishly and softly Marion responded as she pulled out her gray swivel desk chair, "I got married."

Jean at first said, "Oh, that was nice," and then did a double take and said, "You did what? That's a good April Fools' joke. I don't believe you. Show me the ring."

"I can't," she answered putting her hand into her lap, "It's at the jeweler's being engraved."

Unconvinced, Jean said, "Yeah, sure it is. Who's this mystery groom?"

Marion trying desperately to avoid a commotion answered, "His name is Frankie," she said almost convincingly.

Jean put her hands on her hips and said, "How come we work together all day and you never mentioned him?"

Defensively she lowered her voice and responded,

"Because I'm a private person."

Disbelieving and prying further with her voice rising, Jean asked, "How long ya known him?"

Marion simply said, "Awhile," remembering how Gretchen asked the same question.

Pushing further Jean stood up next to Marion's desk and said, "Ya, well how long's a while?"

Guarded she answered, "Long enough." "So 'Miss Secretive,' When's the honeymoon?"

As Marion put her right index finger on her adding machine to begin tallying payments to dissuade nosy Jean, she said, "Later. We can't afford one right now."

Wanting proof, Jean asked, saying it loud enough for the whole division to hear, "So, when do we get to meet this fictitious husband of yours?"

They all overheard and laughed as they shook their heads while Jean sat back down at her desk muttering under her breath, "Marion's wild tale is the best Fools day joke yet."

Embarrassed and feeling judged, Marion lowered her head and immediately began focusing on her job, tallying the backlog of payments from the patients. She did this each day secretly grateful that no one brought it up again until she came to work on April 6th wearing the white gold band engraved inside with the words "til the 12th of never." The inscription was based on the 1964 song by the same name. The rhyming lyrics Frankie selected lent hope for Marion to have eternal love.

You ask how much I need you, must I explain I need you, oh my darling, like roses need rain You ask how long I'll love you, I'll tell you true Until the Twelfth of Never, I'll still be loving you.

Jean noticed first. Pointing at her ring finger she said, "Marion, is that a Crackerbox ring you're wearing to convince us you got married?"

Marion proudly raised her hand and said, "No, Jean.

This is my real wedding ring."

"What are you kidding me? C'mere everybody. I don't believe it, but Marion really did get married. Come see!"

The women gathered around to read the inscription with the help of a magnifying glass. Joking aside, they hugged her and planned an office wedding shower that featured a yellow cake with scrumptious strawberry icing and fruit spiked punch. She was grateful, but uncomfortable when they teased her.

"So, Marion, are you getting laid every night?"

"You do know how babies are made don't 'cha?"

She, inexperienced and shy about discussing sexual activities, averted her eyes and avoided answering them.

Marion barely had time to get adjusted to married life when she developed a constant fever of 104 degrees. Her raw throat made swallowing difficult. She slept eighteen out of twenty-four hours for over a week. Unable to hold her job, Ithaca Hospital Insurance let her go due to her fifteen days' ankle injury absence and the ten days and counting yet to be diagnosed illness. Neighbor Eileen, accompanied Marion, feverish and unsteady on her feet, to the general practitioner's office. Eileen, worried sick, lit up a cigarette in the examining room.

Nurse Mitchell's white rubber soled shoes squeaked as she walked into the room and gasped. Her white starched uniform stiffly moved as her body did. In disbelief she said to Eileen, "What do you think you're doing? You can't smoke in here. If you have to smoke, go out the outer lobby."

Eileen, crushed the cigarette in the palm of her hand as she defensively said, "I'm so worried about Marion I had to do something to relax."

The lab work report later confirmed Marion had mononucleosis with spleen and liver damage. What a start to marriage! A couple of Marion's classmates died two years earlier of the same illness, due to misdiagnosis, so she knew it was serious.

When she called Sarah for the second time in a month, Sarah knew something must be wrong.

Working up her courage Marion propped herself up on two pillows while she painstakingly dialed the number.

She simply said, "Mom."

Sarah, just home from work was in the kitchen stirring instant mashed potatoes to go with hotdogs boiling in the saucepan. Perplexed as to the purpose of the call replied, "Yes. What is it? You don't sound so good.

What's wrong? Is Frankie okay?"

With weakened voice she answered, "I have mono with spleen and liver damage. I'm very sick. Can you please come and help me? Frankie just got a new job working for the same company as his brother Ronnie. He's in training to manage a small grocery store of the chain called Mitchums, so he can't miss work."

Sarah sighed, "Marion, you shocked me when you called two weeks ago to tell me you got married and now this? What's a mother to do? I'll see if Rhonda can stay at her babysitter's. I'll ask work for some time off."

With a little lift in her voice Marion said, "Thanks, Mom. I really appreciate this."

Even in training, the company allowed Frankie to pick up Sarah from the airport.

The first thing Sarah said to Frankie was, "So, what'd you see in my daughter making you want to marry her?"

He thought the question odd, as if she felt her daughter not worthy of him, but he did not want to reveal his real answer. Instead, he appropriately responded, "I love your daughter. She's good to me and I'll take care of her."

Sarah heard all she needed. She could relax as another daughter was married off. So, she didn't get to attend the wedding, but she didn't have to pay for it either. She also did not have to be in an uncomfortable setting with Andy and Mary, his bride of eighteen months.

The problem was where would Sarah sleep? Gretchen and Tim lived a block away, but did not answer the door or the phone when Sarah tried to tell them she was there. Sarah did not have the courage to confront her daughter at work. She assumed Tim kept Gretchen from her and she did not want to make things worse than what they might already be.

Fred and Eileen offered to let Sarah sleep on their couch just as Betty had done before marrying Ronnie. Frankie was his charming self when he came home from work while Sarah cared for his new bride. He was thankful he could escape to a job instead of tending to his sick wife. He avoided sick family members like the plague. He did not tolerate any weak people depending on him.

To avoid giving Frankie mono, Fred and Eileen loaned them a cot which Marion slept on while Frankie slept in their only bed, a single one.

Marion, so ill, yet felt guilty neglecting her wifely duties. She was too weak to initiate sex when Sarah went downstairs to sleep on the neighbor's couch. The doctor warned her that she could give her husband mono, but she vaguely worried Frankie would find someone else to "service" his sexual needs.

Routinely, Sarah cooked in the efficiency apartment kitchen, so tiny the stove and refrigerator door could not be opened at the same time. Marion slept and Sarah read because there was no television to watch.

As Marion started to improve, the newlyweds wanted to take a road trip so Sarah could meet Frankie's parents, Homer and Barbara Finch. The return airline ticket was delayed for a few days. With Rhonda still happy back at home at her babysitter's, Sarah relaxed. The family meeting went so well Sarah was invited back to visit whenever she could make the trip.

After a total of two weeks Sarah returned to Wisconsin. No sooner had she left when Eileen met Frankie in the lobby at the mailboxes as they both returned from work.

"Hey, Frankie how you doing? Did Sarah get home okay?"

Frankie, staring at the bills in his hand said, "I guess so. We haven't heard otherwise."

Eileen started to whimper. Frankie looked up at her perplexed.

"My Freddie didn't come home last night. I think he's cheating on me."

Frankie unsure how to answer said, "I'm sorry Eileen. Maybe something happened. Have you checked at his work?"

"Ya, they say he called in sick today." Looking down at her flat stomach never challenged by childbearing Eileen asked Frankie, "Do ya think I'm still sexy at forty?" Almost in the same breath she added, "What am I gonna do?"

"Ah, I don't know Eileen. Maybe he'll come home tomorrow and explain it all. I gotta go check on Marion. Sorry," as he bounded up the steps before she could utter another word.

When Frankie told Marion about it she had a fleeting anxious moment when she wondered if Frankie might "screw" Eileen given the chance. She vowed then and there the mono had to be over so she could save her marriage of two months. As Marion's symptoms lessened, no matter how tired, no matter how sick, she made sure she did not refuse Frankie sexually. If she ever gave the hint of being too tired, he'd comment, "I'm sure I can find someone out there who wants to have sex with me," guilt-tripping her into pushing her tiredness aside.

Frankie was assigned his own store in Elmira, New York just after the truth came out that Fred was in fact having an affair with his secretary, Josie. He abandoned Eileen to shack up with his new love. Fearful continued communication might test the possibility of Eileen and Frankie getting together, Marion returned their cot and cut off all contact when they moved.

Since moving to Ithaca, she had purposely had minimal contact with Hank, but before they moved she and Hank celebrated their birthdays together with spouses and his children. His was the day before hers. As she hugged him good-bye she whispered in his ear, "This time it is me leaving you."

He smiled and hugged her back. Her feelings for him although suppressed lurked under the surface. Moving she hoped would put that part of her life behind her.

Store managers did not get much time off so Marion had to learn to handle the home front mostly by herself. With the $125 Frankie brought home weekly and groceries only costing an average of $20 they were going to make it.

Her mother had survived on much less feeding a family of five.

The honeymoon period over, it was too uncomfortable now for the two of them in a single bed. Frankie needed his sleep he said to function at the store. He told her, "Why don't you get some blankets and sleep on the floor? When I go to work you can go back to bed so we'll will both get sleep."

She dutifully did so all the while her back aching from the cold, hard linoleum. She chalked up her fatigue to lingering effects from the mono and sleeping on the floor.

A routine established. Frankie would leave at 8:15 in the morning and arrive back home around 9:15p.m. She would climb into the bed after he left and sleep for a couple of hours. Communication with him during work hours was reserved only for emergencies. Marion weekly, meticulously scrubbed the orange and brown kitchen and hallway congoleum on her hands and knees with a scrub brush and bucket of water filled with pine scented Janitor in the Drum. While she scoured the floor, she dreamed of the day when they could afford their own house or maybe have a baby, despite Dr. Carson's prediction that conception was impossible since she did not ovulate.

When Frankie came home he expected dinner to be ready and for her to be at his beck and call. Marriage was not the fantasy she imagined playing dress up as a child. Although food was more plentiful than in her upbringing and the bickering was less than her parents' she still longed-for tenderness in their relationship. Marion believed to atone for her sin of fornication she must become the good biblical example of a wife: quiet, compliant, and obedient. If she did that, then maybe God would fulfill her fantasy to live "happily ever after." In the reconciliation process, she additionally prayed for her love for Frankie to develop and flourish. She had no idea what real marital love looked like not having any positive role models, but she knew she did not want to be the nag her mother was.

"Marion, these Bisquick dumplings are doughy," Frankie said lifting one out of the bowl with his fork. "Can you throw them back in the pot?"

Grabbing his bowl, she said, "I'm sorry, Frankie. It didn't say on the package how long to cook um."

"The Campbell's vegetable soup they're in is fine, they just need to be not so doughy." Trying to butter him up Marion said, "Ok hon, how long do ya think I should cook em?"

"How the hell should I know? You're home all day eating bon bons and watching TV so you should know. That's your job!"

Silently, letting her tears drop into the boiling pot she prayed that she would be able to tell when they're done so he would be happy.

Session Thirteen

Marion walked into Dr. Weinstein's office and noticed he had rearranged the furniture. Uncertain where to sit she asked, "Is there a reason you re-arranged the furniture?"

He laughed. "I sit looking at my patients day after day and miss seeing the sunshine. I moved the chairs around so we both can see sunlight. I have learned from you and others that I must take care of my needs too. Now for some people with an obsessive-compulsive disorder it will take weeks for them to feel relaxed again due to the change. It is good to change things up occasionally, don't you think?"

To this day, Marion wonders if he deliberately rearranged the furniture to have an impact on people expecting things to always be the same. Her take away from that session was that change can be good, even when sometimes it is unexpected.

Eye Opening Reality

A MONTH AFTER the newlyweds moved, Marion felt her strength slowly return. One day she started to say, "Hey, husband," liking the idea of being married, but it came out "hey Hubbles." Frankie turned toward her puzzled as she began to snicker putting her hand over her mouth.

"C'mere," he said reaching out to her. They both fell into each other's arms onto the bed in laughter. The name stuck and Frankie in turn created "Whiffles" as her nickname, which made her glow with the endearment.

A week after he began calling her Whiffles she sat at the table deeply engrossed writing a letter to her mom.

"Hey, Whiffles. Guess what?" Frankie said.

"Huh, what?" she asked, continuing to write.

Scowling he said, "Look at me when I talk to you."

She laid down her pen and looked him dead in the eye and said, "Okay, I'm all ears now. What'd ya have to tell me?"

"The grocery store on Main Street has an opening for a part-time clerk. Go tomorrow and apply. You can walk to work and we can ride home together."

"Ah, okay, but do you think they will hire me with you managing at the other store?"

"Just do as I say and don't turn it into a major event.

Got it?"

Anxious, hesitant to ask any further details, she just answered, "Okay."

In keeping with the norms of the 1970's Marion prepped for the job interview. She donned the same yellow and white shift dress that she wore to her premarital counseling session, cognizant now of how a married lady should sit. She curled her shoulder length hair and walked the two blocks from their upstairs one-bedroom apartment down the wide cement sidewalk, past the YMCA, to the Main Street store. She envisioned herself unloading stock from cardboard boxes onto the shelves like Frankie and smiling as she checked customers out at the register. Patrons walked by as Supervisor Eloise asked Marion a few questions standing in the aisle next to the pay phone.

"Can you run a cash register?"

Marion with a confident smile said, "Yes, I did it for two summers on Mackinac Island."

Eloise, curious, said, "Oh where's that?"

"It's a tourist island in the Upper Peninsula of Michigan. The overpowering smell of horse manure about knocks ya over when you first get off the ferry. I got in great shape riding my bike the nine miles around the Island," Marion said.

"Really? About the only exercise I get is when I lift a fork to my mouth," Eloise said with a nervous, self-deprecating laugh as she tugged on her snug dress to smooth out the wrinkles.

Lacking an appropriate response, Marion, with her eyes of compassion, just stared.

Finally, Eloise broke the silence. "Cool. Well, that's about all I need to know. When can you start, Marion?"

"Tomorrow? What time do you need me and for how many hours?"

"Be here at noon, til six, okay?"

Smiling, Marion said, "Okay, and if you don't mind, what's the hourly wage?"

"The new rate just went into effect this month: $1.85. Don't spend it all in the same place," Eloise chuckled. "On a more serious note there is something I should tell you," she said lowering her voice to a whisper. "The boss, Mason, is rarely here. He stays across the street on the bar stool most of the day, coming in at closing time to tally the day's figures." She wrinkled her nose and made a sweeping gesture as she admitted, "I honestly don't know why the company keeps him. I do all the managing around here and should get paid to do it. Sorry, to bother you with these details."

Cheerfully Marion responded, patted Eloise on the arm and said, "Well, maybe the company will find out and promote you for all your efforts."

Sighing, Eloise said, "Fat chance of that, them putting a woman in charge. It may be the 70's, but women still have a long way to go."

"Yup, you're certainly right about that. Well, I look forward to working with you Eloise."

"Me too, Marion. See you tomorrow. I'll have the tax withholding information forms ready for you to sign then."

"Okay, thanks," Marion said, smiling with a bounce in her step as she exited the store.

Hoping Frankie would be pleased, she walked one block further to his store to tell him the good news.

Frankie was found on aisle six busy stocking Bayer Aspirin bottles onto the shelf. Marion snuck up behind her strapping husband, put her hands over his eyes as he squatted, and said, "Guess who?"

"Santa Claus?" he sarcastically asked as he removed her hands and kept uploading the merchandize from the box on the floor.

"No, silly. It's me, the new employee of the Main Street Mitchums Grocery Store," she announced as she hugged his neck.

"Good, then maybe you can buy some clothes that make you look more like a wife, instead of a high school girl," he said without getting up.

Crushed, she pulled back with an embarrassed bright red face, eying the two cashiers looking awkwardly downward as she dashed into the unisex filthy bathroom with thin walls to cry.

She turned on the faucet and stood whimpering until a knock on the door jolted her to wipe her nose and dab her eyes before turning the handle to leave.

She exited the store down an aisle on the other side of the gondola where Frankie was still working. *All I want is for Frankie to be pleased with how I look, to be proud that I am his wife. Maybe if I shorten the hem on my black skirt, that might make me more appealing to him, at least until I can afford to buy some new "married woman" type clothes.*

On her first payday Frankie said, "Let's go to *Lerner's Store* and see what they have that I like for you."

When they entered the store, he went directly to the blouse rack and began pushing each hanger aside until he stopped. He selected one and held it out for Marion to see, a beige long-sleeved blouse with pleated bodice and plunging neckline. She took it from him and headed to the dressing room. She came out holding the front of the blouse close to her chest.

Frankie said, "Turn around." She did so.

"I think it will look sexier if you go braless."

"Hon, I'm not comfortable going out in public without a bra. I know I may not have much, but I don't like to advertise," she said shifting from one foot to the other.

"Who cares?" he said, grabbing her wrist to pull her hand away from her bodice. "You are wearing it to please me. I like it and that's it," Frankie said, his six-foot-two frame towering over her petite body with his size 17 ½ baby blue cotton twill shirt bulging at the buttons.

He paid for the blouse and a kelly green polyester miniskirt with a wide gold zipper down the back. She felt uneasy imagining wearing the outfit outside the apartment but thought *maybe I need to get over my uncomfortable feeling.*

As they walked to the car Frankie said, "I get turned on when other men look at you. You act like such a prude. Remember, your full-time job is to please and obey me."

She agreed, pleasing her husband was important, but she could not reconcile feeling bad inside while she did it.

"Frankie, pleasing you is important, but my body is supposed to be God's Temple. I have a difficult time going out in public dressed like a whore."

"You're MY whore! When we got married you promised to obey me and when I say you will wear something I like, that is what you will do."

"I remember: love, honor, and cherish, not *obey*, Frankie," she said sliding onto the car seat next to him.

"Then DEAR, your memory is screwed up. It said obey. You took an oath in front of the minister, witnesses and God. You don't intend to go back on your promise to God, do you?"

She had no way to prove or disapprove what he said. She just remained quiet. When they entered the apartment, she went to the kitchen sink and turned the hot water faucet full blast to prepare to wash the dishes, hoping her action would head off any further discussion of the topic.

One evening after both working until 9:00 p.m., they entered their abode exhausted. Frankie sat on the couch and kicked off his wingtips while Marion hastily removed her coat, set down her purse on the breakfast bar and proceeded to start their evening meal.

"When's my supper gonna be ready? I'm starved," Frankie asked as he unfolded the newspaper.

"I am doing it as fast as I can," Marion said gritting her teeth as she reached for the large can from the cupboard door above her head. "We just got home."

Frankie put his feet up on the green vinyl hassock and turned toward her as he said, "You should've planned better before you went to work. I expect my meal to be ready when I get home."

She seethed as she placed the edge of the metal Ravioli container under the lip of the electric can opener. She heated it in a one-quart saucepan as she buttered some white sandwich bread. Her hunger was past the tolerable point. All she wanted was to go to sleep. He pushed the hassock aside as she set his food on the T.V. tray in front of him. Then she went into the bathroom to wash her face and brush her teeth. Frankie's nose was buried in his science fiction paperback as he ate, so he did not even notice that she did not eat. As she emerged in her nightgown he raised his eyebrows.

"Hmm, ready for some night time fun?"

Risking his wrath, she feigned a headache which was not entirely a lie. Her temples pounded due to a twinge of hunger. As she carefully stepped over his stocking feet on the way to the bedroom, he lifted his left foot.

"Stop a second, would ya?"

"What, Frankie? I'm about to go to bed."

"Well, you know I work hard all week, so on Friday nights I'm going out drinking with other grocery store managers in town. We're gonna go to the strip clubs or play poker at each other's home. I'll tell ya when it's your turn to host it at our place. That's it. You can go to bed now."

What about me working hard? What about me doing something for fun? Oh yeah, perish that thought. Women aren't allowed!

About a month later Frankie handed Marion a piece of paper as she put away laundry. She inquired, "What's this?" looking at the list.

He said, "Friday night the guys are coming over to the house for poker. It's a list of things you need to buy."

With a scrunched-up face she asked, "Frankie, how am I supposed to buy this stuff? I don't have any grocery money left over."

Pulling a twenty from the back of his wallet Frankie said, "This oughta cover it."

Perplexed, Marion wondered if he had more money hidden away in other places. She was too afraid to broach the subject, since he handled all the finances, doling out only $20 per week to buy groceries, a little less than a normal amount for 1970.

When Friday night came, Frankie stood in the tiny kitchen. From behind Marion he whispered in her ear, "Remember, don't come out of the bedroom. If I want you to get us something, I'll let you know."

Marion, because she urinated a lot, put a Maxwell House metal coffee can in the closet. She read one of Frankie's science fiction novels curled up on the bed to distract her full bladder. She held it painfully in dancing around until she finally released the forceful stream. Some spilled onto the floor. She quickly mopped it with a towel praying Frankie would not smell it and yell at her for not waiting to pee until after the guys left.

As his wife, she eagerly, repeatedly, tried to gain Frankie's favor, but she felt she missed the mark. In his store the next week, Gwen, a female employee, raised her feather duster from the pink metal display shelf and asked Marion as she collected some needed household items into a plastic shopping basket, "Marion, how ya doing? You and Frankie okay?"

"Yah, why do you ask?" Her high-pitched voice cautiously queried.

Pointing toward the petite dishwater blonde clerk at the register she said, "Well, you've gotta watch out for Dee, 'our resident whore'. She'll steal Frankie just for the thrill of it and dump him like a hot potato. You take care, okay?"

Trying to maintain her composure, Marion said, "Oh, okay. Thanks for the warning. Does Frankie know about her?"

Shaking her head, Hope, the other employee said, "Naw, a guy don't want some woman telling him such stuff."

One Friday night as she left Frankie's store with a package of toilet paper peeking over the top of a bag, she overheard the assistant manager, Judy, on the other side of the store's back wall talking to Frankie in the office.

"Frankie, where we going for that drink after work?"

"The Barn Bar on Smith Street."

She responded, "Okay, good. Are the other managers going too?"

He said, "I think so, but I haven't checked yet."

Marion knew Judy was already having an affair with a married man so she feared her husband to be an easy target for Judy as well. In addition to keeping a watchful eye on Dee, now she believed she had to worry about Judy too. She anxiously crept out of the store, fearful the employees would detect her insecurity and ask her about it. When Frankie came home around midnight, Marion was sobbing on the couch, certain he was unfaithful to her.

Blubbering, her face stained with tears, she blurted out, "I know where you've been."

Aggravated, Frankie kicked off his shoes and, with his voice raised loud enough for the neighbors to hear, said, "What the hell are you talking about? Of course, you know where I've been - out with the guys at the club, just like every other Friday night."

Defensively crossing her arms across her chest, she responded, "I know Judy was with you. I heard her talking to you about it."

The overpowering smell of Jack Daniels on his breath drew her back as he glared at her and said, "She met all of us for one drink and went home. You're acting like a scared kid. You have no reason to be jealous. I'm going to bed. You can stay up all night crying if you want to. I gotta get up for work in the morning."

She dried her tears and laid down on the floor pallet beside the single bed where Frankie, lay asleep. Grandma Finch's wool afghan supported her body. A satin trimmed twin size polyester orange blanket overlaid with a gold chenille bedspread helped comfort her grief while a squishy foam rubber pillow cushioned her head. Her back ached and she chalked up her ever-present fatigue to lingering effects from the mono and sleeping on a cold, unyielding floor.

When her backaches increased in intensity, even after she got extra sleep in the single bed, she thought maybe her period was coming. Since the onset of her menses at age eleven, she never had regular periods so sanitary napkins sat untouched under the bathroom sink, just in case she needed them.

She had stopped the birth control pills to see what could happen, believing pregnancy was impossible without ovulation. One morning after Frankie left for the store, Marion sleepily climbed into bed still warm from her husband's body. Tucking the covers under her chin she closed her eyes in anticipation of some much-needed shut eye. She positioned her body first one way and then another, but her back pain crushed all hopes of any blessed, soft replacement sleep compared with her night-time cold, hard floor. She said out loud, "I can't be pregnant 'cause I don't ovulate. What is wrong with me? Maybe I ought to see my gynecologist to see if I have an infection or something."

Dr. Goodson, the gynecologist, listened as she described her symptoms of nausea, low back pain, breast soreness, and tiredness. He asked if she was using birth control and she told him she had stopped in the hopes of having normal periods now that she was a married woman.

She held her breath as she asked him, "Is it possible I'm pregnant?"

His half glasses rested on his nose as he read her chart. He looked up and shook his head, and said, "No. What you're having is a pseudo pregnancy. You cannot be pregnant due to your history of no ovulation. False pregnancy happens to women who desperately want a baby but unfortunately cannot." He patted her shoulder, turned and walked out of the room. Having a baby had not been in her thoughts since age fourteen when her gynecologist, Dr. Carson, told her it would be unlikely. As she slowly gathered her belongings, she prayed, *God, I know being pregnant is not possible, but if by some miracle, I am, I will take it as you showing favor to me.* She felt silly as she redressed. *How am I going to explain this to anyone? I don't feel right, but he says it's in my head. This sure doesn't feel like it's in my head.*

Nurse Ellen knocked on the door and entered the room. She mentioned no return appointment, or any need for a prescription. She said simply, "The door to the reception room is on the right," pointing with her outstretched right hand.

Marion felt dismissed. The doctor never examined her, or took a pregnancy test, or sent a bill. She tried to ignore her symptoms, but day after day as she got out of bed, the nausea came in waves. Embarrassed, she did not want Frankie's judgment for creating an imaginary pregnancy. She figured when he went to write the check for the office visit, she would tell him it was just a regular visit. After all, when they first met and had discussed kids, Frankie told her he must be sterile. He said he believed that because of all the women he slept with, no one ever came up pregnant. She remembered telling him on the second date that she was told she could never get pregnant.

Whether or not he paid attention to that information, she did not know, it never came up again.

A week later Marion dragged herself off the floor pallet and dashed to the bathroom. Her urge to urinate happened many times a day and even at night now. As she tried to make Frankie's coffee she dropped the metal filter spilling the contents all over the counter. After she swept the coffee granules into the trash can she reloaded the basket and plugged in the Faberware percolator.

Frankie shouted out to the kitchen from the bed, "Marion, where's my breakfast? It's almost 8 o'clock and you know I have to leave in thirty minutes."

"I'll be right there," she said as she stood over the toaster waiting for the toast to pop up.

Entering the bedroom, carrying Frankie's breakfast – two pieces of lightly buttered toast and a cup of black coffee. She gagged.

"What's the matter with you, Marion? It's the same breakfast you've been fixing me for months. You got a stomach bug or something? C'mon. I don't want you upchucking on my food," he said briskly snatching the plate out of her hands as he glared at her.

"I'm sorry Frankie, I don't know what's wrong. Maybe it's the aftereffects of mono, like they said might happen," she said as she sat down bedside him on the bed careful not to jiggle too much so he would not spill his coffee.

"Well, do something, 'cause I can't stand to hear you gagging every morning."

Resigned to do better, she plugged her nose as she brought him his tray the next morning balanced on her left arm.

"Now this is ridiculous," Frankie said. "There is nothing wrong with you, so stop being so dramatic."

Still, a month passed and the illness persisted. As she ironed Frankie's favorite green oxford shirt she wondered, "*I don't understand why I'm nauseated every day. My back aches, my breasts hurt and I am so sleepy. What's going on? Is this just because I want to be pregnant? It feels different than mono. If I go to my regular doctor he will probably say it is in my head too. I gotta shake this off.*"

She finally saw Dr. Swanson, her family physician. He did a gynecological exam. After he removed his gloves, he put his foot on the waste basket lever and dropped them in. He turned back to Marion, smiled and said, "Get dressed and come across the hall into my office."

She dressed quickly hopeful that he had an explanation for her symptoms. She sat down in the red leather chair directly across from Dr. Swanson's desk. Inhaling, she waited.

"I think you're pregnant," he simply said.

With furrowed brow, she asked, "But how can that be? Dr. Goodson said it was just in my head."

"We can't be sure until we get a urine sample. Can you give me one?" he said handing her a cup to pee in.

"Sure, I can," she said taking the container from his hand.

Back in 1971, samples were sent to the hospital lab to be tested, taking weeks to get an answer.

Marion crumbled up the hamburger in the frying pan to make sloppy joes. As the aroma hit her nostrils she could feel the queasiness rising in her stomach. She gave into the urge to eat a carrot, her third that day hoping it would stave off her nausea.

What is going on with this sick feeling all the time and eating carrots like a rabbit? Am I pregnant? If I am, that'd be a miracle. If I'm not, then do I have something seriously wrong with me?

Before answering machines and cell phones were invented, she only hoped she would be home when the call came. Each week day before work she stared at the phone, hoping it would ring. Wednesday morning after Frankie left for work, she sat down on the forest green vinyl couch with wooden legs to read her bible. Fifteen minutes later she awoke to the phone ringing.

"Hello, Mrs. Finch?"

"Yes, this is she."

"This is Dr. Swanson's office. Remember that urine sample you gave us?"

Expecting the results, she was disappointed to hear, "The hospital lost it. Can you come give us another one?"

"Of course, I can stop on my way to work around 11:30 this morning. Will that work?" "Yes, just tell the front desk you're leaving a sample to test for pregnancy."

She felt frustrated having to wait longer for the results. A week later the call came again. "Mrs. Finch? This is Dr. Swanson's office calling again."

Ready and bracing for the results, she cautiously asked, "Did you get the results of my pregnancy test back yet?"

Pausing, drawing in a breath, the receptionist hesitantly said, "You are not going to believe this. The hospital was out of the chemical used for pregnancy tests, so they froze your sample. When they thawed it, it was unusable, too old."

Believing she was never going to find out the results, she asked, after a deep sigh, "So you need me to come give you a third sample, right?"

"I'm sorry, but yes, please."

After she left the sample, they said she should hear from them in another week. It had now been two months since she initiated the whole process with Dr. Goodson, the gynecologist. When home, she again sat by the phone, stared at it and prayed for it to ring. It did not. Friday afternoon she came early to Frankie's store after unloading the groceries at home. She paced the aisle on the creaky wood floor gathering the courage to call Dr. Swanson's office. At 4p.m., her wits gathered, she dropped a dime into the pay phone and dialed the number while patting her expanding waistline.

"Hello, this is Marion Finch. Are my pregnancy test results in yet?"

The receptionist calmly responded, "Let me go see."

Marion waited for what seemed like an eternity.

Finally, the receptionist picked up the receiver.

"Hello, Mrs. Finch, are you still there?"

"Yes," she answered hardly daring to breath.

"Good. I have the report in my hand. Hmm. The result is positive."

Marion, seeking clarification said, "Positive what? I am or am not pregnant?"

Without emotion, the receptionist said, "You are pregnant."

Thoughts racing, heart pounding, Marion thanked her and asked, "Okay, what do I do next?"

The receptionist, Marion suddenly remembered was named Susan, said, "You need an appointment with Dr. Swanson a month from now and you need to start taking prenatal vitamins, and rest as much as you can."

"Susan, thank you. Can you make that appointment for me now?"

"Sure, do you want morning or afternoon?"

Marion excitedly said, "Morning, please." She got off the phone with tears glistening in her eyes. She waltzed into Frankie's office area where he was calculating the store's weekly order on his old oak desktop.

She sat down on a wooden crate beside him and impatiently waited for him to look up.

Frankie, intent on adding up the column of numbers, intermittently chewing on a Number 2 lead pencil, glanced toward her with a bewildered expression.

"Marion, you're grinning like a Cheshire cat. What's up?" he asked as he turned his head back to his task at hand.

Wanting his full attention, she paused to carefully to choose her words as happy tears slid down her cheeks. She reached out her right palm to rest on Frankie's forearm and said, "Well…, I went to see Dr. Goodson two months ago. I thought I was pregnant then, but he said I was not, could not, and that it was just in my head."

Cocking his head to the side without looking at her he said, "And…."

Bursting into happy tears she said, "I'm pregnant! We're going to be parents."

Now, turning to look her straight in the eye with raised eyebrows he said, "This is a joke, right?"

Excitedly she answered, shaking her head, "No, Frankie it's not. Dr. Swanson, our family doctor, did the test and it's positive."

Reflectively, Frankie placed his forefinger on his temple, looked up at the ceiling and spoke as if Marion was not even there, "And to think I thought I was sterile all these years. No other woman that I know of got knocked up. Wow, me a dad. That means I have ta grow up. I'm only 24. I don't know if I'm ready to do that."

Marion interrupted his monologue. "Ready or not, it's gonna happen. Frankie, aren't you excited?"

"I don't know. I need time for it to sink in."

"Well, according to Dr. Swanson's calculations, you've got until August 2nd," Marion said as she kissed him on the cheek.

Frankie did not flinch. She added, "Well, this pregnant body is going home and putting my feet up and relaxing," she said with a big grin on her face as she left him to ponder the news.

Walking on air, Marion did not allow Frankie's lack of enthusiasm or attention to dissuade her elation.

Nesting quickly began for Marion. Thinking out loud, as she regularly did, she made up Frankie's bed, and said, "Hmm, I guess maybe I don't have gas pains, but it's the baby moving inside of me. Wow, what a miracle! Thank you, God." Her eyes went wide. "We can't bring a baby into this small apartment. We need a bigger one, one with at least two bedrooms. I better talk to Frankie about it. Hmm." (She put her finger to her lips and added). "He hasn't appeared too happy about becoming a dad so I'm not sure how to approach him about this."

Later that evening, as Frankie worked on the crossword puzzle in the daily newspaper, Marion took the opportunity to approach him. "Frankie, I've been looking for a new apartment for us."

Chewing on his pencil eraser he asked curiously, "Why? We've only been in this one for six months. I bought another twin bed so you don't have to sleep on the floor anymore. What more do you want?"

She looked down at her rounding abdomen and patted it, as if for good luck. "We don't have room for a baby and all the stuff that goes with a child."

Frankie raised his voice immediately, throwing the paper and pencil onto the floor. "I can't afford more rent! The $115 we pay now is stretching us with my $125 a week salary. Besides, you aren't gonna be able to work long so we'll have less income. You better think this through."

Grabbing the paper off the area rug, he stormed into the bathroom slamming the door behind him. When he came out he appeared more relaxed.

Cautiously, Marion said as he resumed his place on the couch, "I already have thought this through. I found an apartment I want us to look at. It's across town, only ten minutes from work. It's an upstairs two-bedroom for $135 a month. Can we go look at it please?"

Sighing, Frankie quickly learned that arguing with a pregnant woman was futile. She would just disintegrate into blubbering tears so he said, "I guess, but don't get your hopes set on it."

Smiling she hugged him and said, "Thank you, I'll take care of transferring the utilities and stuff."

"Whoa, hold on there. I didn't say we'd move. I said I'd look at the place."

Session Fourteen

Marion looked wistfully out the window of Dr. Weinstein's office while he tended to an urgent phone call. No longer feeling as tense as her first session, she just sat pondering her thoughts.

"Hello, Marion. Sorry, I was delayed. How are you? What have you learned since our last session?" he asked settling into his swivel chair.

"I'm doing so much better Dr. Weinstein. I am realizing that life does not have to be a constant crisis. I am sorry about whatever your client's situation is, but I am very thankful this time that it is not my crisis."

Dr. Weinstein grinned and asked, "You ready to learn and heal some more?"

"Yes, sir. Today I want to cover how my life evolved after my first child was born."

"Go ahead," Dr. Weinstein said.

And Baby Makes Three

ONCE SETTLED IN the two-bedroom upstairs apartment on Walker Street, complete with a furnished, full size bed, Marion looked for a Baptist church to attend. Picking one out was fine, but, as was expected, final approval rested with Frankie's permission.

Marion planned her strategy. She fixed a plate of pasta with heavily seasoned quarter-size meatballs smothered in Ragu sauce. A slice of garlic toast rested on the edge of the Melamine lime green plate. She brought it to him in the living room, setting it down on the T.V. tray with an eight-ounce glass of whole milk.

"Here you go, hon. Your favorite, spaghetti and meatballs."

Glancing up from his science fiction book, he said, "Where's the salt and pepper?"

As he sprinkled the condiments on his pasta he absentmindedly picked up the Italian dressing to pour on his iceberg lettuce and tomato salad. He went to shake it to mix up the spices in the bottle, but unfortunately, oil, vinegar, and oregano splattered across the pocket and dripped down the row of buttons on his favorite oxford green shirt. He cursed, "God dammit woman, can't you even remember to put the cap back on the bottle? Are you really that stupid? How the hell are you gonna buy me a new shirt, huh, tell me how?" Shaking his head, he glared at her and yelled, "You don't think before you do things. I swear you get more incompetent daily."

Marion, shaking in her shoes, did not know what to say. She said, "I'll soak it Frankie, I'm sorry. I'll be more careful next time. I promise. Give it to me." She quickly removed it and his tee shirt over his head and transferred them to a bathtub of warm water and a cup of Tide detergent. Unfortunately, much to her dismay, the stain remained.

She quietly retreated from the bathroom. For the next two hours, she replayed the scene over and over in her mind sitting at the far end of the couch with Frankie at the other end, his anger long ago cooled, lost in his book, oblivious to her consternation. She tried to fathom how she incurred his wrath. *God, I'm trying to please you and Frankie, but I keep failing. Frankie's anger scares me. Please help me to do what he says so he doesn't lose his temper like that again.*

She wanted to approach him about going to church, but knew she would have to wait for the right time. He reached across the cushions around 11:00 p.m. patted her on her right thigh and said, "Come on to bed. I'm ready for my blowjob." She felt relieved that maybe the anger storm had passed, so back in his good graces, she could approach him tomorrow with her request.

She laid awake long after he was snoring. Tears stained her pillow. No more compliments like in Ithaca when she fixed his first plate of spaghetti a year earlier. Frankie had become a ruler commanding his kingdom, telling his subject (Marion) when, where and what meals to bring him, what sex he wanted, how much money she would have to stretch to pay for food and his clothing, and when she could have an opinion or not. She accepted her sentence for giving into lust before marriage, but vowed, *God, if you will help me, I will make Frankie love me and I'll do everything I can to improve my marriage. Thank you, Amen.*

To "warm" him up to her request, the next night she took the scooper out of the kitchen utensil drawer and plunged it into the brick solid container of butter pecan ice cream. Wearing the plunging neckline beige blouse, he bought her, she sashayed over to the couch handing him the treat. He eagerly devoured it while she coyly moved a strand of hair back from her face watching him.

Frankie set the empty dish down on the brown faux, wood T.V. tray in front of him and said, "That sure hit the spot. Thanks, Whiffles."

"You're very welcome," she said as she took the bowl and rinsed it out in the sink. Returning to the couch, she quietly snuggled up beside him under his left arm. He reflexively put his arm around her as he continued to read. She next placed his left hand inside her bra. He folded the page of his book and set it down on the arm of the couch.

Turning to face her he asked, "What's this all about?" enjoying the activity.

"Oh nothing," she coyly said. "Just an appetizer for later."

"I'm glad to see you're interested. I like women who initiate sex, show variety, and are imaginative. One of these days I'm going to shove it up your ass."

"Frankie, I don't like that idea. That'd hurt. Butts aren't made for sex, vaginas are."

"I thought you told me your aim is to please me," Frankie said manipulating her former words.

Changing the topic, afraid to let the opportunity go any longer she said, "Can I ask you something?"

"Sure, if it does not cost me anything." he said as he stared at her breasts.

She cautiously said, "Frankie, I'm going to go to a Baptist church on Sunday. Is it okay with you?"

Briefly looking up at her face, he pulled back from caressing her body and said, "Baptist churches are all hell fire and brimstone. I don't need that shit. I'll tell you what. You can go, but when you get back, you're going to let me fuck you up the ass for being such a nice husband. I don't want to hear any whining about it or you can't go." He picked his book back up and said nothing more.

Marion, in shock, silently slunk away into the kitchen to clean up as her heart drummed and her mind reeled.

She knew she had manipulated him to get him to agree to her going to church, but that plan backfired and now she did not know if he was serious or just testing her. How had Frankie morphed into such a tyrant in the short time since she married him? At times, she thought he was generous like when he bought her the blouse, but then in a split second, with no warning, he switched and became frighteningly scary like the day before when the salad oil spilled on his favorite shirt. How could she obey God, worship at a Bible-believing church, and not incur the wrath of her husband inflicting physical, sexual pain upon her? Somehow, God would have to help her get through the dilemma.

While in church she could not concentrate on the sermon. When she closed her eyes for the pastoral prayer, panic gripped her as she envisioned

Frankie looming over her, inflicting searing pain upon her body. This was one service she did not want to end. Arriving back at their second-floor apartment, she cautiously mounted the steps hoping maybe he was asleep. As she opened the front door, the smell of his Marlboro, burning in the metal clip of the ashtray, flooded her nose. She hesitated. *Do I ask him? Do I just go into the bedroom? Do I pretend like I forgot?* Praying that her obedience would please him and God, she undressed and laid on the bed. The need to please, to not be rejected or yelled at, overrode her panic. It did not take long for Frankie to walk by the bedroom on the way to use the toilet. He saw her naked lying on her side on the bed. A big grin spread across his face.

"Ah, I see the wife has come home to make good her promise," Frankie said triumphantly as he started to unbuckle his pants.

She shut her eyes tight and said nothing as Frankie opened the night stand, scooped up a large glob of Vaseline, and shoved some into her rectum with his index finger to make insertion easier. She held her breath as she said a silent prayer asking God to intervene and prevent the madness about to commence.

Rolling her over on her stomach he said, "Relax, stop clenching your ass muscles because I won't be able to get my dick in."

She tried to relax as much as she could. He weighed 230 pounds and she only 120 at this point in her pregnancy. Breathing was hard with him on top of her, so she turned her head to the side, body trembling to get some air. He didn't appear to notice or to care. To endure it, she focused being on Mackinac Island down by the water where she contemplated major decisions in her life, hoping to make the "Greeking" (anal intercourse) bearable. With each thrust a shiver went up her spine. As painful as it was, she remained silent. It lasted less than five minutes but felt like an hour.

She walked the fifteen steps into the bathroom, turned on the sink faucet and began to weep. Looking up into the medicine cabinet mirror she asked, *God, is this my punishment for not waiting to have sex before I married? If it is, I'm sorry. I want to go to church and worship you, because I know you want me to, but if it means enduring this, I don't think I can do it. Please help me, tell me what I am to do!"*

She dried her tears after she wiped away the blood and went to the kitchen to prepare his Sunday dinner. Frankie, silent, redressed and returned to his "man" chair and resumed reading his paperback where he left off.

Each Sunday thereafter, she dutifully undressed when she came home and put her mind in a faraway place while Frankie had his "way" with her. He did not need her mentally present. There was no affection, no intimacy, just a powerful aggressive act forced on her anally. If she did not cry out, he finished more quickly. The tearing stung for days, but only a tinge of blood stained the toilet paper by the fourth time.

This repeated act added to the quicksand created by all the abusing males in Marion's life. With each succeeding trauma, the viscosity of the quicksand grew thicker. Whenever she tried to escape the muck she sunk only deeper. Her body reacted to the stress. One of the ways was allergic reactions to food, animals, dust, trees, crops, and medications. Since infancy they plagued her. Allergy injections were part of her life since she was twelve. Often, she mentioned how her upper arms and hips felt like pin cushions from all the shots. One Thursday, the allergist had a new bottle of serum and the protocol (mistakenly) called for an increase in her dosage at the same time. She left the office not noticing anything different. By the time she got to the laundry mat to do her weekly wash, her head was itching. By the time the clothes were in the washing machine, her face was swelling. She calmly asked the next-door drycleaner attendant to call Emergency for the ambulance to come. The woman panicked, froze, afraid Marion would die in front of her, so Marion grabbed the phone and called the local emergency number herself and then Frankie. He beat the ambulance to the drycleaners and drove Marion to the hospital with a police escort stopping traffic along the route. She made it in the nick of time. Worried, Marion made sure their treatment could not harm the fetus. Subsequently, a twenty-minute wait in the allergist's office made certain there were no further reactions.

Back at work, two days later, at 5:30 p.m. on Saturday evening, right before closing time, Marion was dusting some stock when Boss Mason walked in which was unusual for him to appear before she left for the day. Eloise left the cash register to go to the basement to assist in tallying the day's deposit. She returned shortly thereafter.

"Marion, Mason wants to see you."

Perplexed, she asked Eloise, "Why, did my drawer not balance?"

"I don't know," she said avoiding looking at Marion's face. "He just said to ask you to come down."

Putting down her dusting cloth, she descended to the musty cellar. She saw Mason hunched over the desk smelling like a brewery, intent on his task of rechecking his math, the adding machine's paper roll unwound as he clicked the handle, punching in the numbers.

"You wanted to see me, Mason?"

"Yah, c'mere!"

Thinking he was going to show her where her numbers were off, she moved closer.

He grabbed her forcefully by the arms and pressed his body against hers, planting a slobbery, whiskey nauseating kiss on her mouth. Trying to pull away, he held her tighter. Lifeless, she was afraid, so she did not to resist. Finally, Mason let go. Shaken, she did not know whether to fight or flee. In the millisecond it took her to recover, Mason spoke.

With slurred speech six inches from her nose he pointed at her chest and said, "You're going to meet me at the Downtowner Motel Wednesday night after work. If you tell anyone, I'll kill ya. Ya, understand?"

Her voice and body quavering she said, "Yes." She believed his threat.

In a daze, her wobbly legs ascended to the top of the stairs. Marion grabbed her gray polyester coat off the metal hook and walked out of the store past Eloise without saying a word. She did not recall walking the block to meet Frankie at his store. She just sat in the car's passenger seat waiting for Frankie to lock up for the night.

Getting into the car, Frankie lit up a Marlboro and asked Marion, "What you got in mind for dinner? We're supposed go to Jim's, the Southside Mitchums Manager's house and meet his wife June and their kids after we eat." Preoccupied she did not respond.

"Earth to Marion, wake up," Frankie said shaking her shoulder. "I asked you a question. Are you deaf, or just refusing to answer me?"

"Ah, I'm sorry Frankie. What did you ask me?"

All she could think about was, *what just happened to me? What did I do to make it happen? Frankie is going to be so angry with me thinking I caused it. I know it.*

Frankie, with raised eyebrows, asked, "What's wrong with you?"

With tears welling up, clutching the dashboard, she breathed, "I can't tell you."

Raising his voice, slamming his hand on the steering wheel, he said, "Can't tell me what? I'm your husband for God's sake. You can tell me everything."

Tears streamed down her face dripping onto her blouse, "It's Mason.

Turning toward Marion, he said, "What about that good for nothing drunk?"

Haltingly, her eyes downcast, she said, "He grabbed me in his office."

Incredulous, he screamed, "HE DID WHAT?" Shaken, her words were spoken fast, "He grabbed me and kissed me and told me I was going to meet him at the Downtowner hotel next Wednesday night after work and if I told anyone he was going to kill me!"

With hands turning white, he gripped the wheel and said, "Oh, he did, did he? We'll see about that."

Fear rising, she asked, "What are you going to do?" she asked eyes wide.

Definitively, he said turning to face her his eyes, ablaze, "Take care of it. That's what I'm going to do. No one messes with MY wife."

Trying to be prepared, she asked, "But what exactly are you going to do?"

Ignoring her question, he said, "First thing you're going to do is call up Eloise and tell her you quit. You understand?"

Trembling in fear she asked, "But, what about Mason? I don't want him to kill me."

Reassuringly he said lowering his voice, "I'll make sure he doesn't harm you. Now, as soon as we get into the house, go call Eloise, like I told you to do."

She began to cry harder. Maybe the tears were because Frankie was showing concern for her. Maybe it was because she feared he may believe she already had sex with Mason and the baby growing inside her was his since Frankie stated more than once that he was sure he was sterile. Fortunately, Frankie did not address the increased blubbering. He just handed her his handkerchief to wipe off the tears and snot plastered across her cheeks.

When she called Eloise to quit, the perceptive woman asked, "Did Mason hurt you? Drunk, he's cornered all of us women, but won't remember any of it tomorrow. Please don't quit."

But Marion did, fearful Mason might carry out his threat. They visited Jim and his family later that evening, but Marion said little, still in shock.

First thing Monday morning Frankie marched down to the basement of Mason's store to confront him. Before a word was uttered, Mason saw the enraged Frankie coming toward him and raised his arms to protect his face. Turning his body to the right, Mason said out of the corner of his mouth, "I didn't do anything to her, honest."

Frankie ignored his feeble attempt to lie and punched the left side of Mason's jaw with his right fist and walked away. For a few days, there were daily hang ups and heavy breathing phone calls to the house phone.

That evening while Frankie sat mesmerized by the news in his green vinyl recliner Marion handed him his plate of macaroni and cheese. Her hands shook so badly that she almost dropped his plate.

"What's wrong with you?" Frankie said irritated, staring at her trembling all over. "You sick or something, again?"

"No, I'm not sick," she said sitting down on the couch beside him. "I'm just so scared Mason will kill me like he said. Every time the phone rings, I jump. I wish I could go someplace to get away."

Frankie said, "Mason is not going to do anything to you." He rolled his eyes. "He's just a drunk bully. If you're really that scared, go to my parents for a few days. I don't think it's necessary, but if it'll stop your shaking so you can take care of me like a wife should, then go get yourself together and get back here."

Marion took the bus to Barbara and Homer's house in Cortland. Frankie's Aunt Evelyn came over to visit her sister Barbara and gave her words of wisdom to Marion. She stood up hands on her hips in front of Marion and said, "You can't let guys do that to you. Kick 'em in the nuts and walk away. By the time they get up, you'll be gone."

Tears streamed down Marion's cheeks as she sobbed, "I was so scared after I told Frankie that Mason would kill me as he threatened if I told anyone."

Aunt Evelyn hugged her and said, "Don't let him know you're afraid. They don't like strong women. It throws 'em off balance, but do it anyway."

Marion, tried to adopt that stance when Frankie came to get her the next weekend.

Feeling empowered by the pep talk, she called the grocery store headquarters to report Mason's actions. Because it was his word against hers, they did nothing. No sexual harassment policies existed in the 70s. Marion, despite her confidence boost, still feared running into Mason, so she avoided downtown for months.

As the crisis passed, she excitedly prepared for motherhood. The grocery chain Frankie worked for did not have maternity benefits so they borrowed money on Marion's life insurance policy to cover the cost of her prenatal care, hospital bill, post-partum visit, and the pediatrician fees. To cut costs, Frankie believed she could borrow some of June's (the Southside Mitchums Manager's wife whom she had just recently met) maternity outfits and return them after the baby was born. The fact that June was much taller and heavier did not sway his thinking. Marion did not feel comfortable to ask, even if they were the same size. He finally, begrudgingly, gave her ten dollars to buy material to sew her own maternity clothes. Searching through the bargain bin she discovered a couple of yards of green large print floral pattern fabric that she made into a matching top and slacks outfit. A black and white paisley designed cotton broadcloth fabric she made into a jumper. She found a polyester brown stretch knit dress in the Salvation Army thrift store. The three outfits would have to suffice. Frankie, after all, had no intention of skimping on his "necessities" of Marlboros or Friday nights out. When Frankie came home Thursday night after work, Marion had straight pins scattered all over the floor and Simplicity tissue pattern pieces positioned on the couch cushions and on the seat of Frankie's recliner.

Frankie stretched his right hand in a broad sweeping motion, his face reddening, "And what the hell is going on here? I hope you don't think you can forget about taking care of me since you are so freaking tied up in becoming a mom for God's sake," he said pushing all the pieces from his chair onto the floor.

"No, Frankie. I'm not neglecting you," she said leaning over hugging him. "I'm saving you money by sewing my own maternity clothes. Remember?"

"Saving money is great, but do you have to be so messy about it? I want to come home to a place where I can sit, eat, smoke, and watch T.V. in peace. This ain't it," he said visually surveying the room.

She quickly gathered up all the pieces and placed the stack in the corner by their bedroom closet and returned to the kitchen to retrieve his tuna salad plate from the refrigerator.

Family physician, Dr. Swanson, agreed to be her obstetrician since the gynecologist misdiagnosed the pregnancy. She went to see him regularly for her prenatal checkups.

"Dr. Swanson, I can't fit into my shoes. I have a headache every day. My wedding ring is so tight I can't even get it off," she said trying to twist it to show him. As she stood up from the examining table she doubled over in abdominal pain. "Is there something wrong?" she anxiously asked.

Patting her on the right shoulder he said, "Now Mrs. Finch, don't you worry. I'll take good care of you. You only have a month to go so I will be seeing you weekly now."

Feeling only a tiny bit reassured she said, "Okay, if you say so."

Marion exhibited the typical symptoms of Toxemia, with elevated blood pressure, albumin in her urine, swelling of her hands, feet, and brain, visual impairment, and excruciating headaches. The most distressing part was Dr. Swanson did not inform her that her blood pressure was elevated or that she had the condition now known as Preeclampsia.

Passing her August 2nd due date, she impatiently waited for her child to make his or her grand entrance. On Monday evening August 8th while Marion brushed her teeth, she felt a gush of fluid spill onto the floor.

Embarrassed and naïve, she thought she just peed her pants.

Cleaning it up, she put her hand on her aching lower back.

By the time she entered the bedroom, she knew labor had begun.

"Frankie, are you ready to finally be a dad?" she gingerly asked as he awaited his night time pleasure.

"Do I have a choice at this point?" he asked half joking.

"Ah, well – you better get ready cause my labor's started."

With fear in his voice he said, "Are you sure?"

"Quite certain, remember, I'm a week past my due date."

Anxiety rising, he asked, "Do we need to go to the hospital now?" he said starting to don his trousers.

"No," she put her hand on his leg. "the books all say to wait til my contractions are ten minutes apart."

No one slept much that night. At six a.m., exhausted, Marion awoke Frankie who had just dozed off. "Frankie, hon, it's time to go to the hospital."

Groggily he answered, swinging his legs over the side of the bed, "Okay, give me a minute to wake up and have a cigarette."

"Okay, but be quick, my pains are ten minutes apart."

Arriving at Elmira's St. Joseph's Hospital, they found all the doors locked. Strange, did babies never come at early hours? The intercom system responded when they rang the bell.

"Hello, how may I help you?"

"My name is Marion Finch and I'm in labor."

"Are you sure it is not false labor? When is your due date?"

Angrily and impatiently blurting out, amid a contraction, "YES, I'm sure. My due date was a week ago, August 2nd."

The door opened and she was whisked to Admitting by the attendants with Frankie trailing behind, feeling left out.

Dr. Swanson arrived by 7:30 a.m. After he examined her he reassured her, "You are only dilated one centimeter so it will be awhile before your baby comes."

She did not know it was unusual for them to continuously check her blood pressure. The enema was uncomfortable during a contraction. As typical, they shaved her private parts for prevention of infection. There was no time to be embarrassed by all the procedures.

The labor accelerated as the day wore on. They kept asking her if she wanted something to ease the pain. "No, thank you," clutching the starched white sheets, she answered between clenched teeth.

They did not know the reason for her rejection of drugs to ease the childbirth process. She heard in church that pain in childbirth was due to Eve's disobedience in the Garden of Eden. To endure the pain was her Christian duty, she felt, and she thought if she did, maybe God would forgive her for her past sinful behavior.

At 4:30 p.m. Dr. Swanson returned and chuckled, "Thanks, Marion for waiting all day to deliver. I did not have to cancel any of my patients. Now Mr. Finch, you go there (pointing to the outer area) to the father's waiting area, 'cause you know dads are not allowed in the delivery room."

About at her wit's end and so exhausted with no food or water in almost twenty-four hours, she gratefully thanked the orderlies for wheeling her into the delivery room. Transferring from the gurney onto the delivery table she groaned pleading with tear-filled eyes, "Please give me something to end this pain."

Dr. Swanson in his soothing voice said patting her arm, "Mrs. Finch, two more pushes and your baby will be here."

Crying in defeat she said, "I don't care," grabbing Dr. Swanson's arm before he let go of hers. "PLEASE PLEASE knock me out!"

As they placed the gas mask on her face, she apologized to God and tried to tell the anesthesiologist she changed her mind, but it was too late. She woke up and looked at the clock on the wall in front of her. It was 4:45p.m., only ten minutes later.

God, I'm sorry. I could not wait. Please don't be mad at me.

With warm blankets surrounding her shaking body, a six pound, little wrinkly-skinned boy was laid on her chest while her head throbbed.

Dr. Swanson added to her guilt for not staying the course, "I was right. It was only two more contractions and your son entered the world."

All she could muster was, "Thank you."

Frankie was finally allowed in to see Marion after she was cleaned up and transferred to the maternity ward to recuperate along with fifteen other new mothers. All the beds were made of iron painted white with a slot at the end to hold the medical chart. Adam, their newborn son, was seen by Frankie through the glass, safely in the nursery after his mouth and nose were suctioned, PKU test done, and imprints of his feet made.

Marion was expected to be in the hospital at least five days, the average time. During that time fathers were only allowed in during visiting hours. Since

Frankie had to work long hours, she rarely saw him. Everything was done on schedule: feeding, bathing, sleeping, and eating, to get the babies used to it.

Marion surveyed the ward of sixteen beds, mothers of all sizes, but mostly young like her. Turning to the bed next to hers she said, "Does Nurse Puckett get on your nerves like she does mine?"

Adjusting her pillow, Milly sat up and said, glancing furtively to see if the coast was clear, "Ya, I was talking on the phone to my husband when she brought me Joey. She yelled at me for not hanging up soon enough."

Marion put her feet over the side of the bed onto the floor facing her bedmate and answered, whispering, "I know. Adam had been with me for over an hour. I nursed him, burped him, and changed him. He fell asleep in my arms. I was looking at a magazine so I wouldn't fall asleep and drop him. She yelled at me 'Mrs. Finch that is not how you take care of a baby. There is no time to be reading magazines!' I felt like a little kid being punished by my teacher. We may be young, but we don't need some old woman yelling at us."

"I agree, Joey's my second baby and I'll be twenty-two next month. I got married right out of high school as did most of my friends. Ut Oh! We better hush," she said finger to her lips. "Here comes Nurse Puckett now."

One day being awakened from a short nap, she looked up to see Dr. Goodson, her original obstetrician, pulling up her chart at the end of her bed. A month before Adam's birth they had received an invoice for the only 'prenatal' visit Marion had at his office. It was stamped final notice. Frankie had written a response to that bill.

Dr. Goodson:
    This is the first bill we have received from you. We would not mind paying it, but you did not examine Marion, or take a urine sample. This figment of her imagination you claimed she had will be born in one month.

Sincerely,
Frank and Marion Finch

Dr. Goodson saw her name on the chart, frowned, set it back down, said nothing, and moved on to the next bed. They never got another bill from his office.

Happy to be home, Marion repeatedly looked out the bedroom window awaiting Sarah and Rhonda's arrival on Sunday evening, hours after the hospital discharge. She was clueless how to care for a newborn and prayed her mom remembered and would teach her. Sarah and Rhonda scarcely put their luggage down in the guest room before they washed their hands in the bathroom sink and excitedly took turns cradling Adam and changing his diaper.

Marion clumsily nursed Adam every two hours.

She sat on the couch with a burp towel covering her breast. With each suck, Marion winced and her sanitary napkin filled with blood. She thought it must be normal. She could not ask her mom, because she bottle fed all three of the Parker girls.

Marion remembered her manners and, looking up from kissing Adam on the top of his head said, "Mom, Rhonda. I sure appreciate your help. I didn't know being a mom was this tiring."

Sarah responded, handing Marion a glass of cold milk to drink, "Yes, it is. Grannie Nellie came after Gretchen and you were born, but was not helpful at all. She said she did not remember how to give a bottle or change a diaper and had no interest in re-learning. By the time Rhonda came, I told her to stay home."

Marion did not know how to respond to that so she said nothing. Frankie was very cordial to everyone while they visited for five days.

"Now Grannie and Rhonda, you be sure to be careful driving home. Two women on the road alone can be dangerous," he said protectively as he loaded their suitcases into the trunk of their pale green '67 Chevy II.

"We will," Sarah said as she hugged Marion and kissed Adam on the forehead saying, "Now that I'm a grandma, I'm going to have to call each Sunday to catch up on how you're growing, little guy."

Marion fell into a routine of napping when Adam did, but set an alarm to get up in time to fix Frankie's supper each evening. After her family left, she felt insecure as a new mom and wondered which of her symptoms were normal. She did not want Frankie to think she could not handle being a new mom, or that she was overreacting, so she only briefly mentioned her symptoms to him. When the blurry vision and pressure headaches did not subside postpartum, she called Dr. Swanson who sent her to an ophthalmologist. Dr. Clark revealed that Toxemia caused the swelling of her brain, affecting her vision.

Pacing the living room, she finally got the courage and dialed her obstetrician's number.

"Hello, Dr. Swanson's office. This is Susan. How may I help you, please?"

"Susan, this is Marion Finch. May I please speak with Dr. Swanson?"

"Mrs. Finch, what is the nature of your call? Can I help? He's with a patient right now."

Marion firmly said, "I need to talk to him about my visit with Dr. Clark."

"Oh, okay, Can I put you on hold until he is done with the patient?"

"Yes, I can wait. Thank you."

She continued to twist the phone cord around her hand hoping Adam would not awaken from his nap before she spoke with Dr. Swanson. Three minutes later he came to the phone. She told him what the ophthalmologist's diagnosis was and asked, "Why didn't you tell me I had toxemia?"

"I didn't want to worry you," was Dr. Swanson's response. "I'm your doctor and I was handling it. That is why I sent you to Dr. Clark. You'll be fine in a few weeks.

The headaches will subside and the vision will clear up.

You're a new, anxious, inexperienced mom. Leave the worrying to me. I'll see you in a month for your six-week check-up and you'll see I'm right. Good-bye."

Being the compliant patient, she did not question his authority and tried not to bother him again until her post-partum check-up.

Frankie, ill-prepared for parenthood, groaned every time Adam, sleeping in the crib next to their bed, woke him in the night. Marion would tip toe out to the living room to lay on the couch to nurse him. Each time Adam latched on, she would cramp and soak her pad. She did not want to be a frantic new mother who called the doctor all the time so she tried to manage it on her own. Being a conscientious mom, she gingerly she put her finger between the diaper and his cuddly skin so not to poke him with a diaper pin. Not wanting the smell to bother Frankie she promptly placed the soiled cloth diaper in the pail in their only bathroom.

Marion's day quickly evaporated into nursing her hungry son, washing diapers, carrying the laundry basket up to the attic to dry them in front of the space heater. A dryer was a luxury they could not afford. On Thursdays when Frankie had his day off, she would drag the basket down the flight of stairs to dry at the laundry mat. The time away was precariously planned around Adam's afternoon nap. Frankie agreed to watch him, if he did not have to change a poopy diaper. If Adam did not cooperate, then she had to take him with her and balance him in his infant seat on top of the laundry basket.

Frankie informed her, "my day off is mine, not a day to turn into helping you. Don't expect me to cook, or clean, or fix anything. You don't work so all of that is your job plus you are to take care of me."

She did her best to comply with his demands to have peace in her life. Each morning after Frankie left she would read her bible and talk to God. *Thank you, Father for saving my soul. Thank you for the miracle of Adam. Help me to be a good wife, and help Frankie be a good husband and want to follow you. Amen.*

She wanted Adam to have the religious influence that could positively shape him into a godly man. Marion took her tiny baby boy to Elmira Baptist Church by herself.

She did not dare leave him in the church's nursery or Frankie said she could not take him. Praying for him to be quiet, she set him beside her on the next to the last pew determined to leave the service if he bellowed.

As the organ played the prelude, *Bringing in the Sheaves*, Sylvia, the head deacon's wife leaning over to Marion said, "Cute little fella. Where's his daddy?" Fumbling with the light blue baby blanket covering Adam's body in his infant seat she said avoiding the woman's gaze, "Ah, he's home. He doesn't like church much."

With Sylvia's glasses positioned on her nose, she looked over them at Marion.

With pursed lips moving she said, "Sounds like you did not pray about it before you married that heathen, or is he just backslidden? Maybe you're not being an obedient enough wife or praying hard enough for him to see the error of his ways and become the spiritual head of his family. Too bad your son there, (pointing at Adam) being so young, won't know what it's like to grow up in a godly family."

Marion held in her anger at Sylvia's judgment. She clutched Adam to her chest and kissed his cheek. She did not respond. On the way home, she silently prayed.

"God, what am I supposed to say to someone like that? I can't make Frankie go to church. Please God, mold his heart."

The next week the sermon was about "God's will for your life." Preacher Wilkins pounded the pulpit as he said, "If there is turmoil in your life, if there is discord in your marriage, then maybe you are not following God's will for your life."

God, I tried to correct my sin of fornication by marrying Frankie. I try to please him and you, but nothing seems to work. You gave me this miracle, sweet Adam, she said looking down at him sleeping peacefully, *when doctors said I could never have kids, so you can't be too mad at me. I can't handle every sermon telling me how I have failed you.*

To avoid more guilt trips, she just stopped going to church. The decision was partly influenced by Frankie's comment on Friday.

"When's your six-week checkup, again?" Frankie asked, looking up from his Isaac Asimov novel.

"Two weeks from Tuesday, why Hubbles?" she asked perplexed picking up his supper plate from his lap.

He said with a wink, "Cause I can't wait to get back to my Sunday afternoon 'Greekings.' I was a good husband to let you have this six weeks off while you got over having Adam, but soon I can have my way with you again," he said rubbing his hands together.

She visibly cringed. On Sunday, he questioned her, "So when you gonna be home from church today?" with a twinkle in his eye, counting down the days til his pleasure resumed.

"Oh, she said cradling Adam. "I'm not going. Adam is too cranky when he wakes up and you won't let me take him to the nursery. I don't want to interrupt the people worshipping God, so I'm not going."

Frankie looked dejected. She said nothing and went into the kitchen to prepare lunch.

Being a mom felt like swimming in uncharted waters. To ease her lack of knowledge and isolation, she interacted with some of the women, also mothers, whose husbands either managed stores in town, too, or were salesmen to the stores. She called June occasionally. "Hello, June. It's Marion. How ya doing?"

"Fine, Marion and you?"

Twisting the telephone cord around her fingers she wondered how to phrase her answer.

"I'm okay I guess, but I have a question. Is it okay to ask you?"

"Sure, ask away. The boys are sleeping so I have time to chat."

"Thanks," Marion said letting out a sigh. "Every time I nurse Adam I flood my sanitary napkin and have cramps. Is that normal?"

"Oh dear, I don't know. I haven't had that experience. How long you been nursing him?"

"He's five weeks old today," she proudly said. Trying to be encouraging June suggested, "Why don't you call your doctor and ask him since your check-up isn't til next week."

"I will. Thanks. I can't wait to see you tomorrow.

I'm glad you're driving me to get groceries since I can't til after my six-week check-up. I'll see you tomorrow at 11:30."

"See ya then, bye Marion."

"Bye, June."

When Marion called Dr. Swanson's office as soon as they opened the next morning, he had his nurse tell her to continue as she was until he saw her the following week. She felt so drained nursing, but did not know if that was normal or not. Dr. Swanson, upon examination, determined her hemorrhaging was not normal. Whatever he wrote in her chart about the cause of the bleeding he did not share with her. He said to stop nursing and pump to see if the same effect happened. It did, so sadly she switched Adam to Enfamil formula. He made the adjustment well and began sleeping longer between feedings. She was glad that at least she had given him six weeks of breast milk to boost his immune system.

She continued daily to pray for Frankie's spiritual condition. About two months after she stopped attending church, he surprised her. She did not know if her prayers were working or being a dad mellowed him. One Saturday evening after work he sat at the kitchen table while she cleared away the dishes. He said touching her arm as she lifted his plate to take to the sink, "Marion, I was thinking."

"Ya, Frankie about what?" She was holding her breath unsure what he might say.

"Maybe we could go to church together."

"Oh, Frankie. I'd love that. That would be good for Adam too," she said smiling squeezing his arm with her free hand.

Frankie told her, "I'll look around and see what I like and then we'll go, okay?"

Excitedly, she said, "Okay, sure." Marion felt this was a step in the right direction.

God was working on Frankie's heart. She had been praying for such an answer. Marion, allowed to voice an opinion on which church to attend, did so, but Frankie made the final choice. He selected a liberal, small, welcoming Lutheran church where any baptized Christian could take communion. Marion, once again hopeful for their future, believed God was molding her husband into the model, God-fearing man he was destined to be.

Being a mom was delightful, even if scary for Marion. Her family was too far away in Wisconsin and Frankie's family, although close, were busy working fulltime. Frankie did agree to vacation briefly in Wisconsin when Adam was two months old to meet Andy and Mary and visit Sarah and Rhonda.

The visit was pleasant spending the first three days at Sarah and Rhonda's house, and then the last three with Andy and Mary. Marion looked tearfully at Andy standing outside the car. "Dad, I don't want to go home. Do you realize this is the first time we ever got to spend three days together since I was a kid?"

Andy hugged Marion tight as tears stained both their cheeks. Andy pulled back and grabbed his handkerchief out of his shirt pocket to blow his nose. "It's okay, I'll miss you too, but I'll call you every couple of Sundays so I can catch up on what Little Adam's doing, okay?"

"Okay, Dad. That'd be great. Love you," she said as she got into the front passenger seat silently replaying the highlights of their visit.

Back from the trip she gradually learned how to take care of Adam as she looked forward to the bi-weekly phone calls from her dad and stepmom. If she wanted to talk to her mom or sister Marion had to initiate those phone calls, because Sarah would not spend money unless it benefited her personally.

On Fridays June and Marion had the rare privilege of driving their one family car. They each met at the Mitchums store at the North edge of town that had a cafeteria attached to it. A meal cost less than a dollar. The rest of the week the car sat outside the store all day in case the husbands needed to go somewhere.

Four families got together on the weekends. Two of the men were grocery store managers. The other two were cigarette salesmen. None of the wives were employed outside the home. The men sat around talking shop and smoking cigarettes over beers. Marion looked forward to having adult conversation with other women. The women stayed in the kitchen, fixed the food, chased after all the children, and replenished the six packs when beckoned.

Marion peered her head around the dining room wall to summon the men out to the backyard where picnic tables awaited them loaded down with fried chicken, deviled eggs, and potato salad. As Marion turned back toward the kitchen Frankie called out to her. "C'mere a minute, would ya?" She did wiping her hands on her paisley apron. Frankie said, "tell the guys how you screwed up the turkey the other night." The men sat silent while he berated Marion.

Irked, she turned and stomped back to the kitchen. She could hear him sharing the embarrassing details of how she forgot to take out the giblets package before she cooked the bird.

After that, abruptly, invitations to gatherings stopped. Marion never knew the reason, but wondered if it had to do with how he treated her in front of the four families or if had he said or done something inappropriate with one of the wives? She was too afraid to ask anyone to know the truth.

Whenever she asked Frankie, "Are we getting together with the gang this weekend?"

His sullen response gesturing wildly with his hands was, "How the hell should I know? Do you think I have a crystal ball or something?"

She continued to have lunch on Fridays with June for about a month and then June called and abruptly said, "Marion, I can't go to lunch on Friday. I'm sorry."

Marion thought it odd, but only said, "Oh, okay, I'll miss getting together."

June offered no comforting word and hung up. She never called back. One Friday Marion saw June in the grocery store with Debbie, a salesman's wife. It hurt her feelings, but rather than make a scene, she quickly and quietly exited the store. Thereafter she just shopped in Frankie's store.

Marion was surprised months later when Frankie took her with Adam to Ray and Debbie's house on a Saturday evening. Marion happily greeted the old gang thinking they were back in their friends' good graces.

"Debbie, I'm so glad you invited us. It's been a long time since we got together," Marion said hugging her.

Debbie pulled back and looked to Frankie as she said, "Marion, we did not invite you. Frankie found out from Harry that we were getting together and invited himself."

Chagrined and angry, Marion grabbed her coat and son to leave, her face flushed. As she turned to Frankie, she said, "Come on. We're going home."

Totally inappropriate, Frankie slammed his hand on the table and stated, "No, we're not! We're here and we're going to stay."

Not having any car keys or money to call a cab, Marion sat down at the dining room table cradling Adam on her lap holding back the tears of rejection and embarrassment all at the same time. Frankie tried to insert himself into the other's conversations. They turned their backs to him.

Steaks and potatoes were cut in half to have enough to go around. Marion did not feel like eating and just sat quiet for what seemed like an eternity until they could leave. Ray, Debbie, Harry, Jim, and June carried on a conversation ignoring Marion and Frankie as if they were invisible. Frankie's squared-back, shoulder posture gave off the impression that he felt he belonged there as he ate in silence.

On the way home, perplexed, feeling totally humiliated, Marion asked, "Why did you have us go when you knew we were not invited and what did we do that was so terrible that they do not want us there?"

Turning to face Marion, he angrily said, "I don't know why, so I decided to confront them. We did nothing wrong and we deserve to be included."

Risking his wrath, she said gesturing with her left palm, "But not when we were not invited. That was embarrassing. Don't do that again."

As anticipated, Frankie pointed his index finger at her and said, "You are my wife. You will go where I say go and you will do as I say do. Do you understand me?"

Head bowed, her voice quavered, "Yes," she said.

They never went back to any more gatherings. She was too afraid to find out the reason and thought it was better to just close that door and move on, but to what? She had no other friends.

Back to her own little nest, Marion, frugal like Sarah, made her budget stretch. She sewed clothes for Adam and herself. Her main function was to make her husband happy and want to come home.

A pattern emerged. Marion entertained herself watching the *Somerset* soap opera while she fed Adam his afternoon bottle. The rest of the day she sang along with the tunes on the Christian radio station. Frankie worked five twelve-hour days seeing Adam awake only on his days off, expecting him to not interfere with his plans to sleep in, have sex with his wife, or meals upon demand. As best she could, Marion complied.

On one such evening when Adam was already asleep, Frankie revealed more of his inner rage.

"Marion, get me a glass of milk would ya?"

Bringing the milk in the twelve-ounce plastic blue glass, she handed it to him. It slipped out of his grasp and he cursed. "God dammit woman, can't you hand me the glass without spilling it?"

Marion knew it was not her fault but did not protest. Heart pounding, she quickly grabbed a towel from the bathroom rack, returned and offered to clean it up for him.

"No, I'll do it myself. Get out of my way," he said pushing past her.

She stepped back, unsure whether to leave, help, or just stand there. As he was about to finish wiping up, he raised his arm to set the glass with the remaining two ounces of milk on top of the thigh high book case, but instead he tipped it over drenching the brand-new set of Britannica encyclopedias.

Throwing the glass against the wall, knocking off the plaster, he shouted, "Fuck it. Now my encyclopedias are ruined."

Then, yelling at Marion, he said, "You need to learn to either lead, follow, or get out of the way."

Unsure how to respond, she just shook her head affirmatively, all the color drained from her face.

He grabbed her head and shook it up and down as he said, "Bobbing your head up and down is not an answer. Can you do as I ask?"

Timidly she answered, "Yes, Frankie," trying to escape his grasp.

"Yes, Frankie, what?" he asked letting go and glaring at her.

"I, I, I will do my best," she stammered while her bottom lip quivered.

He motioned with his right hand, "Just git out of my way and leave me alone."

She crept away as she shook with fear because although he was overbearing and his voice could be angry, she had never experienced this type of his physical rage before, but now could feel anger's waves breathing out of Frankie.

A few days after his anger cooled, needing some social interaction outlet she said, as she purposely handed him a heaping bowl of butter pecan ice cream, "Frankie, I heard about a women's Bible study on the Christian radio station. I wanna go. Okay?"

Not looking up, he said, "I guess so, if your housework is done."

Kissing Frankie on the cheek, she said, "thank you," and walked back to the kitchen.

Excited to have this opportunity, she joined the group. The following Tuesday, Frankie's new day off, he agreed to watch Adam if she was gone only two hours.

The Women's Bible Study met at a welcoming one-story brown wooden cottage decorated with white gingerbread trim, the home of the local Child Evangelism Society, three miles from the Finches' apartment.

Walking into the abode, she noticed six women, average age of forty, all with their long hair pinned up into a knot on the back of their head. Introductions made, the women greeted her warmly. "Welcome, Mrs. Finch, to our bible study. We're so glad you can join us."

Smiling, she answered as she sat at the extended dining room table, "Thank you, I've been looking forward to this for a few weeks. What are we studying?"

"If you brought your King James Bible, open it to Ephesians 5:22. We are studying about wives being subject to their husbands. You are an obedient wife, aren't you?"

Nervously, she fidgeted in her chair as she opened to the passage in record time to demonstrate her adeptness at navigating God's Holy Word. "Yes, I am, but Frankie isn't one to be the spiritual head. He's not really into church and all that."

Clucking, Mrs. Thomas said in a condescending manner, "Really, did you not marry the man God has for you? Did you not pray earnestly for the one God set aside for you? If you didn't, you're in for a life of sorrow, my dear."

Marion sat crestfallen not hearing anything else Mrs. Thomas may have said. Instead she silently prayed, *God, I'm really trying to obey you by studying your word with God-fearing women, but this kind of talk is not helping. I'm really trying to make up for having sex before marriage. Please forgive me and bless my marriage.* Hopeful that God would answer her prayer she vowed to come back the next week.

Marion walked in to find the women deep in prayer with their hands folded on top of their bibles. Quietly checking her watch, she was on time, in fact early. Silently, she tiptoed to the end of the table and attempted to noiselessly pull out the metal folding chair and sit down. Maybe, like her "so called" recent friends, this group did not want her either. Before she could unfold her chair, upon hearing her Mary Jane shoes bump the table leg, the group simultaneously opened their eyes and said, "Amen." "Welcome, Mrs. Finch. The topic today is all about adornment. Would you please read I Corinthians 11:15 out loud?"

"I'd be happy to. 'If a woman has long hair, it is her glory and is given to her for a covering.' Any other verses?"

"No, that is sufficient," Mrs. Peabody, the leader, said.

Marion did not have long hair.

"Mrs. Finch, how come you are not obeying God's Word? Why do you not have long hair and why do you go against Jeremiah 4:11 wearing make-up and jewelry? Don't you know those things are an abomination to God? We were praying for you before your arrival that God would open your eyes to the truth."

She sat quietly through the remainder of the bible study, but did not return. She was becoming disillusioned, gradually leaving behind the religious guilt trips she was fed by so called fundamentalist "Christians". These devout folks actually believed God *told* them to judge others to help the sinners see the err of their ways to avoid burning in Hell forever. Marion began to wonder what, if anything, she had been taught by religiously rigid people was applicable to her present life? She never doubted the validity of her personal relationship with God. It was in fact, deepening, as the band of guilt that suffocated her every action due to the admonitions of her well-meaning judges, was loosening.

Marion spent her days talking to five-month-old Adam jostling him on her knee, singing him the Christian praise songs of her youth, listening to the Christian radio station, and reciting nursery rhymes, but longing for adult interaction.

One day her landlord, Mr. Hershberger saw her struggling to get Adam and the groceries upstairs.

"Let me help you, Mrs. Finch." Holding his arms outstretched he said, "I can hold your little feller while you take the groceries upstairs. Come back down and I will fix you a nice cup of hot tea."

Grateful for the assistance, she shyly said, "Are you sure you can handle a five-month-old?"

"Yes, not to worry. I'm a grandpa now with three rambunctious grandsons. We'll be fine. Go now," he said motioning to her.

She did and thoroughly enjoyed returning for the tea, and gratefully accepted the extra homemade chocolate cake to bring upstairs later for Frankie. But most of all, she relished the conversation with Mr. Hershberger. She jabbered on about this and that, starved to speak in more than one syllable baby babble.

"You're welcome to come down anytime you want some company, Mrs. Finch."

"Please call me Marion," she said smiling. "Thank you so much Mr. Hershberger. This has been so nice, but Adam needs his nap now," shifting him from the landlord's lap to her hip.

That night she excitedly told Frankie about her visit. Frankie stared at her with a fixed glaze, "What the hell were you thinking?" he bellowed.

Perplexed, Marion stood there with her mouth open wondering what he meant.

"You ought to know not to mingle with our landlord. You don't want him knowing our business. The next thing you know he will be raising our rent, or coming upstairs to check on things. I want you to promise me you will not reveal our business to him and will not get chummy with him. You understand?"

Through her sad eyes and frown she said, "Yes, Frankie."

She resumed her lonely daytime routine. The company decided to send Frankie out to reset stores. When the corporation fired a manager, Frankie's job was to reorganize the store in preparation for the new manager to take over. When he went to Scranton, Pennsylvania for a week he rode the Greyhound bus. Marion even missed Frankie's familiar moody nature. Even though she had the car, she had no money to do anything and no one to go visit. Adam gleefully giggled as Marion tossed snow high in the air above his stroller downstairs in the backyard. The outside excursion was short-lived to return to the warmth of the four-room apartment. Frankie called home on Wednesday night.

"Hello, Marion. How ya doing?"

"I really miss you. You okay all by yourself? How's the reset going? When you coming home?"

"Whoa, one question at a time. Yes, I'm okay, but I miss my night time fun with you. I miss Adam even though he's cranky. And as for when I'm coming home, Friday night, I'll catch the bus back. Can you pick me up at 9 o'clock at the bus terminal?"

"Of course, love you."

"Love you too, bye."

The next reset was in Buffalo, NY. It was as cold as the Arctic Circle when for the first time, the family accompanied him on the job in late January. The Finches left their Elmira apartment thermostat set on sixty degrees to conserve costs while gone the four days.

"Frankie, it's sure nice that the company let the baby and me come with you to Buffalo and stay in this efficiency. I really like being all together. Adam isn't used to seeing you much cause he's usually asleep before you come home."

He looked up briefly from his Robert Heinlein novel to say, "Ya, it's kinda nice, but I don't get much lovings with him right here in the room with us."

"Well, when he goes to sleep it'll be okay, right?"

He gave no response as his nose returned to his book. Marion accepted that she got his attention briefly and that would have to do. As the wind howled outside, she lifted Adam out of his playpen, wrapped him in his aqua and white crocheted blanket Grandma Mary had made him, cuddled him on the bed singing "Rock a bye Baby" until he drifted off to sleep. She gingerly laid Adam in his playpen after moving it away from the draft. Luckily, he slept through Frankie's time of pleasure. During the day while Frankie reset the store, Marion entertained Adam, like at home, bouncing him on her knee while singing nursery rhymes to him and imagined where they might move, next maybe to Meadville, PA or Syracuse once he finished resetting stores.

Returning home to Elmira, each night after work she would ask handing him his supper plate, "Frankie, have you heard anything yet? Do you know where you're being transferred since you finished resetting?"

Grabbing the plate from her hand he finally said, "Woman, get off my case. I don't know and quit your bitching about it. When I know, you'll know. Now let me eat and read in peace."

By the end of February, Frankie's supervisor Clyde wanted Frankie to open a brand-new store starting in April, but withheld the whereabouts. Marion was heartsick because she could not tell her family that they were moving. One day she lost it and called him at the store.

"Frankie, I can't take it anymore," and added in rapid succession, "I swear I'm going crazy. I gotta know where we're going and when. I have all these things I gotta do (spewing them out): tell the landlord, pack, find movers, tell our families, change the phone, turn off the power and…."

Exasperated he said, "Marion, what do ya want me to do? I can't make the company tell me."

Shaking her finger at him over the phone, commanding, she said, "I'm telling you – you better come get Adam right now. I'm going crazy."

Resigned he replied, "All right already. I'll be there in a few minutes."

Fifteen minutes later Frankie ran up the stairs and swung open the front door with a frightened look on his face. Marion had never threatened *anything* before.

Obviously tense, he asked, "Marion, what's all this talk about going crazy?"

Strangely rational she said, "Frankie, I've been patient. I haven't told my family, our landlord, or anyone. I can't stare at these four walls in this apartment a minute longer. I gotta get out of here. It's like knowing a bomb is going to explode and I'm sitting on it just waiting for it to happen. It's driving me insane." She handed him Adam and said, "Watch him and I'll be back."

Anxiously he asked holding Adam at arm's length, "Where ya going?"

"For a ride to clear my head," she declared.

Aware that he could not change her mind, he said handing over the car keys reluctantly, "Don't wreck the car. I gotta get back to the store."

Feeling her power, she said, "They can get along without you for a little bit. You're going to be gone soon anyway." She bounded down the steps squealing the tires as she pealed out of their parking spot.

Frankie, uncomfortable caring for seven-month-old Adam solo, turned on the television and looked at his son.

"Well Adam, it's you and me kid. I hope your mom gets back quick. I need a cigarette and to pee."

Adam just stared, observing the dad he barely knew.

Marion drove about two miles down Walker headed toward the outskirts of town and re-thought her plan. "I can't leave Adam with Frankie. He won't know what to do if he starts wailing. *God, please help me to handle all of this and be a good wife. Amen.*

Frankie, paced with his squalling son, frightened that Marion became so bold.

The fifteen-minute drive was just the refreshment she needed. She bounded back up the steps with a smile on her face.

Frankie relieved, said as Marion opened the door, "I'll call Clyde and tell him we gotta know something 'cause we have to tell our landlord."

"Thank you. Keep holding Adam for a few minutes while I go up to the attic to get some boxes dashing past him. She yelled over her shoulder, "I love you and I'm sorry I had you come home, but I really was going crazy."

Session Fifteen

"Dr. Weinstein, since last week's session I can't stop thinking about how what I believed has changed so much since I began to allow myself to view it from a different perspective."

"Marion, when we go through trauma, it is like we are in a container with no escape. It isn't until we are let out or get out that we can see the environment for what it was. Outside looks different than inside. Are you ready to explore some more?"

"I can't wait to do so."

"Where do we start today, Marion?"

"The Albany Haunted House experience," she said. Dr. Weinstein rubbed his palms together and said,

"I can't wait for the adventure to begin."

Haunted House

To Marion's relief, relocation news was revealed the following week. Frankie would open a new store in Albany, New York. Delighted, Frankie ignored Marion's apprehension. She wanted her husband to want her, respect her and be proud to show her off. But her insecurities remained and took root. Albany was the last place she wanted to reside because the family of his prior fiancé, Michelle still lived there. Even though Michelle lived with her husband Jack in Oregon, Marion still had nightmares believing, given the chance, Frankie and Michelle would reunite.

Early on a Monday morning, the first week of April, the Finches drove from their Glendale Ave apartment in Elmira, N.Y. to Albany in their black 1968 Valiant Regal. They spent the night in the Howard Johnson's motel eager to get a fresh start apartment hunting on Tuesday morning. Scouring the newspaper for available housing yielded slim pickings since Albany University classes were still in session. Baby Adam became cranky, sick with continual vomiting, and got on Frankie's nerves.

Red upholstery draped the bench seats of their car. In an era before child car seats were mandatory, Marion sat to the far right and held scowling Adam on her lap as Frankie looked at street names trying to locate an 'apartment for rent' sign.

Being impatient, unused to Adam's behavior, Frankie turned to Marion and said, "Shut the baby up already! I can't stand his crying another minute."

Squaring her maternal shoulders, she said, as she cradled her infant, "I'm sorry, Frankie, but there's something wrong with Adam. He keeps throwing up and he won't eat or drink his bottle."

Irritated, Frankie turned back to face the windshield and said, "His puke stinks. We won't be able to find an apartment anywhere with him squalling like a wild dog. I don't care what you do, but make him stop," he said spewing spit.

With tears streaming silently down her cheeks, she turned her face to the passenger side window and held Adam tighter until, exhausted, he fell asleep. Feeling the warmth on his brow and looking at the flushed cheeks, she timidly said to Frankie, "Adam's really sick. We need to take him to the doctor. I'm very worried about him."

Angry for the interruption to their plans, Frankie turned toward her with a balled fist and said, "You worry too much. Babies get sick all the time. He'll be fine. I don't have money for a doctor with the deposits we have to pay."

Gathering all her courage, Marion boldly met his eyes and stated, "I'm taking him to the ER. Just drop us off. He needs a doctor."

Finally, sensing the seriousness, he said, "Fine," putting both hands back on the steering wheel. "When they tell you it's nothing, and we don't have money for deposits, and we have ta sleep in the car, remember I told you so."

Poor eight-month-old Adam had a bad case of strep throat. She was relieved to know her motherly instincts were on target. Since they now had insurance, the hospital agreed to bill her once they filed the claim. Frankie waited in the car, chewed his fingernails, and chain smoked his boxed Marlboros.

Returning to the car, two hours later, Marion had a smug look on her face. Getting into the vehicle she showed Frankie a prescription.

"Frankie, Adam has strep throat. We need to fill this prescription," she said waving it in his face.

"And what is this going to cost me?" he said grabbing it out of Marion's hand. "I bet they didn't even check him, like Dr. Goodson with you. I'm not going to pay some outrageous doctor bill," he growled.

Letting out a deep breath she replied slowly choosing each word. "They did a throat culture. They're gonna bill the insurance. I'm sure our part won't be much. We gotta get this script 'cause he could get a lot worse if we don't." Pointing, she said, "There's a drugstore, let's stop here."

He begrudgingly paid the three dollars for the antibiotic prescription and sped out of the parking lot while cussing out other drivers.

Under his breath, he muttered, "The wife and kid are always costing me something."

Marion, too afraid to say anything, learned silence was best until his anger passed.

Antibiotics cured Adam's strep throat and they moved into the multi-family apartment house on Catawba Street in Albany. Marion unpacked the last box as Adam, now eight months old, tried to pull himself up in his play-pen. She periodically picked him up and swung him around dancing in their expansive kitchen. The apartment they found was six blocks from downtown Albany, in the middle between the Polish and Italian neighborhoods.

Frankie, home on that first Sunday morning the day before he began setting up the new grocery store, suggested swatting her on the behind, "Hey, Whiffles, can you smell that pizza pie from the strip mall behind us?" sniffing the air. "It reminds me of the Italian pizzeria on Main Street in Cortland. I'd go there after I finished my paper route and gobble down the steaming slice before I walked home to my Ma's home cooked supper. How 'bout we go check it out for lunch?"

"Sure Frankie, we can do that," Marion said nodding her head. "Let me get Adam's socks and shoes on him and the stroller off the porch," she felt hopeful that this move was off to a good start.

As they walked up the steps to reach the street, their next-door neighbor, Francine, greeted them with a plate of homemade chocolate chip cookies. Marion reached out to receive the goodies with a big grin.

"Thank you. They'll be perfect to finish off our meal after our pizza. Come on over tomorrow morning and we can have some tea and eat some, if any are left," said Marion.

"Sure, Francine said. "That'd be great. See ya." The delicious smell of the various shopkeeper's wares wafted into their nostrils as they walked around the corner. The aroma of hot pizza pies combined with the smell of Kielbasa drew customers with watering mouths into the establishments.

The Finch apartment was on the ground floor of a three-family, brown, asbestos sided, century old dwelling. The apartment's kitchen worn linoleum floor sagged in the middle. The white warped wooden cupboards did not completely close. The deep kitchen sink had a singular faucet with hot and cold knobs and a porcelain ridged drain board on the left-hand side of the sink with storage underneath the cabinet. The twenty-year-old gas stove worked adequately. The antiquated heating system combined with high ceilings made the five-room flat hard to heat. The three bedrooms had newer linoleum and the living room had a maroon area rug over a mahogany hardwood floor. The one bathroom, recently remodeled, had a tub, toilet, and shower, but no storage.

The door to the basement stairs was at the edge of the kitchen. The laundry was in the cellar, but the place was so spooky, like her Lodge bedroom, that Marion avoided it as much as possible. She felt someone breathing on her, standing behind her whenever she braved her fear to quickly load clothes into the washer or new dryer. At night, she heard hammering and sawing in the basement at the workbench below the kitchen. It was odd that it stopped whenever Frankie was home. She thought maybe she was going crazy, that no one else could hear it.

One night, Rose and Arthur, friends Frankie knew from the church he attended while dating Michelle, came over. Wanting to make a good first impression, Marion made her famous chocolate-coffee-mayonnaise cake with homemade, sugary chocolate, mocha icing like Grandma Winnie used to make. The aroma of fresh brewed coffee filled the air as they gathered around the kitchen table.

Rose and Arthur's son and daughter occupied Adam in the living room building a block tower. As the adults pulled out the kitchen chairs to indulge in the savory dessert, Rose stopped.

"What's that sound?" she asked.

Pouring coffee into the mugs, Marion said, "Which sound?" Did she mean the kids playing in the other room, the sound of the upstairs neighbor's water running through the pipes, or the siren in the distance headed toward St. Luke's hospital?

Pointing to the far wall in the kitchen Rose said, "That hammering sound. It sounds as if it is coming from inside the wall."

Marion, spilled the coffee on the table top as she whispered, "You hear that?"

"Of course, I do," Rose said.

Arthur chimed in, "You wouldn't think someone was doing construction at this late hour."

Marion smiled as she turned toward Frankie and said pointing her finger at him, "See, I told you I wasn't making it up."

Frankie just shrugged his shoulders.

Joining her guests at the table Marion said, "Frankie never hears it. He tells me that I'm just making it up. I don't know where it is coming from, but I'm going to ask my landlord tomorrow to see if he has a clue. Thank you. Now I know I am not crazy. Thank God."

"Well," said Rose glancing around the room. "I sure would want to know who or what is making that sound. It's creepy."

Marion clearing the cake plates said, "Tomorrow I'm going to find out what's going on."

Frankie just shook his head not understanding why it was such a big deal.

The next day she walked across the street to her landlord's house. Knocking on their screen door, Mrs. Thomas invited her in.

"Mrs. Thomas, is Mr. Thomas home?"

"Yes, dear what's the matter?" she said compassionately as Marion tried to quiet her squirming nine-month-old.

"Oh, hello, Mr. Thomas," she said as he emerged from the bedroom looking sleepy with one red suspender on his shoulder and the other hanging down his leg. "May I please ask you a question?"

"If it's not going to cost me money, sure," he said smiling.

"Can you please explain to me what the noise is I hear every night down in the basement, the hammering and sawing and why I feel like a man is watching me when I do laundry?" Laughing, he said, "Well, that would be, Mr. Perkins. He built the house at the turn of the century and…..well, he died at his workbench in '42."

Taken aback Marion said with a furrowed brow, "Oh dear. Is he dangerous?"

Chuckling, Mr. Thomas assured her, "No he's just curious and wonders why someone is living in his house.

Pay him no attention and he'll leave you alone."

Not feeling very confident she said, "Okay, I guess."

She determined at that moment that their lease would not be renewed in eleven months.

Once she got used to Mr. Perkins' noises, she settled in the apartment. One Saturday evening Frankie came home with a Sears' bag under his arm.

"Hi Hon, what's in the bag? Did you bring me a surprise?" she asked with an expectant grin on her face.

Frowning Frankie asked, "Why would I bring you a surprise? Do you think you've earned one? Since you're being so nosy, open the bag for yourself."

Feeling emotionally punched in the stomach, she had no desire to look in the bag. She started to retreat to the kitchen to warm up his supper.

He grabbed her arm as she walked by him.

"Marion, since you were so fired up about what I bought, I'll show you after you bring me my supper in front of the television."

She did not honor him with an answer. She felt the hot tears sting her face. She brushed them aside not wanting him to see her cry and tell her she was so sensitive she couldn't even take a joke. When she returned with the meatloaf made with bread crumbs, green peppers, and onions, different from what she usually made, she had previously hoped he would like it. Now all she wanted to do was to throw it in the garbage, but she did not. He was unwrapping the package from the bag.

"So, how you like my new golf glove?" he said, holding it up for her to see. "It was on sale for six bucks."

"Oh, when do you have time to play golf? You only take Sundays off."

"If you must know, Miss Nosy, my boss, Clyde, is coming to look at how I set up the store. He wants to go golfing Wednesday afternoon."

"I see," she said, with all the wind out of her sails. Whatever he wanted or needed he bought.

Looking down at her shoes, Marion thought, *I really need a new pair, but how can I convince Frankie of that especially since he just blew money on a glove he will wear only once.* Directly asking would be a bold move that could backfire, she knew, so she planned her strategy.

The next afternoon she handed Frankie a plate while he sat on the living room couch reading Isaac Asimov's book *Mars*. Marion said, "Here Hon. I made your favorite chocolate cake and here's a glass of milk to wash it down with. Adam's taking a nap so when you finish your snack, I have a surprise for you."

Eyebrows raised, he asked with a grin, "Oh, have I been a good boy and earned a surprise unlike you? Could it be a little afternoon pleasure?"

Gritting her teeth, she nodded.

Once the beast was tamed, she took aim. As she pulled her shoe out from under the bed she said, "Oh, pooh! My shoe heel is broken. Can you fix it for me?"

Probably certain he had just been duped into a shopping spree, but enjoying the afternoon delight, he said with a sigh, "Go get $5 bucks out of my wallet and get yourself a new pair."

"Thanks Frankie. I will."

She knew it meant only getting something on sale that would not be of her liking, but grateful to get anything, she acted very happy about it. It took a week to find a pair that was in a bargain bin that sort of fit her and would last a long time. She broke them in sporting bruises on her big toes until they stretched out. While shopping for herself, she decided to see if Adam could get some shoes too. If she skimped on groceries, she might be able to afford some.

While removing Adam's shoes, the clerk commented, "Oh, I don't see many children with their socks darned anymore."

Marion was embarrassed to have someone know that she mended one of the only two pair he had because she could not afford new socks for his ever-growing feet. She quickly gathered Adam up, shoeless, and walked away saying "he needs his nap." At home, she just let him go around barefoot.

Marion, like with her mom, Sarah, never knew from one minute to the next what kind of mood to expect from Frankie. On a rare Saturday that Frankie had off, he and Adam napped while Marion tried to quietly remove the antique cradle from the apartment that they had used for Adam. The next day they were to return the heirloom cradle built by Great Grandpa Finch to Frankie's parents' house. Unfortunately, Marion, all of 110 pounds, dropped it as she was lifting it into the trunk, breaking off one of the rocker pieces. About that same time, Frankie emerged from the house his 220-lb. frame looming over her. "Jesus H. Christ, what the hell were you thinking? You could have asked for help, but no you are too Goddamned independent and now you broke it. Are you happy? How you going to explain it to my family?"

Marion, too afraid to cry with the neighbors within earshot, whispered, "I'll glue it, Frankie. I'm sorry. I was trying to let you rest on your one day off. I'll tell your family I broke it."

Frankie surprised her with his response said, "I never did like the cradle anyway," he said dragging the cradle back into the apartment to be glued.

As soon as the storm rose, it was over. There was no rhyme or reason to the outbursts, no way to predict or prepare. Marion's stomach stayed clenched in a permanent knot.

Frankie worked fourteen hours a day preparing for the grand opening of the store. Marion did her best to single-handedly parent Adam, not yet one, and deal with Mr. Perkins. She remembered the spirits in her childhood home. Apparently, Mr. Perkins was not the only unwelcomed entity who invaded her dwelling.

Over a cup of tea one afternoon Marion with trepidation described the encounters to neighbor Francine. "When I turn on the radio this song called "My Marion Makes Me Smile," plays, but when I call Frankie and ask him to hear it, he says it's not playing on the store radio. It freaks me out. Every time I put Adam down for his nap he screams as if someone or something is torturing him. When I try to take a nap, I get a knocking on my head board with someone calling out my name 'Marion, Marion.' It spooks me out so bad I get up. I'm afraid I'm going batty like my Grandmother Nellie."

"Boy, am I glad to hear I am not the only one," Francine said, squeezing her teabag with a spoon and resting it on the saucer. "I was relaxing on the couch last night and something or someone threw me on the floor. I was so scared I got my bible and started praying."

Marion excitedly asked, "Do you ever hear the ghost, Mr. Perkins sawing and hammering at the workbench in the basement?"

"Is that what it is? I always thought someone was doing construction late at night somewhere in the neighborhood," said Francine.

"Nope, it is Mr. Perkins who built the house, our landlord said. You know what you and I should try?"

"No, what?"

"We should, at the same time, go down to our adjoining basements when we hear the sounds and see what happens," said Marion courageously.

"I don't know if that is such a good idea or not, but we can try."

Before evening when Francine came by to borrow a cup of sugar, the song Marion mentioned earlier was playing on the radio. Francine heard it. "Is that the song you told me about?"

Marion stopped loading the cup midair and asked, "Yeah, you can hear it?"

"Hey, let's call the station and ask them about it."

"Francine, that's a great idea," Marion said handing the sugar bowl to Francine.

The radio station said they were not playing that song and had never heard of it.

"Can you believe that Francine? They've never heard of the song. That is so weird," Marion said, returning the sugar bag to the pantry shelf.

As Francine headed back to her apartment, they apprehensively agreed to meet in the adjoining basement at nine p.m. At 8:55 p.m. Marion with Adam fast asleep called Francine, "You ready to do this?"

"I dunno, but we gotta find out what this is. I'm going to hold my long phone cord in my hand as far as it'll reach down my basement stairs. I gotta be honest. I'm shaking all over."

As Marion landed on the bottom stair step she reached and unlatched the door between their basements. Silence was the only sound. Marion did not know how to talk to spirits or remove entities, so she endured Mr. Perkins and whoever else mutually inhabited the house as she tried to ignore their antics.

On Saturdays, Francine visited her boyfriend Tommy, missing the weekday afternoon tea time she and Marion shared. So, lonely for adult conversation, Marion speed walked Adam in his carriage the three miles to the store arriving as Frankie was finishing his day.

Frankie, never pleased to see her at the store, ignored her most of the time. This day he told her to get some money out of his wallet for a soft drink.

She saw a note from one of his female employees offering to do anything, at any time, he wanted. Marion freaked out, but contained it until they got home.

Sweetly she said, as she handed him his dish of butter pecan ice cream, "Frankie,"

Impatiently he responded with eyes glued to the boob tube, "Yeah, what?

Calmly asking, "Remember when you told me I could get some money for a drink out of your wallet?"

As if bothered, he responded without diverting his eyes from the screen, "Of course I do. Why?"

Hesitating, she gingerly said, "Well, there was this note in there from Freda."

Irritated at her, he turned to face her and said, "So what?"

"It said, 'I'll do anything for you,' Just what does she mean?" holding her breath for the answer.

Admonishing her, he said, "In the first place you got no right reading anything in my wallet. In the second place, it's none of your business. In the third place if you must know, she meant she could work for me any time because she needs all the hours she can get. Satisfied now? Let me eat my ice cream in peace before it melts."

Marion knew he was lying, but she let it go. "Okay, Frankie."

Criticizing her the same as always, he said, "You know you worry too much."

One stretch Frankie worked twenty-three days without a day off. Adam was asleep when daddy left and when he came home at night. The day he finally had off, Adam, now thirteen months old, came to find Daddy in bed with Mommy. He shrieked, frightened because he did not recognize him and wanted him out of mommy's bed.

Frankie declared, "God, my own son doesn't even know who I am. It's time to look for a different job so I can be home nights with him."

Jumping at the opportunity to encourage him she said, "Great, Frankie. You'll be fantastic at whatever job you choose."

Frankie surprised Marion when he told her he wanted to go to church. Sunday was his only day off. She did not like his selection. He took them to the Missouri Synod Lutheran Church, the church he had joined while dating Michelle. It was uncomfortable for Marion to attend even with Michelle absent, because Michelle's family, the Turners, still attended.

I see how the Turners treat Frankie. He's eating it up. He acts so comfy in their home. I never see any pictures of Michelle. I wonder why? Boy, they sure treat Adam good too, but I'm kinda a fifth wheel. Michelle's mother, Olivia, a World War II nurse, was very righteous. Cleanliness, rigid religious rules, and staunch German values shaped her life and all those who wished to be a part of it.

"Marion, thanks for helping me wash the dishes. Here put this capful of bleach in the water to kill any germs you brought with you," said Mrs. T. carefully handing the cap to Marion. "Sure thing Mrs. T.," as she dutifully poured it in the soapy water.

Mrs. T. supervised her work sitting two feet from her at the dining room table sipping on a cup of steaming black coffee. She assumed Marion would comply when she inquired, "When are you going to take classes to join the church?"

Hedging on an answer, she said, "I don't know yet with Frankie's work and all."

Frankie piped in, "Aw, Marion I'll get you there to classes somehow."

So, why is he so gung ho to have me be part of this church? He's never been that way before. I'll bet it's to get close to Michelle's family and find out where she is and contact her.

She snapped back to attention when Mrs. Turner said, "By the time my grandchildren are old enough for confirmation classes, maybe you'll live close enough so the kids can ride together," said Mrs. T imagining it, all planned out.

Reminiscing, Mrs. T went on, "I remember when Oma lived with us and all the girls would gather in her room to hear Bible stories. Do any of Adam's grandparents do that?"

Covering for them, Marion answered, "I'm sure they would if we lived closer to them."

With Mrs. T's church influence, Marion got a part-time job to help financially, working two days a week at the Mother's Morning Out program at the church. Neighbor Francine watched Adam because he was not old enough to attend. Work broke up the monotony and gave her a little spending money.

As they returned from their visit with Mrs. T, Marion found Frankie in a good mood, so she jumped at the chance, "Ya know, doctors have told me, if

I ever want to have more children, I better do it sooner than later, cause the older I get, the less likely it'll be t' happen. It 'd be nice for Adam to have a playmate. Whatcha think about it?"

"I dunno know," Frankie said chewing the left side of his cheek. "I think Adam was a fluke and I'm probably sterile for sure."

She boldly reported with head held high, "I was talking to Dr. Smith at church today, you know the gynecologist."

"Ya, so….?"

"Well, I told him about my problem with ovulating…"

Verbally exploding on her, his face purple, he said, "ARE YOU CRAZY! Airing our personal affairs in front of the church?"

"No, no, no," she said shaking her hand back and forth. "I didn't. Honest. We were talking by ourselves in the corner of the fellowship hall. Anyway, he said he could probably help me and would take me on as his patient."

Frankie pursed his lips and said, "What's this going to cost me?"

She smiled. "He said he would take what insurance pays and charge me no more! Isn't that exciting? I'm going to do it."

"I don't want to hear anything about needing more money for this. You understand?"

She did not allow his restriction to damper her mood. "It'll be fine, Frankie. You'll see."

When Marion went to see Dr. Smith about pursuing fertility drugs to help her get pregnant, he examined her and found she was already pregnant. Counting back, conception occurred on Frankie's one day off!

When she told Frankie that night that she knew exactly when she got pregnant he just shrugged his shoulders and continued glued to the football game on the television. She sighed and went back to the kitchen to wash the dishes.

Oh no, I'm having trouble swallowing. My vision goes completely black but thankfully comes back and these headaches are bad. I'm scared. Is this that toxemia again? I don't dare say anything to Frankie 'cause he will just complain about no extra money to see the ob. doc. God, please make it go away and for this baby to be okay.

When she went for her next prenatal visit, Dr. Smith forbid her to drive.

"Marion, it is unusual to have toxemia with the second pregnancy, but we'll keep an eye on it. If it gets worse, let me know."

Anxious, hoping it would stop on its own, she said, "Okay, sure."

As the alarm clock buzzed, she threw back the warm covers, planted her swollen feet into her fuzzy pink slippers, walked to the dresser, and silenced the alarm while fighting nausea, dizziness, and visual blackouts. She inched her way along the wall, her hand steadying her wobbly frame. In the kitchen, she brewed Frankie's Maxwell House coffee, poured it into his favorite brown porcelain mug, and gagged at the smell. She balanced the cup on a cookie sheet along with his bowl of Shredded Wheat with whole milk as she brought it to him in bed quickly exiting so he would not berate her for gagging over his food.

After Frankie left for work, she would get Adam up, feed him some Cheerios and a banana and take him over to Francine's apartment. All this was done before 9:00 a.m.

At 9:05 a.m. she began the ten-minute walk to the bus stop. The nursery school was three miles to the east of the apartment, too far to walk there fast enough. Needing to save money, she would often walk the hour to home. As she ambled along, she talked silently to herself.

I am so tired. All I crave is spaghetti, but I know it's not good for me to eat so much of it. I wish my family or someone lived close to help me. How am I going to handle Adam and a new baby?

Marion clung to most of her Baptist beliefs. Deeply indoctrinated, she thought her Independent Baptist Church had God's direct blessing and that any other church was second best or less. Frankie wanted her to become a member and raise their children in the Missouri Synod Lutheran church they were attending. Not being a member meant she could not take communion, a very important sacrament to her. The other dilemma was the fermented grapes. The idea of drinking alcohol for communion felt sacrilegious to her Baptist beliefs. Lutheran traditions varied in many aspects from her coveted Baptist ones. If she embraced the Lutheran path, it meant she would allow herself to be labeled a heretic by her Baptist friends. Since she no longer kept in contact with them, each going in separate directions, their opinion mattered less to her now.

The Lutheran priest showed up unannounced one day at her door. She invited him in. He quoted the Catechism and tried to get her to commit to taking classes.

She objected to the part where the priest had the "Keys to the Kingdom," the power to absolve, or not, someone's sins. Only God could forgive sins, not man, she believed.

Father Hoefstede was aggravating, wanting her to affirm his statements, "If you take the classes to be confirmed, you could join the church as a good wife should. You do want to be a good wife, don't you?"

When Frankie came home she told him about the visit after he inhaled his plate of Ragu and pasta.

Expecting some sympathy, she told him, "Frankie, Father Hoefstede came by today telling me I need to take Catechism classes so I can join the church."

Not really paying attention, typical, his nose in a book, he said, as he absentmindedly chewed on the fingernail of his left index finger, "So what'd you tell him?"

Standing two feet from him in front of the sofa, she calmly spoke honestly, "I said I'll think about it." She had no intention of joining the Lutheran church, but she was afraid to say it openly.

Frankie arose off the chair cushion with his nostrils flaring and red face glaring at her as he punched her abdomen with his closed right fist. He then declared, "You will obey me. You will take those classes and become a Lutheran. Do you understand me?"

Reeling in disbelief, fearful and in pain, she tried to fathom what had just happened while struggling to breathe and answer. She finally said, "I'll pray about it."

Satisfied for the present, he sat back down in the chair and resumed reading his Isaac Asimov book, as if nothing happened.

Dazed, she retreated to the kitchen and grabbed onto the edge of the sink. *God, why did Frankie punch me? Why is he so angry? He knows I'm pregnant. Why would he want to harm our unborn child? Please, let the baby be okay.*

Luckily, the baby was all right. She did not tell anyone about it, especially not Dr. Smith, her obstetrician from the church.

Session Sixteen

Settling into her familiar therapy chair, Marion sat quietly while Dr. Weinstein picked up his notepad and positioned himself in the chair across from her.

Marion smiled waiting for his weekly question.

"Where do we venture today, Marion?"

"I always thought family was the sacred jewel. If you had family, you would be completely satisfied. Boy was I wrong."

"Tell me about it, Marion," said Dr. Weinstein, with pen in midair ready to jot down some notes.

"Before we launch into today's story, Dr. Weinstein, tell me, why do people think that geographical cures work?" Marion asked.

"That's an excellent question, Marion. What is more important, is why did you believe they worked?"

Sighing Marion flashbacked to her feelings about moving to Frankie's hometown.

"Maybe if I share with you how a geographical cure failed, I might better understand why I thought it could and would work."

"Okay, Marion. Remember though, even if you think it was a failure, it was part of your journey to get here so it can't be all bad."

"Good point, Dr. Weinstein. I will remember that as I now tell you the story of moving to be near Frankie's parents and brother."

Family is Not Everything

FRANKIE WAS TRANSFERRED again, after eleven months, no more worries about the Lutheran Church. This time they moved to his hometown, Cortland, New York. Relieved, Marion believed having family around would strengthen their marriage. In March, the family of three and three quarters moved into a modern two-family house with no ghosts, a mile north of Frankie's parents, Homer and Barbara's home, and a mile south from Frankie's brother Ronnie and wife Betty's home.

Frankie announced if they had a baby girl she would be named after Marion's mother. Marion had no say in the matter. Baby Sarah entered the world through natural childbirth with minor jaundice in July. A special device called a bili light attached to an incubator healed the condition quickly. It converted the elevated bilirubin so it could be excreted through bowel movements and urine. Nurses covered her delicate eyelids with special shields preventing the light from damaging the retinas. Because the jaundice caused by a substance in the mother's breast milk lead to the high bilirubin levels, Sarah was not allowed to have breast milk for the first ten days of her life. As Marion pumped, she agonized whether like with Adam would she be able to continue to nurse this child once cleared to do so. Sarah latched on well and there was plenty of flow. Life fell into a livable routine. With a newborn and twenty-two-month-old Adam, life was anything but dull.

Gathering up baby Sarah and the diaper bag Marion called for Adam to come from his cousin's bedroom. "Time to go home Adam. Betty, it is so nice to spend time with you with the kiddos. Thanks for lunch. I gotta pick up Frankie in a couple of hours so I better go start supper," Marion said hugging her sister-in-law.

"Hey, Marion it's good to have family. I never thought we'd be related when I saw you at the bus stop that day, but I'm glad we are. Bye. See you Saturday at Homer and Betty's for supper."

Saturday evening When Frankie walked in the door from work he asked Marion, "What time we 'posed be at my parents' tonight?"

Marion answered, "Your mom called. Said to be there at 6:30. We can get in a couple of hands of Pinochle before the kids' bedtime."

Marion sat down at her mother-in-law's table to peel the carrots for the coleslaw. As she did, she watched in awe as Barbara painstakingly turned the knob of the handheld can opener with her gnarled arthritic fingers and then poured the applesauce into a serving dish. She never complained. The aroma of cube steak smothered in brown gravy and onions baking in the oven made Marion's mouth water. Betty chased after the kids in the living room while the men sat glued to the television commenting on the Syracuse football game. Periodically one of the males told the kids to hush. After the delicious meal, Ronnie stacked the dishes from the silver chrome kitchen table into the sink. Homer sat at one end of the table and Barbara at the other end. Marion and Frankie sat beside one another and across from them sat Betty and Ronnie next to the coffee pot. As soon as the players picked up their cards Homer spun his wedding ring around to signal his suit selection to his partner.

"Poppy (Homer)," said Betty laughing, "We all know you're going in diamonds when you do that. We aren't that dumb."

Homer threw down the cards and stormed out when he lost the hand. Marion saw where Frankie's childish temper originated and she hoped her children would not follow suit.

Frankie usually just ignored his father's immature behavior. Men in the 1970s were the head of the household. Men were expected to respect their fathers. Women rarely challenged males. Women were accused of attending college just to earn an MRS. degree. It was okay for women to obtain an art (poetry, dance, ballet, drawing and painting, music), elementary education, social work, or nursing degree. There was hostility was toward women in business, medicine, law, psychology, philosophy, religion, math, and science. Those occupations were thought to be only for men. If a woman pursued those degrees she might be called a bitch or accused of trying to emasculate men.

Thus, Frankie had the ultimate decision again about where the family would to go to church. Thankfully, there was not a strict Missouri Synod Lutheran church like in Albany. Frankie took them first to Evangelical Lutheran Church where he used to attend as a college student, but since his favorite priest left, it was not the same. They did not go back.

Feeling generous he told her, "Okay, I'll go to a Baptist church with you."

Excited that God must be working more on him, she said in rapid response, "Okay, great." Of course, the church was having a revival with much hell, fire, and brimstone preaching. Apparently, Marion's time away from the guilt-trip type message made her less open to fear-based preaching.

"Boy, am I glad to be out of that service. That certainly wasn't what I expected, Frankie. I'm sorry. I don't want to go back there. It's too much of a downer," Marion said shaking her head.

"That guy sure was wound up. I didn't think he was going to ever quit until some wretched sinner confessed," Frankie said laughing.

Marion, placed her hand on Frankie's as they drove out of the parking lot, feeling content to finally agree over something.

Frankie suggested, after much talk back and forth, "I know. Let's visit the church where I grew up. I haven't been there since I was fourteen when my parents stopped going because of the terrible way they treated the new pastor. I wonder if anyone I know is still there."

Cortland Christian Church was a good blend of both of their religious backgrounds. The worship service was simple, no kneeling for prayer on hard wooden benches, no Apostle's Creed, no hell, fire, and brimstone preaching. Pastor Henry was a great sermon writer, but not charismatic in his delivery. The choir performed professionally practiced pieces from the great composers, like Beethoven's *Ode to Joy* opening a whole new world to Marion's limited musical experience.

Marion turned to her son beside her on the pew and said, "Adam, you need to be quiet and sit still. Daddy's going to take up the offering. He'll be right back and then you can go to children's church."

Squalling, Adam wanted no part of behaving. He jumped out of the pew as Marion tried to grab him without dropping three-month-old Sarah. Adam ran to assist daddy passing the offering plate. Luckily, because the congregants thought Adam was cute, Frankie did not chastise Marion after the service that day. Within a month, Frankie, still listed on the roster as active, had been elected a deacon and began serving in many capacities in the one hundred-member church.

Frankie was assigned to the biggest store in the region right on Main Street across from the Cortland Bar and Grill where he ate lunch ritually every day at 2p.m. The employees respected him and he appeared happy in the job. Unknown to Marion, he was stealing cartons of cigarettes from the store, believing he deserved them and somehow thought his management skills covered for the loss. Four months into little Sarah's life, the executives walked in and fired him. The reset crew he once led, walked in as he walked out.

No job, no way to pay the rent, and nowhere to go, he immediately fell into deep depression. He sat in the living room upholstered chair and chain smoked his Marlboros while staring off into space. Marion tried to hide her anxiety fearful of their future.

"I can't believe they fired you, after all you did, reorganizing the store, giving up your vacation, and even working seven days a week," Marion said handing Frankie the morning newspaper.

Sullen, Frankie did not respond. She even wrote a letter of protest to the home office of Mitchums. Their written response said, "We don't discuss the details of someone's termination with family members."

One day Poppy stopped by the house about a week after Frankie was fired. "Frankie, why don't you come work with me? You'd be the second generation of Finch small appliance repair business. You know I'll be retiring when your mom does and you can take it over. What'd ya say?"

Frankie agreed to work for his dad until he could find something more suitable to his college education.

"Come on Frankie, let's go get some doughnuts and coffee," said Homer just as Frankie slipped his work apron over his head and tied it behind him.

"Dad, I just got here." Frankie said with a puzzled look on his face. "Besides, doughnuts aren't good for your diabetes."

"No problem," Homer said his hands shaking due to low blood sugar. "I'll just take more insulin. But since you're so high and mighty, stay here." He slammed the door, spinning his truck wheels as he sped out of the parking lot.

While gone, Frankie cleaned up the work area and drew a couple of designs. He would sell the unique contraptions fashioned out of leftover appliance parts. He also figured out how to create a booster seat for little Sarah out of some excess vinyl from a discarded recliner and a toy box for Adam from some leftover lumber and hinges from an old door. When Homer returned Frankie proudly showed him his plans.

Homer pushed it aside with a sweeping hand gesture as he called to his canine. "Come here, Snoopy. Come see Daddy."

Frankie stomped to the other side of the shop and began noisily hammering tacks into the booster seat cover. An hour later Homer approached him. "You done pouting now, Son? Ya ready for me to teach you a thing or two?"

Frankie scrunched up his face with upholstery tacks between his teeth and turned his back to his dad. Homer set a push mower with a broken blade on the work bench while he let his Alpine cigarette smolder in the ashtray taking puffs in between sharpening the old blades to match the replaced one. In rapid-fire precision, Homer completed his task while Frankie fumed in the corner.

Frankie resented that his dad loved the dog more than his kids or grandkids. It sickened Frankie to watch Homer allow Snoopy, the terrier dog, lick his snot from his nose.

Frankie, industrious, wanted to be busy like when he ran the grocery stores twelve hours a day, greeting customers, running cash registers, and ordering merchandise. Frankie needed to work productively to ease his worry about providing for his family. He had all kinds of ideas of how to grow the family business. Homer wanted no part of any growth. He wanted his arthritic body to coast into retirement. Barbara, the main breadwinner, worked on the assembly line at the Wickmire Brothers window screen company. All Homer needed was enough money for his food, cigarettes, gasoline, and his girlie magazines he kept in the filthy shop washroom. Brooding Frankie began to withdraw. He sat after work staring at a television screen with no awareness of what program he was viewing.

"Hon, you okay? I put the kids to bed, if you want to talk," Marion said sitting down on the couch.

He opened up, his face staring straight ahead. "I'm angry at Mitchum's management for firing me. I'm angry at my dad for the way he treats his dog, better than me. I'm afraid I won't be able to provide for my family and I don't know what to do."

Getting up she placed her hand on his shoulder and sat down on his lap in the recliner and took his hand in hers. "You know Frankie, when I was in a bad place, my mom took me to talk to someone. I fought it the whole way, but the therapist was kind and helpful. Maybe you could do that, talk to someone."

Angrily he retorted, "And just where is the money going to come from to cover that expense?"

"I don't know, but I bet there are some places that charge you based on your income. Do you want me to look for you?"

"I don't know right now. Let me think about it." "Okay, sure," she said kissing him on the top of his head as she got up.

The next week Frankie sat at the table going through the mail while Marion was stirring rice into boiling water. He looked briefly up at her and said, "Just so you'll know, I have an appointment with a counselor this afternoon."

"Oh, I'm so glad," she said stirring a pot of beans. "Who are you seeing? Where do you have to go? What's it going to cost?" she breathlessly asked with the spoon in midair.

Sternly he answered, "This is my business. I don't need you butting your nose into it. If there's something I need to tell ya, I will. Otherwise, don't ask. Don't follow me there or tell anyone about it."

"Sure, okay, if that's what you want," she said and continued to stir the pot.

Whew, I'm so glad he's going. I was afraid he'd end up in a mental institution like my dad.

So, Frankie entered therapy to decide what his path should be. Marion tried to be empathetic, but she was anxious and the atmosphere was tense. She began to understand what her mom went through when her dad was depressed.

Frankie and Homer argued daily. If Frankie had another option for work, he would have taken it. He was too proud to apply for unemployment. In the recession of 1973, gasoline was rationed, and Watergate was in full swing. People were not buying many luxuries like new appliances so fortunately for the shop, many customers wanted to repair their existing ones.

On one such day Marion was in the in-law's apartment over the shop preparing lunch. Adam was downstairs with his dad and Poppy. He came upstairs to use the bathroom leaving the door open. Marion heard the bounce on each step thinking it was Adam descending on his behind. It was baby Sarah! She fell down the sixteen wooden steps and landed head first on the concrete below.

Marion, in the other room, didn't realize what had happened until she heard Poppy's loud gasp. At first frozen, she then ran to the stairs, petrified Sarah was dead and somehow, she was to blame. Initially, no sound came from Sarah's mouth and then she wailed. Marion raced down the stairs and gingerly scooped her up, driving like a maniac to the hospital.

Once at the Emergency Room, she cautiously gave the details. Her sense of guilt must have shown. A month earlier a parent told a similar story taking the child home after treatment. Unfortunately, the child died because of the child abuse. Now the staff briskly removed frightened, squalling Sarah from anxious Marion's arms, strapping her to a board in preparation for full body X-rays.

About this time, Poppy showed up.

Looking around, Poppy asked, "Marion, where's Little Sarah?"

Muffling tears, pointing, she said, "They took her back there and won't let me near her. I think they believe I hurt her."

"Just a minute. I'll be right back," said Poppy in a commanding voice.

He found the people in charge and vouched for her credibility. As soon as the hospital was satisfied that Sarah had not been abused by Marion, the nurse directed her to hold Sarah to calm her down. She could not get to her fast enough. Luckily, she was unharmed. Marion, hyper alert to every move her children made after that scare, did not relax for a long time. A gate at the top of the stairs prevented further tumbles.

A week later Homer sat in his greasy, upholstered, dark brown leather chair in the shop. His dog Snoopy sat in his lap.

"Does Snoopy want to have a bath? You know Poppy loves you," he said stroking his dog's neck.

"Hey Frankie, did you finish repairing those toasters yet? They'll be here at three to pick them up."

Angrily Frankie responded, "No Dad, I haven't.

Why don't you get up and help me finish 'em?" he said glaring at Snoopy.

"Son, if you're going take over this business, you need to manage your time better. You gotta meet deadlines. I won't always be around to work with you, ya know. I'll watch you do it and see how ya do."

Frankie continued to reassemble the last toaster and said, "Dad, I managed a grocery store for years and did just fine."

"Oh really? Then how come you got fired?" Homer caustically asked.

Just then Snoopy jumped off Poppy's lap, perceiving Frankie was a threat to his owner started barking at him.

Frankie kicked Snoopy and he yelped as he limped away.

Poppy yelled, "You Son of a Bitch, get out of my shop. You're worthless. No wonder you got fired."

As Frankie gathered his tools, he yelled back,

"Well, you're a horrible example of a father. You love Snoopy more than any of your family."

He slammed the door on his way out and drove home enraged.

Marion calmed him after he told her the story. She reassured him. "You didn't want to work for him anyway. Go down to the unemployment office and sign up. See what jobs they have. We'll be okay," she said patting his arm, already planning what to do in her head.

He did, and like her mom years before, not having enough money to feed her family weighed heavily on Marion. She gathered her dad's family heirlooms: a set of silver soup spoons, silver salt and pepper shakers, and a green porcelain jar with tiny red roses on it called a hair receiver. Women kept hair gleaned from their brush in it to use to fluff up their buns. With a heavy heart, she walked into the antique shop on the avenue and asked, "What'll you give me for these items?" she said with a wistful look Sighing, the shopkeeper said, "You know, a lot of people are in your same predicament. Times are bad. Selling family keepsake items like yours is hard to do. All I can offer you is $25."

"I'll take it," she said, but under her breath she uttered an oath while clenching her fist, "I will buy these back when times get better. I hope my dad does not find out. He only visits about once a year and I won't mention it in his weekly phone call. This'll buy at least one week's groceries for the family."

Amid their financial nightmare, Marion's stepbrother, Eric (Mary's son), called.

"Hey, Marion, it's Eric, your stepbrother. How ya doing?"

She and he had never met, but she heard about him from her dad and Mary. They told her that Eric and his wife, Agnes, had started some undisclosed business and had done so well that they purchased a brand-new house in New Jersey.

Letting out an audible sigh, with baby Sarah squalling in the background, she said to him honestly, "Eric, it's hard. Frankie's been out of work for months and his own father just fired him from the family appliance repair shop. I don't know what we're going to do. Please don't tell my dad, but I just had to sell some of his family antiques to afford groceries."

"Listen, Marion, I think I have a way to help," he said sounding reassuring.

Disbelieving, she sat down at the kitchen table and fiddled with the white paper napkins lying in the holder in the center of the table as Frankie, hearing only one end of the conversation, was curious. He was irritated that she shared their personal problems, even if it was with her stepbrother. Uncharacteristically, Frankie picked up little Sarah and quieted her.

"So, Eric what do you have in mind?"

"My mom and your dad probably told you we started a business selling products to individuals and teaching them to do the same. I'm ready to expand in your area, and I wonder if you'd be interested in going into business with me?"

Marion was cautious, but intrigued. "Here, let me let you talk to Frankie. He's the business person in the family, not me."

"Okay, put him on."

Frankie spoke with Eric for about ten minutes, all of which Marion could not understand only hearing Frankie's "ah's, oh's, and I sees," as she twirled bouncing Sarah on her hip listening.

In about a week Eric visited and drew the Amway business plan circles explaining how the multi-level marketing plan worked. Frankie and Marion decided to try Amway to hopefully get rich.

A week later, Eric called Marion, saying, "Hey Marion, it's Eric. I never got your check for the order I sent. When did you mail it?"

"Hi, Eric. That's strange. I mailed it from the post office last Tuesday. The products arrived today. What do I do about it?" she asked confused.

Marion, inexperienced with business matters, told him she would get the money from her customer orders and send him a money order to cover the cost.

"That'll be fine, but I can't send any more orders until I get the money for this order."

"Oh, dear. I guess I better get busy and get a bunch of new customers then."

Unknown at that time to Marion and Frankie, Eric did get the money, cashed the checks, and got the money order too. By the time they figured it out, they lost about $1200, an extreme amount on a tight budget. They reported his behavior to the Amway Corporation, but Eric and his wife had disappeared to parts unknown. Marion asked her stepmother Mary about his whereabouts, but she did not know either. They were never reimbursed.

Because Marion believed in the business model, she continued trying to build the business.

To build a successful Amway business each distributor was encouraged to read material to boost their morale and think in positive ways. Marion embraced the concept of a positive mental attitude (PMA). The reading material and cassette tapes lifted Frankie and Marion's morale, despite the unethical practices of Eric. This way of thinking convinced them to set lofty goals as the means to success. To find the money to attend the trainings, Marion would aim to sell enough products to afford the fees. She skimped on groceries and her own eating to pay for the babysitter.

Marion stood beside Frankie as he watched the six o'clock news. During the commercial she said, "Frankie, in *Acres of Diamonds,* I read that everything we need is right where we are in our own backyard. It says to set goals, put them in motion, and go for it. When you do, the path will open. Based on that - we need to go ahead and make the hotel reservation for the Paramus, NJ seminar."

Frankie ignored her. Undeterred, she picked up the phone. "Hello, Janet? It's Marion. Can I come over to show you a product to make your wash the brightest in the whole neighborhood?"

"Sure, wait til tomorrow at two when the kiddos are down for their nap. What is this miracle product?" she curiously inquired.

"I'll show ya, tomorrow. See ya."

After a demonstration of the power of SA8 detergent she asked, "Janet, now that you've seen how it can whiten all your clothes, who do you know that would like to have the same sparkling wash? Oh, did I tell ya, that we go to seminars to learn how to build this business? I have a piece of paper for you to write down some referrals for me. Here's the pen."

The next evening Marion waved cash in front of Frankie as he again watched the news. "Look I got all but $25 of what we need to go this weekend."

Looking up he said, "You sure are gung ho about this. There's a huge snowstorm coming this weekend. What if we get snowed in down there and can't get back? With all this gas rationing it's good that we got an odd last digit on one vehicle license plate and an even on the other so we can buy gas on any day. What worries me is, we go down on Saturday, but don't come back til Sunday. How are we going to get enough gas to get home on?"

Confidently Marion said, "It'll be okay. You'll see," she said stuffing the money into her bra.

As it turned out they did get the snowstorm, making Rt. 81 almost impassable, significantly slowing the journey home. As the gas gauge needle entered the red zone Frankie began to sweat, but Marion, the ever-seasoned manipulator, had a plan.

"Frankie, pull into that station with the open sign blinking and I'll talk to them."

"You're going to get us killed," he said perspiration dripping off his forehead in the twenty-degree weather.

"No, I'm not. I'm going to pull the mother card.

Watch," she said getting out of the car wetting her finger to make fake tears appear on her cheeks.

All gas stations had shotgun attendants to ensure no one without the right last digit for the day could get gas and even if the right day, no more than ten gallons of gasoline.

Marion walked up to the armed guard her arms held tightly across the chest of her blue winter fleece lined jacket. As she drew closer to the armed guard, Marion turned on the tears, wringing her hands. The attendant leaned back against the gas station wall with a rifle across his lap. Marion said, "Sir, we were on our way home. Our babysitter called and said the baby has a high fever. We need to get back to Cortland NOW. Can you please give us five gallons to get home on? We'll pay extra."

The guard, eyed her up and down to make certain she was not hiding a shotgun under her coat. Convinced she was legit he put his hand on Marion's shoulder with tears glistening in his own eyes. He said, "Lady, don't worry, I got kids of my own at home. Our pumps are full of gas. You can get all you need. Go ahead and call your sitter and tell her you are on your way."

Marion, looked over her shoulder at Frankie standing outside the car blowing on his hands to keep them warm. As the attendant started to escort Marion inside to the payphone, Frankie frightened that their scheme might dissolve, took over. The babysitter knew how this couple could be a little bit weird, so calling at 3:00 a.m. did not surprise her.

With the shotgun resting on his shoulder, the man named "Big John" handed the pay phone receiver to Frankie. Dialing the number, Frankie silently prayed Tracey would not pick up. Before completing the connection, the operator said, "Please drop seventy-five cents into the coin slot to reach your party."

Quickly fishing into his pants pocket, he lifted out the three quarters and plopped them into the slot. As quickly as he did, he heard the phone ring. On the third ring a sleepy Tracy answered, "Hello, this is the Finches."

"Tracy, this is Frankie. Is Sarah's fever any better?

We're getting gas and will be there as quick as we can."

Tracy playing along said, "Ah, no, but she's okay right now. I'll see you when you get here."

Smiling, Frankie thanked the shotgun attendant and breathed a sigh of relief when they returned to the warmth of the car heater.

"Marion, don't pull that fast one again," he said chucking.

Marion just giggled. "I told you the mother card would work.

Once home they paid Tracey extra and explained how close they came to not getting home at all.

Attending the hyped-up seminars related to the Amway business spurred Marion on to believe she could accomplish anything she set her mind to do. Through this attitude of prosperity, she believed they would be successful, but it was not happening in that moment. She made a list of goals she wanted to accomplish over the next ten years. As instructed, she visualized what her life would be like when the dreams became a reality. Using the principles from the book, *The Magic of Thinking Big*, they convinced the bank to grant them a mortgage on a two-family modest home, even though unemployed. Frankie's Aunt Evelyn loaned them the money for the down payment.

Marion leaned over Frankie sitting in his recliner and handed him a bowl of butter pecan ice cream. She whispered in his ear, "I pictured us living in our new house by the beginning of the new year. That's just two weeks away. How 'bout we ask our realtor if we can close on December 31st?"

He raised up. "Whiffles, don't get your panties in a wad. We're getting the house and I know if we close on the 31st we can claim the house on our taxes for the year. Lord knows we have enough deductions!" he said as he scraped the bottom of his ice cream bowl. I'll tell ya what."

"What Hubbles? I can't stand guessing," she said hands outstretched standing next to him.

"I'll ask, but don't get all weepy, if they say no."

"Remember, 'anything a mind can conceive and believe in, a mind can achieve.' We're gonna get this on the 31st, you watch," Marion said grinning.

Surprisingly, her mental imaging worked, or maybe it was just coincidental. Moving in after closing on New Year's Eve, they were delighted to be first
time homeowners. They quickly advertised to acquire a tenant to rent upstairs
for $90 a month so they could afford the $192 mortgage payment.

Marion proudly arranged her first house, a yellow wood frame dwelling
with seven hundred square feet on each level and a room in the basement used
for the master bedroom. The wooden two paned glass blue front door welcomed guests. Just inside the entryway was the living room. She knew it was
tiny, but it was theirs. An olive green upholstered fold-out couch sat against
the wall adjacent to the front bedroom. She worked hard on the frugal budget
to decorate their abode in aesthetically pleasing décor. The matching chair
with oak armrests and spindle legs sat against the wall to the kitchen. It was
the chair Frankie often ruminated in, but she believed it would have a new life
now with a happier time. The front 8x10 bedroom was big enough for two
twin beds side by side.

The closet's maple colored solid wood door squeaked when opened. The
two-foot metal clothes bar could support maybe ten outfits, but that was more
than they could afford anyway. Back through the living room to the left was
the entry to the kitchen. The kitchen sink was a farm house design with a wide
basin and a faucet protruding twelve inches above the base of the sink. To give
new life to her antiquated sparse storage cupboards, she painted them white.
The counter tops were gray linoleum, same as the floor. The floor covering
was better than the antique linoleum in Albany so she could live with it until
they could afford better furnishings. The back bedroom off to the right of
the kitchen was next to the only bathroom. The bedroom with sky blue walls
had room enough for the crib and a dresser. The bathroom black and white
square alternating tiles installed in the 1930's contained asbestos, but that was
before anyone knew it was a health hazard. The white porcelain sink with rubber stopper had a rust ring under the faucet by the overflow holes made by a
continuous drip from worn out washers. The toilet needed repair and ran continuously when flushed. The white tub, eighteen inches high was not very deep
nor wide. It sufficed to bathe the children and the shower, although the stream
was weak, got the job done for the adults. To get to the master bedroom,

Marion and Frankie had to descend seventeen wooden stairs through a door in the kitchen, turn left past the washer and dryer into the 10x10 cement block room. Livable in the summer, but cold in the winter, they cuddled to keep warm. Adam and Little Sarah adapted well to their new surroundings, Adam ran from room to room.

Marion, fearful that she would not hear the children upstairs, slept with one ear open, before room monitors were invented. She wanted to keep the basement door ajar, but Frankie insisted it be kept closed so if Adam woke up from his junior bed, he would not fall down the stairs. The neighborhood's cookie cutter houses were built for workers of the Wickmire Brothers window screen company in the 1920s. Each house had been individualized by the owners, but bore the same layout. Marion painted the living room and front bedroom the fashionable orange sherbet color with brown and orange indoor/outdoor carpet to match the walls. The house at 214 Whippoorwill Street was old, but adequate. That winter Frankie and his brother Ronnie went deer hunting for the first time in five years. Luckily, they shot a buck large enough to share the spoils. Marion learned how to fix venison in a variety of palatable methods since they could not afford to purchase store bought meat.

Frankie bluffed his way into a sales job selling commercial lawnmowers, as he lost faith in Amway. Balancing the checkbook at the kitchen table Frankie said, "Marion, we've spent all this money on products, seminars, books, and cassette tapes. All I see is money going out and nothing coming in. The only people getting rich off this scheme is the Amway Corporation and our upline sponsors. I don't trust any of this anymore."

Handing him a cup of coffee Marion said, "Frankie, you may be right, but I think the idea behind Amway makes sense, but perhaps not the way the company does it. I want to attempt to develop the business awhile longer, but I agree, we can't invest any more money without something coming back."

"Suit yourself, *dear*, but I'm out," he said pushing back his chair headed to his recliner.

Marion, uncomfortable presenting the sales plan, just sold the Amway products. They barely met their financial obligations. Frankie's depression and irritability were temporarily abated. Even though he never sold a lawnmower, he learned something. If people believe in themselves, amazing things can be accomplished. Yet, a full-blown oil crisis squelched the notion for anyone who wanted to buy a lawnmower. Frankie knew his sales job was short-lived.

As Frankie stared at the blank black and white television screen, he chewed his fingernails. He did not want to even read his escape science fiction novels.

Frankie yelled upstairs to Marion in the kitchen from his basement recliner, "Marion, where're my silver dollars that were in my dresser? Did you cash them in to buy groceries?"

With Sarah safely plopped into her playpen, she came downstairs because she could not hear what he said.

"What did you say? Adam's firetruck siren drowned out your voice."

Angrily, he repeated, "I asked you if you cashed in my silver dollars."

"No, of course not. Why do you ask?" she said drying her hands on her apron.

"Because they are gone and someone took them."

After they narrowed it down, they figured it was Tracy, the babysitter. Upon confrontation she confessed and worked off the time equaling the value of the coins. Frankie's anxiety over the impending lay off, was contagious.

"Frankie, did you put air in the left rear tire, like I asked?"

"No, I forgot," he said without an apology.

"So, what am I to do if I get a flat when I have both kids with me? I can't afford the cost of a payphone to call someone to come fix it. I worry about it all the time."

"Quit your bellyaching. I'll take care of it," Frankie said motioning her away, exasperated.

To ease the tension and with no excess money for recreation, the family became more active in the church. It did not require cash, just a dish to pass at potlucks. Marion always found a way to sell enough Amway to buy the ingredients to fix a casserole. The Finches were happy to attend because unlike their dinner table, food would be plentiful.

One of their favorite outings was to fellowship at the home of their friend and pastor, Henry. Frankie sat in the basement office of Pastor Henry's while the women set the table for dinner.

"Pastor Henry, how'd you know you were called to the ministry?" he asked while intermittently chewing on his fingernails.

"Well, Son, when God calls you, it is like a nagging cough. It does not go away until you tend to it. Why do you ask?"

"Ah, no reason. I just wondered. We better head back upstairs. The smell of that fried chicken is calling my name."

Marion felt relaxed and hopeful about their future every time she watched the interaction between Frankie and Pastor Henry. Her heart warmed when Frankie even winked at her across the dinner table. She looked forward to the approaching summer and more picnics at their home.

The fifteenth of June Marion got call from her mom, Sarah.

"Hey, Marion."

"Hi, Mom. What's up? You never call," Marion said her brow furrowed.

"Well, I'm wondering when you're planning to have Rhonda come for the summer? She's got church camp next week and then she's free. I thought this was quicker than writing to ask you."

"Sure, mom. I could come up there with the kids over the fourth and get her and you can fly her back in August. Would that work?"

"That'd be great. Talk to Frankie and let me know. Bye."

Marion put a mattress in the back of the station wagon, a loaf of bread on the front seat, a jar of peanut butter and jelly beside her and threw a few clothes and diapers in a duffle bag. She began the adventure on Wednesday, July 3rd. Baby Sarah was a week past her first birthday. Adam was five weeks from turning three. Literally with five dollars in her pocket and a gasoline credit card in her wallet, she naively braved the task. Marion was a woman on a mission – to get to Wisconsin, pick up Rhonda, and to turn around the next day and drive back. She was keeping her promise to her baby sister, "I will come and get you whenever I can and bring you where I am." She attempted to do this each summer since Marion left home.

To prepare for the trip, Marion called Debbie whom she had not seen since Mackinac Island.

"Hey Debbie, this is Marion. How are ya?" "Oh, hi Marion. I had a cold, but now I'm fine.

Haven't seen you in ages."

"Yeah, about that. I'm driving to Wisconsin to get my sister. Would it be okay, if the kids and I slept on my mattress on your floor for one night?"

Debbie said, "You coming by yourself, Marion, with the kids?"

"Yes, I am. Is that a problem?" she asked holding her breath.

"Naw, come on. We'll catch up. Be safe."

The first day Marion drove to Debbie's house in Ohio stopping every 100 miles to use a pay phone to make a collect call asking for herself. When Frankie answered, he said, "She isn't home. Can I take a message?"

Marion then said, "No, thank you," and drove on. It was how Frankie knew she made it each 100 miles.

After spending the night at Debbie's catching up, the next morning at seven a.m. Marion departed heading to Lodge.

The return trip home was arduous. Prior to such luxuries as Google Maps, Marion had to drive and navigate as Rhonda, age sixteen did not know how to direct her sister through Interstate highways. It took them twenty hours, but they made it back to Cortland at midnight. Frankie insisted that Marion service him sexually. Too tired to resist or participate she mechanically performed her "wifely duty," much to his dislike.

Rhonda was a great help with the children, entertaining them so Marion could go grocery shopping or take a rare nap. Marion kept a watchful eye when Frankie interacted with Rhonda. He liked to tease and tickle his sixteen-year-old sister-in-law. Marion said nothing just worried.

The last Sunday of July, engaged in the group conversation around Pastor Henry's picnic table, Frankie opened his mouth to make some comment, but what came out stopped everyone cold. "Pastor Henry, how does one enter into the ministry?"

Pastor Henry's wife, detailing a recipe for Marion, stopped midsentence.

Marion, wide-eyed, asked her elbow sliding off the table, "What'd he say?"

Pastor Henry smiled and said in response to his wife's and Marion's gaping mouths, "I wondered when he was going to ask that question."

Shocked as much as anyone else, Frankie replied, "I honestly didn't plan on saying those words. They just came out."

"It's okay, Frankie," Pastor Henry said patting him on the shoulder. "When God calls you, He doesn't leave you alone until you answer. The first thing you do is to call up United Theological Seminary tomorrow. I'll get you the number. Tell 'em you want to enter and see what they say."

"But, I've a family to provide for. How'll I feed them and go to seminary?" he asked having misgivings for blurting out words he could not retrieve.

"All will get answered soon enough. If God wants you, the way will be provided," said Pastor Henry patting Frankie again on the shoulder.

Marion thought, *oh yeah, I remember now. He told me about the call to the ministry when we were dating. Maybe now God will make him into the man He wants him to be, if Frankie will let him. I can only pray."*

Session Seventeen

"Dr. Weinstein, why is it that life has so many unexpected twists and turns?" Marion inquired.

He replied, "I guess so we don't become complacent. What directional change are you referring to today, Marion?"

She answered, "Just when I had settled into acceptance of life not as I expected, living in my husband's hometown, I was thrown another curve ball."

"So, did last week's session help you understand why you thought geographical cures worked and prepare you to make sense of this curve ball?"

"Yes, I sort of understand the concept of a geographical cure. When a person is dissatisfied with who they are and not in touch with what they need, they seek new experiences expecting it to be different. It is not until they recognize that wherever you go, there you are, that things can ever change. The change must start internally, not externally," Marion said.

"Excellent observation. I can't want to hear what you learn from this curve ball experience," Dr. Weinstein said leaning forward, pen in hand.

Pack up your Troubles in Your Old Suitcase

RHONDA HAD FLOWN back to Wisconsin after that picnic, excited to tell her mom that Marion might move closer to Lodge because Frankie had been accepted into the seminary.

Without so much as a hello, Frankie entered the kitchen from the driveway side door and asked, "Marion, did you call about the U-Haul truck? We move in ten days."

Marion switched Lil' Sarah to her left hip as she stirred the hamburger frying in the pan with the wooden handled metal spatula and pushed the grease to the side. Irritated, she pointed to the packing boxes strewn everywhere and said, "I've been kinda busy and I chased after the two kids all day, but yes, I called to reserve the moving truck. Luckily, we don't have to pay til we pick it up, but where we gonna get the money for that?"

"You know, you worry too much," he said as he stomped down the stairs to plop in front of the television until supper was ready.

"God, I thought you called him to serve you, but he sure does not act like a minister to me! If you're going change him, please hurry it up. I'm exhausted handling all the details."

The sound of Adam's wooden block tower crashing jolted her back to reality. The youngster, just eight days shy of his third birthday, peeked around the corner from his bedroom, "Mommy, who you talking to?"

"Oh, nobody dear. I was just thinking out loud." She reached over and gave him a love pat on the behind and said, "Go wash up. Then carefully go downstairs and tell daddy it's time to eat."

"Okay, mommy." He stood at the bathroom sink on his red wooden folding step stool that Poppy constructed for him to reach the bar of Dial soap and turn on the cold water faucet. He left a trail of water dripping from his hands as he safely navigated the stairs after Marion opened the baby gate and he re-emerged piggy back on daddy.

They ate in silence.

Frankie eagerly gave his notice to the commercial lawn mower company. On his next to last day, he pulled into the Shell gas station off Rt. 81 at the first Wilkes Barre exit. His eyes darted back and forth until he spotted the pay phone next to the free air hose at the far end of the freshly paved parking lot. The asphalt smell made his eyes and throat burn in the seventy-five-degree heat. As he picked up the receiver the operator said, "Number please."

He responded 607-555-1234. "That will be 50 cents, please."

As he dropped the two tingling quarters into the slot he prayed she'd answer quickly so he could get away from the aroma. "I got this feeling again that you wanted me to call home. I don't know what it is you do, but it unnerves me. What'd ya want?"

Chuckling, she wiped her hands on her apron and said, "Guess what?"

"Marion, I don't have time for riddles. I got just enough change to pay for a five-minute call here so say what you gotta say and be done with it."

"All right already. You got a letter from the United Methodist District Superintendent (DS) in Ohio. Do you want me to open it?"

"This couldn't've waited til I got home in an hour?"

"I thought you'd be happy about it, that's all. Never mind. I'll save it til you get here."

"I hate it when you do this, bring something up and not finish it. For Christ's sake open the letter and read it to me."

She ripped the envelope hastily and blew air into it to make the letter easier to retrieve. It informed Frankie that he was appointed the student pastor to two small churches in middle Ohio, a hundred miles from the seminary. When he got home they read it together in fine detail and made a list of questions to call and ask the DS. The family's forks scraped noisily across their plates as they gathered up every steamed pea, fresh from their neighbor's garden. The children were absorbed in a game to see whose fingers could shovel in all their vegetables first. Marion, preoccupied, mentally checked off her list what was left to complete before the move. Frankie interrupted her thoughts.

"Earth to Marion, come in please."

"Huh, I'm sorry, I was deep in thought."

"So, I noticed. Question: I've never been to a Methodist church service; tell me what it's like."

She paused while she changed her train of thought, lips twisted sideways as her eyes looked to the right to access her memory. "Ah, well, they don't believe in being born again. It's mostly a social club, as best I remember. But if you want, we can go to one so you will know what it's like."

"But, there's no Sunday to go to one before we leave."

Lightly she reached across the table to touch his arm, as a smile spread across her face, "Ya know what? I heard about a special service on Thursday nights at the big church on Upton Road. Wanna go?"

"Sure, but what about the kids?" Frankie asked.

"The radio announcement said that a nursery was available."

Apprehensive, as if studying for a final, Frankie took copious notes during the service: Lord's Prayer (check), Apostles Creed (check), Gospel Reading (check),

Hymns (check), Pastoral Prayer (check). He leaned over to Marion and whispered, "I think I got this. It's a lot like the Lutheran service that I'm used to."

Marion smiled back as she breathed a sigh of relief and returned her attention to the sermon.

Greeting Pastor Joe at the back of the sanctuary Frankie requested, "Can I chat with you a minute?"

"Sure son, give me a second to shake the rest of these parishioners out the door and I'll meet you down on the front pew."

Marion gathered the children and waited in the car.

Frankie returned in ten minutes with a lilt in his step.

"He prayed with me and gave me his phone number. Said I could call him anytime. That was sure nice of him to do," Frankie said smiling.

"I suspect he remembers how scary seminary was for him," Marion remarked.

In a jovial mood, he engaged Adam and Sarah in the song, "Into the Air Junior Birdman" including the hand gestures while Marion grabbed the steering wheel and sang along.

By the second week in August, the house they bought only eight months earlier now had two renters. The last remaining expense was the money to pay for the U-Haul truck. They told no one the amount they needed.

Reluctant to say good byes, the Finch family savored their last worship service in their home church.

"Frankie and Marion, would you come down to the front of the church please? It isn't every day the church has a Timothy to send off. We want to pray over you and take up a love offering to help with your moving expenses."

After tearful hugs and well wishes, they made their way to the car. Curious to count the love offering, they emptied the contents of the envelope onto the front seat. "Frankie, look!" Marion said pointing at the pile. "It's $267.50, the exact cost of the moving truck. Did you tell them what we needed?"

"I didn't. Honest," he said shaking his head in disbelief.

Their combined tearful silence confirmed surely that God ordained their plan. Homer and Barbara wanted Frankie and his family to spend their last night in Cortland at their house, but Frankie still had some resentment toward his father choosing his dog over his him. Instead they stayed at Deacon Morse's house and in the morning, the men of the church began loading the moving truck. Marion tried in vain to keep one-year-old Sarah barely walking and three-year-old Adam out of the way as they excitedly wanted to unpack and play with everything. The day passed quickly. Too late to embark on their adventure, they spent another night with the Morse family. At six a.m., they drove the one mile to Homer and Barbara's house to say their tearful good-byes.

The five-hundred-thirty-two-mile trek began at six-thirty a.m. on Tuesday morning The brown 1972 Vega, purchased for Frankie during his lawnmower sales job was securely fastened to the tow bar behind the truck. Marion drove the green wood paneled 1969 Ford station wagon following Frankie. Marion's bladder controlled the stops. Just after the second potty break, she lost sight

Frankie who was leading the way. She realized it happened when she turned around to hand some graham crackers to Sarah. She just prayed.

God, please help me. I can't enter the New York Thruway without him 'cause I don't know the route, have a map, or money for tolls, and I've got no way to reach Frankie. Please have him wait for me before getting on the Thruway. Amen.

It was a welcome sight to see the truck waiting on the side of the road near the entrance to the Freeway. She breathed a prayer of thanks as the toll booth operator handed her the ticket. The radio reception got fuzzy along the northern border of upstate New York, so she absentmindedly made up a song for the journey. "Pack up your troubles in an old suitcase and move them all to Ohio."

Baby Sarah continued to ride in the car with Marion and Adam rode in the moving truck with Frankie. After two hours, Marion needed to urinate again and change Sarah's soggy diaper so she flashed her lights at Frankie and he pulled in the next service plaza.

As soon as they got out of the U-Haul truck, Adam ran up to Marion and spilled the beans: "Daddy moking, Mommy, daddy moking."

Marion gave Frankie a killer look, kicked the dirt under her feet and said loud enough for passersby to hear, "Frankie whatcha think you're doing? You're a minister now for God's sake. We can't afford for you to smoke. You quit six months ago. Or did you?"

Defensively, he said, "I need the cigarettes to keep me awake to drive across the country. Then I'll quit. I promise."

Sternly she shook her finger at him and said, "You better. The congregations are not going to approve of their pastor smoking. You need to trust God on this and quit."

Nervously, biting his lip, Frankie took the cigarettes out of his pocket and slung them in the glovebox.

"I have a good mind to throw them in the trash, but you'd probably just buy more," she said in a condescending manner.

With drooping shoulders Frankie gathered up Adam and whisked him off to the rest room. Sarah, only walking a few months, toddled after them while Marion scurried to chase after her.

The faithful Christian, Marion felt it was her duty to instruct him on how to behave as a proper minister should. Prior to him answering this "call" she always accepted his authority on everything. Now Frankie needed to listen to her to have harmony between them and to receive God's blessing. Marion did not bother to inquire how Frankie thought God wanted him to behave.

They arrived just outside Pleasantville, Ohio to fields of six-foot-high corn, their stalks leaned to catch the breeze in the dry August heat, their silk not yet brown to harvest. The landscape was so opposite the rolling hills of the Southern Tier of New York, Marion felt immediately homesick.

The endless flat miles of Miami County farmland were interrupted by a knoll where the United Methodist parsonage stood. The highest hill in the county was no taller than the rise of bread dough after an hour sitting on the stovetop over a bowl of warm water. But before getting the first glimpse of their new residence, they pulled up to the home of Bertha Polk, their liaison person. As Frankie took the keys out of the ignition he held his breath as if to stop the whole process from moving so rapidly beyond his comfort zone. As they exited the vehicles, their host greeted them.

Extending her hand, Mrs. Polk said, "Welcome to Ohio, Rev. Finch."

Marion gulped and muffled a laugh at the same time. *Reverend? Really? Everything but that in my book.*

After preliminary introductions Ms. Bertha said to the kids, "You wanna go see your new home?"

Shy Adam clung to Marion's shirt and said to mommy, "I want to go to my house."

Reasoning with him Marion said, "It's okay, Adam. It's an adventure. You'll see." As she spun him around, he giggled.

Bertha, hearing impaired, in phone conversations prior to the move, misunderstood their request for information about the parsonage and instead described her own home. Thinking the new dwelling was smaller than their two family one in Cortland, they sold some of their possessions. To their surprise, they drove up to square footage two and half times what was relayed to them. The Finches furniture only half-filled each room.

The next morning there was a knock at the kitchen door leading into the garage. Marion unpacking a box in the family room turned toward Frankie dressed in her pink polyester nightgown and black ankle socks. She whispered, "Who can that be at 7:30 in the morning?"

Perplexed, Frankie went to the door as Marion quickly dashed into the master bedroom frantically trying to find the box with her clothes in it, while the children peacefully slept.

Deacon Smith along with Farmer Rollins extended their hands to Frankie while balancing boxes of food in their other arm.

"We thought you might need a few items, our gift to welcome you as our new pastor," said Deacon Smith.

Mr. Rollins extended an invitation, "The Mrs. is expecting you and your family for lunch at noon. We live just across the creek," pointing out the kitchen window."

"Well, we didn't mean to interrupt. You got a lot of unpacking to do so we'll be going now," said Mr. Smith.

"Thank you, Gentlemen," Frankie said walking them to the door. "See you at noon, Mr. Rollins."

Marion came out of the bedroom to a pile of food, a custom called "pounding" to stock the new preacher's pantry. The tradition went back for generations when a preacher was paid in food, sometimes even Sunday dinner at a church folk's table, if the sermon was worthy of it.

Marion put the flour, sugar, and homemade canned vegetables away in the cupboards and turned on the faucet to rinse off the fresh tomatoes.

"Frankie, c'mere, please. There's no water when I turn on the faucet. We need to call the water department and see if they shut it off after the last pastor left."

Frankie started laughing.

"What's so funny about not having water?" she asked, aggravated at his response to her dilemma.

"Hon," Frankie said spinning Marion around to face him. "There's no water department. We live in the country now. We have well water. It's all electrically pumped. Let me look around for the pump," he chuckled all the way into the basement until he located the pump and reset the switch. He hollered up from the cellar, "try it now."

Crisis abated, they continued to unpack while the kids had a grand time exploring the backyard with cows on the other side of the fence.

At noon, they headed around the pasture outside the fence admiring the Hereford bulls, but not getting too near the cattle. Mrs. Rollins fixed quite a spread for an eighty-three-year old woman. If this was lunch, Marion dared not think what she prepared for dinner. The food was passed around. The meat was shaped like an ear. Unsure what delicacy the Ohioans might have enjoyed, Marion was determined to not eat something that might be an ear. Mrs. Rollins passed the corn on the cob and said to Marion,

"Have a roasting ear, won't you?"

Marion put the corn on her plate and began to pour gravy on her mashed potatoes. Mrs. Rollins then passed the plate of meat to Marion.

Not wishing to offend the hostess, Marion hesitated and, clearing her throat, timidly asked, "Ah what kind of meat is this?"

"Why, that is some of our local farm-raised pork tenderloin, dear."

Marion let out a sigh of relief and put it on her plate. She then asked, "If that is tenderloin, then what are "roasting ears?"

Mrs. Rollins chuckled. "Oh, I get it now. When I said, "roasting ears," I was referring to corn on the cob."

They all had a good laugh and no one ever let Marion live that one down.

The Masters of Theology Program at Ohio Theological Seminary was beginning on Monday, the day after Frankie's first sermon! As he rose to preach, Marion barely breathed, knots forming in her stomach. His sermon highlighted the comic strip, *Blondie*. He rehearsed it for hours on Saturday to the empty pews. What if he said a curse word, a part of his normal vocabulary? What if she was not good enough to be a preacher's wife? In the momentary silence at the end of the service just before the benediction, Adam, used to being in a nursery, said, "Is it over yet?" Marion tried to shush him, her face red with embarrassment.

After the service, tanned Farmer Rollins, age eighty-five, approached Frankie extending his weathered hand and said, "Yep we raise up preachers in this here corn and hog country. I'm up by 5:00 a.m. every morning to tend to my livestock. Since I donated the land the parsonage is on, I'll keep an eye out on ya. By the time you finish your schooling, we'll have you trained to our liking. Until then, we will muddle through as you learn to put together a decent sermon. And by the way, not bad for your first one, son," Mr. Rollins said patting Frankie on the left shoulder.

Frankie, did not know whether to thank him, or resign on the spot. As he shook the last parishioner's hand, he turned to Marion and said in a harsh whisper, "Why the hell can't you keep the children quiet? It was embarrassing to have Adam call out what he did. You know I could be fired at any moment and I have no idea what I'm doing. I need you to control the kids so the church folk don't get mad at us. Can you do that?"

Grabbing Sarah and Adam's tiny palms in hers, she calmly said, "Frankie, the kids aren't old enough to behave in this worship service. I'm used to them being in a nursery or having you beside me in the pew. I don't know how to be a minister's wife. I'm all new at this too."

She vowed to do better. The next week Marion brought Cheerios and matchbox cars to occupy the kids.

Sarah squirmed on Marion's lap biting her mom on the arm wanting to get down. Marion in turn gently bit her to show that was not the thing to do.

Sarah cried out for the whole church to hear, "Ow!"

The women turned and glared at Marion, shaking their heads. Noticing that they were now center stage, Adam decided to get more attention. He began running his matchbox cars on the pew making loud "Vroom vroom" sounds. He let go of one of them and it rolled under the pew all the way to the front of the communion rail. He wailed. Marion did not know whether to get up and leave or just slide down in her seat. She brought out the Cheerios hoping it would divert their short attention span. Instead they delighted themselves dropping the cereal, watching it tumble down the sloped wooden floor to join Adam's red toy car. Feeling Frankie's glare, she pretended to look for a tissue in her purse praying like Adam did the week before, *Is it over yet?*

After church Marion gathered up all the crumbs and toys as Adam and Sarah dashed to find daddy at the back of the sanctuary. Marion, an exhausted twenty-three-year-old mother of two, near tears, felt a complete failure as a preacher's wife.

Mrs. Martin, a plump, sixtyish, gray-headed woman with a tight bun secured in place by a hairnet, had strands of frizzy hair peeking out from under it and a matching mustache. Her brown paisley-design shirtwaist dress was wrinkled on the backside and her brown leather oxford shoes squeaked when she walked. As she approached Marion, she formally extended her hand. "I'm Mrs. Martin. I live up the road from you. I see you aren't too good at controlling your chillins. A guess a big city girl like you doesn't know country ways. We Buckeyes are proud of our state and have expectations of our preachers.

You need to learn to control your youngins so it don't disturb people worshipping our Lord. Can you do that?"

She knew it was a brave move when she puffed out her chest and made direct eye contact with Mrs. Martin while she said, "No, I can't do it by myself, but if you would like to sit with us and help, that'd be great. Thanks."

Mrs. Martin grunted, turned her heel and noisily exited.

The third Sunday Marion brought quiet toys, promised the kids that if they were good they would drive to Walton to the convenience store to buy ice cream. The children squirmed, but were quieter as Marion felt the glares and could see out of the corner of her eye that Mrs. Martin was shaking her head. Marion imagined her saying, "This New York girl will never fit into this Ohio farming community."

As a woman of the times, Marion felt responsible to make her husband look good in public and to oversee their children's proper social behavior. Shortly thereafter, Marion took the children out for children's church before the pastoral prayer. She invited other children to come along. Parents resisted at first, saying children needed to learn to sit through church and behave properly. Being out of the worship service eased Marion's anxiety as it lessened the chance of embarrassment, or getting yelled at by Frankie, or being judged by congregants for not keeping her husband or children in line. On the plus side, the adults without squirming children, could pay better attention to the sermon.

Days, weeks passed as a routine began. As Frankie soaked in the bathtub every Sunday morning practicing his sermon, Marion could hear the splash of the water as it overflowed the tub onto the midnight blue thick carpet. She did not protest because she learned if she kept the kids out of his way, Frankie did not reveal personal information about her in his sermons. She was sort of getting into the rhythm of country life despite how she believed the church women, like Mrs. Martin, thought of her "Hello, this is the Finch residence," she sleepily answered the party line phone at six a.m.

"Good morning Mrs. Finch, this is Albert Smith. I got some maters for you to can for your family. I'll be over at eight."

"Thank you, Mr. Smith," too afraid to say she did not know how to can nor did she have the needed supplies.

As the bushel arrived, she set them in the cool, unfinished basement hoping they would last long enough to figure out what to do with them. When Frankie came home from school, they ineptly tried to make do with a few Mason jars and a dusty blue speckled canning kettle purchased from the local grocer which had probably sat on the store shelf for a decade. Marion's jars all popped open and, over the next few weeks, grew mold. Frankie's did a little better, but that was not as bad as the next spring when they delivered trays of tomato plants, potato cuttings, and assorted other seeds. The farmers did not ask, they just assumed she would tend a garden to feed her family like all the other women in the community.

As Frankie relaxed more, his preaching improved, thankfully not laden with the Baptist form of guilt. He used a technique to awaken the sleeping back row.

"Yep just the other day as I passed by the Rollins farm I saw a calf outside the fence. I didn't know what you're 'posed to do so I got Mr. Rollin's attention on the tractor…"

At that moment, Farmer Rollins jerked awake and the whole congregation including the sleeping farmer chuckled.

Frankie drove four days a week to the seminary.

Leaving at 6:30 a.m. he returned home around 4:30 p.m. On Friday night after Frankie finished his first week of classes Marion tucked the children in and said their prayers.

As she exited Sarah's Pepto Bismal color bedroom, she saw Frankie sitting at the dining room table staring out the window.

She gently touched his shoulder and said, "Hubbles, do you want me to make some coffee?"

As they sipped the piping hot liquid, Frankie sighed, revealing his angst. Turning his palms upright he said, "I have no earthly idea why God called me to the ministry. The other seminarians seem so confident and have grown up in church."

Marion smiled, got up and gave him a hug from behind.

"What matters, Hon is you're doing it, accepting God's call. No one said it would be easy. I promise I will pray for you every day and do what I can to help, okay?"

He hugged her back and said with a wink, "Okay, let's go to bed. I need a little sleeping aide."

Marion developed self-confidence as she singlehanded resolved church crises while juggling childcare and household responsibilities. On the second Sunday in October, Organist Lila played *Just as I am* transporting Marion back to the spring of 1968, when she answered God's call to the ministry while the congregation sang that same hymn. *God, I guess Pastor Gates was right about me being okay to fill the pastor's wife position, but I still feel you calling me into the ministry. I know my call is just as valid as Frankie's! Whenever I hear that hymn, read my devotions, or pray, I feel your presence nudging me, but people don't want to hear what a woman has to say. What can I do about it?*

Each morning as Frankie left for seminary, Marion planned her day: visit Mrs. Rollins recovering from a broken ankle, prepare the devotional for the UMW meeting, fix a casserole for the Ladies Aide Society, call to check on Marsha, the Bush's child who fell out of the apple tree and got a concussion, and read to Adam and Sarah. As it became easier for Marion to do the church work, she became jealous and angry. Why was Frankie allowed to be a minister when his anger erupted without provocation spewing upon the family? To Marion, his continued smoking after he promised to quit, cursing, and throwing things in a fit of rage was anything but holy.

One afternoon Marion combed her hair and put on some perfume at 4:20 p.m. in preparation for Frankie's return from school. Hearing the car enter the driveway, she expectantly opened the door to the garage.

"Hi, Frankie, how was your day?"

Mumbling, he brushed past her to go to the toilet.

"Fine. I gotta a lot of homework. Bring me some coffee, would ya?"

Ten minutes later she entered his office and handed him the cup, kissing him on the cheek to no response.

Adam, hearing that daddy was home, ran the length of the family room to the office. "Daddy, daddy, you're home."

Sarah wore her socks bare as she scooted on her Tyke bike to join her brother. Lifting her feet, she glided into the ajar office door and excitedly repeated what she heard her brother say. Daddy grunted and turned to say a brief hello to the children and pat them on their heads. "Marion, I gotta get this book read by tomorrow.

Take the kids out and keep um quiet so I can read in peace. Bring me my supper in here when it's ready. Go now," as he motioned them out and locked the door.

If there was not a church meeting, Frankie might go hang out at Al's house, a church member, and the local high school principal. Instead of discussing hog farming, Frankie could talk openly about other matters. If he was gone for more than a few hours, she worried. Was he coming home? Was he mad at her? Would his mood be pleasant or irritable? Sometimes, he did not tell her where he was going, just out. If after three hours with no word, she called, aware of listening neighbors on the party line.

Cheerfully she inquired, her anxiety rising in her churning stomach, "Hi, Miranda, is Frankie still there?

Not surprised Miranda said, "Yes, he's finishing his last cup of coffee."

Miranda covered the receiver, but Marion could still hear her say to Frankie, "Marion's checking up on you. You better hightail it home before she sends out the sheriff to look for you."

With sternness in his voice he took the receiver and said, "Marion, I will be home shortly. Kiss the kids good night for me."

Exasperated, she responded, "They've have been in bed for hours already. It's ten o'clock. When are you coming home?"

"Soon."

Before he drove into the driveway Marion primped her hair, smoothed out the sheets on the bed, and quickly straightened the family room piling the kid's toys into the box Frankie had built. She sat down at the dining table ears tuned for the sound of the garage door opening. As she waited she prayed, *God please don't let Frankie be mad at me. I get so lonely here by myself. I just need a hug and reassurance that I'm doing a good job.*

Upon crossing the threshold, she could see his anger as he slammed the door to the garage. She jumped.

He asked hands on his hips, "Why the hell are you checking up on me? Don't you trust me? You make me look bad to the parishioners. Don't ever embarrass me again or I'll give you something to worry about."

The familiar dagger entered her heart; she sucked in all her breath and almost inaudibly answered, "Okay."

If he did not have a meeting or did not hang out with Al, then he stayed in the office until around 11:30 p.m. and then emerged, ready for some orgasmic pleasure. It did not matter if she was too tired to have any enjoyment for herself. He preferred individual oral sex anyway (so much for her former thought that it was only for premarital intimacy). He said it was his sleeping aide. She felt six minutes was not an excessive request to fulfill his night time ritual, but she longed for true intimacy.

As Marion washed up the supper dishes, she heard the office door abruptly open. Frankie stormed into the kitchen with his appointment book in his hand; pointed to an entry and asked, "What the hell is this?"

Cowering, she answered, "I put my name in your book so you could make time to be with me."

Chastising her, he said, "This is ridiculous. You know I have too much to do. My twenty-page paper is due Friday," he said slamming the book.

Apologizing, Marion said sheepishly, "I'm sorry. I just miss spending time with you."

"I can't do it now. Go to bed. I'll wake you up when I come in," he said turning heel back to his office.

If he tried, she did not know it. The alarm went off the next morning as usual at five-thirty a.m. She stumbled sleepily into the kitchen. As the cold water cascaded over her right hand holding the coffee carafe she began to wake up. As the aroma of fresh coffee filled her nostrils she pulled the breadboard out from under the sink and took some of her homemade sliced wheat bread from the freezer. Some of the crumbs spilled onto the floor to be swept up later. Smoothing the peanut butter onto the bread reminded her of the governmental surplus food her family grew up on in between her dad's jobs.

While spreading neighbor Irene's homemade currant jelly on the sandwich, she silently prayed, *thank you God for the provisions you have given us. Please help me understand why I feel like a battery with all its fluid drained out. Is it just lack of sleep?*

Part of God's provisions involved the County Extension agent. One day Mrs. Green came by looking to find families in need. When Marion opened the refrigerator to get Sarah a drink, she commented, "You know, Mrs. Finch, you may qualify for some help to feed your family. I know country preachers don't make much and it is no shame that in doing God's work, you may need some assistance."

"Ya, $5000 a year salary for two churches doesn't go far when we still have a house back in New York State to maintain. What do we have to do to qualify?" Marion asked sucking in her breath sitting back down at the dining room table.

"I've seen enough to know you qualify for government-issued butter, cheese, powdered eggs, milk, peanut butter and food stamps," Mrs. Green said reassuringly.

She felt embarrassed, but knew the children had to eat, so Marion and Frankie drove twenty miles into Pleasantville late in the evening to grocery shop hoping no one recognized them. Frankie went to the car before she checked out.

"Adam, eat your Cheerios and I'll let you watch Sesame Street."

"Mommy, this milk tastes funny."

"I'm sorry. I had to make powdered milk. I'll put some vanilla in it so it will be better, okay?"

He nibbled on his toast and drank some water pushing the cereal bowl aside.

Sarah hollered from the bathroom "Mommy, I'm done."

Marion wiped her daughter's behind and gave her a big squeeze.

"Go eat your breakfast, Sarah."

Rubbing her eyes, the toddler made her way to the circular dark brown dining room table and climbed onto the red vinyl booster seat her daddy had made for her.

Marion sat at the table with the palm of her left hand resting on the side of her head, elbow supported by the table top. She dozed off, briefly jerking awake when her arm slipped off the table. After pouring herself a second cup of coffee she turned on the public television station for the kids to watch their programs. Marion was grateful for a few minutes to make of list of the parishioners she needed to phone. Knowing the party line would not be private, she limited her conversations to general inquiries.

Marion was having more and more difficulty functioning. In the Spring of 1975, (as farmers sprayed fertilizer on the fields), her fever spiked to 104 degrees. Her joints swelled hot and tender.

Around 11:30 a.m. Adam pried open her eyelids and said, "Mommy, aren't you ever gonna get out of bed? I'm hungry."

She sat up placing her foam rubber pillow behind her head and looked at her son. "I'm sorry Adam, Mommy doesn't feel good. Can you bring me the peanut butter and some of the bread from the kitchen counter and I'll make you a sandwich?"

She managed to hobble to the kitchen to make some boxed Lipton's Chicken Noodle soup to go with the sandwiches. Her bladder became so inflamed that she had to urinate often, every hour.

Tired of his wife dragging her feet daily, Frankie finally said, "Here, take this $20 I got from doing the Marshall wedding," handing her the bill. "Go see Doc Nichols in S. Columbus. Find out what's ailing you and get better."

Redressed after the thorough exam, Marion sat up and asked Doc. Nichols, "What's wrong with me? I'm tired all time. My joints ache and I can't get rid of this fever."

This small-town physician did not graduate at the top of his class. He sat in between patients in the reception room in the rocking chair absentmindedly swatting at flies.

His reply was to pull out his prescription pad and start to write something.

Marion interrupted him. "Doctor Nichols. I don't have any insurance and I can't afford repeated visits to you or meds. I just need you to tell me what is wrong so I can fix it."

Not looking up he said, "I don't know," was his simple, unequivocal answer. "Well, since you have no money, I can't send you for lab work. So, here's what ya do. You say you can't tolerate aspirin, right?

"That's correct."

Wadding up the prescription he threw it in the waste basket and said, "I suggest then you drink a little wine for your stomach's sake. It'll ease your pain, help you sleep, and maybe even lift your spirits, pun intended, ha, ha."

That certainly was a waste of $20. I could've figured that out for myself.

All she told Frankie was Doc. Nichols had no idea and that he suggested she drink some to help ease her pain until it either let up or she got insurance to cover the cost of some tests.

Since a little was supposed to be helpful, she felt a larger amount was even better. To obtain her Giacobazzi Lambrusco "medicine," on a tight budget, she became creative. She drove to the convenience store nine miles from home. She cashed a check and went across the street to the liquor store to buy her wine. She went next to the bank and made a deposit of the remaining money hoping to beat the overdraft by selling enough Amway to cover it. Bribing the kids with a candy bar she drove home. Marion hid the wine in a brown paper bag under the kitchen sink.

After Adam and Sarah's nighttime prayers Marion tiptoed out to the kitchen. Frankie, studying in his office did not intrude on her "me" time. She retrieved the bag from under the sink and pulled an empty Mason jar from the pantry. Sitting down at the dining room table she poured the libation into her glass, refilling it until the bottle was empty. As she sipped the burning liquid, it eased her physical and emotional pain. As she could afford to do so this became her nighttime ritual. Frankie, if he was bothered by her booze breath, did not comment.

Quietly lowering her cache of empty bottles into the dumpster behind the convenience store she prayed no one would see her. She could not burn them in the barrel in her back yard because the church took away her trash at the beginning of every month and would find out her little secret.

During the day, she was busied herself being the good preacher's wife. Marion put away the last clean dish and looked over at her son playing with his Lincoln Logs.

"Hey, Adam why don't you bring Mommy your book from school and you can read it to me."

"Okay, Mommy. I know it all. Watch," Adam said crawling up on the couch.

Sister Sarah crawled up next to her brother staring at the words on the page, wanting to read too.

Adam, looked down at his sister and said, "Sary, I can teach you to read too, just like me."

"Okay," she said as he pointed to each word and said what it was as Sary repeated it.

"Kids, let's not get too loud," shushing them with her finger to her lips. "Daddy's doing his homework, just like Adam is doing his. Adam, you read just like Daddy, but he must take a test about what he had read. How about we take Daddy a cup of coffee into the office?"

The kids continued to look at the book while Marion made the coffee. When finished Marion said to Sary, "Here, you carry the spoon. Adam, you carry the napkin and I'll carry the cup."

Off they go tapping gently on Daddy's office door.

"Hello, who is it?" said Frankie knowing full well it was the family.

"Daddy, we have something for you." Adam said.

"Can we come in?"

Opening the door, Frankie picked up Sary and put her on his lap. Adam proudly shows Daddy his reader.

Pointing to it he says, "I read it to Mommy all by myself, just like you read your books."

"Good for you, Adam," Frankie said. Patting each child on the head he said, "Okay Mommy, time for kids to go so Daddy can do his reading. Tell you what Adam, tomorrow is Friday so I'll be home earlier from school and you can read me your book before supper, okay?"

"Yeah, okay Daddy. I'll practice with Mommy after I get home."

"Off with you now," he said gently swatting their backsides. As they ran off he said to Marion, "Since it was your bright idea to interrupt my study time, don't wait up for me," and he closed the door with a thud.

At least he didn't yell at the kids. I want them to grow up with happy memories of times with daddy, not just hear him yelling at me.

All four of the Finches intermittently ran fevers around 100 degrees for the duration of the time they lived there. They just functioned as best they could with the impairment. Years later newspapers reported that farmers were fined for dumping fertilizer into the creek bed that seeped into the water table. Possibly that environmental hazard caused the fevers, the previous pastor's bladder cancer, and multiple neighbors' mysterious health ailments.

In April of 1975, while the kids napped, Marion went to the basement to do laundry. As she leaned over to pull clothes from the washer to transfer them into the dryer, suddenly she felt a sharp twinge in her pelvic region. Ignoring it she finished her task. As she carried the full laundry basket up the stairs, halfway she dropped it, doubling over from a stabbing spasmodic pain, almost tumbling back down the steps. The abandoned basket teetered on the step as she grabbed the rail, struggling to reach the half bath just a few steps from the top of the stairs.

As she clutched her abdomen she said, "Boy, this is going to be some whopper of a period. I guess only having two between Adam and Sarah, this one's gonna make up for that."

Reaching the commode, she hastily pulled down her slacks and under-wear as the spasms increased to a full crescendo and she felt the urge to push. Something plopped into the toilet bowl from her vagina. She looked at it.

"Oh, my God." She clasped her hand over her mouth stifling a scream. "I just miscarried. No wonder I didn't feel good. *I must've been three or four months along from pictures I've seen in Britannica.* Weeping, she apologetically cried, "Oh, little one, I'm so sorry. I didn't even know you were growing inside of me, but I just know you're a boy and I would've named you Mitchell."

Marion stuffed toilet paper into her underwear to temporarily mop up the blood flow. She pulled up her pants, tiptoed quietly to the study door and softly tapped. "Yeah, what'ya want? I'm busy."

As she poked her head inside she saw him pecking out his term paper with his two index fingers on the typewriter keys. Sadly, she said, "Frankie, I just had a miscarriage. It came out in the toilet. I didn't even know I was pregnant."

Without looking up he said, "Well, I guess it's a good thing, 'cause we sure can't afford to feed another kid around here. Anything else? I need to get this assignment done."

"No," she said forlornly as she backed out of the office. She cleaned up the bathroom, retreated to their bedroom and with gut-wrenching sobs, cried into her pillow to muffle the sounds until she fell asleep.

In the 70s there were no support groups for mothers who lost babies through miscarriages, no funerals. Women just flushed away the remains and went on with their life. So, she did likewise, but she never forgot Mitchell.

Realistically they could not afford another child or even birth control, so Frankie announced that he made the decision to have a vasectomy. She did not ask where he would get the money to cover the cost. Marion felt a bitter sweet sadness. Not to worry about getting pregnant was balanced by missing the miracle of life developing inside of her. *Will Frankie be faithful to me if he doesn't have to worry about getting a woman pregnant? Please God, help me be the kind of wife that Frankie wants and needs.*

Marion felt guilty knowing her poor health and recent drinking behavior probably caused the loss of Mitchell. To ease her sorrow, she drank more.

Session Eighteen

Marion looked over at Dr. Weinstein, who was smiling and silently waiting for her to settle in the chair. As she eased her weary body into the chair she smiled back.

"Boy, have I been reviewing what I shared last session," Marion said, then sitting back waited for his reply.

Dr. Weinstein simply said, "How so?"

"I remember how I hoped drinking would turn off the voice in my head that said, 'No, no, no. Don't do this behavior.' It turned the volume down, but the next day my conscience was screaming in my ear. 'I told you not to do ......' In order to drown out that I would drink more. All I got was further into the muck."

"I'm glad you can see that in retrospect. Let's talk about how you navigated through that time," he said.

Inhaling deeply Marion said, "Sure. Here we go."

Libations Lubricate Lasciviousness

ON WEEKENDS, SHE and Frankie joined non-church friends, Sheila and Donald Kemper at the Kemper's farmhouse. The couples met at an estate sale on the edge of the Pleasantville Community. It was nice for the Finches to relax. Since Sheila and Donald enjoyed beer and wine as much as Frankie and Marion, the four got drunk together while playing Clue. After Frankie won the game Donald bribed all the kids ranging in age from ten down to two with three dollars to stay upstairs while the parents continued to get drunk downstairs. Frankie told Marion that she missed out on the pleasure of being with a variety of men and perhaps should gain some experience. She had no desire to engage in such behavior, she longed for her minister husband to set the example of godly behavior, not to encourage adultery.

Frankie said nudging Marion on the arm sitting beside him on the couch, "Go to the cornfield with Donald and make out with him so you can experience a little variety. You might learn something in the process."

Objecting, she said, "I don't want to Frankie. It's not right," pulling back from him in disbelief.

"What are you afraid of? Go only for ten minutes and come back."

Donald, already primed with a six pack under his belt, took her by the hand. Extremely reluctant she followed. Inside, she hoped her compliance would invite Frankie to pay more attention to her.

She could not go through with it. Her insides felt like a blender on high speed, reminiscent of all creepy men of her past. Almost vomiting on Donald, she excused herself and went back into the house.

Frankie sat on the couch sipping another beer. He leered, "Well, what'd ya think, Marion? Did ya learn anything? Did ya get beyond first base with her, Donald? You weren't out there very long."

Defiantly she answered standing in front of her husband, "No, Frankie. I couldn't do it. It's not right." Then she plopped down on the couch with arms crossed.

Frankie stood up. He slurred his words, "You're so uptight. You don't know how to have any fun. I'm going out there with Sheila now."

He grabbed Sheila by the hand and headed for the cornfield, without any protest from Donald. Whether Sheila was a willing participant or not and what they did, she never knew. Marion continued to sit on the couch shaking all over as if hypothermic in the eighty-degree July weather. Her heart was heavy. She was so confused. Tears silently slid down her cheeks. She went into the bathroom to compose herself. An unfamiliar face stared back at her from the mirror.

"Who am I, God? What is going on? Am I the bad wife Frankie makes me out to be? It's supposed to be my full-time job to please my husband and I'm failing, but I don't know what to do. Please help me."

When Frankie and Sheila came back inside twenty minutes later, Marion was sitting on the couch hugging a pillow, not speaking to Donald, just rocking back and forth.

Frankie only said, "You ready to go home?"

After loading the sleeping kids in the backseat, Marion pretended to doze on the nine-mile ride back to the parsonage. She was too numb to formulate any words. In the weeks that followed she tried dressing in a flirtier manner, initiating intimacy more often, but still he seemed bored.

Frankie came home from seminary one Thursday and chuckled to himself as he told Marion the events of his day at school.

"You should see the guys all ogled-eye over this one petite brunette named Vivian. Behind her back, my classmate, Louis whispered as she waltzed by, 'there goes the class whore'. It's hard to believe she co-pastors a church with her husband."

Marion stiffened her posture as she pondered, *such promiscuous behavior signifies she cannot possibly be called by God to be a minister. I better not hear Frankie going around her.*

One day in May before the semester ended, Marion's heart sank into her stomach as Frankie brazenly made an announcement sitting at the dining room table eating a piece of cherry pie Marion had just served him. "Saturday, I'm going to Dayton to see Vivian. I'll drop you and the kids off at the Dayton Museum and come back to get you later."

Incensed, Marion boldly announced grabbing his empty plate from the table, "I'm not going to allow you to go off with that hussy."

Using bully techniques, he said, "So what are you going to do? You've got no college education. You don't know the things I'm studying in school. I'm moving beyond where you are and you're too afraid to try anything new."

Not helping her case, she stood at the sink and cried.

When he returned from being with Vivian, Marion was sitting on a wooden bench near the exit to the museum, haggard and ready to pounce on anyone who spoke to her. She handed cranky Sarah to her smiling, calm daddy.

Marion grabbed Adam's sweaty, filthy palm and headed to the car. Both children were securely fastened in their car seats before she nervously asked, "What did you and Vivian do? Does her husband know?"

Matter-of-factly he said, "We only kissed and it was no big deal."

Crushed, she glared at him and said, "NO BIG DEAL!!!!! Yes, it is!"

Knowing he had her, he said, "If you don't like it, then leave."

Once again that sinking sand enveloped her as she silently ruminated over her situation, fearing losing Frankie 500 miles away from his parents and 600 from hers. With no money, no job and no way to support herself, what could she do? She sat in silence on the ride home.

The illicit relationship only lasted a couple of weeks. Marion suggested to Frankie while he stood at the bathroom mirror shaving, "Why don't you invite Vivian to dinner to celebrate her first time preaching in her husband's absence?"

Marion, strategized, frightened that she would be left on the side of some road without her two kids by her philandering husband. *If I can lay eyes on this tramp to see what makes her so appealing, perhaps then I can model that behavior so Frankie will be faithful to me.*

Marion heard the knock on the inside door to the garage. "Frankie, would you please get the door? I'm stirring the gravy."

Marion cringed as she watched Frankie hug Vivian.

Pasting on a smile Marion extended her hand and said, "Vivian, it's nice to meet you."

Marion, felt dowdy, but acted like the perfect Susy Homemaker hostess complete with the full multi-colored flowered apron slung over her neck and tied at the waist.

She announced to Vivian, "I made an angel food cake for dessert."

"Oh, how'd you know it's my favorite?" Vivian asked, eyes wide.

"Oh, Frankie told me. He told me all about you," he coyly said inviting her to sit down for the meal.

While sitting at the dinner table Little Sarah said, "Mommy, I gotta go potty."

"Go ahead Sary, we'll be here when you come back."

"No, Mommy I can't go," she said shaking her head.

"Why Sary, what's wrong?"

"The cows eat it."

"Huh? What, dear, do you mean?"

"The cows eat my supper, Mommy."

Laughing, Mommy said, "We'll take care that they don't. It's okay now."

As Sarah turned the corner into the bathroom, Marion saw Frankie put his finger to his lips and said, "Shhh."

Marion, quizzically whispered, "What are you doing?" as he lifted Sary's plate off the table and onto his lap.

When Sary returned, she sat up on her booster seat and started to cry. "Mommy where is my supper?"

Frankie said with a straight face, "Cows ate it, Sary. I'm sorry. They came right through the dining room window," pointing at it, and took it."

"Daddy, make them bring it back."

Daddy said, "Okay, close your eyes." She trustingly did so.

Frankie said, "Cows, bring back Sary's food. Look Sary, here it is," he said retrieving it from his lap. Good cows gave it back."

"Daddy, you took my supper, didn't you?"

Everyone chuckled perhaps showing guest Vivian how well the family appeared to function. The cow story has been told and retold for decades, embellishing it each time.

The next week Vivian had a different seminarian on her radar. Seems she did not take kindly to her prey sharing the details of her life with their spouses or seeing their families happily interacting together.

Marion breathed a little easier, hoping he would become content with just her and no more "on the side" frivolity. Frankie surprised her one day riding to Pleasantville to the bank when he suggested, "Spouses can take classes at a discounted rate. Maybe you could attend some, if you can find the money to pay for the tuition."

Excitedly she said turning toward him, "Oh, wow. I'll get to working on it immediately, thank you."

Marion jumped at the chance, thinking she could keep an eye on him at least one day a week and not be left behind educationally as he declared she was. Her hairdresser, currant jelly maker, Irene, who was also a church member, invited Marion to get a free haircut.

Irene told Marion as she styled her hair, "I see you are a God-fearing woman, Marion."

"Thank you, Irene. God has been speaking to me since I was a young child, but not everyone wants to hear that from me, a woman."

Little by little Irene asked more and more questions until Marion shared her the whole call to ministry.

Patting Marion on the shoulder and spinning the chair around for Marion to see her new do, Irene calmly said, "I know someone who could pay that $300."

"Really, who might that be?" Marion asked surprised and expectant.

"I have some money saved that I was going to give to some mission project. I think it would be well-spent on you."

Marion jumped up out of the hairdresser chair and with tears glistening she hugged Irene's neck and said, "thank you, and thank you, God."

Irene said, "Do not tell the church folk about it. It's between you and me and Frankie, of course."

"Yes, ma'am, our secret!"

Marion applied to be a licensed minister of the Christian Church. She had to submit a list of her goals, her church involvement experience, and her call to the ministry. She beamed with pride, but kept it a secret from all but Irene, because the church women snubbed her whenever she mentioned women in the ministry.

Again, with renewed hope for the future, Marion took two classes at the seminary on Wednesdays. She marveled at how the thirty percent ratio of female to male seminarians were treated with mutual respect and value.

Marion, outfitted in her stylish lime green polyester belted mini dress, anxiously drew in her breath as she entered the doorway of Classroom 203.

A slender white male with mousy brown permed hair clasped her hand between his two palms and said, "Hello you must be Marion. I'm Gary. Frankie told me you'd be starting this class. Maybe we can all go out for a drink after class one day."

She answered hesitantly as she stared at the floor.

"Um, okay. We have to get back to the babysitter, but I'm sure we can arrange something." Marion's image of seminarians who prepared for ministry were men who studied their bibles, dressed moderately, did not drink, dance, or curse. This first impression of Gary shattered all those myths. She was not ready to replace her image with something less rigid or so forward. Attending school lessened her need to assuage her sorrows in fermented grapes.

She immersed herself into her studies and she volunteered for anything she could to learn more.

"Do I have any takers who would like to play the part of Rahab, the prostitute?" Professor Michaels asked.

Gary spoke up. "Marion, why don't you do it? You'd be great at it."

Blushing, she agreed. After the role play the professor returned their graded term papers. Gary peeked over at Marion clutching her paper to her chest. "What's wrong, Marion?"

Smiling she handed him her paper. Gary whistled, "Wow, an A-. That's fantastic. I only got a B. No one can say you don't belong here. Good job, Marion."

Meeting Frankie in the hall after class ended she proudly said, "Frankie, look! I got an A- on my paper about Small Town Pastorates."

"Ya well, you are not taking real courses like I am: Hermeneutics or Babylonian History. Yours don't really count," he said.

Crushed, she said nothing as they walked into the cafeteria. Frankie sat down across from two classmates who were one upping each other as to who had the worst thorn-in-the-flesh parishioner. Frankie interjected, making a sideways glance toward his wife, "I can top that. I got a wife who questions my every move as a minister and makes me look bad to my church folk."

Marion, returned her food tray untouched and walked outside to weep quietly in the car.

On the ride home he demonstrated his recently acquired knowledge as he questioned Marion, who had not recovered from the earlier verbal onslaught. "Do you know that the passage that says Mary was a virgin is actually translated meaning a young woman? Do you also know that Jesus was just a normal human man until his baptism when God adopted him and he became the Messiah?"

Wide-eyed she stared at him. "Frankie, that's heresy. Where did you hear such lies? That cannot be right. Are you sure this seminary is teaching you the truth?"

He glared, turning toward her as he said, "You're so Baptist bent you will not even explore the topic. I'm here to learn all I can, but the more I hear, the less I know that what I thought was the truth, may actually not be accurate."

With softened tone, she responded, "I dunno Frankie. I don't want to be left behind in The Second Coming, deceived by the antichrist and be sent to hell for straying from the truth."

Frankie gestured with his right hand, "You know you worry too much. Don't be so afraid to open your mind and see if there are other possibilities to what you were raised to believe."

"I'll pray about that, but it's so scary to think about."

She quietly contemplated what he said for the remaining drive home.

Looking for a kindred spirit, she happily befriended a female classmate also called to the ministry, serving a church 20 miles from them. Tabatha began to ride to seminary with Marion and Frankie on Wednesdays starting in October and within a month was riding to school every day with Frankie. Tabatha's *Charlie* perfume scent remained in the car as Marion emptied out the trash in the front seat. The image of Tabatha's plump 5'7" frame and red blonde hair haunted her. Frankie always told Marion she was overweight at 115 lbs.

"You know, Tabatha told me that her son is dyslexic and maybe a little autistic. That must be hard on her as a single parent in seminary," he shared as if Marion should care when they were putting away groceries in the cupboard.

"Frankie, where is Alex's father?" Marion asked wanting to insert some rational thinking into his new "interest."

More animated he answered, "Oh yeah, Tabatha's parents are well off. They paid for her to adopt him as a single parent. They help quite a bit with him. Tabatha doesn't think she is a good parent, but I tell her all the time that she is."

Marion could see where this was headed and felt powerless to intervene. What could she say to make her husband pay attention to her and no other women?

"Hey, Marion, maybe you could get your hair cut like Tabatha's," Frankie smiled taking a lock in his hand.

She did not honor him with an answer knowing there was no money for even the necessities like shampoo, so she dismissed the thought and turned her head away from him. Anger welled up in her and she vowed, *I will never wear my hair short to be like one of his whores!*

On December 9, Adam, aged five, rode home in the car pool. Mr. Thomas was driving the three kindergarten students in his four-wheel drive Ford F-250 white truck. Approaching the intersection of Pleasantville Rd. N.E. and Cattail Rd. N.E., he hit a patch of ice.

Gripping the steering wheel, Mr. Thomas said, "Hold on kids. We're sliding right toward that ditch."

Unfortunately, the vehicle went over the embankment. The three kindergarteners along with Mr. Thomas all hit their head on the dashboard and were knocked unconscious. Luckily, the dry ditch was only six feet deep and the car behind them saw what happened. Soon the EMTs arrived along with the wrecker. Each child was warmed in the ambulance and checked for a concussion. The sheriff wrote a quick report and the wrecker drove all of them home. The paramedics told the wrecker driver to tell each parent to take their child to the ER to check further for a concussion, in case Mr. Thomas forgot to tell the other parents.

After supper, the Finches drove the twenty-two miles to Fairfield Medical Center in Lancaster. Thankfully, Adam was okay.

Before they headed out the door Frankie said, "Sit here on this bench. I'm going down the street to check on Tabatha. She's having a really rough time and I want to make sure she's okay."

Too exhausted and not wanting to make a scene at 10:00 p.m., Marion said in a loud whisper, "I don't like it. What about the kids? They need to get home to bed."

"They'll be fine. I'll get back in a little bit."

Marion fumed, as five-year-old Adam wailed, still recovering from the car accident, and three-year-old little Sarah fell asleep on her lap on the cement bench outside the emergency room in the hallway near the sliding glass doors. Every time the doors opened, a blast of cold wintery air hit them. Frankie returned quiet and not looking at Marion. Marion was livid and immediately laid into him. "What the hell were you thinking? It's 3:00 a.m.! Adam was just in a car accident and must go to school in a few hours. What were you two doing?"

Without uttering a word, Frankie picked up Adam and carried him to the car while Marion, left behind, slipped and slid in the new wet fallen snow, balanced Sarah on her shoulder trying to make it to the car without falling. The tense ride home matched the frosty air outside.

The next morning Frankie awoke and dialed Tabatha's number from the bed, right in front of Marion. Marion, shaking all over, knew there was something going on between the two of them, but she was too afraid to confront him. She knew the answer.

Taking matters into her own hands, Marion dropped Sarah off at Sheila's and drove the twenty-two miles into Lancaster to the Christian Church where Tabatha worked as an associate pastor to ask Tabatha some questions.

Stopping at the office she approached the secretary who said: "Hello, I'm Nina, how may I help you?"

"Hello, I'm Marion Finch. I'm a classmate of Tabatha's. Is she here?"

"She was a minute ago. Let me call her extension. I'm sorry. She's not answering. Maybe she went home for a bit. She lives two blocks down. Do you know where it is?"

"Yes, I do. Thank you."

Marion walked to Tabatha's apartment.

She was surprised to see Tabatha answer the ringing bell.

"Oh, hi, Marion. What are you doing here? Come on in."

Climbing the mahogany stairs to Tabatha's second floor, five-room apartment, Marion's knees wobbled. Entering the small living room, the hard wood floors creaked as Tabatha led them to and motioned for her to sit in one of the two matching olive-green wingback chairs. As Marion sat down she glanced at the book on the oak barrel-legged coffee table: "Dating a Married Man." She said nothing.

"You want some tea or something?" Tabatha asked as she stood above her.

"Sure, some hot tea would be great. Thank you."

As Tabatha busied herself in the kitchen Marion pondered the situation. *Why is that book on the coffee table about dating a married man? I don't want to think about Frankie having an affair with Tabatha right under my nose. How can I get her to tell me if something is going on and what do I do, if what I fear, is true?*

As the red kettle whistled on the burner, Tabatha placed the yellow rose china cups onto her mother's antique silver tray; the Pekoe tea bags' strings hung over the edge. Pouring the steaming liquid into the cups she then added a sugar bowl, creamer pitcher, and two petite spoons before carefully walking back into the living room to set it all down on the coffee table in front of Marion.

"Cream and sugar?" Tabatha politely asked.

Marion snapped back to reality. "Yes, please. Two spoonsful and no cream. Thank you."

Tabatha's cup remained on the tray. Marion nervously watched Tabatha's every move hoping she would slip up to reveal what was going on between her and Frankie. Marion was afraid to ask directly, because she had no plan, if it was true.

Sipping the beverage, Marion said, "Tabatha, Frankie sure is acting weird these days. You spend a lot of time driving to and from seminary with him. I thought maybe you would know what's causing him to act this way. You know I can't discuss this with any church member. You're my only hope."

Tabatha smiled as she looked Marion straight in the eye and said, "No, I haven't noticed anything. I'll be glad to tell you if I learn something. After all, friends help each other, right?"

"Right, thank you and thanks for the tea. I better be going. Adam's kindergarten car pool will drop him off in an hour."

"You can talk to me anytime, Marion."

As Marion descended the stairs she felt her stomach muscles tighten as nausea waved over her. *What am I going to do? I can't stop Frankie and I don't have anyone I can talk to about it. God, I am so alone and scared. Please help me.*

Marion did her best to keep the house tidy, the children quiet, to offer sex before asked and to anticipate Frankie's every whim before he even thought about it. He became increasingly distant.

"Marion, what do you call this concoction you made for supper? It takes like rubber."

"It's macaroni and cheese, but the oven temperature's not right and it cooked too long. I'm sorry. Let me make you a peanut butter sandwich," she said getting up from the table.

"Never mind. I'm not hungry any more. I'm going into my office to study. Don't bother me."

Marion heard him talking on the phone and laughing. She wanted so badly to pick up the receiver in the dining room, but knew he would hear her and become even angrier. As Marion's actions, more and more displeased him, he paradoxically got compliments from the church members.

"Frankie, that was a good sermon today," said Mrs. Martin shaking Frankie's hand vigorously. "It's just what my sister-in-law needed to hear about God wanting us to develop our talents, not bury them somewhere. Too bad she wasn't here today."

"I'm glad you liked it, Mrs. Martin. Maybe there was a message in it for you too."

"Well, that takes real nerve to disrespect a woman of my age, Pastor Finch!" Mrs. Martin replied as she huffed and stormed out of the sanctuary.

"Have a nice day, Mrs. Martin. Remember God loves you and I do too," he said sarcastically, smiling.

Mrs. Martin stormed out of the church muttering under her breath, "I might have to love that preacher, but it doesn't mean I have to like him."

A week later at the parsonage, Marion received the news that Frankie's paternal grandmother died. Marion left a message with the seminary receptionist asking Frankie to call home. Frankie was scheduled to stay that night in Dayton after his last final.

When he returned her call, he said, "Now I need time away more than ever to process my Grandmother's death, unwind from exams, and return ready for the Christmas rush at the churches."

Pleading, she said, "Frankie, please come home so I can help you with all of those things."

Firmly, he answered, "No, I'm staying at a motel. Don't give me a hard time! I just lost my Grandma."

Questioning, she said, "What motel are you staying at in case I need you?"

"I haven't decided yet. A Day's Inn or Motel 8 (she knew that what he meant was Motel 6) somewhere off Hwy 33." He gruffly cut her short saying, "I gotta go. See ya tomorrow."

Hanging up, she paced the floor wringing her hands, mumbling to herself back and forth from the dining room to the office for ten minutes. "I know he's going to be with Tabatha and there isn't a damn thing I can do about it."

Adam asked her, "Mommy what are you doing?"

Trying to pull herself together, she stopped to hug him and said, "Mommy's cold. I'm trying to get warm and walking back and forth helps me do that."

Satisfied, Adam went back to playing with his Lincoln Logs, while Sarah, mesmerized by Sesame Street on the black and white television at the end of the family room, did not seem to notice her mommy's angst.

Snapping shrilly at three-year-old Sarah, she said, "Turn that down. It's too loud." Sarah started to cry.

Feeling totally rejected and defeated, Marion grabbed a steak knife and headed to the basement.

With each step, she muttered under her breath, *God, what am I going to do? Frankie doesn't want me. Nobody wants me. I can't take care myself, let alone the kids. I hate that bitch Tabatha. Some friend she turned out to be. That good for nothing Frankie. I give him two kids, give up my goals to take care of these two churches for him, and he goes off and screws -Tabatha. God, I wanna to die."* Taking the brown wood handled six-inch steak knife in her left hand she raised it up just above her heart. Tears streamed down her face as she shook, feeling lost, sinking deeper and deeper into the quicksand with no escape. If she plunged the knife into her heart, the pain would end.

Just then the door opened at the top of the stairs. Adam called down, "Mommy are you down here? I'm hungry. Can you fix me a peanut butter and jelly sandwich?"

Snapping back to reality, she said, stifling her sobs, "I'll be there in a minute."

She stuffed the knife into her jeans pocket and gathered her wits. The suicidal gesture was serendipitously interrupted by the innocence of a hungry five-year-old.

At the top of the stairs she hugged Adam so tightly he said, "Mommy, stop! I can't breathe."

Pulling back, she kissed him on the top of his head. She slipped the steak knife back into the utensil drawer unnoticed and turned to see her youngest still weeping on the sofa holding her baby doll.

With her little ones affirming her worth, she felt hopeful for the future.

Beckoning with her left index finger, Marion said, "C'mere Sarah, we're gonna have a picnic right here on the floor with PB&J and your favorite strawberry Quick."

Drying her tears, she raced over, still clutching her doll. As they dined on crustless sandwiches washed down with strawberry Quick stirred into powdered milk they made up silly songs and danced around. It was a temporary reprieve to Marion's sinking sand marriage.

On New Year's Eve, she finally got the courage. She put the kids to bed and returned to the family room where Frankie was watching television.

"Frankie."

"What? I'm watching this New Year's Eve program."

Bravely seizing the moment, she walked over and turned off the television.

"What the hell did you do that for?"

"Because we are going to talk," she said as her back stiffened.

Frankie got up off the couch and came to the dining room table where Marion sat.

Sitting down at the table, glaring at her, he said, "I'm here. So, talk already."

Wanting leverage, she stood up in front of Frankie and looked him straight in the eye. "I want the God's honest truth. Are you having an affair with Tabatha?"

Frankie scraped his chair on the floor as he flung it backward retreating toward the couch. Before he got two steps, Marion grabbed his arm and shouted, "Are you, are you?"

"Yes, I am!"

Marion stumbled backward as she allowed the shock to settle in.

Frankie began to cruelly unfold explicit details. "Tabatha likes it when I fuck her up the ass. She always puts rose petals on the linens before we make love and after, it's weird because she must change the sheets immediately. She can't handle lying on soiled sheets after sex. She's worried about germs. You don't do any of that for me," he said relishing in the tidal wave of emotion that his toxic verbal explosion created.

Pronouncing his decision, he said, "I'm going to send you back to our house in New York. Tabatha and I will raise Adam and Sarah because you obviously can't afford to with no education."

Marion slapped him across the face so hard he temporarily lost his balance. "God, damn you, Frankie. I'm not leaving my children and I'm not going back to our house in New York. I'll tell the District Superintendent what you're doing and you will be out of a job."

Confidently he said, "Go ahead. Tabatha can afford to take care of me and the kids, so you'd be out in the cold."

Fear gripped her as she stormed into the bedroom, slammed the door, unsure of her next move. Once again, she fell asleep sobbing into her pillow. She did not hear Frankie come to bed as she eventually fell asleep due to pure exhaustion.

His proclamation took all the wind out of her sails. Over the next couple of tense days, they only spoke when necessary. Marion continued to make his coffee each morning and brought it to him in bed. She fixed his favorite spaghetti and meatballs. She dressed in a flirty manner while feeling humiliated inside doing it. All her efforts just aggravated him more. He still had sex with her because he wanted to show her who was in charge. Afraid, she did not refuse him.

He casually announced a few days after the confession that Tabatha invited him over for corned beef and cabbage, a meal Marion could not afford to fix.

He said, "I'll be back around 10 and if you don't like it, too bad. You can't do anything about it. Besides, Tabatha knows how to make me happy and sexually satisfied. You don't."

Marion exhibited her normal anxious behavior and paced the whole time, snapped at the kids, and talked to herself again but this time not suicidal. Instead, she became determined to climb out of her quicksand. *What am I going to do? I am losing Frankie with no way to stop him. I'll be damned if I'm going to let Tabatha raise my kids.*

Like her father had done years before, she prayed and made a pact with God, *Please, help me make my marriage work. If you give me the chance, I'll be the best wife ever.*

Before he returned from his dalliance, Marion grit her teeth as dressed up and put on makeup. She hated herself for doing it, but she had to make certain there was no way he could separate her from her children. Inside her gut screamed in anger. *Punch the bastard right in the balls. Tell him you will not stand for this behavior. Stop it or else! Or else what? There was no what else and he knew it.*

When he got home, she offered him the anal intercourse which Tabatha, he said, so graciously gave him. He wasn't interested.

Over the next few weeks for whatever reason, persistence, or with the affair's novelty wearing off, Frankie was not so distant.

The kids were playing in the sandbox in the backyard when Frankie spoke to Marion while she was stirring spaghetti sauce on the stove.

Resigned, as if he were bored, he said, "Marion, I'm going to end it with Tabatha. But she's so fragile. Her son's doing poorly in school; her seminary grades are slipping and the senior minister is unhappy with her performance, so I'll have to let her down gently. To show you I'm serious, I'll take one of the kids with me when I go to see her so I won't have sex with her."

Marion looked out the kitchen window over the sink to check on the children while she protectively said, "I don't want the kids in the middle of this."

"So, you want me to be tempted to have sex with her again because I will, if you want me to," he said. "No, of course not. I don't want you to see Tabatha ever again," she hedged.

Pushing for a decision, towering over her, he growled, "Well, who's going with me, Adam or Sarah?"

With a deep sigh, she said, "I guess Sarah." She prayed that since Sarah was younger than Adam, she would be less traumatized and not remember it. Marion just wanted it to end and for Frankie to want to be with just her.

Much to Marion's consternation, Frankie took his time with the break-up. He took Sarah twice and Adam once to spend time with Tabatha. The children came home excitedly talking about the fun time they had playing with Tabatha's son, Alex.

Frankie announced that his final good-bye to Tabatha would be Wednesday at seminary during the lunch break between their morning and afternoon classes. Marion had no appetite so she skipped the cafeteria and sat outdoors anxiously chewing her fingernails and praying hard. Marion could see Frankie escorting Tabatha into the opening of the woods about fifty yards from where she sat on a cement bench, much like the cement bench at the ER, and the zoo when he was off with Vivian. She could not hear what they said as they disappeared into the foliage. He returned fifteen minutes later. He walked over to the bench where Marion sat with her insides jumbled in a huge knot. Looking up at him she could not tell if he was happy, angry, or what?

"Well, you can stop fidgeting now. It's over," he said calmly.

"How'd Tabatha take it?" Marion inquired, like Gigi of years earlier.

"Not well," he said as he reached in his pocket to get his handkerchief to blow his nose.

"Oh, no."

"What Frankie?" she asked nervously.

"I must've left my wallet back there. I better go get it."

"I can help you look for it, if you want," she offered trying to engage with him somehow.

"No, I need to grieve a bit for what I lost. Stay here I'll be back in a minute."

Her gut ached with that last statement. *What he lost? What about what she lost? What about her feelings? What about the damage to the family, the kids, their relationship?*

None of that was his concern, only his own feelings. Relieved it was over, she just wanted them to drive away and never return.

Once his second "known" affair ended, they focused on graduation and moving which was only three months away. Marion completed a total of four courses over the seminary calendar year: Spiritual Disciplines, Youth Ministry, Small Town Parishes, and Conflict Management. They were not much of a challenge for her even though she had no college. Making two A's and two B's proved a higher education was achievable. The introduction into meditation in her Spiritual Disciple class taught by a Catholic sister paved the way for life-long meditative practices. Meditation was Marion's soothing respite from the overwhelming stresses in her life.

For about a year Marion had been assisting in the worship service reading scripture, helping with the pastoral prayer, and assisting with communion. Marion's ministerial call was clear and unwavering, yet unaccepted by the congregations and women in general.

As usual on Sundays the children were dropped off at Farmer Rollins house to go Sunday school at the larger of the two United Methodist churches while Frankie and Marion conducted worship services at the smaller church. After worship one Sunday Frankie surprised her on the route to the other church.

"Marion, that, by far, is the best pastoral prayer I have ever heard," he said turning toward her beside him in the car.

"Thank you, Frankie. I say what is on my heart," she said pointing to her chest. "I just talk to God just like a human being. No flowery language, no thee or thou, just direct. God doesn't want us perfect. He just wants all of us to surrender to him."

"Now you've gone to meddling, saying that last piece. You know I've apologized to you for my affair with Tabatha, so stop bringing it up. I've put it past me and you need to do the same."

Shaking her head, Marion said, "Frankie, I wasn't referring to that. If you think so, maybe that is your own conscience. I'm talking about me. I ask everyday 'what do you want me to do today, God? Help me to notice when you show me.' If I only give God a part of me then he can't use me completely. I'm just telling you what it is like for me."

"Well, I don't *feel* or *hear* God, like you do. I envy that, your confidence in knowing for sure what you are to do. I don't have that," Frankie honestly admitted.

"Okay, Frankie, I'll pray about it that you might. Would that be okay with you?" she asked smiling, touching his hand.

"Ya, I guess, but don't go trying to change me into something I'm not. We better stop now. Time to go in and do the service here."

Marion was ready to leave behind the seminary, Tabatha, the parsonage, the cold, and especially the female parishioners. As Marion developed her strengths, the church women, feeling threatened by her, avoided her at any of the church gatherings. Marion sat alone at a table at the Ladies Aide meetings drawing on God to help her endure until the Finches could move to a church that embraced God using women. Over time, as Frankie turned a deaf ear to the needs of the church folk, focused on his future somewhere else, the congregants could not wait for his pastorate to end.

Marion began to hear at seminary about a women's movement called the Equal Rights Amendment. It piqued her interest. She could discuss it with female seminarians, but the farmwives in the congregations only followed the tenants of Marabelle Morgan who wrote the book *The Total Woman*. Ms. Morgan said women should wrap themselves naked in saran wrap and only please their husbands. Marion knew firsthand that method had not been working. She was gradually getting bolder in gathering her wits about her to emerge from the quicksand.

Attending a United Methodist Women's monthly meeting, Marion was asked to lead devotions. She chose the story of Priscilla and Aquila, the husband and wife preaching team.

Marion stood up at the head of the dining room table in Mrs. Perkins house to deliver her devotional to the women gathered. She took in a breath and said a silent prayer. *God please make their hearts receptive to what you speak through me tonight.* She opened her bible and read the passage from Acts chapter 18.

"Per the sentence structure of this account, Priscilla would have been the more prominent leader in this preaching duo."

As the women defensively crossed their arms and pursed their lips, Marion knew her opinions were as a minority. After the meeting, as refreshments were served, Mrs. Martin approached her, wagging her finger in Marion's face and said, "Because of women like you, before long all of us farm wives will all have to leave the farm and get jobs."

Marion calmly responded, "Mrs. Martin, farm wives already have full-time jobs working the farm. You just do not receive a salary for it. What you do is important and I am not suggesting you leave the farm. What I am saying is women have just as much right to be treated equally in the work place. That is all."

Mrs. Martin just said, "Humph, that's just some women's libber idea, if you ask me. It's not God's plan." Then she picked up her plate and went into the far corner of the living room.

Marion got an envelope in the mail on Monday, January 10th, addressed to her from the New York State Disciples of Christ office. It said, "After the Committee on the Ministry reviewed your application to be licensed as a minister in the Christian Church (Disciples of Christ) denomination, we have voted to approve you for a period of two years beginning January 2, 1977, (eight days before the letter arrived)."

Marion cried tears of joy and relief. "Thank you, God." She kept repeating over and over. Then she carried the letter into Frankie's office.

"Look, Frankie," she said waving the letter in front of him. "I'm finally authorized to officially begin my ministry. Isn't this exciting?"

"Good for you. Now all we need is to call District Superintendent Johnson to get his approval for you to preach here in the two churches," Frankie said.

Permission granted, Marion spent a month preparing her first sermon. Frankie's two years' experience preparing sermons and her watching how he did it made her debut easier than his first delivery.

Because of the expected rejection of Marion's calling, they did not announce it prior to the actual day of her "coming out" party.

Frank led the worship service as he normally did. When it came time for the sermon he cleared his throat and winked over at Marion. He turned to the congregation and announced. "This morning we are fortunate to have a preacher in our midst who God called many years ago but has not yet delivered a sermon - until today."

The congregation looked first at one another and then turned to the sanctuary doorway expecting it to open any second with the guest preacher. To their surprise, Marion stood up and walked to the pulpit. As she did, chaos erupted. Mrs. Martin led an entourage of angry women up the center aisle to the sanctuary doorway where she turned and announced loud enough for the whole church to hear, "God does not call women to preach. This is work of the Devil. Any of you who stay to hear this abomination are warned that you will incur God's wrath."

To that she and six other women slammed the door as they exited. Marion stood up and led by the Spirit, prayed for "the meditation of my heart and the words of my mouth to be acceptable in God's sight. Amen."

Those who stayed were surprised that "the bear could dance," as they were expecting a circus-type act. Marion's message was not feminist as presumed. She talked about the value of prayer and gave examples how it worked in her life. The men were amused that their wives took such offense to a 115-lb. woman upsetting their traditions. After the service, several young women shook her hand and thanked her for the courage to stand up against such hateful so-called Christian women. As Marion became more certain of her call, Frankie began less certain.

Frankie, sat with his head in his hands in front of his typewriter as Marion brought him a cup of coffee while he worked on yet another term paper.

Setting down the coffee on the book shelf Marion asked, "Frankie, what's wrong? You got a headache or something? Do you want me to get you an aspirin?"

"No, thank you," he said lifting his head. "I'm stuck. I wonder how much of the bible is relevant today. The more I learn about the true meaning of the book of Revelation, the more I think it is just an allegory about Babylon referring to Rome of the day. I'm having a hard time writing this paper because I have more questions now than when I started seminary. I'm not even sure that God called me to be a minister."

"Frankie, I have an idea," Marion said lighting up standing beside him. "Why don't you call Pastor Henry about it? He always seemed to know what to say."

"Maybe that's a good idea. Thanks for the coffee. Do you think it's too late to call him now?"

"I think he'll understand. I'll go out and let you talk to him." She kissed him on the cheek and said a silent prayer as she exited.

God, please help Frankie hear your voice. Thanks, Amen.

He left the office door open. Marion could hear him dialing the number as she stood at the kitchen sink, praying. "Hello, Pastor Henry. It's Frankie. You wanted me to call to plan for my ordination service in June. So, I am."

"Son, you sound down. What's wrong? The stress of completing your studies worrying you?"

"No, it's just I feel like I know less now than when I started. I've been here three years and I am clueless how to lead God's people or even sure I was really called," he said with trembling in his voice.

"Frankie, you're having the normal questioning we've all had. You're finishing a four- year program in three. That's very impressive. God will wax and wane in your life, as you experience new things, but never doubt your calling. How can I help?"

"Thanks, that helps. Could you pray with me right now so I will know God's will for my life and my family?"

Pastor Henry did and Frankie settled down over the next week. He came home excited one day from seminary. Bursting through the door from the garage into the house he said, "Marion."

Emerging from the backyard where the kids were making mud pies in the sandbox she said, "Hi, Frankie.

Did you have a good day at school?"

Ignoring her he said, "Marion guess what?" "What?" she asked rinsing off mud from her hands.

"I found out about this new concept in ministry. It's called a "co-pastorate team." It's where husbands and wives serve together. I decided we're gonna do it."

There was no discussion, but Marion did not hinder Frankie's plans. She did not know where God wanted her to serve, but she felt if Frankie wanted her, then she better jump on it to be the supportive, engaged wife lest he find someone else to take her place.

Session Nineteen

Marion sat in the therapy chair looking at her feet. Dr. Weinstein sensed her down mood due to revisiting the trauma of her life week after week.

"You, know Marion, you can take a break from therapy any time you need to. There is no set course that must be followed."

Tears trickled down Marion's face as she softly spoke. "I wanted so much to live out what I believed God wanted for me and for us. Somewhere along the path, I lost my way trying to hang on to the image of the marriage I desired. I believed God was still punishing me for having sex before marriage and if I tried hard enough or long enough, I would be forgiven. I cry for that young woman part of me for all that pain and sorrow she went through only trying to do what she thought God wanted her to do."

"Yes, it is sad. So many women are led to believe that God will punish them if they fail to be obedient to the church's teaching and their husband's demands. I'm glad that you have been able to know that God is not the angry tyrant you were led to believe. 'Pain that is shared is pain that is divided.' By telling your story it is helping you heal and someday if you tell others it will help them heal too," Dr. Weinstein said.

"It is my hope that from me sharing all this someone else will be spared the depth of anguish I experienced. I am ready now to tell more so I can heal more."

"Good, Marion. Then let's begin," Dr. Weinstein said handing Marion a tissue to wipe away her tears.

Geographical Cure Second Generation

ON A CLOUDY Sunday in January, the temperature hovered just above zero. Eager to reach the warmth of their abode, parishioners hurriedly exited the blood-red brick church. Adam and Sarah clung to Daddy's legs as he quickly shook the gloved hands of congregants. Marion beckoned Irene over to the car, looking around to make certain no one else was within earshot. In a hushed voice, she said, "Irene, guess what?"

Smiling, Irene whispered, sensing the air of excitement in Marion, "What, pray tell?"

Marion touched her arm gently and said in a hushed whisper, "We have an interview for a co-pastorate team position at a church in Marley, South Carolina next Thursday. I'm so nervous yet excited about it."

"That's so cool. You'll have ta tell me all about it as soon as you're back. But, I know. Don't tell anyone. Boy, I'm sure gonna miss you when you're gone, Marion," she said as she hugged her neck. She pulled back and said,

"You're my only female spiritual inspiration who doesn't tell me how to believe in God."

"Yeah, well Irene, you're about the only female who supports me in my call to ministry," Marion said with moist eyes. "I'll miss you, Irene. The rest of the women can't wait for me to move on. Please come visit us wherever we serve."

"That will be my pleasure and honor, Marion," Irene said as she gave her friend and role model another hug and dashed to her own car.

That winter continually pummeled the weary Buckeyes with subzero temperatures. For ten straight days, the thermometer showed minus twenty-three degrees Fahrenheit without the added wind chill factor. The three-minute warning to avoid outdoor skin exposure was heeded by all except the newspaper carrier who tried to finish delivering her papers before the blizzard hit. Her jeep slid into a snowbank and she could not get it out. Since it was not safe to walk in the frigid air she sat in her car hoping someone would come along to rescue her. By the time someone got to her frostbite had already destroyed all her fingers and toes. A three-year-old child died of an asthma attack because no emergency vehicle could get to his home. Two-lane roads became one lane tunnels with ten-foot drifts on either side. This onslaught ironically coincided with Marion gradually thawing the icicles of her frozen broken heart. On February 10th, she and Frankie precariously navigated Route 70 headed to the Dayton airport. A new blanket of snow covered the roadway. As they listened intently to the radio weather report, skidding occasionally on the slippery pavement, they conversed.

"Gee, Frankie what'll we do if the flight is cancelled due to this latest snow storm?"

Frankie, only one month post-Tabatha affair more attentive and less angry said as he gently squeezed Marion's thigh, "Well, if that happens, I guess we'll be stuck in Dayton until we can fly out or have to reschedule it. No matter what, we'll figure it out." After de-icing the plane, the snow ceased long enough for them to take off.

South Carolina's temperature was sixty degrees compared to Ohio's ten above zero. As they approached the airport, red clay dirt graced the knolls beneath them. Stately pine trees dotted the highway along Interstate 20 as they descended. The host family, the Swansons, greeted them warmly speaking in a heavy southern drawl.

Extending his hand to the apprehensive young ministerial couple, offering no time for them to reply, Mr. Swanson said, "Ya'll, Welcome to South Carolina. How was your flight? We're gonna take you to get some good Southern BBQ while you're here, if you don't mind. But first, Mrs. Finch, we'll stop at our home so you can freshen up a bit."

Marion, tired, her face absent of any color, graciously received the make-up Mrs. Swanson, a company distributor for Merle Norman products, offered. She strained to understand their accent, foreign to her. The drastic shift from bitter cold to what would have been their May weather made her sleepy. Dark by the time they headed to the church, Marion's eyelids drooped from weary travel as she fought to stay engaged in the conversation. As they entered Marley First Church, Frankie fumbled in his shirt pocket for his trial sermon, a requirement to "try out" for the position.

He delivered his rousing words to a crowd of fifty eager listeners gathered for this impromptu service.

"Brothers and sisters," Frankie said with a booming voice that needed no microphone and arms open wide with palms up. "We act like Christians who lost the football game of life. We are victorious through Christ," pointing heavenward, "and need to live like winners."

After the service, Mr. Swanson shook Frankie's hand and said, "Interesting sermon, Reverend. Come on in the fellowship hall and I'll introduce you to the church folk."

Frankie and Marion followed behind him and sat down as directed on brown folding metal chairs. People passed in front of them introducing themselves, but Marion overwhelmed, could recall not one name minutes later.

A brassy red-headed single mother of two daughters boldly approached her "future" pastor and said, "Reverend Finch, I'm Mrs. Winslow. You must try my pecan pie. It won the award at the county fair."

Frankie smiled as he accepted the paper plate in his left hand, while holding the fork midair in his right. Another woman, Ms. Mahoney, wearing a plunging neckline denim blouse leaned over Frankie giving him an up close and personal view of her bosom as she began pouring steaming coffee from a carafe into a porcelain cup.

She asked him, "Do you take cream and sugar in your coffee, Pastor Frankie?"

Marion was tended to by Mrs. Swanson while the other female congregants lavished attention upon their thirty-year-old handsome, pastoral candidate.

As the dishes cleared, Mr. Swanson raised his voice above the chatter and said, "Elders, deacons, and deaconesses, come on. Let's get this interview started." Sweeping his arm wide he said to the others, "The rest of you can go home or wait in the sanctuary. Reverend Finch, please sit here at the end of the table. Mrs. Finch you are welcome to sit beside your husband."

Before the Finches accepted the interview invitation, they researched their prospective congregants' lives. The main employer of the town was the Marley Air Craft Manufacturing Plant contracted by the US Government to make planes for the military.

Government-controlled, the plant was like the *Stepford Wives* movie only it was the *Stepford Employees*. Each potential worker was given a personality test to qualify to be hired. Selected males had identical personality types. The acceptable candidate had to keep secret what he did and where on the plant property he worked. As the head of his household, he was instructed to set up a housing account separate from the main checking account for his spouse. The wives did not know what salary the husbands earned or had any knowledge of whether their spouses were exposed to hazardous materials.

Harvey, the chairperson of the Marley First Church board, twenty-five-year employee of The Plant, was first to interrogate Frankie. Dressed in the traditional plant attire, a white shirt and narrow black tie, he asked Frankie, while pulling an ink pen from his pocket protector, "Reverend Finch do you believe in virgin birth?"

Frankie chewed his bottom lip and said, "Yes, of course I do."

Marion lost in thought recalled, *Hmm. I remember that day on the way home from seminary when he said he really believed that Jesus was a normal human adopted by God to be his son at baptism.* She nervously fidgeted in her seat. *How is he going to pull off this charade? This reminds me when I gave Frankie instruction so Pastor Herbert would marry us.* Relaxing her posture, she said, *Oh, I get it now. He's doing this to get hired. So, if that's true, I better play along with whatever he says. I can see the move to South Carolina in our grasp, our geographical cure, much like Mom's move to Wisconsin. The whole Tabatha sinking sand experience will soon be behind us.*

Willy, the curly headed soft-spoken church elder, owner of Flecks Body Shop, asked Frankie, snapping Marion back to the present, "Reverend Finch what is your plan to make the church grow?"

"I will first assess our growth potential based on the community demographics and then I will determine, based on the church's location, what needs of the city we can meet. We will then develop a plan to offer what is not now available to potential parishioners. I will get involved in community affairs so we have a presence people will recognize. I like to visit church folk and see what they want and how they suggest we carry out their plans. Within the first six months I plan to visit every home where I am welcomed," Frankie answered with a wide grin.

Elder Victor, the town accountant, sat quietly throughout the interview but now cleared his throat, and went straight to his point. He stared Frankie straight in the eye and said, "So *Mr.* Finch, this is your first church out of seminary. We know that the school you're graduating from has very liberal ideas. We here in the South have been doing things our way for a very long time. We don't take fancy to some Northerner coming in with crazy ideas that ain't been tried out before. Are you going to do that?"

Addressing Victor in like manner, he replied, "Mr. Milton, I appreciate your frankness. I do not know exactly what we will do until we get here and become involved. I can assure you I will ask for God's direction and will not make decisions hastily nor single-handedly."

Before Victor could reply Deaconess Gladys, spoke up. Batting her eyelashes while adjusting her fur she said, "*Mr.* Finch. I address you that way because you are not ordained yet, are you?"

Quickly learning to address Southern women with high regard, he answered with a smile, "Ms. Gladys you are correct. I will be ordained on June 7th in my home congregation and then I can officially use the title of Reverend."

And another issue Gladys threw in the mix. "Frank, we know the youth are the future of this church. How will you bring them in?"

Frankie unfolded his hands on the table top as he beamed at Gladys. "Ms. Gladys, that is an excellent question. My wife, Marion, here (patting her on the shoulder next to him) is very good working with youth. She tells the children's story each week in the two churches we serve. We work together in the ministry."

Ignoring Marion's silent presence, Gladys said, her glasses resting on the bridge of her nose, "That's nice, but does your wife play the piano or can she direct the choir?"

Face reddening, Frankie answered, "No those are not her ministerial gifts, but she can lead worship, teach Sunday school, preach, and lead women's groups."

Gladys' only response was a guttural, "Humph." Her right index finger pushed her glasses back up as she glared at Frankie and crossed her arms. Frankie met her gaze, displayed a wide grin, rested his hands in his lap, and waited. A deadly silence hovered in the air. Never had a woman been in a church leadership role (deaconesses did not count) so they did not comprehend the meaning of his words. Inexperienced, Marion kept quiet, her hands similarly folded in her lap.

Finally, hearing no rebuttal, Frankie breathed a sigh of relief, breaking the silence.

"Well, Frankie that is about all we need to know for now. We will be in touch with you about our decision in the next couple of weeks. We appreciate you and your wife coming to interview with us. We've had an interim minister for four years and the church is ready to move on," said Harvey shaking Frankie and Marion's hands.

They flew home into another snowstorm grateful for the temporary reprieve from the bitter cold. Marion chatted all the way back from the airport shivering beside Frankie on the bench seat of their station wagon.

"Frankie, what do ya think they will say? Will they want us? I sure would like to escape winter. I hope the kids are okay at Sheila's house. I'm so nervous. I hope I don't spill the beans to anyone before we know for sure."

Frankie inhaled a drag off his Marlboro and quickly switched the cigarette into his left hand holding the steering wheel. He held up his right palm as it to stop traffic and said to his excited wife, "hold your horses. Don't start counting your chickens before they hatch. If they want us, we'll find out soon enough and if they don't, we'll stay put until we find somewhere else to go."

Marion let out a sigh and said, "Okay. I'll try," she said with a big grin.

She stopped by the beauty shop the next morning on her way to the grocery store to tell Irene about the interview. Luckily, Irene was alone.

Rubbing her hands together, Irene chuckling, said, "That is so cool Marion. I can't wait for you and Frankie to have a fresh start where people want your ministerial gifts."

"Me too," Marion responded nodding up and down.

About two weeks later, Harvey sent the contract to hire the Finch Team, but Marion's name was missing so they telephoned him.

"Harvey, this is Frankie Finch."

Excitedly Harvey answered, "Oh, hello Reverend Finch. We can't wait for you to get here. Did you receive the contract I sent?"

With a sigh, Frankie answered, "Yes, but there is one minor problem with it. Marion's name was left off. We are coming as a team, not just me."

Hedging, clearing his throat, Harvey responded, "Oh, okay. I didn't know that part mattered. Just write her name in and it'll be all good. Right?"

"I guess so, if that is what you want us to do, we will."

Frankie assumed that Harvey would inform the other Board members about the contract wording change, but he did not. He did not enlighten anyone that they were coming as a team and did not inform the Finches that no one knew. The date for ministry to begin was three and a half months away on June 1st.

Session Twenty

"Marion, come on in," said Dr. Weinstein holding open his office door. "I'm sorry I am a little late. My wife needed to remind me of an engagement we are to attend after I finish with clients today."

"Thanks for telling me that," Marion said.

Crinkling up his eyebrows he asked, "Why is that?" Chuckling, Marion said, "Because it makes you more human to know you are not perfect and need to be reminded of things, just like your clients."

Dr. Weinstein winked and said, "Do you want to know something else, Marion?"

"Sure. What?" Marion said.

"As a therapist, I learned I was not perfect a long time ago and sought therapy for myself to keep my issues out of the way of doing my work," he revealed.

"Wow, you even get more respect from me admitting that. I knew there was a reason you seemed to understand this process more than just from sitting in the doctor chair," Marion said.

"So enough about me. This is your session. Whenever you're ready go ahead," he said.

"Let me tell you how we made national headlines," Marion said smiling.

"This oughta be good," Dr. Weinstein said as he chuckled.

Husband and Wife Preaching Team Invade the South

ON THE EVE of Marion's twenty-sixth birthday Harvey, the Board chairperson, and George, a 20 something strapping male parishioner flew into Dayton, rented the U-Haul truck, and headed the to the United Methodist parsonage located three miles outside of Pleasantville. Marion fixed sloppy joes served on paper plates with chips and Coke. All the Finches earthly possessions that could be packed were securely boxed, taped, and stacked in the two-car garage. The furniture sat alone in empty rooms devoid of pictures, toys, or nick knacks. That night they slept on mattresses on the floor. At six a.m. the next morning, they rose to the smell of coffee brewing for the last time in the echoing parsonage.

"Marion, do you have all our important documents in the briefcase?" Frankie yelled to Marion a few steps away in the kitchen. She was pouring coffee into Styrofoam cups as he nervously smoked a cigarette in his office one last time.

The church in South Carolina had nothing against smoking, so he could openly nurse his nicotine addiction. "Frankie, relax. I have it all taken care of," Marion said as peeked her head into the office handing him a cup of Joe.

Sheila, her friend of three years, drove in the driveway with her four kids in tow at 7:00 a.m.

Marion, smiled through tears as she said to her friend, "Wow, Sheila you didn't have to get up this early to see us off."

"I know, but it isn't every day that your best friend moves away and you have a big empty hole in your heart," she said with tears trickling down her nose. "Here is a poem I wrote for you, but don't read it until you are on your way, okay?"

Sniffling, Marion answered, "Okay."

The poem spoke of their various antics together, scrimping to feed their families, laughter over children's mishaps, and shopping for garage sale treasures. Marion kept the poem to this day safely secured in her jewelry box.

As they began loading the truck, Irene showed up with four jars of currant jelly and warm hugs for all.

She directed her comment toward Harvey, pointing her finger at him, "Now you take good care of our preacher and 'preachess' here. If you don't, I'm liable to come to South Carolina and tell you a thing or two," she said laughing.

"Ma'am, I have no intention of displeasing you. If Frankie gets out of hand, I know where to send 'um back to get straightened out," Harvey jested.

Irene tearfully told Marion, "stop sweeping already. I'll make sure it's spotless for the incoming preacher. Get on your way now before I start really blubbering."

After one last hug, Sarah and Adam were fastened in their car seats, much like the trip West to begin the ministry three years earlier. Down to one car because the '72 Vega died the last few weeks of seminary, Marion and Frankie took turns driving their newly acquired '74 Buick Electra while the two church men alternated driving the U-Haul. Marion breathed a sigh of relief as the Ohio border gave way to West Virginia. They drove twelve hours, arriving in Marley at midnight, exhausted, yet relieved to embark on this new adventure.

The brick parsonage sat just ten yards from the Marley First Church sanctuary. It took seconds to walk over to the office compared driving to their two former churches in Ohio. One week into the move south, Marion rinsed off a dinner plate at the kitchen sink and absentmindedly stared out the window, thankful all the pain of Tabatha was behind her. *God please bless this move.* The phone rang and jolted her back to the present.

Picking up the handset she said, "Finch parsonage. How may I help you?"

"This is Chuck Milner from WMBF news. We heard you are doing this new-fangled thing at your church – a husband and wife team approach. Is that correct?"

"Yes, sir, it is."

"So how would you two like to explain your ministry to the Grand Strand Community?"

"Ah, let me get my husband and we can talk about it. Give me just a second."

"Okay, I'll wait," said Chuck.

Covering the receiver Marion turned toward Frankie sitting at the dining room table working a crossword puzzle. "Frankie, come quick." Whispering with a big grin she said, "Channel WMBF News is on the phone. They want to interview us about our ministry. Talk to them."

"Hello, this is Frankie Finch."

"Reverend Finch. I'm sure your wife told you that we would like to interview you live on the midday news and replay it on the six and eleven o'clock slots. Would that be okay with you two?"

"Yes sir, provided we are not cornered into an uncomfortable position to defend what we are doing."

"I can assure you, Reverend Finch we just want to inform the public not question your ministry."

"Okay, then we will do it. When do you want us?" "Tomorrow be at the studio at 11:30 a.m. Make sure you wear dark enough clothing. The cameras can make you appear washed out."

"We'll be there. Thank you."

"See you two tomorrow."

Chuck respectfully asked on-air how they felt called to do the team ministry and how they handled people who believed God does not call women to be preachers. Marion felt comfortable on camera and shared her belief that her call in eleventh grade was just as valid as Frankie's. They educated the viewers about an earlier husband and wife preaching couple in the bible named Priscilla and Aquila. Paul talked about them in Romans Chapter 16.

The local Marley Standard newspaper did a follow up interview. Even though the reporter did not get all the facts accurate, it still provided some welcomed publicity for the church. Other newspapers up and down the eastern seaboard picked up the story and published it. People came, curious to see a woman preacher in action. A few, impressed that the novelty could preach a decent sermon, but left disappointed because she did not put on a dog and pony show. Marion only preached unannounced about once every six weeks, but participated fully in the worship service every Sunday. The Finches did not want people showing up only when she preached or avoiding worship if they knew in advance she would be in the pulpit.

A week into her first official career position, Marion walked over to the church office while the children played in the backyard on the swing set. She could hear their shrieks of laughter. The plum and pear trees offered them opportunities to climb up to see the world from a different height. The chain link fence provided protection from Adam and Sarah wandering out to the street.

"Frankie, look," Marion said waving the paperwork in his face. "I just finished the forms to enroll at Coastal Carolina University. I'm so excited. Do you want me to make us some coffee to celebrate?"

"Whiffles, it's 100 degrees in the shade," he said wiping the sweat off his forehead in the un-air-conditioned office positioned between the baptistry and the restrooms, sitting at the desk he fashioned from an old oak door. "Why don't you walk over to the vending machine at the plaza around the corner and get us an ice-cold Coke or something?"

"Sure, you got some quarters? I'll take the kids with me. They'll love this extra treat."

Marion got a brain freeze from quickly downing the thirst quencher. Adam and Sarah complained about having to share a bottle. They guzzled the contents of the Coke equally poured into paper cups, asking for more. After the celebratory refreshment, Marion headed back to the house to fix grilled cheese sandwiches for lunch.

The family settled into a routine. Marion rose at seven, made the coffee and carried it into the bedroom to Frankie on a tray, as she had since they married. Adam and Sarah slept in until eight and stumbled out into living room to ask permission to watch cartoons.

Marion sat at the dining room table reading her bible. She hugged them and said, "Before any cartoons, you must eat your eggs and grits."

"Mommy, what are grits?" Sarah asked pulling out the wooden chair.

"They're made from corn and it's kinda like cream of wheat only with butter on them," Marion said.

Adam tried them, but spit them out. Sarah, eager to watch Captain Kangaroo, scraped her bowl and asked for more. With the children settled in front of the television Marion walked across the parking lot to the church office.

"Frankie, I don't think I can stay awake another minute. This heat is getting to me. We've been here two weeks, but I'm still not acclimated to this Southern climate. I'm going back over to the parsonage to the air conditioning and try to convince the kids to take a nap with me. Your shirt is soaked with sweat and you've only been wearing it two hours. You're going to have to install an AC wall unit in here or you'll die of heat prostration."

Winking, he looked at her as he said, "Tell you what, Whiffles. I know a way to cool me off. Why don't you get down on your knees and give me a blow job? Then go take your nap."

Frowning at him she said, "Have you lost your mind? This is God's house and not a place for sex. What if a parishioner walked in, how would you explain that?"

"Forget it then. You know I like you to be varietious (he made the word up meaning to have variety in their sex life), imaginative, and spontaneous. If you don't want to please your husband, then that's on you."

"Frankie, I am NOT giving you oral sex in the church period," she said as she walked off toward the door where the children now played out in the church yard.

Marion, in a position of authority and earning respect from the parishioners, felt powerful and began to stand her ground including with Frankie.

Marion went to the local library to get a card. The librarian had her fill out a form. It asked for her husband's name. Marion said, "Where do I put my name? I'm a copastor of a church and need my own card, not my husband's."

The librarian peered over her glasses with a sneer, eyeing Marion from the top of her head down to her fashionable mini skirt. In her southern drawl, Ms.

Wilmont, the librarian, said, looking at the form, "Mrs. Finch, around here we do things the way we've done them for decades. Library cards are issued the way names read in the telephone book. Is your name the one listed in the book?"

"No, it is listed as the church," she said flippantly with her hand on her hip.

"Well, **Mrs.** Finch, if you want a card, it must be as Mrs. Frankie Finch or you won't get one at all."

Marion muttered under her breath that she felt she had stepped back in history fifty years as she walked out conceding to the tradition.

One day a church member came up to Marion after worship and asked her, "What do you do at 'that' time of the month?"

Brow furrowing, she said, "I don't know what you mean. What is that time of the month?"

"You know that woman thing," Mr. Sizemore said in all earnestness, with his arms defensively positioned across his chest.

"Oh. Why? Is that a concern of yours?"

He squared back his shoulders and unclasped his arms pointing toward the front of the church and said, "If you serve communion or preach when having your monthly, you will defile the altar and the pulpit."

Holding back the snicker Marion covered her mouth and asked, "Have you noticed anything yet?"

"No."

She reassured him. "I think we are okay then on this matter." She walked away quickly to avoid laughing in his face.

Marion attended college classes every Tuesday and Thursday from 8:00 a.m. to 9:00 p.m. while Frankie picked the kids up from school, fed and tucked them into bed.

"Hon, have you packed Adam's lunch yet?" Marion asked Frankie when she came home too exhausted to even eat.

"No, I figure since I'm the one doing all the work around here that's the least you could do after you sit in Mickey Mouse classes all day and hang out with single college students. You probably wish you were single too."

"Frankie, I'm too tired to argue with you about any of that. I need some help with my Algebra, if you are willing to do so. It may be easy for you, but it isn't for me. I just want to complete my undergraduate degree, go to seminary, and serve God."

Frankie did not help her with Algebra, nor pack the lunch. She tumbled into bed at 10:30 p.m., serviced Frankie, and drug her weary body to the living room sofa to go over biology notes. At midnight, she slid in beside her snoring spouse only to rise again at 5:30 a.m. to study some more.

Tuesday and Thursday mornings Frankie walked Sarah to preschool two blocks away. Adam rode the school bus to Marley Elementary School. One Friday morning while Marion was sipping on her second cup of coffee at the dining room table just about to open her Algebra textbook, the phone rang. She got up from the table and reached around the corner to the kitchen wall phone. Grasping the receiver, she stretched the cord and sat back down as she answered, "Hello, this is Marion."

"Hello, Mrs. Finch. This is Mrs. Watson, Sarah's preschool teacher."

"Oh, is there something wrong? Did my check not clear?" Marion asked apprehensively.

"No, it is nothing like that. It is just that I wonder the reason Sarah is late every day."

"Late, how late?" she asked puzzled.

"It's only ten minutes, but it is consistent every time."

"Let me get to the bottom of this. I will certainly let you know before next Tuesday.

Marion, walked over to the church office peaking her head in the office door and said to Frankie, "I just got a call from Mrs. Watson at the preschool. She says that Sarah is ten minutes late to school every time. Why is that?" she asked, hand on her hip.

Frankie cleared his throat as he said, not looking at his wife, "Yup, I know. We have something we have to do before we can leave for school."

"And what that might be that is so important to make her late for pre-school? Sarah only goes to school on Tuesdays and Thursdays," she said with both hands on her hips. "

He hemmed and hawed mumbling. "Well, Captain Kangaroo doesn't end until 9:00 a.m. and we leave right after it finishes."

"You're joking, right?" Marion said getting in his face.

"It's only preschool for God's sake. It's no big deal," he said turning his head away from her.

Marion marched back over to the parsonage where Sarah was munching on Cheerios in front of the television.

"Sarah, come here a minute, please," Marion said, patting the sofa cushion beside her.

Cereal crumbs clung to her chin as Sarah asked,

"What mommy?" plunking down beside her mom.

She said brushing a loose curl from Sarah's forehead, "I told your Daddy that you have to be on time for school. No more watching Captain Kangaroo to the end and being late, okay?"

"Mommy, I told Daddy, we need to go or Mrs. Watson will get mad at me."

"Well, I think Daddy understands now so you should be okay."

Smiling Sarah said, "Okay, Mommy."

The next Tuesday Sarah came with something in her hand to show Frankie who was glued to the television screen as Captain Kangaroo was waking up Grandfather Clock. "Whatcha got Sary?" Frankie asked.

"Daddy, I want to go to school now. After school, I'm gonna take us to Anthony's Grill and buy you hot chocolate with my own money. See, I have it right here in my hand," she said opening her fist to display the crumbled-up dollar.

"Sary," he said hugging her. "You don't have to do that. Daddy'll buy it."

"No, Daddy, I want to do it, like a big girl," Sarah said.

She did and Frankie made sure she was on time for school for the rest of the year.

One Monday night carrying an armload of textbooks to study for her midterm spring exams, Marion walked past Frankie sitting at the dining room table, "Can you put Adam and Sarah to bed tonight? I have an exam tomorrow." Marion asked, gingerly anticipating the outcome.

He sat reading the newspaper, smoking a Marlboro, flicking the ashes into the ashtray and said, "NO, I can't. I told you I'm watching the March Madness playoffs tonight. You're so called "university" is a Mickey Mouse school anyway. It won't amount to anything when you graduate. I went to a real university."

After setting her textbooks on the kitchen counter she noisily slammed the kitchen cupboard door as she put away the supper dishes.

The next morning, she groggily rose thirty minutes earlier than normal to study and pack the kids' lunches. She hurriedly looked over her biology note-cards while spreading peanut butter on the bread. As she slid the last sandwich into the baggie, Frankie emerged from the bedroom grabbing a coffee cup from the cup hook before she could bring him his tray into the bedroom. He bellowed, "I have to have the car today to go to a meeting across town at 11 so you'll have to find another way to school. I already asked Betsy down the street to take Sarah to preschool and to pick her. So, you don't have to pack her a lunch. Betsy will feed her."

Determined that she would not allow him to sabotage her education, she put Adam on the bus, buckled Sarah in her car seat, and kissed her daughter good-bye as daddy was locking up the house. Without another word, she got her bike out of the garage muttering curse words under her breath and peddled as fast as she could the eight miles to the University, making it just in time to pass her exam with an A. Unconsciously, she knew his need to control her was why he balked at her schooling.

Maybe when I get this education, I can afford to take care of Sarah and Adam myself. Frankie won't be able to control me anymore. God, please help me make it. I'm so tired.

Nine months into their pastorate, the second week in January, Frankie went off to a church sponsored regional retreat. He came back spouting off all kinds of psychobabble, correcting every comment Marion made.

While the kids splashed in their bathwater, Marion warily approached Frankie reading one of his escape science fiction books at the dining room table. "I think you are different since you came back from the retreat."

Laying down his book he said, "You mean you feel scared that I am acting more in touch with my feelings," he pontificated.

Inhaling to gather the courage to respond she said,

"No, Frankie, I think something happened and you do not want to tell me."

"Well, Miss Smarty Pants, if you had gone, you would know what I experienced, but since you didn't, you can't possibly comprehend it. I'm telling you how I feel," he said as he opened his palms. "I feel happy and confident. Feelings are not thoughts. And you couldn't possibly know my feelings," he said pointing to his chest. "They are mine and mine alone and no matter what you do, you cannot make me feel a certain way."

Confused, she did not know what he meant and said, "I have no idea what you are talking about, but all I know is that you are different." Then she turned her heel to tend to the squabbling urchins in the bathtub.

She knew in her heart Frankie had been unfaithful again. Her sexually transmitted Chlamydia infection, discovered a week later, confirmed it. Again, she felt stuck with nowhere to go and no money. She had not yet completed her education. She wrote in her diary and silently prayed for Divine Intervention.

> God, please help me be a better wife so Frankie will not want anyone else. God, thank you that Frankie told me he loved me today and we had a good day with no arguing at the dinner table. "God, I am so tired trying to keep up with school, church work, the kids, and taking care of Frankie. Please help me pass biology and statistics. Amen.

Eighteen months into the church assignment, Frankie entered the sanctuary as choir rehearsal was about to begin. Carlene, a sixteen-year-old high school junior, approached him, "Hey Pastor Frankie, guess what? I got my grades today and I brought up my Chemistry from a C to a B just like you said I could. Aren't you proud of me?"

"Carlene, I am proud of ya, but you better get to your seat now before Myra shoos me out of the sanctuary so she can start practice."

He swatted her on the backside as she passed him. Carlene shocked, turned and looked at him, but said nothing. Marion witnessed the action and pulled Frankie aside in the fellowship hall.

Grabbing his sleeve, she said, "Frankie, I saw you slap Carlene on the butt. It could get you into trouble."

Defensively, he downplayed it as he lifted her hand off his shirt and said, "You worry too much. It was just a playful swat. It didn't mean anything."

Anxiously wringing her hands Marion said, "Go ahead and try to justify your actions to her parents and the church elders."

Deflecting the issue, Frankie turned the tables as he said, "I swear you are critical of everything I do. Get off my case already."

Marion simmered with rage. His actions could damage their ministry. She slammed the door out of the church and headed across the grass to the parsonage.

The next Wednesday evening as Marion instructed babysitter Susan what bedtime snack to feed Sarah and Adam the front door opened. Parishioner Betsy sauntered in with her three-year-old daughter Caitlyn and squalling eighteen-month-old son, Tommy. She set down the diaper bag next to Susan and said, "Tommy needs his diaper changed," and walked out over to the church meeting. Marion attempted to keep her composure as she spoke to Susan, "I'm sorry, dear. I did not know Betsy was dropping her children off. She did not ask me. I'll make certain you get paid extra."

Susan nodded and turned to break up a fight over a toy. When Marion returned from the meeting all four children were asleep on Marion and Frankie's bed. Tommy had soaked through his diaper onto the sheets. Susan apologized as she tiptoed quietly back into the living room. She had fallen asleep reading to them. When Betsy returned to retrieve her children, she helped herself to a Coke out of the refrigerator. After Betsy carried the sleeping ragamuffins to the car with Frankie's help, Marion gently carried Adam and Sarah to their own beds. As Frankie re-entered the house Marion sat at the dining room table sporting a frown.

"What's the matter, Marion?" Frankie inquired. With tears welling up she put her hands in a prayerful pose and said, "I feel like we live in a fishbowl with a flashing neon sign that reads: 'Open Come on in. Free food and baby-sitting.' There's no respect for our privacy and no responsibility to help cover the cost of a sitter or even ask if it is okay to drop off their children. Since when is it okay for parishioners to help themselves to the contents of our refrigerator without asking? I didn't know this position meant the parsonage was a communal living arrangement."

Frankie stood over her half listening as he lit up a cigarette and said, "What'd ya want me to do about it? I'm afraid to rock the boat right now. Can't you talk to Betsy and tell her how you feel?"

Raising her voice, she said gesturing with her hands, "You know how moody Betsy is. If I approach her about it, she's liable to twist what I say and complain to her Board Chair husband. I guess I need to just pray about it."

Frankie, relieved that he did not have to solve the problem, sat down to watch television to unwind while Marion studied.

That Friday as Frankie pounded out his sermon on the portable typewriter with his two index fingers Bonnie, a young neighborhood woman, peeked her head in the office.

"Hey, Frankie. Can I talk to you about something for a few minutes?"

"Ah, Sure Bonnie, but give me just a second to finish this sentence before the thought escapes me."

"Okay, I'll sit right here on the step while you type," she said as she crossed her legs making her hot pants rise even further up her thigh. Her yellow plaid halter top tightly cinched her small breasts together. She batted her eyelashes as she stared at her nails.

Frankie decided to address her behavior, leaving the office door open. Staring first at her chest and then her crossed legs, Frankie blushed and said, "Bonnie, I know you want to talk to me about something and I am glad to do that, but I have a request first. Would you please dress more modestly when you come to the church? I am a normal male," he said then gesturing with open palms continued, "and seeing you dress so provocatively is distracting," staring at her face trying desperately to not look again at her inviting body.

"Well, that sure takes the cake. My pastor is more interested in my body than what I came to discuss with him," she said as she stormed out of the church.

"Bonnie, wait…" but she was gone.

He told Marion about it thankfully, but they both hoped it would not be brought to the Church Board's attention. Any attempt to discuss something privately with a pastor is always considered a request to be counseled. Not knowing the nature of her request to speak with him, he had to assume it was a private personal matter. Such information was held as a sacred trust not to be divulged whether completed or not.

Bonnie went home and told her husband, Eric, about it. Eric decided the way to handle the pastor being attracted to his wife was to give him something else to look at that would publicly expose Frankie for the pervert he was. Eric paid for a *Playboy* magazine subscription to be sent to the parsonage. Eric began his shame campaign by telling his next-door neighbor, Elder Victor, about the office incident, leaving out his part ordering the magazine subscription. Victor told the church board. The mailman, a friend of Board Chair Harvey, let it slip "accidentally" that Harvey's pastor had *Playboy* delivered to his house. Even though Frankie put it in the trash unread, there was no proof he had not peeked at it before tossing it. Eric's plan was working.

Prior to all this coming to a head, Frankie was asked to lead some groups at the local drug and alcohol treatment center. He did and loved it. They offered him a job as director of the Halfway House. Without consulting the church, he accepted the position, believing he and Marion could handle the work of the church and make some extra money.

"Hello, this is the Finch residence," Marion said.

"Marion, this is Harvey."

"Hello Harvey, what's up? The kids and your wife okay?"

Harvey cleared his throat and said, "They're fine. Thanks for asking. Put Frankie on the phone, please."

"Ah, he's not here, but he'll be home in an hour.

How can I help?" Marion hedged.

"Where he is?" Harvey boldly asked.

"He's volunteering right now. Why do you ask?"

Ignoring her question, he said, "Have him call me when he comes in."

When Frankie walked in the door an hour later, Marion told him immediately, "Harvey called and said you need to call him right away. He wouldn't tell me what it is about, but he asked where you were."

"And.....what'd you tell him?" Frankie asked with raised eyebrows.

"I said you would be home in an hour and that you were volunteering," Marion answered apprehensively, nervously wringing her hands.

Frankie slammed down his car keys on the dining room table and shouted, "You shouldn't have told him that. He has no need to know. My off time is mine to do as I please," Frankie said.

When Frankie talked to Harvey, he tried to engage him in sports chatter, "Did you see how the Hoosiers played last night? I can't believe they're undefeated. I got my fingers crossed that they'll go all the way."

Harvey ignored Frankie's attempt to participate in small talk. "Frankie, we've called a special board meeting for tomorrow night. Both of you be there at 7:00 p.m. sharp."

Frankie's tone turned serious, "What's this meeting all about Harvey?"

Harvey simply said, "We'll discuss it in the meeting. Good night."

He hung up leaving Frankie shaking his head wondering what the crisis was about. He told Marion, to make certain they had a sitter because whatever it was sounded serious.

The next night at 6:58 p.m. Frankie and Marion entered the fellowship hall of the church. The elders were already assembled. They invited Frankie to sit at one end of the table and Marion at the opposite end, the same table of their interview twenty-five months prior.

Chairman Harvey with a stern face said, "Frankie, I think you know why we called you in. There have been some rumors about your inappropriate behavior. We need to get to the bottom of it."

Frankie sat motionless, barely breathing. Marion's stomach began to churn. She thought she would have to dash to the bathroom due to diarrhea. She prayed the whole time, *God, please help us.*

Harvey looked Frankie dead in the eye as he asked, "Did you or did you not slap Carlene on the butt in the sanctuary?"

Wringing his hands Frankie lied with sweat pooling on his moustache, "I most certainly did not."

Marion knew better, but bit her lip to keep quiet.

Elder Victor, turned to face visibly shaking Frankie outlining the next rumor.

"Is it also true that Eric's wife Bonnie came to talk to you and you revealed to her that you were turned on by her outfit?"

Frankie stiffened in his seat. He said authoritatively, "Gentlemen, during my ordination I took a ministerial ethical oath. Based on that, I do not divulge who comes to talk privately with me without that person's permission," he said as his shoulders drooped awaiting what would come next.

Mr. Swanson, the final interrogator, scrunched up his face as he began questioning Frankie about the about the third rumor. Clearing his throat, he began.

"We hear you have been hanging out with drunks."

Letting out a puff of air, Frankie shook his head affirmatively staring intently at Mr. Swanson. "Yes, I have been volunteering to lead some groups at the Drug and Alcohol Halfway House."

"Ah, so you admit that you are doing something that we have not approved in your job description."

"I have volunteered in the evening once a week.

Marion has adequately covered any need in my absence."

"That is all well and good, but that is not all. Is it Mr. Finch?"

"What do you mean by that, Mr. Swanson?"

"We hear you have accepted a job there; is that true?"

With a deep sigh, Frankie laid his hands flat on the top of the table as he said, "I have done what I believe God wanted me to do for this congregation to grow. We have gone from an average of fifty, to a solid eighty people in worship. You want to concentrate only on the needs of this church, but I know we need community involvement to grow. My working at the Halfway House could help with the church's growth. Marion and I can handle the responsibilities. This church can be a real presence in the day to day activities of our city, but you're too afraid to try new methods."

Mr. Swanson continued, "Well, Frankie your contract did not have a clause about outside work. Don't you think you should have come to us first, to ask? Nonetheless, we are past that now. You must decide if you are going to be our pastor or work with drunks. You can't do both. What's it going to be, huh, Frankie?"

Frankie's voice spoke with a hint of sadness as he looked down at his feet, "If those are my only choices, drunks or just being your pastor, I choose the drunks."

With a firm tone, Elder Victor said, "Your contract calls for a sixty-day notice. The notice starts today, right now. We want you out of the parsonage by June 1st. You are hereby immediately relieved of your pastoral duties."

Frankie picked up his bible, muttered under his breath something about ungrateful church people, and slammed the door as he departed.

Everyone turned to look at Marion sitting dumbfounded. What was she supposed to do now?

Elder Thomas broke the silence. "Mrs. Finch, we have no quarrel with your church work."

Inhaling deeply, trying to gather her wits about her, Marion said, "So are you saying I can still be your pastor?"

Elder Watson interrupted before Elder Thomas could respond, "We believe your place is with your husband. You are free to leave."

Leave, just like that? Frankie had once again screwed up their life, their occupation, their reputation and now she was free to go. Free to go where, do what? How was her plan to fulfill God's call to be carried out now by Frankie's continual ungodly behavior? With a heavy heart, she left, thanking the church board for their kind words to her and walked out the door to figure out once again how to feed her family, to finish her education, and what to do about her wayward husband.

The church board did not know about his winter retreat infidelities. Trusting no one, she kept Frankie's indiscretions to herself. She only had speculation and antibiotic receipts. It made no difference now. They were fired.

The day after the termination, Marion returned home from transporting the kids now in kindergarten and second grade to Marley Elementary School. Frankie sat at the dining room table drinking a cup of coffee, smoking a Marlboro, staring out the window. The lateness of the hour the night before, precluded any discussion of the final board meeting.

Marion poured herself a cup of coffee and joined Frankie at the same table she had confronted him at in Ohio about his affair with Tabatha. Nonetheless thrilled now as then, she launched into him. "Frankie, now that you got yourself fired, what are you going to do to about it?" she said as she glared at him with stiffened back.

"What'd you mean, 'I got me fired?' Did you forget we are both fired, Miss High and Mighty?"

Standing up next to him she said, "No, Frankie I was not fired."

"What? So, you're still crazy enough to stay here with these fools who don't know a good thing God sent them?" he said as he raised his voice looking up at her standing over him.

"No, that's not the case. They told me I did nothing wrong. The only reason they are no longer having me is because I am married to you. They believe my place should be with you," she said calmly and sat down across from him.

"Well that's a laugh. So, they don't want the guy who taught you everything you know, but they want the inexperienced, non-seminary graduate to lead them?"

"No, Frankie. I'm not the one who got turned on by Bonnie, or swatted Carlene on the butt, or took a job without checking with the Church Board first," she said smugly.

"Oh, Miss Perfect over here who never does anything wrong, yeah right."

"This is getting us nowhere, Frankie. We have to get real and figure out how we are going to afford to feed the family, pay our bills, etc.," Marion said, bringing them back to the matter at hand.

Frankie calmed down and looked at Marion with softer eyes. He sighed, crushed the butt of his cigarette into the ashtray and said, "Good thing the sale of our Cortland house is about to go through. We've got sixty days til we have to be outta here. That should be enough time to figure all this out."

"Okay, but where are we going to live? Are the kids going to go to the same school? I gotta finish my undergraduate degree so I can go to seminary somewhere. I've only got fifteen more credit hours til I finish. If I take classes year around, I can finish next August. Hmmm…."

Holding up his right palm Frankie said, "Whoa, hang on there, Marion. You always have ta get it all planned out. Why can't you just go with the flow and take it as it comes?"

"Because my dear Hubbles, every time I do, you mess up and get fired, leaving me to figure out how to fix the situation," she defensively said with her arms crossed.

Frankie got up from the table without uttering another word and slammed the front door, headed to the Halfway House Director job which paid only sixty percent of what the church position did.

Marion, although exasperated with her erring husband, focused her attention on completing her B.A. in psychology. Without that she could not support the kids should she decide to leave, but at least she would be closer to her goal.

The more she took psychology courses the more she felt her true calling was to be a pastoral counselor rather a pulpit minister.

With unwavering determination, she would eventually earn a doctorate and set up her own private pastoral counseling practice.

The sixty-day departure notice set the tone for many sleepless nights and long talks after Adam and Sarah fell asleep. Marion rehearsed her speech. Before leaving the bed to study some more, she turned to him in his refractory period after sexually satisfying him and said, "Ya know, Frankie, if you work at the Halfway House for just fifteen months then I can finish my B.A. and we can move to North Carolina for me to go to Duke Seminary to get my M.Div. (with a focus on pastoral ministry). If we move to a new church position now, I probably won't have all my credits transfer and we'd have to wait til we've been residents for a while to get in state tuition. No good church would probably accept us as a team without my degree. I don't want the kids to change schools again so soon anyway. What do ya say, huh Hubbles? Can we please stay?"

He did not object, probably because he was half asleep during the first sentence of her speech.

Session Twenty-One

"Dr. Weinstein, can we talk for a minute before I begin telling you the next segment of my life?"

"Certainly, Marion. What do you want to discuss?" Dr. Weinstein asked his client of five months.

"How is it that people can function under such duress and not crumble?" Marion asked.

"Well, when the 'fight or flight' mode kicks in, the person gets an adrenal rush which can carry them through the crisis. They often crash after it is all over when the catecholamine stress hormones do damage to their heart or other body parts."

"Wow, I always wondered how I knew to function during the crisis in the moment, but afterward I would feel drained and would often get sick physically. That helps. Thank you."

"My pleasure, Marion. Are you ready to embark on the next leg of your healing journey?" Dr. Weinstein asked.

"More than ever. Today I am going to talk about survival against insurmountable odds," she said.

"Marion, I am going to continue to take notes of the salient points of your story. Someday I will combine them into a document for you to review your therapy with me. Would that be okay?"

"Yes, I would like to read your objective viewpoint, but I think I will wait until I am further along in my own observations, if you don't mind?" Marion said.

"I agree wholeheartedly, Marion. Let's proceed," said Dr. Weinstein.

Diverted Direction

"FRANKIE, I'M SO happy we are staying in Marley for me to finish my degree," Marion said two months later as they unpacked boxes in their new four-bedroom, fourteen hundred square foot, two-bath, brick home in the lower middle income, south side neighborhood. "I'm sure you'll make it worth my while," he said winking at her and patting her on the behind.

"Careful Mister, that kinda action could get you fired," she playfully jested.

"Fired up for some afternoon delight, is more like it," he teased.

Marion finished her B.A. in Psychology in August the next year. Prior to completion of her coursework she began hemorrhaging. The ceremony for summer graduation was not held until December. Marion had no desire to walk across the stage. She just wanted the diploma delivered to her mailbox carefully rolled up in the cylinder, proof so she could move on to the next degree. Instead of celebrating she prepared to enter the hospital for a partial hysterectomy on August 13th. Her recovery was long and slow. The pelvic pain was unrelenting even after the healing from the surgery. Her gynecologist kept reassuring her that she would feel better in time. She hoped he was correct, but doubted it.

Accepted to enter Duke Theological Seminary starting in August of the next year, they had adequate time to secure a co-pastorate position in North Carolina, except for one small problem. The Regional Minister, equivalent to a United Methodist Bishop, had to endorse the couple so that Frankie and Marion could circulate their papers to churches seeking pastors. The Regional Minister, Gage Jamison, refused to endorse them based on the accusations of Frankie's behavior with church women.

God, now what do I do? I know you want me to be in the ministry, but Frankie's behavior makes it impossible for us to be hired by a church in North Carolina. I'm not commuting every week to stay on the Duke Seminary campus while Frankie is left in Marley to care for the kids. I can't trust him to be faithful to me for the three years. Have you got another idea?

She sadly contacted Duke to say she would not be matriculating in the fall. With a heavy heart, she prayerfully sought God's new direction in her backyard glider much like sitting down on the boardwalk at the water's edge on Mackinac Island.

Like Frankie, Marion, went to work for the Alcohol and Drug Commission part-time. She counseled DUI and Employee Assistance clients. Working half-time with no benefits, she took on additional employment. She became an adjunct instructor at the local college teaching psychology, economics, and public speaking.

Marion walked into in the Halfway House dining room after finishing up with a client.

She smiled as the kids ate cookies and drank some milk at the table with one of the residents. "Hey, Sarah and Adam. How was school today?"

"Fine, Mommy, but Adam pushed me out of the way when I tried to mash the button on the crosswalk pole."

Hugging her daughter, Marion said to Sarah, "Sary, when you get a little bit older, you can walk the two blocks by yourself to the Halfway House, but until then brother is supposed to make sure you get here safely, okay?"

Adam pointed to his sister and said, "Told ya. Ha ha."

Marion chastised him, "Stop it Adam. Sarah will be soon ready to cross herself."

Sighing Sarah pleaded, "When will I be big enough?"

"Soon, too soon," Marion whispered under her breath.

One evening just after Marion tucked Adam and Sarah into bed, the phone rang. Marion got up wearily from the couch answering the white wall phone in the kitchen.

"Hello, this is the Finch residence."

In between muffled tears Marion could hear a faint voice, "John threatened to kill me. I got out of the house with only my purse. Can I come over?"

"Oh, my goodness, of course, Peggy," said Marion to the woman she befriended while they co-pastored the Marley church.

She stayed with the Finches for the weekend nervously biting her fingernails and pacing in the backyard.

After Marion delivered the kids to school on Monday Peggy sat at the kitchen table staring off into space, the coffee in her cup long cold.

"You okay, Peggy?" Marion inquired, placing the palm of her hand on Peggy's shoulder.

Letting out a huge sigh Peggy responded, "I need some of my clothes. Do you think the police would escort me to my apartment to get some?"

"I think so, but is it safe, Peggy? You know, John threatened to kill you."

"Ya, but usually after three days he calms down."

Marion called for the police escort with no knowledge of the protocol for domestic violence situations. She agreed to accompany Peggy.

It took the police twenty minutes to arrive as Marion sat in the car with Peggy downstairs outside her apartment. As Peggy unlocked the door, the police glanced into the apartment to see if John was visible. Peggy called his name. No answer.

Marion stepped cautiously into the living room with Peggy trailing a footstep behind her. The sound of a bottle being set down on the kitchen table could be clearly heard. Marion nervously inched toward the kitchen. As she rounded the corner, inebriated John swung a machete six inches from her face.

Marion screamed as the officers peered into the apartment from the doorway and asked, "Are you okay Mrs. Finch?"

Breathing erratically, Marion jumped back almost knocking Peggy over and said pointing toward John, "Aren't you going to arrest him?"

The deputy, hand on his holster, breathed a sigh of relief and said, "No, we are not. No crime was committed."

Marion faced the policemen, eyes wide, as she asked incredulously, "Are you kidding me? If he had slashed me, would you have then come in and arrested him?"

"Yes, ma'am. We would've," the officer said as he eyeballed Peggy. She went to get her things down the hall. John slumped in the kitchen chair and cursed his wife, too drunk to mobilize. Marion watched him turn the vodka bottle upside down to swallow the last drop.

Marion positioned herself near the front door with one eye on the kitchen opening and one down the hallway where Peggy had disappeared into the master bedroom to collect her possessions.

After safely securing some of her clothing, Peggy exited the apartment complex with Marion, under the watchful eye of the policemen. Marion guided Peggy, obviously still shaking, into the passenger's seat of her car. Marion chased after the men as they headed toward the squad car.

"Hey, wait a minute," she implored. Risking inciting the officer's anger, she defiantly asked with palms outstretched, "Can you please explain to me why you did not come in and arrest John? I just don't get why you allow men to abuse women and do nothing to stop it."

Officer Smith, the taller of the two, quiet until this point turned with his hand on the door handle and answered her curtly, "Ma'am if you want to understand it, talk it over with the Chief. We just follow the law and carry out our orders." With that he opened the car door, slid into the driver's seat beside his buckled partner, put the car in gear, and sped off.

Marion stood speechless, replaying how she could have lost her life and they stood by and did absolutely nothing! Enraged, she took the policemen's suggestion and visited Chief Daniels the next day.

Marion stood at the reception desk of the Marley City Police Department and said to the receptionist reading some report behind the bulletproof glass, "Excuse, me."

The woman in her late forties dressed in a pale blue polyester leisure suit stopped chewing her wad of gum long enough to look up. "Can I help you?" She asked annoyed while she cracked her gum.

"Yes, Ma'am. I'd like to speak to Chief Daniels, please," she said.

"Do you have an appointment?" Ms. Gum Cracker asked.

"No, I don't," Marion said exasperated, "but I'm certain he'll see me cause his officer last night told me to come."

"Oh, so are you bailing someone out of jail? If so, the Chief doesn't handle any of that, you'll have to go to the door on the other side of the building," she said picking her report back up.

Irritated, Marion persisted lowering her voice an octave, "Will you *please* just tell the Chief that Mrs. Finch would like to talk to him and see what he says?"

"All right, all ready," she said slamming the report down. "You don't have to get snippy with me. I'm only doing my job for Christ's sake," she said as she backed her swivel stool out from the countertop.

Marion paced in the waiting area. *God what should I say? What if he dismisses me without a glance? Please guide my steps and words and forgive me for being so short with the receptionist.*

The receptionist returned. "Well, today's your lucky day. The Chief is making time to see you."

The pink steel door buzzed as the impertinent receptionist held it open for Marion to enter the inner sanctum. Silently seething, the receptionist pointed to the door at the end of the hall bearing the Chief Daniels name plate.

"Thank you, Ma'am." Marion said as she confidently strode toward the open door.

Chief Daniels looked up over his reading glasses balanced on his nose and said, "Sit down, Mrs. Finch. I've been expecting you. Officer Smith told me you have questions."

"You're darn right I do. I can't understand why you allow violence against women to continue and don't interrupt it until it's too late," she said sitting on the edge of her seat.

Chief tried to explain. "According to the English Common Law, a home is a man's castle. Unless a crime is committed in our presence or we are invited in, we cannot enter. We figured if you were foolish enough to go in, then you were responsible for whatever might happen to you. Our officers are trained to delay entering domestic violence situations. It has the highest rate of officer causalities."

Breathing out a puff of air, Marion said, "I'm glad I know this, but I wish I knew it sooner. There must be somewhere this woman can safely go, right? A shelter or something."

"To be honest we don't have anything like that. Most women go back anyway," said Chief Daniels looking her straight in the eye, shaking his head. "If you would like to start something, we'll support you."

Marion vowed that day to create something for such situations. She formed an Ad Hoc Advisory Committee with some influential town folk. She persuaded a sociology professor, a physician's wife, a school psychologist, a retired United Methodist minister, the head of the local Hotline, and an attorney to share their expertise, thoughts and ideas.

Wiping her hands on her apron adorned with juicy strawberries of various sizes, Marion answered the phone. "Hey, Dr. Chris. What's up?" Marion asked.

"How fast can you get to the ER? I got a woman here who has a concussion and broken arm, compliments of her irate husband. You gotta get her to safety, outta town, before he finds her and finishes the job."

"I can be there in twenty minutes. Will that be soon enough?"

"Ya. When you get to the front desk tell them to page me and I'll come get you. Ms. White is securely hidden in a locked room at the end of the main ER hallway. I'll have you pull around to the back exit. Don't tell me where ya take 'er, so if her husband comes a looking, I can truly say I don't know."

"Got it."

Using a pre-arranged system, Marion passed the woman off to a trained volunteer who drove her to the women's shelter in Jacksonville, Florida. Marion personally smuggled one terrified woman out of town in the middle of the night to a shelter in Lumberton, N.C., using one of the Ad Hoc Committee member's car. Hiding the woman in Marion and Frankie's house became too risky after three days for fear that the alleged Mafia connected husband would find her.

The Committee appointed Marion the first executive director of the Women's Safe House (WSH) in the town of Marley. Part of her job description involved talking to women in court to offer them counseling services and then following up with them in her office.

One cold January morning a man showed up at the Halfway House seeking Marion. The resident had no idea who he was or what he wanted so the resident just pointed to the back stairs. Marion had a one room office over the outpatient counseling reception room. The stranger knocked on the door. Marion opened it, surprised to see it was not one of the residents.

He pushed past Marion and shut the door, blocking the exit with his back. He growled, "Where's my wife?"

Marion, senses heightening, thought quickly. There was no panic button. She could not reach the phone across the room. She had to think ahead of this angry man.

Extending her hand, she said, "Hello, I'm Marion and what is your name?"

"You know damn well who I am and I demand to know where you're hiding my wife, Mary Peabody," he said slamming his fist into his palm.

"Well, Mr. Peabody, right? Let's sit down and talk a minute," edging closer to the desk where the phone and a chair sat."

Mr. Peabody was not leaving until he had some answers. Marion honestly did not know where she had been transported, so she did not need to lie.

"When is the last time you saw your wife?" Marion asked stalling for time.

"Last night right before she left the house without so much as her coat," Mr. Peabody said in all earnestness.

"Well, Mr. Peabody," she said unfolding her hands on top of the desk. "I have not seen your wife. Have you checked the hospitals or with the police?" knowing full well she was probably safely escorted far away from him by now.

Abruptly standing up he yelled, "I ain't calling no pig. They don't like me. They try to tell me how to run my marriage. I don't need no damn law telling me what I can and can't do in my own home. They got no idea how crazy my ole lady is. She's probably run off with the mailman or sumthing. I saw her making eyes at him last week when she thought I was at work."

"Well, Mr. Peabody. I'm sorry I can't help you.

Do you have someone you can call?" She gingerly asked.

Leaning over the desk he grabbed Marion's wrists and held on tight as he said, "Listen here Missy, if I find out that you know where my wife is, I'll track you down and if you got kids, you'll never see um again. You got that?" he said raising one eyebrow.

Gently removing her wrist from his grasp, she said, "Now Mr. Peabody there's no reason to get angry. I'm sure you'll find out about her soon."

He let go and got up walking toward the door and stopped. "Don't forget what I said," he said pointing his finger at her. "I'll find where you live."

As soon as he was on the other side of the door, Marion locked it and sat down shaking from head-to-toe. It took a few minutes before her wobbly legs could carry her downstairs to Frankie's office.

When she knocked on his closed door, he responded, "Door's open."

She entered the room and saw him at his desk writing up session notes. Looking up frowning he asked, "What'd ya want?" He scolded. "I'm kinda busy here."

She walked over next to his desk and said putting her trembling hand on his shoulder, "I just got threatened, our kids will be kidnapped if I don't tell this guy where his wife is. Luckily, I don't know where she went."

Ignoring her obvious physical reaction, he kept writing as he said, "What'd you expect, meddling in these guys' lives? All they want is for their woman to obey them and then he'll probably treat her like a queen. And what the hell do you think you're doing, endangering the lives of these residents, huh, Marion?"

"I had no idea that any abusive husband would find out where I am. I'm just trying to get these women to safety, away from the violence," Marion responded hoping he'd hug her or tell her he'd protect her from the big bad guys.

"You know yourself that these women go back. These couples are so caught up in the cycle of abuse, that neither one wants out. Besides, these women egg it on, the broads want ta get laid, sit home and eat bonbons, and watch soaps all day. I can relate to these guys blowing up at their wives who don't respect or obey them, just like someone we know," pointing at Marion, cocking his head to the side. "Now get outta here (gesturing with his right arm), so I can tend to what I get paid to do."

Marion backed out of the office fuming, muttering under her breath, "Yah, well you're no picnic to live with either Mr. Halfway House Director." She marched over to the executive director's office. When he heard her plea, he installed a call button that afternoon.

That night at the weekly Halfway House household issues' meeting Marion stood up. "Men, I need you to understand the importance of keeping my office a secret. Someone came in today looking for his wife. He was extremely angry and would have done me harm, if he thought I knew. Here is the phone number to give any male who walks in asking for information about his wife," she said waving an index card. "I'm pinning it to the bulletin board. Write the number down on this tablet that I'll leave on the dining room buffet. Then escort whomever out of the building and come tell me. I don't want you, me or their wife killed. Thank you."

She sat down. Ronnie spoke up. "Marion, we sure don't want anything to happen to you. We'll beat up this the guy up for you. All ya gotta do is tell us where to find him."

"Ronnie, thank you, but that will not solve the problem. I now have a panic button installed upstairs under my desk. It will buzz in Frankie's office. If you hear it and Frankie is away from his desk, go find him or two of you can come upstairs immediately. Open the door without knocking. Thank you."

"Sure, thing. Ms. Marion. We can do that for you," said Ronnie.

One memorable day, functioning in her executive director position of WSH preparing for an evening wine and cheese fundraiser for the shelter, she busily gathered all the supplies needed for the event. She dropped off the plates, cups, napkins, and silent auction items to the Triple Crown Apartment Complex Community Room they rented.

She smoothed the last wrinkle on the yellow plastic tablecloth with her fingers and said, *Okay, I think that's it. Now what have I forgotten? Oh, crap* (she slapped her forehead), *I haven't eaten all day. I totally lost track of the time. I guess the twelve kinds of wine and cheeses will be my supper.*

Being an election year, politicians running for Congress welcomed the invitation to the fundraiser. Marion had no recollection the next day of who she promised to vote for, nor how she drove home afterward with a wine glass in hand. The quantity of alcohol she consumed on an empty stomach while still apparently, functioning, was proof of her alcohol tolerance. Her forgetfulness of promises made was indicative of an alcohol problem that she ignored.

Marion's efforts combined with the Ad Hoc Committee paid off. By the end of 1982 the United Way funded the shelter and counseling center.

Marion proudly listed Executive Director on her resume, but thankfully turned over the reins to Charlotte, the wife of their physician friend, Chris, soon after Mr. Peabody's threat. Marion later realized she did not miss the hob knobbing to garner support for the shelter.

Marion expected her physical health to improve when the stress of the Executive Director position ended, but it did not. Six months after she turned the reins over to Charlotte, in desperation, she saw her gynecologist.

Redressed after her internal exam Marion walked across the hall to Dr. Johnson's office. She sat in the red leather chair as he wrote something on a prescription pad.

She timidly asked, "Dr. Johnson, you did my hysterectomy almost three years ago, and I still have pain. What's wrong with me?"

Looking up at her he said with compassion, "I always wondered why your bladder was beat red when I did your surgery. I think it's time for me to send you to see urologist, Dr. Howe, my colleague. Perhaps he can answer why you keep getting recurrent urinary infections," he said handing her what he had written.

After multiple tests and failed medication interventions, Dr. Howe decided to do an outpatient bladder biopsy procedure. Marion, sent home after the procedure, had to be admitted two days later due to complications and spent two weeks hospitalized recovering. Frankie resented solo parenthood. He played on a church softball team at the time and injured his right ankle. He hobbled on crutches, like Marion did after their car accident thirteen years earlier. Children under twelve were not allowed to visit in the hospital for fear of spreading germs. One evening Frankie snuck the kids up the back stairway painfully jumping up each step.

Nurse Meagan entered Marion's hospital room to administer the nightly dose of Codeine to help her sleep and ease the pain of her swollen abdomen. Glaring at Frankie, pointing toward the door, the nurse said, "Children are not allowed to visit. Get them out of here now!"

"These children have not seen their mother in days. They're scared. They'll only stay for a few minutes, I promise," said Frankie.

"Fine," she said, "but make sure you take them back down those same stairs you snuck them up on, or I could be fired."

"I will. I promise. Thank you."

The nurse softly closed the door as she left to tend to her next patient. The children sat on the foot of Marion's bed and Sarah asked, "Mommy, when are you coming home? I miss you. Daddy doesn't know how to do my hair right and Adam is picking on me all the time saying you're never coming home."

Marion tried to sit up with her swollen belly, heavily medicated brain, and weakened spirit.

"Sary, Momma loves you and I'm coming home just as soon as I can. Adam, stop telling your sister lies and I love you too. Frankie, as much as I want to see the kids, please don't get caught with them up here and get you thrown out for good. Give momma a kiss and I'll talk to you tomorrow."

As they snuck back out, Marion wept. She missed her kids, was in tremendous pain and did not know what was wrong with her. Was she dying? No one had explained any of it to her. Never had – years of medical complications eroded her trust in doctors because no one had properly diagnosed her condition.

Dr. Howe sat down, like her children did, on the end of her hospital bed that Sunday night after rounds and said, patting her leg through the blanket, "Marion, you are one very sick woman. You have gastritis right now, but your bladder had almost completely shut down when you came in through the ER. You were going into uremic poisoning. With this condition, you cannot drink alcohol or caffeine."

Ignoring him she asked, "What exactly do I have?"

"You have a disease of the bladder called Interstitial Cystitis or IC. It is like arthritis of the bladder. It causes it to shrink and harden. You will need ongoing treatment to keep it open and working."

Her voice rose shakily as she tried to reason with him. "Dr. Howe, I need my coffee to get through the day. How can I make it without it?"

"You have been here a week already and not had any, so you are pretty much through the detox from the caffeine."

"Is the caffeine withdrawal the cause of my horrific headache?" She asked as she stroked her forehead.

"Yes. There is another thing Marion, I need to discuss with you."

She interrupted before he could continue, "Oh, okay, but first tell me, is this IC fatal?"

Inhaling before answering he spoke like a caring parent. "No, but it is something you will have to adjust your lifestyle to cope with. There is something else we need to talk about."

Hesitantly she asked, as she raised her palms from under the hospital sheets, "What?"

"When we ran your blood work for surgery, you had a pretty high blood alcohol content."

Defensively she said, "Yeah, so?"

"Well, your elevated blood alcohol content, combined with the anesthetic, made your blood pressure so low we had trouble waking you up. Marion, with this disease you can't drink alcohol. It aggravates it and makes the pain worse."

With tears sliding down her cheeks she said, "I was only trying to deal with the pain of it all."

Patting her on the wrist he said, "I know, but it does not help. I can give you something for pain and the nausea, but you can't drink on top of it."

Letting out a deep sigh she said, "Okay."

After he left she contemplated what he said. *My friends and I either get together to drink coffee or we discuss the world's problems over a bottle of wine. I don't feel like I fit in anywhere. Now this is just one more thing to set me apart from others. I'll bet they won't want to be around me, if I can't join in their fun. Curse IC,* she said as the tears drenched her starched pillow case.

Her first week in the hospital she spent in and out of consciousness with continuous diarrhea. The second week she begged to go home.

Sitting up to show she felt better, she asked, "Dr. Howe, can I please go home? It's my birthday tomorrow and I want to be with my family blowing out my candles, not here!"

All the next day she moped, hoping the nurse would walk in with discharge papers. No such luck. Dr. Howe sent his physician's assistant to see her on rounds that day. She felt he was deliberately avoiding her on her birthday. PA Greg said, "Marion, you still are not emptying your bladder enough to have the catheter out. We'll see how you are in the morning, okay?"

She tearfully said, "okay."

At 5:30 p.m. the dietary services worker knocked on her closed hospital room door.

"Come on in," she said hoping it was someone coming in to cheer her up.

The employee, a black female with one gold front tooth, smiled as she carried in the tray.

"I hear someone's got a birthday today," she said, presenting a cupcake on the tray.

Tears welled up, knowing that someone remembered and showed compassion. She almost hugged the woman. Seeing no candle, she asked like an expectant child, "Is there a candle too?"

"Oh, yeah. Matches aren't allowed in patient's rooms, but I just so happen to have a lighter and candle in my pocket for such celebrations and smokes on my break," she said grinning.

Adam and Sarah had baseball practice that night so Frankie said they could not come wish her a happy birthday. The hospital switchboard was closed by the time they ate and got ready for bed. Marion called on the hospital room phone, but the kids were already asleep. Frankie promised to make it up to her when she got home.

The next day, Frankie's secretary, Connie, finally showed up to take Marion home.

"Hi, Connie. Where's Frankie? I thought he was taking me home," she said with eyes heavy with both emotional and physical pain.

"I dunno know, Marion. Frankie just asked me to come get you on my lunch hour and to bring back lunch to him, so I am."

As Marion agonizingly climbed the three front porch steps to enter the house, Connie held the door open for her. As soon as she plunked down on the couch inside the door, she raised her feet to elevate them with one of the orange and brown throw pillows. She quickly dozed off, too tired to care about anything at that moment. About every forty-five minutes she painfully rose to use the restroom. The bladder spasms wracked her whole body as she doubled over in pain screaming.

At 5:20 p.m. Marion heard the blue Pinto station wagon pull into the driveway. Frankie bellowed, "Sary, come back here and get your bookbag and lunch box out of the car. Adam help her. You know I can't carry it all with these crutches," he said as he waved one in the air balancing on his good foot.

As Frankie hobbled up the steps he precariously held the screen door open and shooed the kids inside. They dropped their belongings on the floor beside the end table just inside the door. Frankie leaned on the door frame peeking his head into the room as Marion lay on the couch pale in a fetal position.

Frankie declared without even a hello, "I've had these kids by myself for two weeks. I'm going to the baseball game with Connie. I'll be back later," and he exited out the door before she could reply.

Marion's heart sank. Was he starting another relationship right under her nose? Marion could not stand up on her own or lift any weight. There was no fight in her. Like when she was a child being ignored by her mom when sick, she felt abandoned again when she needed him most.

She laid on the floor and played a board game with Sarah. This now ten-year-old had resentfully assumed the household responsibility of cooking supper each night during Marion's hospitalization and afterward.

A couple of weeks into Marion's recuperation Rhonda called.

"Guess what Sis?"

Marion, barely able to function had no energy to get excited about any surprise in a monotone said, "What?"

"I can come to help out. My boss at the State Natural Rivers Division says he can manage without me for a week. How long does it take to get there?"

Using every ounce of strength Marion could muster she answered, "Ah, let me ask Frankie. My brain isn't functioning on all cylinders right now." She handed the phone to Frankie and he wrote down Rhonda's travel details. That week Rhonda catered to the needs of Adam and Sarah. She took them to the park, the library, and out for ice cream. Marion could rest and take some heavy-duty pain killers without worry about being unavailable to ten year-old-Sarah and twelve-year-old Adam. Frankie stayed late at the office and hung out with the halfway house residents playing cards after hours.

Within a month, Marion determined she had to fight to be able to get out from under Frankie's control and continual emotional abandonment. She gingerly forced herself to eat better, avoid caffeine, and think about how, with more education, maybe she could combat his abusive hold on her.

Contemplating her options and hoping to prove Dr. Howe wrong, she opened the china closet.

"Darn, the only alcohol left is some Kahlua. Well, since Frankie's facilitating the group tonight while Jerry's on vacation, I'll just finish this up."

Brewing the coffee, she anticipated the sweet taste she remembered. Sipping on the liquid in her Irish Coffee mug she felt smug. *I guess Dr. Howe doesn't know everything.* About ten minutes into her libation, her bladder started to spasm. She laced her arms around her belly as she heaved into the commode. Next, she lay on the floor writhing in pain.

Oh, dear God. What have I done? I can't live in this much pain. If I have to live like this, please take me.

Clearer than any human speaking to her Marion heard, "My dear child. I will take you, if you wish, or I'll help you fight this. It is your choice."

God, if you'll help me, then I will try to fight this. Just then Sarah came in to use the bathroom. Frightened she asked, "Mommy what's wrong? Get up!"

Not hiding her tears, Marion said, "Sary, mommy can't get up. Can you get your brother please?"

Face ashen, the two traumatized children helped get mom to the sofa by the front door. Adam ran to a neighbor's house to get help. The neighbor, Linda handed the long-corded kitchen phone to the couch for Marion to call Dr. Chris.

"Chris, something's really wrong. I took a few sips of some Kahlua and now I'm in excruciating pain, vomiting, and can't stand up. What do I need to do?"

Afraid to incur Frankie's wrath for drinking, she instead called friend Rosemary, to drive her to the ER. The kids stayed at the neighbor's house until Frankie got home. After a Talwin injection for pain and Phenergan for nausea she was doped up enough for Rosemary to bring her back home. She slept peacefully for twelve hours while Frankie angrily tended to the children again.

Since I can't drink any more how am I going to deal with the pain of this IC disease? I better find some way to distract me. If I stay sick too long Frankie may find someone to replace me. I know! I'll go back to school to get my Master's. That way I can support myself and the kids, if I need to. Lord, I know I don't ever want to do ministry with Frankie again. He's too controlling. God, I have really enjoyed counseling with clients. I feel called to do that. Being a pastoral counselor still fills my call to the ministry, right? If I am right, will you please direct me?

Babysitter to the kids, Lindsey worked part-time at the Drug and Alcohol Commission and had a Masters of Social Work. She suggested Marion apply to the School of Social Work in Wilmington, NC. She did and was accepted to begin the fall semester just two months after getting out of the hospital while still barely functional due to an inflamed bladder and frequent urination with ureteral spasms.

Session Twenty-Two

"I know now how courageous I was amid being terrified, Dr. Weinstein. I'm beginning to see God was there even when I could not sense it. It is like the poem that talks about Christ carrying the person with only one set of footprints visible in the sand," Marion said.

"Ah, yes. Feeling alone while being supported underneath. It is mysterious how God is there even when we do not recognize it. I'm glad you do see now that you were not alone," Dr. Weinstein said.

"Another thing I am noticing, Dr. Weinstein. I see now how God brought me to you, to help me sort all this out."

"Thank you, Marion. I believe every patient is sent to me by God, and that I must treat the person as the priceless gift they are. I am grateful you see that through me. It is a privilege to work with you. It is a sacred journey. Are you ready to open the next chapter?"

"Yes, sir," Marion said affirmatively.

The Poverty Escape Route

THE FIRST WEEK in December of 1984, Frankie leaned over Marion and turned off the light as she sat up in bed reading Yaalom's textbook on *Group Dynamics*.

"Hey, why'd you do that? I was studying," Marion said angrily.

"Cause, I'm ready for you to pleasure me," Frankie said raising her nightgown over her head.

She learned it was fruitless to fight him off. Six minutes of pleasure for him and she could go out to the living room and read some more. As she redonned her nightgown and slid her toes into her fuzzy pink slippers Frankie sleepily murmured, "Oh, by the way. I decided you can come to the Asheville Christian Retreat with me next month."

Marion said nothing. She walked out to the living room and sat on the same sofa she curled up on after her hospitalization to ponder what he announced. *Why is he now after six years saying I can go with him? Does he think I'll keep him from cheating on me or that I'll find someone to sleep with so he won't be the only adulterer. I know he's had a "Same Time Next Year" relationship with Tina. I wonder if maybe she's not coming. If I say I won't go, he'll probably tell me that it gives him freedom to sleep with whomever he wants. God, I'm trying to be the 'good wife', but this is asking too much of me. Please help.*

She knew of his relationship with Tina because she read some of a letter he had written left on the desk, much like his diary when he proposed to her. It said, "I sure enjoyed 'our time' together last week. You taught me some new moves. Can't wait to take it to the next level at the retreat next year. Frankie, your 'same time next year' Guy."

It's no good to tell him I found it. Every time I've tried to speak up what does it get me? Nothing, only him angry, saying, 'so if you're so unhappy go ahead and leave, but I get kids. Lord knows you can't support 'um and you're always sick. No judge would award them to you.' Was he right? I can't afford to raise them yet, but by God, I will find a way, if I have to. Maybe this retreat will help our marriage.

She tried to block it all out, but each year after his return her sexually transmitted infections made it all real. Frankie even went to see Dr. Howe. He told him to prophylactically (as a preventative) take an antibiotic before he went on the retreat. Apparently, Frankie had the infection so long it was in his tissues according to Dr. Howe so that although he had no active symptoms, he could still transmit it. Perhaps he sexually contracted a new type of infection that the preventative antibiotic did not treat since Marion continued to acquire new infections after his annual retreat. Was Dr. Howe condoning Frankie's behavior? She did not know whom to trust anymore.

Before embarking on the four-hour drive to the Asheville Christian Retreat Center, Frankie stopped at the liquor store on Highway 17 just outside the Marley City limits to pick up a jug of Jack Daniels and four different bottles of wine.

As they neared Frankie's "long-anticipated" destination, he turned to Marion, dozing fretfully beside him on the front seat and said, "Ya, know what, Marion?"

She opened first one eye then the other, not fully alert. "What? I was cat napping."

Frankie, said, "I'm faithful to you fifty-one weeks out of the year. This is my one week of freedom. If you don't like it, leave, but know that I get the kids."

As if in slow motion, his stinging words took root. She could feel herself sinking into the quicksand again. She thought about jumping out of the moving car. One hundred miles from home, no money to get a bus ticket, no change to even call someone to come get her, and no one to even call if she could. What choice did she have? She responded with silence. He knew she had no means to leave.

Tina spotted Frankie in the reception area, came over and planted a wet kiss on his left cheek. Frankie, stood back. He responded, "Tina, I would like you to meet my wife, Marion."

Déjà vu to Gigi in O'Malley's Bar years before, Tina was not prepared to meet Marion.

Marion forced a crooked smile and squeaked out the words with her body trembling, "Nice to meet you, Tina."

Tina's body stiffened. She scowled at Frankie and said unconvincingly to Marion, "ya, you too."

Tina believed Frankie's lie that he was in an open marriage. Tina did not know if that meant there would be no fun time for her and Frankie alone this week while Marion sampled other wares, or did Frankie expect a threesome.

After supper, walking back to their room, Marion asked Frankie, "I'm going to call and check on the kids at Connie's house. Do you want to talk to them?"

Frankie, well on his way to being totally intoxicated, told Marion, "Naw, you do that. I'm going to visit Tina. I'll be back after while." Without another word, he sauntered off, leaving Marion emotionally kicked in the gut, out of breath, standing in the hallway.

She did not want him to go, but feared he would physically attack her if she tried to stop him, or worse yet send her home where she could not observe or interrupt his behavior and where she had no resources.

Catatonic, with her room key in her hand she stood. *God, what am I going to do? If I anger him, he could convince Director Green to fire me on some trumped-up work issue. I don't have any other job any more. I'm stuck. I can't afford to support my kids on my own until at least I finish my Masters program. I don't have any money to move out. He could convince a judge that I'm emotionally unstable so he'd get the kids. I need to hear Sarah and Adam's voice. It'll ground me. But, on the other hand, I can't call the kids like this and Connie would pick up on something being wrong. For all I know Frankie's screwing Connie too. I feel so all alone. God, where are you?*

She began to shake, fumbling to insert the key in the hole to unlock her room. The image of Frankie screwing Tina flooded her mind. No amount of shaking could wake her from this nightmare or alter it.

The Emergency Room abandonment nine years earlier flashed in her mind. Plopping down on the bed the words tumbled out, "I can't control my husband. He's even screwing Tina right under my nose and I can't do a damn thing about it. I can't live like this. I am NOT going to live another minute in this quicksand. I'm going to get out," she said pounding her fist on the pillow.

Gathering the sheet in her hands she pulled it off the bed and sat down. She twisted the soft fabric between her fingers, rocking back and forth. She cried, *it'll be over soon. No more being left. No more being hurt. No more pain.* She looked down at the sheet and got up. As she tied the sheet to the shower head she felt powerful that she was finally going to escape the suffocation, the quicksand. As she held the other end of the sheet in her hand ready to wind it around her neck, images of Sarah and Adam flooded her mind. She paused. What would her action do to them? How would Frankie raise them? She sat down on the shower floor and wept. As the tears flowed, her internal fortitude rose to the surface. She raised her fist like Scarlett O-Hara, "As God is my witness, I will never (go through this pain again.)" In a still small voice in her head that she recognized as God, she heard, "I am with you. You are not alone."

She was still sobbing when Frankie returned, his clothes reeking of Tina's perfume and sex.

Looking up at him from the bathroom floor with her chin jutted out, tears glistening her cheeks, she said, shaking her index finger, "Frankie, this is it. I'm done with you. I almost hung myself tonight. You can see the sheet is still draped over the shower," she said pointing up to it, "but you know what? You're not worth it. I know what I smell in your underwear. You are screwing Tina and I am not going to put up with this anymore. If you ever do this again, I swear I will divorce you. Do you understand?" she said her body stiffening, voice escalating.

Frankie, shaken, stood in the dressing area outside the bathroom as lies dripped from his tongue like a water out of a spigot. "It's not what you think, Marion," he said in a high-pitched voice with turned away eyes. "I masturbated into my underwear. I did not screw Tina, honest."

Frankie had often told her, "you tell the truth in such a way that no one will believe you." He was semantically correct. He probably didn't screw Tina since coitus was not his favorite sex activity. He said many times before, "Eating ain't cheating."

She had never taken a stand before. Now entering her second year of her three-year Master's in the Social Work program, she felt empowered.

Frankie, still trembling, leaned over Marion crumpled on the floor, untied the white sheet from the showerhead, gathered the end lying lifeless in Marion's hands and repositioned it on the bed, tucking the bottom end under the mattress, as if to erase the horror of that scene. In an instant, the old frightened Marion found her voice, her resolve. She remained on the bathroom floor her knees bent rocking her whole body back and forth. Frankie laid on the mattress, curled up into a fetal position and tried to verbally coax Marion to come and get into bed with him.

She, for the first time in her marriage, did not comply. After twenty minutes, she arose like a ghost and laid herself on the edge of the bed, trying to process what had happened. She eventually fell asleep out of utter exhaustion. Frankie sensed in that moment the wife he bullied, controlled with money and threats, disconnected herself from him.

During the next day's morning session, Marion raw with emotion, followed facilitator Ronald's instructions as he led the participants in a meditation. "Sit comfortably on the floor. Close your eyes. Take in a breath slowly. Count to four. Now exhale. Take in a breath again. This time return in your mind to a time in your life when you felt intense fear. Observe it. Don't relive it."

Squirming on the floor, shifting her weight first from one buttock to the other, Marion started gagging. The smell of semen in her mouth was overpowering. She could hear the gut-wrenching cry of the small infant inside of her finally expressing her emotional pain and terror at the abuse that Grandpa Russell inflicted upon her on that Thanksgiving afternoon decades ago. After the exercise, she felt determined to help that inner child and her wounded betrayed soul to heal.

Upon returning home, her empowerment held as she entered psychotherapy to deal with her childhood sexual abuse, her ongoing physical ailments, and her cheating husband.

Therapy was an eye opener. The therapist, a former Catholic nun, Lois, understood how God called people to special tasks. Marion at age thirty-three, the details uncovered in therapy, called her sister Gretchen.

"Hey, sis."

"What's up? We haven't talked in a month," Gretchen responded picking up the receiver.

"I hope you and Tim are okay."

"Yah, we are. You sound funny. What's wrong?"

"You're right. I'm kinda off. Can I ask you about something from our childhood?" Marion tentatively inquired.

"Sure, but let me go into the bedroom away from the radio program Tim is listening to so I can hear you better. Okay, I'm ready. Ask away."

"You may be surprised to know that I'm in therapy 'cause I got some things from my childhood to get over. There's vague memories, that others might say is impossible for me to remember from such an early age, so I'm hoping you can help me know if they're real or not. Sooooo. Do you know of any instance where Grandpa Parker did anything inappropriate to anyone?" Then Marion breathed a deep sigh waiting in silence for Gretchen to respond.

After a long pause, Gretchen said, "Well, how much do you want to know?"

"You mean something really did happen to others and not just me?" she asked excited.

"Ya, and probably more than we know about."

Gretchen went into detail about her own incident while babysitting, confirming the possibility that Marion's memories were of real events. They commiserated with one another, trying to comprehend the reason their parents never confronted Grandpa Russell. At the end of the call Gretchen promised to be supportive of Marion's molestation recovery.

After many more therapy sessions Marion decided to broach the subject with her dad during one their regular Sunday night phone calls.

"Hey, Dad. How are you and Mary doing?"

"Fine, pumpkin. How you doing?"

"Well, can I tell you something?"

"Of course, you can always tell your ole dad anything. What is it?"

"You may not have known this, but I remember Grandpa Russell doing something sexual to me when I was just a toddler. You and Mom were not in the room and I had no way to tell you what happened."

Andy, quiet on the other end of the phone feigning disbelief that his father was capable of such an act said, "Maybe you just dreamed it and it did not really happen."

Marion dropped the bombshell, "I wish that was true Dad, but Gretchen also remembers what he did to her at Aunt Eileen's house when she babysat that night."

"Oh," is all Andy could muster. "Grandpa has been dead for almost twenty years so he can't hurt anybody anymore. Let's talk about something more pleasant. How are my grandkids doing? Can you put them on the phone?"

Marion knew that was the end to the discussion so she called Adam and Sarah to the phone and hung up telling her dad, "I love you and tell Mary I love her too."

When she brought up the matter to her mom, Sarah was not surprised, never apologized, nor elaborated, just said, "Yes, Grandpa was capable of such behavior."

Therapist Lois helped Marion affirm her worth. She explained how people who were victimized at an early age have a homing beam that other abusers pick up on including future husbands.

"Lois, do you mean my grandfather started this homing beam that Kevin, Hank, Rick, Mason, and even Frankie tuned into?" She excitedly asked as hot tears trickled down her nose.

"Yes, but just as it was instilled like an implant, it can be disassembled. We are going to do a visualization exercise. You will go back to eighteen-month-old Marion and rescue her from grandpa's grasp."

By realizing that from now on she always had choices and as she began to value her own worth, she could deactivate the implant. No man ever propositioned her again. Empowerment mushroomed into all areas of her life. She was no longer a victim and the whole world knew it by her body language and her choice of words. Frankie knew it too.

Yet, even with psychotherapy, her physical issues persisted. The pain from the Interstitial Cystitis caused urethral spasms, the raw inflamed pinpoint bleeding and the ulcers on the bladder wall, combined with nausea and unrelenting diarrhea, plagued her daily. In April, her allergist put her on a yeast free diet and prescribed Lomotil for the diarrhea, a synthetic morphine. Her pain so uncontrollable, she addictively ate the pills like candy in front of her clients praying for at least temporary relief. If scheduled drugs were found in her system, as a drug and alcohol counselor, she would be fired.

Marion had been seeing a client named John for a couple of months at the local jail. Marion sat at the desk catching up on paperwork as he was escorted in by the guard. Marion invited him to sit down. He eyed her and asked, "You Jonesing, Ms. Finch? Cause you sure are a shaking. You need something to bring you down."

"John, I appreciate your concern. I'm having some medication issues right now. It'll be fine in a day or two. Thanks."

Luckily, John did not mention it to any authority figures at the prison. Frankie knew what she was prescribed, but did not monitor the amount she took.

The last week of July Marion asked Frankie sitting at the kitchen table, "Frankie, can you come into the bedroom for a minute?"

He entered looking curious, expecting some play time. Marion laid down on the bed shaking. "Frankie, I've decided I need to go off the morphine. This Friday, after work, will you help me?"

Disapproving he answered, "That's crazy, woman. You know we put people in the hospital to detox," he said hands on his hips.

"Think about it, Frankie. If I did that, I'd lose my job and could not work again in my field," she pleaded.

"Fine, but if you run into trouble, don't expect me to cover for ya," he said.

"I'll be fine. I'll just need you to keep the kids occupied, check my blood pressure, and check on me occasionally."

The cramping, diarrhea, and blood pressure fluctuations were rough over the three days, but by Monday she was feeling more stable. Frankie did as she asked without empathy. She claimed July 29, 1984 as her sobriety date even though she had stopped alcohol June 13, 1983. She used the July anniversary date because even though sober a year, she was considered still in an altered state because she abused the Lomotil prescription. She had to be totally clean and sober to start her recovery journey. Medications are allowed for Alcoholics, but need to be taken as prescribed.

In August Frankie was asked to fill in as a supply minister at the local United Methodist Church. He agreed to work for them on a week-by-week basis. It meant Sunday morning preaching, leading Bible study on Wednesday nights and an occasional wedding or funeral. That extended over a period of eleven years. Marion assisted by teaching Sunday school, telling the children's sermon, leading the youth group, and occasionally preaching. Frankie and Marion weaved the ministry around their already full schedule including their full-time jobs, Marion's Social Work Master's program, and the kid's school and sport activities. A day off was rare.

Frankie acted appropriately in his job at the Drug and Alcohol Commission and as a preacher. He had stopped drinking after Marion's suicidal encounter in the hotel room the retreat.

Eleven months before Marion finished her Master's in Social Work degree she was given the opportunity to become part of a pastoral counseling, psychotherapy group practice. She seized the opportunity before it vanished.

Sitting the family down in the den she explained the proposition.

"If you can manage over the next year to help me out, I can finish my Masters while I get a private practice going, so I'll be able to make a great deal more money and pay for things we can't afford now. Can you all do that?" she asked smiling.

Sarah asked with a worried look on her face, "What if I get sick and have to come home from school?"

"Well," Marion said, looking at Frankie. "Daddy, can bring you to the office, if need be, or I'll rearrange my clients so I can be with you. Will that be okay for a while?"

"I guess so," Sarah said. "Can I go now?"

"Not yet. What about you, Adam. You're being awful quiet."

"I don't need you here. I go to work after school. I'm not home usually til nine anyway. Can I go do my homework now?"

Marion looked over at Frankie sitting in the recliner saying nothing. "Let's see what Dad says before you two go. Frankie, what do you have to say?"

"What can I say? You got your mind made up no matter what I want. So, it makes no difference. You kids can go back to whatever you were doing." He then picked up his science fiction book and the kids departed.

Marion sighed, got up, and went to the kitchen to do the dishes. Fitting in six hours of school work, thirty-seven and a half hours as a drug and alcohol counselor, and ten hours a week building a private practice, while still trying to balance what it took to be a good wife and mother, was challenging. Determined to never be pushed down in that quicksand again, she inched forward. Her confidence soared as she came closer to completing her Master's degree which would allow her to be self-sufficient, if need be. The benefit for her efforts was increased income she set aside in a personal savings account.

About one hundred days from graduation, Frankie and Marion were watching *Hill Street Blues* on television. No sooner did it go off the air than Frankie's speech became garbled. He could not move his left side. Marion called Chris, their physician friend. He told her to have him follow some instructions.

"Frankie, Chris says for you to lift your left eyebrow."

Garbled, "I am." He wasn't.

"Smile."

It was crooked and his face drooped on the left side.

"Stick out your tongue." He tried.

He failed each test. Chris directed her to call the ambulance but not tell Frankie he was probably having a stroke. He was five days short of his 39th birthday.

As the EMT's were wheeling Frankie out on the stretcher, he smoked his last Marlboro and Marion loudly called out, "Adam, Sarah wake up. The ambulance is taking Dad to the hospital. Please go to school in the morning if I'm not back. It'll be all right. I'll call you when I know something."

They both sleepily stood in their doorway and asked, "What? What's wrong with Dad?"

Marion, not wanting to instill alarm, calmly said, "Dad's having some kind of reaction. He'll be fine. Dr. Chris said to bring him to the ER so the EMTs are taking him. I love you, gotta go. Bye."

The diagnosis - a thalamic stroke. Dr. Chris stood over Frankie's bed on the stroke unit and said, "Frankie you're one lucky son of a gun. Usually, fifty percent of those who have this type don't survive, the other fifty percent are in a permanent vegetative state. It's a miracle you're alive. You had your last cigarette, Buddy. You're living on borrowed time now. You could have another stroke if you don't watch out."

Frankie with garbled speech said, "I know. I get it," as hot tears rolled down to his chin.

Marion was so scared. They just purchased a new Oldsmobile a week before. She parked it, afraid she would have to return it. She had one semester to go in her Master's Program. She had flashbacks of her dad having his heart attack when they just bought a new Ford.

Marion, two days later, drove Sarah to middle school sensing she needed some "Mommy time". Adam, as usual, caught the school bus with the neighborhood kids.

"Sarah, I'll pick you up after school so you can sit with Dad at the hospital. I'll come back after seven when I finish completing your dad's monthly paperwork. Mr. Green, (Frankie's boss) said I can do Dad's work along with mine until he's able to go back, so I'm gonna need a lot of help from you kids for a while. Okay?"

"Mom, is Dad going to be okay?" Sarah asked, a worried expression on her face as she grabbed her book bag off the car floor.

Trying to convince herself mostly, Marion said, "Sure thing Sary, Dad has to have physical therapy, to learn to tie his shoes and his tie, to learn to talk and walk right again, but eventually yes, he will be okay." She leaned over to hug her before she got away.

When Frankie came home six days later, friends helped take him to physical therapy. His brother Ronnie came to help for a week. The stroke greatly fatigued him so he only worked part-time until his energy strengthened. Marion designed a weekly family meeting she nicknamed "Flip Group." It was Family Life Intervention Program. The kids hated it.

Marion called down the bedroom hallway, "Sarah, Adam come into the den. It's time for our FLIP group." Groans could be heard as thirteen-year-old Sarah and fifteen-year-old Adam trudged into the room. Marion set the stove timer for an hour. "Come on kids, it'll be fun. You'll see. Let's do this for Dad, okay?"

Frankie spoke in halting, garbled words, "it's …..okay…..if they….don't want…to."

Marion read the agenda: talk about who needed to be where for what school activity, what friend could they ride with, what school projects were due that needed adult supervision. Then she asked questions, "How do you feel about Dad having had a stroke? What are you afraid will happen next? What do you need from Mom and Dad?" No one could pass. Fifteen minutes before the timer buzzed to signal the end of group, Marion announced, "Okay, game time. Adam gets to choose tonight."

As they were about to start the Yahtzee game, the doorbell rang. Marion peered out of the front window curtain and shouted, "Kristen, read the note on the door. 'Adam and Sarah are not available right now. Please do not ring the bell.' Come back at eight."

When the timer buzzed, Marion smiled and silenced it as the family opted to continue playing the game. Crisis averted, Marion grateful for her therapeutic skills she was gaining, breathed a sigh of relief. Her family was still intact.

Session Twenty-Three

Marion sat in the reception room waiting for the client before her to finish his session. When the man exited the office, he walked past her with tears streaming down his face. Marion wanted to reach out and touch him to tell him it would be okay, to not stop the process. She knew she could not fix it for him, but she could fix her life by continuing her own healing journey. Anxious to get the session started, she told Dr. Weinstein, "Today I know I can't fix anyone. They must do it themselves. The best way I can help others is to heal myself, just like you realized entering your own therapy. Let's begin today's chapter. Okay?"

"Certainly. You are learning much and integrating it very well," said Dr. Weinstein.

Recovery

FRANKIE, AT FIRST, was subdued, grateful to be alive and somewhat thankful that Marion managed everything during his recovery. Gaining in confidence, within a year Frankie had recovered his ability to walk and talk without impairment. His left side remained weaker, and his cognitive impairment persisted. Frankie's short-term memory deficit and difficulty searching for words challenged both Marion and Frankie.

"Marion, I want (long pause)," Frankie called to Marion in the kitchen, from the den.

She picked up the dishtowel to dry her hands and entered the room. He was sitting in the recliner. Pointing, she asked him, "do you mean the remote?" He shook his head vigorously from side to side. "Do you want something to eat?"

He said loudly, "No, let me think."

"I'm sorry, Frankie. I was only trying to help," she said sitting down on the hassock in front of him staring at him while he tried to find the missing word.

"Damn it! I hate this. I used to know stuff and now I am so stupid," he said exasperated.

Over time she learned to wait until he either figured it out or asked for help. Eventually like in the past, he would have sudden angry outbursts without provocation. He would not directly tell Marion he appreciated what she did for him, or apologize for his outbursts, but would announce it in front of others. She wondered why he could not tell her to her face, but she was at least grateful he said it out loud within her hearing.

One day after work on the way home he confided in her. Touching her arm as he backed out of the office parking lot he said, "Ya, know Marion, I think my sexual acting out was because of my drinking." Turning to look over at her he said, "Since I've been sober, I can see the alcohol lubricated me and loosened my inhibitions. I think I'm okay now."

"I hope you're right, Frankie, cause I'm sure not going back to that life again," she said while shaking her head to stop the flashback of that shower scene.

The next Friday night Frankie came home from work grumpy. Marion was stirring the sloppy joe mix into the hamburger frying on the stove front burner.

"What the hell are you cooking hamburger again for? You know I wanted pork chops tonight," he said as he took off his brown penny loafers and threw them against the back wall of the kitchen.

Marion answered calmly, "Frankie, the hamburger was about to go bad. I'll fix your pork chops tomorrow night."

"If I wanted them tomorrow night, I would have told you that. You don't respect my needs and wants. You're always doing what YOU want. I'm outta here." He slammed the screen door on his way out.

Sixteen-year-old Adam entered the kitchen with fourteen-year-old Sarah trailing behind him smelling the hamburger frying in the skillet. Adam rubbed his stomach and said, "Smells good, Mom. Where's Dad? What's he so mad about now?"

Taking a breath, Marion said, "Your dad is having his usual Friday night grumpiness. Come on, let's eat. It's ready."

Sarah and Adam giggled as Marion tossed a kernel of corn from her fork into the air mimicking her dad years early. The atmosphere lightened without Frankie's critical attack on whichever child he decided to pick on during that meal. She knew where he went. He always went to play cards with the guys at the Halfway House. After supper Adam, like Marion's sister Gretchen, turned inward. Saying no farewell, he took off on a solo walk.

Sarah hung around the kitchen while Marion cleared the table.

Sarah finally broke the ice while sitting at the table swinging her left foot. "Mom, why *does* Dad get angry with me and leave?"

Marion stopped loading the dishwasher and turned around to hug her daughter. She said, "Sarah, Dad's not mad at you. His temper tantrums are not your fault. He is just an angry person and it is no one's fault, but his own."

"But Mom," she said raising her arms. "He's always criticizing me, and yelling at me."

"You're right Dad does do that. I know he is not really made at you. When I try to point out to him how hurtful his words are, you see how he just gets madder. You're a beautiful girl," she said gently squeezing her arms. "I want you to be happy, have fun with your friends and let me worry about dad, okay?"

"Okay, Mom thanks. I love you," she said with a big grin on her face.

"I love you too Sarah. Now go find your brother in the neighborhood and let's play a game."

In May of 1986, Marion finally earned her Master's degree in Social Work with a 3.8 GPA at the UNC Social Work School. Bill Cosby and Alex Haley were the commencement speakers. Mr. Cosby talked about students "Going Forth," leaving parents and taking on adult responsibilities. Marion knew all about taking on responsibility after three years of commuting to the Wilmington campus. She was excited to finally have Frankie and her kids meet the classmates she developed friendships with over the last three years.

After the ceremony, Marion met her kids climbing down from the stands and hugged them. Frankie stood beside them frowning, biting his cheek with his arms crossed. Marion began to unzip her graduation gown and pointed saying, "Let's go over to there, the School of Social Work reception. My friends Celeste and Tracy want to meet you all."

Frankie stiffened as he lambasted her. "I don't care to meet any of the people you went to school with. You won't see them again anyway. I wanna go home. We'll eat back in Marley."

She gestured with open palms, "But it's important to me. I worked hard to get this degree and the people I want to introduce you to are my friends who want to meet you."

As he turned his back and began to walk away he smarted, "I'll be in the car. Kids, if you want to go along with your mom's ridiculous notion that these people actually care about her, then fine, go with her," he said sarcastically.

Marion introduced Adam and Sarah to her friends with a heavy heart. The classmates said, "I thought you wanted us to meet your husband?"

Marion, sad, just said, "I'm sorry, but ever since his stroke three and a half months ago, he tires easily and he's ready to go home."

Her coveted celebration dinner was not in the fancy Seafood restaurant she envisioned, but back in Marley at the same old Ryan's Steakhouse. No frills, no congratulatory remarks, just Frankie's anger and criticism. Frankie pointed out how she should be grateful. Speaking loud enough for the next table to hear he said, "I'm here. Do you see any of your family coming to congratulate you? Hell, no. Who paid for your school? Did your family pay for your college or Master's degree? Huh, did they? I did. I'm the only support you got and don't you ever forget that!"

She quietly left the table and went to the restroom, embarrassed for anyone to see her stinging tears. *This is what you call support? I would call it criticism and continual harassment.*

Returning to the table she pasted a smile on her face for Sarah and Adam's benefit. She was not hungry any more. She sat in silence. Adam and Sarah ate in silence, hoping this rage would not continue as they went home. The children learned to ignore or avoid Frankie's anger by occupying their time away from home as much as possible. Adam got involved in the big downtown United Methodist Church's youth group. He worked with a local remodeling contractor in the summers and at a buffet during the school year. Sarah became the nighttime receptionist at a therapy practice. In June of 1989, Adam graduated from Marley High School and went off to college in New York State. Although Adam had been a quiet child the house seemed empty in his absence even with Sarah still there. Adam, somewhat an introvert, called home daily, homesick, even though he did not admit it.

Without the children as a buffer, Marion kept busy working many hours in her private practice to avoid Frankie's anger. The tension between Frankie and Marion took its toll on her body. When the medications could no longer manage her pain, she agreed to have Dr. Howe do surgery.

"Hey, Rhonda. How are ya?" Marion asked her sister on the phone, whom she rarely got to see living so far apart and both working full time jobs.

"Hey, Sis. I'm good and you?"

"Well, I know your birthday is next week and I wanted to call before, 'cause I'm going to be getting ready for surgery scheduled for the next day."

"Oh, what for?" she asked bewildered.

Marion filled in the details. So, the day after Rhonda's 33rd birthday, Marion entered Marley Regional Hospital as an outpatient to have simple bladder tack up procedure. In the eleven years since her partial hysterectomy, her bladder had dropped, creating a painful cystocele. Dr. Howe encouraged her to do the surgery to help alleviate some of her Interstitial Cystitis pain. She finally consented, was told it would be a quick recovery. She kissed her children good bye as they went off to school. Frankie dropped her off, planning to return when she was ready to be released to go home. He did not think he needed to be present, so he went on to work.

Marion, used to depending on herself, said a simple prayer as the anesthetic IV flowed into her vein. "God, I put myself in your lap. Please take care of me through this procedure."

The anesthesiologist told her to count back from 100. Ninety-nine, ninety-eight and she was out. Fifteen minutes into the procedure the nurse monitoring her blood pressure announced, "Dr. Howe, she's crashing. Stop."

As Marion's blood pressure bottomed out, her sense of consciousness heightened. With the calmness of a glassy sea, her ethereal spirit rose from the figure strapped to the gurney, and floated effortlessly through the air out of the ceiling into another dimension. A light, like one shining under a closed door beckoned her to approach. There was no pain, no fear, no sadness, and no remorse only an intense sense that she was totally enveloped in a blanket of love so powerful that it exuded from her soul into her surroundings. The walls of the tunnel enveloping her began to part, and a light of the most beautiful shade of yellow shimmered in front of her.

She had no other thought than to be there in that moment. Getting her bearings, she tried to move toward the light. What surprised her was how her thoughts became the vehicle to propel her forward. Emerging from the murky darkness she became aware of a presence beside her. "Mitchell, is that you?" Marion shrieked.

"Yes, Mom it's me. Here I'm okay and you see me as the teenager I would have been had I lived. Do you want to go forward and meet the others?" he asked as if he and Marion had ongoing conversations since the day she miscarried him sixteen years earlier.

"Oh, my dear, sweet baby boy. How I wished I could have held you all these years," she said reaching out for him as he embraced her. Pulling back, curious, she asked, "What others am I to meet?"

"You'll see, come on," he said grabbing her by the hand.

She could feel him, look at him and only marvel.

Was this heaven? She wondered.

Mitchell helped Marion get into a little dark blue rowboat. He stood up paddling in deliberate quick strokes, parting the black lake water while Marion sat on the brown wooden seat holding onto the sides of the craft. She could feel the tepid water brush against her hands.

In less than a couple of minutes they neared the shore. Marion saw the shadowy outline of figures at the edge of the water. She could not decipher any familiar faces. The crowd gathered around the boat as it reached the shallow water and they drug the boat effortlessly to the shore. Stepping out, Marion looked at the myriad of faces all smiling at her.

She gasped, "Grannie Nellie is that you?" Pointing to the twelve-year-old mousy brown-haired young man she said, "Austin, you died when I was in fourth grade." Turning around she stared at another familiar face. "Juanita, you were hit by a car the week before eighth grade. Wow, you all look so good."

Marion spun around looking the scenery and then she shouted, "Hey, wait a minute," raising her left index finger. "I've been here before. I remember it now," she said spinning around, smiling. "That time in July of 1980 when I got stung by four bees and I felt my spirit lifting out of my body. I recall getting a glimpse of this place and then being pulled back. Do I get to stay this time?"

A seven-foot male figure she did not recognize placed his hand on her shoulder and communicated telepathically with her, "*No, we brought you here to show you what is going to happen to you in the future, but you won't remember until each event takes place.*"

One by one the future scenarios played like a video showing work she would do, people she would help, and directional changes in her life. Once finished, the tall spirit figure said: "It is time for you to return. We will be with you always. You can ask for our guidance as needed. Your mission is to tell those who feel unloved that they are loved and for you to love them until they can love themselves."

She did not fathom the implication of her mission in that moment. She asked, "How will I remember to ask for guidance?"

"Remember Robbie and the Indian Chief?" he said as his shape transformed into the Chief. "Like this, we will make ourselves known as events unfold."

"Oh, Okay, thank you," she said, overwhelmed.

Before another word passed, she was sucked back into her sedated body. In the ten minutes, she had been gone, Dr. Howe had stepped back as Dr. Winton, the anesthesiologist, pushed medication into her IV to reverse the hypotension, slowly elevating her pressure, but keeping her sedated. With her spirit returned, the medical staff was finally able to complete the surgery and send her to the recovery room. Even though she was given the amnesiac drug Versed, she recalled every detail of the Near-Death Experience (NDE) except the future events they showed her.

The simple outpatient operation turned into a two-day hospital stay due to fever and infection in the bladder.

When she went for her follow-up after the procedure, she spoke with Julie, the urologist's nurse. "Julie, can I look at the surgical notes from my bladder tack up?"

Sitting down on the swivel stool, Julie looked her in the eye and asked, "Why? Is something wrong?"

Marion hesitated, "If I tell you, you'll think I'm crazy," she said wringing her hands.

Julie put her hand on Marion's wrist and said, "It's okay, just say it."

"Well, during surgery I left my body. I knew I was dying," Marion cautiously said while watching Julie's response. "I wanted to read the notes from the procedure to see what happened."

Julie smiled and told Marion, "You're not crazy. My brother drowned and left his body. Friends pulled him ashore and gave him CPR. He remembers it like it was yesterday and it changed his life for the better."

Marion sighed, relieved. "Yah, ever since, the world is different. It's only been ten days, but I feel more connected to God. I don't fear death any more. The pain of this IC disease doesn't scare me. And weirdest of all, guess what? "I don't know," but tell me Julie said.

With tears welling up Marion said, "I met Mitchell, the child I miscarried at three months. I recognized him immediately and he did me. On the other side, it is so peaceful with indescribable colors and feelings."

Julie got up from the stool and hugged Marion. She said, "Don't let anyone ever tell you that experience is not real, because you know it is. But now, I better get you prepped for Dr. Howe or or he'll be mad."

Marion felt affirmed in that moment and free of her general anxiety present prior to her NDE. Since awaking from her surgery, she could feel her spirit guide's presence even though she did not know yet what to name him.

To further her recovery, she entered psychotherapy again, not with Lois, but with therapist, Dr. Kirk, trained in Native American spiritual techniques. Through hypnosis she learned that the figure she feared, the American Indian, in her bedroom wardrobe was her Spirit Guide, the same figure manifested in the NDE. Spirit Robbie who was with her since a small child and had left when she entered kindergarten was her protector, and the boy on the roof outside her upstairs bedroom was dead, but didn't know it. The fiftyish man who appeared outside her bedroom window at their cinder block house was also dead. Dr. Kirk helped her make sense of her NDE and answered questions about seeing spirits.

"Why didn't the spirits make themselves known when Grandpa was molesting me?" she asked with furrowed brow and palms upturned.

"They were with you, you just did not recognize them," said therapist Kirk, reassuring her.

To release the hold all the abusers had on her psyche, Dr. Kirk directed her through a session of holographic breathing. The process is done to very loud psychedelic music while doing hyperventilating breathing. The outcome is like the experiments done on LSD volunteers. It creates an altered state. A partner sits with the subject to make certain the person does not do anything harmful to themselves or others. The process returned her to the point of conception and then forward. It was very cathartic and she felt lighter afterward. Thus, her confidence and ability to stand up for herself grew even stronger much to Frankie's consternation. She began to celebrate and embrace life.

Marion called Gretchen again to validate what she had experienced in the session.

"Gretchen, hey. I just went through a therapy session to help me recover from some childhood events. Can I ask you a couple of questions?" "Sure, ask away."

"Well, was there a time when I was in a baby carriage and a brick was thrown at me?"

"Wow! You remember that? You were only about nine months old."

"Well, this process we go through, goes back through our memories and helps us uncover stuff."

"Man, that's really deep. Do you want to know what I remember?"

"Ya, if you don't mind, please?"

"Well, I was seven and Mom asked me to watch you in your carriage so she could wash out diapers. She set you in the sun so you wouldn't be cold. Eric, the neighborhood troublemaker kid who lived behind us, picked up a brick and threw it toward you. Johnny saw him do it and stepped in front of your carriage just in time. I chased Eric all the way back to his house and told his mom. Our mom came running out when she heard the commotion and she took you back inside."

"Thanks, I can't believe I could see all that. I'm glad Johnny saved me."

"Ya, me too."

They discussed a few more mundane things before they hung up.

Marion no longer felt like a heavy cloud hung over her head. She laughed more and even socialized with some female friends. In June of 1991, Finches celebrated Sarah's high school graduation. In the fall, Sarah entered UNC where Marion obtained her Master's and where Adam transferred after his freshman year at Albany University. Not having the distraction of children's activities monopolizing Marion and Frankie's off-from work time created an uncomfortable lull. Marion, uncertain whether Frankie would escalate his anger toward her without the buffer of the children, vigilantly monitored his every mood, but no longer felt responsible for his behavior.

She could not find a pattern to his moodiness. She continuously expected his rage to erupt. A pleasant interruption to Marion's monitoring preoccupation came when Sarah visited about once a month. Mother and daughter went shopping, out to eat, and laughed a lot no matter what mood Frankie exhibited. As a result, Frankie would become sullen and pout until Sarah returned to college and then he would unleash his anger.

"So, how much money did you blow on Sarah?

You know that is the reason she comes home," Frankie queried while Marion loaded the dishwasher.

Looking up at him not flinching she answered,

"Frankie, come on. She wants to see her parents occasionally. We aren't the mean ogres any more. Enjoy it, 'cause before long she won't even want to come home."

Rather than respond, he just grumped his way to the couch, picked up the television remote, and did not speak to Marion for the next couple of hours. She did not allow his foul mood to upset hers. A victory since she had the NDE and holographic experience.

Over the next couple of years, as Marion's private group practice became more profitable Marion and Frankie began to enjoy their elevated financial status. Frankie continued to work at the Drug and Alcohol Commission promoted to the Assistant Director's job. To celebrate their success and fill the void of the empty nest, Marion and Frankie started to travel together. As Frankie finished his tenure of eleven years as the part-time pastor of the United Methodist Church telling the congregants, "I've preached all the sermons I have in my barrel. It's empty. You need some new blood. It's time for me to finish my work here." The church sadly accepted his resignation and the District Superintendent assigned a retired United Methodist minister to lead the flock.

Frankie and Marion celebrated and traveled to Australia and New Zealand. Marion did not go as a missionary like she thought she would as imaged as a teenager, but as a tourist.

They both continued their full-time jobs, but took Friday afternoons off. Frankie planned their activities. He stood by the back door ordering his wife, "Marion, get your clubs. It's time to play golf."

Marion, typing on the computer in the den, waiting for a client's return phone call, answered him, "Frankie, I know Dr. Chris told you to play to recover from your stroke, but why do we have to go every Friday afternoon?"

Exasperated, he said, "We have a membership at the country club. I want to use it. You want to spend time with me. I'm going to play. Are you coming or not?"

Inhaling deeply, she answered, "Give me a minute.

I have to finish typing this session note."

"Well, I'll be in the truck. If you're not there in three minutes, I'm going without you." She silently hoped he would go, but she knew his temper would then flare all weekend. She shut down the computer and tied her golf shoe laces as she headed out the door.

Marion felt like a building being erected, each level representing her accomplishments securing her resolve as her income also climbed.

As she got into the truck on the way to the golf course, Frankie told her, "You need to get a real job with insurance and benefits."

Stiffening Marion turned to him beside her and said, "Frankie, I made $63,000 last year, even taking two weeks off to go to Australia and New Zealand. I wouldn't make that kind of money in an agency. Besides, I'm not a good team player. I'm better going solo."

She bought him new Calloway clubs for Christmas, but it only temporarily provided any improvement in his mood. As they sat down to eat at Wendy's after the round of golf, Marion picked up a French fry and looked over at Frankie.

"Frankie, you need to get a haircut. You look like an unmade bed, a shaggy dog."

Running his fingers through his hair he said, "Yeah, well, I remember when you used to love me and respect me and you'd cut my hair."

"I don't have time to do that now. I have more important things to do in my life," she said flippantly.

She no longer asked for his permission to do things, or go places and would schedule events for herself. There was a growing unrest in her life she couldn't quite pinpoint. Despite the success, she was not happy, something was missing. She had always wanted to earn her doctorate, but Frankie said it was unnecessary. Maybe the third degree was the missing piece.

Before Marion could explore the possibility of earning her doctorate she began to daily meditate. It deepened her connection to the God of her understanding which changed drastically since her Near-Death Experience. She no longer feared God's judgment. One night in early spring of 1993 she had a dream. She found herself wandering through the waiting place where people go after they die. People around her aimlessly moved as if lost in unfamiliar territory. Each did not recognize they died or that anyone else was present. A voice from above her ethereal form spoke to Marion, one she recognized later as her spirit guide, Natir.

"Marion, we brought you here to offer you an opportunity. You can make a spiritual leap progressing far ahead where you have traveled. If you decide to make this jump you cannot ever return to where you were. You cannot discuss this dream with Frankie, if he chooses not to join you. Do you understand?"

Frankie was wandering in the abyss like her and did not hear the voice. In the dream, she looked at her lost husband and asked, "Do you want to jump with me?"

"Sure," he said as she leapt upward.

But he did not leap, instead rode her coat tail, behind, not beside her.

When Marion awoke, she looked over at Frankie already awake. She asked, "Did you have a dream?"

"No, why do you ask?"

"Ah….okay, then. Thanks."

"What is going on? Did you have a dream or something? Level with me."

She swiveled her legs over the edge of the bed to head to the bathroom and said, "I can't discuss it with you."

He grabbed her arm and said, "I'm your husband for God's sake. Tell me!"

She pulled her arm away and attempted to skirt his question, but he stood up between her and the doorway.

"I'm not letting you out of this room until you tell me."

Now what do I do? If I tell him that is going against what my spirit guide told me, but if I don't I'm gonna pee my pants right now.

Reluctantly she did expecting lightning to strike at any moment. It did not. Frankie said, "I would 'a followed you."

That is exactly what he did. Grabbing onto whatever spiritual discipline she explored, he drained her energy wanting the benefits without doing the personal labor. Marion deepened her meditation practices even being able to travel to other places and speak other languages as her body slept. Her communication with her spirit guide became more conscious and regular.

Over Thanksgiving weekend in 1993, Frankie, Sarah, and Marion went to visit Adam in Washington DC where he was studying at preparing to fulfill his own call to the ministry. He heard God's call while serving as a volunteer with a youth group at a United Methodist Church close to the UNC campus in Wilmington. Settled in their hotel room after a long day of sightseeing Marion quickly fell asleep. She awoke to a shimmering light standing by her side of the bed.

As she rubbed her eyes she stared. Her Spirit Guide spoke to her telepathically standing next to her on the rug beside the bed. The guide was translucent, but she could not see through him.

"It is time for you to set up a holistic psychotherapy clinic," the Spirit declared.

"Huh, what'd you say?" she asked unafraid, sitting up. "How can I do that? I don't even know where to start or why I should," she bravely stated.

"Remember us showing you things to come?" he said stretching out his arms.

"Ah,… You mean when I saw Mitchell during my surgery mishap?"

"Yes, we told you we would let you know when you needed guidance and the time is now." The figure then vanished.

Marion sat up on the side of the bed, perplexed, trying to comprehend what it all meant. Was she just dreaming? No, this was real. She groped around for the pen and pad of paper next to the phone. Quietly she curled up in the chair in the corner of the room and made some notes. She looked at the clock. It was 3:15 a.m. Where would she find an office, colleagues, money to set it all up, business licenses, etc. Exhausted, she crawled back under the warm covers and waited for daybreak, too excited to sleep much. When the sun peeped through the heavy curtains she smiled, stretched her arms and got up. Coming back with two cups of coffee from the reception area, she told Frankie about her visitation.

He listened, but played Devil's advocate. "Where the hell are you gonna find money to do that? Why would you want to do that when you're making good money in the group practice where you are? I think you got a wild hair up your butt and this is just a fabrication to make me think your fantasy is real."

"Frankie, I don't care if you believe me or not. I'm going to do what I feel led to do. If it is supposed to happen, it will, and if not, it won't. Don't stomp on my dream."

Frankie sulked the rest of the day. Whatever activity she was interested in pursuing on their mini vacation, he found some reason to object to it. But she was determined to not allow his foul mood to dampen her spirits.

In two weeks at the weekly group practice staff meeting, she announced her plan as they each went around the table sharing whatever news they wished. She cleared her throat and said, hesitantly, looking down first at her hands and then making eye contact with each of the four colleagues, "Well, I have decided to leave the practice and go out on my own. I know it will be hard and you may not all be supportive of my decision, but I hope you will be happy for me."

Ted spoke up. "Marion, that's wonderful. We will miss you. When you leaving?"

She slowly answered, looking for a response on her colleagues' faces, "In ninety days."

They congratulated her and wished her well. She expected the owner of the group practice to object or have a non-compete clause because her exit would diminish their cut of her income. Their acceptance confirmed her vision must be valid. In eleven weeks by February of 1994, she had an office, a partner, and three other professionals sharing the space. It was her dream, but it still was incomplete. She wanted a doctorate so she could be certified to do more holistic techniques.

She sat down in the living room next to Frankie on the couch while he watched the History Channel on television. When the program ended, she asked, "Can we talk about something, please?"

"What's wrong now?" Frankie asked, glaring at her as he pushed the mute button on the remote irritated for the interruption to his planned evening of mesmerized television watching.

Drawing in a breath she started. "I have decided I want to go ahead and get my doctorate."

Looking down his nose at her he said, "Oh, you have had you? Why do you need all these ABC letters after your name? I think it is just for your fucking ego."

She crossed her arms and said, "No, Frankie. I want certification to do more holistic modalities, to be respected as a credible practitioner."

In a stern voice, he asked, "And just where are you going to get the money for this unnecessary wild hair of yours?"

Sitting up straighter she uncrossed her arms and said, "I can afford to pay as I go."

Opening his palms, gesturing, he said, "Why can't you do your so-called holistic crap without more school?"

She responded in a strong voice, "Because doing things like acupressure, meditation, hypnosis, visualization, and healing touch all require certification at an accredited school. If I get my doctorate at a school that teaches all of this, then I have all I need."

"I do not approve of this. You are on your own. It better not cost me anything extra," he said loudly folding the newspaper, open to the crossword puzzle, on his lap.

Marion sat up straight to bring home her point. "Frankie, I pay more than my share of the expenses around here. Since my practice has grown, we have taken nice trips and I purchased new clubs for you, a new truck, and got you your "midlife crisis" stick shift sports car. I am a good wife and you know it."

Muttering under his breath, "I remember when you were nothing but a high school graduate. Without me, you would still be working back at Ithaca Hospital. No sir, no one should have to pay for their wife's third degree. That spells divorce."

Marion ignored his muttering because her mind was made up. She got up off the couch and sat at the kitchen table pondering her next move. *I just need to find out where I want to go and finagle a few expenses to afford a doctoral program.* The more excited she got, the more withdrawn, depressed and angry Frankie became. She persisted on toward her goal undeterred by his mood and criticism.

A year after Marion's hotel spirit visit, Sarah said, as she passed the mashed potatoes during the Thanksgiving meal, "Mom, Dad I want you to meet some-one. His name is Chuck. He owns a moving business. He's smart and I think you'll like him."

Marion took the mashed potato dish from Sarah and looked over at Frankie who said nothing. Marion took the lead. "That's great Sarah. When do we get to meet him?"

"He's coming in from Raleigh tomorrow. He's my friend Sandy's boy-friend's brother. Is it okay if he comes for supper?" she asked with a pleading look.

Marion asked Frankie, "You got any plans tomorrow for supper?"

"I do now," he said. He asked Sarah, "Is he Mr. Right or Mr. Right now?"

"That's not very nice," Marion chimed in.

"What's wrong with that question? Is a father not allowed to ask my daughter's intentions?" He pushed his chair back and headed to the television without waiting for a response.

Chuck had a troubled past, but seemed to be on track for living a better life, so Frankie and Marion welcomed him into their lives, optimistic that people can and do change for the better.

Sarah and Chuck's relationship progressed to the point of marriage. They were living in a rental house about five miles from Mom and Dad.

While Sarah was at the house to do laundry, Marion asked her, "Hey, Sarah. I have an idea. Wanna hear it?" Marion asked as she was loading the dishwasher while Sarah was doing laundry on the other side of the kitchen door.

"Sure Mom, what is it?" she asked with a quizzical frown, peeking around the corner.

Beckoning her daughter, she said, "Come sit down at the table and I'll tell ya."

Sarah set down her laundry basket with the dryer door still open and came to the table.

Marion smiled as she patted Sarah's hand and said, "Well, you know that your dad and I are planning a twenty-fifth anniversary celebration complete with renewing our vows."

Sighing deeply, acting bored she answered, "I know, Mom, you have talked about it like a bazillion times already."

"Yes, my dear daughter, that's correct. But what if we combine your marriage ceremony with us renewing our vows? It would save some money and the relatives would only have to make one trip down South to witness both."

"Mom, I don't care. If you want to do that, it's fine with me, but I'll check with Chuck just to be sure.

Marion excitedly started planning the double event before Chuck even agreed to it. She called her daughter two nights later. "Sarah, when do you want to go shopping for your wedding dress? I budgeted $900 for it."

"Whoa, Mom. Hold on. I haven't even talked to Chuck yet about the whole idea. He does want to marry me, but maybe he's not ready yet."

"Ya, I get it. I'm jumping the gun, but the celebration is 100 days from now and we have a lot to do."

"Mom, don't get your panties in a wad. I'll talk to him tonight about it. You're stressing me out, so let up already, okay? I love you Mom. Talk to you tonight."

Chuck thought it was a great idea. He did not have to shell out money for a wedding, since his family could not have contributed.

Marion may not have had the family present when she eloped, but she would make this renewal even better than her long ago dashed wedding fantasy. Marion decided that the reciting of vows would wipe the slate clean since Frankie had supposedly not had an affair in ten years. They could stroll into retirement together hand in hand, mellowed over the years.

Marion met Sarah at the florist to pick out flowers for the wedding. Marion was looking at the various options in the thick binder when Sarah entered.

Looking up Marion said, "Hey, Sarah. Sit down," she said pulling out the chair beside her. "I've been looking at bouquets based on our budget. What do you have in mind? You like red roses or pink? Your dress kinda has an ivory tint to it so either color will look pretty."

"Mom, I don't care. Pick what you think looks best," Sarah said sighing.

"Dear, what's wrong?" Marion asked looking concerned.

"Nothing," she said unconvincingly, turning away. *Don't people see I am recreating the wedding I never had? It is all crumbling and no one seems to care, but me. God, I've been faithful to you all these years and paid my dues sticking it out with Frankie and raised two terrific kids. I wanted this renewal to be a fresh start, a clean slate after all of Frankie's sexual indiscretions. Can you please help me here?*

They chose flowers and went to lunch. Sarah lightened up so Marion just assumed she had wedding jitters.

The long-awaited day soon arrived. Chuck had just changed jobs two weeks earlier. The new boss, owner of a home improvement store, refused to give him time off to attend the rehearsal. A gay guy friend of Sarah's stood in for Chuck. The soloist developed laryngitis so someone else had to replace her at the last minute. The caterers never got the check for the down payment on the reception. Marion refused to let any of it get her down on what she selfishly wanted to be a day she finally walked down the aisle to the watching eyes of all her family and friends.

On the day of the wedding, a family golf tournament was arranged for whomever wanted to play. Peter, the husband to the caterer who was also Frankie's friend, pulled Marion aside at the fourth hole. "Marion, why do you let Frankie talk to you that way? He's so disrespectful calling you crazy in front of your family, even if he is joking. I hurt for you."

Laughing, she waved her hand in the air and said, "Oh, Peter, I don't even notice it any more. It is just how Frankie is. He's unhappy with himself and takes it out on me. I just ignore it."

United Methodist Church, where Frankie had pastored was filled with a hundred guests, both family and friends. Marion wore a teal rhinestone studded two-piece brocade satin dress with a white orchid wrist corsage. Andy, her father, twenty-five years late, escorted her down the maroon carpet center aisle. Sarah, adorned in a long-sleeved antique white lace wedding gown with V-neck carried a bouquet of red tea roses. Frankie asked his daughter before they began their grand entrance, "You sure about this? We can leave right now with no judgment."

"Dad, stop. The music is playing. It's time to go. Remember preschool? Well, this is the same. From here on I can handle it myself."

She kissed Frankie on the cheek, encircled her arm around the crook of his arm, opened the outer door coaxing him to begin their walk down the aisle to Chuck, her beaming groom.

Marion teared up as she watched her smiling youngest clearly recite her vows. Frankie wiped a tear as well.

To be economical, Marion purchased plain black suits and tuxedo shirts for all the male attendants. Just when they would ever wear the shirts again was not considered. Adam officiated the renewal for his parents but did not yet have his elder's orders to preside over his sister's nuptials. Jerry, an ordained colleague of Marion's performed the young couples' ceremony. It was just as Marion imagined; a fun, family celebration.

The reception was held three miles from the church at the Marley Country Club where Frankie and Marion had a golf membership.

"Mary, how is your phlebitis doing?" inquired Grandma Sarah coming over the table where Mary was seated with her leg elevated.

"If I don't kick up my heels and cut a rug, I'm fine. Thanks for asking," Mary joked.

"Sarah, sit down. Take a load off. I heard you tripped over your vacuum cleaner and that's why you have the cast on your leg, right?" Mary said pointing to the cast. "That's pretty scary when you live alone."

"It was," Sarah remarked patting her cast. "Thankfully, the kids got me a new-fangled contraption called a 'cell phone'. From now on I will carry it with me in the car and keep my handset charged up in the house and always with me. It was frightening to lay on the floor for two hours wondering when someone might find me. Luckily, my neighbor came when I did not show up to go to the movies. Thankfully, she had a key and drove me to the ER.

Van Morrison's song *Have I told you Lately that I love you* blared in the background as DJ 'Tiny Tom,' a three-hundred-pound giant with sweat droplets poring on his forehead, announced, "Please welcome Frankie and Marion Finch, parents of the bride to the dance floor."

As the couple took center stage Andy watched from the sidelines beaming at his beautiful daughter. As the song ended he wiped away a tear and
grabbed two cups of fruit punch from the Libbey glass bowl positioned on
the round table next to the three-tiered soon to be sliced butter frosting wedding cake. Andy walked back to the table where Mary sat. She was deep in
conversation.

"Can I join your conversation, ladies?" Andy asked, grinning, precariously
holding the two cups of punch in his withered hands.

"Sure, if you don't mind talking about the pitfalls of getting old," Sarah
quipped.

"Have you heard the one about the retired rabbi, priest, and monkey row-
ing in the boat?" Andy joked setting down the glass cups in front of his present
and former wife.

Both Mary and Sarah simultaneously said, "Yes, Andy, many times."

No one ever heard the end to the joke, because Andy could not recall it.
He used it as a conversation diversion. They all laughed.

Gretchen and Tim sat in the back of the room watching the festivities,
reserved but smiling. They did not engage in the dancing, an unacceptable
Christian behavior by their belief system. They observed the interaction between Sarah and Andy and Mary, but made no attempt to join in the conversation. Whomever approached the couple were warmly greeted. After the first
hour of festivities, Gretchen tapped Marion on the shoulder as she was talking
to a colleague of hers. "Hey, Sis, what are the plans for supper?" Gretchen
asked. "Tim wants to go soon."

"Leftovers from the reception up at the house. When you get ready to
head in that direction, let me know and I will give you the key so you can
transport some of the food, okay?"

"Sure." She turned back to her husband and said, "Tim, why don't you
start gathering up our camera and my sweater and we can go on."

"Yes, dear," Tim obediently responded as he stood up from the circular
reception table.

Marion breathed a sigh of relief, *Well, God we did it. Daughter married off, clean
slate for Frankie and me. Life is good. Thank you.*

But the contentment of the day was short-lived. Sarah called Marion early Saturday morning six months after the wedding.

"Mom, can you come over, please?" Sarah pleaded sobbing.

"What's wrong, Sarah?" Marion asked apprehensively.

"Chuck did not come home last night. I think he is seeing someone else," she whispered, (her heart breaking.)

Marion immediately turned off the waffle iron, told Frankie where she was going, unsure what she would discover, and drove the ten minutes to hug her grieving daughter. A mother's worst fears were confirmed. With puffy eyes, Sarah admitted Chuck had also hit her. With broken hearts over their daughter's pain, Frankie and Marion jointly invited their distraught daughter to move back home. She did, sad but much wiser. She stayed for a few months and then started a new life in Columbia working for an accounting firm launching a successful career for herself.

Things were not good in Marion and Frankie's renewed marriage either. Marion wrote in her journal on June 10, 1996.

Frankie criticizes my golf. When I yell back he gets angry. He even left me at the course in my golf shoes and headed home. I started to walk the five miles, but he came back, drove up beside me and waited for me to get in. He did not speak to me for hours. He will not discuss finances with me and continues to spend money on what he wants but tells me I must pay off my credit card debt. He asks if I've had a big money day with clients because he has a new toy he wants to buy. When I try to read devotions and pray he won't even put down the newspaper. God please help me know how to make my marriage better. Amen.

Session Twenty-Four

"Can you believe this is your 24th session, Marion?" Dr. Weinstein asked.

"In some ways yes, and other ways no. I am so far removed from the scared ninety-six-pound weakling I was when I first entered your office, but I know there is so much more to uncover, and I am anxious to get on with I," Marion said.

Dr. Weinstein nodded and said, "You're in the driver's seat as you have always been, but didn't know it. Take us where you need to go."

Don't Get Too Comfortable

August of 1997 turned out to be a pivotal month of cataclysmic proportion for both Marion and Frankie related to their jobs. Frankie, had worked for the Alcohol and Drug Commission for eighteen years, first as the Halfway House director, then outpatient treatment coordinator, and finally the assistant director over the whole agency. When his boss, Mr. Green, left, Frankie temporarily became the interim director until the Board of Commissioners would decide if he or someone else should be the new director.

The meeting to vote for the new director was scheduled while Marion and Frankie were to vacation with Rhonda and her husband Don at Hilton Head using one of the Finches timeshare exchanges.

Frankie turned to Marion chewing on his index finger sitting in the screened in porch. "I think I'll get it over with and call the office to see how the vote went at the Commissioners' Meeting last night."

Marion, empathetically said, touching his arm, "I hope Dear, it's good news, but if it isn't we'll figure it out, okay?"

"Yah, sure we will," he said flippantly going into the condo.

"Hey, Kurt. It's Frankie. How'd the Commissioners meeting go last night? Did they choose the new director?" he asked with baited breath pacing.

He knew the chance of him being hired permanently were between slim and none. If he was not hired, he also knew no king wanted any contender to the throne in his domain.

"Hey, man. Ah…..Well, they did vote last night."

Impatiently Frankie inquired, "And…?"

Attempting to find a way to soften the blow, Kurt finally answered. "Ya know, nepotism is alive and well in this county."

Frankie's shoulders sagged as he plunked down on the barstool at condo where they were staying for the week. After he let out a sigh he asked, "So they hired Nick, the commissioner's nephew, right?"

"I'm sorry Frankie. Yes, they did. What are you going to do now?"

Reaching into his left shirt pocket as a reflex action to retrieve a cigarette, a habit put down eleven years earlier, he said, "I have no earthly idea. Thanks for leveling with me. I guess I will see you Monday, unless they call and tell me they don't need me anymore."

"Okay, see ya, Monday. We'll get a cup of coffee and chat."

"Ya, sure," Frankie said unconvincingly.

Upon return from the vacation that following Monday a woman came to see Marion. She suspected that her ex-husband's girlfriend was abusing her daughter. The woman (the mother) was the non-custodial parent. She asked Marion to talk to her daughter. Marion agreed to see the seven-year-old. Upon assessment Marion determined after visually observing teeth indentations on the girl's arms and legs that the mom should take the child to be examined by a doctor to verify the alleged abuse. The mother did so.

The following week Marion received a letter in the mail from the social work licensure board. It stated that the custodial parent had filed a complaint against Marion for not seeking permission of the father to have a session with his child.

Marion called the licensure board. She was told that an investigation into the complaint was on-going that they must investigate the claim thoroughly. Marion sought legal representation uncertain what the outcome of the investigation would be.

While Marion fretted over the outcome of the case, Frankie prepared for his job termination. The Commission offered to allow him to stay for one more year or to receive a severance package and to additionally get health insurance for eighteen months. He chose the job for a year and the insurance, because he had nothing else to fill his time and no desire to go elsewhere. Prior to the new "ruler," Frankie's expertise was sought by the whole staff.

"Frankie, can you come down here?" Amanda asked over the intercom. "I can't figure out how to get my computer screen to unfreeze. You're the only one here who can do it."

"Sure, give me about ten minutes. I'll be down as soon as I reconcile the office checkbook."

As soon as he returned upstairs Ramona poked her head in Frankie's office doorway and inquired, "You got a minute Frankie? I need to consult with you about an Employee Assistance Program (EAP) client who keeps missing appointments. Can I notify his employer or am I breaking confidentiality?"

"Sure Ramona, come on in. Let's break this down. We'll look at company contract," he said as he opened the filing cabinet. "Yup," pointing to the clause, "The EAP contractor can report absences of mandatory clients per the release the client signs upon the commencement of treatment."

"Gee, Frankie you're the best. I sure am going to miss you when you're gone in a few months," Ramona said touching his shoulder.

As the time approached for Frankie's termination, the new director told the employees in a meeting that Frankie was intentionally not invited to join, "Staff, I know you are used to going to Frankie for all your problems, but that is now different. Anything you would have taken to him; I want you now to bring to me. Is that understood?" as the employees looked at one another fearing their job security all responded, "Yes, sir."

As fewer and fewer people asked anything of Frankie, he isolated himself in his office and his depression reared its ugly head again. Marion's hearing was held the first week in June. The Board was her accuser, judge, and jury. The result of the hearing: The Board determined that the custodial father did have the right to permit or refuse treatment for his daughter, but since in fact abuse was founded by the Department of Social Services, then the non-custodial mother had the right to seek medical treatment for her daughter. Marion was ordered in the future, if such a case presented, that she should find out who the custodial parent is first, get that person's permission to have the session, and if that was not possible, then notify the

Department of Social Services or law enforcement before sending the child for medical examination. She was ordered to take a graduate level ethics course to be clear on how to handle such future situations. She was put on probation until she completed an approved course. The Board would then determine if the coursework was sufficient or whether they would revoke her license.

Making the best of it, she decided to welcome the opportunity to see how she would handle going back to school and working.

Fearful that they may permanently revoke her licensure, she looked at other options. She applied to finally be ordained as a Disciples of Christ minister, having served for twenty-three years as a licensed minister in good standing which meant she had to be supervised by someone all that time. Frankie had voluntarily taken on that task. The Commission on the Ministry Committee invited her to come present her request.

Sitting down on the cold brown metal folding chair at the eight-foot table, she looked around at people she had directed as the chairperson of the same committee in the last decade. Smiling, putting her hands on the table, she met the gaze of ministerial colleagues and elders from various churches in the Region. She said, "I want to be ordained. Please tell me what you require of me to complete the process."

The Regional Minister, Anthony spoke, "How about you step out of the room for a few minutes and we will discuss it?"

"Okay, sure," she said heading for the rest room then to the carafe of the decaffeinated coffee brewing on the hotplate. In less than ten minutes they called her back in.

Marion, surprised, said, "That didn't take long."

Anthony laughed and asked, "Marion, how long have you been serving churches?"

Taking in a breath she answered, "I was first licensed in 1976." Counting on her fingers she said, "Since then I've served as a pastor, I've been the head of this Committee, I've been Moderator for our Regional Assembly, I've also been a short-term Interim minister twice for churches looking for a pastor and have done supply preaching when and where needed."

Anthony looked at her and said, "That is sufficient. We voted and decided we believe you are ready now to be ordained. When and where would you like the service to be?" he asked smiling.

As tears glistened in Marion's eyes she said, "Oh my, thank you. Since I have served the whole state of SC I think I would like to do it at our State Regional Assembly (Annual Statewide Conference) in September. Would that work?"

Anthony said, "It hasn't been done there before, but I think that would be great."

She excitedly called Adam and Sarah when she walked in the door of her house. "Adam, Guess what? I finally got approved to be ordained in September. Can you come and participate please?"

Adam always the even toned responder said, "Of course, Mom. I'll be happy to come and lay hands on you. It sure has been a long journey for you, huh?"

"You got that right. Thanks, we can talk more later. I know you need to prepare for church tomorrow. Love you."

"Love you too, Mom. Bye."

"Bye."

Frankie overheard the conversation. "What's this? You didn't think to tell me first. What am I chopped liver? Why'd you pick the Assembly to do it at? Now not all the people who want to come, can. It'll be too far to drive on a Saturday afternoon. You should've discussed it with me first. After all, who taught you all you know about ministry all these years? Did you even think to ask me? No, Ms. Independent."

Marion's lip started to quiver. She turned her face away so he would not see it. Taking in a deep breath with her stomach knotted, she turned back and said, "Frankie, Anthony said it would be okay. So that is when it will be."

"Well, Anthony doesn't live with you and know that you make decisions without even considering how it negatively impacts other people's lives," he said looking at her as if he was disciplining a disobedient child.

Marion tried her best to give Frankie some slack knowing he was feeling unwanted and unneeded as the time approached for his position termination. She attempted to include him in her ordination celebration plans but he just gestured for her to leave him alone and told her, "if you really wanted my input you would have asked for it before you planned the whole ordeal. You're on your own on this one."

So, she slunk off to the bedroom and made a list of what she wanted for the service with a heavy heart.

On the last day of his employment, Marion arranged secretly with the staff to have a reception downstairs in the conference room. The director, Nick knew about it and politely refrained from attending. Balloons, a banner, and a huge cake that read "We Will Miss You Frankie," greeted him as he was escorted blindfolded into the room. Kirk presented him a plaque that thanked him for his now nineteen years of service. Marion stayed in the background watching Frankie's pain silently oozing from the inside out. Her heart ached for him to find a new purpose, a place where he felt he belonged, a place that needed him as much as he needed it.

Marion offered to have him join her private practice. He did, paradoxically counseling the abusers referred from the abused women's coalition and private clients, but he missed interacting with staff. Seeing clients all day drained him emotionally. Lost, with no clear focus, he became sullen and angry like back in the 70s, taking it out verbally on Marion. She knew where it could lead, but she was stronger now and did not have kids she needed to raise. The more her practice income increased, the more Frankie's anger rose. Marion knew he was angry at himself, but she could not allow him to take it out on her.

Marion locked the inner door to the office when she walked over to the post office. Frankie came in to work, unbeknown to Marion.

As she walked back into the outer office, Frankie was yelling, throwing the reception room magazines on the floor.

"Frankie, what's the matter? Why are you so angry?" she said, fear rising.

"I'll tell you why the hell I'm angry. You are so goddamned sure of yourself, you don't think about anyone else. I come here to work where you're in charge. You have no respect for me. You tell me everything I should do. I'm sick of it, just sick of it," he said glaring at her, eyes wide and his hot breath breathing down on her, towering over her.

"I don't know what you're talking about Frankie," she sincerely said.

"I'll show you, Ms. Perfect. This door is locked," (turning the knob of the inner office). You didn't even think that I need to get in. You really don't want me working here, do you?"

Shaken, she unlocked the door as she said, "Frankie, I'm sorry. I usually don't lock the inner door. I thought you were coming in much later this morning. I'll go have a key made this afternoon. I did not do it on purpose, honest."

He said nothing more, brushing past her he went into his office and slammed the door. She had to pull herself together to greet the next client in five minutes. She desperately wanted him to be happy. Maybe him working there was not the best answer. Her heart was heavy as she tried to figure it all out.

Frankie decided to enroll in a Clinical Pastoral Education program doing chaplaincy work in a hospital. He thrived in the hospital setting. He applied and was accepted to a hospital in Florence driving the 135 miles round trip a day, commuting like when he was in seminary. The program, only a year-long, gave him a stipend, health insurance, and free psychotherapy. It was the boost he needed.

Marion learned to function at home by herself when Frankie was on call staying overnight at the hospital. All but one household responsibility was hers so it was not much different.

Since Frankie's been handling laundry for twenty years, I haven't thought much about it. Let's see how much laundry detergent does the box say to add?

If she complained about him shrinking something or mixing colors, he told her, "If you don't like how I do it, then take it over yourself, Ms. Smarty Pants."

She mostly tolerated his methods, but if she had something that needed special handling she would wash it separately. While he was away she watched Hallmark movies, went to bed when she chose, and ate frozen microwavable meals. It was freeing and as her independence developed apart from Frankie, he did not like it. A joy interrupted the tension in July of 1998 when Adam, now ordained, himself married a lovely woman he met at seminary named Gwen and together they pastored United Methodist churches.

Unsure if completing her probation requirements would allow her to continue to be a licensed social worker she anxiously contemplated how she could return to pulpit ministry, if she had to do so. On September 19th at the State Assembly of the South Carolina Christian Churches held at the Myrtle Beach Christian Church many fellow ministers, colleagues, and family members placed hands on her head to complete her ordination service.

Well, God it only took me thirty years to complete the process of my call to the ministry, but we did it. Thank you for never abandoning me. Now if I can't be a therapist I can still serve your people.

The engraved clock Sarah purchased to commemorate the occasion still proudly sits on Marion's desk.

By the time, Marion finished the Ethics course in March of the following year, she was convinced, earning an A, that she could obtain her doctorate at Argosy University over the course of the next few years, providing an altered path towards pastoral counseling, a possible alternative to licensure as a social worker. The anxiety over still not knowing if her license would be revoked hung heavy like a gray cloud over her head threatening to empty its acid rain on her at any moment. Finances were the only drawback to the doctoral program. Less new client referrals made it difficult to afford the tuition.

On April 19th as Marion placed their chef salads on the large oak coffee table in front of the couch she was careful to replace the cap tightly on the Ranch dressing before handing it to Frankie sitting beside her.

"Here you go, Hubbles, the dressing for your salad. I had a very productive day today. Got my clients' insurance paperwork all sent off."

Frankie, deep in thought, shook the bottle holding his index finger on the cap for good measure. As he poured a thick ring of dressing over his lettuce he remarked, "I am tired of Marley. We have been here for twenty-three years. I am leaving and I don't care if you come with me or not."

"What did you say?" Marion asked, dropping her fork.

"You know darn well and good you heard me. I'm finishing CPE in August and I am going to move away, somewhere."

Her voice escalated as she stood up, hands on her hips and asked, "What about my practice here? What about my doctoral program?"

"You said yourself Marion, you're tired of working so hard and since the complaint was filed against you, referrals have dropped off. We could have a fresh start and go somewhere as a co-pastorate team again. You could have a small private practice and we could downsize and enjoy life more. I happen to know of a church opening in Mt. Pleasant and I am going to apply for it."

Her mind reeled with this news. She did not respond further. There were no words. He told her to call their realtor and see what the house was worth. She was not sure she wanted to do any of this, but thought just finding out the worth of the house did not mean she was going through with it. She slept only three hours after their discussion ended at 2:30 a.m.

A week later Marion had a dream that Frankie was having an affair. She wrote in her journal about it.

God, am I imagining this or are you trying to warn me? God, please show me. I'm so torn about moving to Mt. Pleasant. Frankie is right that the referrals have dropped off. He's promising me that I can finish my doctoral program, that we will work less, spend more time together, and we'd share the church responsibilities. I just don't know. The last time we did was such a disaster, but what if they revoke my license. I must do some sort of work. I enjoy the ministry, just not Frankie's constant criticism about how I do things. God, please show me what to do. Amen.

As Frankie applied for the church position, he put their house on the market. She tried to be enthusiastic for his needs and wants.

Marion sat down at the kitchen table to eat the crockpot stew that had been simmering since she left for work hours earlier. She blew on her forkful and said, "Frankie, I am going to miss this house that I planned to stay in until I couldn't climb the stairs any more. In just fourteen months the mortgage will be paid off. I don't want to go into major debt again. I want a smaller house in Mt. Pleasant. We don't need much with the kids off on their own now. We don't even use our upstairs in this house."

He responded without looking up from his science fiction novel, making no promises, "We'll see what happens."

"I know this move to Mt. Pleasant is good for you, but I am sad leaving my friends, my colleagues, and clients behind," Marion admitted freely, sighing as she absentmindedly put a spoonful of stew into her mouth.

"Yeah, but they'll forget all about you and do just fine when you move away," he said looking up as got up with his glass in hand.

As Frankie poured a glass of water from the refrigerator outside spout, he reminded her, "I stayed here these twenty-three years for your career. Now it is time to move for mine."

He had a valid point. She wanted to be supportive of her husband's needs, but it still scared her. She was used to being able to buy the clothes she wanted, go out to eat when and where she wished and now all those amenities would disappear. She had vowed she never wanted to be destitute again, but it seemed to her that the path Frankie chose was headed in a negative direction.

She did not recall during her Near-Death Experience seeing Mt. Pleasant in her future. Since no spirit stood beside her bed to tell her not to go along with Frankie's plan, she began following his lead with a sinking feeling, believing, despite her lack of vision, she had to trust that God was leading Frankie in a direction that would be for their good. As she allowed Frankie to direct their steps, her sadness multiplied. The holistic clinic, called The Healing Path, only five and a half years old, shrunk as each colleague had each in turn found a new direction and left the practice in the last year. Marion solely bore the overhead expenses in her 1500 square foot office. She did not know if the Social Work Licensure Board would end her probation or revoke her license permanently due to the complaint. The anxiety over not knowing led her to seriously consider returning to co-pastorate ministry with Frankie, an insurance policy in case she lost her license.

"Frankie," Marion said as he was about to fall asleep after his nighttime ritual of oral sex.

"What, can't you see I was just about asleep?"

"I'm sorry. We can talk in the morning," she said turning away toward the wall.

"Damn it, Marion. I hate it when you do that. Tell me what you were going to say, for God's sake," he said turning her over.

"Well, I have decided I will go along with going to Mt. Pleasant, if I can still work on my doctorate," she said pensively.

"Is that it? Can I go to sleep now?"

"Ah, it's okay, then?" she hedged.

"I suppose."

"Thank you, thank you. I love you, Good night."

"Good night, already."

Talking to a local Marley psychiatrist, Marion agreed to share office space with him as she downsized her practice over an eighteen-month period to restart a new one in Mt. Pleasant. She was heartsick, but felt as a wife, it was still her commitment to try to bring some peace for her husband.

She did not want to leave, but did not want to be alone either. She agreed to sell the house and move to Mt. Pleasant. As she started downsizing her Marley practice, she started building a new one in Mt. Pleasant.

That August the movers arrived – church members from Mt. Pleasant. Once the moving truck was loaded, the church members led the way back to Mt. Pleasant.

Marion wandered each empty room, her voice echoing. She plopped down on the only remaining piece of furniture, a twin bed, flush against the south wall of the master bedroom burying her head in the pillow.

God, what have I agreed to? This was my dream house. My vision to set up a holistic clinic is now unraveling. I don't know what you want me to do. I don't know if I'll even still have a license in six months. My heart is so heavy, God. Just when I thought everything was secure, it's all whisked away. Are you punishing me? I don't want to be poor again. Please help me. I feel like I'm sinking in that quicksand again with no hope of ever escaping.

Their cedar-sided Cape Cod style dream house on the wooded lot built after Frankie's stroke finally sold on their anniversary the next spring. She wept the whole time signing the papers, knowing she made a mistake, but there was no turning back now.

After the sale, she moved their travel trailer behind the psychiatrist's building. At seven p.m. Marion poked her head in her colleague's office.

"Good night, Dr. Millikin. I'm going to go get something to eat and settle in my camper for the night."

"Marion, be careful. This isn't a very safe neighborhood. That's why we don't put a sign out front. We're afraid thugs will break in looking for drugs," he said as he waved to her.

She popped another *Lean Cuisine* frozen dinner in the camper microwave, her second such meal for the day. A huge piece of fudge topped off her evening. Too tired to read, she just worked and slept. On Wednesday night, she called Frankie before leaving the office on her new-fangled cell phone.

"Frankie, I'm leaving in a few minutes. I should be home by 11:30."

"Are you bringing more stuff from your old office? You know there's nowhere to put it. You've got the garage and spare bedroom full," he said exasperated.

Sighing she said, "Yes I bring more each trip I come. I'll leave it in my car until the morning and figure out what to do with it. It's so desolate driving through the back roads coming home. I hope I don't have any car trouble," she revealed apprehensively.

"You worry too much, you know that. I'll see you when you get here, if I'm still awake," he said hanging up. She lived a dual life – single Monday through Wednesday, a confident, competent therapist in a private practice, but Wednesday nights, as she drove to Mt. Pleasant, anxiety enveloped her. Thursday through Sunday she co-pastored the church, built a new practice, and squeezed in doctoral work, all while trying to impossibly please Frankie.

Session Twenty-Five

"Do you believe if I had today's awareness back then the outcome would have been different in my life, Dr. Weinstein?" Marion asked as she started the session.

"It does not matter what could have been. That is past. What is important is knowing where you are now and making conscious decisions based on your present knowledge. Who knows looking back years from now you may say, 'I wish I had known thus and so and I would have chosen differently.' Reviewing what led up to your choices helps you to see patterns and understand motives. Examining your behavior can change it," Dr. Weinstein explained.

"Thanks for explaining all that, Dr. Weinstein. I feel better. Let's move on," Marion said.

The Mt. Pleasant Disaster

WHEN MARION WOKE up on Thursday morning, refreshed from her drive from Marley, she shuffled to the kitchen in her pink terry cloth gripper socks. She spilled coffee on the kitchen floor while pouring it into her stainless-steel mug.

Frankie, sitting at the dining room table, watched her in disbelief. He cleared his throat and then laid into her. "Ya know Marion, when you come to Mt. Pleasant, you're coming to my (rented) house, my rules, my ways. You need to stop being so messy and wipe up that spill."

Marion set her coffee cup down on the table and turned her head to the side and asked, "Gee, what got you so grumpy this morning, Frankie?"

"This is where I live now," he said pointing to his chest. "I'm establishing a routine, making friends and getting the congregation to open up to new ideas and what do you do? You come waltzing in here like you own the place, making a mess, and then leave three days later to go back to your high and mighty life as a therapist. I'm just as important in my job as you are in yours. You need to be brought down a notch, all but ABD (all but dissertation) fucking Dr. Marion," he said, spewing spit as he raged."Furthermore," he said turning back around, "since we are into this co-pastorate ministry I have the final say. Since you did not complete seminary, I will decide what gets preached and you will read your sermon to me each week to make certain it is biblically sound. You got that?" he said hands on his hips.

What could she say? Her heart hurt. Her blood throbbed through her veins. She wanted to bolt and run, but where, to whom? She could feel the sand pulling her down, down into the abyss. Rather than respond she just picked up her car keys and silently got in her car to go grocery shopping.

Flashbacks to his aggressive sexual behavior and punching her in the stomach when pregnant with Little Sarah, flooded her mind. She feared if she challenged him that he would become violent again. If he got angry enough to tell her to get out of "his house" she had no where she could afford to go.

They toured multiple homes for sale. Marion crossed her fingers hoping that a new dwelling jointly selected would lessen his territorial hold over her. They disagreed on all the possible houses. She wanted to downsize into a fresh, compact, and simple abode. He wanted large and projects to piddle on.

She anxiously awaited an answer from her licensure board about her probationary status and if the course she took was sufficient. Tallying her monthly expenses, she attempted to make the funds stretch to cover traveling back and forth to Mt. Pleasant.

Frankie, looked over her shoulder standing above her. "You know Marion you screwed up. It's your fault, if you lose your license to practice. You should've known better."

"Hey, where's my support, Frankie?" she said looking up at him. "Didn't you ever screw up unintentionally, huh? Well, believe me I have replayed that scenario over in my head a thousand times. If I could take it back I would, but I can't," she said slipping under his arm, retreating to the bathroom to solitarily lick her wounds.

Not knowing if she would be career bankrupt she was reluctant to sign on the dotted line for a thirty-year mortgage. In desperation, she told Frankie when she emerged from her self-imposed timeout, "if you'll let me continue with my doctoral studies and get a hot tub I'll agree on The Lakes Subdivision house."

"Since I'm such a nice husband who has put up with your shit for over thirty years, I'll agree to that, but you have to agree to get a part-time job.

She looked him straight in the eye and said, "I am getting a small private practice going here in Mt. Pleasant as I close out mine in Marley. That should do it."

"Hell no, it won't," he said slapping the rolled-up newspaper on the table. "I mean a real job with set hours, a schedule and maybe even health insurance."

"Fine, I'll look, but remember I don't play well with others in employment settings. I do better solo," she said firmly.

"That's a crock of shit and you know it, Marion. You're just so god-damned independent that you don't want to work for anyone," he said and then he stormed outside to go for a walk.

She reluctantly agreed to sign a thirty-year mortgage, putting them back in $100,000 debt, secretly planning when she completed her doctorate. she could afford to leave, if needed. Conniving ways to do that meant she gave in to some of his demands.

As they settled in the three-bedroom, two bath home in The Lakes Subdivision, Marion noticed her chest was tight and she wheezed when she slept in the master bedroom. She went to see Dr. Chris when back in Marley.

"Marion, your lungs don't sound so good and you look depressed. Your weight is down five pounds. What's going on?" her physician friend inquired.

"Well," she said sighing, "You know that complaint against me is still not over. I don't know if I will eventually lose my license. I can't sleep well and I'm driving two and half hours each way back and forth to Mt. Pleasant. Ya know Frankie's still depressed having lost his job at the Commission. So, to answer your question, a lot is going on."

Taking her hand, he looked at her, eyeball to eyeball, "Marion, you look anorexic. You're down fifteen pounds in the last year. You're depressed with good reason. I'm going to give you something for depression and something to help you sleep. I really suggest you talk to a professional about all these stressors."

"I really appreciate all this Chris, but I don't want to gain all the weight back. I worked so hard to get off these pounds over the last eighteen months. I worked with Dr. Jenkins to get my blood pressure, cholesterol, and weight down. I'll take the medication and think about talking to someone in Mt. Pleasant." Hugging him she took the prescriptions with her as she checked out at the front desk.

As Marion returned to Mt. Pleasant each week the humid weather triggered her asthma and a month after seeing Dr. Chris she developed pneumonia. One morning while Marion was hacking up green phlegm into a tissue, Frankie who was looking over the mail slammed his palm on the table in the new house causing Marion to jump.

He looked over at her as threw the Kleenex into the trashcan and said, "You're always sick. We can't do anything because all our money is going to doctors who don't help. You need to tell yourself this is crap and get over it. I'm not paying this stack of doctor bills. It's on you."

Then he stormed out of the house and drove off in the car. Marion did not have a chance to respond. She sat down at the table to look at the bills and said a silent prayer.

God, I don't want to be sick. I don't know what's wrong with me. Please help.

Marion's ill health continued. She tried to refocus by preparing for her mom Sarah's move to North Mt. Pleasant away from the cold Wisconsin winters. Grandma Sarah purchased a condo in November.

"Marion, why are you so consumed with your mom's move here? We have a life too, you know. I hope she doesn't occupy all your time and you forget about me," Frankie said as they were preparing to get into bed.

"No, Frankie you can be sure I won't neglect you," she said as she prepared for the nightly ritual to satisfy his sexual needs.

Grandma Sarah arrived in Mt. Pleasant ahead of the moving van. She stayed with Marion and Frankie for three nights.

"Mom, aren't you excited to finally get into your new place tomorrow?" Marion asked sitting at the kitchen table sharing bagels and cream cheese with Sarah.

While chewing a mouthful of blueberry cream cheese on a piece of her cinnamon bagel Sarah smiled and some of her contents oozed onto her lip. Marion wiped it away and giggled.

"Mom, we're going have a good time together." Sarah nodded as she continued eating.

The next day as Frankie helped Marion unpack her mother's belongings he asked Sarah, "Grannie, (he loved to call her that, because he knew she hated it since her mom was called Grannie) you have enough clothes for three women. Why do you need so many?"

Marion defended her mom, "Leave her alone, Frankie. She didn't have much growing up and skimped when we kids were coming up, so she buys clothes. So, what?" Frankie slunk off to Grannie's recliner and ignored them.

Hmm. He doesn't equate buying every new gadget that suits his fancy as the same thing.

The first Thursday in February, Mary, her stepmother called. "Marion, this is Mary," she said sounding down.

"Mary what's up? You don't sound so good."

She started to cry. Before she could answer Marion inhaled quickly and then said, "Oh no, something's happened to Dad, hasn't it?"

Between sobs Mary said, "Your dad grabbed his head and slummed over standing next to the pantry in the kitchen. I called 911 and they came right away. It's a stroke and they say it's bad."

"Mary," forming plans as she spoke rapidly. "I'll reschedule all my clients and I'll get there as soon as I can. What hospital is he in?"

"They flew him to Charlottesville. He's on the same floor as Christopher Reeve when he had the horse accident."

"Mary, don't worry. I'm sure Little Sarah will come too. We will probably get there by tomorrow night, okay?"

"Thank you. Your dad loves you girls and will do better when you get here."

The next day daughter Sarah and Marion drove the eight hours to Virginia. They checked into their hotel and went to his room about nine p.m. Rhonda flew in from Wisconsin arriving the next morning.

Andy's condition was bleak. He could not swallow, eat, follow commands, see, or respond. He was obviously in pain because he kept rubbing his forehead. Marion went to the nurse's station.

"Excuse me. I need someone to give my dad some pain medicine. He is obviously in discomfort."

The nurse, charting, sitting at the desk, looked up. "What room is your dad in?"

Exasperated Marion said, "He's in room 204. He's in pain."

The nurse dismissively said returning to writing her notes, "Your dad had a massive stroke. He can't feel anything."

Marion leaned over the counter and glared at the nurse. "I don't care what the hell you say. Come to his room and I'll show you."

The nurse looked over to CNA (Certified Nursing Assistant) gathering supplies to bathe her next patient and said, "If the Director of Nursing comes by, tell her I'm going to educate the family in 204." With that she followed Marion into her father's room.

Marion leaned over her dad and said, "Dad, if you're in pain, squeeze my hand." She felt a gentle squeeze.

"I think that is just a coincidence, a reflex action," the nurse said in a condescending tone.

Marion raised her voice, grabbed the nurse's sleeve, and tugged while pointing to the door. Once in the hallway Marion poked her finger into the nurse's chest, "I don't care what the hell you think. You are going to give my dad pain medicine or I'm going to call an attorney and sue you for patient neglect and suffering! You got that?"

Removing Marion's finger off her uniform the nurse stated clearly, "I can't make that decision, but I will page his physician to see what can be done."

"Thank you. That is all I ask," Marion said exhaling.

Andy received pain medication and his body relaxed. His hand stayed at his side. Marion saw that her dad's adult diaper was soaked. It was shift change time. The nurses were doing the report to hand off the patient updates to their nighttime counterpart. Marion started to push the bedside call button then stopped. She knew it would be at least thirty minutes before someone would come in the room, even if they answered the intercom. She grabbed a diaper off the side table and began to lift her dad's frail body to change it. As she did her dad started thrashing.

Marion understood. Whether verbal or not, her dad was embarrassed to have her change his diaper. She soothingly spoke to him as tears slid down her cheeks.

"Dad, you changed my diaper many times when I was little. Now it is my turn to help you. I love you and I'm not embarrassed. It is a way to show you that I care and I don't want you to be wet, or suffer any more discomfort."

With that his body relaxed and he laid still. To Marion it was a sacred moment between the two of them, one she never forgot.

The next morning Mary alone sitting in the chair, crocheting, next to her husband of thirty-two years looked up when Dr. Westover came in the room on his morning rounds. He looked at Andy and back to Mary and plainly said, "I need to put a feeding tube in so your husband can get nutrition."

"But, Dr. Westover, my husband clearly said in his signed paperwork here," pulling it out of her purse pointing to the clause, "he does not want any heroic measures. I can't go against his wishes as much as I want him to live," she said with tears welling up.

"I cannot in good conscience let him starve to death, that would be cruel," he said staring at the chart avoiding her gaze. "So, I'm scheduling the procedure for today at 2:00 p.m.," then he briskly walked out of the room, not waiting for a response.

When Marion and Rhonda entered the room after eating breakfast in the hospital cafeteria Mary told them what was to happen. Gretchen was not present nor intended to come.

Rhonda said, "But Mary, Dad would not want that."

"I know, but what can I do? He's the doctor," she said wringing her hands looking woefully at Andy, finally resting comfortably.

Marion went into social work action. "Let me go find a hospital social worker or chaplain to see what we can do." She took off before anyone could object.

Without involving a judge, the family was told nothing could stop Dr. Westover. They spoke clearly to Andy believing he could understand their words.

"We're sorry Dad, we know you do not want this, but we cannot get Dr. Westover to listen," Marion said holding her dad's hand.

The chaplain said a hasty prayer with the family surrounding the bed before an orderly wheeled Andy down to the operating room.

The man who lived to talk, eat, and laugh could now do none of these things. The family grieved each of those losses. Marion, Sarah, and Rhonda returned home the day before they transported Andy to a nursing facility because Mary could not care for him at home. Marion called daily to get an update and check on Mary. On Grandma Sarah's seventy-fourth birthday, Andy peacefully passed away.

All the family congregated at Mary's house before and after the funeral surrounding her with love and support, all except Gretchen and Tim. They did not attend any family events. They felt no connection to Andy since he divorced Sarah and did not acknowledge the stepfamily. Even ex-wife Sarah sent her condolences.

After the funeral Marion received word that her probation was lifted. The victory paled in comparison to the depth of grief due to the death of her father. Unable to financially recoup her losses in Marley from lessened referrals, due to the complaint, she opted to move forward.

She closed out her Marley dream practice by the year's end and continued her doctoral studies from Mount Pleasant. A few clients opted to continue therapy with her, commuting the distance to Mt. Pleasant. New clients, along with some seasoned Marley ones, all abused as children, learned together to claim their own empowerment.

In the process, Marion disclosed to this women's sexual abuse survivor group her own experience with Hank on the Island.

Kim listened intently and asked, her palms resting on her chin, "Marion, you've helped each of us prepare to confront our abusers. How did you confront this man?"

Marion hesitated before answering. Taking a deep breath in she looked around the circle at each of the five women and then said, "actually I haven't yet. I don't know where he is. But you know what?" she said, her hands in a prayerful pose. "I think I'll see if I can find out and practice what I preach."

The women all nodded in agreement. In her heart, she believed he probably negatively shaped more than just her young life and perhaps was even listed on a national sexual offender list. Websites, arrest records, and sexual offenders' lists yielded nothing, so she hired a private investigator. Her intention, if all her suppositions were true, would be to confront him, at least over the phone, about his behavior and how it affected her all through the years. Herself empowered, she would finally take charge of the naïve teenager trapped inside of her. In hindsight, the adult Marion saw how Hank groomed that inexperienced seventeen-year-old to gradually trust him, only to be later confused by his actions and to ultimately feel rejected and abandoned by him. Found in less than forty-eight hours by the PI. she sent him a letter and asked if they could talk. While she was not home, he left her a voicemail message to call him. She went to her church office on a Sunday afternoon and quietly closed and locked door while she gathered her courage, stomach churning.

She said a brief prayer, "God, please direct my steps. Thank you, Amen." The phone's receiver laid in her hand as she nervously dialed the number, "May I speak with Hank, please?" she asked as her hands shook.

"This is Hank."

"Hi, this is Marion Parker Finch," she said with a quavering voice, biting her fingernail as he spoke

"Oh, hi. How are you?" he asked pleasantly.

She delved in. "I called you for a reason. I wanted to talk to you about something."

Pausing, "Ok, what?"

"Do you remember how you told me one day I might be mad at you?"

"No, but okay," he said in a condescending manner.

Drawing in a breath and then letting it out slowly she said, "Well, through the years since we had our relationship on Mackinac Island, it has affected me. I have been to therapy about it, different times in the last thirty years."

He said, "I knew you were a troubled teenager. I hope the therapy helped you."

Defensively, she raised her voice as she said, "You kissing me and fondling me was not right. You were a twenty-seven-year old married man for God's sake and I was just a naïve seventeen-year-old."

He rejected her claims, denying the veracity of them. He said, "I don't know what you are talking about. I did not do anything wrong. You were a disturbed young woman."

Raising up in her chair and squaring back her shoulders, she confidently said, "I just want you to know how what you did affected me. Did you ever reveal any of your escapades to your wife or tell her about the affairs you told me you had apart from our relationship?"

Ignoring the question Hank answered, "Sally and I divorced amicably years ago, and I have been married to Helen for ten years now. We own a Bed and Breakfast Inn here in Wisconsin. If you ever want to talk again, let me know. I wish you well."

Angry, Marion, hung up. Although she did not get the response she wanted, she prided herself in confronting him. Maybe, just maybe, he would think about what he did and have some guilt about it or maybe think before he did it to someone else.

When Marion drove home, she played the scene over and over in her head. When she entered the house, Frankie was watching a golf tournament on the television. Marion sat down on the couch beside him, quiet, waiting for a commercial. She asked him if she could talk for a minute while the Nike commercial played. Turning to face him she said, with tears in her eyes, "Well, I talked to Hank."

Impatient to return to his program he said, "And, what? I haven't got all day for you to drag this out. What did he say?"

Marion's stomach became as hard as a rock as she, in fits and starts, tried to put it into words. "He said I was a troubled teen and nothing happened." Then she paused waiting, hoping for some reassuring statement.

Grabbing the remote to unmute the commercial he said, "I don't see what the big deal is. He only kissed you and fondled your butt. It's not like he fucked you. You were seventeen not seven for God's sake, you weren't his student, and you probably led him on!"

Marion got up from the couch and stood in front of the television and said, "I'm not going to argue this with you. You are not a female so you don't get what it is like to be treated like you're an object and only for the gratification of the guy." With that she walked away into the study and shut the door. It was an eye opener for her, one unfaithful husband joining ranks with a fellow cheater.

Boy, my chest is tight. I guess the stress of all this, clients, church work, and school is too much. I better go see my allergist and pulmonologist just in case it's not stress. Frankie will be so mad, me spending money on doctors again. 'What a waste,' he'll say. Like Mom, 'it's just your nerves. There's nothing wrong with you'

Dr. Futuro, the pulmonologist sat her down in his office. "Marion, your O2 sats are really low, in the 80s. Look at your nailbeds," he said lifting up her hand. They're purple. That's not good. I'm going to order you to have oxygen at night while you sleep. You need to see your allergist, Dr. Nixon."

Wheezing as she spoke in a hoarse whisper she responded, "What's causing all this asthma problems? I haven't had it this bad since I was 12."

"Some people don't do well in the humid Mt. Pleasant climate. You may be one of those," he said with a sigh.

When she saw Dr. Nixon she got more bad news. Turning off the exam room light the doctor put the X-ray up on the light box and said, "Marion, look at this X-ray of your lungs. It's like you smoked for twenty-five years. Did you?"

"No, Ma'am. I never did, but my husband did for fourteen years of our marriage until he had a stroke," she answered.

"See these dark spots on the X-ray?" she said pointing to them.

"Yes, what does that mean?"

"You have pneumonia in both lungs. That is why it is so hard for you to breathe. What did Dr. Futuro tell you to do?"

Scared, Marion told her and felt her anxiety rising making the breathing even more difficult. Antibiotics were prescribed for ten days for the bacterial pneumonia.

It took a week to get the order for the oxygen to be delivered. The condenser positioned beside her side of the bed whined all night long.

"Marion, that noise is deafening. I can't sleep. I'm going out to my recliner."

"I'm sorry Frankie, but if I don't use it, I could stop breathing permanently," she said as she hacked up more green phylum into a tissue on the night stand.

Returning for a follow-up visit, Dr. Nixon spoke frankly to her, "Marion, you live in a house with a crawl space, right?"

Puzzled Marion asked, "Yeah, why do you ask?"

"Well, ever since Hurricane Hugo in '89, houses with crawl spaces are prone to hold mold. People with your asthma are greatly impacted by those situations. It can be life-threatening," she said as she patted Marion on the knee.

A couple of weeks before the 9/11 attack and just sixteen months after buying their house in Mt. Pleasant, Frankie agreed for them to move to a smaller vinyl sided/faux brick patio home on a slab to help Marion's breathing difficulties. In the process of selling their home the prospective buyers paid for an inspection. It revealed as Dr. Nixon predicted, mold in the rafters and floorboards probably acquired from Hurricane Hugo damage. Unfortunately, that damage was not discovered when the Finches bought it or they could have avoided some of the physical effects on Marion and the cost of an environmental clean-up fund for the subsequent buyers.

Fifteen months into living in the slab house, Marion wrote in her journal.

We had a great Thanksgiving Day yesterday with fourteen people. We went shopping at six a.m. then played golf. I beat Frankie. Boy, was he mad. Last night in bed he began to complain. When you give me a BJ, it feels mechanical. I want to shove it up your ass once a year. God, his guilt trip is so strong. I feel a hit in my stomach and a sinking feeling like I'm going deeper into quicksand. Frankie wants to move to a new place. I know God, it'll be no different. He will tire of it soon and want something else. I've gone along with it all these years. He tells me one minute how grand I am and the next he's complaining that he never gets to do what he wants. I want to remain in my adult state, not the scared little kid state. I do not want my gut to hurt. Help me stay firm and headed straight ahead. Thank you, God. Amen.

After that entry, Marion became emotionally numb. Any time Frankie criticized her, she just went somewhere else in her head and blocked it out. Frankie noticed.

"Earth to Marion. Are you even here? Your eyes are glazed over and you didn't even jump when I slammed the door," he said when she sat staring out the window in the living room.

Marion snapped out of her daze and turned toward him, "Hmm, what'd you say?"

"Never mind. You're obviously not interested in anything I say or do anymore. Go back to that wasteland inside your little mind," he said, tapping her left temple as he walked by out into the garage to start a load of laundry.

In January, seventeen years to the day of Frankie's stroke, Grandma Sarah entered the hospital with congestive heart failure. The on first Monday in February, doctors performed a double coronary bypass. Frankie's fifty-sixth birthday was three days later. The next day, Frankie's mom, Barbara, struggling for seven years with COPD died, ten years after Poppy had died from Alzheimer's. Rhonda flew into Mt. Pleasant to care for Grandma Sarah while Marion and Frankie flew out to Cortland for Barbara's funeral. Marion had promised her mother-in-law she would perform the service and did. Exhausted, Marion was surprised at the number of compliments given as she headed out the door to join the funeral procession to the cemetery.

Frankie held the car door open for Marion. Walking around to the driver's side he got in and buckled his seat belt. Turning toward her he said as she drew in a breath and collapsed into the passenger seat, "You did a fairly good job, Marion. You only messed up one thing."

Too tired to care, Marion said, "Really? What did you find that I screwed up?"

"You quoted mom, 'Barbara always said, anyhow', but actually it was anyway."

"Frankie, I got one, minute part wrong. People who know your mom knew what I meant. People who did not know her well wouldn't know I got it wrong," she said, motioning with her hands as she spoke. She sat silent for the rest of the drive to the cemetery. After the graveside portion of the service she got into Adam's car, saying nothing to Frankie and rode back to Ronnie's house to meet up with the rest of the family.

With the inheritance from Frankie's mother, they purchased the condo above Grandma Sarah's to rent out. They hoped to control the noise level by carefully selecting the right tenants to not disturb or keep Sarah awake. Owning rental property was an uneasy endeavor for them. Marion spent Mother's Day painting the condo preparing it for possible tenants to view. Her mom, reconciled with Gretchen since Sarah's wedding, spent the holiday in Ithaca, New York happily visiting her oldest child. Frankie, never even wished Marion Happy Mother's Day, saying, "It's just a made-up Hallmark money maker. You're not my mother, so I am not doing anything for you." He did not do anything for his mother either. If any gift was bought, Marion did it. The kids each sent Marion a nice card.

Frankie grumbled whenever she approached him about anything lately. Walking out of her church office into Frankie's, Marion told him, "Our tenant Laurie just called. She said the A/C isn't working right. It's ninety degrees in the apartment. Can you please go by on your way home and check it?"

"I don't know anything about A/C units. Call her back and tell her to just wait awhile and see if it cools down. Maybe she put it on heat instead of air," he said not accepting the responsibility, eyes not moving from his computer screen.

Marion stopped on her way home. It was even hotter now in the upstairs two-bedroom apartment. Exasperated, she did not know what to do. Finally, she called their realtor, Mo and asked for a good A/C repairman. A hundred bucks later it was repaired. Marion was relieved that the crisis was abated, but Frankie was furious.

"I would've taken care of it. Why'd you have to call Mo and pay for a repair?" he said enraged. "You're always costing me more money," he said, flinging his wrist in the air.

"Frankie, it was your idea to get the condo, not mine. I don't know how to be a landlord. Maybe we should hire a property management service to take care of things," she cautiously suggested.

"Naw, I don't need any more money going out for something **you** can handle," he said as he stormed into the guest bedroom slamming the door.

The two churches they co-pastored at this point were forty miles apart. Tuesdays Frankie spent the night at the smaller church. Marion, once again relishing the time apart, could freely relax with her mom. Frankie did not want to share his wife with his mother-in-law, so this arrangement worked to everyone's benefit. Sarah sipped on her tea while Marion put her feet up in her mom's condo. Looking over at her daughter finally relaxing, Sarah asked her.

"Marion, I just don't understand why the Mt. Pleasant Church doesn't grow. Your sermons are spot on and related to the current world. I even admit that Frankie delivers a good message. The people are so stuck. I don't know how you can stand working so hard for people who don't appreciate anything you try to do."

Marion sighed, setting down her cup on the coffee table and said, "I know, Mom. When I preach what I believe God wants me to say (*and Frankie approves of*) the people either ignore it or feel they know better than God. They are so afraid to grow, because of being hurt in the past by preachers who promised them the church would flourish and it did not. Frankie's so frustrated that he's ready to quit, but we can't. I'm not done with school and I believe there's hope that they'll grow."

"Well," Sarah said. "I've decided to attend mass. I can't watch what they do to you and keep my tongue. If I spoke up, it might hurt your ministry and I don't want that."

"I understand Mom, and don't blame you. I'll explain it to Frankie. I doubt the members will even notice. I'm sorry."

Frankie did not comment when she told him. Maybe he was happy to not have to preach to his mother-in-law.

One Wednesday morning Marion walked into the church front office to get the mail. Routinely, she turned on the computer to start her day. Clicking the AOL icon, she stopped, putting her hand over her mouth out of shock. There in front of her was a picture of two naked women with obviously enhanced breasts in a seductive pose. Her face reddened as she clicked the off the monitor.

She stepped into the doorway yelling down the hall,

"Frankie, come here, right now!"

As he approached he said, raising his voice,

"What's so urgent that I had to stop what I was doing and come right now?"

Pointing she turned on the monitor, and angrily asked, "Frankie, what the hell are you doing looking at pornography on the church computer? You know I file insurance claims on this system. If it's monitored, we will get fired and I will lose my social work license for sure."

He shrugged his shoulders, and said, "Marion, you worry way too much. It's no big deal. I'll remove it. I'll erase the cookies. You don't respect me anymore and are always critical of me. A man has a right to some privacy."

"Not on the public church computer. This behavior is committing professional suicide. I am so angry with you right now!"

"You made your point already, so shut up about it," he said as he closed out the browser and erased the cookies.

She marched back to her office and did not speak to him again until supper time.

Days later she courageously inquired what he had done to get rid of the evidence. "Problem solved," he simply said.

"How may I ask?" Marion quizzed him, hands on her hips.

"I took the Internet off the front office computer," he said nonchalantly.

"Well, I better not find it again. It's filth, that is all it is, disgusting filth," she piously proclaimed as she went back to reading her assignment for her doctoral statistics course.

I'm sure he is still looking at pornography, but I have no desire to play detective and find out. I am so angry that his brother got him started looking at porn when he visited him on his solo vacation in August. It makes me feel dirty when he has sex with me. I know he's thinking of those slutty women he ogled on the computer screen.

One night as Frankie and Marion soaked together in their hot tub sitting on opposite sides, Marion assembled her courage and asked him, "So is this how it's going to be all the time now? You verbally taking out your anger on me?"

"Yes, what do you want to do about it? You betrayed me. You took out student loans and did not tell me. It affected our credit and ability to get a loan for this house," he said pointing his finger toward the dining sliding glass door.

Glaring at him, she said, "You told me I could continue my doctoral schooling when we moved here. I asked for your help to pay for it. You told me no, so I found a way to pay for it myself. It is for $27,000 and I have fifteen years to pay it off over time starting in May of 2005. I always meet my obligations, so you do not have to worry about it."

"You used to trust me and do what I said. Now you do not even listen to me. You think now you are Miss Smarty Pants because you are getting the fucking doctorate. And for what, so we can be stuck paying for it instead of being able to retire? Did you think about our credit score when you messed up our credit? Did you, huh? I don't think so."

He stopped talking, got out of the hot tub and went to sleep in the guest room. They still had an A+ credit rating even with her loans.

The next evening Marion finished loading the dishwasher and wiped her hands on the dishtowel. She picked up her notebook and walked into the spare bedroom to work on the computer on her dissertation. Frankie followed her close behind.

Surprised, she looked up to see him glaring at her as she sat in her desk chair. Her back stiffened, prepared for whatever he was about to proclaim.

"You have your papers strewn all over in this room," he said sweeping his hand across the bed knocking them all on the floor.

"Hey, why did you do that?" she said her voice rising. "I had them all organized as to how they fit into my manuscript," she said, nostrils flaring as she began to pick them up.

Towering over her by thirteen inches he said with hands on his hips, "I'm sick of this goddamned doctoral program occupying your every waking thought, your every spare moment away from the church and client responsibilities. Where do I fit in to the equation? You used to care about what I thought and needed. Now you just criticize my every move. If you don't straighten up, there's gonna be a major change around here. I'm warning you, mark my words," he said as he left the house, driving off in a huff.

She reassembled the papers in proper order as she tried to fathom what just happened. *God, do I really have tunnel vision? Am I missing what you want me to do? Am I the horrible person Frankie paints me to be? I've got no time to ponder any of this. The defense for my thesis is due in a couple of months. I'll worry about Frankie when it's over.*

Even though she was making more money than he was by building her private practice in addition to her church duties, it was not enough to support herself. She could not move out and felt stuck just like in Ohio when the kids were small. She went to see a therapist. The therapist challenged her, "change the pattern with him. Instead of him storming out of the argument, upend him. You leave."

She tried. One night after she spent four hours reviewing her literature review, she came back into the kitchen area to get a snack, feeling proud of her accomplishment. Frankie saw it differently.

"So, is the all but ABD fucking psychotherapist done for the night ignoring me?" he said as he turned off the television.

"I'll come bed in a minute and you can have your night time orgasm so you won't feel neglected," she said pouring the milk into her cereal bowl.

Frankie got up from the couch and slammed the Interpreters Bible he was reviewing for his sermon on the dining room table as he said, "I don't need you to patronize me with my night time perfunctory blow job. I'm sure I can find someone that appreciates me and wants to be with me since you obviously don't."

With that he went into the bathroom to prepare for bed. Marion thought about it for a second and then it dawned on her. *This is my opportunity to do as my therapist suggested.* She put her bowl in the refrigerator, quietly grabbed her purse and keys and slipped quietly out the front door.

It was eleven p.m. Frightened to embark on this new behavior at such a late hour, she just sought the solace of her church office. She pulled out the sleeper sofa in her office preparing to depart early enough for the church secretary not to suspect she spent the night. Frankie called on her cell phone continuously. She finally answered it.

"Where the hell are you?" he demanded.

"I'm somewhere safe where I plan to spend the night," she sighed feeling a little powerful.

Frankie caved as he pleaded, "Please come home so we can talk about this."

"So, you can yell some more and threaten me? No thanks."

"I promise we will talk, just come home."

Reluctantly she did, hoping her therapist's instructions had turned the tide in the huge wall of ice that formed between her and her disgruntled husband.

Unfortunately, it did not.

As she re-entered the house he was sitting in his recliner chewing his fingernails. She walked in and said nothing. Walking toward the bedroom, he got up out of his seat and put his hand on her shoulder. She pulled it away and entered the doorway of the bedroom. After undressing she slid under the covers and turned toward the wall away from him. He clutched her unrelenting body toward him wrapping his arms around her chest. She did not move.

When Marion awoke the next morning, she slid out from under the covers without saying a word to Frankie. She went into the bathroom and closed the door. As Frankie was getting dressed to go to the church office he announced loud enough for Marion to hear him through the bathroom door, "I've decided that I'm not going to have sex with you again until you let me fuck you up the ass."

Drying off after her shower she said opening the door, "fucking me up the ass is not sex; it's power manipulation and I will not stand for it."

"Fine then, I will just have to go find someone who wants to be with me and respects me." He went to the kitchen to get the morning coffee she had set the timer to brew the night before.

While Frankie was out of the room, Marion fell sobbing onto the bathroom floor, "God why is this happening to me? Why did you ever send us to Mt. Pleasant, this God-forsaken place where the people do not want us and Frankie has become meaner than ever to me? Why?"

"Oh, by the way, just for the record, God did not send us here. It was my idea. I decided it was what I wanted to do," Frankie said as he stuck his head back into the bedroom doorway seeing her weeping in a disheveled heap on the bathroom floor.

Marion scowled at him and pounded on the floor as she said, "I trusted that you prayed about it and God told you to come here. Why didn't you tell me? We're having all this misery because it was what you wanted to do? Are you crazy? Don't ever drag me where God doesn't lead us again."

He grabbed her off the floor by her wrists and dragged her to her feet. He said, "Get dressed and in the car. We are supposed to already be at the church for our normal office hours. Do you want me to call the secretary and tell her we are delayed because of your temper tantrum?"

Nauseated and shaking, she robotically donned her clothing and then sat mute on the ride to the church. When she entered the educational wing, she headed to her office. She could not even greet the secretary, knowing her eyes were red and swollen from tears. She did not know how the strife between them was going to be resolved, but knew it would not be good.

God, the only way I afford to escape this quicksand existence is to complete my doctorate and get a good paying position somewhere, but what about the churches. I can't abandon the people. I can't continue to live this way. I need some direction. I don't remember any of this scenario in my Near-Death Experience. Where are you God? I'm lost and sinking deeper. Is this situation my punishment because I told Frankie about my spiritual leap? I'm afraid I will never escape this hell.

To complete school she believed that she had to play along with Frankie by initiating sex to calm the beast and allow her time to work on her dissertation. As quickly as she could she would try to get things back to a normal dysfunctional routine. That meant playing along with his wants, needs, and ideas until she could not stomach the charade any further. Frankie picked up on the dichotomy.

As they ate lunch at the Chinese Buffet restaurant after attending a ministerial meeting Frankie was all smiles.

"Marion, aren't you excited to go to Louisiana with me to trade the motorhome?"

"Frankie, sure. It will be a great time away from the church," she said pasting a smile on her face.

"Now that's not very convincing. You're shaking your head yes, but your arms are crossed defensively. Your body and words don't match."

"Ah, well Frankie, I was thinking about the meeting with my Defense Committee coming up and wondering how will I work on my dissertation on the road," she lied.

"Sure, you are. That is all you think about twenty-four seven," he said raising his voice.

The energy to live this deceptive existence drained her. It reached its pinnacle after their Louisiana trip. Marion developed a series of physical reactions she thought from the non-responsive churches, the criticalness of Frankie, the tension between her mom and husband, researching and writing her dissertation, attempting to develop a private practice in her "spare time," and financially finagling paying all their combined expenses. As the deadline grew close to complete her doctoral program, she could not remember people's names or important dates from her past. Her swollen feet, achy body, and head-to-toe itching constantly plagued her. The symptoms appeared after an insect bite on the trip to Louisiana in July. She remained hopeful that her symptoms would dissipate once she completed her dissertation.

Agreeing with Dr. Rosen, her rheumatologist prescribed anti-inflammatory medication and upped her dosage on Wellbutrin to see her through to graduation. Frankie only noticed Marion's lack of response to him. As he stood at the kitchen sink he asked her, "Marion, how about turning on the news?"

No response. She continued reading the article about stress and hearts attacks for her dissertation research.

Frankie walked from the kitchen to the couch ten steps from the sink, grabbed her chin and forced her to look up at him.

"Marion, I asked you to turn on the news. What is wrong with you? Something definitely is. You don't hear me or listen to me when I try to talk to you. You start saying 'no' before I even complete a sentence. I think you are getting Alzheimer's or something."

Moving her head out of his grasp she looked him straight in the eye as she said, "I'm afraid, too. I know something's not right, but I do not know what. I'm willing to find out though."

Frankie stiffened his posture as he turned, picked up the remote to turn on the television and said, "I don't care what you do, but if you become incapacitated, don't expect me to take care of you."

That night when they sat in the hot tub, Marion approached Frankie about his anger. She wrote about it in her journal.

> I asked Frankie, "Are you afraid I'll leave you either by death or mental illness? Is that why you're pushing me away, to leave now?" He said, "I guess so." Help me God to be healthy, do the right things, and not give in to things that are harmful to me, including Frankie's fears and anger. Thank you. Amen.

She had to know, so if she was failing cognitively, then she could prepare. She saw a kinesiology chiropractor who told her she was gluten intolerant, but her Fibromyalgia symptoms could be alleviated. She had intelligence and memory testing done. Tests showed she had an IQ of 128, but she had processing delays and some short-term memory deficits. An MRI revealed three brain lesions thought to be a normal part of aging. The results explained that what Frankie thought was her not listening, not hearing what he said, was her just trying to process what he said.

Ah ha. I thought all this was just stress. Boy was I wrong. It's funny, but I am glad to know. Now maybe I can do something about it. I'm NOT crazy, imagine that! But, Frankie won't believe me, I know. How am I going to break it to him? In the hot tub? Naw, he'd be too preoccupied with his fun time after the tub. Maybe while we're eating breakfast? Guess, you gotta help me here, God with an opening. Please?

The next morning Marion busily typed notes on the computer as Frankie yelled at her from the adjoining bathroom. When she did not turn around, he sauntered over the desk and said right in her face, "Woman, open up your ears. Any adult can understand what I say. I speak in plain language. Do you want to go to the Chinese Buffet or the Seafood Buffet? It is not rocket science, just give me an answer."

"I'm sorry Frankie, I was deep in thought typing away. What did you ask me again?" she asked with a perplexed facial expression.

For Marion, each time he interrupted her attempts to process what he asked, adding more words, the processing stopped and she would have to start over.

He spoke again deliberately and very slowly, "Doooo youuuuu wanttttt tooooo goooo toooo theee Chineseeee buffetttt orrrr theeeee Seafooddddd buffetttt forrrrr lunchhhh? Was that slow enough for you?" he said with a smirk on his face.

Marion pulled out the test results from under her textbook and showed him.

He said throwing them back down on the computer table, "I don't believe any of that shit. You just don't want to listen to me or respect me anymore."

She learned it was best to not try to defend her position because he could fire back retorts so fast she was unable to formulate an adequate comeback. To calm the waters, she simply said, "Seafood Buffet for lunch is fine."

Marion was relieved that the psychological test results verified that she was not crazy, but living with Frankie's constant anger made her question if he could drive her crazy.

A month later she approached Frankie cautiously again about her test results as he sat reading the newspaper at the kitchen table.

"Frankie, could you stop reading the paper for a minute, please?" she asked setting down her coffee cup in front of her.

Looking over his glasses at her he said, irritated, "Why, what's so important that I have to interrupt finishing the word jumble?"

"Please accept my spatial tracking deficit. It is documented by the neuropsychologist. I try really hard to respond when you ask me a question, but when you add more to it before I have a chance to process what you first asked, I get flustered and lose the whole conversation."

"You done now? Or did I ask too long of a question? It's not rocket science you know or maybe it is for your so-called diminished brain function."

His queries were the very example of what she just requested he not do. She could not process the information quickly enough to form a response. He said nothing else, picked up the newspaper and resumed working the puzzle. She felt defeated by the one person who is supposed to be supportive. In the past when she processed things after a conversation had grown cold and tried to come back to the discussion, he would chastise her, "Why are you bringing that up now? That was two days ago. I'm not mad about it anymore, but I can get mad again, if you want to revisit it."

She returned to Dr. Rosen and showed him the results of her testing. He diagnosed her with Fibromyalgia and added Flexaril to help with the pain and sleep. He sat down on the brown swivel stool in front of her and told her, "Marion, when you complete your doctoral degree, remember, you'll probably have less stress and pain." Then he patted her on the knee and tore off the prescription from his pad and handed them to her.

Next, she saw a dermatologist to address her continuous itching, thought to be related also to her stress level. The dermatologist did a biopsy on the bug bite and declared it was an arachnid bite, but the origin of the species not identified. Maybe the bite had something to do with all her symptoms, especially her incessant rash and itching. It would take another seven years before she had the answer.

Marion explored methods she was learning in her doctoral studies that could assist the congregations to become motivated to grow spiritually and hopefully increase in number. One congregation averaged eighteen people on a Sunday and was financially solvent. They had no interest in mission work. The other larger church averaged forty people on a Sunday. Once a thriving congregation, now barely met its expenses. The transitioning neighborhood around the Mt. Pleasant church was an impediment for the potential to draw in new homogenous people to match the existing members. The idea of meeting the needs of their new multi-cultured neighbors was abhorrent to the congregation. Both congregations claimed to want growth, but even a specialist brought in from the denominational headquarters to do some mission planning remarked that she had never seen such unmotivated congregants. The churches were not verbally hostile to the preachers, but their apathetic behavior spoke volumes. The congregations were happy to have Frankie and Marion create programs, do visiting, and be a witness in the community. But the parishioners had no desire to expand their own involvement beyond Sunday morning worship and maybe a Wednesday night Bible study if the Finches led it.

Frankie and Marion began a community healing service held on Thursday nights. Church members refused to come. The pastors led the service right from their book of worship. The service mirrored the one that Episcopal Churches use which involves anointing a person with oil on their forehead making the sign of the cross and placing hands on the top of their head while praying over them. Based on the bible passage from James 5:14, "Are any among you sick? They should call for the elders of the church and have them pray over them, anointing them with oil in the name of the Lord." People from the community who came felt blessed. In July one of the elders attended. After the service, he approached the ministers cornering them at the sanctuary door leading into the church library.

"Frankie and Marion, can I talk to you privately?" he said his voice in a hoarse whisper.

"Sure Henry," they said, hopeful that he would praise their acumen for creating this community service, as walked into Marion's office and closed the door.

As Frankie and Marion sat down on the couch in her office they smiled inviting Elder Henry to sit in the chair opposite them. He chose to stand shutting the door behind him. Leaning over to the couple he pointed a finger at Marion's chest raised his voice saying, "Just what do you think you're doing here? We did not grant you permission to have this holy roller service. This is work of the devil. I have a mind to get you fired over this," he said flailing his arms in the air.

Dumbfounded, Marion and Frankie were at first speechless. But slowly they regained their voice. Marion spoke up, looking up at him towering over her. She spoke calmly. "Let me show you where this anointing with oil healing service comes from in our Book of Worship," she said standing up to reach it off the book shelf above her head.

"I don't need any book other than the Bible. I know what a holy roller service is, getting people to fall out and pulling demons out of 'em. I saw enough of that quackery when I grew up with my missionary parents. You better not do this service again, or I'll have your jobs!" With that he stormed out of the office and slammed the door to the parking lot.

On Sunday morning when Marion stood up to preach after welcoming visitors to the congregation, Elder Henry got up from the pew and spouted off without waiting for permission, pounding his Bible as he spoke.

"I'm here to inform this congregation of the unauthorized holy roller service these pastors are leading. Church, if you are with me on this, you will fire these imposters that call themselves our pastors and return the church to what it should be, the way we have always conducted ourselves. Who is with me on this?"

Everyone sat motionless waiting for Marion to react. Marion broke the silence.

Voice level, speaking affirmatively, she said, "Elder Henry. If you'd like to discuss this in a private meeting, I will be happy to do that, but right now I have a sermon to preach."

She told the congregation to turn to Matthew Chapter Seven.

Elder Henry got up from his pew, walked out the sanctuary door never to return. After his outburst, three major financial contributing families asked to speak with the Finches privately. With heavy hearts Frankie and Marion agreed to meet them at the parsonage.

Before the meeting Henry's son left a voice mail message on their home telephone answering machine. "Frankie, Marion, this is Steward. I am informing you that my family can no longer tolerate the tension in the church. I need a Bible-based environment where my boys can grow up in the Lord. Bye."

Sitting down in the Finches' formal living room Bart spoke first. "Frankie, Marion. Today was the last straw. Going to church used to be a joy. When you two came, we were so inspired. Elder Henry's temper tantrum was the final act. I can no longer participate in a congregation that acts so childish, is afraid of their own shadow, and will not even hear any new idea you want to try. We love you guys, but we will be looking to worship elsewhere."

The second family, the Williamsons, smiled as they shared their news. "Frankie, Marion, we have no quarrel with you," Mrs. Williamson said. "We have good news for our family, but sad for you," she said exhaling. Pointing to her husband beside her on the sofa she said, "Mr. Williamson just got a new job in Virginia with a start-up IT company. We're moving in three weeks. We're sorry to leave."

Marion tried to display a stiff upper lip, but the wind was knocked out of her. She suggested they pray for direction for each of them and the church. They even prayed for Elder Henry. In the weeks that followed, Frankie and Marion went through the motions pastoring the church, but felt so defeated. They tried to discuss it with the Regional minister, Anthony, but he was accepting a position at the national headquarters and preoccupied with his departure.

The tension impacted not only Frankie and Marion, but also Grandma Sarah. She started psychotherapy in the summer of 2003 to deal with all her losses and transitions.

She asked for Frankie and Marion to come to a session.

Frankie would not. Marion did.

Therapist Susan said, "Marion, your mom is depressed. She feels belittled and ridiculed by your husband. She is unhappy and feels like you side with your husband against her."

Sighing deeply Marion wrung her hands and said, turning to her mom, "Mom, why didn't you tell me this? I try very hard to keep the peace. You know Frankie is a bear and is angry at life and takes it out on everything and everyone around him."

Susan asked, "Isn't your husband a minister?"

Marion crossed her arms. "Yes, but he's human and has issues he needs to deal with. I am not his keeper. I can't fix him. He has to want to live life differently."

Susan asked, "Why are you defending him?"

Exasperated, Marion said, raising her voice stiffened, sitting on the edge of the chair, "I'm tired of people telling me I am not doing what they want or need. I work very hard to help each person get their needs met while neglecting my own. I can't keep doing that. I'm sorry Mom that you think Frankie is so mean. I don't know what to do to change that. You need to find a way to talk to him about it. Maybe Susan can call and ask him to come in for a session."

Susan turned toward Sarah and said, "Tell your daughter how you feel about Frankie."

Sarah was hesitant, her bottom lip quivering,

"Marion, I'm afraid of Frankie. He yells if you or one of the kids tries to talk to him. I don't want him getting angry with me," she said.

"Mom, what do you want me to do? I can't make him not be angry. He's very mad at me for working on my doctorate. He thinks it is a waste of time and money."

"Ya, Marion. I don't get that. I thought he would be proud of you for all your hard work."

"I don't know Mom. I don't have an answer. I'm sorry."

Marion sat in silence waiting for the session to end. She hugged her mom as she left feeling like a failure as a daughter and as a wife.

Her parting words were, "Mom, I'll try to talk to Frankie, but I make no promises. Okay?"

With eyes downcast Sarah said sadly, "Okay."

She wanted to just run away from all the stress and tension. She tried to broach the subject with Frankie as they were eating dinner together, a rare occasion for him not to be reading during the meal.

"Frankie, Mom had me come to a therapy session with her today."

"Yah, so?

"Frankie, she feels you don't like her, that you criticize her and resent her being here."

He picked up a forkful of rice as he said, "Your mom is too sensitive. I tease her. That's all."

"Well, she sees it differently. Could you please let up on her some?"

"You Parker woman are all overly sensitive. You don't know how to take a joke." With that he got up from the table and turned on the television.

Marion felt she was left with no solution and her food sat like a rock in her abdomen.

The daily drudgery to function in her marriage, stimulate her congregations to grow, see clients, work on her doctorate, and keep the peace between Frankie and her mom was compounded by the Mt. Pleasant's church environment. The mold inside the larger Mt. Pleasant Church became so bad that it affected Marion's asthma. She began to wheeze just entering the building. A mold remediation team came in to fix the problem. Frankie and Marion boxed up the moldy library books that sat for fourteen years untouched on the shelves damaged by the water from Hurricane Hugo that hit on September 21, 1989.

Marion had to vacate the building for the six weeks of remediation. Church members appalled, that the pastors would remove these "sacred" books from the library without Board approval, carted the boxes to their own homes, intent upon returning them to the shelves once the Finches no longer served them. The member's disgruntled action only intensified Marion's strife and the negative effect on her body. She tried to re-engage the members in a joint goal.

Sunday morning Marion enthusiastically approached the pulpit of the Mt. Pleasant Church. "This morning, parishioners, I have a proposition for you. We are going to multiply the loaves and fishes, to expand our talents. We are going to raise the money to put on our new roof to demonstrate to this community that we are an alive, involved church. In my hand are envelopes. In each one there is a $5.00 bill. I want each family to take that seed money and creatively come back with some method you used to multiply it. The money will go toward our roof fund."

As Marion passed out the envelopes people frowned. "We're retired," said the Kittle family. "On a fixed budget. We can't do this," as they tried to hand it back to her.

Marion patiently smiled and said, "I believe if you pray about it, God will bless you and show you what to do." With that said, she walked to the next pew. A month later the fruits of their labors were presented. Some bought ingredients and made pound cakes and sold them. One bought material and sewed some clothes and sold them. The remainder of the families brought the envelopes back. "Here, we couldn't think of anything. Here's your money back."

Marion shrugged her shoulders and said with a heavy heart holding the offering plate in front of them,

"Okay, I'm sad that you did not have enough trust in me to at least try the process."

On the next Saturday night Marion exhausted from her studies, church duties and few private practice clients printed out her sermon. She came into the living room to go over it with Frankie. She sat down on the couch next to him ready to read it to him.

"I'm ready Frankie to go over my sermon with you. Are you ready?" she said looking up at him reading, sitting on the foot stool in front of his recliner."

He nodded, putting down his book.

She read the opening paragraph and he stopped her.

"Where the hell did you get that information? It's not sound," he lambasted her.

Defensively she responded stiffening her back, "I took it off a couple of biblical websites and I did a little poetic license after reading the *Interpreter's Bible*."

"You can't do that," he said grabbing the papers out of her hand. This is what you need to say…"

A lump formed in her throat as she tried to accept his criticism that did not at all feel constructive. She bravely broached a related topic. Inhaling, she began, "Frankie, last Sunday David noticed something at the Mt. Pleasant Church."

"Ya, what, pray tell would that be?"

He said, "that he has been paying attention to the selection of scriptures and he sees that what I preach is the passage before the one you preach, but a week later. I couldn't tell him that you decided to have us each only write two sermons a month and that we preach each one at one of the churches. Do you think we should start writing a new one each week? I don't want them to not be spiritually fed or disappointed in our leading them."

"Woman, I swear you worry too much. Has David ever complained about my preaching? NO! So maybe it is just you," he said and got up and went into the guest bedroom to watch television away from her.

God, what am I supposed to do? I can't please Frankie, you, and the churches. Please help me. I'm sinking here.

A reprieve from the discord came in February of the next year when Adam's first child was born, a son named Joshua. The long-awaited grand-child was a welcome relief to Marion and Frankie's tension-filled marriage and in a church career position where there was no hope for improvement. Marion relished being called "Grandma." Grandma Sarah embraced being a great Grandma. Marion relieved some stress sanding and refinishing a crib much to the liking of the new parents. She began to buy little trinkets to bring to her grandson whenever she could manage to get time off to drive the six hours to visit him.

Frankie, assured that neither congregation had any desire to change, be-lieved a geographical cure would again solve all the problems in his life. The five years in Mt. Pleasant had only brought misery, disappointment, and cre-ated a wider rift between Frankie and Marion.

Marion's journal entry summed it up.

God, since I get tongue-tied when I try to explain to Frankie how I feel I will write about it. All day today my chest hurt, a burning in the middle, a heavy feeling like my heart is breaking. There is a deep, deep sadness and anger. When I try to say why I do the things I do, I feel like they get twisted. This morning when I read devotions I was near tears the whole time. Frankie sees that I do things against his wants. Please help me God, to know what to do. Amen.

"Marion, I'm done," Frankie said as they got into the car after the Church Board meeting on a Thursday night. Gripping the steering wheel, he said, "You know good and well that the Board voted to put on that new roof. You raised the money to do it and now they want to wait and do it later." Looking up as if to implore God he added, "I want to serve a congregation that is not afraid to critically explore what the scriptures say, a body of believers that walk what they talk. All these people want is to return to the good 'ole days when the church and the coffers were full."

Lowering her voice to instill calm she said, "Frankie, I know you're upset. I am too, but I understand their anxiety. They've nursed this church for so long just doing crisis management that they don't even know they're doing it. Look at how they dress, their homes. They buy nothing new, recycle the old. They're afraid and that fear is keeping them captive. If I just had a little more time, maybe all the stuff I'm learning in my doctoral program will turn the tide. What do ya say, huh, maybe?" she said tilting her head while smiling.

"No, I'm done. I am putting out my papers this week to go to a church that wants to grow and is willing to try new things. There has to be one somewhere," he said chewing on his index fingernail.

She had just finally fixed her mom's condo the way Sarah wanted it. After evaluating the aftermath of the move from Marley to Mt. Pleasant, Marion feared leaving now would just duplicate the same scenario.

The next Sunday Marion witnessed an encounter that tipped the scales. In a congregational meeting after worship, Hilda stood up from her pew and began her verbal rampage with hands on her hips. Patricia, the nine-year-old acolyte, the only child left in the church, sat next to her mom, wide-eyed with her mouth open.

Ms. Hilda proclaimed, "I don't believe how disrespectful the new members are. They know we have been doing communion the same way for fifty years," she said with arms waving. "Deacon Ralph shows up in a Hawaiian shirt and flip flops to serve at the table. That is so disrespectful to God. And another thing, our acolyte doesn't even know how to bow properly. I've showed her at least ten times," said Ms. Hilda exasperated.

Marion infuriated, could hold her temper no longer. "Ms. Hilda, with all due respect, God doesn't care how we dress to come to church. God wants us to just come. And another thing," she said pointing her finger at Ms. Hilda, "how dare you criticize this loving child who, out of the goodness of her heart, volunteers to be our acolyte. I'm so frustrated that no one here wants to even ask, 'what does God want for this church?' I'm done," she said as she walked off the platform, went into her office and wept.

When she got home she told Frankie to go ahead, to circulate his papers. He filled them out that afternoon sitting at the computer desk where she had done her doctoral studies.

As his finger hovered over the send button on the email to the denominational search and call office, Marion raised her monogramed coffee cup to her lips and said, "I'm glad you're circulating only your papers. I don't want to ever work with you again. Your critical attitude and lack of shared responsibilities, I will not miss."

With that he pushed the send button and then retorted, "Now that you have your doctorate, you think you're so smart, Marion, but I know better. You only did it for your fucking ego."

"I'm paying off my debt and my doctorate will be useful to my career," she said reassuring herself.

"We'll see. So far all it has gotten me is a bossy, disrespectful wife and $27,000 more debt," he said as he got up from the desk and headed toward his recliner to watch some Sunday afternoon football.

That night Marion had a dream. It revealed that what she learns from dreams comes from her spirit guide and as she gets healthier she is to share her gifts, her jewels with others. She meditated and asked, "How am I to do this and with whom?" The answers did not surface then. Frankie flew out to an interview in Mississippi. That Sunday was annual event where old members were invited back called "homecoming" at the Mt. Pleasant Church. The smaller church thought Frankie was attending the event. Marion did not mention to the Mt. Pleasant folks that he was not at the other church. Both the Finches hoped no one would figure it out. Pastors in the Christian Church (Disciples of Christ) tradition had to secretly interview for a new position because a minister could be fired from the present position if they suspected the minister wanted to depart. An expression in clergy circles commonly heard is, "you are only as good as your last board meeting," meaning a clergy person could be fired at any time the Board met.

Marion walked into her office at 1:30 p.m., the designated time for him to call. She shut her door hoping no stragglers would wander in. Frankie called. She picked up the receiver apprehensively. He said, "Marion, I have good news."

Holding her breath, she asked, "Ya, how did the board vote?"

"My new appointment starts in just six weeks, on January 1st. They voted six to one to hire me. Aren't you excited to move away from the Mt. Pleasant mess?"

Twisting the phone cord in her hand, the same phone she confronted Hank on years earlier, she sighed.

"Frankie, I don't feel like our job is done yet. Are you sure God is calling you to this place? I don't want another Mt. Pleasant Disaster."

Perfunctorily he said, "Yes, dear. I prayed about. Can't you just be happy for me?"

Happy for him, yes, but all that was now involved preparing to move was overwhelming. The most pressing issue was to inform her mom.

"Hey, Mom do you want to go to Shoney's for breakfast today?"

"Sure, what's the occasion?" sensing something was up.

After filling their plates from the breakfast buffet bar, they sat in the booth and Marion said grace. Marion sipped her coffee but barely touched her food. Twisting her fork in her left hand she plunged in.

"Mom, remember how I explained to you that the churches we pastor do not want to grow?"

"Sure, that's why I stopped going and go to mass at the Catholic Church. It's too painful to watch how the people treated you."

"Well, Mom, (pregnant pause to delay the news) um, Frankie says he has had enough and he is ready to move."

With a furrowed brow, Sarah asked, "Where?"

"It's in a town called Murphy, Mississippi, near Olive Branch."

With the weight of the news sinking in, Sarah started to cry wringing her hands. "What about my condo? I just got it fixed the way I want it. What about Frankie begging me to move close to you guys for years and when I finally do, now he wants to move?"

"I'm sorry, Mom. Ministers do move, but I thought it would-be years from now. You can always stay here, if you want."

Marion felt so torn. She wanted her mom to be happy, to be settled. She wanted Frankie to be at peace with his work. Whichever way she turned, someone felt rejected and left out. Marion surely felt her needs were not even part of the decision-making process.

Session Twenty-Six

Settling comfortably into her familiar therapy chair Marion turned to face Dr. Weinstein with a smile and said, "here's my takeaway from my sessions thus far: I have observed that people act a certain way in their twenties to rebel against their parents wants and wishes. In their thirties people are afraid they are going to miss out on careers, so they pursue that aspect of their lives like a ravenous animal. In their forties they don't care so much about what their parents' think or want. In their fifties often one of the parents dies and the person begins to see some of the traits of the parent in themselves and it does not seem so repulsive any more. I think we are all just trying to survive the best way we know how and we do not intentionally set out to damage others unless of course the person is sadistic or a psychopath," Marion stated.

"Great overview of your perceptions, Marion. I am certain that others would agree with you as I do. Now it is time for you to take over and teach me more," Dr. Weinstein said with a big grin on his face.

Detachment

As Marion announced to the larger congregation the impending departure of the co-pastorate team she could see sadness on some of the parishioners' faces. A handful of the forty church members believed the Finches were their last hope for the survival of the congregation. Now they were faced with the death of their last hope. Abandoning ship was not a singular event as many members had already departed. Before the pastors moved on, these same members threw two parties for them. One party celebrated Marion earning her doctorate with a 3.9 GPA and the other a farewell gathering.

In the fellowship hall at her doctoral celebration, Frankie stood up. He raised his cup of red fruit punch to make a toast. He cleared his throat and said, "My work here is done. Marion does not need me anymore. She has outgrown me." Then he sat down.

Ms. Hilda patted him on the shoulder as she said, "Pastor, Marion still needs you. Getting her doctorate's, a good thing. You'll see."

He just shrugged and walked out of the hall to his office while the party continued. Marion noticed but did not go after him. It was her party and she was not going to cater to his needs like she did at her Masters graduation celebration.

His anger, due to his fear of being abandoned, now made sense. He kept her controlled all those early years for many reasons, most prominently because she had no education and thus could not afford to raise the children without him. With each succeeding degree, she became more independent, more detached from Frankie. She stayed married to this man by choice. With a doctorate, she could eventually afford to leave him when she secured the right position. Even though it was not verbalized, they both knew she could now leave. Marion believed he tested her to see if she *would* leave. She wanted to prove all the naysayers wrong, who believed their marriage could not last, only knowing each other for seven and a half weeks before they married.

Marion did not want to be divorced like her mom and dad. She intended to be the martyr and outlive Frankie, but the stress of coping with his moods and anger might do her in first.

On December 9th, she wrote in her journal.

It is 28 years since Adam's car accident and the start of Frankie's affair with Tabatha. I looked at the cookies on Frankie's computer this morning to search for a site, I recently visited.

I saw where Frankie went to a porn site. I looked to see what it was. It was a young girl having sex with an older man. I got nauseated and quickly shut it down. He broke his promise that he would not go to those sites any more. When I woke him up this morning I asked him about it. He said it is my fault because I'm not sexual enough with him.

He only goes to it to relieve himself when he feels horny. He asked how that hurt me. I told him it felt like it was more important than me. He said it wasn't. He said accept him as he is by doing what he needs me to do. God, how can I honor you, and do the things he asks that I feel are against your ways? Please help me. Amen.

The day of the move arrived on December 26. The Murphy Church with an active membership of one hundred people sent four deacons to load up the Finches and bring them to Mississippi. Traditionally, in the Disciples denomination, each hiring church either pays for movers or volunteers to transport the incoming pastor's belongings to the new location. It had been that way from Indiana to Marley, from Marley to Mt. Pleasant, and from Mt. Pleasant now to Mississippi. Marion was to finish up with her clients and arrive in Murphy on January second. Frankie was supposed to follow behind the movers in the motorhome. Hours before the volunteers arrived Frankie checked all the gauges and lifted out the motorhome's battery to service it. While lifting, he turned left instead of right wrenching his back. He could not sit, stand, or lie down without searing pain. As the workers settled in for the night, Marion drove Frankie to the ER to have pain medication administered.

Three hours after she returned home, Frankie was fast asleep, but the workers were up, ready to start loading. Frankie was too medicated to function. Marion took over. Orchestrating the move, she had them loaded and out the door by noon. On next to nothing sleep she drove the twelve hours to unload, and in two days, turn around and come back to finish her last Sunday service and to perform a wedding.

Everyone agreed that Frankie would stay behind for two days until he finished his pain medication. Bullheaded and fully medicated, Frankie instead drove to Mississippi the next day with his friend, Leonard. Marion was furious.

"Frankie," Marion said pulling him aside from the parishioners who were helping her unpack, "what do you think you're doing showing up under the influence of pain meds? This is NOT a good first impression for the congregation."

He shrugged his shoulders and walked past her, a grin on his face as he said to the guy unloading his tools in the garage, "Thanks for helping. I know I won't remember yet, but remind me your name again?"

Patting him gently on the shoulder he said, "Calvin's my name. I heard about your back. I've got a chiropractor who can help. Go sit down and I'll call him to get you in."

Frankie, visibly in too much pain to protest, sat down at the dining room table. The furnace was not working, so after they got Frankie an appointment, Calvin called his furnace repair guy. He agreed to come early the next day, hopefully before Marion started back to Mt. Pleasant. As promised, the furnace guy had it all under control by eight-thirty the next morning so Marion loaded up her suitcase and she and Leonard headed out. The Finches were ready to begin this new adventure, hopefully with God's in the forefront this time.

On January 2, her last Sunday to lead worship for the larger congregation, the worship leader, Mr. Watson led the congregation in the hymn *In the*

Garden. As Mr. Watson stepped down from the chancel area to his seat in the second row, Marion rose from the burgundy velvet pastor's chair beside the communion table and approached the pulpit. Raising her arms wide she said, "this church has been in labor for a couple of decades. The life expectancy of a congregation is twenty-five years. Then either the next generation picks up the baton and moves forward or the dwindling members die or move and the closes its doors. You can with God's help use the tools Frankie and I taught you to become a thriving, new baby church, or you can deliver a still birth and be forever in grief over the loss encountered. It is up to you. Whatever the decision, please support your new pastor. Pray for him or her, invite your minister to dinner. When they suggest an idea, hear them out. God does not want this church to die. You have great potential. I will miss the friends I've made and will cherish the direction God gave me to lead you. I will be honest. I will not miss the dissention. Thank you for allowing me to be your pastor these last five and a half years. I love you all. Amen."

The congregation stood on their feet and clapped. Marion teared up as she hugged her congregants and wished them well. *Where had that response been the last five years? Why now, too little, too late? Maybe they will better support the next pastor. My work here is done.*

She drove back to South Carolina the third week in January this time to take the Mississippi State Social Work Licensing Exam. When she registered to take it, she had no idea when they would move so she scheduled it at one of the approved sites: Marley Technical College Campus.

Passing the licensing exam, she could now see clients in Mississippi and build a practice once again. She retained her South Carolina license until the renewal ran out so she could periodically return to see clients still there. She was relieved to not have to be under Frankie's authority directing her church work and previewing her sermons for scriptural soundness. She did not miss the board meetings or the twenty hours it took her each week to prepare an acceptable sermon.

Frankie did say to her periodically in Mississippi, as in the past, "Why don't you get a real job, with benefits and a set salary?" She reminded him she did best working on her own and he had agreed she could build a private practice again – her fourth time beginning from scratch, each time successfully.

They both knew developing a strong clientele took five years. She reached that point in Mt. Pleasant and now had to start fresh in Mississippi.

Three months after the move Grandma Sarah, lonely for family interaction, was ready to sell her condo and move to Mississippi. Marion was relieved, but Frankie was irritated, not wanting her around. He claimed she was too self-centered. Marion just shook her head in disbelief.

Marion talked only briefly to her sisters about the move. She could tell that they were unhappy with the whole exodus from Mt. Pleasant, which by their opinion meant Marion and Frankie abandoned Sarah after encouraging her for years to come to the warmer climate. Marion was in such turmoil. As much as she attempted to point out the advantages to their mom moving to an apartment, she knew she had failed her mom. To please her mom meant Frankie would be mad at her. To please Frankie meant her mom and sisters would be mad at her. Adam and Little Sarah only saw their grandmother if she happened to be where Frankie and Marion lived. They witnessed their Dad harassing his mother-in-law in Mt. Pleasant with statements like, "Hey, Grannie. Is that another new outfit? You have more clothes than any woman I ever knew." Little Sarah would say to Frankie, "Dad, leave her alone. She buys clothes, so what? You buy a new guy toy every month or trade your vehicle every six months. You're no different." With that statement, Frankie would sulk off to the bedroom and slam the door.

Because of all the upgrades and improvements to Sarah's condo, it sold quickly. In April Sarah flew Marion back to pack her up and await the movers. The condo closing was scheduled for eleven a.m. the next morning. Frazzled, Sarah tearfully sat down in her olive-green arm chair and said, as her hands rested on her chin, "Marion, you're pushing me too fast. I don't know if I want to keep that pile of stuff or not. I don't know about anything in my life right now."

Marion set down the packing tape as she turned to her mom and said in a sympathetic tone, "Mom, I'm sorry that I'm so task-oriented right now, but the movers will be here at 8:00 a.m. and I have to have everything ready to load. Tell ya what. Why don't you go sit on the patio and let me just pack it all up?

In Mississippi, we can then sort through all the boxes and donate what you no longer want. Will that work for you?"

Sighing, Sarah said, "I guess so."

Marion opened the sliding glass door and said, "Your deck chair awaits you, Madame," as she guided her mom to the seat and returned to quickly wrap the fine china and carefully slide it into protective sleeves to put in the box slots. The loading up and closing went through without any delays. Heading west to Mississippi, they stopped first at the Sonic for an ice cream Blast.

Sarah's new home was a two-bedroom apartment around the corner from Marion and Frankie's home. Depressed that she was no longer a homeowner, Marion explained how at age seventy-nine, it was time to enjoy life and let someone else worry about maintenance, repairs, and taxes. Marion helped her to methodically go through the boxes at her own pace reminiscing over all the years of memorabilia.

On Tuesday nights Frankie joined a bowling league at the invitation of one of the church members. Marion used the time, like Mt. Pleasant, to be with Sarah. The two women fixed up her apartment, went out to eat and enjoyed one another's company.

Sarah joined a local ballroom dancing club. She was happy. When the grandchildren came to town to visit, the family atmosphere was lighter. Daughter-in-law Gwen confronted Frankie when he was inappropriate. Although he resented it, he kept his cool. Frankie was respected in the church so he had less anger to take out on the family. Sarah chose to attend mass at the local Catholic Church. Marion had a vision during the night of December 9th, on the 29th anniversary since Adam's car accident which was the same date Frankie started his affair with Tabatha, and the day Michelle broke up with him thirty-seven years earlier. The prophecy revealed that Frankie would have an affair with some blonde woman with the initials CL, that the church would find out about it and he would abandon Marion. Shaken she tried to function normally throughout the day attributing the experience to just being coincidentally related to the past trauma on that date. She wrote it in her journal but kept it to herself.

To celebrate Sarah's eightieth birthday, Rhonda and Marion planned a huge celebration inviting the dance club, new friends she made, and all Frankie's church members. Rhonda set up an armchair in the church fellowship hall where they held the party. The daughters lovingly put a princess crown on their mom's head and a sash over her shoulder that said, Happy Birthday. She was glowing with all the attention. Gretchen chose not to attend.

Still glowing from all the personal attention Sarah sat in her recliner with all her birthday cards neatly in their envelopes on her lap when Marion picked her up for a colonoscopy a week later Sarah had been complaining of indigestion and bowel difficulties so the gastroenterologist scheduled the test.

Dr. Patel came into the family waiting area about ten minutes after they took Sarah to the procedure room. "Family of Mrs. Parker?"

"Yes," Marion stood up and walked over to him standing by the door from the surgical area.

"I'm Dr. Patel," he said holding his surgical cap in his left hand. "Your mom has some obstruction. I can't complete the colonoscopy. I need you to take her to Olive Branch Hospital Imaging on University Dr. so they can do a CT scan."

As he handed her a handwritten order, Marion attempted to get more information, but he quickly disappeared back through the "no entrance" door.

Multiple tests later, the diagnosis was confirmed. Breast cancer had returned after a twenty-five-year hiatus and metastasized to her colon and throughout her body. Paradoxically, just after a celebratory eightieth birthday her life stopped when she was given between two weeks to two months to live.

Rhonda's husband Don drove his wife back to Mississippi after she had been home only a week after the birthday festivities. In the hospital, Sarah distraught that her life was so quickly ending asked Marion to call Gretchen. Rhonda had handled the family communication up to this point, including initially notifying Gretchen about her mom's terminal condition but Marion was not privy to that conversation. Now Rhonda and Don were resting back at her Sarah's apartment.

Stepping out into the hospital hallway, Marion did as asked, pacing outside her mom's room. "Hey, Gretchen, Mom asked me to call you. She wants to see you one last time before she dies. When can you get here?"

"Ahhhh, I can't come," she said almost in a whisper.

Incredulous, Marion screamed loud enough for her mom to hear while flailing her right arm, "What do you mean you can't honor your mother's dying wish? What is so terribly important that you can't get here? You were with your mother-in-law and father-in-law until the end. Have you forgotten we are still family?"

"Stop," Gretchen said, obviously sobbing. "It's too stressful, Tim can't handle being around death and he won't survive if I come by myself."

"Fine. Then can you at least say good bye on the phone, or is that too stressful for Tim too?"

Gretchen agreed to talk to her mom once last time. Marion carried the phone back into the room and handed it to her mom, now crying as well. Marion, still fuming, stepped outside so they could have a private conversation.

Gretchen and Tim never spent a night apart in their entire marriage. He did not attend to his parents or their affairs when they were dying, or after their deaths. There was no funeral. Gretchen cared for Tim' parents by herself. Like Marion, Gretchen chose to give into her husband's needs and wants, closing off her own feelings. Gretchen and Tim only visited Sarah in her home once since they married. The visit lasted for less than twenty-four hours back in the late 1990's.

After Rhonda and Don returned to the hospital Marion told them how angry she was with Gretchen.

Rhonda assured Marion that the two of them would handle Mom together.

Dismissed from the hospital after a colostomy and procedure to drain fluid from her kidneys, Sarah was moved to a nursing home until the best course of action could be decided. Marion, sleep deprived, completely exhausted kept seeing clients. Rhonda and Don drove back to Northern Wisconsin. After a few days in the nursing home, Marion saw how Sarah, obviously unhappy, could not perform the necessary physical therapy to qualify to stay there so she moved her back to her own apartment initiating hospice care. A hospital bed in the living room made it easier for her to look out the window to see the birds flock to the feeder that her dance group bought.

In just four weeks Sarah had gone from a woman joyfully celebrating her eightieth birthday to an emaciated woman with pasty skin breathing oxygen through a cannula. No food stayed down and the colostomy bag leaked fecal matter onto her clothing. The smell was so nauseating that anyone within the room gagged. Marion hired a morning and afternoon sitter to administer her mom's oral meds, change her diaper, and read to her when asked. Marion took the night shift. Listening to her mom's irregular breathing, expecting each breath to be her last kept Marion awake. Three hours of sleep each night sustained her for a couple of weeks. Rhonda returned for a third time in a month for an extended time to help and relieve Marion. The hospice nurse pointed out the mottling on Sarah's feet, a sign of organs shutting down. Informed that death could come in days or up to two weeks made the death vigil interminable.

Sarah, in and out of deep sleep, aroused a little to ask for a sip of water. Leaning over to gingerly place the cup up to her lips, Marion put her hand on her mom's back to support her half sitting up. Lying back on the pillow she pitifully asked her daughter hovering over her, "how long does it take to die?"

Rhonda and Marion turned to one another and answered simultaneously, "We don't know."

Therapist skills and faith engaged, Marion sat down beside her mom and held her hand. Stroking her fingers on her mom's withered palm she said, "Mom, sometimes people have business to finish before they can go to God. When it is close to time, someone may come from the other side to help you cross over."

Sarah pulled her hand away and said, "I sure hope that it's NOT my mother."

Marion spoke soothingly to her mom, "Mom, when the time comes it will be a good transition that you don't have to fear."

Rhonda leaned over and kissed her mom on the forehead and said, "Marion's right, Mom."

Easing her daughter's tension Sarah responded,

"I'm not afraid, but I still have things I want to do." With that, she fell back into a deep sleep and Rhonda and Marion tiptoed into the guest room to sort through mom's belongings. Since Rhonda was task oriented and wanted to be helpful, to save Marion from all the aftermath, she arranged for some of her mom's things to be donated to a church or to Goodwill. Her piano was going to a church that served the homeless.

Months before Sarah's cancer diagnosis, Marion and Frankie were scheduled to go on a cruise with some friends to the Bahamas. They could have gotten their money back, but Rhonda insisted that they go.

She said, "There's nothing to be done here. You need a break. I'll call the cruise ship when she dies. She's being cremated and we have the service all planned. It's paid for so leave the rest to me."

Feeling tremendous guilt, aching for rest, Marion went. She checked the ship-to-shore phone whenever they went back into the stateroom. Finally, Marion could wait no longer and called Rhonda on Wednesday, halfway through the cruise.

"You're never going to believe this. Mom is not ready to die. She woke up out of the near-death state and wanted to go on a picnic."

Marion had mixed emotions. "Great," she monotoned. "I wonder if this is a temporary reprieve or if mom is going to live for a while now?"

"I don't know, but she is definitely not dying today!"

"Ut oh, what about her belongings that we donated?" Marion inquired.

"Ah, we'll discuss that when you return. Gotta go. Love you."

Marion, of course was grateful her mother was alive, but then worried how would she manage mom's care, work, and tend to her marriage?

Rhonda went home after the cruise since Sarah was not only alert, but up and moving. Marion decided the best option was to move mom into her home. Stretching mom's funds by not paying rent, or having to coordinate around the clock sitters, Marion could rest more. Getting Frankie to agree to it would be the biggest challenge.

On Thursday evening, April 27th, just six weeks after Sarah's diagnosis, Marion dragged her mom's six large rubber maid containers of winter woolen clothes up the attic stairs before Frankie returned from the church men's monthly meeting.

Getting Sarah settled in the guest room, Marion said, "Mom, I'm only putting your summer things in the guest room closet. I don't want Frankie making comments to you about how many clothes you have. This will be our secret. He rarely goes into the attic so he won't see them and tease you about it."

Despite Marion's best efforts, Sarah was miserable the whole two months she stayed there. Frankie walked down the hall to the master bedroom holding his nose. As he shut the door to the bedroom he complained, "God, Marion can't you do something about that wretched smell of your mom's colostomy bag? I can't handle the smell of shit every time I walk by the hall bathroom."

Sitting up against the headboard reading, Marion said, "Sh…she'll hear you," putting her finger to her lips. "She can't help it. I'll spray more air freshener in there."

Sarah heard what he said. The next morning after Frankie left for the church, Marion came out of the bedroom headed to get a cup of coffee. Sarah was sitting at the dining room table staring out into the backyard with tears streaming down her face.

"Mom, what's wrong?" Marion asked putting her hand on her mother's frail one.

"I heard Frankie complaining last night. I know he doesn't want me here. I don't want to be here. He doesn't even say hello or good-bye. I'm not wanted anywhere," she said as the tears escalated to sobbing.

Marion inhaled deeply as she sat down. "Mom, I don't know what to do. I want you happy, but I want you safe for whatever time you have left. Let me see what I can find out about assisted living facilities. You'd have a very small apartment, but it would be yours."

Smiling through her tears Sarah said, "I would love that, if you can do it for me. Thank you."

When Frankie and Marion had a quick dinner with church friends while a neighbor sat with Sarah, friend Cindy said, "Frankie, don't criticize Marion for forgetting to pick up your dry cleaning. She's tending to her dying mom. You should be more supportive and understanding. Can't you see she is exhausted?"

Marion looked over to Frankie. She knew he feared getting old and feeble. Watching Sarah die was too much for him. He said, "If I get like her, just shoot me."

Marion found an assisted living facility which allowed hospice to come in to care for her mom. Sarah, ecstatic, hugged Marion.

A daily routine was established. Marion stopped every night after work to visit her mom. She arranged a volunteer to come and take her out for ice cream. She managed mom's finances, paid off her credit card debt, and helped her make final arrangements.

On September 23rd, five months after her diagnosis, Sarah met friends she had not seen in a long time for dinner and went shopping earlier in the day. She was not feeling well, so Marion stayed at her apartment with her. She called hospice to see if it was okay to give her some morphine drops since the facility nurse was off duty for the night. They told Marion yes to give the drops every couple of hours. After the first dosage Marion watched television while mom rested. When Marion heard her mother moaning, as instructed, she gave her a second dose. Sarah was quiet. Marion was relieved to see her resting. About 11:15 she turned away from the television to see if mom needed more and to put her under the covers. She was not breathing. She called the night supervisor who brought a mirror to check for signs of breath. Having none, Marion called Hospice.

Marion had no tears, no sadness, just relief that she cared for her mom to the end in a loving manner. No longer would Marion have to balance pleasing mom while staving off Frankie's anger. Her task, her life's purpose, as the NDE guides told her was to love those who felt unlovable until they could love themselves. She believed her mom felt loved. For forty-three years of Marion's life, she had been her mom's confidant, caretaker, and supporter to the end. Now Sarah rested in peace.

Marion called Frankie, "it's over. Mom's gone. You can go back to your normal life now," she callously said too exhausted to care how the words stung.

"I'll ignore your caustic remark. Do you want me to come, or not?" "Um, yes, please."

He showed up, friendly with the staff and hospice folks, but did not say much to Marion. The prearranged funeral home arrived and took away her body.

Marion waited until the next morning to call Adam and Little Sarah since there was no sense waking them up late at night. Rhonda was out of town without a contact phone number so she left her a voice mail message. Gretchen, when called, coldly replied, "Thanks for letting me know."

In a moving tribute, the unique memorial service included Sarah's favorite waltz danced by two of her ballroom friends. Family participated in planting a portion of her ashes under a butterfly bush in Marion and Frankie's yard. The remainder – a portion shipped to Canada to be buried along with her relatives in the church cemetery and a final portion sent home with Rhonda.

Most of the inheritance Sarah acquired, savings from her state accounting job, was distributed prior to her death which made Marion's job as executrix easier.

Marion hoped with her mom gone Frankie would be kinder to her, but with Sarah out of the picture, the wall of ice between Frankie and Marion thickened. A year earlier as a birthday present to herself Marion consulted with a Medical Intuitive physician. She only gave the doctor her birthdate. The woman accurately described Marion's life. "You are in a marriage by yourself. You will get divorced and remarry." That frightened her. She did not want to be divorced. She wanted Frankie to change, to be nicer to her, to respect her, to treat her as a woman he was proud of, not criticize every decision she made.

Marion's twenty-thousand-dollar inheritance made her feel like she had some power over Frankie, keeping him guessing at what she would do. She secretly relished giving him a taste of his own medicine. Despite Frankie's increasing distaste for anything Marion did, she opted to prove the intuitive reading wrong and to stay in the marriage. The familiar dysfunction was less scary than embarking on a journey alone.

Sarah was visiting for the weekend in Murphy. Marion fixed a very nice breakfast complete with scrambled eggs, grits, crisp bacon, and waffles. As Marion called them to the table, Frankie remained in his recliner doing his crossword puzzle. Sarah and Marion quietly waited for him to say grace and begin eating. After five minutes Sarah asked, "Dad, you coming? We're waiting on you. Mom's fixed a really nice breakfast."

"Naw you go ahead; I want to finish this puzzle."

When the breakfast was cold and as the two women sipped their coffee chatting away, Frankie sauntered over and sat down. Poking his fork at the eggs he said, "These are runny."

Marion uncharacteristically picked up his plate. Frankie thought she went to go make him more eggs. As she started to dump the whole contents into the trashcan, Sarah stopped her.

"Mom, wait," Sarah said stretching out her arm. Then she turned to glare at Frankie and said, "Dad, you're an ass and you know it. Mom worked hard to have a nice meal and you criticized her. She should have dumped it."

Sarah brought the plate back and set it in front of him. He ate in silence as the women left to go shopping. During the car ride to Kohls, Sarah said, "You know Mom, you gotta stick with Dad. No one else would want you with all your health issues. If you dumped his plate he would have retaliated and it would have been worse for you. I know Dad's a royal pain, but he is all you got."

Marion said nothing, her heart breaking and her mind reeling. Her stomach felt like a rock exploded in it and that the quicksand sucked her deeper into the muck. Taking to heart what her daughter said, she took a portion of the inheritance and remodeled her kitchen, put some on her student loan. The group practice she joined a year earlier closed. She took the needed amount and set up her own practice for the fifth time in her career. Splurging, she paid a down payment on a three-year lease on a BMW. Frankie said it was a "fucking waste of money," but she felt she deserved it. Doing without all those years justified her desire.

On Mother's Day nine months after her mom's passing she had a dream. She saw her son Mitchell in the afterlife playing with other children happy and free. Her mom walked toward her healthy and happy. Marion smiled as she reached out for them. She awoke from her afternoon nap feeling her mom pat her leg. Comforted, Marion knew she was not alone.

Session Twenty-Seven

"Dr. Weinstein, why are people so threatened by other people's hard-earned success?" Marion inquired as session twenty-six began.

"Marion, people sometimes want what the other has, but are not willing to put in the effort. Others are afraid that the success will mean they will be left behind," Dr. Weinstein answered.

"Hmm," is all Marion said and then added. "I never would have imagined that I would be where I am today, sitting in your office telling my story and healing in the process," Marion revealed.

"We may not foresee our future, but as it unfolds it is like the back side of a tapestry," Dr. Weinstein explained.

"What do you mean?"

"Did you ever do cross stitch, Marion?"

"Yes, why?" she asked.

"The backside is a jumble of knots and threads going every which way, but when you turn it over you see a completed beautiful design intricately interwoven thread by thread. That is your life. You don't see the complete picture while in the weaving, but looking back you can. That is what you are doing in therapy, examining the tapestry of your life. You see the stops and starts, the tangled messes, and the beautiful redirected paths. It all comes together little by little," Dr. Weinstein said.

"I love that description. Thank you. It gives me hope for the future. Let's examine some more twists and turns," Marion said.

The Price of Stuffed Emotional Pain

IN JULY, ANOTHER blessed event took place. Adam's wife Gwen gave birth to twins Mathew and Michaela. Marion considered it a reprieve from the constant strife and tension between her and Frankie. In the fall, a year after Grandma Sarah died, Marion became anemic, nauseated, dizzy, and extremely fatigued like when she was in kindergarten, fifth, and eighth grade. Her internist sent her to a hematologist to order a bone marrow biopsy looking for Leukemia like suspected years earlier. The undetermined cause of the symptoms persisted, observed over several visits in a year's time.

One day Marion went to the laptop on the desk in their home office to look up her symptoms on Web MD. As she clicked on the Internet Explorer Browser icon a window opened. It was some sort of a story. She read the first few lines, shocked to discover it contained a salacious story about teenage girls. She could feel her blood pressure soar. She gritted her teeth, dreading the confrontation with Frankie. It was a replay of the Mt. Pleasant church computer all over again. She marched into the living room and stood over Frankie with her hands on her hips while he chewed on an eraser working the daily crossword puzzle from the Olive Branch Times.

"Why in God's name are you putting pornography on **my** computer? You have your own computer. I thought you quit looking at pornography. Or was that a lie too? I don't want to know about it, see it, or even think about it. Get it off my computer today!"

"It's only stories. There's no pictures."

"Oh yeah? I read some to see what was on my screen before I knew what it was. It involves teenage girls!"

He said nothing and reached for the remote turning on the television to drown out Marion's voice.

What she had read sickened her. Often, he had wanted her to tell him stories of family members having sex while they shared intimacy. She refused and he would become angry and degrading in his treatment toward her.

Marion never checked her "cookies" again to see if he visited any sites or erased the files/links or not, because if he did not, she had no plan of what to do. She could not fathom what was going through his perverted mind, but she wanted no part of any of it. She desperately felt the need to hold on to the marriage since her own daughter said no one else would want her. With Frankie, she knew what to expect. If she left now, all the inheritance spent, it meant sleeping in her car since her office lease said no sleeping allowed.

There did not seem to be any rhyme or reason to Frankie's mood swings. When he generously bought her new clothes to his liking or brought home Ghirardelli chocolates, she assumed she must have pleased him in some way, but was never certain. When he discovered that he had Type II diabetes, she assumed his moods were related to his blood sugar level, but that did not consistently correlate. She always prayed that his good mood would last. When it dashed, she would be surprised, caught off guard. She became hypervigilant, startled at every loud noise or unplanned movement.

Marion masked her emotional pain by focusing her energies in a positive direction, working with very complicated client situations. She instituted innovative ideas like joining with her psychotic clients in their psychosis to help bring them back to reality without their psychiatrist increasing medications. It worked. Clients no longer needed inpatient treatment. In fact, dosages lessened. Some could live independently. She continues to this day, to keep in contact with people she counseled decades ago, affirming their worth and validating that each person is not their diagnosis. The person's present therapist knows of this interaction and approves of it. Marion's holistic methods began to be noticed by the local social work unit. Attending the annual meeting she was floored to be recognized at the Olive Branch, Mississippi's Social Worker of the Year.

Those accolades infiltrated her mind when Frankie berated her actions. Deep down she knew she could exist outside of the quicksand without Frankie, but she did not want to have to do so.

Frankie had been going on an annual summer mission trip with Adam since the early 90s. It gave her a week of peace and time to indulge in her wants. In 2004 Adam organized a trip to Georgia. Marion began attending annually that year in support of Adam's mission work. The fifth year of the mission trip took place in a small South Georgia town where Adam and his wife were serving three United Methodist churches. A woman, Clarissa, from the church in Murphy was on the same bowling team with Frankie, came along with her teenagers and other church members. She made a strange comment one day at lunch. She looked at Marion and then turned to Frankie and said,

"For our next date you need to dress better."

On the ride, back to the work site Marion looked over at Frankie driving and asked, "What was Clarissa talking about?"

"Huh, what do ya mean?" Frankie asked bewildered.

"Weren't you listening when she said, 'for our next date, you'll have to dress better.' Everyone else heard it and stared at her."

"I have no clue. I'm sure it was just a joke," he said chewing the side of his cheek.

Frowning, Marion said, "well whatever she meant, it isn't right. You better watch out for her."

Frankie said in a condescending manner as he glared at her, "You worry too much, Marion. I have enough to deal with being married to you. I don't have time to worry about what some woman making some offhanded comment to me. It means nothing."

Marion kept her guard up and her eye on Clarissa. She did not trust her at all as she pulled Frankie aside each evening for a private chat while the mission workers sat around the campfire. Marion did not intrude because Frankie was Clarissa's pastor and hoped he would behave ethically in his interactions with his parishioner.

In July, Cliff and his wife Cindy, the same couple who confronted Frankie about how he criticized Marion when her mom was dying, invited them to go to the Chinese Buffet and afterwards the local baseball game. While at dinner

Frankie got a call. He briefly spoke and handed the phone to Marion, "It's Clarissa. She wants to speak to you."

"Hello."

"It's Clarissa. I'm sorry to bother you at dinner, but do you mind if I come along to the baseball game?"

Thinking it odd to be asked such a question, Marion answered, "That's fine. See you there."

"Frankie, why is Clarissa asking me for permission to come to the game?"

"I don't know. I guess she does not want to intrude."

"Whatever."

The game was slow so Marion and other church members prepared to leave early.

Frankie said, "I want to stay and watch the game. Do you mind if I have Clarissa bring me home?"

"That's fine with me."

Frankie got home about ninety minutes later. He shut the front door with a big grin on his face. Marion looked up from the HGTV show she was watching and asked, "What's got you so happy?"

He sat down in his recliner and said, still beaming, "I just had the best time talking to Clarissa. She respects me, looks up to me. She cried telling me about her troubled marriage. It was so refreshing communicating with her in a way that you and I no longer do."

Marion's guard up, she muted the T.V. remote and turned to him. "Can't you see how she is conniving? She's weaseling her way into your life. It's another woman about to blossom and you always fall for that kind. Remember, I was once that kind of woman and now you say, I no longer need you?" Shaking her finger at him she said, "You're walking on dangerous ground. I told you Clarissa is ripe for an affair in an unhappy marriage, having had a hysterectomy, and her oldest going off to college. Watch out!"

"You're crazy. She just needs to talk to her pastor."

He got up and went to bed not even saying good night.

Marion always feared that some woman would come along and take Frankie away from her. Just when they were supposed to celebrate their sunset years coasting into retirement, traveling, and enjoying the grandkids. Clarissa came along threatening to destroy that fantasy. Marion planned to outlive Frankie due to his poor management of his diabetes. She planned to be the faithful martyr to the end. Now that position was threatened by Clarissa's behavior.

Frankie invited Clarissa and her husband Walter along for walks with Marion. Clarissa would intentionally prance in front of Frankie sashaying her derriere. Frankie's eyes were glued to her butt and Walter, totally oblivious to the whole affair developing in front of his eyes, just naively followed the entourage.

The church secretary let it slip that Clarissa was volunteering in the office three days a week, "helping" Frankie with a variety of projects. Marion discovered the diabetic appropriate lunches packed for Frankie were put aside to often have fast food lunches with Clarissa.

Marion was hypervigilant to catch Frankie and Clarissa in inappropriate behavior. Frankie threw her off track one chilly Sunday afternoon as she handed him a cup of Joe in front of the fireplace preparing to watch a movie.

"Thanks for the coffee, Whiffles. Ya know I was thinking," he said as she sat down beside him.

Marion braced herself, never sure what would come next, "What Frankie?" Cliff, Cindy, Sandy, and Devin on going on an Alaskan cruise in August. How 'bout we go too?"

With a furrowed brow she asked, "Really? Okay, if you want to."

She hoped his infatuation with Clarissa was waning as they prepared for the trip. A few days before departure, Marion and Frankie were in the bedroom. Frankie sat on the bed reading the Sunday comics. While unzipping her suitcase to begin packing, Marion asked him, "What are you going to do with our dog, Sampson while we're gone?"

Nonchalantly he answered, "Oh, Clarissa is going to watch him. Sampson will get along fine with their dog."

She stamped her foot and glared at him. "What the hell did you say? I can't believe you're that stupid. I told you to stay away from her, she's trouble. You are going to get yourself fired over the amount of time you spend with her. It looks suspicious. Don't think I don't know about it. Cause I do and I don't approve."

"Well, you don't respect me anymore. She listens to me and thinks I'm smart. We aren't doing anything wrong. Remember, I warned you, if you didn't start respecting me again and doing as I say, I'd be outta here."

Storming out of their bedroom into the master bathroom she announced vehemently, "I am seeing an attorney first thing Monday morning. I told you back in 1984 if you ever did this behavior again, I was divorcing you. Now I am!"

"Wait a minute. You don't have to do that," he said calling after her.

Turning back to him she said, "Fine. Then you call Clarissa right now in front of me and tell her you cannot continue like this with her. It is not right as her pastor."

Exhaling loudly Frankie said, "Fine."

He sat down on the edge of the bed with Marion beside him. He slowly, painfully dialed Clarissa's number sighing deeply.

"Clarissa, this is Pastor Frankie. Marion says that I need to change how I am relating to you. I am your pastor and need to be in an authority position and not continue a friendship like we have."

Marion could not hear any response. He quietly hung up. Franked looked up at his wife anxiously pacing, breathing heavy.

"Calm down. No need to go to an attorney," he said. Defending his behavior, he said, "You have not respected me for a long while. I just got caught up in someone listening to me. Our cruise to Alaska will be a fresh beginning. Okay? Come here," he said as he patted the bed, meaning he wanted oral sex.

Orgasm calmed the wild beast, wiped the slate clean, made it less likely that he would stray, and created a more harmonious atmosphere.

Marion reluctantly agreed to go on the cruise with him since the threat of Clarissa replacing Marion seemed to be temporarily abated. To keep things from causing him to lose his job, she told no one.

God, what is going on? Why has Frankie returned to old behaviors? Am I to blame? Did he really stop his affairs twenty-three years ago? Am I overreacting? Please help me God, I'm sinking deeper in the quicksand and feel no lifeline.

On the cruise, she acquired a whopping pelvic infection. It was so bad she had to go to the ship's doctor to get pain medicine. Frankie offered no compassion only anger that her pain was inconveniencing him, yet again.

As Frankie and Marion wandered in and out of the little shops in the Skagway tourist district Frankie pulled her by the arm into a jewelry shop.

Pointing at an item in the glass case he said, "Hey look at this blue sunflower necklace. Do you like it? What do you think about me getting one for you and one for Clarissa for taking care of Sampson for us?"

Incredulous, Marion said her brow wrinkled, "I can't believe you even asked that question. Why would I want to have something you want to give to the dog sitter?"

She walked out of the store and headed back to the cruise ship with deep sobs welling up in her chest. Frankie bought Marion the necklace and earrings to match and bought a key chain of lesser value for Clarissa. Marion was not impressed, but did accept the necklace. Her heart ached still knowing that he wanted someone else. The remainder of the cruise she pasted on a smile while dining with church members, but inside the cabin she sulked and inwardly disconnected from reality, staring off into space. Frankie ignored her and read his novels.

In October, they went camping in a state park near Russellville, Mississippi. Sitting in the camper in the middle of nowhere with again no money in her pocket, he cornered her as she sat at the dinette doing a Sudoku puzzle.

Frankie sat across from her and stared at her. She looked up and said, "What?"

"I was just thinking," Frankie said.

"Oh yeah, about what?" she asked frowning, never sure what might come next.

"I wonder what's happened to you since your mom died? You're a nervous wreck. You ignore or criticize me. When I start to ask a question, you shake your head no before I even finish. You need to go back to therapy."

Slamming her Sudoku book down she yelled pointing her finger at him, "I'll tell you what is wrong with me! It's your behavior. I know something is going on with you and Clarissa and you're trying to hide it. You ride to hand bell practice with her, after I explicitly asked you not to. You together lead a Bible study class. Right in front of church people you go for walks together. It is opposite everything I teach churches to protect against. You are unfit to be a pastor."

Frankie stood up and towered over her, his hot breath blowing on her cheeks. "You, crazy woman, are the reason I spend time Clarissa. She is everything you are not. If you don't get some help, I'm out of here. Oh, and by the way you also need to get another job to pay off your student loans. Because of your fucking selfish actions, I can't ever afford to retire." He stormed out of the camper and went for a walk not speaking to her the rest of the night.

The tension mounted between them. They spoke only as necessary. Marion felt her breath squeezed out of her as she sank deeper in the quicksand.

While Frankie was in the shower one morning after they returned home, she heard his phone beep, indicating a text. Since phone privacy had never been an issue with them she read the text. Perplexed she carried it to him now drying off.

Raising the phone up, she said, "Who is Lisa and why is she texting you?"

He turned sideways away from Marion to dry his back. "Ah, it's Clarissa," he sheepishly said.

Grabbing his towel, yanking it off him, she asked,

"Why the hell is she texting you as Lisa? I thought you cut off communication with her?"

"Clarissa knew you did not want her communicating with me, so she decided to use the name Lisa so you wouldn't know," he said sheepishly.

"I'm done. I'm going to the elders and tell them you are unfit for duty."

"Go ahead. I don't care anymore what you do," he said as he dressed and left.

When she returned home that evening she called the elders to come together. She wanted to inform them of Frankie's past so they could become aware and monitor his current inappropriate behavior toward Clarissa.

Careful not to reveal too much, the next night Marion addressed the elders sitting around a conference room table. Sitting at the head she rose and haltingly said, "Thank you for meeting with me. I have a concern to share with you."

They sat motionless, staring at her hands in their lap, waiting for her to reveal her news.

"Years ago, Frankie became depressed while serving a church. He escalated his drinking and displayed behavior unbecoming a pastor. He is not drinking, but I fear that his depression is surfacing again. I know he is not fit to serve this church right now." Then she sat down.

Elder Josh spoke first, "Marion, we appreciate your concerns. As far as I know we have not noticed any behavior that would cause us to question his ability to serve this congregation. Perhaps you are premature or overreacting to a situation. We know you have been through a lot with your mom dying a while back."

Marion sat dumbfounded. Could they not see what was right under their nose? She had no concrete proof and she did not want to falsely incriminate Clarissa and destroy her family.

Elder Michael spoke next, "Marion, I've noticed some tension between you and Frankie. Maybe a professional could help you sort this out. Why don't you try being more supportive of his ministry and see if that helps?"

Fighting back tears, Marion mumbled her insincere thanks and left. She sat in her driveway sobbing before entering the house. Frankie watching a Monday night football game, looked up as she came in. She said nothing. She walked quietly down the hall, shut the door to the master bedroom and cried herself to sleep. Frankie, delighted that no elder called him in for a meeting continued spending time with Clarissa.

One of Marion's functions was to be a psychological resource to their denominational state office. She trained congregations around the state to prevent churches from the very thing happening in front of her, pastors that prey on parishioners. She talked to the state minister about Frankie not being fit for duty, being depressed, without revealing her suspicion that he was having an affair with Clarissa. Reverend Lucas was compassionate, but did not pry. She did not want to reveal what she suspected because it could impact her reputation in the denomination. She wanted to do damage control, for someone to alert Frankie to how his actions could damage people and cause him to lose his position and throw them once again into a financial disaster.

She needed some objective viewpoint that would hear her side of the story so she entered psychotherapy with a pastoral counselor with whom she could tell the truth. He revealed what she has been afraid to say out loud, "Frankie is either having or preparing to have an affair with Clarissa and you must decide what you are going to do for yourself."

Marion knew she was not going to tolerate his adulterous ways anymore. Even if she had to live in her car, it was better than living with his cheating ways. She knew of at least nine affairs before Clarissa and there were probably more she did not know about.

When Marion looked in the mirror she did not recognize herself. The worry lines etched in her forehead made her feel old. "I don't know who I am any more, God. I don't know what to do. Please guide me."

Session Twenty-Eight

"Wow, Dr. Weinstein. I didn't realize how I lost myself during all that chaos that I shared last session," Marion revealed as she sank in the therapy chair.

"It is pretty daunting when you realize that after the fact, isn't it? I'm so glad you found your way back, Marion."

"Yeah, me too. The funny thing is, the core of who I am is nothing like what I was back then. My experience of being married to Frankie has been like a stone bombarded by water continually washing over it, hardening it, shaping it," Marion said.

"Great analogy, Marion," Dr. Weinstein said picking up his notepad.

When the Last Parent Dies

WHEN THE PHONE rang at eight p.m. on Saturday, December 6th, Marion was surprised to hear her stepsister, Ellen's voice. They had minimal contact over the years since their parents married. Usually visits to Andy and Mary's home included time with Mary's adult children and their respective families. Since Andy died visits were scarcer.

"Hey, Ellen what's up? We haven't seen each other since August."

Marion could hear the anxiety in her voice. "Ah…Mom is in the hospital. She has pneumonia."

"Oh, dear. How bad is it?" Marion asked, twisting the phone cord in her hand.

"Dr. Winston says we'll know more tomorrow after he takes an X-ray of her lungs. She was too weak to do it tonight."

Marion was very concerned. Her stepmom had not rallied since Andy died eight years earlier. She was lonely, without purpose, no one needed her anymore.

"I'm sorry Ellen. Do you think I should call her? If she's having trouble breathing, I don't want to make it worse."

"How 'bout when I go up to the hospital tomorrow I call you from her room and then you can talk to her?"

"Sure, if you think that is okay and can wait."

"I think it will be all right. We'll let her rest tonight. I'll call you about 4 tomorrow afternoon. Would that be okay?" Ellen asked.

"Sure, we'll be back from lunch after church by then. Talk to you tomorrow. I'll be praying for you mom. Bye."

"Bye, Marion."

Unfortunately, it was not okay. Mary died in the night when none of her family were present. Ellen harbored the guilt for years that her mom died alone. Marion reassured her that often people choose to cross over when the family is not sitting in a death vigil. Over time Ellen forgave herself.

Marion promised to do her stepmom's funeral just as she had her mother-in-law Barbara's. When she announced the sad news to Frankie, he said, "I know you don't want me to go with you, so I won't."

The tension between them was as thick and suffocating as black smoke so much so that she could not fathom him offering her any support anyway. She flew to Virginia alone.

When she returned five days later, she sat next to Frankie on the couch watching the news.

"Frankie," Marion said turning toward him, "You know my theory about people having affairs, don't ya?"

"Huh, why are you bringing that up?" he asked as he continued to avoid her gaze.

"Because I'm watching your behavior. I know that people have affairs after a parent dies. You've heard me talk about it concerning my clients many times."

"So, again I ask, why are you bringing this up?"

"I bring it up because you're acting strange. You defend Clarissa whenever I point out her seductive behavior, like sashaying in front of you when we went for a walk. People have affairs because they don't want to look at their own mortality or deal with their grief. I see you're depressed. I know the signs. I'm watching you."

"So, what the hell are you saying?" he said as he got up off the couch to let Sampson out the door to the back yard.

"I'm saying you're depressed and angry at me and there is something you need to do before it turns into an affair, cause I'm not going to go through it again," she said as she got up and went to the kitchen to make herself a cup of decaffeinated coffee.

Knowing what she habitually did this time of night he said, "If you make it, I'll drink some."

It was their private ritual to have coffee together in the evenings and talk about their day before they undressed. The discussion would continue in the hot tub. On this night, as Marion set the cups on the dining room table even before she put the steaming hot liquid to her lips, Frankie put his hands around his mug and said, "You're right about one thing, Marion. I am depressed. I don't know what I want to do with the rest of my life. You and I are growing further apart. You don't seem to care what happens to me. I've decided that I want a six-week sabbatical from the church to go away and ponder my navel or something," he half-joked.

Marion raised her cup to her lips with the steam rising to her nostrils and said, "If you need a ministerial sabbatical, I'm all in favor of that and am willing to fill in for you while you're gone. With one stipulation."

"Yeah, what's that?" Frankie asked with raised eyebrows.

"Wherever you go, Clarissa is to have no contact with you. If you genuinely want to sort out what you want, she is not to be in the picture. I don't trust the woman for a skinny minute. If she thought she could have you, she would."

"You worry too much about everything. I'm not agreeing to any terms. I'm her pastor. She is a good supportive friend who inspires me, lifts me up, and listens to me, none of which you do anymore."

With that he got up from the table and walked to the bedroom to get undressed for the hot tub. After a twenty-minute soak he slithered into bed awaiting his oral sex nightcap.

Marion sat at the table pondering what was happening in her life. The more she tried to confront the gap between them, the further away Frankie emotionally moved. She felt like she was digging her fingernails into the dirt at the edge of the quicksand pond desperately trying to claw her way out of the muck. She knew she could not gather the elders again to address this devious plan for a sabbatical. Like before, they would just chastise her.

Except for sex, Frankie withdrew from further engagement with Marion. As it was in Ohio, she complied, afraid to let go of the only connection they still had.

One night late, when Marion got home from her second job, working part time assessing drug and alcohol clients at the local in-patient rehabilitation center, she found Frankie sorting his CDs, putting some into boxes. Perplexed Marion said, "Hey, whatcha doing?"

"I've decided I want to downsize into an apartment. I'm getting too old to handle all the yard work. I'm getting these CDs ready to sell at a yard sale."

It took a minute for the enormity of his announcement to sink in.

She put her hand on his over the box as she said, "Wait just a minute. I remodeled the kitchen to my liking. You just beautifully completed landscaping in the backyard and now you want to move again?....I'm not ready to move."

Frankie took her hand off the box and said, "So can you afford this house without me? I don't think so." He grabbed another box behind him and began filling it.

Marion stormed off to the office and just sat there staring at her laptop screen.

God, what is happening here? Where are you? I'm sinking deeper and don't know any way out, please help me.

Besides her private practice, Marion was working all the extra hours she could to pay off those student loans as he requested, not knowing that while she was working, he was busy with other activities at their home. She began to lose weight due to lack of appetite. Her five-foot frame shrunk as she scaled down from 137 lbs. to 99 lbs.

One night Marion reached for her beach towel to take out to the hot tub. There was an unfamiliar blue one lying across the tub.

Holding it up to Frankie undressing in the bedroom, she asked, "Where did this towel come from?"

Frankie shrugged his shoulders as he said, "I don't know. Maybe Ted left it last week when he brought us that casserole dish he made."

She purposely let it slide. Marion, unable to dissuade Frankie, tearfully signed the real estate contract to list the house. The Mt. Pleasant and Marley pattern of reluctantly selling her cherished home repeated. Too depressed to express her needs and wants, she just robotically went through the motions of doing only what had to be done, to stay in a quicksand marriage.

On Sunday morning, she sat in the car waiting on Frankie. Usually he made them late to church. She used to beep the horn and try to gather all he needed so to be on time. Now she just sat in the passenger's seat staring out the window. When Frankie finally emerged from the house, she did not even flinch when he loudly closed the truck driver's side door.

On the way to worship he asked, "Where do you want to eat after church?"

Lost in her own world she did not answer. He finally said, "Fine, don't answer. I'll go somewhere without you."

Marion averaged about four hours of sleep a night as her mind churned over and over with the fear that she was losing Frankie right in front of her. He, although cruel and mean to her, was the ice flow of her life that she clung to, but it was shrinking and breaking apart.

After worship, Clarissa's family opted to join the Finches at Texas Roadhouse. Frankie blew the paper from a straw across the table at Clarissa. Marion, nervously laughed while her stomach felt like dynamite about to ignite. She picked at her food. No one said anything. When they got in the truck for the ride home, she commented on his behavior.

Marion deeply sighed before turning toward Frankie driving and said, "Frankie, that looked pretty inappropriate, you acted like you were a teenager around Clarissa. People are going to talk, ya know? It could cost you your job."

Frankie turned glaring at her, "Ya, know I've had just about enough criticizing from you. I don't care anymore if I lose my job. Your bitching is driving me insane."

She sat silent the rest of the way home.

Frankie arranged for a garage sale. He started selling things Marion wanted to keep. She stopped him as a buyer picked up a Rachmaninoff CD to purchase. "Hey, I want that. Don't sell it," she said.

"I bought and paid for it and I can sell it if I want to." Without another word, the customer put it back down and she returned it to the house.

That night Frankie said to Marion as he undressed, "So the five grand I paid for this hot tub was a waste of money. You never get in it anymore with me."

"Frankie, I told you that I think the bacteria in it is making the sores on my body get worse. They itch like crazy ever since that bug bite in 03. I changed the water like you said and sanitized it, but I still itch."

"Whatever you say, DEAR. You know you just don't want to be with me anymore."

He closed the door to the deck and slid into the hot tub. She could hear the water slosh over the top of the hot tub.

She sat on the bed contemplating her options. She finally undressed and went out to the tub. She silently slid into the tub. Frankie said nothing.

Reminiscent of a similar conversation in their Mt. Pleasant hot tub, she inquired, "Frankie, you seem so angry all the time. What is going on?"

"You are what is going on. You are depressed, critical of my every move. You undermine my authority at the church and you do not respect me. Maybe you will commit suicide and I will collect your insurance."

Taking a millisecond to process that last comment, she said nothing, grabbed her towel, climbed out of the hot tub, crawled into bed and said not another word to him that night. The next session with her therapist, Dr. John she brought it up.

"Dr. John," Marion said sitting in the blue wingback client's chair wringing her hands. "Last night Frankie told me maybe I'll commit suicide and he'll collect my insurance money. That makes me so mad. Why would he say that?"

Dr. John fixed his gaze on Marion's face and with a caring empathetic tone he said, "Marion, it sounds to me like he is either having the affair with Clarissa or about to, blaming you. What do you want to do about it?"

As if she stepped into a meat locker, she began to shake all over, "I am not going to stand for it. I do not know how I will make it on my own, but with God's help I will."

"That's the right attitude," Dr. John said reaching over to pat Marion's knee. "Let me know what you decide. I will support you in your decision."

Frankie and Marion began apartment hunting when they had a contract on the house. Marion said that if she had to downsize, she wanted to be in a nice place. Frankie looked at dumpy apartments because he claimed she did not need much while he was on sabbatical. Then he slipped up. While walking through a beautiful high-end apartment in a gated community Marion said, "I really want to live here. It feels right."

"If you get this apartment, I can never afford to leave you."

"If you are going to leave me, I deserve a nice apartment."

Frankie signed the lease and they moved in the first of March. For reasons, unexplainable, unwittingly, Marion did not add her name to the lease and Frankie did not question it.

On March 10th, at 3:00 a.m. as Frankie got up to use the bathroom, he passed out due to low blood sugar, his chest hitting the shower stall. Refusing to allow her to call an ambulance, she convinced him to let her drive him to the hospital.

X-rays revealed five broken ribs and a punctured left lung. Surgery drained the blood and re-inflated the lung.

Marion sat on the chair beside his bed anxiously mulling over whether she would need to preach for him that next Sunday, or if he would be permanently impaired because of the fall. Her thoughts were interrupted.

Frankie said, "I don't want you here. I want you to leave."

Firmly, she stood up and planted her feet squarely in front of him as she said, "You are my husband and I am not leaving and Clarissa is not allowed to come."

Frankie demanded, "Hand me my phone and bring me my computer."

"No, I'm not going to do that. You need to rest and not be worried about those things."

Wincing in pain he said, "Look, I am in no shape to argue this with you. Bring me my computer!"

Marion had no fight left in her. She called Elder Roger to have him inform parishioners and to call the trained elders into action to handle the day-to-day activities until Frankie was well enough to return.

Just as Marion was getting ready to go home to get his computer, Frankie's phone rang. Marion grabbed it before Frankie could reach for it. It was her!

"Clarissa, Frankie needs to rest. I do not want him to have any visitors. Please respect my wishes and stay away."

"Of course, tell him I will be praying for him. Let me know if I can help in any way."

"The best way you can help is to stay away and let him rest."

Marion hung up the phone and handed it to Frankie.

"There I took care of that interference. Now just rest. I'll be back with your laptop in a couple of hours."

The pain medicine was kicking in so he said with garbled speech, "Ya, okay."

Believing she derailed Clarissa's intentions, Marion drove home, fuming all the way.

"Once again I am cleaning up Frankie's messes. I'm sick of this."

Session Twenty-Nine

"Dr. Weinstein, do you believe in Karma?" Marion inquired.

"Why do you ask, Marion?"

"Because I like to believe that we reap what we sow and that we get punished for the harm we do to others," Marion admitted.

"Oh. I see. So, do you believe you are being punished because you had sex before marriage?" Dr. Weinstein asked in a calm voice.

"No, not anymore."

"Marion, I think people suffer consequences due to their own actions. Is that Karma or God punishing them? I don't believe so," Dr. Weinstein said.

"Hmm. I'll have to ponder that one," Marion said. "Let's begin today by talking about how truth got revealed."

Drugs Reveal the Truth

MARION EXITED THE Olive Branch hospital parking garage at 7:45 a.m., mind absorbed on her task to reschedule her clients before the first one arrived at 9:00 a.m. If she looked over at the incoming cars, she would have seen Clarissa entering the hospital parking lot in her white two-door S-10 standard cab pickup truck. Clarissa's grip on the steering wheel and her eyes staring keenly ahead focused on her mission to get to Frankie as quickly as possible was just as tantamount as Marion's mission to keep Clarissa away from Frankie.

After contacting all six of her Wednesday clients, Marion returned to the apartment and collapsed on the bed to rest, but sleep eluded her. Like the gears in a grandfather clock, her mind clicked pieces into place. *Oh, my God. They ARE having a full-blown affair! No wonder Frankie didn't want me at the hospital.*

In a frenzy and before she lost her courage, Marion sent this text to Clarissa: "I know what you and Frankie are up to. I am telling you to stay away from my husband." No sooner did she send the text to Clarissa, when Frankie, all doped up on pain medication, called. "Why are you harassing Clarissa?"

Her fuse blown, she yelled into the receiver, "and why the hell are you defending her? I know what is going on and I'm going to get to the bottom of this."

"Whatever," was his only response. Then he asked, "Are you bringing my computer or not?"

She did not grace him with a response. Instead she hung up on him and frantically looked for her keys and his laptop. As much as Marion was unhappy in her marriage, she did not want someone else coming along and taking it away right out from under her. She viewed Clarissa like a weasel, the animal that lives in abandoned dwellings of others. Marion had no intention of being pushed out of her marriage. If she chose to go, that was a different matter. She needed to know the truth so she could choose her next step. She abhorred being made a fool of, that Frankie sadistically emotionally manipulated her so he could ingest some forbidden fruit.

Clarissa serendipitously stepped out of Frankie's room to go to lunch or a nasty confrontation would have erupted. Marion, with no time for pleasantries opened the hospital room door and walked over to Frankie's bed putting her face four inches from his and hissed, "You might as well tell me the truth, because I know it anyway. How long have you and Clarissa been sexual?"

He gave Marion a blank stare. Then with glassy drugged eyes, he laced his fingers together on top of the covers, obviously pained as he inhaled each breath over his five broken ribs, "um, we started having sex when we got back from the cruise."

Marion yelled out of frustration motioning with her hands, "You broke your ministerial and marriage vows; you wrecked Clarissa's marriage, you lied to her husband, damaged her kids, and forever hurt the church. Are you out of your ever-loving mind, getting senile or what? What's this, fling number 10? Why now? Why her? Are you serious about this affair or is it like the others, just a passing fancy? Huh, Huh??? Can't you see you're repeating your same old pattern? You've fallen for a tall dumb blonde who can offer you nothing but stroke your ego and your cock. I thought you said all your sexual affairs were due to drinking or was that a lie too? Or are you drinking now also? I'm not cleaning up this mess. You're on your own."

With slurred speech, he said, "Marion, I did not wreck their marriage. It was already broken before I came along. I don't know what I want. I am so doped up on medications and in so much pain, I can't think straight."

"Well, I'll tell you what Lying Cheating Ass of a husband," Marion said as she gathered up her purse and phone dropping his laptop at the end of his bed relishing that he could not reach it without assistance. Pointing her left forefinger at him she said, "Until you know what you want, you're on your own. I told you I would not go through this shit again. I want no part of this chaos. GOOD BYE and good riddance," she said as she tried to unsuccessfully slam the door.

The nursing staff charting on the other side of his wall heard her ranting. Marion went to nurse's station to ask to speak with Ms. Reynolds, Frankie's RN.

Beckoning, she asked the nurse to step out into the hallway. She did. Speaking in a loud whisper Marion said with trembling lips, hands shaking, "Ms. Reynolds, my husband Frankie Finch in room 204 just confirmed that he's having an affair. I refuse to be a part of his craziness. He's on his own. If he needs something, don't call me. Call our daughter." She quickly scribbled down Sarah's number and handed it to her. Then she tromped off in a daze before Nurse Reynolds could even react.

Marion left him to heal from his injuries, to deal with the loss of his job, and to explain his actions to Clarissa's husband. She left it all in his lap and went back to her office.

She functioned on autopilot. She planned to catch up on paperwork, but she could not focus. After returning from the restroom she saw a missed call on her phone. It was from Clarissa's husband, Walter. Her heart hurt for him. What could she say to him to ease his sorrow when she was reeling in her own? Looking at her watch she decided to get it over with before his lunch hour ended.

As she dialed his number, she silently prayed, *God, please give me the wisdom to know what to say to him. Thank you. Amen.*

"Walter, this is Marion. I'm returning your call," she said trying to sound professional to give authority to the wisdom she was about to impart to him.

She could hear the despair in his voice as he asked, "Why didn't you tell me they're having an affair?"

Releasing a heavy sigh, she answered, "Walter I didn't want to think it was true. I tried to protect you and the church from him. I'm sorry."

She recognized the role she played in the cycle. Like many in addictive and/or abusive relationships, first the role of the victim, then the persecutor, and ultimately the supporter of the abuser. She naively believed she was doing damage control if she could stop Frankie's destructive behavior, to avoid further victimization of innocent people. Stopping his behavior meant she would return to status quo – a dysfunctional marriage, but one she was used to. Her attempts to get the elders to intervene had backfired so she thought it was her responsibility to control her husband.

Preparing for his exodus since November, Frankie had his resignation letter written in detail, covering all the bases. The Church Information Technology officer immediately shut down Frankie's access to the computer and printed the needed documentation of email exchanges between Frankie and Clarissa.

Clarissa's husband used a tracking device to glean email correspondence between Frankie and Clarissa. Marion had a copy given to her for legal purposes.

Since the high-end apartment complex would not allow recreational vehicles in their parking lot, Frankie parked the camper at the church awaiting Board approval to begin his sabbatical living in the camper. Something told Marion to go look inside it. She found a box of Clarissa's pictures of her children and important documents like her birth certificate and passport. Frankie had similar items stashed inside including his passport and a check book to Region's Bank with only his name on it. Still in shock she decided to see what monies he had used to open the account. Entering the Olive Branch Credit Union, she showed her ID and asked to speak with a customer service representative. Behind closed doors she revealed Frankie's plan to run off to parts unknown with his mistress. The customer representative sympathetically told her that she had the right to empty out the account, if she chose because her name was jointly on it. She removed a substantial amount and put it into her business account at a different bank. She did not inform Frankie of her actions, just as he did not inform her.

Marion smugly said to herself: *Huh, I guess Frankie couldn't continue his secret life, awaiting his imminent escape plan with Clarissa. It all came literally crashing down around him when he fell in the shower. Karma's a bitch.*

Frankie decided to enter a week-long program for wayward ministers to find his new path. Before he departed Marion called a meeting at the local Burger King of Frankie, Clarissa, Walter and herself. She wanted to confront

Clarissa face-to-face. A part of Marion felt this woman was duped into falling for Frankie and the other part believed she beguiled Frankie into her black widow's web.

Within earshot of the restaurant employees Marion, unabashed, asked, "Clarissa what are your intentions? Are you ready to be done with this affair?"

Clarissa, obviously under the influence of chemicals, answered sheepishly with downcast eyes, nervously fidgeting in her seat, "No."

Walter, visibly shaking with tears glistening in his eyes, looked at his estranged wife and said, "You asked for time apart. I've paid for you to stay in a hotel for this whole past month and all the while you were fucking our minister. And you Frankie, all holier than thou, counseling me on how to keep my marriage together while you were screwing my wife! You are an asshole and a fraud for a minister."

Frankie, heavily sedated, turned toward Walter and said, "I'm sorry, Walter, I did not mean for the affair to happen, but I am not the cause of the breakup of your marriage. Trouble existed for a long time. I'll go to the minister's week-long program and figure out what to do."

Taking advantage of the opportunity for a drug induced, truthful response Marion asked, "So Frankie what do you want?"

"I don't know."

"Okay, since you don't have a clue, I am taking myself out of the equation. You decide for yourself. If you want some input for your therapists while you are at this week intensive therapy program, sign a release and I will fill them in on the details. If not, let me know what you decide when you do know. As for me, I'm done!"

Because, Marion found Frankie had in fact brought Clarissa to the new apartment as well as her home, she did not want to stay at either place. While he was in treatment, she called their friend Jim, "Hey, can I ask a favor of you?"

"Sure, Marion what can I do for you?"

"Well, I'm moving my things into storage while Frankie's in treatment. I can't get the frame of the guest room bed apart. Could you help me with that? If you feel uncomfortable helping me, being Frankie's friend too, I'll understand. No hard feelings."

"Are you kidding me, Marion? Of course, I'll help. I'm so shocked by Frankie's behavior that I have no words. When do you want me to come?"

It took less than fifteen minutes to disassemble the frame and cart it off to storage. Marion was a nervous wreck packing up things. She had not heard from Frankie so she did not know when he was coming back from treatment and what his reaction would be when he discovered the half-empty apartment. She drove to daughter Sarah's in Dothan to spend the weekend before Frankie was due back. She did not want to be in town to incur his wrath.

He called as she approached Montgomery, Alabama. She inhaled deeply before she answered on the third ring. "What the hell gave you the right to empty out the apartment while I was gone to treatment?"

"Frankie, I only took my things," she calmly answered.

"I have rights. I am a human. You can't do that to me!" he said with his voice quavering. "I'm still in pain. I don't know what I want. Couldn't you have waited to discuss it with me? Did you have to do it when I had no defense?"

"Frankie, did you discuss with me before you decided to fuck Clarissa? No, you didn't. You said you did not know what you wanted. You still don't. I told you that I'm choosing to take me out of the equation. I told you I would not be a part of this chaos. This consequence is due to your choices." She felt good about speaking up.

"You had no right to do that."

"Frankie, I'm not going to argue with you about this. I'm going to hang up now," she quietly said.

"Oh, hell no. You're not hanging up on me." She did.

She lived minimally, with her clothes stashed in her office closet out of sight hopefully of her clients. Each night after the last client left she would sit down to type up session notes at her desk while absentmindedly picking at a microwavable meal. About 9:00 p.m. she grabbed an outfit for the next day as she headed to Elder Harold's house to sleep in his guest room. She functioned on pure adrenaline, losing clients over the public knowledge of her situation in the small town.

In about three weeks Clarissa returned to Walter. Marion found out while at the worship service with some mutual friends. A text was circulating between the attendees. Marion wondered what all the gossipy whispers were about. After the service, Becky pulled her aside.

"Marion, I thought you should know that Clarissa just went back to Walter so Frankie might contact you.

He's distraught."

Sighing Marion said, "Thanks for the heads up." *I know what this means. He'll be crushed and wanting someone to make him feel all better. That has always been me. He always turned to me for solace and like a dummy I fell for it nine other times. I felt needed, but not this time.*

Marion hated that Frankie's choices negatively affected the lives of so many people while she sincerely worked at meditating and putting her life together without all the chaos. On the drive to Elder Harry's house her phone rang.

Sure enough, it was Frankie. How ironic. The first person Frankie called to discuss his broken heart was with Marion, the very person whose heart he broke, whom he said did not respect him, nor listen to him anymore which supposedly drew him to Clarissa.

"Marion, can we talk? Clarissa went back to Walter. She said she could not leave her kids. I'm so lost. I need to talk to someone."

"Have you called your friend Cliff?"

"He's not available."

"I'll talk to you briefly, but nothing else." She knew not to trust him, to be manipulatively drawn back in under his control. The only reason she spoke with him was because she picked up on his suicidal state. If he acted on that impulse, facing her children knowing she did not talk to him, would haunt her forever.

Session Thirty

"I learned from you and this process that I am not ready until I am ready. Everyone has a different timetable and path. I can only be on my own path. I cannot convince, cajole, or coax someone to live their life to my specifications," Marion said when Dr. Weinstein asked about her "A-ha" from her therapy thus far.

"Those are words of a very wise woman, Marion."

"Thank you. It is because you have given me the space to tell my story a piece at a time in the order that I chose that has given me the confidence to move ahead," Marion responded.

"It has been a delight to be on this journey with you, but it is not over yet, is it?" Dr. Weinstein asked.

"Not by a longshot," Marion said smiling.

She Does it her Way

FRANKIE HAD TO have someone in his life. He could not be alone. He compulsively called Marion every day, anxious to hear they were on track to reconcile. She made no such promise. No longer employed as a minister, he worked an eight-hour minimum wage job at a local call center. He had abundant free time to mull over how to get what he wanted. Marion with a full-time psychotherapy practice did not have much down time. When she did, she continued to do activities, she wanted to do, like visit the National Civil Rights museum. Frankie, perplexed because the old guilt trip mechanism used to manipulate Marion, no longer worked, as if the quicksand soil was hardening allowing her to slowly climb out.

To soothe his anxiety, he needed his home base to be secure. Like a child trying to earn brownie points, Frankie reported his good behavior.

"Marion, I went to two recovery meetings yesterday. I am working on a fourth step about my sexual addiction. Please pick up the phone and talk to me. I really need to hear your voice."

She called him back two hours later between clients, knowing not to jump at his command as in the past.

"Frankie, it's Marion."

"What took you so long to call me back? I really needed to talk to you. After all; what can be more important than talking to your husband? Did you listen to my message?"

"I did listen," she said in a composed tone. "Ya know. I think what you are doing is great for you, but I don't know if it is in my best interest. You have things you need to work on. I've been dealing with my own issues with Dr. John."

"Don't patronize me with your tone. I'm working hard here to show you I'm serious. Can I at least get some atta boy for my efforts?"

"Frankie, there's a reason you returned to having affairs. I don't know why and am not supposed to be the one to help you figure that out. Do I care about what happens to you? Yes, but I'm not going to throw caution to the wind and pick up where we left off. I'll tell you what…."

"What, Marion don't leave me hanging here, I'm desperate."

"I see Dr. John tomorrow. I'll call and ask him if he will talk to you for a portion of my session to suggest what therapist you will do well with to work on your addiction issues."

"Can't I just see him regularly?"

"No, because he would not be objective for both of us individually."

"Oh, so you spend your sessions judging me? You know damn well you have major issues."

"No, I actually don't. I work on me and how I relate to you," she said calmly undoing his criticism.

Dr. John briefly spoke with Frankie with Marion's permission to assess his sincerity at wanting help. He could not tell for sure, but believed miracles were possible since Frankie was still a sober after twenty-three years. Maybe if Frankie went to a therapist whose specialty was dealing with clients' sexual addiction issues and to continue attending Sexaholics Anonymous, both could help him.

Those were Marion's terms: go to therapy and continue SA and then they would talk.

Sitting down for a burger together after work, Frankie pulled out his copy of *The White Book*. He read her the checklist on page 8 of the Sexaholics Anonymous book.

"Marion, I am amazed that I fit seventeen of those twenty characteristics of a sex addict."

Staring at him with a smug expression she answered, "Ya know Frankie, none of this is news to me. I've been seeing it, living with your addiction for 38 years. I'm just glad that you are now aware of it. That will help you to change it."

Frankie excitedly added with a big grin raising his hands in exclamation, "Yes, change it for us!"

Marion was reticent to join in his enthusiasm. She was not convinced that he was just playing along until she gave in and moved back in with him.

One night without provocation while they were sitting on Frankie's apartment porch he said, "I think it's time for me to come clean, to do a ninth step with you."

Marion had not braced herself for the gush of information unloaded into her lap.

"Remember all those years I went to the winter retreat before I invited you?"

"Only too well," she sighed. "I fretted at home knowing you were unfaithful and I would pay the price with another STD upon your return."

Ignoring her remarks, he launched forth in an excited tone, "I got inebriated enough to overcome my introverted personality. I'd get on the dance floor looking for a woman to seduce. It was so easy with so many women starved for attention. The first year was Marcia, it was just a trial run, no sparks. The next year was Sharon, and then Tina, the keeper," he smiled reminiscing. "I always felt bad the next day, but would drink again and by nightfall be ready to risk a little more. Now I understand that I'm addicted. It never filled my emptiness. I always wanted more. I'd be faithful to you for fifty-one weeks thinking that was enough, that I deserved some 'on the side' for good behavior."

Marion, traumatized by the confession sat dumbfounded while Frankie looked relieved. He had no comprehension of how his narcissistic unloading wounded the one person he was needed to appease to secure the home base. Before, with home base secured, he could wander off free to return at will. Not now, but he did not consciously recognize Marion's lack of empathy. He wanted to be rewarded for being such a good boy coming clean.

Pushing the envelope Marion inquired, "Frankie all that is history. You were supposedly faithful for twenty some years, except of course for your pornography addiction. But how do you justify your affair with Clarissa? I saw her flaunting herself in front of you, pointed out the warning signs, but you ignored them? Why?"

"Clarissa is a good woman. I am still grieving over the loss of that relationship. She loved me unconditionally. She did not criticize me like you did. She listened to me and valued my knowledge. You stopped caring about our marriage. Your doctorate became more important than I was. I took you from a high school graduate and paid your way through three degrees and what did I get in return, an angry, bitter, vindictive woman for the past three years. You drove me to Clarissa."

"Really?" How about the thirty plus years I put up with your overbearing, controlling, angry, abusive behavior? My reaction to all those years was to verbally retaliate. You belittled every step forward I made. You tried to keep me from accomplishing anything that would help me be able get away from you," she said gritting her teeth and stiffening her body.

Frankie, with a look of a deer in the headlights just stared at her. Finally, he asked, "When did I ever abuse you? I never touched you!"

"How about punching me in the stomach when I was pregnant with Sarah because I wouldn't agree to become a Lutheran?"

He stood up. "I never did that. You're making it up."

Marion called after him as he opened the door to the house. "I don't have to defend what I said, because you know it's true by your very reaction. I'm going back to Elder Harry's house."

Marion continued her own private therapy to change her codependent behavior, to stop making excuses for Frankie's behavior or to try to control his behavior. Frankie saw a therapist trained in sexual addiction. Over the next two months they both attended 12-step support groups for those in recovery from sexual addiction. Marion did telephone call-in group sessions called COSA and Frankie attended SA. On Sunday nights, they together joined a telephone couples' recovery group.

"Do you think this couples group applies to us?" Frankie asked looking bewildered when the call ended sitting at the dining room table. "I haven't paid prostitutes to service me like those other men mention."

"Frankie, you may have not paid prostitutes, but there are many other sexual behaviors you revealed to me. Why don't we listen in a few more times before we decide if this is the right resource for us?" she answered anxiously.

"Fine, if you want to, but it's a waste of time to me. We do better talking to each other, in my opinion."

She admitted to herself that he was opening up, in fact gushing information, but she liked the structure of some source outside of their own efforts.

When the sale of their house fell through they contemplated moving back into it. So, Frankie paid a hefty sum to get out of the apartment lease and they moved back into the house.

"I don't understand why you insist on sleeping separate, waiting to have intercourse til we go to Memphis. We're already married for God's sake."

"Frankie, you may not get it that I have been through tremendous hurt and betrayal. I want to go slowly to make sure this is the right thing for both of us. I don't want to feel pushed."

"Ya, but what about me? I've been honest with you, doing what you want, when you want. I don't know what more you want from me. I'm still depressed and grieving."

"Do you even comprehend how much pain I feel when you allude to losing Clarissa? It's as if she was your one true love and I am a boobie prize. Frankie, I've referred to you as my Velveteen Rabbit these last two months. You've been honest and forthcoming. I didn't have to wonder where you were or what you were doing."

"It's really hard for me to be present," he said tearing up. I'm so used to thinking about sex every few seconds that living a mindful life is foreign to me. Please give me some slack for trying, but not being perfect at it yet."

"Frankie, I'm trying too to be present, not critical, supportive and to respond in a timely fashion when you ask me a question. I think our trip to Memphis is a new beginning, a fresh start."

Sighing, Frankie kissed her good night on the forehead and went back reluctantly alone to the master bedroom.

As they registered at the Regal Inn in Memphis the next weekend, Marion anxiously imagined how she would be intimate with Frankie and if he would be mentally present with her or be thinking about Clarissa. Too afraid to bring it up, she just unpacked and waited. Frankie made no move to initiate any physical action. *That's odd. He couldn't wait to get back into my pants. What's going on with him? He's so quiet. Is he having second thoughts?*

Looking up from reading his Sexaholics daily devotional book he asked, "Are you ready to go eat supper? I saw a seafood restaurant over by the mall."

"Sure, let me get my purse."

Throughout the meal, Frankie stared off into space. When they returned to the room Frankie laid down on the bed channel surfing. Marion did not know how to read his behavior. She finally broke the ice, standing in front of the television screen. She said with soft eyes, "Frankie, you don't seem to be having a good time. How come?"

He put down the remote and patted the bed beside him. In the past, it meant he was ready for some orgasmic behavior. She did so, uncertain if the behavior now had a different meaning. Turning toward her Frankie said, "I'm scared Marion. I am afraid this won't work. I don't want to be alone. We've been together so many years when no one thought it could work and now what if it doesn't?"

Breathing a sigh of relief, she took his hand in hers and said, "Frankie, we won't know unless we try. If it doesn't, we can walk away knowing we did everything we could. What do ya say? Are you willing to try?"

He stared up at the ceiling so vulnerable, so raw, so real that she began to kiss him on the forehead and cheeks and then his lips. At first holding back he gradually reciprocated. After orgasm, they laid in one another's arms, silently. Marion prayed that the path ahead would be less treacherous than the one behind.

The first two weeks back home set a routine. Marion saw her clients and Frankie worked at the call center. Schedules overlapping, neither had much to say to one another. The following week Marion, scheduled since February, prepared to attend Adam's annual mission trip, but minus Frankie. He and Clarissa were banned due to their affair.

Clarissa's daughter went. Emotionally drained from all the drama, Marion did not want to be around her. It hurt too much. Characteristically, she sucked up her feelings and dealt with it. She knew it was not their fault.

Seventeen-year-old Winnie came up to Marion while she and four teenage girls were watching *Wheel of Fortune*. "Ms. Marion, can we talk outside for a minute?"

"Sure, let me find my shoes."

Sitting down at the picnic table on the back porch deck Winnie revealed her dilemma. "I'm angry with God, Frankie and my mom and dad. Can you please explain to me why Pastor Frankie had to wreck our family?" she said wringing her hands with her head down.

In the empathetic therapist voice, she said, "Winnie, there is not a simple answer to that question. I do know though, that it is not God's fault."

Tears dripped off Winnie's chin as she went on. "My mom doesn't even talk to me. She just stays in her room with the door shut. I must have done something wrong to make her do that and not want to be around me."

Gently hugging her Marion said, "Oh, Winnie. I'm so sorry. None of this is your fault. Let me talk to your parents about it okay?"

"They'll be mad at me."

"You can listen in if you want while I call them," Marion said reassuringly.

"No, if it's okay with you, I'm going to go back and watch television with the other girls."

"Of course. I'll let you know what your parents say."

Winnie said, "thanks for talking with me," got up and walked back into the hunting lodge.

Marion continued to sit at the picnic table her head in her hands. *God, what do I do now? Why is this dumped in my lap? How come Frankie doesn't have to deal with this?*

Marion reluctantly called Winnie's home phone number, "Walter, I need to tell you something about Winnie. She's angry with you, Clarissa, Frankie and God because of the situation."

Marion could hear her voice take on it professional tone.

"Let me put Clarissa on the phone," sighed Walter.

"Just put the phone on speaker and she can hear everything I say," Marion wearily said as she paced back and forth in the moonlight.

"Okay, go ahead, she's listening."

"Clarissa, because of your and Frankie's actions, Winnie is affected. She needs to talk to a therapist about everything."

Walter said, "I think she'll be fine." Clarissa was silent.

Inhaling loud enough for them to hear Marion said, "Okay, I've informed you. Now the next step is up to you two."

Walter said, "I understand. Thank you. Bye."

"Bye."

Marion called Frankie. She blurted out without any greeting, "Just thought you oughtta know that Winnie's angry at God, you and her mom for what you have done. I should not have had to but I did talk to her. I am exhausted and angry that I have to be the one to handle this, to once again do damage control due to your actions," she said pacing on the porch.

Defensively Frankie retorted, "So what am I supposed to do from here? What do you want me to say?"

"What I want is for you to take ownership for the damage you've done, for me to not have to be the one to deal with your victims when I am a victim too."

"How do you suggest I'm supposed to do that without causing any further damage to Clarissa or her family?"

Softening she said, "I don't know. Maybe you could discuss it with your therapist on your next visit."

"I don't have a next visit. I'm not seeing Dr. Howard anymore."

"What?" she said raising her voice loud enough for the mission participants to hear inside the lodge. Lowering her voice, she asked, "Why didn't you tell me this before now?"

"Because I made the decision after my session yesterday. I don't feel the need to go anymore. He's not really helping me anyway."

Exhaling, she finished with, "We can talk about this when I get home. Just so you'll know, I called Walter and Clarissa listened in on the speaker phone. I suggested they talk to her. This is one of the costs of your actions," she said in an exhausted monotone.

"I don't need a guilt trip," Frankie shouted into the receiver.

"Fine. I'll see you Saturday." She hung up not waiting for him to say anything further. When she returned home, Frankie was distant, did not appear glad that she was back. He did not even ask about the work the team did. She was too physically exhausted to bring any of it up. On Monday morning, she returned to work. Walter called that afternoon.

"Can I come talk to you?"

"Sure, it's 2:30 right now. How about 3p.m.? Is Winnie all right?"

"I'll explain when I come," said Walter.

Her next client was not until 3:30 p.m., time enough to hopefully listen to whatever Walter had to talk to her about.

She greeted him in her reception room sharply at 3:00 p.m.

"Hey, Walter have a seat," she said pointing to the upholstered metal armed straight back chair. He had an envelope in his hand.

"Hey, Marion how ya doing?"

"Okay, I guess. What's in the envelope, Walter?" She anxiously asked. "Is Winnie all right?"

Taking in a deep breath he said, "I think you better sit down."

With wobbly knees, she sat beside him and asked in a quavering voice, "What do you have to tell me? Just say it."

"Last week while you and Winnie were on the mission trip I became suspicious that Frankie and Clarissa were sneaking around again, so I put the device back on the computer to track her online activity. I found out they were meeting up Olive Branch Park this morning. I left work with my camera. I caught them in his truck in the parking lot. I took pictures. They saw me. They know I am showing them to you now. Here they are."

He spilled them on to her lap. As they slid onto the floor she stood up with her voice rising.

"That's it. It's over. I will go see a lawyer tomorrow. I have put up with his behavior way too long. I am sorry, Walter, this is being done to your family, your marriage. I know this is at least his tenth affair. I thought I could help him, but he doesn't want it. Clarissa has no idea the quicksand she has stepped into."

Walter stood there weeping and shaking. She could not tend to his needs right now; her mind was reeling. She had a client coming in ten minutes so she had to compose herself and think things through rationally, an impossible task.

After a blur of a session with her client, Marion went home to Frankie sitting on the couch looking like a convicted felon awaiting sentencing. All she said was, "I have the pictures." They had planned to go walking in the mall. Marion asked him, "What do you want to do?"

Frankie avoided her eyes and said, "Let's go walk at the mall."

Exiting the car, they headed for the mall entrance. Marion turned to Frankie and said, "I want to talk to Clarissa." She wanted to hear it from the mistress' mouth who re-initiated their contact. Had they had sex again or just talked?

"Fine," Frankie said.

Marion dialed the number on her cell phone outside the South entrance to the mall while Frankie sat on the wrought iron bench two feet from her staring at the ground. Marion paced while she waited for someone to answer.

"Walter, this is Marion. Put Clarissa on the phone."

"Hey, Marion. She's right here, but she won't come to the phone."

"Put it on speaker, then," Marion commanded.

"Clarissa, I want to know who restarted this affair, you or Frankie? Have you had sex again?" Silence.

Walter said, "She won't say anything. I've asked her the same questions. What I can tell you is, it's mutual by the texts and emails I've intercepted."

Her parting words to Clarissa, "You are a conniving bitch. You don't know the damage you have caused, but someday you will regret this. Walter, I'm sorry," and she hung up.

Turning to glare at Frankie, he looked at her, sighed heavily and said, "I just want to go home now."

Returning home Frankie sat motionless on the couch. They were supposed to go camping together the next day over the 4th of July holiday. Instead of discussing their plans, Marion locked herself in the master bedroom rocking back and forth on the bed as she called daughter Sarah.

With a detectable shaky voice, Marion asked, "Hi, Sarah. What do you have planned for over the 4th? Can I come visit?

"Mom are you okay? By yourself?"

"Yes, by myself and no I'm not okay."

Exhaling deeply Sarah said, "I told you not to reconcile with dad since I first learned about this affair. I knew he would hurt you again."

"I know, but I had to do it my way. I wanted to be the one to leave, not be the one left."

"I understand. Be careful driving here and you can tell me or not tell me the details when you get here."

"Okay. I'll leave first thing in the morning and be there by 4:00 p.m. Thanks. I love you."

"Love you too, Mom. See ya tomorrow. Bye."

All night Frankie held on to Marion for dear life while they slept. Frozen in position, she did not reciprocate his embrace or sleep much. Knowing Marion was detaching, he panicked.

At 8:00 a.m., as Marion wheeled her suitcase to the kitchen door he asked her, "Aren't we going camping?"

"I'm leaving. I'm going to Sarah's for the weekend."

Frankie grabbed her and held her close and said, "I'm sorry. I did not mean for our marriage to end this way."

She limply stood there until he let go of the embrace. His gaze locked onto her stoic face and he asked, "So when do you want me moved out?"

"I want you gone by the time I get back Sunday night," she said with no emotion. Then she shook the sand from her feet and crossed the threshold into her new life.

Session Thirty-One

Dr. Weinstein clapped as Marion sat in the chair across from him. Smiling Marion asked, "Why are you clapping, Dr. Weinstein?"

"Because I am so proud of you for the progress you have made, the insights you have gained into your behavior, and the actions you bravely took when the odds were against you," he said.

"It certainly did not feel brave at the time. It felt like out of control anger fueling my actions," Marion said.

"Anger can be a good tool to propel us to do insurmountable tasks, like you did. Well done, Marion."

"Thank you, Dr. Weinstein. I still have more to reveal," Marion said eager to begin the session.

No Turning Back no Matter What

FRANKIE MOVED THE camper to live at Olive Branch Campground. Marion let out gut-wrenching sobs Sunday night when she returned to the empty house. Frankie had only taken a few clothes. She managed to muddle through the next week, gathering her wits to have a consultation with a divorce attorney. Her body vibrated, stress hormones continually pulsing through her bloodstream like she had consumed twenty cups of coffee. Her fight or flight mode locked on to steadfast determination to end the hell of thirty-nine years.

Before the papers could be signed, she felt ill. She was down to ninety-nine pounds. Her abdomen hurt and there was pain when she had a bowel movement. Convinced her symptoms were stress-induced, she tried to ignore them, but they got worse. In final desperation, she called her gastroenterologist for him to do an endoscopy and colonoscopy. He told her there was no need as nothing was physically wrong with her, just stress. Three years earlier her colonoscopy was clean, but to appease her, he did both tests. The endoscope was fine, but the colonoscopy discovered a tumor on her hepatic flexure. Awakening from the procedure Marion heard Dr. Peterson and daughter Sarah discussing where to refer her for surgery. Sarah's plan for only a weekend trip became majorly extended, since she only had the power of attorney to handle her mom's affairs since Frankie moved out.

Someone leaked the news to Frankie. His response, "The bitch is playing the sick card." When Sarah confirmed the validity to her dad, he was so concerned he wanted to pray over her. Marion refused. In the past, people

Frankie prayed over, tended to die within forty-eight hours. She did not want to become one of his casualties. The realtor had a good offer on the house, but Frankie declined to accept it. He wanted to hold out for more, an action that delayed the cash Marion desperately needed to cover her now unemployed status.

Tumor removal surgery with a colon re-section was scheduled for the first week in September. On August 29th, she woke not able to see out of her left eye for forty minutes. She chalked it up to stress with all the preparations needed to close her psychotherapy practice and prepare for surgery. Her second of five TIA's (Transient Ischemia Attack – minor stroke) occurred on August 30. She lost sight in her left eye again for thirty minutes. On Sunday, September 6th when Sarah went for a walk, Marion noticed her left arm started aching and felt tingly. When Sarah returned from her morning stroll, Marion was shaking her arm.

"Mom, why are you doing that?"

"Ah, well…. I can't get my arm to wake up and I have a pain in it."

Panicking Sarah said, "Why didn't you tell me before I left? We need to get you to the ER stat!"

Feigning the severity of the numbness she said, "I'm sure it will go away like the vision problems did these last few days."

"WHAT?????? Get your shoes on. We are leaving now."

"I think it's just stress. They'll send me home. It's a waste of their time and my limited funds."

"Mom, I don't care. We will let them decide if it's serious or not. You know how dad was when he had the stroke. I'm not taking any chances on my watch."

Marion, was in fact, having a series of small strokes. She had two more after she was admitted to Olive Branch Hospital. The team of surgeons consulted to determine whether the colon cancer resection surgery should be first after removing the tumor, or the right carotid artery clean out to remove the plaque. The re-section performed on the 9th went well, but she hemorrhaged afterwards due to the blood thinners, which were given to prepare for the carotid artery surgery. On the 16th they did the second surgery placing her in

ICU for twelve hours. Although she developed an e-coli and staph infection, they still released her on September 19[th.]

The tumor was a T3 because it went through the colon wall, but had not reached nearby organs. It was Stage C on the Duke's Scale which meant it spread to at least one lymph node near the bowel. The colon surgeon said they would have done chemotherapy, but due to her minor strokes they could not. They told Marion her five-year survival rate was 60% without chemotherapy.

On the 23[rd,] with Rhonda supporting her wobbly ninety-six lb. frame, Marion entered the lawyer's office to sign the divorce papers on the third anniversary of her mother's death.

Frankie sat at the conference table with tears streaming down his cheeks and said, "Marion, I don't want to be divorced. Are you sure you want to go through with this?"

Staring straight ahead her hands folded on top of the conference table she emphatically answered, "Yes, I do. I am sure."

The divorce finalized on October 30, thirty-nine years, seven months and one day after they were married, a bittersweet day.

To celebrate the legal uncoupling, she went out to dinner with her friends. They were all applauding her success while inside she was an emotional wreck. She had been determined to never be another divorce statistic like her mom and dad had been. Even though Marion and Frankie's short courtship doomed the longevity of their marriage, she still felt she failed.

Session Thirty-Two

"If my daughter had not come to my rescue and if I had not found S-Anon I know without a doubt I would not be alive today," Marion tearfully announced.

"I am so glad both of those support resources were available to you. Just think, the richness I would have missed not getting to hear your story and watch you heal," said Dr. Weinstein.

What to do with the Rest of her Life

DISABLED, DEPRESSED, AND nearly broke, Marion moved in with daughter Sarah in Dothan to recover from colon cancer and her five minor strokes.

God, I'm so angry, lonely and sad. I'm sleeping in little Sarah's guest room on the same bed my mom slept on three years ago, dying from colon cancer. I have no job, no house, no marriage, and my friends live 400 miles away. I feel like a fifth wheel, a piece of unwanted furniture like mom felt around Frankie. Please help me to move on and regain hope. Amen.

Before Marion's cancer diagnosis, her 12-step recovery group helped her funnel her anger and begin to focus on her emotional recovery from nearly forty years of deception, abuse, and broken dreams. A new good therapist helped knit the pieces of a shattered woman back together.

Marion contacted Walter to offer some advice. He answered on the second ring.

"Hey, Walter. How ya doing?" Marian asked sitting down at the computer desk still dressed in her pajamas at five in the afternoon.

Sighing he said, "I'm making it slowly. I'm still so angry though at Clarissa and especially Frankie for being such a hypocrite and lying all the while he was telling me to hang on to my marriage."

"That's what I want to talk about. You open to hearing some words of wisdom?" she asked.

"Are you sure you're well enough from your cancer to do this?" Walter inquired.

"Actually, this will help my recovery knowing I was able to stop something potentially harming your children."

"Okay then. I'm all ears."

"Well, if Clarissa is all gung ho to get a divorce I suggest you stipulate that she be granted it only if she agrees to not have your daughter around Frankie," Marion stated plainly.

"Ah, and why is that may I ask?" Walter said.

"Bluntly, because he likes teenage girls, if you get my drift. I worry about him approaching your daughter and what he might do in front of her. I'll be glad to put it all in writing for your attorney. I don't know if you'll want to hear all the details, but your attorney will have them."

"Marion, I'm so sorry you are going through all this."

"Me too, Walter. I hurt for your family. Clarissa has no idea what she has gotten herself into, but I did try to warn her that night in Burger King."

"Well, I'm done with her no matter what and moving on."

"Good for you Walter, good for you. Email me your lawyer's email and I'll send the document to her."

"Thanks for doing this. I know it's hard for you, Marion."

"It is Walter, but it's the right thing to do. Bye."

"Bye, Marion. Get better."

Marion wrote a guide for churches to help them deal with such betrayal when a minister has an affair, is a sexual predator, or has a sexual addiction. Writing was healing for her to outline a way for others to avoid the trauma she endured. The guide was a preventative damage control tool to help congregations, the ministers' families, and all the victims.

To enhance her healing, she journaled:

I no longer have the farce of a marriage. Every time I feel sad I am reminded of the hurtful things Frankie said, 'I didn't expect the marriage to last. I would just ride it as long as I could.' Maybe you'll commit suicide and I'll collect your insurance.' 'You're just angry with me because I got the realtor to give me a house key after you changed the locks. I let Clarissa into your house, to use your computer and sit on your couch.' 'I didn't want to be stuck with that nice apartment cause then I could never leave you.' 'You don't look good in glasses.' 'I had a dream that you had a fatal illness and I was angry that I couldn't leave you.' 'I was just playing along when we were reconciling. You were turning me an emasculated shell of a man, that I hated.'

As she ruminated over her loss, she noticed something. Her fatigue was increasing and other symptoms surfaced which were not present before her surgery. She wondered if her nausea, unsteady gait, sweating, low blood sugar, fever, and achy joints were cancer-recovery-related or if they meant her cancer had spread. Her oncologist told her that she did not need chemotherapy or radiation because of the placement of the tumor. A PET scan showed no cancer spread, so her symptoms did not add up.

Blindly, she kept waiting to feel better.

One day she met a man, Pat, at the grocery store whom she had known in Mt. Pleasant.

"Pat, what are you doing here in Dothan?"

"Oh, hey, Marion," he said hugging her neck. "I haven't seen you and Frankie in five years. How'd you get here?"

"Well, it's only me. I divorced him a few months ago, I got cancer and had to close my practice and move in with my daughter. What brought you here?"

"I'm sorry about all your troubles. I was bitten by a tick and got Lyme disease while working back in South Carolina. I got too sick to work so I came here to live with friends. I found a clinic here that has helped me. Maybe they could help you." His symptoms and Marion's had similar traits. She made an appointment with the same practitioner.

Lab results confirmed Lyme disease, with multiple co-infections, heavy metal toxicity, Hashimoto's thyroid condition, pre-diabetes, multiple vitamin and mineral deficiencies, a benign brain tumor, and brain lesions. As she got educated about the effects of long term, untreated tick bites, she realized she probably had Lyme disease for over thirty years.

Now understood was the Fibromyalgia symptoms, the high fevers, the swollen joints, the cognitive decline, the nausea, the dizziness, and balance issues. She almost called Frankie to say, "I now know what was wrong with me. I really was physically sick. It was not in my head (well, brain yes, but not psychosomatic)."

Her therapist cautioned her to not fall into the trap of inviting him into her life again only to be disappointed. Frankie contacted Marion by text one day to ask how she was doing.

"I am still having a major Herpes outbreak after four months but the treatment for the heavy metals is helping."

"How did you get the heavy metal poisoning?"

"From the Wicker waste in the water in New York, farming chemicals in the water in Ohio, and the industrial waste from South Carolina."

Although never discussed, Frankie knew where she got the Herpes – from him and he from Clarissa.

In January of the new year she applied for Social Security disability, approved in April. Her prior experience helping clients get approved for disability paid off. Now the real recovery could begin. Waiting another year before she could qualify for Medicare meant she had to draw on her retirement funds to pay the $900 a month insurance premiums and exorbitant medical expenses.

Living with daughter Sarah had its challenges. Marion never had quiet kitchen manners. Mornings started at 5:00 a.m. as she got up to begin her regime of taking her forty different medications spaced throughout twenty-four hours, designed to rebuild and heal her body. She thought she quietly closed the dishwater after retrieving a clean glass. Sarah hollered from the bedroom adjacent to the kitchen wall, "Mom, can't you be quieter? I need to sleep." Marion, tearful, tiptoed back to the guest room. Unsteady on her feet she tripped over the threshold plate leading to her room, making another loud noise. Luckily, she caught herself on the doorframe, but so fatigued she just plopped onto the bed and cried.

Sarah sat her down at the dining room table after work.

"Mom, I think it's time for you to get your own place. I have a colleague at work that has a duplex less than a mile from here. Do you want to look at it?"

Marion was only paying her daughter $400 a month. How could she afford more? The place was a two bedroom, two-bath duplex, just her size. Going over the numbers Sarah showed her how she could afford the place.

"Mom, do you want to look at any other apartments, before you decide?"

"Sarah, I am not in a good mental state to make any decisions. If you think this is good for me, then I'll do it. Having you just across the woods from me helps me feel more secure about it," she said her hands shaking from fatigue.

She moved in, grateful to not be interfering with anyone's life, to have the freedom to go to bed when she wanted and to bang around in the kitchen as loud as she wanted. A light in the darkness emerged when Sarah, like Marion, who was told she could never get pregnant, announced her pregnancy, a baby due in February. Sarah always told her mom she was not having a child until her mom was around to help. The time had arrived.

Baby Ethan was born on January 30th. Each evening Marion came to Sarah's to help. Ethan bonded with his grandmother. Marion assisted with chores and Ethan gave Marion a reason to get up each morning. On the weekends, she traveled to Georgia when able, to get healing hugs from her three oldest grandchildren. All of them were the light of her life.

In the fall Marion had a health setback. She had a fever of 102 for two weeks. Her abdomen was hot to the touch and she was nauseated and dizzy. She feared that cancer had returned. Unable to walk erect due to abdominal pain, she groaned in agony, lying in bed. Her fatigue was so intense that her arms and legs felt like they were made of cement. Three trips to the emergency room yielded no diagnosis. Finally, her nurse practitioner made the correct diagnosis after consulting with her oncologist. She had MGUS the beginning of Multiple Myeloma (blood cancer). Her bone density scan revealed she had moved from Osteopenia to Osteoporosis meaning her bones were more likely to break.

Marion had treatment options. She could continue to take an injection every six months called Prolia for her bone loss. She could take a monthly injection called Gamma Globulin to boost her immune system, meaning she had to avoid crowds and sick people for the six months of treatment. An easy decision to make, she used the time to re-assess all her involvements. Whom did she still want in her life and who was she done with? Her 12-step meeting met in her home.

The recovery meeting once a week was the total of her live social interaction with the outside world except her doctor visits and time spent with her children and grandchildren. She blocked Frankie on her phone and in her email.

Her virtual social interaction time was a whole other picture. Voice America an Internet radio company contacted her after seeing her profile online. They offered her a radio program, an hour once a week. She would do a thirteen-week pilot for $3000 and then sign a contract if she got sponsors to underwrite the show to continue it. She was still too sick to undertake such a task. When they asked her again in six months, she hesitantly said yes.

The show ran for two and a half years covering multiple topics from health to wellness to spirituality. She virtually met people from all around the world. Being still cognitively challenged, she laboriously wrote out and practiced each show's script repeatedly to get it down to the exact time frame. To prepare a broadcast took her twenty hours, but through the process she regained her confidence and connected with many helpful healing modalities. She used some of those methods herself and with her future clients. At the highlight of the show, in one month she had forty thousand listeners. Not bad for a disabled, housebound, sixty-year-old woman.

Session Thirty-Three

"What a transformation you have made in yourself, Marion," Dr. Weinstein said reviewing his notes as Marion sat down.

"It is pretty amazing even to me. There are just a couple of chapters left to catch you up to date. Are you ready to move forward, Dr. Weinstein?" Marion asked.

"Yes, Ma'am. Full speed ahead," he said laughing.

Time to Move on

AFTER FOUR YEARS of being single, she decided to venture out into the dating world. Absent forty-three years, the whole scene seemed foreign to her. With Sarah's help she posted her profile. She was just going to email men back and forth and someday get the courage to meet one. Uncomfortable communicating with all fifteen men who showed an interest, she eventually narrowed her choices down eventually to three. Sarah's opinion mattered. Her caring daughter pointed one out on the screen and told her, "That's the guy to pick."

As she became more relaxed through written communication, she entertained the idea of meeting this guy. Being very cautious, she did a background check to make sure he was not on a sexual offender list. Passing her test, she met Carl at a Natural Food's coffee shop. Initially, she just wanted to consult about marketing techniques for her radio show because he had experience. After a successful meeting, he asked for a real date. She agreed.

Carl and Marion saw the movie *The Great Gatsby* for their second date. From then on, they were inseparable calling themselves "two peas in a pod" due to their similar interests.

In July, two months after their first meeting Marion, well enough to work some, began seeing psychotherapy clients at the clinic where she continued her Lyme disease treatment. On her first day, Carl surprised her with a bouquet of mixed flowers to congratulate her new position.

When he came to pick her up to drive her home, she beamed. She hugged his neck after setting the vase down on the reception area side table, "Oh, Carl, they're beautiful. Thank you so much."

"Where would you like to dinner, my love, to keep the celebration going?"

"Carl, you are so good to me. Let's go to the Mexican restaurant, okay?"

He winked, "Sure, if we can stop for ice cream on our way home," their favorite treat to share.

Marion had never experienced such attention to her needs. She relished all the attention. They married in December front of forty family members and friends, a true celebration.

Prior to the wedding, Marion requested Carl get medically checked out since he had prostate cancer years before and had a heart stent put in. She wanted a healthy husband to enjoy many years together.

In fact, PSA lab results revealed his prostate cancer had returned, but not yet spread to the rest of his body. An easy fix the four consulted specialists agreed. Daily radiation for eight to nine weeks usually cured prostate cancer. To access this treatment meant making the one- hundred-mile round trip five days a week, arriving with a full bladder. After multiple attempts, he figured out the exact amount of liquid to consume on the way to be ready for the procedure without overfilling the bladder.

Treatment began the end of January, the first month into their married life. Marion, still not feeling well squeezed in her weekly IV therapy to boost her immune system. Carl commented throughout those first few months, "I've not been this happy in years." Marion radiantly smiled as she experienced the amazing difference true love made in a person's health and mental state.

In June, Carl had cataract surgery first on one eye and then the other. She asked him how his sight was after the first procedure. He said everything looked brighter, clearer.

"So, do I look any prettier?"

"Not possible."

Beaming she said, "Honey, that is the right answer."

He told each new healthcare professional he had seen more doctors since he met Marion than he had in twenty years. She lovingly clarified. The long-term issues should have been dealt with long ago, but no one pursued it with him.

As they made an appointment for him at the clinic where Marion worked to get some IV therapy to help with his unregulated blood pressure, he hung back, reluctant to add another medical cost to his stretched budget.

She turned to him as she wrote down the appointment on a card for him, "Honey, I do this for you because I want you around for a long time and as healthy as possible."

"Oh, I will be," he said smiling and winking at her.

Together they restarted a business he previously had. A hired seamstress made head wraps worn by bikers, surgeons, cancer survivors, and people with alopecia. They had a ball going to motorcycle events dressing in matching patriotic outfits to capture the attention of potential customers.

They stopped at every Wal-Mart to find reasonable priced fabric to make the "doo rags," as they were called. Their trip to Wisconsin the end of September to attend Marion's 45th high school reunion became a buying trip. The car loaded down with fifty-four yards of assorted fabric could potentially yield $4000 in profit that would pay for entry fees to events, and more fabric.

The second weekend in October was a two-day event in Nashville. At most events, vendors knew not to be set up past dark because the drunk night-time customers only spent money buying beer mugs commemorating the occasion. On this day, the rain closed them down early, a good thing because Carl's left elbow was swollen twice the normal size and his blood pressure was elevated. Carl protested going to the ER.

"Honey, I know you think I need to go, but they will not do anything for me. Going wastes our time and money."

"You may be right, but your blood pressure is very elevated too, and I don't want anything to happen to you."

"Okay, but if they just send me home with nothing, we will know I was right."

What a throwback to forty-two years earlier taking Adam to the ER for strep throat, and Frankie to the ER five years earlier with a punctured lung. Marion was grateful for Carl's more pleasant attitude toward her about it.

Three hours later they emerged with the diagnosis. A pain shot eased the throbbing, but the Allopurinol prescription for gout went unfilled because a full bottle awaited him at home on the over the commode medicine shelf. Carl's only complaint was the long wait to be treated. Marion, breathed a sigh of relief that it was nothing more serious.

On Thursday, October 8th, Carl received *Glucocil*, a new natural supplement in the mail supposedly to help lower his blood sugar.

Picking up the bottle on the kitchen counter Marion turned toward Carl sitting at the dining room table eating his cereal and said, "Honey, did you tell your VA doc or your nurse practitioner about this supplement to make sure it doesn't interact with any of your medications?

He turned to look at her and smile. He said, "No, but it'll be fine. Don't worry about it. I'll tell them next time I go, if it works."

Session Thirty-Four

"I know I am going to cry today, Dr. Weinstein. So, have the tissues ready Okay?"

"Sure thing, Marion. I might even cry along with you. Let's begin," Dr. Weinstein said.

The Unthinkable Happened

On Monday night October 13th around midnight Carl and Marion did their bedtime ritual. They faced one another in their queen-size bed and said, "I love you, sleep well, good night," and then turned their backs to one another and promptly fell asleep. Marion awakened at 5:15 a.m. by the sound of Carl falling out of bed. She thought he was on his way to the bathroom and fell due to low blood sugar (a scenario she remembered only too well).

"Honey are you okay?"

No answer. She quickly ran around to his side of the bed. He was on the floor mumbling trying to get up and looking very frightened. Marion knew immediately this was a stroke like Frankie had.

Kissing him on the forehead Marion said, "Dear, I'm not leaving you, but I have to go unlock the front door and turn on the porch light while I call the EMTs."

She raced to open the front door while grabbing her phone and dialing 911. She was not sure how long before the Rescue Squad would arrive, but knew time was of an essence. In less than the thirty seconds it took her to open the door, dial the number, and get back to Carl, he had managed to get himself halfway up between the floor and a standing position. Fearful, if she lowered him to the floor he may break a hip and never recover, she wedged her left shoulder under his right arm while pulling out the folding chair beside the dresser with her right foot. How she managed to elevate his 235 lbs. to get him seated compared to her 120 lbs. she does not know, but love has Herculean strength.

Hugging and holding Carl she thought:

Should I grab Carl's unsigned updated will on my desk and help him sign it? No, that wouldn't be right. Boy, I'm glad we signed our Advance Directives at the bank ten days ago. I shudder to think what would happen if we didn't. I know we discussed donating our bodies to science for their research to help others, but now is not the time to even think about such morbid things. Thank goodness, our prenup. protects me in a case like this, in case he goes to a rehab facility I can still live in the house. Oh, what a relief, I hear the sirens coming.

By the time the volunteer firemen entered the house not five minutes later, Marion was in the bedroom still hugging Carl, seated in the folding chair, telling him she loved him, and was not leaving no matter what, while tears trickled down her cheeks. As the First Responders took Carl's blood pressure and talked to him, Marion stepped out into the hallway outside the master bedroom. Two of the three rescue workers lifted Carl onto the gurney while the third man spoke into the crackling walkie talkie with Dothan Hospital Emergency Room physician.

God, I know this doesn't look very good. Please help Carl be okay and for me to know what to do to help him. Amen.

While the volunteers professionally tended him, she gathered his blood pressure readings they had been keeping for months, his medication list, driver's license, and insurance card. Due to bad weather, the ambulance drive was lengthened. Unsure if Carl had a stroke and when, the four-hour window to treat him with clot-busting medication was closing.

Marion arrived at the hospital unable to see him while they initially worked on him. She envisioned he coded and they did not tell her. The doctor and nurses let her into his room as soon as they could. By the time she entered the room, the doctors were already huddled, comparing their opinions and options.

Although confused, Carl could nod his head some. He smiled and tried to wink when Marion entered the room. In no time at all his two daughters and Sarah arrived. The CT scan revealed a blood clot. The assumption was his C-pap mask probably slipped off in his sleep, and when he quit breathing, the lack of oxygen caused his heart to go into A-fib. When his heart got back into normal rhythm he threw a blood clot to his brain. Since doctors did not know when the stroke occurred, they could not do the medication to dissolve the clot.

The family all agreed to surgery to remove the clot and it was successful. Placed in ICU, they anxiously watched for signs of improvement or decline due to the risk of a brain bleed from the procedure. He began to show signs of pain and lessened ability to respond. The family requested a second scan to see the results from the clot removal. All, including the doctors, were devastated to find he now had a brain bleed. The surgeon showed the family on the computer screen the area of the brain affected by the bleed, breaking the news that Carl was not going to recover. He could no longer communicate, move at will, swallow, or understand commands.

Since the advance directive paperwork was freshly signed, Marion knew his wishes. As the family discussed Carl's wants, the staff read his healthcare directives that clearly stated no heroic measures. Marion and the daughters gave the go ahead for him to be removed from all life-saving treatments including no hydration, no insulin drip, only pain medication as needed. The offer was made for him to enter Hospice House to live out whatever time he had left with grace and dignity.

He was wheeled out of ICU at 5:00 p.m. on October 15th. By 6:30 p.m. the family gathered around his bed at Hospice House. Since ice cream was his favorite food, his daughter, with the approval of the staff, gingerly placed small spoonfuls of the frozen delight on his tongue to melt. In no time at all he reflexively licked his lips. They wondered if the doctors were wrong, could he really swallow, and could he get better?

The foretold symptoms developed quickly - the gurgling in his throat as fluid filled his lungs and the visual swelling in his skull. At this point they were giving him morphine every fifteen minutes at any sign of discomfort or moaning.

The family continued to congregate around his bed. Each had their alone time to say good-bye as the nurses said death was imminent. Volunteer musicians came into serenade him across the threshold into eternity. The family sang along, tears streaming down their faces.

At 10:15p.m. on October 16, Carl took his last breath as all held their own. The staff ushered the family out to prepare his body for final viewing. A bath, clean bedclothes, and a warm multi-colored dark comforter greeted them when they each came in to say their final good-bye.

Marion came in last. As she stroked Carl's hair, her tears dripped on to the squares of the comforter. She spoke softly to him, "You are now in the presence of God. I shall miss you, my dear husband of only ten months. You loved me well. You taught me that I was worth loving and through that I learned to love myself. I will be okay. Thank you for the gift of yourself to me." Kissing his forehead already cold and gray she said, "I'll see you on the other side, but you'll always be right here," as she pointed to her heart.

After a silent prayer, she walked out of the hospice room into the arms of family and friends waiting to comfort her and to share their own sorrow.

The End

Session Thirty-Five

"Dr. Weinstein, this has been quite a journey. I don't know what I will do every Wednesday morning at eleven now. You have become such a rich part of my life. It is not so much what you have said, because you say very little. It is mostly your presence that has validated my story, my perceptions, my send of worth," Marion tearfully said as she leaned forward to grab a tissue off the table between her and Dr. Weinstein.

"I am going to miss our sessions too. The ebb and flow of your life has affected me in profound ways. I, too, got to see the Hand of God throughout your journey. As promised here is the collection of my notes and observations. As your last entry what do you want to say about this whole process?"

"In keeping with the process of my psychotherapy treatment with you I am going to respond to your question as the narrator of Marion's life."

Epilogue

Through all the tragedies and despair in Marion's life, including the abuse and the broken dreams, she learned to trust herself, to emerge from the quicksand, stronger, more resilient. She did not resent Sarah or Andy for not giving her a better childhood. They gave out of what they had to offer. Her Near-Death Experience put the pieces together. Marion's life purpose was to love those who felt unlovable until they could love themselves. Mom-Sarah learned to do that. Frankie did not. All Marion's actions to demonstrate love toward Frankie did not penetrate his self-loathing. She knew in the end that he must choose to resolve his own issues. Shaking the dust from her feet, gave Frankie the opportunity to face his demons, absent the security of Marion's presence as his home base. To exit the marriage Marion had to accept that the medical intuitive was right, "she was alone in her marriage." Stepping out, she discovered she could be alone without being lonely.

As for the shortened time with the man of her dreams, Carl, she is not even bitter about that loss. He taught her to love again and to know she is worth loving. He accomplished with Marion the very thing that she had been commissioned to do with others. With his help, she healed from her former marriage and now looks forward instead of backward in her life. She gains strength from her triumphs, and never, never, never gives up because the best is yet to be.

Biography of Author

The Rev. Dr. Melanie J. Barton Bragg is a holistic psychotherapist. She has a Master's degree in Social Work and a Doctorate in Pastoral Counseling. Dr. Barton is a licensed independent social worker and a member of the National Association of Social Workers. She is an ordained Christian Church (Disciples of Christ) minister. This is Melanie's second book. Her first, The *ABC's of Children's Sermons* is available on Amazon. Dr. Barton had a radio broadcast for two and a half years. You can listen to the archived episodes at www. thedrmelanieshow.com. She currently lives on the Gulf Coast of Florida and enjoys spending time with her children and grandchildren.

31655520R00296

Made in the USA
Columbia, SC
02 November 2018